J. DANIELS

THE SWEET ADDICTION SERIES COLLECTION
ISBN: 978-1-68230-543-0

This book is a work of fiction. Names, characters, places, events, and other elements portrayed herein are either the product of the author's imagination or used fictitiously. Any resemblance to real persons or events is coincidental.

Cover design ©
Kari March, Kari March Designs

Interior design and formatting,
Christine Borgford, Perfectly Publishable
www.perfectlypublishable.com

Sweet Addiction

J. DANIELS

For my love, my amazing husband,

who puts up with my craziness.

Chapter One

"SHIT. SHIT. SHIT. JOEY? I need you!" I'm flustered and running late as usual, frantically trying to zip up my new black strapless dress and failing miserably. "Damn it, Joey."

Throwing my hands in the air in frustration, I step into my favorite black pumps and run downstairs into the bakery, my bare back completely exposed. Joey, my assistant and dear friend, is leaning his tall, perfectly tailored, suited frame against the doorway and watching me, clearly amused. A winning smile spreads across his face, and if I weren't so rightly irritated, I would have stopped to appreciate just how handsome he looks.

"What the fuck? Can you zip me up, please, so we can go? The cake should have been delivered over an hour ago."

He pushes off the wall and moves toward me, his expression softening. "No, dear, it's already been delivered."

My back straightens as the cold metal of the zipper slides up my spine. "What? No it hasn't."

"Yes, it has." His hands grip my shoulders and spin me. "I dropped it off myself because I knew you would be freaking out up there getting ready and making us late."

"Really?" I ask, staring up at him unconvinced.

He nods. "Really, cupcake."

Smiling and reaching up, I kiss him quickly on his freshly shaven jaw. "You're the best, you know that right?"

"I know." His eyes run down my body and I feel my cheeks heat up. "You look *amazing,* Dylan. Seriously," he wiggles his brows at me, "if tits did anything for me…"

I hold up my hand to stop him, but teasingly mold my breasts and plump them up. "Yeah? They do look fantastic right now, don't they?" He smiles down at me, his one dimple sucked in tightly.

"You ready for this?" he asks as he brushes my hair off my shoulder. "We can still back out. I'm all for ditching this shit and going bar hopping instead." His brow arches as he searches my face, waiting for my response.

I exhale forcefully and grab his arm, leading him toward the door. "No, we can't ditch. Juls will be pissed if we don't show up. Besides," we halt at the door and I grip his massive shoulders, "I thought you wanted to do bad things with men we'll never see again?" Slutty wedding sex awaits and I am more than ready to experience it.

His eyes quickly light up with mischief. *There's the naughty Joey I know and love.* "Oh, fuck yes. Let's do this, cupcake."

FAYETTE STREET IS BUZZING WITH people, all wandering in and out of shops on this beautiful June day. I lock up and spin around, seeing Joey stomping his foot irritatingly in the direction of our transportation.

"Seriously, Dylan? Do we have to take the van? This suit is *way* too nice for that thing, and you know what kind of cars those rich bitches will be rolling up in." He motions to his outfit with a sweeping hand as I walk toward the driver's side.

"I'm sorry, but do you have another suggestion? Your car is in the shop and this is my only mode of transportation at the moment." I open the door and step in, standing on the ledge and looking over the roof at his scrunched up face. "And be nice to Sam. He's been through a lot lately."

He lets out an exhausted breath. "If I ruin this nice suit… and please explain to me why you named this stupid thing. Who names their delivery van?" I ignore his last comment and start it up, glaring at him as he climbs in to ward off any further insults.

"Don't make me put you in the back," I warn as I pull away from the curb toward an evening of inevitable awkwardness.

"HOLY SHIT. THIS PLACE IS fantastic!" Joey shrieks as I pull onto the driveway leading up to Whitmore Mansion, following a long line of expensive vehicles. I wince and rub the steering wheel, preparing Sam for the looks he will undoubtedly receive. "Oh, for Christ's sake. See. I fucking told you we would stand out like idiots. Do you realize we're sandwiched between a Mercedes and Lamborghini. A fucking Lamborghini."

I swallow loudly. Joey's right. My delivery van, which is adorned with swirls of cupcakes and icing splashes on both sides, is completely out of place here. I'm fairly certain we will be the only non-luxury vehicle in the parking lot. My ringtone startles me and I quickly pull my phone out of my clutch, hitting the speaker phone button.

"Hey, Juls."

"Are you here yet? I'm dying to introduce you to Ian and his entourage of insanely hot friends. HEY. What are you doing? You should be rounding up the groomsmen. Jesus, do I have to do everything around here?"

I giggle at my best friend as we slowly inch closer to the parking attendants. She's usually very calm and collected, until it's close to show time.

"Please, for the love of Christ, tell me one of Ian's ridiculously hot friends prefers cock to pussy. I need to get laid, and I needed it to happen yesterday." Joey is practically bouncing in his seat as I chuckle at him. There is nothing he likes more than a wild, no strings attached hook up, and weddings offer the best situation for such thing. Especially weddings where there is free booze.

"Actually, his friend Billy didn't once glance at my boobs when

I was leaning over Ian, so you might be good to go there, JoJo." With that information, he pulls his visor down and begins fixing his already perfectly coifed blond hair.

"We're at the valet guys now, so we'll be right up." I hit end and stop in front of three young boys who eye up Sam questionably and glance between the three of them, silently asking who wants to drive it. I step out with my purse and walk toward them. "Here, the clutch sticks, so don't be afraid to be rough with him." Tossing the keys to the one closest to me, I loop my arm through Joey's and watch as the two boys who don't have to drive Sam snicker at the one with the keys.

"It smells like cupcakes in here."

My head falls back and I laugh with Joey at the valet attendant as we follow the crowd into the venue.

To describe this place as beautiful is an extreme understatement. Entering through rustic doors, the floor plan opens up to a massive foyer with dim lighting given off by Tiffany-inspired glass chandeliers. Stained glass windows surround both doors, and antique furnishings and artwork fill the room. Guests are making their way down the hallway, which leads into another large room, most likely where the ceremony will be taking place. A grand staircase, wide enough for ten people to walk side by side, leads up to a second level, and as I inhale, the scent of old wood and calla lilies fill my lungs. *Damn it.* This wedding is going to be beyond chic.

"There you are. Holy shit, Dyl, you look incredible. Is that dress new and when can I borrow it?" My beautiful best friend is adorned in a navy dress with an empire waist, her dark chocolate brown hair pulled back into a chic bun. "Justin is going to shit a brick when he sees you," she whispers against my ear as she ends our hug. I'd prefer it if he just dropped dead at the sight of me, but I'm not that lucky.

"Thanks. You look amazing as usual. How's the bride?" Her fingers fluff my blonde waves that fall past my shoulders, and she leans in and gives Joey a kiss on each cheek.

"Annoying. Come on, you both need to find seats and quickly. We're about to start." She grasps my hand in hers and I pull Joey behind me as we walk straight back and into the room labeled The

Great Hall.

"Okay, where are all the hot boys at?" Joey searches the room, practically bouncing on his feet. The boy is on the hunt and has a predictable, one-track mind.

I shake my head at him. "Could you please try and keep it in your pants during the ceremony? You are technically *my* plus one, and can wait to get all freaky with some lucky man at the reception."

"I make no promises, cupcake." He smoothes his suit and wiggles his brows at me as Juls extends her hand, pointing toward the left side of the room.

"See the man sitting five rows back on the end, with the ponytail?"

I laugh and her eyes widen. "Ponytail? You didn't say Ian had a ponytail."

"Well, he does. And he lets me tug it when I'm coming."

"Hot damn. Get it, Juls!" Joey begins fanning his face and I know I need to do the same. My cheeks suddenly feel like they're on fire. Although, I shouldn't be that surprised at my best friend's comment. Between the three of us, we're all entirely too obsessed with the male appendage.

"Anyways," she continues with a tone, "the three equally delicious looking men next to him are all his colleagues. And Billy," she meets Joey's anxious eyes, "is the one next to the two empty seats. You guys better hurry up and grab them before someone else does. Oh, shit." She glances down at her watch and pushes us forward into the room. "Sit. Hurry." She clicks away on her heels as I stare down the center aisle where the bride will be walking down any minute. *Shit. I can't walk down that aisle to my seat. That has to be some kind of weird karma to walk where the bride of your ex-boyfriend is about to walk. No, thank you. I do not need that kind of bad luck.*

"Come on." I grab Joey's sleeve and pull him with me toward the left side of the room, walking quickly up the rows of chairs until we stop at the fifth row. Ian, Mr. Ponytail, glances up and smiles at me. *Ooohhh, he is cute*. "Excuse me," I say softly. I step between his long legs and the chair in front of him, trying to quickly make my way to the two empty seats. There isn't much space to wiggle through, and I inwardly laugh at the thought of my six foot two, muscly assistant doing the same shimmy right behind me. The lights start to dim, indicating the ceremony is about to start, so I move faster, Joey pushing up against my back.

"Oh, shit." My heel slips on the arm of a suit jacket that is hanging on the back of a chair and I fall backward, crashing straight into the lap of the man sitting two seats down from Ian. His hands quickly grab my waist and I gasp at the contact. *Oh, great. Good job, Dylan.* Glancing down slowly, I see the sexiest pair of hands I've ever laid eyes on. They're big, and his long fingers tightly grip my hips. Slightly tanned skin contrasts beautifully with my black dress, and I hear a few muffled laughs coming from behind and both sides of me. My eyes flick up to meet Joey, who is grinning widely and glancing behind me amusingly at whoever's lap I am sitting in. I stand up quickly and spin, getting the first real look at the man my ass is now acquainted with. "Oh, shit," I gasp, seeing a small smile form at the corner of his perfect mouth. *Oh, God, I want those lips on me.* Full and pink with a predominant slit running down the middle of the bottom one. His tongue darts out and slowly licks it. *Whoa.*

"You already said that, love." *Holy fucking shit, that voice. Are you kidding me with that voice?* Low and sweet, I can almost taste it. My eyes quickly scan the rest of his face as Joey nudges me in the back, urging me to move forward. *Fuck him. He can wait a second and allow me to marvel at this spectacle in front of me.* His body is fit, built, and definitely makes good use of a gym membership. Perfectly disheveled, dark brown hair that is slightly grown out, striking green eyes that are glued to mine and a strong jaw. *Jesus, is this guy for real?* He could be a fucking model with these looks.

"I… uh… I… sorry." Swallowing loudly after my poor attempt at a sentence, I move quickly and fall back into the chair closest to the aisle, my chest heaving rapidly in my dress.

"What the fuck was that?" Joey whispers as he sits down next to me, blocking my view of the hottest guy I have ever seen in person.

"I don't know. I fell."

"You are such a whore; you did that on purpose. Christ on a cracker, he's hot." Joey leans back a bit and I meet the man's eyes briefly before I drop my head, my cheeks instantly flushing. “Did he get hard? Is he huge? He looks huge.”

I cover my mouth after a loud gasp escapes. “Jesus, you have zero filter. Thank God, we aren’t in a church. He does look huge though, right?” We giggle and make crude gestures at each other as the wedding party music begins to play.

“I bet he’s bigger than Justin,” he teases and my eyes widen.

“Are you serious? The ring bearer is probably bigger than Justin.”

His mouth falls open. “I fucking knew he had a little dick. You never admitted it.”

“Yup.” I wiggle my pinky finger at him and he cracks. “We should have gotten Sara a dildo as her wedding gift. She’s gonna need it.”

Oh, my God, Joey mouths as I glance up to the front of the room. My eyes instantly fall on Justin, who is now standing next to his groomsmen. *Fucking hell, he looks good. I was hoping he got fat.*

“You okay?” Joey whispers and I nod, slowly turning in my seat so I can see the bridesmaids walk down the aisle. They’re all wearing peach-colored dresses that sweep along the floor with each step they take. I smile at the flower girl as she sprinkles petals along the path and settles up front with the rest of the party. The room is beautiful, everything in white and coral. Tall crystal cylinders line each row of chairs and small, lit votive candles float in the water they hold. Calla lilies are spread throughout the room in vases, on tables, and each bridesmaid clutches one. With the change of the music, the guests all rise to their feet and turn their heads toward the back of the room. My eyes meet Juls’ immediately as she stands by the door.

“You okay?” she mouths.

“Whatever,” I reply. She steps up and opens the double doors, allowing Sara to walk through with her father.

I spend the rest of the ceremony staring down into my lap at my fingers. They are freshly painted a deep plum color and I smile at the sight of frosting, which is smudged on my left ring finger knuckle. Popping it into my mouth and sucking, I moan softly at the sweet taste of sugar as Joey weeps like a baby next to me. To my surprise, I'm not emotional at all. Weddings usually turned me into a blubbering idiot, but today, at this particular wedding, I'm emotionless. I guess a part of me should feel a bit sad. Not because my ex-boyfriend is getting married to someone other than myself, but because I wasted two years of my life on a relationship that almost broke me, and seeing him again is a reminder of all that time wasted. An annoying reminder. *Why the hell did I even stay with him for that long?* It definitely wasn't because of the sex. Sex with Justin was bland and boring. He never once brought me to orgasm. Not once. I would have to finish myself off after he rolled out of bed and stalked into the bathroom. Of course, I always let him believe he got me off. I had to give the guy something. Raising my head, I glare at his profile. *You're welcome, dick.*

"And now it is with honor that I present to you, for the first time ever, Mr. and Mrs. Banks. You may now kiss the bride." Everyone stands up and cheers and, of course, I follow suit. It would be rude not to, and I'm not bitter, so, whatever, I cheer. Justin and Sara share a lingering kiss and earn a few whistles from the audience. I feel Joey's hand squeeze mine and I glance up into his big, blue eyes.

"I cannot *wait* to go drink my weight in booze," I whisper to him.

He bends and presses his lips to my ear. "And I can't wait to get my hands down the pants of this playa next to me. Maybe play a little just the tip."

"Jesus. You would." Everyone is watching the bride and groom walk down the aisle, but I'm lost in silly conversation with one of my closest friends. I'm giggling so hard that tears are starting to fill my eyes. And these will be the only tears shed from me today.

"Come on, Dylan, you know you want to slip off into a dark corner with your mystery man whose lap you accidently fell into. Maybe do a little something else in that lap of his."

I raise my eyebrow and lean back, seeing piercing, green eyes flick to mine instantly. A small smile pulls at the corner of his mouth. *Sweet Mother, he is gorgeous.* I quickly lean forward and try to play it off, but fail miserably as a wicked grin smears across my face. "Hell yes, I do. I fucking love weddings."

Chapter Two

THE GUESTS FILE OUT OF The Great Hall and up the grand staircase to the second level. Once Joey and I reach the top, we stand there a moment to take in our surroundings. The entire second floor is the reception hall, and ridiculously decked out in coral and calla lilies.

"Holy hell. Are those ice sculptures?"

My eyes follow Joey's gesture toward the right side of the room. "Isn't that a bit over the top? Ooohhh, there's the cake."

"Told you I delivered it. I feel you doubt my capabilities as your trusted assistant."

I nudge his shoulder as we walk to the place card table. "And I feel *you* really love Sam and are just afraid to admit it."

Tilting his head back, he laughs loudly. "How badass would it be if we started doing our deliveries out of a Lamborghini."

"Badass and extremely impractical. Maybe when we make our first million we'll splurge on a luxury delivery vehicle." I grab our place card. "Come on, we're table twelve."

I don't really care what table we're at, just as long as we aren't in direct view of the bridal table. Justin still hasn't made eye contact and I'm hoping to keep it that way, and with this many people in attendance, avoiding him shouldn't be a problem. Round tables cover three sides of a large wooden dance floor, the bridal table elevated on a platform and overlooking the guests. The tables are draped in white linen with coral ribbons running along the edges and beautiful calla lily filled centerpieces. The DJ is already playing music and a few people are dancing while others mingle around the tables, talking and enjoying themselves.

"There you two are." Juls comes skittering over to us in her dangerously high heels and grabs onto our forearms as we admire the sculptures. "How was it? Be honest." I cock my head to the side and scrunch up my nose as Joey rubs the back of his neck, seemingly in pain. Juls panics, her eyes bug and her fingers immediately rub her temple.

"It was brilliant!" I yell as relief washes over her, followed by a stern *I'm going to kick your ass* look.

"As usual, you are one badass bitch, Juls. If I ever get married, you'll be running that show." Joey rubs her bare shoulder and she winks at him.

"Well, I only have a few minutes to spare before I have to get the bridal party lined up to come in so," she steps in between us and loops her arms through ours, "let's go introduce you to some hotties." *Oh, shit. I almost forgot about hot lap guy. Almost.*

"Oh, my God, Juls, you missed it," Joey says through a laugh.

I lean back and hiss. "Shut up, Joey."

"What? What did I miss?" She flicks her head back and forth between the two of us as I stare him down.

Don't you dare. I'm still your boss and will fire your ass right here. He must have read my thoughts because he never finishes his sentence, or maybe it's because we're now standing in front of the hot, Chicago, man candy club. The four of them are standing near a table conversing amongst themselves, but all conversation comes to a halt as we walk up. All of them, and I mean all of them, are way too attractive to properly function around, and now it's suddenly feeling a thousand degrees hotter in this room.

"There's my girl." Ian reaches his hand out and Juls steps into him, placing a quick kiss on his cheek before she steps back. I keep my eyes on Ian, not wanting to drift to the man whose eyes I know are on me. I can feel them burning a hole into my profile.

"Boys, I would like to introduce my very best friend, Dylan." Her hand grabs mine and pulls me forward as I glance up and run my eyes down the row of men, stopping on the one closest to me. *Damn, he keeps getting better looking.* "And this is Joey, the hottest gay man in Chicago."

"Oh, please, Illinois, bitch. Let's not downplay my sexiness." Joey straightens out his tie as I try not to laugh. My assistant has no modesty.

Juls glances down at her Tiffany watch and her eyes go wide. "Crap. Ian, will you finish the introductions? I need to take care of some shit."

"Sure thing, babe. Be quick though." He holds onto her hand tightly, making her tug away playfully before his smile lands on me.

"Christ, you're so pussy whipped." The blond man standing next to Ian says softly. I glance at him quickly, smiling at the idea of Ian being completely caught up in my best friend. The two of them started dating a few months ago and she's already head over heels for him. Due to our busy schedules, this is our first time actually meeting, and from what I can tell by the way he looks at her, he seems just as infatuated.

Ian glares at the blond who laughs around his drink before he turns back toward me. "Dylan, it's nice to finally meet you." He holds out his hand to me with a genuine smile as I shake it. Ian is tall and built, very muscular with nearly jet black hair that is barely long enough to pull into his pony. His brown eyes regard me kindly.

"Yeah, you too, Ian. I've heard such lovely things from Juls."

He shakes Joey's hand and exchanges some pleasantries while my eyes strain to not look at the man standing directly to my left. "And these are my work associates and mates, Trent, Billy, and Reese," he says, motioning down the line of men. *Reese. Of course that's his name. A guy looking like this wouldn't be named something not sexy, like Ted or Joe.* I shake Trent and Billy's hands as they say how nice it is to meet me. Trent, who made the pussy whipped comment, is the shortest of the group with almost white blond hair that curls at the ends. And Billy, who only has eyes for Joey at the moment, has sandy blond hair that is kept super short, and diamond stud earrings in both ears. I begin biting the inside of my cheek as I turn my body toward Reese.

"Dylan, I believe we've met briefly." He extends his hand and I place mine in his without hesitation, feeling his callused fingers tickle my skin. I have to look up into his stare, even though I'm wearing one of my tallest pair of heels. He's got a torso that stretches on for miles, one I'd like to wrap myself around. His perfectly tailored, dark gray suit frames his hard body almost unfairly, and as he smiles, the tiniest little lines appear next to his eyes. I sigh. His attractiveness is a bit unnerving.

"Yes, briefly. I'm so sorry about that." *Not really.*

Still holding my hand, he leans in a bit, his breath warming my face. "I'm not. Let's go get a drink."

I stumble a bit at the closeness of his face to mine, but somehow manage a quick nod in agreement to his request. Finally dropping my hand, I meet Joey's eyes and he winks at me before I turn and walk side by side with Reese to the bar. I want to reach out and slip my hand back in his, but I don't. That would be weird. *Stay strong. Resist the urge.*

"What can I get you?" the young bartender asks and I realize, after a long silent moment, Reese is waiting for my order, staring at me with an amused grin.

"Oh, umm, jack and coke please."

Handsome next to me raises his eyebrows at my drink selection. "No girly drink for you?"

I shake my head and brush my hair behind my ear. I've never been the type of girl who orders martinis and fruity drinks that cost eight dollars apiece.

"I'll have the same." His fingers strum the counter as I try not to stare at his profile, which is an extremely difficult task. The man is too beautiful *not* to stare at. I'm handed my drink and immediately take a large sip. "So, I don't think I've ever met a woman named Dylan before. And I *definitely* don't think I've ever had a Dylan fall into my lap." His lips touch his glass and I stare a bit longer than I mean to as the liquid slips into his mouth. *And I am now suddenly jealous of his beverage.*

I shift on my feet, flicking my stare back up to his eyes. "Oh, um, my parents were a bit obsessed with the singer. They had picked the name Dylan before finding out the sex and decided that no matter what, that was going to be the name. So, here I am."

He smiles. "Yes, here you are. Do you like any of his music?"

I think for a moment before replying. "I like that American Girl song."

Smiling slightly, he leans against the bar, his tall frame towering over mine and the bartender's. "That's Tom Petty," he corrects me, his lips curling up in amusement.

"Oh, then I have no idea if I like any of his songs or not." I wrap my lips around the tiny straw and his jaw tightens, a small twitch appearing at the sharp angle of it. He clears his throat and runs a hand through his hair, making it even more of a perfect mess. *God, even his hair is sexy.*

"So, bride or groom?" I ask, watching his confusion turn into realization.

He smiles behind his glass. "Bride, sort of. I don't really know Sara, but I've worked with her father. He invited the four of us." His hand motions toward Ian and Trent who are sitting together at their table. I shake my head as I realize Billy and Joey are already missing. *Predictable Joey. We've been here for a whole five minutes.* "You?"

I roll my eyes. "Groom, unfortunately."

He steps closer, brushing his suit jacket against my bare arm and tilting his head down toward me. "Really? Why, sweet Dylan, does it sound like you *really* know the groom?"

Sweet Dylan? Oh, my. I glance up into his eyes. "Because I *really* know the groom. He's my ex."

His eyes widen and he leans back. "Seriously?"

I nod. "Cheating ex to be specific."

"Fuck. That sucks. I mean, isn't this awkward for you? Why are you even here?"

I laugh slightly and point through the crowd toward the dessert table with my free hand. "Do you see that beautiful, five tier, deliciously constructed, wedding cake?" He nods and searches my face. "I made that. That's why I'm here."

"No shit? So, you're a baker?"

I proudly smile as the DJ softens the music.

"And now, ladies and gentlemen, I ask everyone to direct their attention to the front entrance. The party has arrived!" The crowd cheers and whistles as each bridesmaid and paired groomsmen line up at the door. I feel a pair of lips brush against my ear and freeze, my pulse instantly racing.

"You interested in watching this?" His face is dangerously close to mine and I almost stumble at his scent, which is now filling my lungs. He smells like citrus and I have a sudden urge to bury my face into his neck and inhale him deeply.

"Not really," I softly reply, glancing up into his green stare. Nodding once, he grips my elbow and pulls me through the crowd, stopping in front of the dessert table.

"So, what do we have here?" He tilts his glass and takes a sip as we both admire my work. I smile and beam at my creation. It really does look fabulous.

"Well, the cake itself is an orange sponge cake with Grand Marnier whipped cream and marmalade filling," I gesture toward the peach colored pearls and calla lilies cascading down the side, "and the little dots and lilies are made of sugar so it's all edible."

Leaning forward, he admires the flowers with a furrowed brow, studying it closely. I greatly appreciate his interest, considering they were a bitch to make, and can't help but giggle quietly at his look of deep thought. I've never even seen a groom react this curiously to a cake I made.

"Wow. I thought the flowers were real. You can really eat those?"

I smile proudly. "Mmm mmm. They are insanely sweet and practically dissolve on your tongue once the heat of your mouth touches the sugar."

He raises an eyebrow at me as he straightens up. "Christ. You make that sound so dirty," he says with a low raspy voice. I shrug as if to silently portray I always made things sound dirty, which seems ridiculous even in my head. *No big deal, just how I talk.*

"So what do you do, Reese?" I take a generous sip of my drink and watch his eyes go to my mouth, my teeth clamping down on my straw.

After a moment's hesitation as his eyes linger, he replies, "I'm a CPA with Walker and Associates."

Nearly choking at his admission, I clear my throat as his eyes widen. "Get the hell out of here. You're an accountant? You?" *He must be joking. Beautiful and highly intelligent? I feel like I've found a unicorn.*

He simply nods and studies my face with a small grin. "Does that surprise you?"

"Yes. The guy that does my taxes has psoriasis and looks more like my father. There's no *way* someone as hot as you is an accountant." *Jesus, Dylan.* I close my eyes and shake my head, hearing a small chuckle from his direction. When I open them, finally, I lock onto his curious stare, his lips slightly parted as if he's about to speak. The DJ comes over the speaker system and halts him.

"And now it's time for the bride and groom's first dance."

I turn my body toward the dance floor, which has suddenly opened up to allow Justin and Sara into the center. Sara looks beautiful in her strapless gown with intricate beading and Justin looks decent in his suit. Okay, maybe a little better than decent, but that doesn't say much. I've always thought all men look better in a suit, no matter what they looked like before they stepped into it. A familiar song softly plays overhead and I cringe.

"Jesus Christ. You have *got* to be kidding me." I down my drink and place it on the dessert table as Reese steps closer to me.

"Do you not like this song?" he asks. Everyone is watching the couple adoringly and I'm staring at Justin like I want to punch him in the throat. *What a tool.*

"No, I love this song. I loved it so much that I made it *our* song two years ago." I laugh. "Of course, I shouldn't be surprised Justin failed to be original here. He was never one for change or originality, especially when it came to our sex life." My eyes flick to Reese who is now sucking on a piece of ice. He bites it hard and lets it slide down his throat as he leans down, his nose brushing against my temple. I freeze.

"Really? Tell me." I swallow loudly and close my eyes, wanting to block out everything around me that isn't him in this moment.

It's only his breath on my face, his scent, and the slightest contact of his skin against mine. "Did the two of you ever sneak off at a wedding and fuck each other's brains out?"

Holy hell. Did he just say that? My eyes shoot open and my mouth drops. *Can I honestly respond to that? Would he like it if I told him exactly what I want to say, which is I only want* ***him*** *to fuck my brains out at this wedding, or any wedding for that matter?* I shift on my feet and search my head for the appropriate wording when Joey appears at my side, out of breath.

"Cupcake, I need a moment." He grabs my hand, smiling flirtatiously at Reese and pulls me toward our table, planting me firmly in a chair.

I glare at him. "This better be an emergency for me to allow you to pull me away from *that* conversation. He just basically insinuated he wanted to fuck me into tomorrow, and I'd very much like that." My eyes flick back to Reese who is talking to one of the bridesmaids now, her hands playfully pushing at his chest as he speaks. *Oh, please, you look so desperate.*

Joey straightens his tie and pulls his jacket off, slipping it on the back of his chair. "Good lord, he's direct. But back to the important matter at hand, Billy just gave me the best blow job of my life."

My eyes narrow at his beaming face and he shrinks a bit in his chair. "Seriously, Joey? *That's* what you had to pull me away from Reese for? You couldn't have waited until *after* I had an orgasm to tell me this?" I lean forward and his eyes widen. "And for shit's sake, what guy hasn't blown you that you aren't quickly trying to give the title of best mouth in Chicago to?"

"That's not all I needed to tell you." He moves in closer to me, his hand brushing my hair back to reveal my ear. "On our way to our secluded hook up spot, I saw the bride with her lips wrapped around the best man's dick."

"WHAT?" I clasp my hand quickly over my mouth as I feel hundreds of eyes on me. "Are you fucking serious?" I manage in a much more appropriate tone. He nods just as Juls storms up to our table.

"You two bitches are so fucking loud. What's going on?"

"Nothing," Joey and I say in unison.

I'm not sure we should make Juls aware of the situation just yet. I'll let her get paid first, and then drop that juicy bomb in her lap. She'll want to rub it in Justin's face how he got what was coming to him, and that might result in a canceled wedding reception and a loss of her commission.

I brush my hair off my shoulder and smile sweetly at her. "Are you done with your wedding planning duties now?" I ask, wanting to change the subject.

"Yes, finally." She rolls her eyes. "That fucking wedding party was a disaster. I'm pretty sure they were all in some giant orgy back there before they walked into the reception." I meet Joey's eyes and we both try to keep a straight face. The music picks up and Juls jumps on her heels, reaching out for our hands. "Ooohhh, I love this song! Come on. Let's go show these rich snobs how we shake it in downtown Chicago."

"You know it, girl," Joey says as I shuffle quickly behind them.

She makes a quick stop at Ian's table and my eyes lock on to Reese who gives me a playful smile behind his drink. The other boys are talking amongst themselves. "Wanna dance, babe?" Juls asks before Ian grabs her and pulls her into his lap, kissing her passionately in front of everyone. I can't help but blush and glance quickly at Reese, who notices and winks at me. My heart beats roughly in my chest at the gesture. *Relax, it was just a wink.*

"Jesus Christ. Get a fucking room," Joey says, pulling me in the direction of the dance floor.

"Wait." I pull my hand out of his and quickly walk around the table. I stop in front of Reese and lean down, pressing my lips to his ear as he lifts his face to mine. His fingers curl around my arm and the contact makes me momentarily dizzy. "Keep your eyes on me," I say, and he sucks in a breath. Our eyes are locked and our faces inches apart.

"How could I not?" he replies softly. I straighten and see the lingering intensity in his stare as Joey reclaims my hand and pulls me out onto the floor, which is now packed with guests.

Beyoncé's "Naughty Girl" is bumping through the speakers, the bass vibrating through my body as I begin to move. Joey and Juls dance next to me, the three of us trying to out dance the other.

My hands move up my body, brushing over my stomach, up my chest and up around my neck as I close my eyes and let the music take over. I love to dance, especially with my best friends. My hands run through my wavy hair and I feel the hem of my dress rise a bit, brushing the middle of my bare thighs. "Go girl!" Joey squawks and my eyes flash open to see him spinning and twirling around me, as only Joey can do. For a man so tall and muscular, he can move his body as if he were professionally trained. I sway my hips and move in the most overly flirtatious way possible, hoping and praying Reese is watching me, but not having the balls to glance over and know for sure. I squeal with Juls as Rihanna's "S&M" comes on overhead. A pair of strong hands wrap around my tiny waist from behind, and I still, feeling hot breath in my hair.

"Don't stop, Dylan." Reese's voice sends a chill up my spine and goose bumps along my exposed skin. His hips move against my back as he pulls me against him, his hands slipping around my stomach. Juls' eyes widen and she goes to reach for me when Ian appears by her side and grabs her hand, spinning her into him and dipping her for a kiss. I close my eyes and feel his hands move up my rib cage, his thumbs brushing along the bottom of my breasts as I rub my ass against his crotch. I haven't danced like this with a guy in years; in fact, I don't know if I've ever enjoyed it this much before. My pulse is hammering in my throat and I can feel my face heat up from the contact. We're moving together in perfect rhythm as I reach up and around his neck, feeling his breath on my bare shoulder. His hands spin me and my chest presses against his.

"This dress is killing me," he says, brushing my hair out of my face and tucking it behind my ear. We continue to move against each other, his impressive erection digging into my stomach and my hands gripping tightly around his neck while he holds on to my hips. Our lips are so close — open as our ragged breathing brushes each other's face, sharing the same air. If either of us were to move in slightly, we would be kissing.

"Were you watching me?"

"Depends. Were you dancing just for me?" I lick my lips and nod. His eyes widen before he drops his hands from my waist and grabs my hand, pulling me away from the dance floor. *Holy shit.*

This is it. I'm actually going to have slutty wedding sex with the hottest guy on the planet. I inwardly high-five myself as we move quickly between the guests.

I follow closely behind him, my heels preventing the faster walking I would have preferred as we move down the staircase and down the hallway that leads to the bathrooms. My chest is rising and falling rapidly and my nervous energy has kicked in, causing me to practically bounce on my feet. He pushes the men's room door open and drops my hand.

"Wait here." Disappearing behind the door, I stand outside the men's room and pray to God no one is in there. I'm so wound up right now, I can't imagine what would happen if we didn't follow through with this. I've never felt this turned on in my life.

I lick my dry lips as he opens the door and smiles. "You don't mind a bit of an audience, do you?"

My eyes widen and I swallow loudly, seeing a small smirk form on his lips. "I hope you're joking." *I'm not having sex in front of people. No fucking way.*

"I am. Come on." He grabs my hand, but I stay firmly planted in the doorway.

"You don't have a girlfriend, do you? Because if we're about to do what I think we're about to do, it's not happening if you have one."

He raises his eyebrows at me, seemingly unprepared for that justified question. "No, no girlfriend. I haven't had one of those since college." He tugs me against his chest. "Any more questions before I ravage you?"

I shake my head slowly with a flirtatious smile.

"Good." He pulls me into the bathroom and locks the door behind us before he pushes me up against it. His hands grab my face as his lips softly brush against mine, tasting and teasing me. My bottom lip is pulled into his mouth and I moan, granting him full access as I part my lips and his tongue sweeps inside.

"Fuck, Dylan." He moves his tongue against mine, biting and licking my lips. *Holy hell, this guy can kiss.* His mouth expertly explores mine for what seems like hours, and I slowly feel a pull building in my core. This kiss actually makes me feel bad for all of the other kisses I may get from guys in the future. The bar is being set ridiculously high here, certainly unattainable by the majority of the male race. My hands rake through his hair, holding his head to mine as my body responds to his touch with moans and whimpers. There's no controlling myself here; I'm completely abandoning all my reservations and giving in to everything I'm feeling. I'm suddenly picked up, my legs wrapping around his waist as he carries me over to the vanity, our mouths still working each other's. He tastes like spearmint and liquor as I lick him off my lips while his mouth moves down my neck.

"You taste so sweet. I bet every part of you tastes like this."

I groan at his words as his lips brush against the swells of my breasts, which are poking out from my dress. My hands tangle in his mess of hair. His lips move along each collarbone and over each shoulder, tasting and nibbling every inch of exposed skin.

"Reese."

His hands hike up my dress and trail up the insides of my thighs. His fingers slide along the length of my panties and his eyes meet mine. They're the greenest eyes I've ever seen, no other color mixed in. It's almost hypnotizing staring into them. Deep pools of emerald. My panties are quickly slid down my legs; my eyes widen as he tucks them into his pants pocket. *Shit, that's hot.* My fingers work frantically at his suit jacket, prompting him to slip it off and place it next to us. I'm practically clawing at his dress shirt, fumbling with the buttons with my shaky hands. I need to see him bare in front of me. I want to see his muscles contract as he moves inside of me, and by the way his shirt stretches across his chest, I know without a doubt he'll be unbelievable to look at.

"This has to be quick, love. I don't think we have time to get completely naked before someone tries to come in here." He presses his forehead against mine and I growl as he brings his mouth back to mine. Two fingers slip inside of me and I cry out.

"Oh, God."

"You're so wet and really fucking tight." His lips move along my jaw. I'm panting against him, arching into his touch. "Does that feel good, love?"

"Yes. Please, I need you," I beg as his free hand pulls a condom out of his back pocket.

He hands it to me. "Hurry."

I hold the wrapper with my teeth as my frantic fingers work his button and zipper, my legs helping to slide his pants and boxers down to his mid-thigh. My eyes widen at his length, and I groan loudly as he works me with his fingers, his thumb circling my clit. "Am I distracting you?" His lips move against my neck and I can only nod and moan my response. I swallow against his lips and feel them curl up on my skin. I'm getting close already, but I want him in me; I need him in me. Going without sex for a year has been worth it if it leads to it happening with Reese.

Regaining my focus, I rip the wrapper with my teeth and slide the condom down his length while he stills in my hand. His heavy breathing mixed with mine fills the room. I stare, fascinated by how much it has to stretch to form around him, and trail my fingers underneath, hearing him inhale sharply. He's long and heavy, my fingertips barely touching as I grip him. The man is gifted. Crazy gifted. *Will he even fit in me?* My mind scrambles at the thought. *Well, wouldn't that be a nice fuck you from karma. Here, Dylan, feast your eyes on this magnificent penis that you can't even handle.*

Pulling out his fingers, he wipes a line of my arousal on the top of my breasts and immediately licks if off as I lift into him. "You taste fucking amazing." He leans back and locks eyes with me, licking his lips. "I need to be in you. I can't wait anymore." His hands wrap my thighs around his waist as he enters me in one deep push, a loud groan escaping both our mouths.

"Reese!" His thrusts are deep and quick as I hold onto his neck with one hand and the edge of the vanity with the other, my knuckles stark white. Our eyes are on each other's as he slows his movements, guiding his length almost completely out of me before he rams it back in.

"Dylan, holy shit." He continues the slow torture as a bead of sweat drips from his hairline down to his jaw. Darting his tongue out, he licks his bottom lip before pulling it into his mouth, biting on it as I stare, mesmerized.

Rocking my hips into his thrusts, I feel him deeper than I have ever felt anything in my life. His green eyes are burning into mine, full of intensity and desire. His words to me echo in my ears as he tries to control our quickly climbing orgasms. "So good. So fucking good, Dylan. Let me hear you. Scream for me." No guy has ever talked to me during sex, and it's probably the hottest thing I've ever heard. His fingers dig into my hips and I think he might bruise me, but at the moment, I don't care. The slight pain he's inflicting on me is actually fueling my need for him.

"I'm close. Come with me," I grunt, seeing his eyes light up. Sliding his hand between us and under my dress, his thumb presses against my clit and begins to move, bringing my climax to the surface. My nails dig into his neck as I throw my head back and erupt. "Reese. Oh, God."

His free hand grips my neck and pulls me into his thrusts, which are now so powerful I think I might split in two. "Fuck!" he cries out. I reach up and pull his hair as he comes. His eyes never leave mine and my name escapes his lips at his release. I thought most guys closed their eyes when they climaxed, but not this one, and something about him watching me, letting me see him completely unravel, makes this even hotter somehow. He stills inside me and pulls my face toward him, bringing our lips together. His kisses are soft and sweet, going from one corner of my mouth to the other. My lips are swollen and chapped, and I couldn't care in the least. I'd kiss this guy until my lips actually fell off.

"What the fuck was that?" he asks, my eyes flickering open and searching his face. *Amazing. Mind blowing. Beyond anything I could have imagined.* I want to say these things, but don't, not really understanding why he would ask me that question or what the hell he means by it.

He shuts his eyes and pulls out of me, tossing the used condom before he pulls his pants up and tucks himself back in. Turning his body toward me, he picks up his suit jacket and slips it across his broad shoulders, his face completely impassive. *Ah. The awkward aftermath of sex with a stranger*. I avoid his eyes as I hop down and turn to fix my dress in the mirror, realizing he still has my panties in his pocket. *Fuck, is he going to give them back? Or does he expect me to ask him for them?* I meet his eyes briefly in the mirror, breaking the contact almost immediately at the sight of his tight jaw and creased brow. *Fuck that. I'm not asking him anything.*

The door rattles. "Shit." His voice is clipped and irritated as he glances at me before turning toward the door. "I'm really sorry," he says as his fingers slide the lock back and he opens it, allowing two men to enter as I stand at the sink.

"Well, well, well. What have we here?"

I shake my head and push past them, my shoulder brushing against Reese as I walk down the hallway and quickly up the stairs, leaving him in the restroom. *Jesus Christ, what was his problem? What the fuck was he sorry for? He came didn't he?* I'm fuming, my hands clenched tightly at my side as I storm through the crowd. I make my way to my table where my two friends sit, picking at the food on their plates. Their eyes both lock onto my face and Joey grins wide while Juls studies me questionably.

"I need to get out of here," I say, grabbing my clutch that I had left on the table, and trying my best to avoid their stares.

"And where the hell have you been?" Joey asks, pushing his plate away as Juls stands up and walks over toward me. "Please tell me you just got thoroughly fucked."

"Yes, Dylan, where were you? You missed the cake cutting."

Goddamn it. That's the only thing I really wanted to see.

"Don't ask." I glance to my right and spot Reese as he walks toward his table, his eyes meeting mine briefly before flicking away. He looks thoroughly fucked as well, his hair a sexy disheveled mess.

"Oh, Christ. Please tell me you didn't do what I think you did with him?"

I bend down and kiss Joey quickly on the cheek, ignoring Juls' questioning. "Are you coming with me?" I ask.

"Nah, I'm going to spend some more alone time with Billy." He pulls me closer to him. "I want every fucking detail tomorrow."

I roll my eyes at him before I turn and walk out of the reception area with Juls. I make it down the stairs and to the front door before she stops me and demands answers.

"Well?"

"Well what? I forgot your question." *I didn't.*

She crosses her arms over her chest and glares at me. "Did you fuck Reese? Dylan, please tell me you didn't."

"Technically, he fucked me and thoroughly freaked out afterwards. Can I go now please?"

Her mouth drops open. "Fucking motherfucker. Dylan, he's married."

I have to grip the wall to prevent myself from falling over. "What? But he said he didn't have a girlfriend." My mouth drops open. "Oh, that asshole. I bet he thought he was really clever, telling me he hasn't had a girlfriend since college. I suppose a wife isn't technically a girlfriend." The tight sensation in my gut from my previous orgasm is now instantly replaced with nausea and an intense urge to punch Reese in the nuts. "How do you know he's married?"

Juls runs her hands down her face. "Ian told me he was married when I met all of them briefly for drinks last week. Wow. What a scumbag." *Indeed. Scumbag doesn't even come close to describe him at the moment. I'm thinking douche-bag, tool, asshole, fucking prick.*

Pinching the top of my nose with my thumb and pointer finger, I quickly replay the hottest sex I've ever had over in my head. I drop my hand and clench my fist. *I could kill him.* "And no fucking wonder he couldn't get away from me quick enough afterward. How the hell was I supposed to know he was married? He wasn't wearing a ring."

"Dylan?" We both turn our attention to Justin who is standing at the bottom of the steps, eyes wide and full of shock as he looks at me. *Well, this night just keeps getting better.*

I snap my eyes back to my best friend, ignoring the cheating loser on the stairs. "I'm leaving before I get arrested for homicide. I'll call you tomorrow," I say to Juls and Juls alone.

I open the door and walk out to the valet attendants, reminding them I'm the owner of the delivery van as they laugh amongst themselves. I'm fuming and so not in the mood for this shit. "You're working a fucking wedding, so I know you're not riding around in a Lexus. Just go get my fucking van," I snap at them and they immediately shut up. One scurries away quickly toward the parking lot.

"Dylan, can I talk to you?" Justin's voice comes from behind me.

"No. Congratulations, Justin. The ceremony was lovely." I

feel his hand on my shoulder and I turn quickly, stepping out of his grasp. “Don’t touch me. Shouldn’t you be upstairs with your wife?”

He snickers and steps closer, his gray eyes full of mischief. “Well, if I heard correctly, aren’t married men your thing now?” *Oh, no, he did not just say that.* My hand comes hard and fast, slapping him across his face as he stumbles back, wide-eyed and smiling.

“Fuck you,” I snap. Seeing Sam pull up to the curb, I walk quickly to the driver’s side. I can’t pull away fast enough; tires spinning as I quickly make my way down the long driveway and away from my complete fuckup of a night. I should have never come to this stupid thing. *Hooking up with a married man at the wedding of my ex-boyfriend. Jesus, Karma, you are one hateful bitch.*

Chapter Three

SUNDAY WAS A COMPLETE BLUR. I spent the entire day in bed, unless I had to use the bathroom or get something from the kitchen. After several missed calls and texts from Joey, I finally turned my phone off and kept it that way the rest of the day. Juls probably made him aware of Reese being married, but whereas she was into lecturing me about the topic, Joey would high-five me, insisting I tell him every juicy detail about the hook up, and I wasn't in the mood for either. I didn't want to think about the best orgasm I'd ever had. I didn't want to think about the way his lips felt against mine, against my skin, the taste of his mouth, his smell, the way his face looked when he came, the sound of my name on his lips, the way he looked at me as he fucked me against the sink, or how ridiculously huge he was; because he was married. He was fucking married and a complete tool for hooking up with me behind his wife's back. I can't even have a one-night stand without it blowing up in my face. Then there was my jerk of an ex-boyfriend. Following me outside and putting his hands on me like that when he should have been glued to his new wife's side. Talk about a scumbag. Of course, he did get cheated on at his own wedding, which could not delight me more. That bastard got everything he deserved and whatever else is coming to him. I hope he doesn't find out about his wife's indiscretions for a while and thinks he's in a loving marriage. When in reality, she is out fucking anything that moves.

MY ALARM ANNOYINGLY WAKES ME at five a.m. on Monday, as usual. I like to get a run in every morning before I open up the shop, mainly because of the large amount of sugar consumption that happens regularly between Joey and me during work hours. Dressing in my running gear, I grab my phone and keys off my nightstand and go downstairs into the large kitchen. I live in a small loft above the bakery and have since I opened the place three years ago. It's practical for me living at my job since some days I'm required to get up in the middle of the night to work on something for a client. My loft consists of one large room, which I separated into two with a decorative screen, giving my bedroom area some privacy from the living room and kitchen. It is small, quaint, and cheap. Renting the room above the bakery only costs me eight hundred and fifty dollars a month, which is relatively inexpensive for the downtown Chicago area. Below the loft, the stairs dump out into the large kitchen/work space, which I spend the majority of my time in, with a doorway that leads out to the main bakery. I make my way through the doorway and smile at Joey's face, which is pressing against the glass, peering inside. He never misses a run. I step outside and lock up behind me, seeing his angry expression glaring at me as I spin to greet him.

"Well, thank God you aren't dead. What the fuck? I called you a million times yesterday." He stretches his back by twisting from left to right. "I believe I told you I wanted details."

I bend down and reach for my toes and he does the same. "I'm sorry. I needed to mentally check out yesterday. The wedding was a bit much." *Understatement of the century.* Stretching my hamstrings, I stand up and press my hand against the window of the bakery to steady myself.

"And are you going to just stand there and *not* tell me what the fuck that means?"

"I'm sure you already know everything, you gossip queen. Hasn't Juls spilled the big surprise?"

We start jogging down the sidewalk together, our feet hitting the pavement at the same time. It's already hot as hell outside and that just ups my annoyance level.

"What big surprise? Juls spent the rest of the reception sucking Ian's face and God knows what else, and I ate my weight in cake after I saw Billy flirting with a waiter."

"Oh, shit. I'm sorry, Joey. That really sucks."

"Whatever. He ended up driving me home, and I did him in the back of his Denali as punishment."

I push his arm, but he doesn't budge. The man is a mountain of muscle. "Jesus. Well, I guess you showed him."

"Oh, I did. Now, what surprise?"

We make our usual trek down Fayette Street on the deserted sidewalk, Joey initiating the pace as he always does.

"Reese is married." *God, it still sucked today saying it out loud. And why did my heart physically ache at the sound of it. I couldn't be that affected by a wedding hook up, no matter how good the sex was.* I stop running and look back at Joey who is frozen on the pavement, his blond curls already sticking to his forehead with sweat.

"He's what?" He starts up again, momentarily stunned, and I move with him.

"You heard me. Fucking married. Of course, he didn't mention this before, during, or after our hot as hell sex in the men's bathroom. He just simply asked me 'What the fuck was that?' after he came, told me he was sorry, and went on about his business." I push my legs faster as we run up a small hill, feeling the burn in my thighs.

"What a dick. Are you sure though? I mean, I didn't see a ring and you know I hunt that out first thing."

"Yeah, so do I. Apparently, Ian told Juls that he was married. He probably didn't wear his ring so he could fuck me blind. Oh, and I almost forgot, to top the night off, Justin followed me outside and alluded to me fucking *him* since married men are my thing now." *Asshole.*

Joey snaps his head toward me, eyes wide. "Are you fucking serious right now? Where the fuck was I when all this was happening?

Oh, that's right. I was eating my goddamned feelings." He picks up his pace as I struggle behind him.

"Slow down! Your legs are miles longer than mine."

"Crap, sorry." He returns to my side. "I'm sorry about Reese, cupcake. I really am. But—"

"Don't fucking say it, Joey." I know exactly what his next words would be.

"I'm just saying—"

"Shut it, Holt," I grit out as he spins around to face me, effortlessly running backward.

"You could be the sexy mistress. If the sex was *that* good, why give it up?"

Now *I* start sprinting and hear a squeal from him as he catches up within seconds. "Are you mental? I am not going to be his fuck buddy on the side. I don't care how amazing the sex was or how hard he made me come. Fuck that shit." I wipe my forehead with the back of my hand, the sweat already starting to build on my skin.

"Ooohhh, how hard *did* he make you come? Was he huge? Please tell me it didn't have some weird hook to it like Billy's did." He shakes his head quickly. "I'm not quite sure how I feel about that yet."

"Jesus Christ. It is way too early to talk about dick sizes and which way they curve." I pause. "But for the record, he's massive and as straight as you pretended to be in high school."

"I fucking knew it. You lucky bitch."

We run in silence the rest of the way around the neighborhood, the only noises coming from us being our breathing and the sound of our shoes striking the pavement. I run fast and hard, desperately trying to push the memory of Reese and our hook up out of my mind and hoping to run away from it. But that isn't going to happen, at least not today, and it isn't happening for my running partner either. I can almost hear Joey's mind working as we run, most likely coming up with all the possible secret rendezvous scenarios between Reese and myself. Needless to say, the five-mile trek today is both mentally and physically exhausting.

I shower and dress for the day after saying goodbye to Joey, so he can do the same. He only lives a few blocks from the bakery and will be back before we open at seven a.m. He is my only employee at the moment, seeing as I haven't gotten around to hiring anybody to replace Tiffany after I fired her. I'm not entirely sure I need anybody else to work for me; Joey and I seem to manage just fine on our own. I grew up with him, going to high school together, and then to college where we both studied business. He was more than supportive when I dreamed of opening my own bakery and insisted on becoming my assistant so we could stay close. Although, deep down, I think he just wanted to sample all my new creations. Thank God for our daily runs, otherwise, I'm certain we would both be as big as a house.

I tie my favorite apron on and begin pulling the pastries, muffins, cupcakes, and cookies from the back racks and bringing them up front to the display cases. The house specialty is my banana nut muffins, which I spent five years perfecting the recipe on. They're insanely delicious and it's a struggle not to eat every one myself straight out of the oven. I sell out of them every day by noon and nothing makes me prouder. At a few minutes before opening, Joey comes hustling through the door carrying two coffees and his award-winning smile.

"I'm dick talked out, so don't even," I say as I open the register and count the money.

"Cupcake, there's no such thing, trust me. I had them put in an extra shot of espresso for you this morning, figured you might need it," he says, walking around the counter. "Although, perhaps you'd prefer hard liquor with your coffee today?" He hands me my piping hot cup and I smile weakly. He is handsomely dressed in dark jeans and a bright blue polo shirt that brings out the color in his eyes.

"Thanks and, yes, liquor would be my preferred beverage this morning, but I don't think the sight of me stumbling around the shop wasted off my ass would be good for business." I take a sip and let the hot liquid run down my throat, instantly perking me up as the front door swings open. "Good morning. And how are my favorite regulars today?"

Mr. and Mrs. Crisp live around the corner and come into the shop every morning for two of my banana muffins. They are beyond adorable and always start my day off with a smile when I see them.

"Well, besides the fact that this one kept me up all night, snoring, we are just fine, Dylan." Mrs. Crisp motions toward her husband who smiles sweetly at her.

"You love it, dear. I'm sure you told me once how my snoring helps you sleep." Mr. Crisp lovingly rubs his wife's back as she bats him away playfully.

"Oh, that's ridiculous, Harry," she huffs. I pull out their muffins as I smile and place them in a bag, grabbing the money that was placed on the counter. "And how was the wedding, dear? You stick it to that nasty, no good ex of yours?"

I roll my eyes after handing Mr. Crisp his change. "Not the way I would have liked to." I cross my arms over my chest and lean against the counter. "Whatever, I'm just glad it's over with. The cake looked amazing and was apparently delicious." I motion toward my assistant who is nibbling on a muffin. "This one ate an entire tier by himself."

He snorts loudly at my declaration. "It was not an entire tier. Well, actually, yeah it probably was." The four of us all laugh together as he devours his breakfast. The man can put away the sweets.

The front door swings open, getting our attention, and an older gentleman carrying a white box walks in and up to the counter. Mr. and Mrs. Crisp wave their goodbyes and slip out.

"Can I help you?" I ask, staring at the box questionably. It doesn't have any labels on it, giving no indication as to where it's from.

He places it in front of me with a smile. "Good morning. Delivery for a Ms. Dylan." My eyes widen as Joey steps next to me.

"What the hell did you order?" he asks as I sign the slip for the man.

"I didn't order anything, I don't think. Who sent this?" The man just shrugs and takes his clipboard, pushing the box toward me on the counter and walking quickly out of the bakery. We both stare at the box, glancing up and meeting each other's eyes.

"Well, aren't you going to open it?" he asks, arching his brows at me.

I study it suspiciously before replying. "I don't know; don't bombs come in unmarked packages?"

"Who the hell would try to bomb you?"

"Well, for starters, a certain wife of a certain someone who banged my back out Saturday night," I huff. He makes a face at me and pulls the white ribbon that is tied on the top, lifting the sides of the box to reveal a folded brown card on top of white tissue paper. I open the card and quickly scan the handwriting.

Dylan,

I fucked up. I'm so sorry. I would love to see you again.

X Reese

My mouth drops open. "You have *got* to be kidding me." I hand the card to Joey and hear him gasp after a fleeting moment.

"Holy shit. He would love to see you again? Dylan!"

Snatching the card back, I pull apart the tissue paper and cock my head to the side as I stare at the contents of the box. "What the hell?"

Joey leans in and gawks. "*Oh, my God.* This has to be the sweetest thing I've ever seen."

I pull out a pound of flour and drop it on the counter as he squeals next to me. "Why would he send me flour?" I am beyond confused right now while my assistant is bouncing around like a bunny. You would think by the way he's reacting that I'm currently staring at an engagement ring instead of baking supplies.

"Don't you get it? Instead of *flowers* he sent you *flour* since you're a baker. Shit, that's romantic."

I shove him and he doesn't budge. "Romantic? A married man just wrote me saying he wants to keep fucking me on the side. He's married, Joey. This is not romantic. It's sleazy and disgusting." Picking up my coffee and stepping away from the counter, I stare at the flour and take generous sips. *This is insane and my assistant is an idiot.*

"You're missing some key adjectives there. A *hot* married man wants to keep *rightly* fucking you on the side. You must have blown his mind, girl. Plus, he sends you presents? I want him as my secret boyfriend."

I shake my head. "What a pompous asshole. He must think I'm some two-bit whore to willingly submit to this joke of a request. Fucking douche-bag." I pick the card up and toss it in the trash as Joey lunges for it. "Leave it."

"No. At least keep it for a day. You might change your mind."

"You are high off your ass if you think I would actually consider this."

"I fucking wish I was high right now. That would be an excuse for my insane case of the munchies." He throws his hands up dramatically.

We both giggle at each other and the situation. Of course, this is my life. I couldn't have some hot guy, who gave me the best orgasm, be interested in me. No, that would be too normal. He has to be a hot *married* best orgasm giver with a mouth I would pay to have on me again. *Figures.*

THE MORNING WENT BY QUICKLY with the steady flow of customers. Mondays are always busier in the bakery, mainly with walk-in specialty requests, which I enjoy immensely and Joey hates. He prefers that I'm not tied up in consultations all day so we can chitchat and gossip. It's close to noon when Juls walks in, looking as chic as ever in her tight pencil skirt, white blouse, and heels to die for. I really need to raid her closet someday. Besides the height difference between us, we're similarly built and could swap clothes easily. We're both slender yet toned, given how religious we both are about our exercise routines.

"Hello, lovies. And how is everyone's Monday going?"

I moan as Joey smiles big, showing off his lonely dimple. "You look hot, Juls. Got a meeting with an annoying couple?" I ask as I straighten out the remaining red velvet cupcakes in the display case.

"Actually, I was just about to head over to Ian's work to have lunch. You know I gotta look good for my baby."

I perk up. *Perfect. I could tell him off in person.* "Mind if I joined you?"

She tilts her head to the side as Joey gasps dramatically. "Are you going to confront him?" The excitement in his voice is almost palpable.

I nod firmly. "Hell yes, I am. If he thinks he can proposition me to be his dirty little secret, he is seriously mistaken."

"Excuse me? What the fuck have I missed?" Juls brings both hands to her hips and stares at me, waiting for an explanation. Of course, before I can speak, Joey opens his big gay mouth.

"Well," he rests his chin on his hand, "Reese sent our sexy friend here a note with some flour saying he was sorry about fucking up and would love to see her again." His grin cracks his face open. "Isn't that fantastic?"

She stares at us with a furrowed brow. "Are you serious? Oh, damn it, I meant to confront him at the wedding after you left, Dyl, but he actually disappeared pretty soon after you did. Besides," she straightens out her skirt, "I was a bit preoccupied. Wait, did you say he sent you flour? As in baking flour?" I nod and she raises her eyebrows, her mouth slowly forming an O. "Ah, instead of the traditional flowers. That's actually pretty clever."

I stomp my foot. "Oh, for fuck's sake. Why am I the only person who didn't get that? And it wasn't clever. It was stupid, because he's stupid."

"Wow, you're really gutting him with that insult," Joey states sarcastically as I pull my apron off. I throw it at his face.

"Well?" I ask, turning to Juls.

"Well what?"

"Can I come with you?"

"Oh, hell yes. I would love to see you chew him a new one. I can't stand cheaters." We both move toward the door as I nod in agreement.

"Hey! What about me?" Joey yells.

I turn my head. "You need to stay here and man the shop. What, did you think I was going to close down for this?"

"Goddamn it! This is why we need another employee, Dylan. I fucking miss everything."

"Don't worry; I'll give you all the details *after* I cut off his testicles." Juls and I walk out of the shop together and toward her car as I give myself a mental pep talk. *Yell first then remove balls or remove balls then yell? Hell, does it matter?*

I'M SLOWLY BEGINNING TO LOSE my edge as we walk into the crisp sleek foyer of the Walker & Associates building. Juls' heels are clicking on the marble and I inwardly curse myself for not changing my outfit before I so bravely decided this was a good idea. I'm wearing a pale blue button up shirt, skinny jeans that are dusted in flour, and my favorite ballet flats. This would have been so badass if I was wearing something sexy and revealing, showing Reese what he will never touch again. *Damn it, Dylan. Think next time.* At least my hair and makeup are on point. We step off the elevators onto the twelfth floor and I follow closely behind her, unsure where to go.

"Nervous?" she asks as she walks up to a small reception area.

"Nope, but he better be." She throws her head back and laughs as I wiggle my brows.

"Julianna Wicks for Ian Thomas, please," she says to the pretty receptionist who smiles and picks up the phone, talking softly into it. She ends the call quickly.

"Go right in, Ms. Wicks."

She shrugs playfully. "I fucking love this shit. My man is so important that I need to check-in with someone before I barge in." I giggle at her and follow her through a closed door after she knocks quietly.

"There's my girl. I've been waiting for you." Ian stands up and walks around his desk, pulling Juls into his arms and smothering her with quick kisses. *Christ, they are annoyingly adorable*. "I'm starving and not just for food," he whispers before his eyes flick to me. "Dylan. Are you joining us for lunch today?" he sweetly asks as he plays with the ends of Juls' hair. He sounds sincere, but I have a feeling he'd much rather spend his lunch alone with my best friend.

I clear my throat. *You can do this, Dylan*. "Actually, I was wondering if Reese was here. I need to speak with him." Juls is too busy frantically working at loosening Ian's tie to even remember I'm in the room. I'm sure she would have snuck in a bitchy remark had she been paying attention.

"Oh, of course." He smiles wide. "Just continue down the hallway until you see the redhead at the reception desk. She'll point you in his direction." I nod and turn on my feet, giving Juls one last glance as I step out, closing the door behind me.

He's married. He's married. He's married. Who cares how fucking insanely hot he is. He's married. My thoughts are so loud in my head; I'm sure the redhead, who I am now standing in front of, can hear them. I smile weakly at her.

"May I help you?" she asks in a rather snippy tone.

"Um, yes. I would like to see Reese, please."

She cocks her head and narrows her eyes. *Jesus. Retract the claws.* Picking up her phone, her eyes run slowly down my body. "You mean Mr. Carroll? And who may I say is asking for him?"

Mr. Carroll. Oh, how fucking formal. I glare down at her. "Dylan."

"Just Dylan?" Her tone is borderline bitchy and I am beyond over it at this point. *Sweetie, this is not the day to test my patience.*

"Yes, just Dylan," I snap back, hands fisting at my sides.

She rolls her eyes and speaks softly into the phone, slamming it down with more force than is probably necessary. "Go on in, just Dylan." She motions with a quick swipe of her hand toward a door that stands at the end of the hallway. *What the hell is her problem?*

"Thank you. Have a nice day," I reply extra cheerfully to pluck her last nerve. She scowls. *Mission Accomplished.*

Not bothering to knock, I open the office door and step inside, stumbling a bit at the sight of the man behind the massive desk. *Yup, that's what he looks like. Completely perfect.* His eyes slowly come up to mine from his computer screen and soften.

"Dylan, this is a pleasant surprise. I assume you received my package?"

I close the door behind me and cross my arms. "Yeah, cute pun. Do you have a minute?"

He smiles and I stumble a bit. "For you? I have several."

Standing up, he gracefully moves his body around the desk and sits on the edge, crossing his long legs in front of him at the ankles and bracing himself on his hands. I shake my head at his cockiness. *Damn it to hell.* If he wasn't so gloriously attractive, this would be so much easier. He stands before me in a light blue dress shirt, gray plaid tie, and khakis, his hair a perfect mess and his green eyes freezing me where I stand. He raises an eyebrow, waiting for me to speak. I could speak. I had a lot to say. But right now, I want to either throw him down and fuck him right on his desk or slap him so hard across his face that he will feel it next week. *Hmm, I could do both. Oh, Christ, Dylan. No. Slapping him. That sounds satisfying.* I move quickly, his eyes widening as I stop just in front of him and strike him across his face, a loud crack echoing throughout the room.

"Jesus Christ," he almost yells, his hand coming up and rubbing his now reddened cheek. "What the fuck?"

"You fucking prick. Who the hell do you think you are?"

He stands up, towering over me in my flats. *Fuck, he's as big as a tree.* "Okay, I probably deserved that." His tone is sharp, but he doesn't sound angry. He seems more concerned than anything. "Look," he pauses, rubbing his cheek, "I'm sorry I kind of shut down after the bathroom. I'm not used to sex getting to me like that, and I handled it like an asshole."

I see red. "Are you serious right now? *That's* why you're sorry? Because you freaked out afterward?"

"Yes, well, that and the fact those men saw you in there with me. I'm sure they knew exactly what we'd been doing." He steps closer to me. "Why the fuck else would I be sorry? I'm not sorry it happened. Are you?"

I push against his chest, but he doesn't move. *Damn it, I need to start lifting weights.* "Yes, I'm sorry it happened. I do not fuck married men, Reese!" I'm shouting now and my throat begins to ache, but not enough to make me stop. However, his current look of confusion is taking away some of my fire. *He's a smart guy. Why isn't he grasping this?*

"Okay, that's good to know," he says with a furrowed brow.

"Great. Now you know. So stay the fuck away from me." I go to leave, but I'm stopped by his grip on my arm, turning me around to face him.

"What the fuck are you talking about?"

I step out of his grasp and look down at his left hand, narrowing in on his bare finger. "You asshole. Why don't you wear your ring? Hoping to get your dick sucked behind that massive desk of yours by some girl who *doesn't* know you're married?"

His look stuns me. I expected him to get angry with me for slapping him, maybe a bit disappointed in me for not wanting to pursue this any further, but the amused look on his face is not what I expected. He runs his hands down his face and laughs, stopping only when he sees my hardened expression.

"Married? Who the fuck told you I was married?"

I step back. "Juls. Answer my question. Why don't you wear your ring?"

"Really? And where did Juls hear I was married?"

I throw my hands up in frustration. "What the fuck does that matter? From Ian. Who else?"

He grabs my hand and pulls me with him toward the door, swinging it open and storming down the hallway.

"Where are we going? Let go of me."

"Shut up, Dylan." My fighting is useless. He is clearly on a mission as he walks toward Ian's office door, dragging my infuriated self behind him. "We're settling this right now."

"Settling what?"

"Mr. Carroll, Mr. Thomas told me to hold his calls."

"It's fine, Jill," he grunts at the nice receptionist as he swings the office door open, pulling me into the room with him.

"Fuck. What the fuck, Reese?" Ian's voice causes me to shriek, and then I focus on what is happening in front of me. My eyes widen at the sight of Juls bent over Ian's desk, completely naked and getting fucked from behind. Ian quickly moves and covers her up as Reese and I spin around and shut the door to keep the curious eyes from the hallway from getting a show.

"Shit. Uh, sorry, man. This will only take a minute," Reese says as we both stare at the door.

"Jesus Christ, Dylan. I was so fucking close," Juls growls.

I hold my hands up. "This was not my idea. Blame the asshole next to me." His head flicks toward mine and I stare him down.

Yeah, that's right. I said it.

"Well? What the fuck is it?" Ian asks, still out of breath.

"Why the hell did you tell Juls I am married?"

He laughs. "Uh, I didn't. You? Married? That's fucking hilarious. Babe, who told you Reese was married?"

"*You* did. Last week when we all went to The Tavern after work. Right?" She sounds nervous and suddenly unsure of herself.

"This is so fucking stupid. Can I go please?" I ask and Reese's arm shoots out and prevents me from grabbing the door handle. I try to push it away, but my efforts are useless.

"Babe, I think you've mistaken Reese for Trent. Trent is married."

My stomach drops.

"Oh. Oh, fuck, you're right. Dylan, I'm so sorry. Shit, I really thought it was Reese. Honest mistake though, right?" She giggles nervously and clears her throat.

I drop my head into my hands. "Jesus Christ," I groan, hearing a muffled laugh coming from my left, and suddenly I want to hurl myself out the nearest window. *Oh, God, this is awkward.*

"Well, now that there's no confusion, can you two love birds please get the fuck out so I can finish?" Ian utters through a laugh. "And lock the door behind you."

"Yup. Uh, meet you downstairs, Juls." I quickly open the door, beginning to make my way toward the elevators when a pair of hands grab my waist and spin me.

"Oh, no. I don't think so," Reese states, gripping my elbow and leading me back down the hallway and straight to his office. *Shit. He's not married. Now what?*

Chapter Four

I'M COMPLETELY UNPREPARED FOR THIS turn of events. Everything was executed perfectly on my side. I slapped him, called him out on his infidelity, and didn't allow his blinding good looks to deter me in any way. I felt powerful storming into his office and telling him off the way I did. But now, now I feel like a meek little church mouse as I cower in the corner of his office. He isn't married. That's not something I was expecting to discover, and definitely not something I was prepared to have to contemplate. I mean, what did we share together other than a hot fling at a wedding? There isn't anything deeper going on here, is there? No, surely not. No one develops relationships from slutty wedding sex encounters. That's not how those things work. If they did, Joey would be in a new relationship every other month. My eyes slowly trail up his long, lean body and stop on his eyes, which are curiously watching me. He's regained his perch on his desk and hasn't said a word as I fidget with my fingers, debating on where to start. *Fuck. I owed him a major apology.* I clear my throat and step closer to him, seeing him shift a bit on his desk.

"So, I was wondering if it was at all possible for you to

completely forget that I came storming in here like a crazy person and assaulted you. If not, I'm not entirely above groveling."

He tilts his head and strokes his jaw with his hand. Pushing off the desk, he bridges the gap between us. "Well, you did think I was a married man who was fucking around behind his wife's back. I think that slap was justified from your point of view." His hand brushes my hair off my shoulder, the small gesture causing my stomach to knot up. "Besides, I would hate to *completely* forget how incredibly sexy you look all feisty and pissed off."

I laugh slightly. "You thought that was sexy?"

He nods and licks his lip as he stares at my mouth. I step into him, feeling his hands grip tightly onto my jeaned hips. "Well then, I could rip you a new one for acting like a total dipshit after you fucked me. It's your call." His chest heaves rapidly as I run my hands up his arms and stop on his biceps, squeezing once before flicking my eyes up to his. Hard muscles tense against my hands.

"Do your worst," he whispers.

My fingers trail up the length of his tie. Yelling at him to make him want me is tempting. Really tempting. But he has, technically, already apologized for his behavior, and right now, I don't want to yell. Not unless he's fucking it out of me.

Gripping his tie in my fist, I pull him back behind his desk and push him down into his chair. "I choose groveling," I declare as his eyes widen. Kneeling before him and steadying my fingers, I slip them into his belt, loosening it and unzipping his khakis.

"Dylan."

My hand grips his length and I pull him out. Flicking my tongue across the head, I glance up into his eyes, which are now glazed with lust. My tongue swirls around the head and down the shaft, licking every inch of him. I trail soft kisses along the seam as his eyes stay glued on my mouth, his lips parting and his breath coming out in quick bursts.

"That's so hot, love. Suck it hard."

I smile and wrap my lips around him, guiding him to the back of my throat as he lets out a hiss. I want to take him completely, but that isn't going to be possible. Not with what this man is working with. Wrapping my hand around the base, I stroke him with my mouth, sucking and licking as his hands find my hair.

"Jesus. Just like that. Don't stop."

His hands guide me at the pace he wants. Up and down, licking around the head before I take him in as far as I can. My hand strokes him tightly, gliding up and down his slick length as my mouth follows its path. His fingers brush down my temple, along my cheek and across my jaw. I keep my eyes on his face, seeing the muscles in his neck tense with each suck and his head fall back onto his chair when I lick the tip. He moans, thrusting his hips into my movements as his hands hold my head in place. I never was a huge fan of blow jobs, but the noises coming from Reese right now are making this insanely hot. I'm not just getting him off; I'm getting myself off. My thighs are pressed tightly together as I kneel in front of him and I know without a doubt that my panties are drenched. He pulses against my tongue. Sucking hard, I pull him deep and let him hit the back of my throat as I relax my muscles.

"Fuck. I'm gonna come."

I pump him with my hand and feel his hot release shoot into my mouth, swallowing and feeling even more powerful in this moment than I did when I stormed into this office. His legs tense under me and his throaty grunts cause me to suck harder, pulling every bit out of him. He loosens his grip on my hair and gently brushes it out of my face.

"Holy fucking shit."

I sit back on my heels and smile at my minor victory. He's still desperately hard and I want to do it again, and again. Making him come apart with my mouth has been one of the hottest things I've ever done. Plus, he tastes good. Really good. I glance up into his eyes as his breathing steadies, his chest pulling at the buttons on his dress shirt.

"I'm not sure what's sexier, you yelling at me *or* you groveling," he says through a grin that's as infectious as it is adorable. I smile and bite my lip as my phone beeps in my pocket. I quickly slip it out.

Juls: I came. Did you? Time to go, sweets.

"Thanks for lunch," I say playfully, his smile still on his face as he resituates himself and stands, offering me his hand. I place mine in his and stand on my wobbly legs. *Holy crap, I felt like I just came.*

"That was incredible." He presses his lips against mine softly, lingering for a moment as my phone beeps again.

"Shit. Sorry, I have a bakery to run. Later, handsome." I pull away from him and turn to see him shaking his head. "Oh, by the way, I'd like my panties back." I keep my hand on the doorknob while waiting for his response.

"Would you?" His voice is thick and causes me to clamp my thighs together. My urge to throw him back onto his desk and ride him is stronger than ever.

I nod and regain my composer. "Yes, I would. That pair happened to be a favorite of mine."

He runs a hand through his hair as he smoothes out his tie with the other. "Too bad, they're also a favorite of mine." He arches his brow and I grip the doorknob tighter. *Holy fuck.* "I suppose I could get you another pair. Although, I'm not accustomed to perusing lingerie shops, and I might get the wrong ones. Maybe you should go with me."

Oh, man. The thought of Reese buying me panties is unbelievably hot. I can picture him, walking around and studying each pair with his curious stare, his hands raking through his hair when he can't find the ones he's looking for. I smile at the image, but quickly shake it off. I shouldn't seem too affected by this guy. "I'm sorry, aren't I standing in the office of a CPA? You're a partner right?" He nods, crossing his arms over his chest as he watches me. "Then a smart guy like you, who I'm assuming didn't fuck his way to the top, shouldn't have a problem finding them on his own. Unless, you *did* fuck your way to the top?" I cock an eyebrow and grin as he shakes his head, trying desperately to hold back his smile. "You can send them by way of your flour delivery boy." His grin bursts through as I quickly exit his office, my cheeks burning from my flushed state.

"WELL?" JULS ASKS AS WE make our way back to the bakery.

"Well nothing. He's not married, apparently." I keep a straight face, but feel like I'm radiating from the inside out. Giving Reese a lunchtime blow job has made my week, and I can't get his reaction to it out of my head. His widened eyes as I pulled him out. His face when he came. The feel of his hands in my hair. I shake my head and snap out of my stupor.

She laughs. "I don't know who you think you're talking to here. But I'm your best friend, Dylan, and I know that face. You like him."

"I'm sorry, did you get the sense fucked out of you back there? I do not like him. He was my wedding hook up."

"First of all, yes, I did get the sense fucked out of me as I always do with Ian. The man is an Adonis."

"TMI," I chuckle.

"And secondly, you *totally* like him; otherwise, you wouldn't have cared if he was married or not."

I shake my head. "Please. The only reason why I cared was because the idea of sleeping with a married man was eating away at me. Now, that feeling of shame is gone."

She pulls up in front of the shop and puts her Escalade in park. "And now that feeling of shame has been replaced with love?"

I bark out a laugh and open the door. "I'm afraid you're mistaken. We still on for drinks tomorrow night?"

"Hell, yes. Give JoJo kisses for me."

I wave to her before stepping into the shop, spotting Joey pacing behind the counter.

His hands are continually tugging at the ends of his hair and he looks thoroughly stressed and irritated. Turning toward the sound of me entering, he drops his hands dramatically. "For fuck's sake. I have been dying here while you two whores played castrate the adulterer. What happened?"

I walk behind the counter to join him and down my now completely cold coffee. "Calm down, you queen. We didn't castrate anybody."

He raises a brow suspiciously. "Well, why the hell not? Wasn't that the whole point of storming over there?"

I'm about to answer when the shop door opens. Joey straightens up and sharply turns toward the door. "We're closed," he barks at the customer as I fold over in laughter.

"Joey." I nudge him and he smiles. "He's just kidding, sir, how can I help you?"

The gray-haired man smiles and moves up to the counter. "Good afternoon. Do you have any tarts? I love tarts and haven't had one in years." He eyes up my display case and taps lightly on the glass with his hands.

"I'm a bit of a tart, sugar," Joey says in his overly flirtatious voice.

"Good Lord. No, sir, I'm sorry, I don't make tarts. Although, maybe I will. What kind do you like?"

He smiles sweetly as his eyes light up. "Oh, all kinds. Strawberry, blueberry, kiwi, they're all delicious."

I giggle at his enthusiasm and pull out a notepad, scribbling down a reminder. "I'll tell you what; I will personally make some tarts and have them in the shop ready for you by the end of the week. How does that sound?"

"That's perfect. Thanks, sugar. I'll stop in sometime on Friday." He winks at me before turning and leaving the shop, the door dinging closed behind him.

Joey shakes his head at me. "Do you have to be so accommodating all the time? We do enough special requests as it is."

I place my notepad on the counter and put my hand on my hip. "Hey, special requests are what make Dylan's Sweet Tooth different from all the other bakeries around here. You can't just walk into Crumbs Galore on Main Street and ask for something they don't make. I like being approachable and accommodating. It gives me an edge." He rolls his eyes but smiles at me, knowing I'm one hundred percent right. Word of mouth about how customers can pretty much request anything in my shop has gotten me a ton of business over the past three years. I shrug and continue, "Now, would you like to talk about how awesome we are compared to our competition, or would you like to talk about how Reese *isn't* married?"

His eyes widen and he stumbles. "Isn't? As in he's single? As in you can continue to fuck him?"

My eyes rake through the display case and I straighten up.

"Hmmm, hold on. We need more black bottoms." I move toward the doorway that leads back to the kitchen when Joey grabs me by the shoulders.

"Fuck the fucking black bottoms. You owe me at least an hour of uninterrupted gossip." His face is red and his eyes are bugging out at me.

"And I'll tell you every juicy detail, after I grab a tray of black bottoms." He lets out a string of curse words and allows me to step in to the back.

I honor what I promised and spare no detail with Joey as I place the cupcakes into the display case. He stands back, completely enthralled by my rundown of my lunchtime office visit. I tell him about how I caught Juls being nailed by Ian on his desk, and about how she had mistaken Reese for Trent. I mention how Reese thought my angry tirade was sexy, and how I was going to yell at him again, but opted for a blow job instead to properly apologize for my face slap. And I wrap up with his words to me when he apologized for his freak out behavior at the wedding.

"He said he's not used to sex getting to him like that? What the hell does that even mean?" Joey asks as he wipes down the glass of the display case.

I shrug and nibble on a muffin. "I don't know. I was hoping you had some words of wisdom. It's not like I'm an expert on this shit or anything."

He silently thinks for a minute, his hand holding his rag still on the glass. "Maybe he means that *you* got to him. Like he was only going into it as just being what it was, slutty wedding sex, a one-time hook up, a sexy romp with a bridesmaid—"

"I wasn't a bridesmaid," I interject and his hand comes up to silence me.

"You know what I mean. He expected it to be a one and done deal, but what he wasn't expecting was *you*. Oh, my God, you're a game changer. He wants more than just slutty wedding sex."

Going through the motions of rolling my eyes, I stop. *Is that what Reese meant? Did I affect him to the point of freak out? Is that even a good thing? No. There's no way.* I shake my head.

"I think you and Juls are still drunk from the wedding. That guy is way too hot for me. Yes, I managed to somehow seduce him after he had *several* drinks I'm sure, but in normal daily life where alcohol isn't free flowing and I'm usually covered in pastry flour and icing, he is way the hell out of my league." I finish off my muffin and toss the wrapper in the trashcan. "Besides, he told me he hasn't had a girlfriend since college, which I'm sure is by choice. Look at him."

Joey walks around the counter, grabs my hand, and kisses the back of it. "Yeah, he does have that whole unattainable bachelor vibe going on. And I'm sure he gets a lot of ass, but right now, he wants *your* ass." He arches his brow playfully. "For the record, I happen to like you covered in pastry flour. And you are *just* as hot as he is."

I smile sweetly at him as he drops my hand and gets back to cleaning. My two closest friends are crazy, rightly out of their minds, and between the two of them, I'm sure my wedding to Reese will be planned within the next month.

I SLEEP FOR SHIT THAT night. Images of Reese's orgasmic face keep entering my thoughts, while I try to focus on anything but him. It's a useless act. No matter what thoughts enter my mind, whether it's searching my brain for what exactly is in a tart, or the anniversary cake consultation I have Tuesday morning, his beautiful face pops in uninvited. Tossing in my bed and now completely drenched in sweat, I sit up and glance at my alarm clock. Three fifteen a.m. *Jesus, I have to be up in less than two hours for my run and haven't slept a wink.* I slam back on my pillow. *This can't happen. I cannot let some hook up affect me like this. I'm never going to get a good night's sleep. You can forget about my morning runs with Joey and functioning properly in the shop. I'll lose my business and everything I've worked so hard for. No. Fuck this.* Hopping out of bed, I throw myself into a freezing cold shower and jolt myself even more awake. Sleep is for the weak. There's no way I'm getting any tonight, so I might as well bake. After dressing, I grab my phone and descend the stairs two at a time.

I know exactly what I'm going to make. It's what I always make when I can't sleep or need a distraction. My mocha cupcakes with espresso butter cream frosting. The perfect combination of caffeine and chocolate, both of which I could consume in massive quantities right now. I open my tattered recipe book and thumb through it until I stop on the familiar handwriting. It's a recipe of my grandmother's that she used to make when I was a little girl, stumbling clumsily around her kitchen as she baked all day long. She made them weekly and always let me help her, my big brown eyes watching her with complete awe as she cracked her eggs with one hand and never needed a measuring spoon because "A real cook will always trust her taste buds over anything else." My mother hated when she would make this recipe with me because I would consume them in mass quantities and be on an insane sugar and caffeine high for hours. My crash would be swift and hard, usually resulting in me passing out in the middle of the living room floor. I always think of my grandmother when I make these. She passed away ten years ago and it makes me sad to think she will never get to see her influence on me now. After pulling together all of my ingredients and starting the coffee maker, I create a group text message with Juls and Joey.

> *Me: Just so you are both aware, it's 3:30 a.m. and I am making my mocha cupcakes. Yes, you read that correctly and yes, it's because I haven't slept at all. Don't bother asking me to go for a run, Joey. That ship has sailed.*

Once the coffee is brewed, I mix in the espresso powder and set it aside to cool while I whip up the remaining ingredients. The smell alone perks me up a bit and I'm not feeling like a completely pathetic, sleep-deprived loser anymore. This is what I know. Baking. I'm good at it and I can practically do it in my sleep. Which I guess right now is ironic considering my current zombie-like state. My mind begins to drift as I whip the batter, watching the electric beaters mix the eggs and sugars. *I wonder if Reese likes mocha cupcakes? Or maybe he's a cookie guy. Shit.* I turn the mixer off and put my bowl onto the counter as I rub my eyes. *Focus, Dylan. You could lose a fucking finger.* I combine the egg mixture with my batter and whip it quickly before dividing the batter evenly into my cupcake liners.

After I shove the trays into the oven, I get to work on the icing.

The icing is made of espresso powder, vanilla, butter, and powdered sugar. It's ridiculously sweet, and one of my favorites. I could live off this stuff if I had to. Because really, is there anything better than icing? *Sex with Reese, his lips, his hands touching me, his sounds...*

"UGH," I yell, slamming my hands down onto the cool counter. This is insane. What the fuck is wrong with me? I've never been this affected by a guy before. I was with Justin for two years and could go days without talking to or seeing him and not even miss the asshole. Which I guess in hindsight should have been a dead giveaway. I mean, shouldn't you want to see your significant other nonstop? But I didn't, and that was at least a relationship. This, whatever it is that Reese and I are doing, or were doing and I may be completely crazy to assume we will continue doing it. This is not serious. And I need to get my shit together and stop acting like it is. I pull the cupcakes out of the oven and lay them on the counter to cool while I test the icing.

"Mmmm. Perfect." I'm half tempted to say fuck the cupcakes and grab a spoon and retreat back upstairs with my bowl. But I yawn instead. And yawn again. Glancing at my phone, the blurred numbers read four twenty-seven a.m. as my eyelids refuse to stay open. With a third yawn, I pull up a stool and prop my head on my fist as I sit and wait for the cupcakes to cool. Then I can ice them and get ready for my day. Yup. That's exactly what I'm going to do. I don't need sleep. Because with sleep came dreams of Reese, and I don't need that. My eyelids fall shut and my breathing steadies. Nope, definitely don't need sleep. Or Reese.

Chapter Five

"CUPCAKE, I THINK YOU NEED to wake up now."

My eyes slowly flutter open and the bright sunlight beaming through my window makes me close them tight again. "Shit." I roll over and cover my head with my pillow, hearing Joey's soft giggle.

"Seriously, Dylan, you're going to sleep the day away if you don't get up."

Sleep the day away? I push back onto my shins to look at the clock.

"It's three thirty? In the afternoon? Fuck." I shoot out of bed and run into the bathroom. "Joey, why the hell did you let me sleep this late? And how did I even get up here?" He follows me into the bathroom and leans against the door as I brush my teeth and unruly hair.

"First of all, I came in this morning to find you passed out face down on the workbench. So, being the nice guy that I am, I carried you up here and put you to bed."

I splash my face with cold water and dry it with a towel, turning to smile at him. "Oh, God. I bet I was a sight." He shrugs and steps aside as I walk into the bedroom and begin getting dressed.

"And secondly, I've been trying to wake you for the past four hours."

I roll my eyes at his statement. Of course, he's been trying to wake me up and I've slept through it. What the hell don't I sleep through besides my alarm? I slip on my jeans and a black tank top before I walk out from behind the partition. "Four hours? Jesus. Oh, shit." My stomach drops. "I missed my consultation."

He smiles sweetly at me and I want to punch him. *What is he, mental? That's money lost.* "Relax, I took care of it. Mrs. Frey was more than happy to meet with me since you were suffering from a stomach bug. You're welcome."

"I love you. You know that, right?"

He wraps me up into a big hug and kisses the top of my head. "You better. Come on, I have something to show you."

I follow him down the stairs and into the bakery. Everything is in perfect order, which I knew it would be. Joey is more than capable of handling shit while I sleep my life away. "God, I'm starving. I feel like I haven't eaten in days. Ooohhh, and you iced the mocha cupcakes." I pull a blueberry muffin out from the almost bare display case and begin nibbling on it while spacing out the remaining treats. Joey emerges from the back carrying a familiar looking white box. *Oh, God.*

"Of course I iced them. And they have been selling like crazy too, along with everything else today. We've been slammed." He places the box on the counter in front of me and I swallow loudly. "But who gives a shit about cupcakes or anything edible right now. You have no idea how hard it has been to not open this." He pushes it closer to me. "Now get to it."

My heart begins beating so hard in my chest I think for sure it will crack my sternum. "Maybe later." I push it away from me easily. *Hmm. Definitely not flour.*

"Fuck that noise. Since you aren't going to freely tell me why you couldn't get any sleep last night, which I'm just going to assume was because a certain someone was on your mind, you *will* open this right now." He pushes it back in front of me and pulls the ribbon.

"Same delivery guy?" I ask and he nods. Not that I really had any doubt. Placing my half-eaten muffin down, I open the box, grabbing the brown card that is lying on top of the tissue.

"Read it out loud," he squawks.

"No. What if he's confessing to a murder? I would hate for you to be an accessory." Joey mumbles something under his breath as I unfold the note and step back, giving myself the illusion of privacy.

Dylan,

Next time I go to Agent Provocateur to replace something of yours, you will be accompanying me.

X Reese

"Fuck me." I throw the card at Joey and riffle through the tissue paper, slowly pulling out the pair of purple lacy panties with the tiny ribbons on the sides.

He slams his hand down on the counter. "Jesus Fucking Christ. He bought you panties?"

"Yeah. I mean, he took the ones from the wedding and I jokingly told him he had to buy me a replacement pair." I stare at the panties, my face instantly heating up at the realization that Reese actually went lingerie shopping for me. *Christ, this is seriously hot.* "I was totally kidding though."

Joey re-reads the note several times before he turns to me, fanning his face with the card. "This has to be the hottest note I've ever read. Like, I could seriously have an orgasm from reading this." His mouth drops open and he steps closer to me, admiring the panties in my hand. "Wait a minute. What do you mean he kept your panties from the wedding? You went home without panties?"

I snatch the note back and slip it into my pocket. "Oh, hold off on the judgment please. Like you haven't gone without your delicates before." He looks toward the ceiling for a memory and smiles as I laugh at him. "Shit, Joey. How hot is this?"

"Wickedly hot. Sweet Lord, you need to fuck him again and

fast before I drug him and drag him over to my side."

I laugh until my side hurts and am only interrupted when the shop phone rings.

"Dylan's Sweet Tooth." I giggle into the phone as Joey studies my panties like a weirdo. "Give those back, you perv," I whisper away from the phone.

"Dylan?"

My back straightens and I almost drop the phone. *I know that voice.* Clearing my throat and pretending I don't, I answer after a beat. "Yes, this is Dylan."

"It's Reese."

"Oh, hi." I swat at Joey to get his attention and mouth *it's him*. He drops my panties on the counter and quickly snatches the phone away from me. *What? No!*

"Reese. You *stud* you. My girl is dying for you to impregnate her."

"GIVE ME THE PHONE."

He grins and nods as I jump up and try to snatch it. *Damn it to hell, he's tall.* "Yup. She just opened your package. Speaking of packages, just how big *is* your dick? As memorable as she says?" *I am going to kill him. Slowly.*

Grabbing the phone out of his hand, I punch him as hard as I can in his shoulder as he laughs at me. "Asshole. Shit, my hand. You're fucking dead, Holt." I shake my hand in the air and bring the phone up to my ear. "Hello?" I say through a wince of pain. *Oh, God. Please tell me he didn't hear any of that.*

"Hi, love. What's this about you wanting to carry my children?" I can hear the smile in his voice, obviously enjoying himself immensely. I, on the other hand, want to hurl myself into traffic.

"Sorry. Joey drinks." *This is mortifying.* "Can I help you with something?"

"Is your hand okay?"

A customer walks through the door and Joey gets to work helping her. After flipping him off, I watch him giggle at me as I slip into the back for some much needed privacy. "Yes, it's fine, I think." Making a fist to stretch it out, I smile at my next move. *He sends me a naughty note; he's going to get naughty Dylan.* "How's *your* hand?"

"My hand? And why would something be wrong with my hand, sweet Dylan?"

I sigh. *Sweet Dylan. Lord, help me, this guy is smooth.* "Well, I just assumed you jerked off repeatedly at the image of me in each and every item in that store today. In fact, I'm counting on it." The sound of coughing comes through the phone and I chuckle. "So tell me, why exactly would I accompany you to Agent Provocateur? I'm there enough as it is."

After a brief moment of just his breathing in my ear, which is making the hair on my neck stand up, he speaks. "Do you own any garters?" His voice is low and taut. *Christ, he sounds seductive, even at work.*

I can feel my pulse hammering in my neck as I bite my bottom lip. "Maybe, why?"

"Wear one tonight."

Tonight? I'm going out for drinks with Joey and Juls tonight. Of course, where Juls goes, Ian goes. And Ian must have told Reese. I suddenly can't wait for drinks.

"You know those cost a pretty penny, don't you? I would hate to lose such an expensive item of clothing when you decide to steal it." Even though I wouldn't mind it entirely. He can confiscate every article of clothing I have for all I care.

"Who said anything about you taking it off?"

I grip the workbench and close my eyes, suddenly feeling like I could combust.

"Reese."

"Dylan."

I glance down at my shirt, my aroused nipples highly visible now. I moan softly into the phone before I answer in a whisper, "I'm so wet right now."

A loud crack rings through the receiver and I know he's dropped it. *Ah, sweet victory.*

"Are you serious?" he murmurs and I chuckle at his response. "Shit. You can't tell me that when I'm stuck at work."

I run my hand up and around my neck, feeling the clamminess of my skin. "Well, I am. That voice of yours does that to me."

Joey pops his head through the doorway and I immediately freeze. "Cupcake, we need more éclairs."

I nod quickly, eyes wide as Joey's grin gets bigger. "I guess I'll see you later then?" I ask, moving toward the pastry rack. I know my face is beet red, and I feel like I've just been caught masturbating. Shit, I practically was.

He breathes heavily into the phone. "I'm counting on it." The call ends, allowing me to grab the container of éclairs with both hands after I place the phone down on the worktop.

Turning quickly, I see Joey watching me, arms crossed. "You look all hot and bothered," he says slyly through his smile.

"I am. And I'm not sure how I feel about it either."

Pushing past him, I walk to the display case and fill the tray of pastries. He leans against the doorframe. "What does that mean? He wants you, obviously; you want him, again, obviously, so what's the problem here?"

I close the case. "No problem. This is just sex. Really fucking good sex. So, no problem." I brush past him and shake my head, silently communicating this conversation is over. Because this *is* just sex. And even though I've always been a relationship kind of girl, I am more than capable of handling hot casual sex. *Right?*

JOEY AND I ARRIVED AT The Tavern at eight thirty p.m. after I spent over an hour debating what to wear. I've settled on my cream summer dress that hugs my curves in the most sinfully way possible. It bunches in the front, accentuating my cleavage, and falls just above my knees. Paired with my matching heels, and feeling my garter cling to my thighs, I feel secretly sexy. My hands shake as we step through the door, Joey leading the way through the packed bar. I have no idea why I'm so nervous. I've already had sex with the guy. And now I know for sure he enjoyed it as much as I did and doesn't regret it. But for some reason, my heart is pounding in my ears and my stomach is clenched tight. *Come on, Dylan. You can do this. He wants you and you sure as hell want him.*

I follow Joey to the bar where Juls is perched on a stool, messing with her phone. With no members of the Chicago man candy club in sight, I breathe a sigh of relief.

"Finally. Holy hell, Dylan. That dress. Shit, that might actually kill him." She grins wickedly and runs her eyes down my body.

I twirl quickly as Joey whistles. "You bitches annoy me with your hot little figures," he grumbles, motioning for the bartender.

"Joey is buying because he's a shithead who steals phones out of people's hands," I say as Juls hops down from her stool.

"Excellent. I love it when Joey is a shithead. White Zinfandel for me, JoJo."

He glares at her and then at me.

"Don't you dare look at me like that. Telling Reese I wanted to have his babies. You're lucky I'm only making you buy us drinks." I cock my head to the side and stare him down.

"Ha! Oh, my God. You would have the prettiest babies," Juls squeals.

"I know, right?" he echoes.

I roll my eyes. "You're both mental."

Juls grabs my hand and tugs me through the crowd, stopping at an empty tall table. My eyes scan the room as I settle on my stool. I quickly tap my fingers on the table and bite the inside of my cheek.

"You're nervous," she states as my eyes meet hers across the table.

"I don't know, maybe this is a bad idea."

She arches her brow at me.

"I feel like I'm trying too hard. I mean, I'm wearing a fucking garter under this for Christ's sake."

"So am I. High-five, sweets." I can't help but giggle at her naughty enthusiasm as I humor her and slap her hand. Of course, Juls is wearing a garter. Between the two of us, I'm sure we've accumulated one of every item in Agent Provocateur.

Joey returns moments later with our drinks. "Well, in case Billy is a no show, Ty the bartender is available for my licking."

I grab my drink and take a sip as Juls snickers. "What *is* going on with Billy? Have you spoken to him since the wedding?" I ask.

He takes a sip of his beer before answering. "He's texted me a few times. You know me though, always gotta have one waiting for me in the wings." He's being evasive. Joey is never evasive.

"I love how you think *that* answer is going to satisfy us. And since when are you tight lipped about your hook ups?" I say as Juls nods in agreement.

"Seriously, JoJo, who the hell do you think you're talking to here? I happen to know from a very well hung, reliable source that you and Billy saw each other last night. And pretty much every night since the wedding."

"Ian told you that? Christ, he is whipped. Your pussy must be like some fucking nirvana or some shit."

My mouth drops open as Juls smiles and shrugs playfully. "Oh, is that right? I thought you weren't sure how you felt about him and his curved penis?"

He looks quickly around the room and takes a sip of his beer. "It's growing on me."

"I bet it is, on you *and* in you," Juls barks and we fall into a fit of giggles as her phone lights up. "Ooohhh, they're here," she squeals excitedly.

My back goes rigid and my pulse begins to race. As if my body is somehow wired to his, I look up at the doorway just as he walks through behind Ian. I listen to my heavy breathing as he moves like liquid through the crowd of people. Eyes dark and hooded in the amber glow of the bar, hair perfectly messed up, making my fingers ache to touch. And that sexy as hell mouth that is glistening as if he just licked it. *Good God, he is glorious to look at.* Needing the liquid courage, I down my drink and earn myself a wide-eyed look from Joey as the men walk toward our table.

"Hey, babe," Juls says as Ian wraps his arms around her back. He smothers her in quick kisses as she moans softly against him.

"Dylan, Joey, it's nice to see you both," Ian says.

I raise my glass at him as Joey does the same, my eyes locking on to Reese. He walks around the table, his gaze never leaving mine as he comes and stands next to my stool.

"Hi." His voice is low and soft as his hand rests on my lower back, claiming me in front of everyone. *Yes, that's right. I'm with him. Move along, ladies.*

"Hi, yourself." I turn my body and cross one leg over the other, the hem of my dress rising up on my thigh and quickly catching his attention. I admire him while he admires my legs. He's looking as hot as ever in a dress shirt and tie, which is partially loosened, and regarding me sweetly, with soft eyes and parted lips.

"You look..." he runs a hand through his hair and I smile, his eyes slowly scanning my body. "...I like your dress. A lot."

"Thanks. Wait till you see what's under it."

Stepping closer to me so his leg is brushing against mine, he slowly trails his hand up my thigh under the table and stops at the metal clips of my garter. His neck pulses as he swallows and slides his hand back out, pulling down my dress.

"Per your request," I say as his lip curls up in the corner.

"So, Dylan, how's the bakery business going? That wedding cake you made was really fucking good, right, Joey? Didn't you have like six pieces?" Ian says as he steals Juls' stool before pulling her into his lap. She runs her fingers along his collar, blissfully oblivious to anyone but him.

"Whatever. I burned it off later with Billy."

"Well, I'm glad you guys got to enjoy the cake since I didn't. I was a bit preoccupied with my own drama." My eyes quickly flick to Reese who is watching me, studying me with a small smile. I give him a quick wink before I turn back to Ian. "But yeah, business is good. Busy as we usually are in the summer. I think I have a wedding every weekend to bake for until September."

"Yeah, we're crazy busy. And when she's not whipping up wedding cakes, she's floating on cloud nine all over that damn shop from the love notes and deliveries she's been receiving." Joey sighs dramatically as I tense in my seat. "It's all very romantic."

Reese's hand moves on my back, his thumb rubbing the material of my dress.

I quickly shove my chatty friend and spill some of his beer on the table. "Remind me why I hired you as my assistant?"

"Because I'm gorgeous and can sell anything to anyone," he replies playfully.

"Please, you say that like my treats don't sell themselves." I twirl my ice in my glass. "If anything, you're more of a liability to have around. Just how many sexual harassment suits are pending against you this month?" Not that he really has any, but it wouldn't surprise me with the way Joey flirts daily with customers. He rolls his eyes as Juls giggles against Ian.

"Jesus Christ. You two fight like you're married," Billy says as he approaches the table with three beers, passing two of them to Ian and Reese.

"We practically are, and before you ask, I'm the man in the relationship," I reply, sucking on an ice cube before dropping it back into my glass. Reese laughs quietly next to me and I glance up at him, meeting his stare.

"Baby, do you hear what I have to put up with daily? Tell Dylan to be nice to me." Joey strokes Billy's arm, and I see my opportunity.

"Hey, Joey, would you like me to get you anything from the bar? Another beer, some food, your balls maybe?" Juls slams her hand down on the table and laughs as Billy's face lights up. Ian and Reese both chuckle as Joey glares at me.

"Bitch," he murmurs.

"Anyway," Billy stretches out before his eyes flash to Reese and then quickly to mine. "Reese tells me you thought he was married. That's probably the funniest thing I've heard all year."

"Fuck off," Reese mutters against his glass.

Billy chuckles and sweetly rubs Joey's arm. "Oh, come on. You? Tied down?" Billy's eyes shift from Reese to mine after I register Reese's slight head shake. "It was even funnier when we heard how you slapped the shit out of him for it."

"Shit yeah it was," Ian chimes in and kisses Juls quickly on the cheek. "I would've paid to see that." I shrug and glance up at Reese who seems to be thinking of something, his eyes staring off past the table.

"You should have seen how pissed she was in the shop. I actually thought she was going to return back to work with your balls in her purse," Joey directs toward Reese, and I shift in my chair, feeling his eyes on me as I slowly glance up and meet them.

"Well, I happen to be very fond of my testicles, so I'm glad that shit got cleared up." He looks around at everyone before dropping his eyes back to mine. Leaning in, he holds my neck with one hand and whispers into my hair, "Come home with me."

I shake my head slowly and smile, glancing quickly around the table. Joey and Billy are now in deep conversation as they both walk toward the bar together, and Juls is straddling Ian's lap. *Sweet Jesus, get a room is right.* My gaze goes back to Reese. His eyes narrow as he picks up my glass and slips an ice cube in his mouth, slowly sucking on it and making my skin tingle. I swallow loudly.

"Why not? I want to take you to bed, immediately."

I blink slowly, suddenly feeling drunk from his voice and the intensity behind it. "No beds," I say flatly, seeing his expression shift to curiosity. I explain myself. "Beds are intimate. And we're just having fun. Keeping it casual. Right?"

He studies me as he places my empty drink down. "Of course."

"Sex in beds leads to sleepovers, and I think it would be better for me if we didn't take it there." This has to be said. If I'm going to attempt to just have casual sex with Reese, I can't do anything that would lead to me getting attached. I'm already losing sleep over the man and we barely know each other.

"Are you telling me that I'm restricted to fucking you in public places only?"

"You say that like it's a bad thing."

"No, love, fucking you *anywhere* could never be a bad thing. I was just dead set on getting your hot little ass in my bed." His eyes burn into mine as his hand lightly trails down my shoulder.

I smooth his tie down as his fingers trickle down my arm. "I just think this is how it needs to be. Besides, I'm sure there are at least a handful of hard surfaces in here that you've already thought about throwing me up against."

His infectious laugh pulls me in and I join him. "Yes, you're right about that." His hand holds the side of my face and he leans in, brushing his lips softly against mine before pulling back an inch. "But I want to get you naked, and I'd prefer it if I did it without an audience. Are you opposed to fucking in vehicles?"

After swiping my tongue across my lip to taste him, I grab my purse and stand up. "Not at all. Lead the way, handsome."

We say our goodbyes to Juls and Ian who pay us little attention. They're practically having sex at the table now anyway and couldn't care less what we do. He grabs my hand and pulls me through the bar and out the door, leading me down the sidewalk and stopping in front of a vehicle that makes my jaw hit the pavement.

"Holy shit. You drive a Range Rover?" I ask as he pulls his keys out and hits the unlock button.

"Yes. Is that okay?"

"Don't these things cost like ninety grand?" My eyes rake over the car with amazement.

He laughs and opens the back door. "Something like that."

I squeal as I'm lifted off my feet and pushed into the back seat. Reese slides in behind me and closes the door. Pulling me into his lap, I straddle his waist as his hands slide down my sides and hold tightly on to my hips. His thumbs press against the front of my pelvis and I feel my core constrict.

"Are you sure I can't convince you to let me take you to my place? I want to slowly devour you, and I feel like this venue won't allow me to appreciate it as much."

I laugh against his mouth, slowly licking his bottom lip until he opens for me and tangles his tongue with mine. *Christ, I forgot how good he was at this. Just kissing.*

I somehow manage to break away for a second. "Mmm, devour me, huh?"

He nods, tilting my head up with his hand and kissing down my neck. My hem is hiked up with his other hand and his fingers graze my stockings where they meet my garter.

"Would you be able to devour me on a couch?"

He pulls back and I drop my head. "Couches aren't intimate?"

"No, not at all. And I want to be devoured on yours. Slowly." His forehead is resting against mine and we're both panting. I've given in easily to the idea of going home with him, really easily. But honestly, this man could convince me to do anything at this point. I'm fairly certain that if he asked me to commit a major felony with him, I would do it willingly and with the same fucking smile that I'm wearing now.

His eyes widen and he slides me off his lap. "Fuck yes. Let's go, love."

Chapter Six

STANDING IN AN ELEVATOR WITH Reese Carroll in a massive building full of luxurious condos is one of the most surreal moments of my life so far. I can't believe what I'm doing, or what I'm about to do with this man. Well, I mean, of course I knew going out tonight was going to lead to sex with him, but I had firmly decided on not leaving with him. I figured we would sneak off into the bathroom at The Tavern or into a dark and secluded corner to hump like rabbits. But here I am, riding the elevator of his building to the tenth floor with him watching me from across the small space. It's taking every ounce of self-control to not drop to my knees on this pristine marble floor and suck him off right here and now. I feel green eyes on me as I stare ahead at the numbers on the panel, loving the fact he hasn't stopped looking at me since we got out of his car.

"See something you like?" I ask playfully as he leans against the mirrored wall.

"Very. But why are you standing so far away from me? Afraid I might violate you before we even get to my couch?"

I swallow loudly. *Violate me? Yes, anytime.* The elevator pings and the doors open before I have a chance to answer.

We're barely in the door of his condo when it's kicked closed behind us and I'm being pinned against the wall. His mouth is hot and needy against mine, sucking and tasting every dip and corner as our tongues move together. I grip the back of his head and pull his tongue into my mouth and suck it slowly, drawing a long groan from his parted lips. His hands move over every inch of my back and down to the hem of my dress.

"Take it off," he orders as he grips my hips and moves backward, leading me out of the entryway and into a giant living room. My eyes widen at the sight of it.

"Whoa. Your place is really nice." I quickly glance all around me. We've stopped in front of a long black leather sofa that faces a fireplace, with a giant television mounted on the wall.

"Dylan, take the dress off."

I smile and look up at him from under my lashes, slowly turning around and gathering my hair over one shoulder. "Unzip me please." Startling a bit at the touch of his hands on my bare shoulders, he keeps one there while the other slowly pulls the metal zipper down my spine, stopping just above my backside.

"Thank you," I say softly as I stay facing away from him and pull my arms out of the sleeves, letting it drop to the floor and hearing a sharp inhale of breath from behind me. *And this is why garters were invented.* I smile without him knowing.

"Holy shit. Turn around." *Mmm, I like bossy Reese.*

Taking a little longer than he probably would have liked, I turn on my heels and step out of my dress, standing directly in front of him in my cream-colored lacy bra, matching panties and garter, and my sheer stockings. His chest is moving rapidly inside his shirt as he slowly trails down my body with his eyes, and even more slowly back up to my face. I see his Adam's apple roll in his throat.

"Be gentle," I whisper, and for a brief moment, something flashes in his eyes. Something I've been feeling and hope he can't see. *Is he nervous?*

"You're so fucking beautiful," he says. I melt on the spot. No man has ever called me beautiful before. Sexy, hot, and I even got "good enough to eat" one time. But never beautiful. *Shit, why did he have to say that?* He steps in to me and wraps his arm around my waist, pulling me against his chest as he slowly lowers me down onto the couch.

"Oh!" I yelp at the cold leather as it touches my bare skin.

Kneeling next to me on the floor, he grabs my one leg and hooks it over the back of the couch and brings the one closest to him up to rest over his shoulder. I begin to shake against him, knowing exactly what's coming. He trails light kisses up my inner thigh. "I've been dying to taste you again. It's all I've thought about." He moves to my other thigh and repeats the action, causing me to tremble. "You have me so fucking wound up here, Dylan. You *will* come in my mouth several times before I fuck you."

"Jesus, you keep talking like that and I'm gonna come before you touch me." My body arches toward his mouth as he laughs against my skin. I know he's right. I know he'll bring me multiple orgasms tonight because he's *that* good. His hot breath warms me against my panties and I moan, feeling his finger slide the thin, sheer material to the side ever so gently.

"Oh," I groan loudly.

His first lick is slow and lingering, ending with a sharp flick of my clit and causing an involuntary tremble of my body against his mouth. Throwing my hands over my head and digging into the arm rest, I look down my body and meet his eyes. His tongue licks in between every fold, and swirls around and inside of me.

"Oh, my God, you're so good at that." My chest is rising and falling rapidly as he works me. I've never had oral sex feel like this, not even close to this. A strong urge begins slowly building in my gut as he brushes hard against my clit and pulls it into his mouth, sucking relentlessly.

"Feel it, Dylan. Feel what I can do to you." Darting his tongue inside me and fucking me with it, my leg that is hooked over the couch begins to slip as I buck against him. His hand darts out and pushes it back over, leaving me wide open for him to expertly explore with his mouth.

"Oh, God," I cry out, tightening every muscle in my body.

Two fingers take the place of his tongue as he licks above his hand, giving extra attention to my swollen nub. He moves slowly, stretching me with his fingers as I begin rolling my hips against his face. My orgasm hits hard and fast, sending me spinning off into orbit as I scream his name and reach down to hold him right where I need him.

"Mmm," he moans against me and the vibration shoots up my body and hits every nerve. His fingers slow their torture as he continues licking me, bringing me down slowly, but not quite enough to ease the throbbing.

"Oh, God. Reese, please."

I know begging him to stop is of no use. Plus, do I really want him to stop? I've never had an orgasm from a guy's mouth on me before, and I know my next one isn't far behind. I moan loudly and bite my lip as he glides one hand up my body, massaging my breast as he licks between my legs.

"You taste amazing. I could do this for days, love."

I groan and arch away from the couch, his hands lifting my ass into the air. "Don't stop." My skin ignites and the fire that has been barely doused comes roaring back to life inside me. The only parts of my body touching the couch now are my shoulders and my head. Reese is supporting everything else as he moves his fingers quickly, slipping a third one inside and pushing with the perfect amount of pressure against my clit with his thumb. His mouth nibbles on the tender skin of my thigh and I cry out.

"Reese. Oh, my God."

"Give it to me, Dylan," he growls.

I come again and it's even deeper than my last one. The leg that was hung over the couch is now resting on his other shoulder and I grip my thighs tight against his head. He sucks on my clit and rides out my orgasm with me, finally allowing me to touch back down after my trembling stops. Slipping my legs off his shoulders, he places them gently on the couch, and this time, the cold leather feels welcoming on my now glistening skin.

"That was... that right there... was..." I have no words. No words have been invented to describe that. My breathing is so strained I can barely speak, even if I *did* have the words. I open my eyes and see him standing next to the couch, slowly pulling at his tie with his amused expression.

"Epic?"

I quickly swing my legs over the side and stand up, stumbling into his arms. "Jesus, you've rendered me crippled."

"Lie back down. I'm nowhere near done with you, love."

I slowly raise my eyes to his and lick my lips. "I figured, but I want to undress you."

He arches an eyebrow and licks my arousal off his lips as he holds his arms out to me. I step out of my heels and drop down a few inches, the top of my head now falling just below his nose. Reaching up slowly, I pull at his tie and slide it off from around his collar, dropping it at my feet.

"I've been dying to see you naked. It's all *I've* thought about," I say as my fingers begin working at the buttons on his dress shirt. "You're wearing way too many clothes for me." I'm fumbling nervously, the anticipation of getting his clothes off causing me to fidget a bit, but I don't care. I focus in on my task.

"Yeah, I know the feeling. You look incredible, but I can't wait to get you *out* of that."

I glance up at him from under my lashes and part my lips, seeing his eyes on my chest. I haven't thought about the fact that he hasn't seen me naked yet. I'm still wearing everything I had put on earlier underneath my dress. Bringing one hand behind my back, I quickly unhook my bra while the other stays firmly planted on his chest. I slowly slide it down my arms and let it drop to the floor, hearing a soft moan escape him. My heavy breasts bob freely and tingle in the anticipation of his body on them. He brings his hands up and rakes them through his hair. "Problem?" I ask, continuing the unbuttoning of his shirt.

He shakes his head, his eyes lingering on my chest. "No, no problem. Those could never be a problem."

I smile and push his shirt over his shoulders and down his arms, reaching quickly for the bottom of his T-shirt and pulling it over his head. *Holy shit.* My breathing picks up as I run my hands over the sharp outline of his chest and down to his abs, tracing the lines of his six-pack. *Or eight pack? Jesus.* Never have I ever seen or touched a body like this. He's hard and defined, but his skin is smooth and it tenses as I graze over every inch of it.

"You're so beautiful," I say softly, licking my lips as I begin tugging at his belt. A soft laugh causes me to look up.

"Can I please be something a little more manly? Beautiful should only be reserved for you." He brushes the back of his hands up my stomach and trails the underside of my breasts.

"Handsome then? Superbly handsome?" I smile up at him and he nods, the corner of his lips curling up.

His thumbs run over my erect nipples. *Fuck the slow touching. I need him now.* My fingers spring to life and I unbutton and unzip him quickly, pushing his pants and boxers down, and stagger back at the sight of his erection. *Yup, just as massive as I remember.* A crazy thought enters my mind as he pulls his shoes and socks off, stepping out of his pants. Not crazy, fucking insane. But before I can think where the hell this thought came from, my mouth opens.

"I'm not sleeping with anybody else," I say quickly, my eyes running over his naked body. His waist is narrow, the prominent V staring me right in the face. Long muscular legs run on for miles. Even his feet are perfect. *Jesus, his body is deadly.* I glance up at him and see his expression. He's watching me, studying me. "I just, I know this is just sex and nothing else, but I'm not going to be sleeping with anyone but you." I'm talking so fast, I'm unsure if he's catching any of what I'm saying. *Where the fuck is this coming from?* "I want to be monogamously casual, or casually monogamous. Fuck, is that even a saying? I don't know. We don't have to be. I mean, if you want to sleep with other women, then that's fine. But if you don't—"

"Dylan."

"I'm sorry." I cover my face and feel completely mortified, but I don't stop. It's like word vomit at this point. "It's just, I want to feel you. Just you. I've never done it without a condom before and I'm clean. I've only been with one other guy, and we always used protection. And I've been on birth control for years." *Fucking hell, I'm an idiot.* "Christ, never mind. Forget I said anything. I'll go grab a condom out of my purse." I drop my hands and turn to walk toward the entryway where I dropped my purse in the heat of passion. His hand grips my wrist and stops me.

"Why are you so nervous all of a sudden? We've already had sex and you've had two orgasms tonight already. You should be completely relaxed with me."

I look anywhere but his face. Yearning to touch his chest, his broad shoulders, and his cut arms. I feel his hand on my chin as he lifts it to meet his eyes. "I don't know, you're naked." I motion to the wonder that stands before me. His tight body is definitely making my brain scramble. "I'm having trouble thinking straight."

He muffles his laugh. "Relax. I *was* sleeping with someone else up until the wedding, but I ended it. It wasn't serious anyway. I don't usually do serious." *Okay, that made sense.* "I think monogamously casual is a saying, and if that's what you want to be, then that's what we'll be." He pauses and I step closer to him, granting him access to my body. He snakes his arms around my waist and holds me against him, skin to skin. The sensation warms me instantly. "And I've always used condoms. Always. If this is what you want and you're sure—"

I brush my lips lightly against his, cutting him off mid-sentence. "It can't just be what I want. If you don't—"

"Dylan, of course I want it too. Do you think I haven't thought about it?" His hand comes up and strokes my cheek as I trace the outline of his chest. His face is completely serious, and I'm suddenly grateful for my extreme case of verbal diarrhea.

"Okay." I step back out of his arms and hook my fingers into my panties. I watch him watch me slowly pull them down my legs and step out of them, leaving me standing in only my garter and stockings. If it's even possible, he gets harder. My eyes bulge in my head as he sits down on the couch, pulling me toward him. *Oh, God, he wants me on top?* I slowly, almost hesitantly straddle his waist as he watches me, his eyes never leaving mine. I brace myself on my knees. "Umm, I'm not used to doing it this way. I don't really know if I'll be good at it like this."

The corner of his mouth twitches. "You can't be bad at it, love." His big hands cup my breasts and begin to slowly knead them, my nipples scratching against his rough palms. Moving closer and relaxing down a bit, I gasp when he brushes up against me, rubbing me in the most perfect way imaginable. He moans softly. "See, whatever feels good for you will sure as hell feel good for me."

"Oh. Oh, wow," I groan as I move against him, up and down in my wetness as his hands slide down my sides and grip my hips. He controls my movements, not allowing me to speed up when I want to or hover over him to allow him to penetrate me. I grip his head between my hands and lock eyes with him as my body responds to his.

"Reese, I need you."

"Mmmm, I love it when you say that." He closes his eyes tightly, a low growl emanating from his throat before he opens them again. "Fuck, you feel incredible against me. Can you come this way?" He slowly trails kisses along my jaw.

I know I can. This feels almost as amazing as his mouth on me. He is unbelievably hard and I'm completely drenched. Plus, at this angle, our faces are inches apart and I can see just how much he's enjoying this. Soft deep groans escape his slightly parted lips and his forehead is glistening with sweat.

I groan before I answer. "Yes, but I want you in me. Please, please let me fuck you."

He moves in and pulls my bottom lip into his mouth, urgently swiping his tongue against mine. He tastes like me, like my orgasm, and it's surprisingly hot. I moan and put everything I have into this kiss. I can't get enough. His mouth can please every inch of my body, and I want to surrender to him completely. *Shit, at this rate, I should just sign the rights to my body over to him now and be done with it.* No other man will ever make me feel like this. My thighs shake against his and I move quicker, gliding up and down against his length, which is now soaked from me. My hands grip his head, tangling in his hair as my body begins to pulse against his.

"Please, I need you."

As his one hand holds my hip tightly, his fingers digging into my skin, he positions himself under me and drives his hips up and into mine. We cry out together. He's so deep in me this way, deeper than anything I have ever felt. "Reese." I go to rock forward on him when his grip on me tightens.

"Shit, don't move." He closes his eyes and drops his head back onto the couch. I stare wide-eyed as his Adam's apple rolls in his neck, the veins along the sides pulsing against his skin.

Oh, crap. What happened? "Is it okay? I mean, does it feel okay?" I'm suddenly wondering if I'm completely screwing this up and way the hell out of my element. But it's a justified question. I really have no idea what I'm doing here.

He tilts his head up and looks at me curiously, brushing my hair behind my ear. "Is it okay? I'm struggling to not blow my load in you right now and you're not even moving." My eyes widen and I can't contain my smile. *I'm making him lose it. Yes!* "Just give me a minute."

"Okay, take your time." I'm completely giddy as he resumes his position, closing his eyes and leaning his head back. I stay perfectly still on top of him, my hands slowly trailing down his neck to his shoulders. Molding my hands against him, I take this opportunity to feel his every muscle. I run my palms down his arms and back up again, softly massaging his biceps and triceps. Skating down his chest, I trace the lines of his abdominals, which are clenched tight and seem to firm up even more from my touch.

"That feels really good," he says as he lifts his head and watches me.

"What? You in me or my hands on you?" I keep my eyes on him as I rub him, wanting to feel every inch of his skin underneath my hands. It feels amazing, touching him like this, feeling his body react to mine and seeing him relax from my contact.

His hand comes up to my face and he strokes along my jaw. "Both," he replies, his green eyes burning into mine.

I wink at him as my fingers trail up his sides and back to his chest. "What does it feel like?"

"Being in you like this?" I nod and he continues. "Warm and really soft." His eyes drop down between us and he stares at me. There. I swallow loudly. "It feels like I fit in you perfectly. Nothing has ever felt like this, for me anyway. Have you ever felt like this before?"

I stare at him, unable to blink as he studies my face. *What did he mean by that? Was he just referring to the sex? Or did he mean just being with me? The two of us together? Shit.* His question is fucking with my head. *I've sure as hell never felt anything like this, in both ways. I'm drawn to this man. The undeniable tangible pull between us is electric. But I'm sure it's one-sided. He's just referring to the sex.*

"Never. Can I move now, please? I'm dying here." I've never been on top during sex and suddenly have a strong overpowering desire to do it and do it well.

"Please," he answers as he keeps one hand on my hip, digging into my skin.

Gripping onto his shoulders, I rock my hips forward against him, moaning loudly as he slides out of my wetness. I push back and continue riding him, back and forth, up and down, bringing him almost completely out of me before taking him back in.

"Holy shit. Just like that, love." He clenches his teeth and rocks into me as I drive against him, pushing himself deeper and deeper with each move. One hand teases and massages my breast while the other holds my side. "Jesus, you feel incredible. So fucking good, Dylan." He keeps his eyes on me as he leans in and pulls my nipple into his mouth. I throw my head back and scream his name as the fever begins to spread throughout my body. He sucks and bites me as I still my movements, arching my back to give him full access to my breasts. I look down and meet his eyes as his mouth stays latched around me, pulling my nipple into his mouth and flicking it with his tongue.

"I love your mouth."

A small smile pulls at his lips as he moves to the side of my breast and sucks hard, leaving a very prominent red mark on my pale skin. His eyes study mine for approval.

"Do that again."

He licks over to my other breast that is now being teased with his fingers. Sucking on the skin just above my nipple, he pulls back after a few seconds and admires his work. I'm marked by him, where only his mouth has pleased me and it's the hottest thing I've ever seen. He's claiming my body and I'm willingly letting him have it. His hands move to my ass and he grips me tightly, picking up my pace.

"Yes. Oh, God. Oh, God." My stomach clenches and twists as my pussy aches. He slides one hand around my waist and down my stomach until his thumb is working my clit. My fingernails dig into the leather as he rubs me in the way that only he knows how. I'm pulsing, shaking against him. My climax is already on the brink before I crash down on top of him. The feel of him inside me with no barrier and now working me the way he's doing, pushes me quickly over the edge. I throw my head back and give in to the release. "Reese, I'm coming." His hand grabs my face and tilts it down, forcing me to look at him. His eyes burn into mine, capturing me as he grunts loudly.

"Dylan, oh, FUCK." I feel his orgasm burst inside me, warm and lingering, and I never want anything more than I want him in this moment. This is amazing. Everything about him is amazing. He pumps once, twice, three times and stills, his eyes staying on mine and giving me the satisfaction of watching him come undone. And then I collapse on top of him, my head hitting his chest as his hand comes up and holds me there. I've never felt anything like this. Not even close. He has officially ruined all other men for me and I am perfectly fine with that.

Chapter Seven

I AM WRECKED, RUINED, AND completely okay with it. I stay in Reese's arms for what seems like hours after we both climax. He holds me, never asking me to move or shift in any way. I can feel him slowly getting hard again inside me, but he doesn't push for us to do it again. He seems as content as I am, just softly stroking my back as my head nuzzles into his neck. I relish in his scent, the smell of him after sex. He still smells like citrus, but it's mixed with sweat and I know right then that nothing will ever smell this good. Or feel this good. Which I hate myself for thinking. His air is the only air I want to breathe now, and it does me no good to think like this. But I can't help it. I'm officially screwed and I know it.

We spend an hour on the couch together, laughing and talking as he holds me against him. I feel terribly embarrassed for not knowing minor details about the man who brought me the most pleasure I've ever experienced. Like the fact that he is thirty-one years old. He grew up in South Side and graduated from the University of Chicago when he was twenty-six with a Bachelor of Science Degree in Accounting and a Master's in Business Administration. He made partner when he was twenty-eight which sounds like a major feat for someone so young. The man is as smart as he is attractive, and I feel completely relaxed listening to him talk about college and his family. He has a younger sister who lives in Detroit who is married with two kids, and his parents are still married after thirty-eight years and live in Maywood. I tell him about my parents and how they encouraged me to open my bakery. Being an only child, they are immensely proud of me and speak of me like I've invented a cure for cancer and not a fabulous white chocolate truffle recipe. We talk about how close I am with Juls and Joey, and how Juls and Ian are practically living together now. Inseparable and mad for each other. I tell him about my morning runs and how most days I wish I had an iPod to drown out Joey's bitchy rants, but other days I enjoy them.

It is an amazing night, and not just because of the sex. I've never enjoyed just talking with someone the way I do with Reese. I don't want to move at all. I could stay in his arms all night, but I know I shouldn't. No sleepovers. After a few hours, I ask him to drive me home, and the look on his face when we pull up in front of the bakery is priceless. He had no idea I live here. *Of course, he wouldn't know that; you aren't dating, Dylan.* I kiss him briefly goodnight, wanting more than anything to invite him inside to see my place, but I don't. I manage to be strong in this one moment. This is just sex, and if I want to keep doing this with Reese, I need to remember that.

I haven't seen or talked to him since our amazing fuck fest on Tuesday, which is making things easier and harder at the same time. Easier because I'm realizing he sees this for what it is and it's making me keep myself in check. And harder because a part of me doesn't want him to see it this way anymore. I spend all day Wednesday staring at my cell phone, waiting for a text or a call from him, until I stupidly realize he never actually got my number from me. The one time he had called me, he'd called the shop directly.

Thursday, Joey and I are slammed with four consultations, two weddings, an anniversary cake, and a birthday cake request. The wedding consultations both take forever because the brides have decided to include the grooms' inputs and no one can decide on anything. Luckily for me, Joey is great at getting people to compromise, a trait that I love more and more about him with each passing wedding consultation. After I've finished up with my meetings, I spend the rest of the evening in the kitchen throwing together the tarts I'd promised the gentleman on Monday. They're relatively easy to make after I fuck up the first one royally. I end up using strawberries, kiwi, and mangos, and then top the tarts with an apricot jam. After managing to only eat one of them, I pass out in my bed and dream the same recurring Reese sex dreams, which keep getting better. I've stopped fighting it. It is useless really. Besides, the sleep I'm now getting is some of the best I've ever gotten. Especially when I wake up from an orgasm.

STANDING BEHIND THE COUNTER AT eleven thirty a.m. on Friday, I let my mind wander to what Reese is doing at this exact moment. I can picture him strikingly sitting behind his desk, working on some audit or whatever and doing it in a way that only he can make sexy. His hair is a right sexy mess, his green eyes are narrowed in on his task, and his massive erection is waiting for me. The shop door opens and I shake my head to clear it.

"Something or someone on your mind, cupcake? I know that look." Joey strolls in, returning from our favorite little sandwich shop down the street and placing the bag of the best chicken salad sandwiches in Chicago in front of me. My mouth begins to water at the smell and I suddenly realize that all I've eaten the past few days has been predominately sugar. *I'm going to develop diabetes if I don't watch myself.*

"No, nothing on my mind except for this sandwich that I'm about to destroy." The bell on the front door dings and I glance up, my heart thumping hard against my bones at the sight of the delivery man.

Joey hurriedly scurries to my side. "Ooohhh, goody. Today has sucked ass and I need something romantic from my favorite numbers guy." The delivery man smiles and places a small brown envelope onto the counter, handing me a slip to sign on his clipboard.

"*Your* favorite numbers guy? And what about Billy?" I ask, handing the man back his paperwork and staring at him suspiciously when he doesn't exit the shop.

"He's not a numbers guy. He's a lawyer. A hot ass lawyer who is taking me someplace uber fancy tonight."

"Awesome. Did you need something else?" I ask the man who stands patiently waiting.

"I've been instructed to wait until *after* you've read the letter to leave," he states nonchalantly.

"Oh, okay." I turn to Joey who looks at me like he has no idea what is going on either as I open the envelope and pull out a small card. My heart begins hammering in my chest and I automatically reach up and place my free hand over it.

Dylan,

It's come to my attention that the only number I have for you is the bakery number. Now how am I supposed to send you text messages saying I want you to sit on my face? Or I can't stop thinking about the way it felt to be inside you? OR I want to see you sometime this weekend if you're free. Please be free.

x Reese

P.S. If you would like these sorts of messages, please give your number to Fred.

Oh, man. I sigh loudly as Joey snatches the note out of my hand. Finding my notepad under the counter, I bite my cheek to stop from smiling so much as I scribble down my cell number and hand it directly to Fred, the delivery man.

"Thanks, Ms. Dylan. Have a great day," he says, turning quickly and walking out of the shop.

"He wants you to sit on his face? Well, that's it, Billy needs to take lessons from Reese on explicit letter writing." He hands me back the note and I place it back in its small envelope, putting it under the counter where I'm now storing them in a small tin. "You know you're practically swooning over there, right?" he says to me as I pull my hair up into a high messy bun.

"Swooning? Who the fuck says swooning? What are you, ninety?" I pull a few stray pieces out and tuck them behind my ears.

He pulls his sandwich out and hands me mine and we start digging in. "So, what did he mean by 'the way it felt to be inside you'? I mean, you've already had sex with him, so why would he... oh... oh, my God. Did you fuck him without a condom?" He spits bits of chicken salad at me as he shouts hysterically.

"Jesus. Close your mouth. I'd prefer to not be covered in your sandwich." *Crap. I really didn't want Joey to know about this, but I manage to forget how fucking insightful he is sometimes.* I grunt loudly before I answer. "Even though it's none of your business, yes, I did." I make a face and wipe a hunk of mayo off my apron that had managed to hit me in the middle of my shop logo.

Slamming his hand on the counter for dramatic effect, like he needed it, he finally speaks after chewing and swallowing his bite. "That's fucking huge and really fucking serious. *I've* never even done that. Shit, how was it? Good enough to swear off condoms permanently?" He smiles wickedly at me as I nod slowly.

"With him? Yes, absolutely. It was perfect."

"So you two are officially a couple now? Fuck yes. That's what I'm talking about, bitch." He holds his hand up for me to high-five him. I shake my head as I chew up my bite. *Damn it. Thanks for the reminder.*

"No, we're not a couple. We're monogamously casual." I take another bite of my to-die-for sandwich.

"What the fuck does that mean?"

I swallow my bite and stare at my sandwich, avoiding his judging stare. "It means we're not serious, but we're only sleeping with each other. So it's still casual and only about sex." I feel a sharp pain in my chest. "Now that we both have established that we'll only be with each other in that way, we don't have to use condoms. Besides, he was my first and I was his." *And that part right there eases that pain.* I glance up at him and see his unconvinced expression.

"Umm, okay. Honestly, I think you're both delusional if you think it's casual for either one of you. *You* light up when you talk about this guy and *he* writes you love letters. Fuck the casual bullshit." He crumbles up his wrapper and shoots it into the trashcan. "On another note, I think it's really sweet that you were each other's first times without it. I'm sure it meant just as much to him as it meant to you."

I grumble loudly, "Shut up, it's just sex. And he doesn't write me love letters. He sends me flour and panties with tiny notes."

"Yeah, you keep telling yourself that. Want something to drink?" he asks, moving toward the kitchen as my phone beeps in my pocket.

"Please," I reply, pulling it out and seeing an unknown number.

Unknown: There you are. Now I don't have to worry so much about Fred intercepting my letters to you.

I smile and type frantically.

Me: Here I am. And I happen to like your letters so I hope you don't mind the risk of Fred intercepting them.

Reese: The risk is worth it, love. Can I see you this weekend?

Me: I think I can squeeze you in somewhere. I have a wedding cake to work on tonight, but I'm free tomorrow night.

Joey returns with two sodas and places one in front of me on the counter.

"Thanks. So, where are you and your hot ass lawyer going tonight?" I force myself to keep my eyes on Joey and not the phone that is in my hand.

He notices the struggle instantly. "Some ritzy Italian joint. And you don't have to hide your enthusiasm about Reese texting you. I'm done trying to convince you it's more than you're both letting on." He takes a sip of his soda and pulls his phone out, pointing to the clock on the wall and smiling wide.

"Sweet. Dance party time," I squeal, setting my phone down on the counter as he docks his phone onto the speaker station and flips to a song.

Every Friday at noon, Joey and I dance and sing along to one song in the shop. It doesn't matter if customers come in and it doesn't matter how busy we are. We always make time for one song on Friday. A few months ago, I had an entire wedding party in here dancing along to "Locked out of Heaven" by Bruno Mars. It was awesome. Justin Timberlake's "Love Stoned" blares through the speakers as I spin around and begin dancing and singing along to the lyrics with Joey.

I'm on a serious roll when he cuts the music and stands, staring at the shop door, the familiar *hot guy in the building* look on his face. Spinning around to see what the fuss is about, I see a very amused face staring at me. Smiling in a suit and tie, the attractive blond steps forward and tilts his head.

"Well, thank Christ I decided to stop in here during my lunch break. Otherwise, I might have missed that hot little show." He steps closer to the counter and presses his hands on the top, causing me to stumble back a bit.

"Sweet Mother. You're like a sexy man-magnet lately," Joey mutters to me softly.

I clear my throat and smile. "Sorry about that. Can I help you?"

"I hope so, Dylan." His eyes drop to my nametag and then flick back to my face. *Good, but didn't have the same effect as my name coming out of Reese's mouth.* He's tall and blond, hair cut short and spiky with chiseled cheekbones and thin lips. "My father came in the other day and requested something. He's not feeling well, so he sent me to come pick it up." He glances down at the display case and then back up at my face. "Do you have any idea what I'm referring to because he wasn't specific?"

I think for a minute before it dawns on me. "Oh, the tarts." I shuffle quickly to the kitchen and bring out the container of treats. "I'm sorry to hear he isn't feeling well."

The man smirks. "Yeah, well, I can't say I share your sympathy. His illness did bring me in here to see you." He smiles wide, showing perfect teeth and winks at me. I shudder a bit.

"Jesus," Joey utters as he steps behind the register. I ignore him and the comment from the man.

"Umm, well, the tarts are three seventy-five apiece. How many would he like?"

"I don't know, three I guess? Can I get your number?"

I freeze midair as I'm reaching into the container to pick out the tarts. *Jesus, Joey was right. I don't think I've ever been this popular with men before.* Quickly shaking off his question, I pull four tarts out of the container and place them into a pastry box as Joey rings him up.

"I'm seeing someone. Here you go, the fourth one's free." I push the box across the counter and meet his eyes. They're the strangest color, a mix between mustard yellow and pale blue. It's a bit unsettling and I quickly glance away.

"Well, that's too bad. If he fucks up and you stop seeing him, give me a call." He smiles and pulls a card out of his pocket, sliding it across the table. I glance down at it briefly before flicking my stare back up to him. There's something about this guy that I find to be a major turn off, but I can't quite put my finger on it. "Thanks for the tarts," he says, turning and exiting the shop as I pick up his card.

"Bryce Roberts. Well, he was disturbingly forward." Spinning around, I toss his card into the trashcan and dust my hands off, brushing the creepiness off my skin.

"Excuse you. Why are you throwing out a hot guy's number? I thought you and Reese weren't serious?" Joey pries as my phone beeps.

I reach excitingly for it and hear his quiet laugh. "I have the *hottest* guy's phone number. I'm set."

Reese: I'll come to you. 8:00p.m.?

Me: Sounds perfect.

I WORK ON THE CAKE for the Smith/Cords wedding all night, finally passing out a little after two a.m. It's one of the prettiest cakes I've made yet. The bride has requested edible cherry blossoms along the base of each tier, and I've surprised myself at just how realistic they've turned out. I snap a close-up picture of one before sending it to Reese, since he seems to appreciate my work. His response is nothing short of swoonworthy. Yes, now that word is being thrown around in my vocabulary as well.

Joey texts me early on Saturday and tells me he isn't feeling well, thinking he had some bad food at the restaurant with Billy and is being taken care of in bed all day. I'm sure that means not just in a *bring you chicken soup and popsicles* kind of way. This means I'll be making the cake delivery on my own today. I'm a bit nervous. I haven't done this in years, the last time being when Joey spent a weekend with a very hot Greek guy he met at a club. They fucked and fought while I busted my ass trying to carry a six-tiered cake up a huge flight of stairs. He paid for that one for weeks.

I stare out at Sam through my shop window. The van is pulled up in front of the shop, back door wide open and ready for me to slide the cake inside. It's almost noon and I need to leave now if I am going to make it to the reception hall to drop off the cake in time. Traffic is always a nightmare on Saturdays, and I know it's going to take me longer than I would like to get there. I'm stalling, not really wanting to attempt to carry the cake by myself and possibly have a major mishap. "Damn it, Joey." I grab my phone out of my pocket and scroll to my favorite wedding planner's contact info.

"Hello, sweets," she sings with her chipper *I'm going to keep everybody in this goddamned wedding party calm* voice. I chuckle into the phone.

"Hey. I'm just now leaving to drop the cake off, so I might be a bit late."

"We're running late as it is, so no worries. This fucking bride is driving me insane." She sighs dramatically. "I seriously feel bad for her groom. Pretty sure he's in for a lifetime of annoyance." I hear commotion in the background and can only imagine what Juls is dealing with. She's had some doozy brides.

I sigh in relief. "Thank God. I'm flying solo today since Joey is playing house with Billy. I really hate doing deliveries alone."

I hear her gasp dramatically. "What are you doing? Go find the preacher. He's been MIA for twenty minutes. Sorry, I gotta go, Dyl. This wedding isn't going to start at all without me. Hey, are we still on for a much needed girls' day tomorrow?"

I jump in excitement, almost having completely forgotten about the massages and facials we booked weeks ago after declaring how little we see of each other. "Yes. I'm so ready for the spa and my Juls time. Good luck with your nightmare bride."

"Thanks, I'll need it. Bye, sweets."

I click end and turn around, staring the cake down as it sits on my side table that I do consultations at. "All right, it's just you and me. Don't fucking piss me off and I won't eat you. Got it?"

I prop the front door open and drop down, carefully and oh, so slowly picking up the cake and carrying it out to Sam's back door. Setting it down on the ledge, I ease it inside while holding my breath and saying every prayer I can think of silently. After successfully putting it where I want it, I close my eyes tightly and force the air out of my lungs. *Okay, half the battle's over.* Moving the holder in place that keeps the cakes from sliding all around the back of the van, I secure everything tightly and close the back doors. Spinning around to walk to the driver's side, I'm halted immediately as I run straight into a brick wall of a chest. *Oh, terrific.*

"Jesus Christ, Justin, you scared the shit out of me." I push away from him as he lets out a small annoying laugh.

"Sorry, Dyl pickle."

Ugh. I hate when he calls me that. I haven't been able to eat a dill pickle in two years.

"What do you want? I'm running late and really don't have time to chat." Nor do I want to. I move to step around him when his arm shoots out and grips my waist. "What the hell? What are you doing?"

"Oh, come on, baby. I saw the way you looked at me at the wedding." He pins me against the van, grinding his erection into my hip. I'm struggling against him, but his grip is firm. Really firm.

"You still want this. I can tell."

"Are you insane? Get the fuck off me!" I yell, whipping my head from side to side at the dead street around us. Figures, any other time of day people are bustling up and down the sidewalks. "What the hell is wrong with you?"

"I know you prefer married men now. Give it up, baby. It's all good. Sara apparently likes to fuck around behind my back, so I can do the same to her." His breath reeks of alcohol and my shoulders begin to burn where he's squeezing me, pressing my body into the side of my van. He runs his tongue over my ear and I buck against him. "Still sweet."

I continue pushing against his chest, trying to back him off a bit. "You're disgusting. I'm not interested. I'll never be interested again. Fuck, you're hurting me, Justin. Let go!" His fingers are digging into my skin and I want to cry, but I somehow manage to hold it in. I've cried enough over this asshole.

He pulls me toward him and then slams me once more against the van, this time knocking the air out of my lungs and dropping me to my knees. I fall over onto my side, gasping for air as he bends down and leans his face into mine. "Your loss," he whispers and storms away as I finally take in enough air to calm my screaming lungs. I cough and wheeze, clutching at my chest as I struggle to pull myself up onto my feet. *What the fuck? What just happened?* Justin turned psychotic; that's what happened. My entire body is in pain and I want to go back inside and nurse my wounds, but I can't.

"Fucking hell," I whimper as I climb into Sam and start him up. I pull the visor down and quickly try to recover my appearance so I don't look like I just got molested in the street. My hair is a mess, completely unraveled from my bun and my face is streaked with makeup. I wipe under my eyes, removing my mascara, and clean up the rest of my face. Peeling my top down to reveal my shoulder, I wince at the bright red fingertip-sized marks that are highly visible. "Jesus Christ. That fucking prick." I pull my shirt back up and cover them up quickly, resting my head back and taking in several slow deep breaths. *That bastard. I'm going to dismember him the next time I see him.* I shake my head and fix my hair. I can't deal with this right now; I have a job to do and I need to fucking do it. I push the events that just transpired out of my mind and pull away from the curb and to a wedding where, hopefully, the only dick the bride will be sucking will be her husband's.

Chapter Eight

EVERYTHING INVOLVING THE CAKE DELIVERY went smoothly. Everything except for what happened before the actual cake delivery. Soaking my sore muscles in my tub, I run through the events that transpired several hours ago in my head. Justin was never aggressive with me when we were together. He never put his hands on me like that before. So I can only chalk up his fucked up behavior to him discovering his wife's wedding indiscretions and dealing with it like a lunatic. I find it rather perfect that he's getting what he deserves, as long as he doesn't deal with it at my expense. One thing is for sure, if he touches me again, he won't have a dick to cheat on his wife with. I'll cut that shit off and make him eat it.

My phone beeps and I sit up in the tub, pulling it off the sink and reading the message.

Reese: We still on for 8:00p.m., love?

I sigh heavily and stare at his message. I'm beyond excited to spend the evening with Reese, but I don't want him to see the hideous marks that grace the skin of my shoulders and my upper back now. And spending time with him and not fucking is going to be a challenge. Of course, I could convince him to do clothes *on* fucking like we did at the wedding. That was still insanely hot. I nod at my decision as I type.

Me: We better be. I'm in the tub right now getting ready for you.

Reese: Prove it.

So many options here. I slump down so the tops of my knees are sexily poking out of the water and press them against each other. I take a quick picture and send it to him.

Reese: I love those legs. Especially when they're wrapped around my head.

Me: I especially love that too. Now stop distracting me. I have an incredibly hot CPA coming over in less than an hour.

Reese: Lucky bastard.

I dress in my favorite pair of skinny jeans, which make my ass look higher and tighter, a tight black T-shirt that has a wickedly plunging neckline, and my black pumps. For casual wear, I have to say I am looking pretty doable. My wavy blonde hair falls smoothly past my shoulders and I stick with minimal makeup tonight, just some tinted moisturizer, mascara, and some lip-gloss. A soft tapping on the glass door downstairs sends me carefully hurrying down the stairs and through the kitchen, stopping in the doorway at the sight of my date in the window. *Shit, not a date. Not a date, Dylan.*

I walk through the dark bakery up to the front door, waving sweetly at him as his smile grows. Reaching up to unlock it, I see his eyes roam down my body, taking in every inch of me before they finally return to my face. I hold my hand on the lock as he studies me.

"Hi, handsome," I say, still not turning the lock to allow him entry. His green eyes are soft and warm and I'm dying to let him in. But I'm going to wait.

"Hi, love. Are you going to open the door or are you expecting someone else? Another incredibly hot CPA maybe?" He places his hands on either side of the door and tilts his head to the side, arching his brow at me. *Oh, how I love playful Reese.*

"No, just you. How well can you see me from out there?" The sight of him in jeans and a fitted gunmetal grey T-shirt, hugging his body perfectly the way I want to, is making me feel scandalous all of a sudden.

"Uh, pretty well." He narrows his eyes at me. "What are you getting at?"

I step back a few feet and stand still. It's dark outside already, but a street lamp that is on the nearest corner is illuminating Reese. His tall frame is the only thing I can see through the glass. I smile widely at him. "If I'm right here, can you see me okay?"

He nods. "Not as well as I'd like to, but yeah. What's up?"

I pull my bottom lip into my mouth as I hold up a finger, indicating for him to wait a moment as I disappear into the kitchen. Carrying out a wooden chair, I sit it down in the middle of the room where I had just been standing and turn my eyes toward him. He's studying me curiously, his eyes indicating he has no idea what's coming. Or who is coming for that matter, because someone will definitely be coming.

"Is the sidewalk busy tonight?" I ask, moving gracefully into the chair and facing him, legs crossing in front of me and my heeled foot drawing circles in the air.

He scratches his head and glances to his left, then to his right before turning back to me. "No, I think I'm the only guy out here waiting for you. You are going to let me in, right?"

And that is the only confirmation I need to get the show started.

"Yes, in a minute." I uncross my legs and spread them, my feet firmly planted on the tiled floor as I lean back against the hard wood. I keep my eyes on him as I slowly trail my hand down the front of me, gliding over my breasts and stopping at the top of my jeans.

"Dylan, what the fuck are you doing?"

Taking both of my hands, I pop the button of my jeans and slide my dominant hand into my panties, letting out a loud moan as I begin moving two fingers against my drenched clit. Reese braces himself against the glass with wide eyes and an open mouth.

"Dylan. Holy fucking shit. Love, let me in." His one hand grips his hair while the other pulls at the door handle repeatedly, the glass shaking slightly.

Tilting my head back, I bring my free hand up to my breast and squeeze, pulling at my erect nipple through my sheer bra and thin shirt. My fingers dip lower, spreading my wetness around and up to my enlarged hot spot as my breathing becomes loud and jagged. He begins pacing outside the window, never letting his eyes leave me or what I am doing.

"Reese, oh, God. I'm pretending it's you touching me." This is absolutely true. I can't touch myself anymore and not imagine it isn't him.

"Fuck. Let me in and I *will* be touching you."

Closing my eyes, I move my fingers in quick circles. I think of the first time he touched me at the wedding, the way his hands slid up my thighs. The way he gripped my hips and pulled me against him, meeting his thrusts with such force that I thought he would break me. His eyes, his lips, the way he filled me completely on Tuesday and the feel of his skin against my skin. How he kept his eyes on me when he was devouring me between my legs. I'm moaning loudly, working myself up, and then I feel it. The pull. The heat. Slow and steady pouring over me and flushing my entire body. I pulse against my hand, coming long and hard all by myself.

"Reese." Bucking against the chair, I hold my fingers still but apply enough pressure to give me what I need. My eyes are closed and my head is thrown back, but through my moans I hear several bouts of pounding on the glass going on and know he's dying out there. I don't know why, he'll definitely be getting his in a minute.

Lifting my head slowly, I push myself out of the chair and calmly button my jeans before I move to stand directly in front of the door. I smile slyly at his appearance. I feel amazing and he looks completely frazzled, hair sticking out all over the place, eyes wide, jaw tightly clenched. I bite my cheek and giggle.

"You're going to kill me. You know this, right?" he says as I slowly slip my fingers into my mouth and suck on them. He runs his hand through his hair while the other one grips the door handle.

"Dylan, if you don't let me in right now, I'll be replacing your door tomorrow."

I snicker and pull my fingers out of my mouth, quickly reaching up and unlocking the door as he barges through and pulls me against him. Picking me up and wrapping my legs around his waist, he turns and locks the door behind us with his free hand before he brings his mouth to mine, his other hand holding me up.

"So fucking sexy, love. But don't do that again," he says between kisses, and I pull back, seeing his serious expression.

"You didn't like my show? It was just for you." He carries me over to the counter and sits me down on top of it, settling his body between my thighs. His hands run up my arms, brushing lightly over my shoulders and up my neck as he slowly traces my throat with his fingers.

"I loved your show. But I don't like not being able to get to you. I was dying out there." I smile and press my forehead against his as he trails his fingertips down my neck and over the top of my breasts. "You look beautiful by the way," he says softly before pressing his lips firmly against mine. I open for him, allowing his tongue to dip softly into my mouth. His kisses aren't urgent this time. They're slow and lasting, as if he's savoring this moment with me. Swallowing my moans, his breath comes out in hot spurts and fills me with my favorite minty flavor. I press my chest against his as his hands wrap around my waist and slowly stroke my back, my hands clamped behind his neck. We both break away at the same time, our foreheads reclaiming their spot against each other's and our uneven breathing surrounding us.

"Missed your face," I say, regretting it instantly because he didn't need to know that. *Crap. I have an orgasm and drop my guard like an amateur.*

"Just my face?" he asks playfully. He brushes my hair behind my ear and runs his fingers through the waves.

I shake my head and begin slowly scratching the back of his neck. His eyes close and a tiny sound of pleasure escapes him, making me smile. "I missed your face too," he replies as he reopens his eyes and traces down the sides of my temples, across my cheekbones, and down to my lips where I kiss the tips of his fingers.

His words warm me the way they shouldn't and I know I need to break this moment before I say something I really don't want him to know. I'm not only weak when it comes to sex around this man. He is slowly infiltrating every part of my soul. "Want a tour?" His lips pull up in the corner and he steps back, holding out his hand to help me off the counter. I quickly drop my hand out of his before I become too familiar with the sensation and walk through the doorway that leads to the kitchen. Flipping on the lights, I walk around the large workbench, feeling him watch me from where he stands.

"Okay, so this is where I spend my time whipping up my fabulous creations and trying desperately not to eat them, which I usually fail at miserably." I motion around the room and hear a soft laugh from his direction. "Storage, fridge, freezer, and oh, shit." I spot a vat of icing that I'd made earlier this morning when I was testing out a new recipe. Grabbing the bowl I'd placed on the shelf, I stick my pinky finger into the hot pink frosting and slip it into my mouth.

"Mmm, yummy," I say as I flick my eyes up to Reese who is perched against the wall. His arms are crossed over his chest and he's watching me with concentrated interest, which I'm beginning to notice is a pattern of his. "Oh, I found this recipe for chocolate peppermint frosting and had some extra time this morning to play around with it. Until I realized I *didn't* have extra time, and I stupidly left it out." I lick my lips and his eyes widen. "Wanna taste?"

"Sure," he answers, moving toward the workstation. I hop up on top of it and wait patiently for him to stand in front of me, as his hands rest lightly on my thighs.

I dip my finger into the frosting. "Open," I command, holding my finger in front of his now slightly swollen lips. They curl up into a small smile before he opens his mouth, his tongue wrapping around my finger and pulling every last bit off. *Jesus, he could probably get me ready for sex just by licking an envelope in front of me.*

"Good?"

"Very, especially coming off you."

"I love mint chocolate. I think it's the perfect union of flavors." I dip another finger into the frosting and pop it in my mouth as he licks his lips.

"I think you're the perfect union of flavors," he responds,

causing me to grin even wider.

"Want some more?" I go to reach my finger into the bowl when he grabs it, taking the bowl out of my hands, and placing it next to me on the workstation. Dipping his own finger into the bowl, he runs his tongue along his bottom lip as he swipes the hot pink frosting down the side of my neck to my cleavage. I whimper as his tongue licks off the line of frosting he's drawn, paying extra attention to the dollop that is now dripping between my breasts.

"Lift your arms," he whispers, grabbing the hem of my shirt and tugging it over my head after I obey him. His eyes enlarge and flick from my face to my shoulders, his face hardening instantly. *Oh, fuck.*

"What the hell? What happened to you?" His fingers trail the small fingertip-sized bruises that graze over my shoulders and I wince at him. Moving my hair out of the way, he leans around me and I hear a soft grunt as he discovers the bruises on my upper back. *Shit. I meant to keep my clothes on. This conversation could have been easily avoided. Damn him and his ability to cloud my judgment.*

"Why the hell are you covered in bruises?" He moves back in front of me and eases in between my legs again, commanding my attention.

"Uh..." *Do I tell him? What would he do? Would he go after Justin? Is that something your casual sex partner would do or is that strictly a boyfriend move? Did I want him to care?*

"Dylan."

My case of word vomit suddenly rears her ugly head again. "Justin came by when I was loading Sam today to go deliver a wedding cake and he came on to me. He'd been drinking and he wouldn't let go of me even though I was screaming at him, and then he threw me up against Sam." I watch his expression shift right in front of me to anger. His teeth clench tight, causing the muscles in his jaw to quiver and his nostrils flare. I move back a bit. *Damn. Angry Reese is intimidating and sexy as hell.*

"That asshole put his hands on you?"

"Yes, but—"

"And who the fuck is Sam? Did he bring another guy with

him?" He slams his hand down on the worktop next to my thigh and I jump. "They're both fucking dead," he says, turning away from me. I grab his shoulders and prevent his escape.

"Don't, just wait a minute." His eyes meet mine and he raises his brows. "Sam is my delivery van. Yes, I named it. It's stupid, I know. And yes, Justin did this, but he's never put his hands on me before. I don't think he would've actually forced himself on me. He was probably just upset that his wife cheated on him." *What the fuck? Now I'm making excuses for that asshole?* I run my fingers down his arms and pull his hands into my lap, squeezing them gently.

"Are you fucking serious?" His voice booms throughout the kitchen. "I don't give a shit if he was drunk, upset, or whatever the fuck. He touched you; he's dead."

"Reese, please, what would you do? You can't hurt him. He could press charges against you. I mean, it's not like it's self-defense or something. Please, just let it go. It really looks worse than it feels." That is a complete lie. It hurts like hell. But I am absolutely terrified Reese will end up getting into trouble over this, and that will hurt a hell of a lot worse than the bruises.

He runs his hands down his face before he reaches out and holds mine, his expression softening. "You should have called me. Why didn't you?" His thumbs stroke my cheeks as he studies me.

I shrug. "I had to go deliver the wedding cake and I was already running late. Besides, I wouldn't want you to do something that could get you into trouble. He isn't worth it." I reach up and hold his hand to my face. "Promise me you won't do anything."

He steps closer to me, bringing our bodies only inches apart and allowing me to wrap my legs around him. "I'm sorry, I can't do that."

"Reese."

"No, love." He kisses me quickly, shutting me up before he continues. "I can't and I won't let anybody hurt you. He'll never touch you again. *That* I can promise you."

I nod slightly. The truth of the matter is, I like that he cares about me enough to want to protect me. And Reese is smart. He won't do anything that could fuck with the career that he's worked so hard for. I shouldn't worry about this.

"Okay, but can we go back to the frosting now?" I ask, seeing his eyes light up at the memory of it.

He nods slowly, the desire sparking back into the green pools that glare at me.

Oh, this is going to be fun.

Chapter Nine

I'M LYING COMPLETELY NAKED ON my workbench, my thighs clamped tightly together in anticipation as Reese continues to remove his clothing. I've never realized until now just how sexy it is to watch a man undress. But I'm quickly realizing that whatever this man does, he does it in a very sexy way. I bite the inside of my cheek as I watch him pull his T-shirt off with one hand, revealing his brilliantly sculpted upper body. I moan softly at the sight of him and catch his attention, seeing his lips curl up in the corner. His boxers come down with his jeans and he steps out of them, grabbing the bowl of frosting that he had placed on a nearby stool before he moves toward me. His free hand grips my thigh, spreading me open, and giving himself room to settle between my legs. I feel the tip of him push against my clit and I whimper.

"Now, where should I begin?" His eyes run down my body and he smiles wickedly.

"You can begin with sticking that big dick in me," I answer, wiggling against him to give me some relief. *Christ Almighty, he feels amazing.*

He chuckles and bends forward. "Somebody's greedy. Did you

not get yourself off well enough?" He drops his head and kisses between my breasts. "You should have let me in when I told you. I would have made you come so hard you wouldn't be begging for my cock just yet." He holds out his hand to lift me so I'm now sitting up, my eyes doing a quick rundown of his body and seeing him notice it.

"Yes, you caught me, I was looking, but I can't help it." I lean back onto my hands and stick my chest out. "Now, get busy."

"Are you always so bossy?" he asks as he dips his finger into the frosting and spreads a generous amount onto each erect nipple. I try to keep still as best I can but am quickly getting worked up. *But let's be honest here, I've been worked up from this man since I fell into his lap.* He looks so focused, so meticulous with his pattern he's drawing on me that it makes me vibrate with silent laughter against his hands. "Stop squirming." He scoops another glob out of the bowl and trails it down the center of my stomach, swirling the pink sugariness onto my clit. I bite my lip to keep from jerking, watching him set the bowl onto the wood next to me and step back, admiring his creation.

"You like?" I ask, my eyes glued to his massive erection, which I am aching to jump on.

His hand strokes his jaw as he studies me. "Fuck, yes." His eyes flick up to mine and I clutch the edge of the workbench with my hands. *Shit, his sex stare could melt me like a candle.* Moving quickly to bridge the space between us, his hand grips my head and crashes my mouth against his. He's rough, swiping into my mouth with his tongue, his breath hot and minty on my face. We're all lips, tongues, and bursts of air as he sucks and bites my lip, the tiny pain of it fueling my desire for him. Breaking away to ease me back onto the wood, his tongue darts out and licks the icing off my left breast.

"Oh, yes." I tangle my hands into his hair as he strokes my nipple with his tongue, pulling it into his mouth and sucking hard before releasing it.

"Mmmm, you taste almost *too* good." His mouth moves to my right breast where he licks it clean before flicking my nipple. He sits up and stares down at me. "Now what?" he asks, and I know the look on my face is one of pure delight. *Am I in control of this?*

"Lick me."

"Be specific, love."

I sit up quickly and wrap my hand around his cock, hearing a sharp gasp from him as he grabs my neck. He shakes his head and removes my hand gently, causing me to frown.

"Not yet." He guides me back down onto my back and I playfully try to reach him as he bats my hands away. "You were telling me to lick you, and I want to know where."

I smirk. "You know exactly where."

He shrugs and slowly begins tracing my belly button, moving the icing around and causing my stomach to clench. "Where, Dylan?" *Good Lord, the man is persistent. I wish I found that to be anything but a major turn on.*

Okay, I can do this. I clamp my eyes shut. "Reese, please lick my pussy until I come in your mouth, and then fuck me until I can't walk." Slowly peeking one eye open, I find a very amused man staring down at me with the biggest grin I've ever seen on his face. I can't help but laugh. "You're a pervert."

"So are you." Dropping in front of me, he latches onto my clit and sucks hard. I groan loudly and arch my back, feeling his hands grip my ankles and plant my feet flat down on the wood. I'm completely open to him and go to drop my feet off the sides when he holds them in place.

"Move and I stop."

I stare down my body and look into his bright green eyes. "Seriously?" I shake my head quickly. *Crap. I feel so exposed like this. He can see everything.*

He keeps his eyes on me as he trails sweet kisses on my inner thighs. "Do you have any idea how beautiful you are, Dylan? Every single part of you. Especially here." His hand brushes between my legs and I whimper. "I want to see you like this." *Well, in that case.* I drop my head back and firmly plant my feet, letting go of my anxiety and opening up to him and his extremely talented mouth.

"Oh, yes." I move my hips against him as he slowly strokes up my length and around my clit, licking off every bit of icing. I want him to pull me into his mouth and suck hard, knowing full well that when he does, I will surely lose my mind. But he doesn't. He keeps up the rhythm of deep caresses, swiping just over or just under my clit and driving me insane. He only dips his tongue into me just enough to make me grip his head with my thighs and then he slowly removes it.

"You're so close, love."

"I know that. Why aren't you letting me come?" My climax is there, right there, and he's toying with it. My body is shaking on the hard wood, the slight chill of it cooling down my heated skin.

"I can feel you pulsing against my tongue. I want you to come, Dylan. I really do." He gives me slow even laps with his tongue, swirling and dipping. Brushing just over my clit, I bring my hips up to make him go where I want him, where I need him, but his hand quickly clamps down on my stomach and presses me to the table.

"Please. I need… please just... little lower. No higher. Please. What the fuck?"

"Are you not enjoying this?" *Lick.* "Because I sure as hell am. In fact," *Lick,* "I think I'll do this for the rest of the night."

Oh, God, he's trying to kill me. Fuck that. If he won't get me off, then I'll fucking do it. Quickly dropping my hand to my sex, I go to rub my two favorite fingers on my spot when he grabs my hand, forcing it back down to the wood and holding it there firmly. Letting out a string of colorful curse words, I finally let myself go limp on the table and give up.

"Why are you doing this?" I whimper as he continues his torment.

His breath warms me between my legs. "Because you wouldn't let me touch you. Do you have any idea how close I was to breaking through your window?" He licks my clit quickly and I pant. "I want to be the only one to give you pleasure, Dylan. Your orgasms belong to me." *Holy shit. I am completely fine with that. Yes. Absolutely.*

"So I can't touch myself anymore?"

"No, you can, but only if I am there to help you. You'll never come as hard as when I do it anyway." Another lick and I shake. "You know that, don't you?"

"Yes," I agree, knowing he is indisputably right. The orgasms I give myself are bland compared to his. Even this anguish he is currently inflicting on me is better somehow. I moan loudly. "Please, you're the only guy who's ever made me come."

He stops, completely frozen between my legs. I feel his hot breath against my skin, but nothing else. *Shit, was that not something he should know? Awesome. No Reese style orgasms for me tonight. Good job, Dylan. Brilliant.*

"Really?" His question hits me after several long seconds of silence.

I nod and cover my face with my hands. "Really. It's just you." Oh, those words rip through me in a way I don't need them to. I'm going to fuck this up, and it'll be entirely my fault. I open my mouth to say something, anything, when he wraps his lips around my clit and pulls it into his mouth. "Oh, God," I cry out. Sucking hard, then harder, he growls against me and I go off like a missile.

"YES." Mid-orgasm, he stands up, and before I can protest the sudden change of direction, he charges straight into me. "Reese."

"Dylan. Holy fuck, you feel incredible." His words are barely audible over my cries as the first orgasm rips through me and another comes up close behind. His hands mold to my breasts as I grip the edge of the workbench and hold on for dear life.

"Tell me again. Tell me I'm the only man who's ever made you come." He pants as his powerful hips crash against my legs. My eyes are glued to his broad shoulders, which are flexing with each drive.

I release my lip that I've been biting and look up at him. "You're the only man. And you're so fucking good at it." My eyes are locked onto his face, his chest, his neck as it pulses with each thrust. His gaze drops to between my legs and I know he's watching himself enter me over and over, stroking me hard and deep. "So sexy, love. Christ, I'm close." Pulling his bottom lip into his mouth, his hands dig into my hips and pull me against his pelvis. I fall, giving him another orgasm as I arch my back off the workbench and clench around him. He groans loudly and pulses inside me, giving me his release with my name on his lips.

"Holy shit," I pant between quick breaths as he splays his body on top of mine.

"Yeah, holy shit," he says into my neck. I wrap my arms around his back and hold him to me. I've missed this. The feel of his chest against mine, the way my skin warms instantly against his. Having him killing me slowly between my legs with his mouth is worth it if it allows me to be this close to him. At the movement of his head, I glance down to see his eyes turn up to mine.

"Handsome," I say, smiling as if I'd just won the lottery. He winks at me and quickly kisses my breasts before he stands up and glances down at our hot pink covered bodies.

"Love, I think we need a shower." He arches his brow at me and I quickly sit up, nodding frantically. *Shower with Reese? Hell fucking yes.*

"This way." I hop down and grab my clothes off the stool as he retrieves his, trailing behind me as I start up the stairs.

"Ah!" After a quick slap on my backside from him, we make it to the top and I turn around to face him, backing farther into my living space. "This is me," I say, watching him take it in. It doesn't take him long. There isn't much to look at. He peers around the partition and wiggles his brows at me when he spots my bed. *No way, buddy. Not happening.*

"I like it. It's tiny though," he states with a smile as he follows me into my bathroom.

Turning on the shower, I place my clothes on the sink top and catch a glimpse of myself in the mirror. I am flushed and covered in sticky frosting, and I love it. Coming up behind me, he places his clothes next to mine and wraps his arms around my waist, pulling me back against him. Rolling my head back to rest on his chest, our eyes meet and he smiles at me. I will never, not ever, get tired of his smile and the little lines it brings out next to his eyes.

"Are you mad at me for what I did?" he asks, causing me to narrow my stare a bit but cracking when his eyes bulge. The bathroom begins to fill with steam and I turn in his arms, lightly pressing a kiss to his jaw.

"No, however, if you would have kept my orgasm from me, you would be purchasing a new ninety thousand dollar vehicle because I would have keyed the shit out of the one you have."

He chuckles, "Noted. Now, let's get wet."

I grin deviously and open my mouth to say something dirty, *of course*, when he stops me with his finger to my lips.

"Pervert."

I'VE NEVER SHOWERED WITH A man before, and I must say, I'm pretty sure that's the best way to go. I am completely pampered. He laughs at my fifty thousand shampoo, conditioner, and body wash choices, which are stacked against the wall, and studies several before choosing the ones he says smell like me. He picks the scents I use most often and I beam inside at the idea of him knowing what I smell like. He insists on washing my hair, taking his time and giving me an amazing head massage as he lathers me up. Washing my body, his face hardens as he carefully rubs my shoulders and my back, but gets back to playful when he washes between my legs. *That* he spends a little extra time on. After I rinse clean, he drops his head and freshens up his marks on my breasts as I moan softly against his mouth. He seems just as happy about them being there as I am.

When it's my turn, I skip the loofah and squeeze the body wash directly onto my hand, wanting to feel every inch of him as I wash him. His muscles relax against my touch and I rub his arms the way I did on Tuesday, seeing his eyes close and his head fall forward. The only muscle that doesn't relax, and seems to not be able to at all during our entire shower together, is my favorite muscle of his. I stroke him long and hard, the lather building as he holds onto my waist and buries his face in my hair. He kisses me deeply, almost lovingly when he comes in my hand. The feel of his hot liquid against my skin is exhilarating and I want to fuck him again, but don't. More than that, I want to get out of the shower and nuzzle against his chest, breathing my favorite air. But Reese has other plans. He wants something besides frosting in his stomach.

I perch myself up on the counter and watch as he raids my fridge, his hair wet and fuckably messy. "Where is all your food? The only thing in here is milk, some weird cheese, and jelly." He closes the door and glowers at me. I'm busy pulling my damp hair up into a messy knot on top of my head when his question finally hits me.

"Oh, I eat out a lot. And what weird cheese?" I hop down and stick my head in the fridge, following his finger to the second shelf.

I quickly close the door. "That is not cheese. Maybe it was at one point, but now, I'm not sure what it is."

He laughs and pulls his phone out of his pocket, kissing the top of my head. "All right, well, I need to eat something besides you. What do you want? Chinese?"

I shrug. "I don't care. I'm not really hungry."

Pressing the buttons on his phone, I study him as he licks the slit running down his lip and brings his cell up to his ear. I reclaim my spot on the counter as he moves between my legs. This is becoming a regular position for us. My fingers slip under his shirt and I trace the hard lines of his stomach.

"Yeah, I want to place an order for delivery. Dylan's Sweet Tooth on Fayette. Yes, one order of General Tso chicken and one order of shrimp lo mein. Nope that's it." He moves the phone away from his mouth. "What's your last name?"

My jaw drops open. "You don't know the girl's full name who you are currently fucking? That's just awful. I know yours, Carroll." I cross my arms over my chest and push my boobs up, seeing his eyes flick down and linger for a long second.

"Dylan."

I shake my head in disapproval. "It's Sparks," I huff.

He chuckles in amusement. "Wow. That's ridiculously fitting." Before I can ask him what the hell that meant, he looks away from me and pays attention to the call. "All right, thanks." Placing the phone back in his pocket, he kisses me quickly on my nose and I groan in protest.

"Why is Sparks fitting?"

His lip twitches. "Because, you're like this little firecracker." I laugh as he plants a kiss on my forehead, running his hands up and down my arms. "Dinner will be here in twenty. Oh, before I forget, we're having this big meeting with some clients on Tuesday, and I was wondering if you would like to provide some of your treats for it."

I run my fingers through his damp hair, causing it to curl a bit at the ends. "I'd love to. What kind of treats?"

"I don't know. It's at ten a.m. so I guess breakfast treats?" His forehead creases as he looks past me and thinks it over. *Lord, he is adorable.*

I smile and play with his T-shirt, bunching it up in my hands. "Well, I happen to make some mean breakfast treats. How many people am I providing for?"

"Twelve."

I nod. "Okay. I'll make sure to have enough for everyone to have three, that way if they don't get eaten, which is absurd, then you can have the extra."

"Great. I'll pay you in orgasms." *Well, that is way too tempting.* His smirk lingers as I carefully think about his offer, looking up at the ceiling for my answer.

"Eh," I finally reply and he wraps me up, kissing me once and then once more, longer and softer as I melt.

We sit in comfortable silence as we eat our dinner on the floor in my living room. Reese makes sure to point out that I am indeed hungry, watching me with amusement as I tear into both of his orders. And I make sure to point out that he is the one who ate *most* of the frosting. I exhale heavily and lean against the partition, resting my hand on my belly as he sticks the leftovers in my fridge and returns to sit across from me.

"Full?" he asks.

"Very. That was crazy good though. I haven't had Chinese since Joey and I ordered it on Easter weekend and we puked it up in my bathroom after a night of binge drinking." He motions with his hands for me to elaborate. "He got dumped by this guy through a singing telegram."

"Jesus, that's really shitty. I didn't realize those things were still around."

I nod and laugh slightly. "Me either; it was awful. The telegram came to the shop and he sang in front of all these customers. Joey was so embarrassed." I brush the tendril that is tickling my cheek out of my face. "So in typical *you just got dumped and your best friends are going to cheer you up* fashion, Juls and I bought all this alcohol and we played drinking games all night. It was really fun until we all got sick." I shake my head at the memory. "And *that* is why Tequila and I are no longer on speaking terms."

He laughs, resting back on his hands, his long legs stretching in front of him brushing against mine. "I can't imagine you drunk. Do you get even feistier or are you an angry fireball? Because, honestly, I can kind of see both."

I giggle and rub my bare foot against his leg. "Neither actually. I get really loud and start giving people nicknames, and then I usually get emotional which is always fun for everybody." I laugh and he smiles at me. "What about you? Do you get extra flirty or do you start hitting people? Cause I can kind of see both." He moves closer and pulls my foot into his lap, rubbing it and causing me to moan softly.

"I don't get drunk. Well, at least I haven't since I was seventeen. I don't usually have more than a few drinks at a time." He pauses briefly and narrows his eyes at me. "How old are you?" His weird line of questioning causes me to give him a strange look. He notices it and continues, "I just realized I have no idea."

"Jeez, good thing I'm legal." He smirks at me and I shake my head disapprovingly. "I'm twenty-six. So, why don't you get drunk?"

He seems to mull over my answer with a smile. "I don't want to, so I don't. I think drinking specifically for the purposes of getting drunk is bullshit."

"Well, *you* haven't had someone break up with you through a musical number." I pull my foot out of his grasp when he starts tickling it, quickly tucking it under my other knee. I try to stifle my yawn but give in to it, rubbing my eyes with the heels of my hands. I am thoroughly exhausted from all my orgasms, and my full belly is making me sleepy. Reese stands up and holds his hand out to me and I allow him to help me to my feet. This gesture will also never get old.

"I should probably go," he says, running his hands up my arms and holding me at my elbows. I yawn again. *Damn it, I really don't want him to leave, but he can't stay. No fucking way. No sleepovers.* "What are you doing tomorrow?"

I lick my dry lips and place my hands on his chest. "Juls and I are having a girls' day. We're going to the spa to get massages and facials and talk about boys." He smirks at me and I give it right back to him. "I feel like I haven't had her all to myself since she met Ian, which I totally get. She's crazy about him."

His hands grip my hips. "I'm sure the feeling's mutual. He talks about her constantly and I give him all kinds of shit for it." I smile at his admission. *Definitely telling Juls that tomorrow.* After a brief moment, his face scrunches and he runs his hand through his hair quickly, looking a bit unsure of himself. "Uh, when you get massages, is it a girl who does it?"

I roll my eyes. "And you call *me* the pervert?"

"What? Oh, no that's not what I meant. Pervert." He snorts and I shrug. *Yup, that's me.* "I mean, is a guy going to be giving it to you, because I don't think I'm okay with that."

Wait, what? I answer honestly. "Actually, I have no idea. Juls booked them weeks ago. But, why does it matter? It's a massage; it's not sexual."

"It just does. If you want a guy to massage you, I'll give you a massage. I'd prefer it if it was a girl and not for the perverted reasons your mind is thinking."

I step back and stare at him. *Seriously?* "Okay, well, I just don't understand why this bothers you." *If this is just casual, then it shouldn't. Right?*

He throws his hands up and looks exasperated. "You're right. Never mind, it doesn't bother me. I should go." He leans in quickly and kisses me on my temple before turning for the stairs.

"Reese." He looks over at me, stopping on the stairs. My head is full with things I want to say to him. I want to ask him to be honest with me, to tell me exactly why it bothers him to have a man massage me. I want to ask him if this is becoming more for him than how it started out. But I don't. I don't ask him anything. "Goodnight."

He smiles slightly and continues walking away. "Goodnight, love." I watch him disappear down the stairs and hear the door close shut behind him as I'm left to ponder what just happened.

Chapter Ten

I WAKE UP FEELING JUST as confused as I did before I passed out last night. Plus, on top of that fun emotion, I'm also completely exhausted after the shitty night's sleep I got. His words played on repeat in my mind, seeping into my dreams and leaving me full of questions. Questions I want desperately to have answered by him, but don't have the guts to ask. I don't get it. Why would me having a massage from a man bother him? Massages aren't sexual at all in that setting. I'm sure they could be if Reese was to give me one, and the thought of that gives me chills, but at the spa I'm currently driving to with Juls? No fucking way.

I've had men give me massages before and I enjoy them a bit more than from women because they are stronger and their hands are bigger. I like my muscles to be worked deeply, and not with little dainty woman hands. But never, not ever have I once felt anything during a massage from a man other than pure relaxation. Christ, most of the time I pass out and have to be woken up, drool sticking to my face and looking like a hot mess.

I grunt as I look out the window. I'm tense and anxious and I need to fucking relax.

"You're awfully quiet, sweets. Not looking forward to our day of beauty?" Juls asks after giving me my alone time to contemplate what the hell happened last night. Not that it helped any.

I sigh heavily. "Something strange happened last night with Reese and I'm not really sure what to make of it." I turn my attention to her. "Do you know if my massage is booked with a man or a woman?"

She laughs a bit. "Uh oh. Did someone voice his opinion of not wanting another man touching you?"

"Sort of? I don't know. He said he'd prefer if it was a woman and when I asked him why it mattered so much because it wasn't like I was getting a happy ending out of it, he said it *didn't* matter and then he left." I rest my head back and rack my brain. "I just don't get why he cares if this is just sex between us."

She makes a sound of amusement before answering. "You, my lovely best friend, are an idiot."

"What? Why?" The car slows as she pulls into the parking lot of Tranquility Day Spa and my stomach tightens. *Fuck. Do I really want to go through with this if it's booked with a guy and I can't switch it? Do I even want a massage anymore?*

She pulls into a parking spot, shuts the car off, and turns toward me in her seat. "Dylan, seriously? What if Reese was the one getting a massage and some fucking hot chick was rubbing her hands all over his body and giving him pleasure. Would *you* be okay with that?"

Well, shit, I didn't think about it like that. "No, I definitely wouldn't be okay with that." I cover my face quickly and rub it. "Damn it. I'm such an asshole."

She laughs and pulls my hands down. "No, you're not. You're expecting him to not care about you because what you two are doing is what you keep foolishly referring to as *casual*. But you're very hard not to care about." Her thumb softly strokes my hand and I smile weakly at her. "Even if you guys are just having fun, he's allowed to want to keep you to himself and so are you." *God, I miss these talks with Juls. She always makes perfect sense out of any situation.* She stops lovingly caressing me and slaps my hand, causing me to shriek. "Now buck up and put your girl talk game face on. You are mine today."

THE MASSAGE IS, OF COURSE, booked with a man, but I quickly protest and am able to switch to an available woman who had a client cancel on her. I relax immediately after that is taken care of and enjoy my facial first, laughing with Juls as we lie next to each other on a doublewide table and get pampered together. I hadn't realized she has made it so we will be attached at the hip all day, but am instantly grateful. As we are left alone to let our masks dry, I take her silence as my opportunity to spill my juice.

"So, Reese told me last night that Ian talks about you constantly. Just thought you should know." I crack a smile and hear her react next to me, a soft gasp coming from her lips.

"Oh, man, I think I love him, Dylan. Like totally head over heels, I want to spend the rest of my life with him kind of love. Is that crazy? I mean, we've only known each other a few months and I've already picked out my fucking wedding colors."

I let out a hearty laugh and grab her hand, squeezing it tightly. "And what color will I be wearing? If you say something pastel, I'm pushing you off this table."

"Oh, fuck no. You know I've always dreamed of a fall wedding." She grunts in annoyance. "Jesus, why are we even talking about this? It's not like Ian is anywhere close to proposing to me. He hasn't said he loves me, if he even does, which he probably doesn't. And I am not going to be the fool who says it first and stands there like an idiot waiting for his response. No fucking way."

"Maybe he's just waiting for the perfect moment. You said he's romantic as hell. Maybe he wants to make sure you're ready to hear everything he has to say."

The door opens and our two estheticians return as I scrunch my face up and feel the mask crack. Juls sighs. "I don't know, maybe. Whatever, I refuse to say it first, that's all I'm saying."

"Me, too," I respond without any thought at all and hear a loud gasp from my right. *No. No way. I am not in love with Reese. Nope.*

"Oh, my…" she starts, but I squeeze her hand tightly and hear a yelp instead of the rest of her sentence.

I stammer, "That's not what I meant. I didn't… I mean, I don't. Shit." I turn my head and see her wide eyes, a smile cracking open her face. "You mention a word of this conversation to Joey and I will tell Ian myself that you've picked out the names of your children." She begins to silently giggle and I slowly join her. *Jesus Christ. Note to self, don't go to spa days with Juls anymore because you lose your fucking mind.*

WE SETTLE IN FOR OUR massages and once again, I completely forget about the state of my upper body after I strip and sprawl out on my stomach, waiting for my masseuse. "The fuck is that?" My best friend screeches as she settles in next to me. I grunt into the open headrest I'm staring at the floor through. *Well, I might as well spill it since her reaction can't be any worse than Reese's.*

I exhale loudly before I explain. "Justin stopped by the shop yesterday, drunk out of his mind, and came on to me. I wasn't very receptive and he didn't handle it well." I can feel her body tense next to me as I keep my head down. *Here it comes.* If you haven't had the pleasure of being introduced to hurricane Juls, consider yourself lucky.

"WHAT THE FUCK, DYLAN! That sorry ass motherfucker will *wish* he was dead when I'm done with him!" Her voice is so loud; I'm certain every person at the spa is getting a taste of this.

"You sound like Reese."

"Fuck that. Reese can have him *after* I get my hands on him first. No guy should ever put his hands on a girl." She pauses and I hear her tense breathing. "He hasn't… Dylan, please tell me he's never done this before."

I push up and rest on my elbows. "Are you serious? He has *never* touched me before, ever. I would have killed him and you know it. Now can we drop this please? I want to relax and you freaking out next to me isn't helping."

"I'm going to cut his balls off and mail them to his mother."

Juls scowls at me as the door opens and two older ladies come in. She settles down on her stomach and curses under her breath.

"Oh, my. Honey, those bruises." The one masseuse states and I grunt, resting my head back down.

"Yeah, yeah. Just work my lower back and my legs please," I say flatly and in a way to let everyone in this fucking room know I am done talking about this. Because I am. If Justin ever touches me again, I won't have to worry about Reese getting into trouble for retaliating or Juls ripping his heart out of his chest, because I will end him myself.

"I WANTED TO MAKE A quick stop before we went to lunch. That okay with you?" she asks after pulling onto the highway. My eyes are heavy and I feel completely relaxed after our day together, which is nice considering how stressed out I was when the day started.

"Yeah, I don't care. Hey, have you heard from Joey at all? I know he's spending the weekend with Billy, but when the hell have you ever known him to not call one of us immediately after he gets nailed?"

She laughs, "I think Joey does the nailing, right? Isn't he the man in his relationships or whatever the fuck?"

"I don't know. Do they switch it up?" I glance out my window at the passing cars. "I mean, do they take turns doing the nailing?"

"I don't think so. Wouldn't it be like you switching with Reese or me switching with Ian?" She pulls off the highway and down a familiar street, turning into a large parking lot that overlooks a view of athletic fields and basketball courts. Pulling behind a tree, she puts the car in park and turns to me, smiling wide.

"Yeah, I guess you're right. Umm, what are we doing here exactly?" I gaze out the front window and see the crowds of people in front of us. There is a large playground filled with kids and their parents, a soccer game going on in the middle of the large field, and a group of men playing basketball. My eyes widen and I grip the seat. *Oh, my.*

"I thought we'd stop and enjoy this beautiful day for a second before we stuff our faces. See anything you like?"

I spot him right away, almost instantly. Shirtless in loose fitting black running shorts, Reese dribbles the ball between his legs while Ian guards him, stepping back slightly before gracefully pushing the ball into the air and whooshing it through the net. *Fuck me, he looks edible.* I hear my breathing quicken as my eyes take in his gleaming muscles, drenched in sweat and practically calling out to me. *Touch me, Dylan. You know you want to.*

"Holy hell." I slam my head back and hear her giggle. "I can avoid lunch entirely if you'd like. Who the hell needs food anyway?" My voice is thick and it takes me a minute to swallow the lump in my throat.

"Seriously, what the hell *is* food?" she says through a laugh and I feel my body temperature rise as Reese steals the ball from another guy and goes up to dunk it. "Wanna get a closer look?"

My eyes widen. "I don't know; he's so pretty from right here. I think if I get any closer I might pass out." *That and the fact it will probably take an army to pry me off his body.*

"Yeah, I know what you mean. Christ, look at Ian. If he keeps moving his hips like that, I might come right here next to you." She unbuttons the top of her blouse and sighs heavily. "How's the sex with Reese anyway? Amazing?"

"Amazing doesn't even touch the surface with him." I moan softly as he goes up and blocks another man's shot. "It's like his body is specifically wired to bring me to orgasm, and I mean *every part of his body*." My eyes go straight to his lips as he bites on his bottom one. "His mouth is insane."

Juls covers her mouth and giggles. "Fuck, I know what you mean. Ian is obsessed with eating me out. He has to do it every time he sees me or it's like he can't function properly. And, Christ Almighty, is he good at it."

I glance over at her. "Who would have thought a bunch of accountants could write a book on oral sex." My eyes flick back to Reese as he dunks the ball again. "Jesus Christ, he's good looking. It really is unfair to the rest of the male population."

"Ooohhh. Send him a text message. That way we can see his

face when he reads it. I fucking love that. Seeing a guy's reaction to you when he doesn't know you're looking. So fucking hot."

I smile and pull my phone out of my purse, thinking for a moment before my thumbs begin to move.

> *Me: Hi, handsome. Just so you know, I had a wonderful massage from a very strong woman named Betsy today. However, I would like another one from you if you're still offering. Does yours come with an orgasm?*

I press send and watch as Reese, after a moment, turns toward a pile of clothes that are tucked against the chain link fence. Holding up a finger, he jogs over to it and searches around before he lifts out his phone. His chest is rapidly rising and falling and his hair is drenched, sticking out all over the place. I can only see his profile and bite my lip as his turns up slightly.

"Ah. Look at that. So worth it," Juls says and I completely agree.

Dropping his phone on his clothes, he jogs back over to the game with his beautiful grin. My phone beeps and I hold it up for us both to read.

> *Reese: Hi, love. I'm glad you enjoyed your girls' day, and yes, the massage from me that you will get very soon definitely comes with an orgasm. Pervert.*

I giggle and turn to see the strangest look on my best friend's face.

"What?" I ask, seeing her eyes beginning to water. *Oh, Christ.*

"He calls you love? Ah, hell, Dylan, I don't know who's more romantic." She wipes under her eyes and I feel mine well up. "You better hold on tight to that one, sweets."

"Yeah, tell me about it," I say and blink rapidly, trying to dry mine up.

Juls backs out of the parking space and drives through the lot, slowing down and staring past me through my window. "Hey, isn't that one of the desk girls from their work? She looks really familiar."

My eyes follow hers and I recognize the girl immediately, the hair a dead giveaway. She's sitting on a bench partially obstructed by a tree and staring in the direction of the basketball game. "That's Reese's receptionist. Fucking bitch. She was so rude to me when I went to kill him on Monday, acting all possessive and catty. Why the fuck is *she* here?" Part of me wants to hop out of the car and run straight into his arms, declaring in front of her and whoever else wants to watch, that he is mine. But I don't. Instead, I just glare at her profile.

"I don't know, but she's staring at them like a creep. Redheads freak me the fuck out."

"Me, too. Come on, let's go eat."

Now that I seem to have not completely blown it with Reese, my appetite is back with a vengeance. Although, it is still a bit unsettling seeing his receptionist eye the lot of them up like she wants to eat them. *Maybe she's dating one of the other three guys?* I make a mental note to ask Reese about it next time we see each other, which I decide will not be until Tuesday. I can't see him every day. I'm already struggling with keeping my feelings and emotions out of this thing between us enough as it is.

MONDAY MORNING COMES QUICKER THAN I would have liked. I pass out early on Sunday and sleep soundly, not hearing my phone ring when Joey calls in the middle of the night. Noticing the missed call when my alarm goes off, I dial him quickly, putting it on speaker phone as I get into my running gear.

"I have news, cupcake. I'm on my way though, so meet me out front."

"Okay." I end the call and slip on my sports bra, tank top, and running shorts before popping into my Nikes. Grabbing my phone and my keys, I run downstairs and out the front door, locking up behind me as I begin to stretch.

It's already humid out and my top begins to stick to me in the most uncomfortable way possible. Summers in Chicago can be brutal, and when you start sweating immediately after stepping outside in the early morning hours, you know you're in for a hot one. This is one of the reasons why I don't understand the appeal for a summer wedding, at least not here anyway. Maybe somewhere with no humidity that doesn't turn your hair into a frizz fest after spending hours on making it look nothing less than perfect. I attended an outdoor wedding a few summers ago where I appallingly watched my beautiful three-tiered white chocolate creation melt in front of everyone at the reception. It was awful. Luckily, the bride thought it was hilarious and didn't care one way or the other because she was so deliriously happy to be married to her husband. Juls worked that wedding with me and told me the couple had only been dating nine weeks before he proposed to her, and at the time, I remember thinking there was no way in hell that marriage was going to last. How could anyone know without a doubt that they wanted to be with each other forever after only being together a few months? Juls agreed with me, saying the bride had mentioned how strongly her family was against the marriage, but she didn't care. She told my best friend she didn't want to wait any longer to start her life with him and that when it's right, it's just right. The past three summers on their anniversary, I've gotten a thank you card from the bride for helping make their day so special. And now look at Juls. She's only known Ian a few months and is crazy in love with him. *And look at you, Dylan. No, don't look at me. Nothing to see here.*

My eyes flick toward the pavement as Joey's tall frame comes jogging in my direction. Stopping in front of me and pulling his knee to his chest, he looks giddy beyond his usual giddy self.

"Are you going to make me ask?" I question, stretching my arms over my head.

He smiles and switches legs. "Billy asked me to move in with him."

Whoa. "What? Are you serious? That's crazy. What did you say?"

"Yes. Obviously." He jumps up and down on his feet and motions to me that he is ready to start running.

"Obviously? Joey, do you even really know this guy? He could cut out your organs and sell them on eBay. He could have a weird fetish."

He shakes his head. "I know him as well as you know Reese

and you're in love with him."

Fucking Juls. Jesus Christ, I need some new friends. "I *cannot* believe she told you that. I will cut a bitch next time her skinny ass walks into my shop." Realizing Joey has stopped running, I glance back and see his expression. *Motherfucker. He is one sneaky bitch.*

"I fucking *knew* it. You love him, Dylan. Oh, my God, this is fantastic." Running up to me, he grabs my shoulders and pulls me against his already drenched shirt.

"Gross, you're all sweaty. And I am not in love with him. Juls told me she was in love with Ian and I said something about maybe, possibly, doubtfully one day being in love with Reese. That's it. End of discussion."

Stepping back and holding me at arm's length, he studies me for a moment before he speaks. "Okay, whatever. But I think I'm in love, so can we focus on that fucking weirdness for a second?"

We hit our stride and I let Joey tell me all about how he's seen Billy practically every night since they met at the wedding and how he's never felt anything even close to this before, which I knew already. Joey is never shy about his feelings toward his hook ups and always shares more information than I would care to know. He tells me how they were hanging out at Billy's last night, lounging and watching television together when he just came out and asked Joey to move in and without hesitation, Joey said yes. He says he didn't have to think about it; he knows he wants to be with Billy every free second he has and he has never been this happy before with just one person. I'm speechless. I am literally without speech. This is Joey Holt we're talking about here. The man who went through other men like he was going for some kind of record. He once hooked up with three guys in one night at a club and did it without them knowing about each other. His longest running relationship was five minutes. And now, after a little over a week of knowing somebody, he's wifing up? I'm not sure whose wedding I'll be getting fitted for first, Juls' or Joey's.

I call Mrs. Frey that afternoon, confirming the details of her anniversary cake she wants me to create for her since I missed our meeting on Tuesday. She sweetly asks me how I am feeling and tells me how excited she is to be celebrating fifty years of marriage with her husband. Fifty years. I can't even imagine. She's a bit undecided about her cake flavors, knowing only her husband wants a chocolate cake, but not having any other preferences. I smile to myself when I ask her if the two of them like mint chocolate and she squeals into the phone. Suggesting my newly discovered chocolate peppermint frosting and telling her how absolutely decadent it is, she settles on her cake and I reassure her it will be ready for pickup on Friday.

After ending her call, I slip my phone out of my pocket and scroll to the contact info of a certain icing lover.

Me: Guess what kind of cake I get to make for someone's anniversary? I'll give you a hint. It's a flavor you seem to be quite fond of.

I walk into the back as Joey helps a customer, and begin pulling out ingredients. I have a good amount of baking to do tonight to prepare for the meeting I'm supplying tomorrow and want to start on it as soon as possible. I decide to make an assortment of muffins, blueberry, poppy seed, and my banana nut ones, some apple turnovers, and a variety of fruit and cheese danishes. The excitement of seeing Reese is almost palpable at this point and I need to stay busy. Placing my mixer on the worktop, my phone beeps and I run over to where I've laid it down on the other side of the table.

Reese: Could it be a cake with a certain hot pink frosting that I licked off you?

Me: That's the one. I don't think I'll look at that frosting the same again. Or my worktop for that matter.

Reese: Well, I'll definitely never look at my couch the same. How's your day going?

I giggle and pull the baking flour, sugar, and salt off the shelf.

Me: Good. Busy like every Monday. I'm going to be slammed all night making the breakfast treats for tomorrow. How's your day?

Reese: Full of meetings that I'm having trouble focusing on. My mind is elsewhere.

Me: Oh, is that right? And where is that dirty mind of yours right now?

I grab several mixing bowls and baking sheets and spread them out in front of me as I let my own mind wander elsewhere.

Reese: Well, it's imagining you spread out in front of me wearing a dress with nothing underneath it, your legs open and my face buried between them. But earlier, I was fucking you on my desk, against my window, and in my chair. I've had a very unproductive day.

"Shit." Note to self, never read a dirty text from Reese while opening a bag of flour, which I am now currently covered in. "Nice one, Dylan."

"You all right, cupcake?" Joey yells from up front as I quickly dust myself off.

"Yeah. Reese is also really good at the explicit text messaging. Like *really* good."

"Goddamn it, Billy."

I laugh under my breath at Joey's comment as I sweep up the flour I've just spilled everywhere. Wiping my hands off on my apron, I grab my phone and quickly reply.

Me: Well, I think we should be able to make at least one of those things happen tomorrow. That big dick better be ready for me.

Reese: My dick and I can't wait. See you tomorrow, love.

Chapter Eleven

JOEY AND I LOAD UP Sam on Tuesday at nine thirty a.m. with the breakfast treats, leaving me with just enough time to run back inside to give myself a quick once over before it's time to go. I've picked out a pale pink summer dress and paired it with some strappy sandals, pulling my hair up into a bun before I run downstairs and lock up the shop. Joey is perched against the van and messing with his phone when I finally emerge.

"Okay, how do I look? Professional with a hint of playful? Do you think the dress is too much? Maybe I should wear my apron. Should I wear my apron?" *Christ, why the hell am I nervous? I've supplied tons of business meetings with treats before. Of course, I wasn't banging any of the men I supplied for until now.*

He smiles and slips his phone away. "The only way I would suggest for you to wear your apron would be if you were to *only* wear your apron. You look great, cupcake."

"Thanks. I think Reese likes me in dresses." I walk around to the driver's side and hop in as Joey gets in on his side.

"Hmmm, I wonder why?" He laughs as my phone beeps. I quickly slip it out of my purse.

Reese: Counting the minutes. (19 to be exact)

I giggle.

Me: Oh, come on, Mr. CPA, I'm sure you can do better than that.

Reese: 1140 seconds. Also, I met you roughly 823,447 seconds ago. Now get your sweet ass here safely so I can kiss you.

I hear a muffled laugh from my right. "Are we going to be driving to the Walker & Associates building or are they coming to us for the meeting?" Joey asks as I put my phone in the cup holder, grinning like an idiot.

"Smart ass. Does Billy know you can get testy in the morning?"

He laughs as I pull away from the shop. "Oh, he knows, cupcake. He knows. By the way, this Saturday we're having our coming out as an official couple party or whatever the fuck, Billy's idea. Seven p.m. at his place, I mean, our place. Ooohhh, I love the sound of that."

"You're adorable. What should I bring? Booze?" I ask, weaving in and out of traffic.

"Obviously, bitch, and a housewarming gift for yours truly." He sneaks in that last part under his breath and I laugh. I'm giddily excited to go to this particular party, and not just because I get to see Billy and Joey together and the home they will be sharing, which I'm sure is insanely chic. Joey has impeccable taste, and even though I've only seen Billy a few times, the man can dress. But I'm also excited because a certain numbers guy that I'm crushing on will most likely be attending with me. And the thought of that makes me drive a little bit faster toward our destination.

I MAKE JOEY CARRY THE bulk of the load as we walk into the foyer, across the marble floor, and to the back of the lobby to the row of elevators. Riding up to the twelfth floor, I shift anxiously on my feet as I hold my two boxes of muffins in my hands, glancing over at the top of Joey's head that sticks up behind his seven boxes. Trying to muffle my giggles, I hear him grunt and make tiny noises of protest as the elevator stops on our floor and I walk behind him, placing my hand on his back.

"If I drop this, cupcake, it'll be your fault. This is once again a perfect reason why we need another fucking employee."

"Stop bitching, we're almost there." I walk down the long hallway, guiding Joey along with me, and stop at Ian's reception desk. The young blonde looks up and smiles warmly.

"Ms. Sparks?" she asks and I nod.

"That's me. Where should we take these?"

Joey turns his body so he can see the girl. "Seriously, where, honey, cause I'm about to drop all of these, and those sexy businessmen can eat them off the floor for all I care."

She laughs a bit. "First door on your right. Go on in. Mr. Thomas and Mr. Carroll are expecting you." I smile at her and walk with Joey to the tall door, opening it with my free hand and allowing him to walk ahead of me.

We step into a large conference room, which has a killer view, tall floor to ceiling windows that overlook the bustling city, and a long rectangular table. A few men, all in nice suits, glance up from their seats as they flip through files while another group of men stand in the corner by the window, conversing together. My eyes find Reese like a homing missile. Standing in a dark gray suit with a two-button jacket and a light and dark gray patterned tie, he stops mid-sentence as his eyes fall on me. I feel it, that familiar pull in my gut that makes me want to drop my boxes and spring up into his arms. The man rocks a suit better than anyone. But instead of acting on impulse, I settle for a smile.

"Hi," I say softly as he moves toward me, his long legs bringing him to me quickly. I hear a laugh coming from the corner and think I recognize it as Ian's, but can't be positive. Right now, the only other person in the room with me is Reese.

"Hi, yourself. Here, let me take that." He grabs my boxes and places them on the table while Joey mutters something under his breath.

"I can't wait to dig into these, Dylan. My girl talks about your creations nonstop and I'm starving," Ian says as he walks up to the table and opens a muffin box.

"Well, I hope you enjoy them. The banana ones are my favorite. Oh, nobody has allergies, right?" I ask and hear a round of muffled "Noes."

"Will someone take these from me already? For Christ's sake, Reese," Joey says and I cover up my mouth quickly to hide my laugh.

Reese takes his gaze off me and grabs several boxes off the top, revealing a very red-faced Joey. "Sorry, man," he apologizes and spreads the boxes out at the end of the table. Joey shakes his head in frustration, placing the remaining boxes on the table in front of the businessmen and opening them.

"Gentlemen, please help yourselves to the treats provided by Dylan's Sweet Tooth. We'll get started in five," Ian announces. Shuffling of papers and footsteps fill the room and I watch as Reese turns away from the table and walks toward me. Joey steps aside and pulls out his phone, smiling at something and giving me the indication that the something he is smiling at is Billy related.

"Handsome," I say softly as Reese stops just in front of me, his hands rubbing softly up my arms.

"Love, you look so pretty. I love you in dresses." My chest constricts as he leans in and plants three gentle kisses on my lips.

"And I love you in suits. I'm about to say fuck your meeting and take you right here on this table in front of everyone."

He laughs and looks at me wickedly. "I wouldn't object. This meeting is going to bore the hell out of me. Maybe I'll make you stay to keep me company."

I play with the buttons on his jacket, pulling him closer to me. "If you think for one second that I could stay in this room with you looking like that and not wrap my lips around you, you're crazy."

His hand grabs my face and he leans into my hair, brushing his lips against my ear. "Pervert. I love that dirty mouth of yours." He glances down briefly at his watch before grabbing my hand. "Come with me."

I look over at Joey who sees me getting pulled toward the door. Before I can speak, he grins and winks at me. "Meet you downstairs, cupcake." I blush instantly as I nod at him.

"Don't you have a meeting to run?" I ask as Reese pulls me down the hallway toward his office. My stomach is doing flips in anticipation of getting him alone.

"The meeting can wait. I need you." My heart squeezes at his words as we walk into his reception area. *Stop interpreting things the way you shouldn't, Dylan.* Scanning the small area as we walk toward his door, I lock onto the redhead behind the desk who glares in my direction, her eyes going to my hand that is in Reese's and her jaw clenching before she looks back up at my face. "Uh, Mr. Carroll, you have that meeting."

"Not now, Heather."

Her face hardens as he pulls me into his office and closes the door behind us, locking it before he presses me against it.

"Fucking hell, I need more than five minutes, Dylan. I don't like rushing with you." His lips find mine and I part for him, stroking my tongue against his as he reaches down and wraps my legs around his waist. I moan into him as his erection digs right where I want it, rubbing me right where I need it. My hands grip his head and hold it to mine as his one hand slips in between us. He undoes his belt, unzipping and unbuttoning his slacks and pulls himself free.

"This is going to be hard and quick, love."

"Please hurry, I need you." My panties are moved to the side and the touch of his finger between my legs makes me gasp. A low grunt escapes his lips as he buries his face into my neck and pushes inside me. He growls loudly, his one fist coming up and banging the door above my head.

"You're so wet. I love how ready you are for me," he says between muffled sounds as he pounds into me. I hold on tightly around his neck, groaning as he strokes inside me with the perfect amount of pressure. I won't last long and I know it. I've been primed for him all morning. My legs tremble around his waist as his hands hold my ass and pull me toward him to meet his thrusts.

"Reese, oh, God." I throw my head back and bite my lip to quiet my sounds. I want everyone to hear us and I don't at the same time. Part of me doesn't care that I am being fucked hard against his door with his secretary just outside, but the other part of me wants it to be just us in this moment. He licks up my neck to my ear and bites down lightly, pulling the tip into his mouth as his one hand comes around me and holds my face. His lunges become harder and I dig my nails into his neck and pull him closer, needing him as close to me as I can get him.

"Dylan."

My name on his lips pushes me to the top. The burning sensation shoots through my body and I lose control willingly. "I'm coming." I strain and arch into him, giving him the angle we both need to get him deeper. He growls and I feel him twitch inside me as I erupt around him at the same time. Warm release fills me and I pull his head back to allow me to watch him. "Look at me."

His eyes fixate on mine, wide and dilated as he stills and exhales sharply. Blinking heavily, he drops his head. "Jesus Christ," he says. His forehead is beaded with sweat and his hair is a right hot mess, which makes me smile. No one can pull off the *I just got fucked* hair like Reese. I am placed down on my feet and have to keep my arms around him to steady myself.

"Wow. You might have to carry me out of here," I say through a laugh. He grins and studies me as he tucks himself away, watching me pull my dress down.

"I could do that." He moves quickly to his desk and grabs a few tissues, dropping down in front of me and wiping between my legs. He discards them in the trashcan and returns in front of me, brushing the strand of hair that fell from my bun away from my face.

I'm certain I look thoroughly fucked, but don't care in the least. This man owns my body and I will let him use it wherever and whenever, and the thought suddenly frightens me. I swallow loudly and back up a bit. "I think your meeting may have started without you." I make sure my dress is covering everything, glancing behind me quickly. His hand stills on the door handle, getting ready to turn it when he looks over at me.

"I want to see you tonight." His voice is low, his eyes hooded as if he's bracing himself for my reaction.

I study him for a second before I respond. "But you just saw me." I want to see him too. I want to see him every second of every day, but I can't. I'm not strong enough for that.

He moves closer to me. "I know. Is there a rule that says I can't see you twice in one day?"

"Shouldn't there be?" My question hangs in the air between us for a moment before he nods in agreement. And then I see it, the shift in his expression that makes my stomach tense. He looks nervous and uneasy. *Is he struggling with this as much as I am? Isn't this what he wants?* I don't ask, but I hate seeing him like this, so I step in closer and slide my arms around his waist, planting a kiss on his jaw as he holds me against him.

"I just… I don't want to get too attached." *Because I'm falling in love with you and it will kill me when you're done with me.*

He clamps his lips together and nods before planting a kiss on my forehead. "I know. Come on, pretty girl. I have a meeting to run." I stand on my toes and plant quick kisses on his lips as he laughs against my mouth. *Serious conversation over, playful Reese back.*

Swinging his office door open, he places his hand on my lower back and ushers me out into the reception area and down the hallway. My eyes briefly fall on little Miss Uppity, her expression cold as usual, but I don't linger. I laugh under my breath and Reese looks down at me. "Something funny?" He stops in front of the conference room door and turns to me.

"Your receptionist is kind of a bitch."

He chuckles. "Ignore her." Pulling me in for a lasting kiss, the door opens, but I don't register it until after he has broken our contact. I wobble. This man can make me weak in the knees if I even cared about *having* knees anymore. The sound of a throat clearing causes us both to look into the room at the table full of men, Ian standing at the door and wearing his biggest smile. "Caught ya. Come on, man, we need to get started." I feel my face flush as Reese straightens his tie quickly and grabs the back of my head, pulling me into him for a quick kiss in my hair.

"Bye, love," he whispers.

"Bye, handsome. Go crunch some numbers or audit something or whatever the fuck it is you do." He shakes against me with laughter and pulls back, winking before he walks into the room. My eyes quickly scan the table for my empty bakery boxes when I stop on a familiar smirk that is plastered on the face of the man who had picked up the tarts for his father last week. His eyes rake over my body, slow and sleazy like, and I suddenly feel dirty as Ian clears his throat, earning my attention.

"Bye, Dylan," he says and I wave awkwardly, turning on my heels and hearing the sound of the doors close behind me.

What the fuck is that guy doing here? And why the hell did he stare at me like that? I ride the elevators down and march purposely through the lobby as my mind races. I find Joey outside in the van talking on his phone as I hop in the driver's seat and start it up.

"Okay, baby. I love you, too. Bye." He ends his call and lays his head back dramatically onto the seat. "I'm in deep, cupcake."

"I can tell," I reply playfully. "You are *not* going to believe who I just saw sitting in the meeting." After waiting a minute for effect, Joey motions with his hands for me to hurry the fuck up with my information as I drive down the street. "That guy who gave me his card the other day in the shop. The cocky one who picked up the tarts."

I hear his sharp breath intake. "Are you serious? What the hell was he doing there? Does he work there? Holy shit, are him and Reese co-workers?"

These are the same questions that are running through my mind. "I don't know; I didn't get to ask. I really hope not though. Asshole stared at me like he wanted to eat me." I feel a chill run through me at the memory of it.

"That's probably because he does. He wasn't shy about wanting you last week, and I'm sure seeing you again with Reese's dick in your mouth didn't help."

I scowl at him. "Christ Almighty, Joey, he just saw me kiss him." *In fact, everyone saw me kiss him.* "Okay, so you're kind of an expert at the whole casual sex stuff, right? Have you ever seen a guy who you are just fucking more than once in the same day? I mean, do you space out the times you spend together or do you just say fuck it and see him whenever you both feel like it?"

Joey chuckles before he answers. "Honestly, when I've done the *just sex* stuff before, we saw each other often because we wanted to fuck often. I think as long as you both can keep yourselves from getting too wrapped up in it, there shouldn't be that many rules." He slips his phone out of his pocket and begins messing with it, ending our discussion.

I contemplate Joey's explanation to me as we drive to the shop. There shouldn't be too many rules? I feel like rules are extremely necessary, at least for me to be able to do this successfully. There are certain things that just can't happen between Reese and me. Like sleepovers and meeting each other's families and doing anything too romantic or intimate. Keeping myself from getting too wrapped up in him is the biggest struggle of my life, but immensely worth it. I want to do this with him more than anything because I love being with him. The alternative, ending this because it's too hard for me, sends a pain through my body at the very idea of it. If anyone is going to fuck this up between us, it's going to be me. He isn't going to interpret things the way they aren't meant to be interpreted, and he isn't going to get too attached, so neither should I. He's used to not doing serious, and even though I'm not, I can keep up. I'm determined to make this work and I will. I just need to stop acting like a stupid girl about it.

I close up the shop on Tuesday night at six p.m., saying goodnight to Joey after he helps me put any uneaten goodies away. My mind has been on Reese all afternoon, and I'm aching to be with him, and not just for sex. I want to talk to him and play with him. I just want to see him. And he wants to see me. I had originally planned on spending my night watching television or taking a long bath, but neither one of those options sound appealing anymore. I stop fighting it and quickly make up my mind. Slipping off my apron and grabbing my purse and keys, I lock up the shop behind me and stroll toward Sam.

Driving to Reese's building is an easy route from the bakery. He lives in Printer's Row, which is just south of downtown Chicago, a mere five minutes away. I'm very familiar with the area, having catered to several businesses in the trendy upscale neighborhood. I like this part of the city, and tell myself I really should come down here more often as I park Sam down the street a bit and lock him up, beginning the short walk to the front of the condos.

I practically sprint off the elevator and down the hallway,

stopping sharply in front of Reese's door and looking down at my flustered state. You would think by the way my skin is tingling that it has been days since I last saw him. Slipping my phone out of my pocket, I smile and quickly type a message.

> *Me: I really want to see you tonight. Is there any way you could stop whatever it is you're doing and come to my place?*

I wait patiently and then a thought hits me that makes me feel like a complete jerk off. *What if he isn't home? What if he's at his office or out somewhere and is going to leave to go to the bakery and I'm not there? Shit.* But just as my blood pressure starts elevating to a crazy height, his door swings open and I smile at the sight of him typing on his phone with one hand, his keys in the other. My phone beeps and he quickly glances up, his lips parting and a sharp breath escaping at the sight of me. I'm still in my pink dress from earlier, but now my hair is down and it frames my face in soft waves. As his eyes take me in, it hits me. Reese had stopped whatever it was that he was doing to come to me, and I know I would have done the same if he had asked. And I am done trying to convince myself otherwise.

Chapter Twelve

"DYLAN, HI. I DIDN'T… I thought—"

I lift up my hand to stop him. "Hold on, I just got a text from this crazy hot guy. It might be important." He leans against the door and beams at me as I swipe across my screen and fail miserably at holding back my ridiculous smile.

> *Reese: I'll always stop whatever it is I'm doing to come to you.*

Oh, man. I tilt my head and step toward him, kissing him briefly on the lips before I turn away from him. "Got my fix. See ya," I say and yelp as his hands grip me around my waist and lift me up, pulling me back against him as he carries me through his doorway. "Put me down, you barbarian." I laugh and he shifts me so I am now hanging over his shoulder, my face in his perfect ass. I smack it loudly and feel his hand pinch mine as he walks me through his condo, which I am now getting my first real look at; of course, it's all upside down at the moment. Stopping finally, he slides me down his body and places my feet on the floor.

"You're here," he states as I give him a quick once over. He's wearing sweatpants and a T-shirt and looks entirely too snuggly. I reach up and run my fingers through his hair as he smiles down at me, the little lines popping out next to his eyes.

"I am, and, thank God, so are you. I panicked that maybe you were out on a hot date or something."

He looks at me curiously and runs his fingers along my jaw. "No hot date tonight, I'm afraid. And what exactly are *you* doing here? I thought we shouldn't see each other more than once in the same day?"

I shrug and step back from him, glancing around the massive living area that we are standing in. This has to be the nicest condo I've ever been in. "I was feeling rebellious. What were you doing before I got here?" My eyes fall on the couch that I am very fond of as his hands wrap around my waist, pulling me back against him.

"Watching TV on my favorite couch." He reaches around and plants a kiss on my ear. "Would you like to join me?"

"I thought maybe we'd play a game. Do you have any cards?"

He releases me and disappears down the hallway and into a room while I turn and sit on the armrest of the couch. Re-emerging moments later, he tosses me the deck and I stand up and walk to his round dining table, pulling out a chair and sitting in it. He sits across from me and I blow him a kiss.

"Handsome." I pull the cards out and begin shuffling them.

"Love, what game are we playing?" He leans back in his chair, his shirt tightening across his broad chest. *Who the hell looks this good in sweats?*

I think for a moment before I reply. "I actually don't think it has a name, so I'll just explain it to you." I stand up and walk around the table, pulling my chair so that it is now next to his, and sit down. He turns his body toward me and begins lightly running his fingertips over my bare knee. I place the stacked deck face down on the table in front of us.

"So, we take turns drawing cards, each suit representing something different. Hearts are kissing, diamonds are oral, clubs are stimulation using your hands, and spades are massages." His eyebrows raise and he licks his grinning lips. "The numbers on the cards represent how many seconds you get to do that activity, for example." I pull the top card and turn it in my hand, showing the five of hearts. Leaning in, I press my mouth against his and swipe my tongue across his lips as he moves with me. I savor his minty taste for five, well worth it, seconds and then break away, placing my card down on the table. "Oh, and I've kept the jokers in. You pick one of those and you get to fuck me."

He rubs his hands together eagerly. "No time limit on the fucking?" Dropping his hand on top of the deck, he waits anxiously for my response with a raised brow.

"No, but I would like to play a little before we get completely lost in each other, so I'm hoping neither one of us draws one for at least a couple turns."

He looks like he is about to respond, but quickly shakes his head as he picks up a card. I dance in my seat as he shows it to me. "Diamonds are what again?"

"Oral." I lean back in my chair and spread my legs as he amusingly kneels down in front of me. He looks just as enthusiastic about this as I am.

"Count it out," he says, slipping off my panties and tucking them into his pants pocket.

"I will be getting those back before I leave," I state, praying he'll actually refuse me.

"Good luck with that." Burying his head between my legs, I wait to start the count until I feel the first lick.

"Oh, wow. One, two, threeeee." He sits up and licks his lips as I reach the end of my count. "Stupid. I should have removed all cards with numerical values less than ten."

"You should have. Three seconds between your legs is not nearly enough time for me."

Picking my card, I stand up and walk behind him as I drop it into his lap. "Count please," I say as I begin massaging his upper back and shoulders.

"Mmmm. One, two, three, four, five…" His numbers trail off as I rub down his arms, digging into his muscles and offering the perfect amount of pressure. I will never get tired of touching him. He's extremely responsive to every little movement of my hands. I move around front and take my seat, pulling his hands into mine and kneading his palms with my thumbs. "Ten." Slowly opening his eyes, he looks at me, completely relaxed and borderline sleepy. "I love it when you do that."

I kiss each palm before I drop them. "I know you do, and I love doing it. You look so freaking cute when you're relaxed like that."

He picks his card and quickly sticks it back into the middle of the deck.

"Hey. What was that?" I ask through a laugh, trying to grab the deck as he brushes my hands away.

"Something I'm not ready for yet. Back off, Sparks." Drawing another card, he flicks it at me and it lands on my dress face up. "Hands?"

I nod through a closed lipped grin. Reaching out and pulling me into his lap in one quick motion, my back against his chest, his fingers run up the inside of my thigh and between my legs. "Reese." I let my head roll back against his.

"Count, love." He slips two fingers inside me and begins rubbing my spot with his thumb in his perfect rhythm.

I swallow loudly. "One, two, Jesus Christ, three, six, Reese." He laughs into my ear and slowly pulls out as I groan in protest. "I fucking hate this game. We should have just played strip poker." I cross my arms over my chest after reclaiming my seat.

He quickly sucks on his fingers before he picks another card and hands it to me. "I like it."

I snatch the card away from him and glance at it quickly, smiling at myself. "Not for long. You're about to hate this game as much as I do, Carroll." Turning the card in my hand, I reveal the four of diamonds. "Pull it out; I don't have all night."

His eyes widen as he reaches into his pants and pulls out his cock, holding it at the base. He's impossibly hard already as I kneel between his legs. Leaning in and planting a kiss on the head, I hear his breathing quicken at the anticipation.

"Count please," I say before taking him in as far as I can. I moan against his skin and feel the muscles of his lower body tense.

"FUCK, one, two, Dylan, oh, God, please don't stop at—"

"Four," I say as I give one last kiss to the head and sit back into my chair.

"Fuck this game," he grunts and pulls me onto my feet, turning me around so I'm facing the table, his chest to my back. "I want this dress off."

Reaching down with shaking hands, I grab the bottom of my dress and pull it over my head in one quick motion, leaving me standing completely naked. His hands reach around and cup my bare breasts, pulling at my nipples as I arch into his grip.

"I need you."

"God, Dylan. Do you have any fucking clue what you're doing to me?" His voice is strained and his breath is hot against my hair. One hand leaves my breast and grips my hip. I feel him between my legs, positioning himself at my entrance. I'm completely soaked and ready for him, but he doesn't enter me. Placing my palms flat on the table, I lean forward and feel his mouth on my back, his tongue and lips caressing the skin on my spine. My elbows are shaking and I can barely hold myself still.

"Reese, please." I need him in me, and wiggle against him, feeling his hitched breath against my back. His hand that is holding my breast runs down my taut stomach and rests between my legs.

"You're all I think about," he whispers so softly that I barely hear it over my panting. But I definitely hear it. His thumb begins moving against my clit as he rubs against my entrance with his erection. "Dylan."

"You're all I think about, too." I drop my head down, somehow feeling even more exposed than just being naked in front of him. His hand grips the back of my neck and rolls me forward, giving him the angle he needs to push into me. We cry out together at that first drive, and he starts moving, harder and harder, faster against me with such force I think I might snap in half. Both hands move to my hips and pull me against him, allowing himself deeper entry and hitting every nerve in my body.

"Reese. OH, GOD." I shake against him, pushing against his every thrust. One arm wraps around my waist and pulls me back to him. He's still wearing his shirt and it slides against my skin, rising up with each movement so more and more of his bare chest is felt against my back. His tight muscles flex against me, the arm holding my waist contracting against my stomach. I reach above me and wrap my one hand around his neck, the other gripping tightly onto the arm around my waist. He's so powerful, every part of him, and not just the way he moves during sex. He's in complete control of every part of me and everything we do together. Fuck feminism. I need Reese more than I need my next breath. His words ring out around me, telling me how good I feel, how nothing has ever felt like this, how he can't get enough of me. Everything he says gets me closer.

"Come for me, love."

"Oh, God, YES." My core ignites and strikes every nerve inside of me as we release together, his name on my lips as I fall forward and sprawl out naked onto his table. He stays in me, his head resting on the middle of my back as his breath warms my already heated skin. We remain just like this for minutes, neither one of us pulling or pushing away from the other. The only sounds filling the condo is our breathing. I finally begin to wiggle against him and he kisses me quickly on my back before pulling out, allowing me to stand and stretch my muscles.

"I was getting the worst cramp. Would have been totally worth it though just for the record," I say as he picks my dress up off the floor and smiles down at me. Studying it quickly in the most adorable Reese way, he holds it over my head and allows me to slip back into it, kissing me quickly on my lips as my head pops through the top.

"Stay here," he orders before turning and walking down the hallway and through a doorway. He walks back out and steps into another room, but now with something in his hand. The sound of running water peaks my curiosity and I'm about to follow him when he re-emerges, carrying a wash cloth in one hand and something else folded up in the other. Dropping to his knees in front of me, I yelp at the chilled cotton as he wipes between my legs, cleaning off what he gave me. "Here, step in." I glance down as he holds open a pair of his boxers.

"Well, this could have been avoided if someone didn't have a panty fetish." He shimmies the cotton blend up my thighs and winks at me. Gripping the waist band, I roll them until they become very short and look like tiny boy briefs. *Mmm, please let me keep these.*

"Yes, but if I wouldn't have taken them, I wouldn't be standing here looking at your hot little ass in my boxers." He reaches around and smacks me. "Hungry?" he asks just as my stomach growls.

I embarrassingly push against it and he smirks. "Yeah, well, I didn't put much thought into dinner since I rushed over here; so technically, it's your fault I didn't eat." I walk over to the couch and plop down sideways so my bare feet are resting on the cold leather.

"Oh, is that right?" he says as I hear movement in the kitchen. I decide not to look and let him surprise me as I grab the TV remote and begin flipping through the channels. I stop on a cooking show and watch with interest as the host begins flattening out pastry dough. "Do you like spaghetti?"

"Yes, I love it. Are you actually going to cook me dinner?" I rest the side of my head on the leather and play with the hem of my dress.

"I'm going to heat it up. Oh, by the way, the guys at the meeting today loved your treats." The microwave dings and I smile. "Those apple things were insane. I ate like four of them."

I radiate from where I sit, and then the thought of the meeting brings back the smirk I'd received before I left. "Hey, there was this guy in your meeting today who came into my shop last week." I close my eyes and try to picture his business card. "Umm, weird first name. Cocky. Thinks he's way hotter than he is."

Reese rounds the couch with two bowls and hands me one before he sits down next to my feet. "Bryce?"

I nod as I take in a mouthful of spaghetti, moaning softly around my fork.

"What about him? 'Thinks he's hotter than he is,' that's funny."

I roll my eyes and chew up my bite. "This is really good. Did you make this?" He smiles and nods as he takes a massive forkful. "Anyway, he doesn't work with you, does he? I mean, if I were to come and see you at work, would he be there?"

He chews up his bite and shakes his head. "No. He's an investor, and I have to deal with his stupid ass occasionally, but he doesn't work in my building. Why, did he do something? If he fucking touched you, Dylan—"

Slurping in my noodles, I hold up my hand to stop him. "No, he didn't touch me. Jesus, Hulk, relax." I earn myself a stern look and quickly swallow my bite. "He just came into the shop last week and asked me for my number, which I didn't give him, and I didn't like how he looked at me today."

His eyes narrow and his fork stills in his bowl. "Did he look at you the way *I* look at you?"

I swallow my bite. "No. You don't make me feel like I'm being mentally taken advantage of. But he doesn't work with you, so don't worry about it."

His eyes quickly flick to mine. "If he comes into your shop again, I want to know about it."

My eyes widen. *Oh, for fuck's sake.* "Don't you think that's a little extreme?" I place my bowl into my lap. *Is he seriously going to injure every man who looks at me twice? Is he always this possessive with his flings?*

"No." He puts his bowl back down. Turning his body toward me, he pulls my feet into his lap, and his green stare burns into mine. "I have a huge fucking problem with guys putting their hands on you or making you feel uncomfortable. Don't ask me not to react to that."

I lean forward and grab his bowl, seeing one side of his mouth curve up as I get a fork full and hold it out to him.

"You're not going to fight me on this?" he asks suspiciously before taking the bite off the fork.

"No, I get it. I would slap a bitch if she put her hands on you or made you uncomfortable." His mouthful muffles his laugh as he grabs his bowl from me. "But just so you know, I can handle assholes like Bryce. I just didn't want to have to run into him when I come see you at work. *If* I come see you at work." I grab my bowl and pull another bite into my mouth, wiggling my feet in his lap.

"If? No, I don't think so. I like when better."

"You only say that because both times I've been there, you've gotten off. It must be nice to have orgasms during your work hours." I move my foot and rub it against him, feeling him twitch under me.

He arches his brow. "You know damn well that if I could escape my office to make you come behind that bakery counter of yours, I'd do it. And I don't just like you coming to my work to blow me or get fucked against my door." I loudly slurp a noodle into my mouth, making him laugh. My ringtone sounds through the condo and I hop up, grabbing it off the kitchen table and exhaling noisily at the name on the screen. *Oh, great.*

"Hey, Mom." I plop back down on the couch and squeeze the top of my nose. I have an awful feeling that I'm going to regret answering this call right now.

"Sweetheart. How are you? I've been meaning to talk to you since the wedding, but your father—"

"Her father what, Helen? Her father what?" *Oh, Lord, help me.* My parents are notorious for both staying on the line during our conversations. "You know damn well what, Bill. Anyways, dear, are you home because we're only five minutes away."

"Mom, I'm fine. The wedding was fine, but no, I'm not home right now." It has been a few weeks since I've seen my parents, and I do want to catch up with them, but now is not the time. Not while I sit next to Reese.

"Just fine?" he asks beside me, earning himself a right shove. "I'm sure when you were screaming my name it was more than just fine in that moment."

"I'm going to murder you," I mumble through clenched teeth as he eyes me up with his wicked grin. I can feel my heart beating rapidly and curse myself for not letting this shit go straight to voicemail.

"Well, where are you? We're in the neighborhood and want to see our only child. Are you at Juls' house? We know where that is," Mom says and I hear the sound of traffic through the phone.

"No, Mom, I'm not at Juls' house. I'm at…" My eyes flick to Reese who is anxiously waiting for my explanation, devouring his spaghetti with a playful grin.

"Would you like *me* to tell your mother where you are?" he asks, reaching for the phone.

I quickly turn away from him and get out of his reach. *Well, this is just perfect.* "I'm at a guy's house. Can I call you later?"

"A guy? What guy? Oh, honey, did you meet someone? What's his name? Can we meet him? Is it serious? What does he do, Dyl? Oh, I'm so glad you found a new boyfriend."

"He's not a democrat is he?" my dad adds. I want to crawl into a hole and die. My mother has been trying to marry me off since I was nineteen. She wants grandbabies and she wanted them yesterday.

"Oh, my God, can I please call you back?" Before I can comprehend what's happening, Reese grabs the phone out of my hand and stands up, placing it to his ear. *Oh, God, no.* My eyes widen and my jaw hits the couch as I slowly watch my world implode.

"Mrs. Sparks? This is Reese Carroll, your daughter's boyfriend." I run at him and knock him off his feet, sprawling him out on his back as he holds me at arm's length. *Does the man have a death wish?* He seems completely unaffected by my move and just gives me a sly grin. "Oh, and, Mr. Sparks. It's so nice to talk to you both."

"Give me the phone, Reese." I grunt and try to move around the arm that is holding me away from him. *Jesus Christ. Why does every male in my life think it's okay to take the phone away from me?* "Give it." My efforts are useless, only making me out of breath while he beams up at me like the gorgeous god that he is.

"Yes, she is very special, isn't she?"

"You are never getting laid again."

"That sounds wonderful." He laughs into the phone. I glare at him and he winks at me. *Jerk.* "I'll tell Dylan to set it up. I look forward to meeting you, too. Okay, here she is." He smiles in his minor victory over me and holds out the phone. "Here you go, love."

Snatching it away from him with one hand, I give him the finger with the other, as I stand up and begin to pace. He stays on the floor, tucking his hands behind his head and follows me with his eyes.

"Hello?" I ask and brace myself for my mother's rant. I sit down on the arm of the couch and rub my temple with my free hand.

"Oh, my. He sounds lovely, sweetheart. And so polite."

I shake my head. "Well, I wouldn't get too attached if I were you. I'm plotting his slow death as we speak." Reese stands up and moves toward me, brushing his hand over my chest before he walks down the hallway. I shudder at the contact.

"Oh, hush. Anyways, darling, since you're busy with your

boyfriend we'll have to see you another time. Love you lots."

"Love you, sweetheart," Dad says.

"Bye, love you, too." I press end and slip my feet back into my sandals, walking myself over to the table to retrieve my keys. *Great. My parents think Reese is my boyfriend. They'll want to meet him now. Just fucking great.* My head is spinning and it's officially time to go home before he decides to go through *all* my contacts and explain our situation to each and every one of them.

"Please tell me I didn't piss you off to the point of you leaving?" His voice washes over me as I turn and see him walking slowly toward me. His sweats hang loosely on his hips and the tiniest amount of skin is now on display under his T-shirt. *Damn him and his body.*

"Why the hell would you tell my parents you're my boyfriend? Are you insane? Do you have any idea the amount of phone calls I'm probably going to get now? Since Justin, I've been able to limit my mother to once a week check-ins. But *now,* she'll never leave me alone."

Stopping in front of me, he pushes my hair back and grips my head between his hands. My face is stuck in scrunched up hate Reese mode, but it is quickly fading due to his softness, and his hotness, and his overall Reeseness. *Stay strong, Dylan.*

"What should I have said? That I'm casually fucking their daughter and not in a relationship with her? That sounds terrible."

"I don't understand why you had to say anything, but fine. Every time she calls me, I'm just going to give her your number and *you* can deal with her." Crossing my arms over my chest, I stare him down as he backs up and shrugs.

"That's fine with me. I can dig for some Dylan dirt." *How is he completely calm and collected over this? Why the hell would he want my parents to think I'm seeing him in that sort of way?*

Flipping my keys in my finger, I turn toward the door. "Everyone has gone crazy. It's decided. I'm the only sane person left in Chicago."

His footsteps follow behind me and I feel his hand grab a hold of mine. "Hold on, I'll walk you out." He turns toward the pair of tennis shoes that are by the couch and slips them on quickly.

Stopping in front of Sam, I glance over at Reese who is staring peculiarly at my vehicle, no doubt hurting my precious Sam's feelings in the process. *Good Lord, we can't all drive Range Rovers.* "Why the hell did you drive your delivery van over here?" His finger traces the cupcake design on the side as he studies it in his usual Reese way.

"Um, because it's my only car." I open the driver's side door and hop in as he moves to stand by me.

"You don't own a regular vehicle?"

I shake my head. "No, Mr. Money bags. I used to drive an old Corolla, but it broke down and I never really had the money to get a new car, so I just take Sam everywhere. It pisses Joey off, but I don't mind." Reese runs his hand through his hair and I sigh. "Don't you dare hate on Sam. He's been the only man in my life that has never let me down besides my father."

He squints at me and leans in, brushing his lips against mine. "And me, I hope."

"Humph. The jury's still out on you, handsome." I feel him pull back to allow me to leave when I grip his T-shirt and pull him close to me again, nuzzling my head into my favorite spot on his neck. "Just give me a minute." I hear a tiny laugh as his hand comes up to hold me against his body. Even though I'm a little irritated and a lot confused, everything seems to melt away when I'm close to him like this. I inhale deeply, allowing his smell to run through me and, hopefully, rub off enough to take some of him home.

"You can stay with me and do this all night if you want," he says softly. I close my eyes and shake my head against him. "Fine, but just so you know, I'm not a fan of this bullshit 'no sleepover' rule."

I pull away from him and rest my forehead against his, seeing his serious expression. "I should go," I whisper and he grabs my face and plants kisses all over it as I try to contain my euphoria. Playful Reese is hard to let go of, but I somehow manage. Closing my door, he walks to the curb and watches me as I pull away, his incredible build slowly getting smaller in my rear view.

My mind is racing as I drive home. So many things happened tonight that I wasn't anticipating and don't quite know how the hell to react to. Between him dropping everything to come to me, telling me I'm all he thinks about, and declaring himself my boyfriend, I feel completely unprepared for what to expect out of him next. Fuck my rules. Reese has his own set that he is playing by and I'm completely oblivious to all of them.

Chapter Thirteen

IT POURS DOWN RAIN ALL day on Wednesday, preventing our usual steady flow of walk-in customers from making the trek down Fayette Street. I stay busy in the kitchen all day, which I tend to do most rainy days, while Joey rifles through my planner to make sure we're prepared for all upcoming orders. I have one wedding this weekend and the Frey's anniversary cake to make, which I've decided to get started on after lunch on Thursday. In between mixing the ingredients, I scroll over the last several text messages between Reese and myself that had transpired yesterday. He really is an expert at the flirty text messages thing. I've just managed to slip the cake into my double oven when Joey's voice comes ringing through the shop.

"Cupcake, you have a delivery," he sings and I move quickly past the worktop and through the doorway. Fred is standing in front of the counter and smiles at me, his gap-toothed grin spreading across his face.

"Hi, Fred. How are you today?" I ask as he steps up to the counter. Fred is the only other man who makes my heart flutter at his appearance, and it's only because he always comes with something from Reese.

"I'm great, Ms. Dylan. Here you go." Sliding a brown envelope across to me and holding out his clipboard, I sign for it and hold up my finger to him. I grab a bakery box and fill it with some apple turnovers, slipping one into a separate small bag and handing them out to him.

"Would you please give this box to Mr. Carroll for me? The one in the bag is for you," I say and his smile manages to grow.

"Sure. Thanks, Ms. Dylan. See ya, Joey," he responds excitedly, turning on his feet and walking out the door.

"Bye, Freddy," Joey replies in his flirty voice, earning himself an eye roll from me.

"Seriously? He's like sixty."

"Age is just a number, cupcake."

I open the envelope and pull out the tiny brown card, my heart beating so loud I'm sure Joey will give me shit about it.

Dylan,

Have you heard the song "Do I Wanna Know?" by the Arctic Monkeys? I can't listen to it anymore without thinking of you, not that I'm complaining or anything. Miss your face.

X Reese

Oh, I miss his face terribly. Handing over the card to Joey, I watch his expression get all weepy while he digs his phone out of his pocket.

"I don't think I know that song," I say as he docks his phone and hits a few buttons. Music begins playing through the speakers, music that instantly reminds me of sex. *Holy shit.* I can actually picture Reese thrusting into me at the tempo.

"Jesus, is this it?" I ask and Joey nods through a grin.

"Yup. I fucking love this song. You should listen carefully to the lyrics, cupcake. I think he's trying to tell you something," he replies as he hands me back the card and starts organizing the display case. I lean against the counter, listening to the song as the front door swings open and Juls comes barreling through.

"Hello, my lovies. Ooohhh, I fucking love this song. Reminds me of sex." She echoes my thoughts as I nod in agreement.

"Reese said it reminds him of Dylan. What you think about that?" Joey asks, and her eyes widen.

"Damn. I think he wants to fuck you sideways, Dyl."

I giggle and smooth out my apron. "Well, naturally." I glance over at my best friend who is standing in the middle of the shop, rubbing her eyes and looking positively glowing. *On a Thursday?* "What's up with you?" I ask.

"Nothing, I just have something in my eye," she replies, as she keeps wiping below her lashes with both hands. She's really going at it and I look over at Joey whose mouth has dropped open.

"JULS!" he yells and startles me so bad I have to grip the counter.

"Jesus Christ, Joey. What?" I ask, my eyes falling on Juls who is now only holding up her left hand. My eyes flick between my two best friends, back and forth, still feeling completely lost until something sparkles and catches my attention. My jaw drops as I finally focus on what Joey has seen. Her delicate hand is now adorned with a shockingly large diamond and I scream. Joey screams. Juls screams. There is a lot of fucking screaming going on.

"You're engaged?" I shriek and she nods frantically, her hands coming up to cover her face as Joey and I round the counter and charge at her. "Oh, my God." The ring is beautiful and totally her. Massive and sparkly, the princess cut diamond is surrounded by smaller delicate diamonds and gleams brilliantly. Tiny diamonds run along both sides down the band as well. "Holy shit, it's gorgeous. When did this happen? How did it happen?" I ask as Joey studies the ring closely.

"Seriously the most beautiful ring I've ever fucking seen. Damn," he chimes in as he holds her petite hand in his.

She wipes the tear that has streamed down her face and shuffles excitedly on her feet. "Last night. Ian took me to Grant Park for a stroll after the rain had let up and he dropped down in front of that massive fountain. I died, right there on the spot." More tears come down and she quickly rubs them away. "He told me he's loved me for so long and he'll love me forever. God, it was so fucking romantic."

My waterworks are now free flowing and turning toward Joey. I see he is as much of an emotional wreck as I am. "You're going to be the most beautiful bride," I manage through sniffles. "I'm assuming we're looking at next September or October for the big day?"

"Fuck that noise. I am not waiting a year to marry that man. We've decided on September seventeenth." Joey gasps and I'm pretty sure I do also. I'm stunned, completely shocked. *Is she crazy?*

"That's like three months away," I say as the shop phone rings.

"Oh, please. Have you forgotten who you're talking to here? I could plan a fabulous wedding in a month if I had to." I dash behind the counter and grab the phone on the fifth ring. She is right though. If anyone could pull off a spectacular wedding in three months, it's Juls. Besides, I'm fairly certain she's already planned most of the details without Ian's knowledge of it.

"Dylan's Sweet Tooth," I chirp into the phone as Joey and Juls excitingly talk about the wedding.

"Hi, sweetheart." My mom's voice instantly sends my back rigid and I squeeze my eyes shut. *Oh, great. It's starting*

"Hi, Mom. What's up?" I ask casually. Please, Lord, let her be calling to tell me someone died or something else non-romance related. *Maybe she's forgotten all about Reese.*

I hear muffled noises in the background, most likely the sounds of my father getting shushed. "Oh, nothing much. So how exactly did you meet Reese? I'm dying to know all about him and Google only tells you so much."

"You Googled him?" I didn't even think my mother knew how to use the internet. Now she's googling the man I'm sleeping with? *Hmmm, maybe I should do that.*

"Yes. Good grief, he's handsome. Now tell me, how did you two meet?" *Oh, you know, he nailed me up against a bathroom sink at my ex's wedding. Crap.* I need a distraction and the sight of my bouncing best friends gives me inspiration.

"Mom, Juls is engaged. Isn't that great? And she's getting married this September." Nothing like wedding news to get my mother sidetracked. She's a sucker for hard gossip, especially when it involves my friends.

She gasps dramatically. "That's wonderful. Oh my, that's so soon." I hear her hands clapping together through the phone. "How lovely. Juls will make such a beautiful bride. You know who *else* would make a beautiful bride?"

What? Shit! I scramble around the counter and grab Joey by the hair, a loud scream emanating from him followed by a string of curse words directed at me. "Oh, shit. Gotta go, Mom. Joey's having a gay emergency. You know him. Love you." I end the call quickly before she can throw out any questions. *Whew. Crisis Averted.*

"What the fuck, Dylan? That hurt. And why does it have to be a *gay* emergency?" Joey rubs his scalp, his face scrunched up in pain as he glares at me.

"Ha! Like there's any another type of emergency involving you," Juls laughs.

"Sorry. Really, *really* sorry about that. My mom knows about Reese and I'm trying to avoid her at all costs." I exhale forcefully. "You know how she is." I decide to keep the 'Reese telling my parents that he's my boyfriend' news to myself. I would never hear the end of it.

"Oh, yikes," he states. "Actually, that reminds me." He quickly combs through his hair. "You remember how Billy thought it was hilarious that you thought Reese was married?" I nod as Juls moves next to me and faces Joey, her arms crossing over her chest. "Well, I thought that was weird. I mean, why is that so fucking funny? He's gorgeous. He could have been married."

"Joey, is there a point to this?" I ask

He huffs in annoyance. "Yes. I asked Billy about it and he said Reese is completely against getting serious with a girl. He won't do it." My stomach rolls. "When they start getting clingy, he moves on to the next one."

"Joey, that's enough," Juls says.

I blow my breath out. "It's fine. I figured as much." But I wasn't expecting it to hurt this bad to hear it out loud. *Shit.* I feel like my heart has been shoved into a vice.

He moves closer to me and grabs my hand, stroking the back of it with his thumb. "Dylan, I'm sorry. I just, I don't want to see you to get hurt." He squeezes me gently. "I like Reese, I really do, and I like him for you, but I don't know if he'll ever want you for more than just sex."

Juls steps in between us and grabs my shoulders. "Don't listen to him, Dylan. *I've* seen the way he looks at you. I don't care how many girls are lining up for him. He only sees you." She speaks softly, her hands applying light pressure to my tense shoulders. He is *currently* only seeing me; I want to correct her. But I don't. I manage to paint on my most convincing *I'm not affected by this* face and smile.

"It's fine. I'm fine. I wasn't expecting this to become a fucking relationship or anything more than what it is so, whatever; I'm fine." Juls studies me closely as Joey manages half a smile. "Anyway, where are we headed tonight to celebrate?" My change of topic catches on and they both start rattling off names of bars. "You two discuss it. I have some work to do."

My stomach churns as I walk past my friends and into the kitchen. Images of hundreds of women walking into Reese's office, closing the door behind them, and then re-emerging moments later looking rightly fucked pour through my head. *How many girls have blown him in that office? How many has he fucked against that door?* The thought of Reese screwing anybody besides me makes me instantly queasy. "God, what the fuck am I doing with this guy?" I say to myself as I check on the cake.

Juls pops her head through the doorway. "Six p.m. at The Tavern, sweets. Love you." She waves with her blinged out hand and I giggle.

"Love you," I reply with genuine enthusiasm just as my phone begins to ring. Reese's name flashes across my screen and I hit decline. I can't talk to him right now. I have work to do and staying busy is my best defense at keeping my mind off him. Walking over to the shelf, I grab the ingredients I need for the chocolate peppermint frosting and place them on the worktop. I reach for my mixer next as my phone rings through the kitchen. Leaning across the worktop, I see his name again and huff loudly as I press decline. "No," I state firmly. Perching myself up on a stool, I begin rifling through my recipes. I really need to organize these better. And rewrite some of them. My grandmother's chicken scratch handwriting is beginning to rub off and most are borderline illegible. Hearing the text message alert on my phone, I wipe my hands on the front of my apron and reach for it.

Reese: Are you ignoring me?

No, Mr. Persistent, I'm just putting some distance between you and my heart. The sound of the song, which Joey has apparently put on repeat, seeps into the kitchen and I soften. A song reminds him of me. A song that I need to remember to look up the lyrics to. My thumbs get to work.

Me: No, just really busy. Juls stopped in and showed off her massive engagement ring and now I'm behind on some baking. What's up?

I press send, pleased with myself for not berating him with questions about previous lovers and office sex romps. I'm about to place my phone down when his name flashes on my screen with an incoming call. *Damn it. I can't just ignore him again; he knows I'm not too busy to text.* I swipe the screen.

"Not feeling the text messaging today?" I ask through a smile that I inwardly curse myself for having. He hasn't even spoken yet and I'm glowing.

"Not when I can hear your voice instead. How are you today, love? Any new favorite songs?" The sound of crunching comes through the phone and I suspect he's received my special delivery just for him.

"Maybe. And I'm okay. I'm just still in shock over the engagement news." I swallow the lump in my throat. *Christ, cheer the fuck up, Dylan. This hot man has chosen you over all other women in line to play with. He chose you.* "So, are you coming out to celebrate with us tonight? I have a few nicknames I'd like to throw at you once I get all kinds of tipsy." The timer on the oven sounds and I walk over to it, clamping my phone between my ear and my shoulder to retrieve the cake.

He laughs softly and I can picture my favorite smile lines next to his eyes. "Yeah, but probably not till late. I have some stuff I need to take care of first." He pauses and the sound of crunching fills the receiver again. "Should I be concerned you're going to get shitfaced without me there? Because a part of me is concerned. Actually, isn't there some rule that says you can't get drunk without me?"

I laugh and poke the center of the cake with a knife, pulling it out clean. The idea of seeing him in a few short hours has blanketed all of my stupid girl concerns and I'm now my usual drunk on Reese self. I wouldn't even need alcohol tonight. "First of all, I'm not going to get drunk. If I did, I would completely blow my chances of riding you later on because I would pass out." I turn the oven off and grab a mixing bowl for the frosting. "And secondly, my friends know how to handle me and know when to cut me off. I think you forget that I'm twenty-six and not twenty-one. I've been doing this for a few years you know."

He grunts and I automatically roll my eyes into the phone. "None of what you just said gives me any comfort. I'll just make sure to get my shit done quickly so I can cut you off myself."

My hand not holding the phone goes to my hip. "If you storm into that bar and throw me over your shoulder like some caveman, Carroll, we will be having words when I sober up."

"Hmm, thanks for the idea, Sparks."

"Reese." The sound of the dial tone blares in my ear and I stuff my phone back into my pocket. *Oh, for Christ's sake.* He would do something embarrassing like that. I can just see myself getting hauled out of there tonight with my face stuck in his ass again. Well, two can play at that game. If he's going to manhandle me in front of my friends, then I'll just have to make sure I'm wearing something to make him lose his shit. That's my only defense really, causing him to stumble at the sight of me and giving me, hopefully, enough time to run away from him. But do I even have an outfit that could pull that off?

"Joey, we're closing up early so we can go shopping." I begin throwing the ingredients for the icing together into a bowl. I register his elated response and focus on my task at hand. Finish making the frosting, ice the cake, and blow Reese's fucking mind. I grin mischievously at myself. He has no idea who he's messing with.

AFTER PERUSING THE RACKS AT La Bella for over an hour, I finally settle on a sleeveless coral dress with a deep v neck and exposed back. It isn't too clingy, allowing me for movement and hiding the lines of my white garter with matching bra and panties. But it is short, really fucking short. I had decided on the garter immediately after our phone call ended; that and the fact I would be picking out some sort of dress for the evening. Reese looks at me differently when I wear dresses. He still has that raw animalistic stare that could melt the panties right off me, but there is also this sweetness behind it, a gentleness that I see when I wear them around him. He looks at me like I'm delicate, and I like that.

Joey has gotten his car back from the shop and drives us to meet Juls at The Tavern, not failing to remind me that we both look better in his ride than in mine. *All this Sam hate.* I'm already two rum and cokes in when Ian and Billy show up, my heart pounding at the anticipation of Reese's arrival.

"I would just like to say, Ian, that you did an amaaazziinngg job on the ring. Like fucking brilliant, dude. You're like the lord of the rings now. Ooohhh, you're Frodo." *Yup. I am definitely in the nickname giving stage of my night.* I bop around on my stool, tapping my hands lightly on the bar in rhythm with the song playing overhead.

"Wow, how many drinks have you had?" he asks as Juls wiggles in his lap. She can't stop looking at her ring and it's absolutely adorable. I'm certain she's shown it to me fifty times since we've arrived, as if I haven't seen it already.

"Psst, like none," I reply. "So have you two thought of a honeymoon spot?"

"Fiji!" Juls yells and Ian barks a laugh.

"I don't really care, just as long as I get my sexy wife in a bikini, and then quickly out of it," he says and I feel my face flush. "I can't *fucking wait* to marry you." He speaks so low, I almost don't hear him. But I do. Tears fill my eyes and I meet Juls' rapidly blinking teary-eyed stare.

"Ladies room?" I ask and she nods.

"Babe, will you get me another drink please?" she shouts back at Ian who gives her a quick wink. We walk arm in arm to the bathrooms and slip inside, the sound of the bar crowd dying down as the door closes behind us. Stepping in front of the mirror, I smooth my dress out and fluff up my hair as Juls reapplies her lipstick.

"By the way, this Saturday I'm holding you hostage after your cake delivery," she says as she hands me the tube she's just used. I take it and shake my head, slowing applying the nude color onto my lips and then quickly wiping it off.

I grunt in annoyance. "I can't pull off lipstick. It makes me look like a hooker. And why am I being held hostage on Saturday?" I hand her back the tube and she sticks it into her purse.

"Excuse you. Maid of honor duties." I screech and jump on my heels. "We've got some dress shopping to do." She wraps me up in a hug as we giggle against each other.

"I'm going to lose it when I see you in a wedding dress. Fair warning," I say as we let go of each other.

She grabs both of my hands and beams, taking in a deep breath before she slowly lets it out. "I'm so happy, sweets. I can't believe he chose me." She pulls her bottom lip into her mouth and bites it to stop it from quivering.

I squeeze her hands with both of mine. "Who wouldn't choose you?" I drop her hands and turn back toward the mirror, wiping under my eyes. "Is, uh, Reese in the wedding party?" *Please say yes.* The sight of him in a tux is something I would pay to see.

"Of course, he's the best man, which means you two will be paired up. You're welcome." She giggles at me and I watch in the mirror as my cheeks burn up.

We exit the bathroom together, Juls walking ahead of me and blocking my view, but it doesn't matter. I could have been blindfolded and I'd have known he was here. I always feel his presence before I see him. As she steps through the crowd, my eyes lock onto

Reese who is standing at the bar talking to Ian. My stomach tightens and I clench my fists as I walk slowly, studying him and waiting for him to notice me. He's in his work attire, dress shirt and tie with khakis, his hair sticking out all over the place, and I decide that walking slowly is for morons. Pushing my way through the crowd, his eyes turn to mine and he smiles sweetly before his mouth drops at my appearance. I pick up my pace and run straight at him, jumping up into his arms and hearing Juls and Ian's collective laughs as I cling to him like a vine. His smell hits me and I softly moan.

"Handsome," I whisper into his ear as I squeeze him tightly, no intention of letting go any time soon. "I thought you'd never get here."

"I came as soon as I could, love." He inhales me deeply, holding my body against his as I keep a solid grip around his neck. Shifting me against his body, he turns and lowers himself onto a stool, pulling me into his lap. I lean back and study him. Green eyes blazing, parted full lips, and smile lines. *Man, he is lethal.* He opens his mouth to speak when his eyes trail down my body and stop on my thighs.

"Fuck, Dylan." I glance down quickly at what's possibly caused his outburst and curse loudly at the sight of my exposed garter. *Shit. This dress is not meant to be sat down in.* "What are you wearing?" I'm quickly placed on my feet in front of him as he begins tugging at the material, frantically attempting to bring it down to a more appropriate length. The giggling from me comes naturally at his flustered state.

"Are you trying to give me a heart attack? What the hell is with the dress?" he asks through clenched teeth as I quickly scan the red faces of Ian and Juls who are watching in amusement. Joey squeals on the dance floor as Billy dips him and kisses him deeply in front of everyone. The relentless tugging of my dress brings my eyes back down in front of me.

"You don't like it? I thought you liked me in dresses," I tease.

"This shouldn't be allowed in public. Seriously, what the fuck? You've been here for how long in this shit?" He glowers at me and runs his hands down his face, bringing my attention to his right hand that looks like he's spent the night dragging it against bricks. His knuckles are cut up and slightly swollen and dried blood stains his skin.

"Jesus Christ. What the hell happened to your hand?" I reach for it to examine it more closely when he quickly pulls away from me.

"Don't worry about it. The dress, Dylan. Why are you wearing that?"

Oh, no fucking way is he going to react like this and not give me any answers. I grab my clutch off the table and make to turn away from him. "Fuck you. I wore this for you, you stupid asshole." His hand grabs my elbow, but I somehow manage to snatch it out of his grip. "Let go of me. How dare you come in here with your hand looking like you beat the shit out of somebody and give me a hard time about my outfit. You have no fucking right to act like that." *What the hell? This is not the reaction I was hoping to get out of him for wearing this.* I push through the crowd of people and see the exit, but feel his hands on my waist before I can get very far. *Figures. Engage barbarian mode.* I am turned sharply and pulled against his chest, his mouth pressing firmly to my temple.

"I have *every* fucking right to act like this," he growls.

"No, you don't. What the fuck happened to your hand?" I push away from him and take a step back, sternly staring him down for an explanation.

He steps closer to me, eliminating the gap I just created. "Your ex is what happened to my hand. I told you I'd make sure he never touched you again, and I fucking did. Now explain to me why the fuck you're wearing that? You knew I wouldn't be here until later, so don't fucking say it was for me."

I move quickly, there is no thought behind it, just pure shock, and slap him hard across his face. The sound of the crack echoes through the bar, but no one seems to pay us any mind, except for Juls and Ian. Apparently, lovers' quarrels are common in establishments like this.

"Are you *actually* trying to insinuate that I'm wearing this for somebody else? Fuck you. You drive me fucking crazy." I bring my hand back again, but Reese reaches out and stops it, bringing it down to my side and pulling me against him. His chest is heaving rapidly and when I press my lower body against his, I feel his need for me digging into my hip. *Fuck, he's turned on by this?*

"You drive *me* fucking crazy. Now, say your goodbyes so I can take you home and fuck some sense into you." I catch my breath at his words, but know right then, even before he said it, that I want it just as much as he does. He knows how and when to push my buttons and he does it better than anyone.

"Juls, I'm leaving. Love you," I yell, but keep my eyes on Reese.

"Holy hell. That was crazy hot. Bye, sweets," she yells back, and before I can object, I'm being dragged out of the bar by a very hot and bothered CPA. *But who am I kidding here? Like I'd ever object.*

Chapter Fourteen

"I HOPE YOU REALIZE JUST how pissed off I am at you right now," I say as I sit in the passenger seat of his Range Rover, watching him weave easily in and out of traffic. We've been driving in silence for eight long-ass minutes and my annoyance level is through the roof.

He turns the radio down and clears his throat before glancing over at me. "Why, because I don't want other men looking at you? Tough shit. That dress should be illegal." His hand grips the center console and I stare at his red cut up knuckles.

Crossing my legs and letting my dress ride up on purpose, I cross my arms over my chest and stare him down. "What happened? You didn't kill him, did you? I'd prefer it if I didn't have to visit you in prison." *Although, a conjugal visit with Reese might be worth Justin's demise. Mmmm, he could rock the hell out of some jail attire.*

Stopping at a red light, he flexes his injured hand before he reaches over and slips his finger under my garter, snapping it against my skin and making me yelp. "No, I didn't kill him, but he probably wishes he was dead right now. He won't bother you again." I bat his hand away to keep him from pulling at it as the red light turns to green. "Did you have fun tonight?"

Forcing out a laugh, I turn to him and see a hint of teasing in his set profile, his lip twitching slightly. "Oh, yeah, I was having a blast until this crazy man showed up and freaked out over my wardrobe selection, which, by the way, *was* for your eyes only. You owe me multiple orgasms for that little tirade."

He lets out a laugh as he pulls into the parking garage of his building. "Oh, I think I'm the one who is in need of multiple orgasms. It is *my* birthday after all." *Wait, what?*

"It's your birthday? Today?" He nods with a smile and parks the car, stepping out as I stay frozen in my seat. My door is opened for me and his hand grabs mine, pulling me quickly out of the vehicle. "Is it really?" The man could be lying just to get his multiple orgasms.

He reaches in his back pocket, pulls out his wallet and hands it to me. I flip it open and stare at his license, which of course contains a picture of him looking annoyingly good. *Who the hell takes a good driver's license photo?* Focusing on his birthday, I confirm what he has just revealed to me.

"Why didn't you tell me?" I ask, handing him back his wallet as we walk into his building. His hand rests on my lower back as he walks me toward the elevators, nodding politely at the people we pass.

"I just did," he replies, pulling me into the elevators and pressing the tenth floor button. I wrap my arms around his neck and press my body against his as we ride up to his floor. His scent fills my lungs and I swoon.

"But you should have told me sooner. I would have made you a cake. It's what I do, you know."

His hands grip my waist as he presses quick kisses into my hair. "Well, you can make me a cake now." The doors open and he quickly pulls me with him down the hallway and into his condo. *Jeez, is he in a rush?*

Flipping on the lights, I follow behind him as he sets his keys down on the counter and walks into the kitchen. I slip out of my heels, set my purse down, and begin rummaging through his cabinets, praying for ingredients.

"Do you have any flour?" I ask as he closes the fridge and hops up onto the counter. Unscrewing the cap, he takes a sip of his water and looks to be in deep thought, his eyes staring at the cabinets. "You're in my spot," I say as I watch him with amusement.

"Umm, no. I don't think I have any flour. And yes, I am in your spot. But it's my birthday, so I'll do whatever the fuck I want." He smirks at me and I give it right back to him, turning and glancing up on a high shelf.

"Can you reach me the Bisquick please?" I ask as I open the fridge and pull out the eggs. He hands it to me with a kiss and hops back up.

"Are you making me birthday pancakes?"

I pull out a bowl and grab a fork. "Nope, I'm making you my four ingredient banana cake that I used to whip up in college. Juls and I roomed together and I would create desserts out of whatever crap we had lying around. Bisquick was always on hand because she's a breakfast junkie." I grab the sugar bowl and set the oven temperature. "You've given me little choice here. I'd be set if I wanted to make you a cake made out of ramen noodles and chunky soup." He watches me intently as I mash up the banana and begin mixing the ingredients together in the bowl, occasionally glancing up and seeing him studying me. He always seems so fascinated by whatever it is I'm doing, and I wonder if he looks at every girl like this. *Ugh.* The thought makes me whip the eggs viciously.

"So you're thirty-two today," I state, sucking the batter that has splashed up onto my knuckle off with a soft moan.

"I am." My eyes go to his and he winks. "I'm six years older than you now. Does that bother you?"

His question baffles me, so I decide to really give it some thought. Our age difference doesn't bother me at all. If he was ten years older than me, I wouldn't care. Scrunching up my face and thinking hard, I see his grin widen as he waits for me, a soft breathy laugh escaping him. I shake my head. "Nah, but that's mainly because you act half your age." His eyebrow arches. "Besides, I have a thing for older men." Tipping the bowl, I pour the cake batter into his one and only baking dish and shuffle it to even out the distribution.

He hops down and comes up behind me, his hands spreading across my stomach. "Do you? I had no idea," he says as he pulls my hair over one shoulder and kisses down my neck. I close my eyes and grip the baking dish tightly. *Lord, this man knows how to wind me up in no time.*

"Well, I have a thing for you," he growls into my ear, his hands sliding up the front of my dress and molding to my breasts. My head falls back against his shoulder and I groan. "I need to put this in the oven." He grumbles in protest but finally steps back, allowing me to place the dish into the oven and set the timer.

"Okay, birthday boy, you've got twelve minutes to play with me until it's ready." I turn to see his wicked grin and he wastes little time, grabbing my hand and pulling me into the living room. Stopping in front of the couch, he pulls me into his arms and runs his hands up my spine as his face drops to bring our lips together. He opens my mouth with his and snakes his tongue around mine, coaxing me to move with him and I obey. My hands fumble with his tie, loosening it and dropping it to the floor as his mouth assaults mine, teasing and tasting every inch of me. I feel his arm muscles flex around me and then the sound of a loud rip comes from behind me as the fabric of my dress is torn from my body.

"Did you just… I can't believe you just did that." I spin around quickly and step back and out of his arms, seeing the handful of material clutched between both fists before he drops it at his feet. *Are you fucking serious*? "Dick. Do you have any idea how much that dress cost me?" I step into him and deliver a sharp poke to his chest with my finger. *Yeah. That'll show him.*

He cocks his head to the side and narrows his eyes at me. "If you say more than five dollars, you got ripped off. That thing was the size of a handkerchief." His arms wrap me up and he tosses me onto the couch like I'm some sort of rag doll. I yelp in protest as the cold leather hits my skin, but am only momentarily chilled before his body is pressing against mine, warming me instantly.

"You are ridiculous. What the hell am I supposed to wear now when I leave?" I grumble between kisses. His mouth meets mine the moment he relaxes down on me. I moan as his tongue dips into my mouth, delivering long strokes against mine and filling me with his minty flavor. "Fuck, I'm so mad at you." I grunt as he laughs against me, moving his lips down my neck and licking a trail to the top of my breasts. *Stay mad, Dylan. Don't give in. Don't lose it. That was a two hundred and fifty dollar dress.*

"I love it when you're mad at me. You're so fucking sexy; I can barely contain myself here." He molds his hands over my breasts and pulls my bra down, slipping a nipple into his mouth as I grab his head. "Mmmm, these are always on my mind. So fucking beautiful." He licks and sucks me, drawing loud moans from my mouth. Brushing his nose against the mark next to my left nipple, which is slightly faded, he sucks on the small patch of skin. My hands grip his hair and hold him against me. I hate that his marks are fading on me and am more than happy to let him bring them back out. Moving to my other breast, he freshens the mark there and then plants a soft kiss to it before he glances up at me. His smirk makes me grunt.

"You're an asshole," I groan as he moves lower, licking and nibbling at my stomach. Wrapping my legs tightly around his waist, I push him up and grip his dress shirt with both hands tightly before I rip it apart, tiny buttons flying out in every direction. My hands push it off his big shoulders and down his arms, pulling his T-shirt quickly over his head.

"Impatient much? We have all night, love," he says as he works his belt, sitting back between my legs.

"You started it." *All night?* My hands stretch out and rub his ripped chest, brushing down his stomach along the tight muscles. *God, I love touching this man.* My index finger plays in the patch of hair that runs below his belly button. "What do you want for your birthday?"

He reaches into his pants, pulls himself out and leans forward, rubbing himself along the length of my wet panties. I groan and dig my nails into his back. *Wasn't I mad about something?* "You in my bed," he says against my mouth. Our lips are close, our heavy breathing mixing together and I tremble against him, his words bringing out my fears. "Nothing has to change. This is still just sex. I just need to have you in there."

Seconds, minutes go by and he stills against me, waiting for my response. I don't know what to do. I want to do this for him, for me, more than anything. Being in his bed, surrounded by his smell and imagining what it would be like to stay there with him is a thought that is constantly running through my mind. But can I do this? He said nothing has to change, but can I keep it from changing for me? I think long and hard and make my decision. Yes, I can. Because this is worth it. He is worth it. I close my eyes tightly and nod, hearing a small sound escape him and I'm quickly lifted to my feet. We round the couch together when the oven alarms, causing me to dash in and pull the cake out.

"Jesus, you should only be allowed to wear *that* in my kitchen," he says as I insert a knife quickly into the top and pull it out clean. Glancing down at my attire, I smile at him as I meet him in the dining room where he stands waiting for me. My hand is placed in his as he leads me down the hallway and opens the last door on the left. Stepping aside for me, I walk ahead of him and take in my surroundings.

His bedroom is big and spacious, containing a large four-poster bed with one nightstand on each side, a tall dresser and a chair in the corner next to a small bookshelf. I scurry over to it and glance at his reading material, all educational and way the hell out of my depth. "Wow, you're a bigger nerd than I thought." Pulling out a massive textbook with the words *Corporate Accounting* on the front, I sit in the chair and flip through it, feeling his eyes on me as he moves into the room. The sound of his clothing removal catches my attention and I glance up at him from under my lashes. He is now standing completely naked and staring at me, holding out his hand and arching his brow.

"I'm reading," I mutter through a grin and am quickly yanked from my chair, book crashing to the floor in the process as he lifts me up and tosses me on the bed. The smell of him hits me like a truck and I whimper. *Crap, this is going to wreck me.* Wrapping his hand around the back of me, I am moved up the bed so my head is resting on his pillow, his body settling between my legs. I watch intently as he slides my panties down and tosses them, leaving my garter on and tracing the clips with his fingers.

"So fucking sexy," he says against my thigh, kissing the skin along my garter. "You're so soft, love, and you always shake when

I'm right here." His lips brush against the skin of my inner thigh and I gasp, trembling on cue. "I love how I do that to you."

I quickly remove my bra and reach out for him. "Come here. I need you." I grip his shoulders and pull him up as he shifts above me, pushing straight into me in one quick motion.

"I've dreamed of this. You, in my bed. Fuck, Dylan." His words ring through my ears as he strokes me with long slow movements. Pulling almost all the way out before he glides back in. My legs tighten around him and I pull his mouth to mine, needing his kiss, needing his breath on me and in me.

"Me, too. Oh, God."

He groans loudly and I pull his lip into my mouth, dragging my teeth along his skin. My hands are brought over my head and held above me with one of his. His eyes burn into mine with such raw emotion that it rips through me, crippling me. I turn my head to break the contact.

"Look at me," he grunts, his hips thrusting hard and fast, slamming against mine and pushing me up into the headboard. His grip around my wrist tightens and I arch off the bed, pushing my chest against his. "Dylan, I need to see you." I turn back to him, giving him what he wants and letting myself feel it. Heat spreads across my skin, radiating from deep within me as his free hand holds the side of my face. "Don't pull away from me," he pleads, but even if he hadn't said the words, his eyes are telling me the same thing. They show every emotion, every unspoken thought. I am completely lost in his green stare, completely lost in him. Everything about him holds on to me, keeping me right with him in this moment and there isn't a single part of me that wants to pull away, that will ever want to pull away. I can do this. I'm strong enough for this.

My body is quickly on the brink, undeniably responsive to his and I want him there with me. I pull my lip into my mouth and clench around him, seeing his eyes widen and halting his thrusts.

"Holy fuck." His eyes clamp shut and I do it again, contracting my muscles and feeling him react with a jerk. "Jesus Christ. Love, if you keep doing that..." And I do. I do it again, this time holding it, and his eyes open and lock onto mine.

I clench around him once more and he grunts loudly before he starts to move. I moan and bring my hips up to meet his charges, giving him deeper entry and pulling a low groan straight out of him.

"Come with me, love." His mouth comes down and devours mine, pulling my tongue into his and sucking hard and deep. I come fast, my body shaking and pulsing, my screams swallowed by his mouth as he gives me his release. Warmth runs through me, clinging to me, to us. Our bodies fit perfectly together and I pray he'll never get tired of me, of this. Because I never will.

Our breathing steadies as he stays on top of me, pressing my body into his mattress. He's heavy, but not uncomfortable and I find the weight to be the perfect amount of pressure against my body. My fingers trail lightly along his back as his hot breath bursts across my neck. My touch deepens and I rub his hard muscles, working up to his neck and firmly digging in. I giggle at his tiny moans of pleasure. He loves it when I touch him, and right now, that's what I want to do. I wiggle underneath him and his gorgeous face turns up to gaze at me.

"Let me up. I want to give you a birthday massage."

He quickly and with great enthusiasm pushes himself back onto his knees and allows me to move around him. Grabbing a few tissues off his nightstand, I'm wiped clean of his release and the trash is quickly discarded. As he settles back down on his stomach, I straddle his waist and admire the view. He has the sexiest back I've ever seen, broad and built, but not overly muscular. I hate big bulky guys, and Reese has the perfect muscle to leanness ratio. After giving one quick smack to his perfectly sculpted ass, I begin rubbing up and down his back, gauging his reaction to find the amount of pressure he wants. A few soft moans indicate I'm pressing him just how he likes, and I move to his shoulders and start working him.

"Tell me something I don't know about you," I say, wanting to find out every little detail I can. Reese seems really open after sex and I'm going to use that to my advantage.

He moans, "Mmmm, I hate cats." His muffled answer makes me belt out a laugh.

"That does not even count. Come on, Carroll, you can do better than that. I totally hate cats too, though. They're so smug." My hands work his upper arms, pushing and pulling his muscles until they loosen. His breathing is peaceful and steady underneath me.

"I don't know; it's hard to think when you're touching me like this. Why don't you just ask me a question?" He turns his head and rests on his cheek, eyes closed with his long lashes brushing his cheekbone. *Jesus, I would kill for lashes like that. Why do guys get the best lashes?* "Dylan."

"I'm thinking." I have questions, so many questions. But am I brave enough to ask them? I bite my lip and decide to start slow. "Do you hook up with a lot of girls at weddings?" That isn't too bad. It's not like I asked him how many girls he's slept with, which I *am* very curious about. His eyes open for a moment and then he closes them again.

"I'm not sure what classifies as a lot, but yes, I've hooked up with women at weddings before." He moans as I press my thumbs deeply into his upper back. "I'm sure I wasn't your first either."

"Yes, you were," I blurt out, seeing his eyes pop open again. He blinks rapidly before he flips under me, holding me still so I'm now straddling his stomach. His hands run up my thighs and play with my garter as I begin rubbing his chest. "Well, you were my first slutty wedding sex. I've had a few drunken make out sessions at weddings before." I haven't, that's a total lie. I've actually never done anything with a stranger at a wedding besides dance with them. But the way Reese is staring up at me right now, eyes full of wonder, I feel the need to not sound like such an angelic virgin hovering over this experienced player. I clear my throat and massage down his arms, seeing his eyes close again and giving me the opportunity to stare while he isn't watching me. "Have you called other girls 'love'?"

A small smile forms on his lips as his eyes remain closed. "No, just you."

I feel my heart swell. *Hmm, I like that.* "Were there a lot of girls before me?" I speak without thought and clamp my eyes shut, bracing myself for his answer. The same image runs through my mind of the hundreds of girls in his office and I pray for a low number. A really low number.

"Dylan, do you really want to go there? Can't you just ask me what my favorite movie is or some shit?"

I slowly open my eyes and see him staring at me, green eyes blazing. *Jesus, is it that big of a number that he doesn't want to tell me? I think I have the right to know.* "You know my number; it's only fair. Just tell me if it's in the triple digits or not." My hands rest on his abdomen and I get a shocked expression.

"Jesus Christ. Triple digits?" He scrubs down his face with both hands. "I don't know, close to twenty probably. Does it really fucking matter?" His hands return to my thighs and I glare at him.

"Yes, it really fucking matters, otherwise I wouldn't have asked." Sliding off his body, I kneel next to him on the bed and grab a pillow to cover myself with. He quickly takes it away. "Give me that."

"No. It's my birthday and I want to look at you." He tucks the pillow behind his head. "Now, tell me why it matters?" I shake my head and get off the bed, walking toward the doorway. "Where are you going?"

"To get some cake. It's not like I can leave or anything. You destroyed my dress and I don't have a car," I call out behind me as I walk down the hallway. My mind is racing. *Close to twenty? I've been with one guy besides him. One.* I walk around the couch and pick up his dress shirt, slipping it on and letting it hang open since all the buttons had been ripped off. I bring the collar around my face and inhale deeply. *Oh, man. Please let me keep this.* I slice two pieces of cake and place them on plates, grabbing some forks and heading back down the hallway. Reese is now sitting up, his back against the headboard and the covers pulled up around his waist

"Wow." I stop at the end of the bed and stare at him after he speaks, his eyes fixated on my attire. "You look beautiful in my shirt. Keep it."

I smile and climb up on the bed, handing him his plate. "Here, happy birthday, handsome." I lean in and give him a quick kiss with his cake, lingering for a few seconds as he moans against my lips.

He smiles at me and takes it, grabbing a huge bite with his fork. "Mmmm, this is really good." Watching his perfect mouth work the bite, I see his Adam's apple move as it slides down his throat. "You can make this for me every year."

My fork hovers in the air as I'm about to take a bite myself.

His eyes fix on mine and I quickly look down and pull the bite in. *Every year?* I moan softly around my bite and relish in the delicious banana flavor. This cake is too easy to taste this good. I watch in amusement as he devours his cake quickly, leaning over and placing his empty plate on the nightstand. The muffled sound of a ringtone rings through the bedroom.

"Shit," he says as he hangs over the side of the bed and pulls his phone out of his pants. He shakes his head quickly before he answers it, exhaling and leaning back against the headboard.

"Hi, Mom. Thanks. Yeah, I'm good, how are you? How's Dad?"

Now usually, I would just sit back and enjoy my dessert and not think of anything devious to do in this situation. However, the memory of Reese stealing my cell phone and giving my mother unwarranted information creeps into my mind, along with a brilliant idea. I sit up and lean across him, feeling his eyes on me as I place my plate on the nightstand next to his.

"Oh, yeah? That sounds like him. When's he trading it in?" Grabbing the sheets with both hands, I yank them down and quickly crawl between his legs, my mouth enveloping his partially erect cock and feeling it come to life immediately. "Shit. Uh, nothing." I smile around him and grip the base, holding him tightly as I lick up his length. His thighs clench and his free hand fists the sheets. "Mom, can I call you back?" I pull him into my mouth and slide up and down his length, hearing small throaty grunts from above me. "No, I'm just in the middle of something. *Oh, fuck.*" My hand glides along the wetness and meets my mouth. He pulses against me as I suck him hard, then harder. "I'll call you back." The phone is chucked off the bed quickly and his hands grip my hair.

"God, yes. Just like that."

I groan against him, my free hand reaching under and holding his sac. "Tell me how good it feels," I say as I lick the tip. My hand pumps him, long even strokes as I glance up at his expression. Eyes dark and powerful, brow creased and jaw clenched.

"So fucking good. Your mouth is incredible." He jerks and I slip him back into my mouth. His hands grip my head, pulling me up and down at the rhythm he wants, and I let him. It is his birthday after all. His hips thrust up and he fucks my mouth as I tame my gag reflex. He's so deep in me, hitting the back of my throat and making my eyes water. His soft praises keeps me going even though my jaw is beginning to ache. "Dylan, so good, oh, God, I love your mouth." I feel a pulse and know he's close. Increasing the pressure, I suck as hard as I can and cup his balls, feeling them tighten in my hand. He groans loudly and twitches. I squeeze every last drop out of him and swallow, savoring his taste. My eyes flick up as I lick him and see him watching me, always watching me. I've missed the look on his face at his release, but the look he's giving me right now makes up for that loss. He's in complete wonderment. He brings his hands up and runs both through his hair.

"Damn, that was unreal. Come up here."

I wipe my lips with the back of my hand and move up his body until I am straddling his waist. "Do you like it when I do that?" My hands rest on his arms and I squeeze them gently.

His laugh warms my face. "Are you kidding? Did I not just come in this pretty little mouth?" His finger runs along my bottom lip and I kiss it lightly. "Do you like doing it?"

I nod quickly and we both laugh. "I love it. I used to hate it, but with you, I love it." He smiles sweetly and runs his hands down my arms. "Have you always liked eating pussy?"

My question causes him to stumble back a bit and he shakes his head at me, giving me a strange look. "Uh, I'll always like eating *your* pussy. Let's leave it at that." He narrows his eyes at me, seeing my unsatisfied expression. "Dylan, really?"

"What? I'm just curious. Why do you like mine so much?" I glance up at him from under my lashes and see his eyes trail down to the topic of discussion. "Don't all women taste the same?"

He licks his lips and smiles, causing me to bite the inside of my cheek to hold in my grin. I have no idea why I'm so curious about this, but I am. His eyes meet mine and he shakes his head. He trails his finger down my stomach and dips into me. "Yours is the sweetest pussy and the only one I want. I'm a bit obsessed with it." I moan softly as he moves around before slipping out of me.

"Good," I state as he pops his finger into his mouth and smiles around it. *Good Lord, that's hot.* He engulfs my face in his hands and moves in slowly, planting the sweetest, most gentle kiss he's ever given me. Pulling back ever so slightly, we study each other. There are no words, just the sound of our breathing as my eyes examine every inch of his face. He looks completely relaxed right now. No furrowed brow, no tension in his jaw. Just slightly parted lips and soft green eyes. My finger runs down the prominent slit in his bottom lip to his chin, feeling soft stubble along his jaw. I sigh. The sight of Reese with a five o'clock shadow would surely cripple me. Trailing his fingers along my skin, he brushes over my eyebrows, down my temples and across my cheekbones.

"What are you thinking right now?" he whispers and I lean in, pressing our foreheads together and closing my eyes. *God, what wasn't I thinking?* That I love being with him like this in his bed, that I am so wrapped up in him, and at certain moments, I think it might break me. That I'm scared, terrified, of my feelings for him and his possible lack of feelings for me in the same way. I need to give him an answer so I do.

I open my eyes and connect with his. "That I'm scared I'm going to fuck this up," I reply, so soft, so low that I think maybe he misses it, until his eyes widen. I swallow and continue. "I don't really know what I'm doing. I mean, I've never done this before." His hand brushes my hair back. "You make this look so easy, and I just… I feel like I'm struggling." My voice breaks at the end. I sound weak. Pathetic even. His silence eats away at me so I shift down a bit to lay my head against his chest in my favorite spot, nuzzling his neck. I need his scent right now. I am anything but relaxed after that admission and I know it will soothe me.

"I think you're amazing," he pronounces into my hair, his hands wrapping around my waist and holding my body against his. *Amazing? At this? Really?* I exhale slowly and feel all the tension leave my body. That is all I needed to hear. If he thinks I'm amazing at this, then I must be doing something right. Closing my eyes, I concentrate on his breathing and let his smell wash over me. His hands dip under his dress shirt and stroke my back lovingly, just like he did last week on his couch after our long talk. And once again, there is silence between us. But this kind of silence, the kind where no words are welcome because just being together, holding each other, is better than anything that could possibly be said. This kind of silence is perfect. And then I pass out from my favorite form of intoxication. Reese Carroll.

Chapter Fifteen

I'VE ALWAYS SLEPT SOUNDLY IN my bed, wrapped up in my nine hundred thread count sheets and down comforter. My feather top mattress gives the illusion of sleeping on a cloud and once I lay down on it, I'm out for the count. Dead to the world. I can usually sleep through anything except my daily five a.m. alarm. I once slept through the commotion of two fire engines and several ambulances when a building across the street caught on fire. I had no idea. When I eventually woke up mid-morning on that Saturday, I was shocked at how loud the sirens were that I had slept through. So most mornings, even when I have to wake up at five a.m., I feel extremely well rested and ready for the day. A good night's sleep is very important for your body to properly function and I usually achieved one nightly. But this morning, as I slowly shift my head from side to side, eyes still closed and the feel of something heavy on top of me, I feel like I've been sleeping for days. I've never felt this revitalized. Slowly fluttering my eyes open, I spot a wild mess of dark brown hair spread across my chest. Hot breath blows across my breast, tickling my nipple, and it takes me a minute to process what's in front of me, or really, what's on top of me. My eyes shoot open and I turn to the alarm on the table next to me. Seven twelve in the morning it flashes. *Seven twelve? Fuck!*

"Reese. Get up." I wiggle underneath him, but he's not budging. He's not even shifting his weight at all. He's clinging to me like Saran Wrap, his head nuzzling between my breasts and our legs tangling together in the sheets. I almost don't want to move because being under and wrapped up in him this way feels amazing. But it's morning, and I fucking slept over. "REESE." Gripping his shoulders and snapping back into my sanity, I push with everything I have and he grumbles, rolling over onto his back and slowly opening one eye. That one eye scans my body and he smiles.

"Morning, love." *Whoa.* I'm momentarily stunned by his deep groggy bedroom voice. Low and throaty, it sends a chill through me. I glance down quickly, noting that I'm still wearing his dress shirt, which is completely open, and my garter and stockings. Darting his arm out, he pulls me close to his body and wraps around me again.

"You look wildly sexy right now, in my shirt and in my bed." His hand runs down my stomach and brushes between my legs. I involuntarily moan, knowing full well that I do not have time for this. But my body belongs to this man and I can't help how it reacts. "You're so wet. Were you dreaming about me doing this?" One finger dips in, then two, and I throw my head back and arch my body off the bed.

"Oh, yes, right there." My head falls to the side and my eyes meet the clock again as his fingers move in perfect rhythm. It's after seven. The bakery opened at seven a.m. "Fuck. I'm so late." I bat his hand away and try to sit up when he slams me back down, moving on top of me and pressing me into the mattress. "Reese, seriously, I don't have time for this. Joey is probably freaking out right now." He rolls his hips against my pelvis and I moan at the sensation. *Bakery? What bakery? Who the fuck is Joey?*

He kisses me hard, darting his tongue into my mouth and I taste toothpaste. *Toothpaste?* I shake him off me. "Hey, why do you taste like you've brushed your teeth? Have you been up already?" If he says no, then the man even has perfect morning breath, which would not surprise me. My eyes widen as his smell hits me. It's his usual decadent scent, but it's stronger. Fresher. His wicked grin beams down at me and I grit my teeth and grunt. "Reese, did you already take a shower this morning?"

"You're not the only one who gets up at five and works out. And Joey is not freaking out." He plants a quick kiss on my lips. "I called him and explained the situation." Another hip roll catches my breath. *Focus, Dylan. It's just a penis. The best penis, but still, just a penis.*

I glare up at his giant grin. "Are you telling me that you got up at five and didn't wake me? Do you *not* realize I have a business to run? And what time do *you* have to go to work or are you *that* important that you can come and go as you please?" I groan as he rolls again. "And stop doing that." My hands frantically push against his body to remove him off me but nothing happens. *Shocker.* He leans off a bit and grabs my arms, bracing them on either side of my head. Dropping his head, he rests his forehead against mine.

"So feisty. You make me want to keep you here all day just to see how mad I can make you." I open my mouth to protest and his tongue slips in, capturing mine and slowly sucking on it. *Oh, Lord, help me. I have no will power when it comes to him.* He releases me all too soon. "But I won't because I do have to make it into work sometime today. And just for the record, I did try to wake you up to go for a run with me, but you were in a coma." I grunt loudly and make a face at him. *That I can definitely believe.* I wiggle underneath him and he arches his brow, moving his hips up to rub his length against my clit.

"Oh, God," I whimper, clamping my eyes shut.

"Now, you have three options here. You get to pick how I make you come before I take you to work." He wiggles his brows at me and I giggle. Playful Reese is impossible to say no to.

"I don't have time for this," I plead weakly. His eyes narrow at me and I issue him a smirk.

"Who are you trying to fool here, Dylan?" Hip swivel and I groan. "I could make you come in two minutes if I had to." *Yeah right. He's good, but not that good.* "Hands, mouth, or me."

Holy hell. I'm trying desperately not to allow my smile to crack my face in half, but I'm failing miserably and hardly caring. I jerk my hips up against him and see his eyes widen. "You." He licks his lips and releases my arms, reaching down and wrapping my legs around his waist. He enters me in a quick thrust and I cry out, my head rolling back and my arms reaching above me to grasp the headboard. "Yes, oh, yes." My hands grip the posts and I push down with my arms, meeting his movements and forcing him deeper inside me. "Reese."

Gripping my thighs, he brings my legs to his front and rests them on his shoulders as he pummels into me. His groans are loud and throaty. "Feel it, love. Feel what only I can do to you." He arches back and holds my legs as he drives into me. "Nobody will make you feel this good, Dylan, just me." My eyes are glued to his and I can't look away. I want to tell him he's right, that I know no other guy will ever make me feel like this and I never want to give one the chance. But I don't. Instead, I just feel him. Every stroke, every push, I feel and take everything he gives me.

Deeper, deeper, harder and he's relentless. I'm close, so close that I can't believe I actually doubted what he does to me. Clearly my insanely good night's sleep has rendered me stupid. His hand trails down my leg as he thrusts and his thumb finds my spot. With the slightest twitch, I'm done.

"I'm coming. Oh, fuck." I close my eyes and scream so loud my voice breaks. I hear his loud cry and flick them back open to see him glued to me. Green and piercing, he captures me and I watch him fall apart. He pulls his bottom lip into his mouth and bites down as he pumps into me, giving me his release. Turning his head, he presses his mouth to my leg and pants, his jagged breath bursting across my shin. He stills inside me as we slowly come down together.

"Jesus Christ." I feel and see his lips curl up around my skin. My legs are dropped from his shoulders and he moves off the bed, lifting me up into his arms. He carries me down the hallway and straight into the bathroom. I'm placed on my feet in front of the vanity and glance at myself in the mirror. "Oh, shit." My hair looks rightly fucked, but not in the unbelievable Reese hair sort of way, my lips are swollen, cheeks flushed, and my breasts are beautifully tainted with his marks. My fingers frantically comb through my hair as he smiles behind me. "I need something to wear out of here. Any suggestions, or would you like me to just wear what I have on?" I arch my brow and crack a smile as his fades. *Oh, Mr. Possessive is back.*

His hands come up and rake through my hair, messing up what I've just tamed. "You're hilarious. Would you like to take a shower with me?" he asks as he walks over and turns it on. His bathroom is far nicer than mine, massive even with a shower that could probably fit ten people. *Nine women and Reese possibly? Ugh. Don't go there.* I shake the thought out of my head.

"Yes, but it has to be quick. No funny business." I bend and begin unhooking my garter, sliding my stockings off my legs. He disappears after I catch him watching me for several long seconds. Always watching. He reappears moments later as I slip into the shower, a pile of clothes in his hands. "You don't have conditioner?" I ask as the warm water cascades down my body. The only thing in his shower is shampoo and his body wash, which I grab quickly and take a sniff of. I close my eyes and let the citrus scent run through me, opening them to find Reese standing in the shower with me and smiling.

"You use that and you'll smell like me." He smiles, pulling it out of my hands and squirting some into his palm. "I think you like how I smell."

"I *love* how you smell," I reply as his hands work into a rich lather and he begins rubbing them over my body. "And now I won't even have to see you again today to get my Reese fix." He laughs softly and I watch his concentration as he washes me, starting at my neck and moving down each arm. He covers every inch of skin in suds and I giggle as his hands work my breasts, meticulously washing them for several minutes. "I think they're clean."

"I'll be the judge of that." His hands move down my stomach and around my waist, dropping to my ass and working the lather there as I squirm against him. "So, since you've survived a sleepover with me, that means we can have them all the time now, right?" he asks playfully, his eyes twinkling with mischief.

"Absolutely not. I never intended on sleeping over, in fact, I think you let me fall asleep on you on purpose and tricked me into it." He kneels in front of me and washes between my legs, lingering with a grin before he moves down. He massages my thighs and my shins, bringing each foot up and washing them thoroughly as I grip the shower wall. I'm terribly ticklish and he knows it. I think about what he just asked me. Sleepovers all the time? There's no way I can do the sleepover thing again, let alone all the time. Even though I did get the best sleep of my life, and the sight of him wrapped around me this morning is a memory I'd like to hold onto forever. "That was a special birthday treat." I hold on to his head to keep my balance.

He stands and grabs his shampoo, squeezing some into my hand and doing the same to his. "Honestly, I had every intention of taking you home last night. But I think we must have fallen asleep at the same time. The last thing I remember before passing out is you lying on my chest." We begin washing each other's hair together, my eyes closing as I enjoy the scalp massage. He really is good at this. "And then when I woke up at five and couldn't get you awake without a fog horn, I called Joey and told him you accidently fell asleep and you'd be a little late today. He didn't seem surprised." Our hands drop and I back up into the water, rinsing my hair and smiling at the scent that is now going to be on me all day. I've honestly never smelt anything better, and I live in a fucking bakery.

"Do you always want your flings to spend the night?" I move out of the water and switch spots with him, allowing him to rinse his shampoo out. I grab his body wash and squirt some into my palm. *Shit. Do I really want to know the answer to that? No, I don't.* "Never mind. I don't want to know that." My hands begin to wash his body as his eyes study me. "It doesn't matter. I just don't think we should make a habit out of it." He moans softly as I move over his shoulders with pressure, down his arms, his chest, and his stomach. I get nice and close to reach around and wash his back, inhaling him deeply while I do it.

I kneel down and wash his legs, his erection staring me right in the face. "Dylan, we're casual and everything, but I think you're more than a fling at this point. I don't usually fuck my flings repeatedly." I stand and look up into his eyes as he rinses the soap off himself. His jaw is tight and his brows are furrowed. "Okay?"

I swallow and nod slowly. *Okay. So I'm above his fling status, but still casual, nowhere near the girlfriend zone. And according to*

Billy, he doesn't do girlfriends, so with Reese, there isn't a girlfriend zone. I guess he does care about me more than his other hook ups.

"I'm all clean, feel like getting a little dirty?" I ask and his eyes widen instantly. He reaches for me just as I slip quickly out of the shower. "Sorry. No time for that this morning." I wrap a towel around myself and quickly grab the clothes he placed on the sink, making a break for it toward his bedroom. I hear his laughs behind me as I drop the clothes on the bed and examine what he's picked out for me. Sweatpants, a T-shirt, and a pair of his boxers. W*ait, where are my panties?* I glance around the room, looking all around the bed when Reese walks in with a towel wrapped around his waist. I look up at him and my eyes widen. *Sweet Lord.* I've seen the man naked several times already, but the sight of him in just a towel makes me clench my thighs shut.

"Like what you see?" he asks, winking at me as he walks into his closest, momentarily stunning me.

I drop to my knees and glance under the bed. "Panties?"

He's not long and re-emerges with a dress shirt, khakis, and tie, shrugging at me and barely holding in his smile.

I stand and grip my towel. "You have them, don't you? What, are you starting some weird collection of my lingerie?"

He drops his towel and begins dressing, causing me to look away quickly before I jump on him. "I have no idea what you're talking about, but I believe I provided you with some boxers to put your sexy ass into, so I'm not sure what the problem is." He slips on his boxers and pulls his white T-shirt over his head.

"Humph, pervert," I reply and his smile spreads across his face as I drop my towel. I feel his eyes on me as I step into his boxers, rolling them as I did before to make them fit me better. Next, I get into the sweatpants, which I also have to roll several times at the waist. Slipping on my bra, I pull the T-shirt over my head. It's an old University of Chicago shirt and has apparently been worn repeatedly. *Did he give me one of his favorite shirts?* I glance at him as he stands in front of the mirror hanging on his wall, putting on his tie. He looks devastatingly handsome and oh, so yummy in the morning, freshly fucked and showered. He eyes me quickly and I smile before I walk out of the bedroom, needing to leave his presence before I rip his clothes off. Grabbing my purse off the dining room table, I slip into my heels and shake my head at how ridiculous I look in them with his sweats.

"Ready?" He walks down the hallway toward me and stops when I turn to him. I let out a heavy sigh at his appearance as his eyes fall onto my feet. "You look beautiful," he states as if it's obvious, and I run at him, meeting him in the hallway and wrapping my legs around his waist. "Whoa. Hi, love."

"*You* look beautiful. I look rightly silly. Now come on, I'm late enough as it is and you're making me want to throw you back into your bed." He turns me around and starts back toward his bedroom as I giggle into his neck. "No. We can't."

He grunts in protest as he carries me toward the door and we finally leave with me still in his arms.

AFTER STOPPING TO GET A couple coffees, we drive down Fayette Street and pull up in front of the bakery. I glance out the window and see Joey standing behind the counter. "Did you have a good birthday?" I ask as I unbuckle my seat belt and turn to see his eyes on me.

He smiles sweetly and reaches out, pulling my hand into his and lifting it to his lips for a quick kiss. "I had the best birthday." *Oh my.* He drops my hand and I lean in, pressing my lips against his and lingering there for a moment. I suddenly don't want to get out of his car. Not after last night, not after this morning, and definitely not after what he's just admitted. He's minty and delicious, he smells heavenly, and he's dressed way too good right now.

I lean back a bit and his eyes open. "Make out with me," I say in my best flirtatious voice.

He licks his lips. "Isn't that what we were just doing?"

I shake my head, wrapping his tie up in my hand. "No, that was a goodbye kiss. I want you to devour me."

His hands reach around me and he pulls me toward him, sliding me sideways into his lap. "You mean, like this?" he asks and brings his mouth firmly to mine. His tongue twists in my mouth, moving with mine, stroking, licking, and tasting every inch of me. I'm panting so heavily that I'm certain the windows will start fogging up any second.

"I fucking love kissing you," I say as I manage to break away briefly and kiss down his neck to his collar, relishing in his scent.

"See, we could do this every morning if you'd sleep over more."

I move back up and latch back onto his mouth, silencing his ridiculousness. The man is crazy. After several long, totally worth it, minutes of sucking face, I somehow manage to pull away and lick his taste off my lips. "Have a great day, handsome." I open the door and hop out, turning back after nearly stumbling from the make-out session.

"You too, love," he replies. I glance down and notice his erection, reaching in quickly and rubbing against it. His hand clamps down on mine and he moans, pulling his bottom lip into his mouth and shaking his head at me. "Go, before I throw you back in here and take you to work with me to finish what you've started." I shriek and hear his laugh as I shut the door and wave. I'm floating, completely high off him as I make my way into the shop, ready to start my work day.

Chapter Sixteen

"MORNING," I SING AS I walk into the shop and get a massive smile from Joey. I quickly rush upstairs and change into more appropriate work attire, smiling as I fold up Reese's clothes and stick them into my dresser. *I will definitely be wearing these again, and often.* I slip on jeans and a blue blouse and pair them with my favorite pair of strappy black sandals. After throwing my still damp hair up into a messy bun and applying some makeup, I re-emerge into the bakery and see Joey tapping a familiar white box on the counter.

"You have so much to tell me about *after* you open this," he says with a grin. I think he looks forward to my deliveries from Reese as much as I do.

"Did that just get here?" My eyes rake over the box as I pull it close to me. *How in the hell did he have time to send this to me already? He's probably just now settling in at his office.*

"Actually, it was waiting out front this morning. I guess he wanted you to have it as soon as you got here." He sighs. "So fucking romantic. Goddamn it, Billy."

"Oh, leave poor Billy alone, not all men can be as perfect as Reese Carroll." *Jesus, did I just say that out loud? Is Reese perfect?*

I think silently for a moment as I stare off into space and decide yes, he is perfect. Catching Joey's *hurry the fuck up* stare, I excitedly pull the white ribbon and open the box, my eyes widening as I hover over it and glance at the contents. "Holy fuck." I pull out several pictures of an orgasmic Reese. Literally, I know this face, the face he makes when he climaxes. "Oh, my God." I rifle through the box and see pictures of him from the waist up, someone obviously having taken them as they were riding him until he came, waiting for that exact moment to capture it.

"Jesus Christ. Is he… is that… he sent you these?" Joey squeals and grabs a few of the pictures. I allow it only because there's none containing anything from the waist down. *I can't believe this. There's at least a dozen in here. He sent me pictures of him fucking someone else? Or to be more specific, someone else fucking him?* My heart drops as I stare at his face. He's looking at the camera, looking into the eyes of the person taking the picture as she brings him to orgasm. His jaw is clenched, crease in his brow, piercing green eyes. *I'm going to be sick.* "FUCK." I snatch the pictures out of Joey's hand and shove them all back into the box. "I can't believe him. Why the fuck would he send me these? WHAT THE FUCK, JOEY?" My scream causes him to stumble back and he holds up his hands.

"Christ, I don't know. I mean, these are pictures of him having sex with someone, right?"

"Yes. Did you not see his face?" My eyes fill with tears and his face softens. "Why would he send me these?" I drop to the floor. "Oh, God." My hands cover my face and I sob as Joey moves around me. I'm expecting him to drop to the floor with me, but he doesn't. And his voice tells me why.

"Yeah, Reese Carroll please," he says and I glance up to see him holding the shop phone to his ear. *Oh, fuck.* "I don't give a flying fuck if he's in a fucking meeting. Put his ass on the phone now."

"Joey." I stand and try to grab the phone out of his hand, which I realize is useless. We've been down this road. His eyes widen and I see his jaw twitch.

"You stupid fucking prick. What the fuck is wrong with you?"

I can't move and my tears are still falling down my face. I should stop Joey. I can handle my own battles. But right now, I can't form a single thought in my head.

"Don't play dumb, Reese. Dylan got your fucking delivery, you fucking asshole." I stare at the box that's practically screaming at me on my counter and grab it, dropping it into the trashcan. I feel dirty all of a sudden and have a strong urge to go jump in a bath of hand sanitizer. "What delivery? You fucking know what. Why the fuck would she want to see something like that? Fuck you. Don't fucking come near her again." He slams the phone down, his breathing erratic as he turns to me and pulls me into his arms. I cry against him into his chest, letting go and convulsing in violent shakes. My phone begins to ring in my pocket but I ignore it. I know exactly who it is. "Jesus, I'm so sorry." The shop door swings open and we both turn to see Mrs. Frey walk in. I quickly push away from Joey and wipe away my tears.

"Mrs. Frey. Hi, how are you?" I ask as her eyes search my face.

"Dylan? Oh, sweetie, are you all right? Is this a bad time?" She moves toward the counter and I frantically shake my head.

"No, no, not at all. Umm, boy drama." She nods in appreciation and smiles at me as I force a friendly expression. "Let me grab your cake." I walk in the back and pull her cake out of the fridge, placing it on the worktop to give it a final once over. My phone rings again in my pocket and I once again ignore it. *Fuck him.* I open the cake top and glance at my creation. The chocolate peppermint frosting messes with me and the tears come again. "Pull your shit together. You're at work," I say to myself quietly. I can't let this affect my job. I was warned about Reese, multiple times actually. I shouldn't be surprised. It's my own fucking fault for reacting this way. I quickly close the cake box, plastering on a smile as I walk back up front.

"Here you go. One double chocolate peppermint cake. Happy Anniversary."

Mrs. Frey beams at me. "Oh, Dylan, it looks lovely. You even scrolled our names on it. Bless you, dear." She leans in and gives me a quick hug before she waves at Joey and turns to leave.

As soon as the shop door closes, my fake expression drops and I crumble. "Joey, I need a minute." I quickly run into the back, up the stairs, and hurl myself into my bed.

I'm immediately reminded of waking up with Reese as I wrap

myself around my comforter that doesn't smell like him. However, I do. *I* fucking smell like him. I used to love this comforter, but right now, I hate it. I used to love everything about this bed, but not anymore. Not after last night. Last night was obviously some sort of a fucking joke to him since he decided to remind me ever so sweetly this morning of all his other hook ups. *What were his words? Close to twenty probably? What a whore.* My phone beeps a text message alert in my pocket and I pull it out and chuck it across the room, sending it crashing against my wall. I close my eyes and think back to last night when I hear commotion coming from below me. Familiar commotion. *Shit.*

"Reese! Do not fucking go up there!" Joey's voice screeches and I panic, flinging myself out of my bed and running toward my bathroom as I see his head quickly emerging up my stairs.

"Dylan!" he yells, panicky, but I make it to the bathroom and slam the door, locking it quickly. The door shakes as he pounds on it. "Dylan, what the fuck is going on?"

I back away from the door and sit on the edge of the tub. "Go away, Reese." The tears sting my cheeks as they stream down at a faster pace. My eyes are locked on the door as it shakes furiously. "Go the fuck away!" I hunch over and cover my ears the best I can. *Where the fuck is Joey?*

"Dylan, what happened?" The banging stops. "Please talk to me. I don't know what delivery you got, but I didn't send you anything today. I fucking swear to God I didn't." *He didn't send me anything? But it was in the same box. The white box.*

I stand. "You didn't send me anything?" My broken voice stings my throat.

"No, love, please open the door. I need to see you." I hear the sound of a light thud and picture Reese dropping his head against the door. My mind scrambles. *If he didn't send me anything, then who did?* "Dylan?" I quickly wipe under my eyes and turn the lock, opening the door and looking up at him. He immediately grabs me and pulls me into him and I don't protest. I let him hold me until I remember the pictures, which only takes me a few seconds.

"Let go of me!" I yell and push past him, feeling his hands on my waist and spinning me around.

"Love."

"No. You may not have sent me those pictures, but someone sure as hell did. I can't fucking believe this." The images are burned into my mind and I'm fuming.

"What pictures? What are you talking about?" I go to walk downstairs, hearing Joey's voice and someone else's, but Reese holds on to me.

"Let go of me and I'll fucking show you."

He does, but not before I hear him mutter something under his breath that sounds an awful lot like *drives me crazy.*

I march into the bakery and see Ian pinning a very red-faced Joey against the wall. "Jesus Christ. Let him go, Ian." He does and Joey shoves him hard before turning toward me.

"Are you all right?" he asks, flicking a glare toward Reese who has followed close behind me.

"Yes. No. I don't know." I reach into the trash and pull out the box, thrusting it into Reese's chest. "So glad I got to see these. Really made my fucking day." I walk over to Joey and make sure he's okay.

Ian walks up to us both. "Sorry, man. I just needed to give my boy a chance to talk to his girl and knew you wouldn't let him."

Joey smoothes out his shirt. "You're lucky you're marrying one of my best friends; otherwise, I would have hurled you through that window. Asshole."

"Fuck," Reese says and we all turn to him and see him fishing through the box. "That fucking bitch. Dylan, I'm so sorry you saw these." He moves closer to me and I step back, putting my hand up to stop him.

"Who sent them?" I ask sternly. His eyes flick to Ian and I move in closer. "Reese, who the fuck sent these to me?"

He swallows loudly. "The girl I was last…"

"Fucking?" Joey fills in.

Reese nods.

"Classy," Joey adds.

Ian's eyes widen. "Shit, man. I knew she was pissed that you fired her, but I guess she was way past pissed. And clearly unstable. Fuck." *Fired her? Oh, please don't tell me.*

I shake my head and feel all three pairs of eyes on me. I rub my temples. "Let me guess, bitchy redheaded receptionist?" Reese and Ian's eyes both react the same way. I run my hands down my face. "Wow, nice, Reese. Have you fucked every girl in your office or do you just have a thing for the ones who give your current hook up access to you?" He doesn't answer that and it's probably for the best. I can feel my blood pressure boiling and I want to hit something. I need to hit something. "One of you better fucking volunteer or I'm slapping all three of you."

Joey immediately backs up. "Fuck that. What the fuck did I do?"

Ian looks at Reese who quickly steps forward, holding his hands out to me. I step in and slap him hard, harder than I've slapped him before and yelp as my hand begins to sting. "Shit." I shake my hand and feel Reese grab it, looking at it as his reddened cheek glares at me. *That looks like it hurts. Good.*

"Jesus," Ian says and Joey muffles a laugh. The redhead pops into my mind and so does the image of her sitting on the park bench last weekend. "Oh, my God. I knew that bitch was psychotic." I yank my hand out of Reese's as he begins to rub it.

"What are you talking about?" he asks.

"Juls and I saw that whore staring at you guys while you played basketball on Sunday. It was really fucking weird." My eyes flick from Ian to Reese and I see a small smile pull at Reese's lips. "What the hell are you smiling at? You *do* realize I have another hand to slap the shit out of you with, right?"

"You were watching our game?"

Oh, damn it. "No," I snarl and his smile widens. I hear a muffled laugh from Ian. "Maybe. That's not the point. She was staring at you guys and it was really fucking creepy." I grit my teeth. "That stupid bitch. She better pray I never see her face again, otherwise I'm going to break it." I know my face is blood red and see all three men smiling at me in amusement. "Shut up," I snap and turn at the sound of the shop door opening. I freeze as Justin steps into the bakery and possibly also into the room he will die in.

"Fuck," Joey and I say in unison as Reese moves quickly, grabbing me with one arm and pulling me behind him.

"What the *fuck* are you doing here?" he blasts as my eyes stay glued on Justin. He looks fucked up, seriously fucked up. Eyes are swollen, his nose is jacked up, and he has a massive cut in the corner of his mouth. I briefly feel sorry for him until I remember his hands on me last week. His mouth is hanging open and his eyes widen at the sight of Reese. Clearly, he wasn't expecting him to be here.

"I told you to stay the fuck away from her!" Reese shouts, loud enough that I think the glass window rattles.

Ian moves to stand between the two men. "Justin, this isn't the best time, man," he says as he keeps his hand on Reese's heaving chest.

This is not what I need right now and I'm angry enough to deal with this asshole myself. I move quickly out from behind Reese and step in front of Justin, feeling Ian's body tense. "I suggest you leave now before I cut your dick off and feed it to you." His eyes widen as he backs up slightly. I step closer and close the gap. "I'd say I'd make you choke on it, but let's be serious, that thing never once satisfied me." My eyes flick quickly to his crotch before I smirk back in his face.

"HA!" Joey laughs behind me and I want to turn around and high-five him, but I don't. I just watch my ex shrink a few inches in front of me.

"Jesus Christ. I just wanted to apologize for what I did, Dylan. I'm sorry, okay?" His eyes flick to Reese. "Really fucking sorry."

My body relaxes a bit and I nod once before flicking my eyes to the door. "Good, now get the fuck out."

"Whatever." He turns sharply and leaves the shop and I force all the air out of my lungs. *Fuck, I feel like I need a drink.*

"Shit, Dylan. Remind me never to cross you. You're a bit terrifying." Ian laughs behind me as I spin to see two very amused expressions and one that isn't so amused.

Reese looks a right mix of angry and apprehensive. "I need to get back to work, but we need to talk about this."

I cross my arms over my chest. "Talk about what? That one of your twenty hook ups sent me pictures of her making you come? Nah, I'm good." I push past him and feel his hand on my arm, spinning me back around.

"We *will* fucking talk about this," he growls and puts the box under his arm before he pulls me in and kisses me forcefully on the lips. I hear a soft moan in my throat and try to swallow it down. *Damn it, stupid body. Stay angry with me.* He pulls away and turns toward the door. "Let's go, Ian."

Joey and I stand in the middle of the shop and watch as the two hot CPAs walk out the door and pile into the white Range Rover parked out front.

THE REST OF THE DAY goes by without a hitch. No more obscene deliveries and no more mangled ex-boyfriends coming in with overdue apologies. This day started out so great and turned awful within a matter of minutes. I'm miserable and bitchy and Joey is paying for it because he's the only person I can yell at right now. I'd never call Reese at work and cuss him out, no matter how pissed off I am at him. I'm much more of a show up and barge into his office type of girl. But I won't do that today either because I really don't want to see him. The man is hard to stay mad at in person, and right now, I need to stay mad. Juls is wrapping up with a bride all day, dealing with last minute wedding preparations, so she's off limits too. So my poor assistant has been dealing with my mood swings, and they have been a doozy.

Mainly because the memory of the amazing night and morning I had with Reese keeps filtering into the memory of the photos I received. And I get it; it's not his fault the photos were sent to me. He obviously didn't send them. But he allowed them to be taken and had to have known they could possibly be leaked or shown to somebody. I've never let anyone take pictures of me like that or taken ones of myself and sent them to anybody. So why did he let her do it? Did she mean something to him? Was she special in some way or did he allow all of his hook ups to take pictures of him like that? That thought makes me want to drink myself into tomorrow. And then there's the quantity that I received. There had to be at least twelve different shots of him having an orgasm. Twelve separate times they fucked and she made him come. Were there more than that? Did she only send me the best images? His words from our shower together run through me. *I don't usually fuck my flings repeatedly.* So she obviously wasn't a fling. She was more than that to him. Just like me. Maybe she got too clingy and that's why he ended things with her. She was the girl he wasn't really serious with before the wedding. And he's not really serious with me. How am I any different than her?

"Cupcake, you all right?" Joey asks as I put the finishing touches on the cake for the Brown/Tucker wedding. Even though my mind has been elsewhere, I'm still able to put together a beautiful, four-tiered, white chocolate creation with sugared Gerber daisies cascading down the side. "Dylan?"

I step back and admire my work. "I'm fine. Come look at this, will you?" Joey shuffles back into the kitchen and I hear his reaction, causing me to smile. I turn and see his adoring expression. "Looks pretty good, right?"

He moves next to me and puts his arm around my shoulder, pulling me against him. "Gorgeous. You never cease to amaze me, cupcake." He plants a quick kiss into my hair as my phone beeps. Somehow, even though I had hurled it with all my strength against my wall earlier, it managed to survive the assault. I reach quickly into my pocket after wiping my hands off on my apron.

Reese: I need to see you tonight.

I show it to Joey. "Well, you knew that was coming; the boy is persistent." He leans in and checks out the flowers. "What are you going to do?"

I stare at his message before I answer. "I don't know. I think I need a night with my two best friends and no boys. Can that happen?" He smiles and pulls his phone out, quickly messing with it. I'll deal with Reese tomorrow when we both attend Billy and Joey's party.

His phone beeps and he turns toward me. "Juls is in, cupcake. No boys." I nod and smile weakly as I reply to Reese.

Me: I can't tonight. I need some time to think.

Joey walks back up front while I await his response. It doesn't take long.

Reese: Don't pull away from me.

He guts me with his words, the same words from last night. Is he *that* worried I'll end this? Or he is just worried I won't give him the opportunity to explain the situation. I type quickly.

Me: I'm not. I just think I need some space. You have no idea what this feels like for me.

I go to press send, but don't, my thumb hovering over the button. *Shit. Do I really want space from him?* Hitting the back button, I shorten the message before I send it.

Me: I'm not.

JOEY DRIVES US TO JULS' house after we close up shop and make a quick liquor store run. There is no way in hell I'm not drinking tonight. I'm actually surprised I didn't dive into the vodka bottle that's been in my freezer for months at some point today. But I'd never drink at work, no matter how hurt or pissed off I was. Reese hasn't sent me any more messages or tried to call, which I'm grateful for. But it also surprises me. He is so damned persistent about everything that I half expected him to barge into the shop before closing, throw me over his shoulder, and take me home with him so we could fuck, talk, and fuck some more. And I hate that a chunk of me wishes he would have. But tonight isn't about boys. It's about spending time with my two best friends, laughing and hanging out like we did before the three of us fell fast and hard for members of the Chicago man candy club.

Joey parks outside Juls' building and we walk inside together. She lives in Hyde Park, which is about fifteen minutes from the bakery, in a two bedroom apartment. She's lived here since graduation, and it occurs to me as we walk up the flight of stairs to the second floor that she will only be living here for a few more months. She will surely move in with Ian after the wedding, and the thought of her not living in this place that holds so many of our memories saddens me. I sigh and catch Joey's attention as we step out onto the floor.

"Come on, cupcake, we're here to have fun, not sulk." I follow him to Juls' door and he opens it without knocking, in true Joey form. Once he's been to your house, he feels like he lives there along with you.

"I'm not sulking. I'll just miss this place once Juls moves in with Ian." We spot her in the kitchen opening a bottle of wine and she beams at us. "Do you remember that time we threw that eighties party here and you dressed up like Vanilla Ice?" He blushes at my memory as we plop down in front of the television on the floor.

Juls walks over with three wine glasses and hands them out. "That was fucking hilarious. You knew the entire rap from Teenage Mutant Ninja Turtles," she says. I giggle into my glass and take a few large sips.

"Christ, I will never live that shit down. Thank God no one took any video of that mess."

"That party was insane," Juls says behind her glass. "Dyl, remember how pissed off you got at Justin because he was the only person here *not* dressed up?"

I nod and picture the memory, rolling my eyes at it and taking a sip. "What an asshole. He spent the entire party bitching about the music selections. It was a fucking *eighties* party. What did he expect?"

Joey laughs around his glass. "I think he expected you to just leave with him and not have an amazing time. But you have never been that girl, cupcake, and he should have known that. What a waste he was." Juls and I mumble in agreement.

"A waste that ended up getting *exactly* what he deserved. Prick," she adds, tossing us each a pillow so we can sprawl out on the floor. "Are we going to talk about the pictures, sweets?"

"No," I quickly reply.

Joey rolls onto his side. "You can't be mad about girls he's fucked before you. That's not fair. He didn't even know you when those pictures were taken."

"That's not why I'm mad." I sit up, glaring at both of them. "Well, okay, yes it bothers me that he's been with other women. And I know it shouldn't because I wasn't a virgin when we started this thing between us, but I've only been with Justin." I put my glass down. "Reese gave me a ballpark figure of close to twenty girls and that's a fucking lot. Which is fine, whatever. I can deal with that as long as it's not thrown in my face. But it was." I close my eyes and picture one of the images from the box. Grabbing my glass off the small table, I down it quickly before I continue. "I'm not even mad at him about this. Not even in the slightest, which is what's making this so fucking confusing. The only thing he did wrong was allow for the pictures to be taken of him and not confiscate them after he ended it with her. He didn't send them to me. He doesn't talk about other girls he's been with. He tells me *I'm* amazing and *I'm* all he thinks about." I sigh heavily and throw myself back down onto my pillow. "But now I have to deal with psychotic ex-hook ups and I'm not sure I'd do well in prison. I'm too hostile." This is true. I'd probably end up permanently in solitary confinement after getting into too many fights or disobeying orders.

I glance over and see the bursting smiles on my two best friends' faces, desperately trying to hold in their hysteria. I motion for them to let it out and the three of us fall into a fit of giggles.

"All right, so I have a question," Joey says and I shake my head, preparing for the worst here. "How the hell did you wind up spending the night with him last night? I thought you were against sex in beds and sleepovers and anything too intimate."

"You slept over at his house?" Juls asks.

"It was an accident. He wanted to fuck me in his bed for his birthday, so I let him, and then we passed out together. I'm not letting it happen again." I glance over and see Joey's mischievous grin and Juls' teary eyes. "What?"

"You were his birthday present? Oh my," she says and blinks rapidly. *Good Lord, she's emotional lately.*

I glare at Joey. "And what's up with you?"

Crossing his hands behind his head, he continues after a dramatic pause. "I just think it's cute that you *think* it was an accident.

I mean, he could have woken you up and driven you home, but he called me instead and told me you would be late today. It was no accident, cupcake. He wanted you there."

My eyes widen and I sit up. "He called you this morning, right?"

He shakes his head and grins wide at me. "Nope. He called me last night after you passed out."

I shuffle over and sit on top of him, hearing him squeal underneath me. "What the hell do you mean he called you last night? Are you serious?" His grin answers for him and I glance over at Juls who is laughing hysterically. "I can't believe this. He lied to me."

"Oh, relax, sweets. I think it's romantic that he wanted you to spend the night with him. How was it anyway?"

The memory of last night runs through me quickly and I feel my lip curl up into a smile. I shrug and play it off. "It was okay." *Wow. I don't even sound convincing to myself.* I roll off Joey and lay back down on my pillow. "I sure hope he enjoyed himself because that shit is never happening again."

"Hmm mmm," my two best friends say in unison. I bite my lip to contain my laugh but crack, letting it out as they fall apart next to me. This is how the rest of the evening plays out. Laughing and joking on the living room floor in Juls' apartment as we polish off two bottles of wine. There's Juls and Ian's wedding talk, Joey and Billy's moving in together talk, and mine and Reese's crazy fight hard, fuck harder, non-relationship talk. It's a much needed gab fest among three friends who used to only rely on each other. After several hours of gossiping and alcohol consumption, I pass out in the middle of her living room and slip into my Reese coma.

Chapter Seventeen

AFTER A FAST BREAKFAST WITH Juls, Joey and I return to the bakery and put the finishing touches on the wedding cake before loading it up into Sam. The reception hall is thirty minutes away and traffic is a nightmare, but we make it on time and drop the beautiful, white chocolate, Gerber daisy cake off without any issues. I shower and dress after saying my goodbyes to Joey and lock the shop up, deciding to sit outside on the bench, which is a store down from mine, while I wait for Juls. Today is dress-shopping day and I'm not sure who is more excited about it, her or me. I've never been in a wedding party before and am delighted to be a part of Ian and Juls' special day. Plus, I *would* have the hottest date on the planet. Of course, that's if we are still doing this thing between us in three months. The thought unsettles me and I scroll through my phone while I sit on the bench, pulling up his last text message.

Reese: Don't pull away from me.

What the hell does that even mean? I'm sure it doesn't mean the way I'm interpreting it, which is in the most gigantic scheme of things way possible. I'm sure he's only referring to my justified freak out over the pictures I received yesterday. *Shit.* The thought of them makes me queasy. His face, the face I had hoped was only reserved for me, clearly isn't because it's been captured by another woman. I sigh forcefully and jam my phone into my jeans pocket. How stupid of me to think he only looks at me like that. That I'm the only woman he watches intently as he's coming. I close my eyes tightly and the sound of a car approaching causes me to peek them open. Juls' black Escalade pulls up to the curb and the passenger window rolls down as I stand up.

"Let's go, sweets."

I smile, pushing all of the Reese drama to the very back of my mind. I can't think about this shit right now. Today is about Juls, and I'm going to keep my mind occupied with all things maid of honor like.

WE'VE ARRIVED AT CHRISTIAN'S BRIDAL Shop, and after a few moments of quick hysteria over the fact that we are *actually* shopping for Juls' wedding dress, we walk around the store and peruse the selections. Juls' sister Brooke, who will be the other bridesmaid next to Joey, met us here shortly after we arrived. I haven't seen her in a while and she's been talking my ear off nonstop about the lack of men in her life and probing for information on mine.

"Oh, come on, Dylan. Tell me all about this guy who works with Ian. I'm dying for some hardcore gossip and Juls won't tell me shit," she says from the dressing room next to me. We've been handed a few dress choices and I'm currently slipping myself into a chocolate brown strapless number that feels and looks incredible. *Damn. Would it be weird to buy this if Juls doesn't pick this for her big day?* I zip up the back and open the curtain.

"There's nothing to tell. He's just a guy I'm having fun with." I step out and hop up onto the pedestal in front of a massive mirror, seeing Juls' reflection as she stands behind me.

"Holy shit. I love that one. What do you think though? Is it comfortable? Do you think we should go for something more cheery, like maybe a burnt orange color?"

I spin around to face her. "Burnt orange? How the hell is that more cheery? And are you trying to make us look like pumpkins?"

She bites her bottom lip and eyes up my dress as Brooke walks out in the exact same one. "I love this one. Juls, pick this because the other three are fucking hideous and make me look like I'm six months pregnant."

Juls moves to stand by her sister and runs her hand over the material. "Yup, this is it. You both look amazing in it and I love the color." She smiles and bobs her head. "Well, that was way too fucking easy. Now it's time for the real fun." She wiggles her brows and walks to her dressing room while Brooke and I stand and gaze at our reflections.

"And what do you mean you're just having fun with this guy? Are you telling me it's strictly a sex thing between you two, because if you are, I think that's bullshit. Guys can make that shit work, but I don't think girls can. We're too emotional." *Jesus. Did she hit the nail on the head or what?* Leave it to Brooke to be exceedingly insightful when she hasn't even met the guy I'm just having fun with yet.

"I'm keeping my emotions out of it." *Or, at least, I'm desperately trying to.*

"Ha! Yeah, okay, good luck with that. How's the sex?" I glance over at her and issue my wicked grin. "Damn. I need to start checking out office buildings for smart men. You and my sister are making bank."

My phone beeps in my dressing room and I hop down quickly, racing in to pull it out of my discarded jeans. My heart sinks a bit at the message sender.

> *Joey: Party is postponed. My baby has the stomach bug that's going around. How's the dress shopping going?*

> *Me: Oh no! Tell Billy I hope he feels better. We just picked out our dresses and Juls is trying hers on now. I'll send you a pic.*

Well, shit. I guess I won't be seeing Reese tonight at the party after all. My disappointment quickly gets blanketed by the realization that it might be a good thing to go a few days without seeing him. Between the accidental, but not really accidental, sleepover to the photos I received, I have a lot of shit to think about. I hear a gasp from Brooke and I quickly slip out of my dressing room and let my eyes fall on Juls who has just emerged from hers. *Holy shit.*

"Holy shit. Juls… oh my, that's… oh, wow." There are no words to describe the woman I'm staring at right now. She's beautiful, exquisite even, in a strapless tight laced bodice and ruffled skirt, her tiny waist accented with a deep brown sash that falls down her back and onto her train.

"Wow. You look amazing," Brooke states as her sister takes her place on her pedestal and begins to twirl slowly.

"It's beautiful, right?" She shakes her hands out by her side and I can tell she's nervous.

"What is it?"

"I don't know. Is it weird that I have no desire to try on any other dresses? I mean, this is the first one I put on and I feel like this is it. I can see myself marrying Ian in this. Maybe I should try on more."

"Fuck that. Who cares if it's the first one you try on. You look amazing in it. Like crazy amazing. I can *totally* see you marrying Ian in this dress," I reply and see the tension leave her shoulders. Leave it to Juls to worry about the standards of bridal gown shopping. Her smile widens in the mirror and I can tell she's on to something. "What?" She quickly hops down and slips back into her dressing room.

"Damn it. I wanna get married. There better at least be some hot groomsmen for me to fool around with at this thing," Brooke grunts.

"The best man is off limits, just so you know," I reply and she squints at me.

Juls re-emerges with another gown in her hands and walks over to me, thrusting it into my arms. "Here, try this on."

"What? Are you crazy?" *She must be if she thinks I'm slipping into a wedding gown.* "I am *not* trying on a wedding dress."

"Why not? This would look amazing on you, right, Brooke?"

Oh, for Christ's sake.

Brooke steps up and admires the gown. "She's right, Dylan. It's a halter and you always look amazing in halter dresses with those boobs of yours. Remember prom? God, I fucking hate you both."

I back up. "You are both nuts. There's no way I'm putting that thing on or any other wedding dress for that matter. I'm pretty sure I'd seal my fate as being perpetually single if I did." This is an honest fear. Karma has been increasingly hostile toward me lately and I can see her crossing her arms and stomping her foot at me now, daring me to push my luck.

"Oh, come on, Dyl. Brooke will try some on too, right, Brooke?" We both look at her sister who is sulking on her pedestal.

"Whatever. I fucking hate weddings."

I shake my head and turn back to Juls who is staring me down. "No."

She stomps her foot and grits her teeth. "Excuse you, but as maid of honor you're supposed to do everything I ask."

"And that includes trying on wedding gowns? Are you mental?"

She frowns big time at me and I melt. *Damn it.* "Fine, give me the stupid thing." I rip it from her hands and march with fury to my dressing room as she squeals in delight. *This is insane and completely ridiculous.* After stripping out of my maid of honor dress, annoyed, I step into the wedding gown and slowly zip it up, my eyes widening as I gaze down at myself. "Oh, shit," I whisper, obviously not low enough because Juls rips open the curtain.

"Wow. You look incredible." She pulls me from my room and pushes me up onto the pedestal as Brooke walks up behind me.

"Damn, Dylan. Would it be weird to put that shit on hold indefinitely?"

I smile subtly at her comment and gaze at my reflection. My chest tightens at the sight of myself. Me, in a wedding gown, and I look amazing. *Crap.* I'm covered in lace from my detailed halter down to my train. I was never a fan of lace, but right now, standing in this dress, I'm a *huge* fan. A clicking sound comes from behind me and I turn to see Juls taking a picture of me with her phone. "What the hell?"

"Oh, relax. I won't send it to any sexy CPAs or anything. It's just for us." I can't imagine what would happen if Reese got a hold of that picture. He'd probably freak the fuck out and end things for sure. *Talk about being clingy.* "Seriously, Dylan, look at us." Juls hops up onto my pedestal and grabs my hand, linking it with hers. Besides the fact that we are both standing in wedding gowns, humorously, we're complete opposites in appearance. Juls with her dark brown, straight hair and me with my uber blonde, naturally wavy mess, her piercing blue eyes contrast with my wide brown ones that seem to take up the majority of my face, and she's a good three inches taller than me as I stand up on my toes to bring me up to her five foot nine height. "Goof. I'm getting married, Dyl."

"You are and I'm not, so I'm getting the *fuck* out of this thing." She giggles as I hop down and slip back into my dressing room. But before I take it off, I admire myself alone for a brief moment. I've never given much thought to getting married. Having only been in one serious relationship, Justin never appealed to me as the marrying kind, which now seems ironic since he *is* married. Just not happily, or faithfully. But standing in this dress right now, for the first time in my life, I can picture myself walking down the aisle toward the one person I want to spend my life with. And before I can put a face to that one person, I slip out of the dress and back into reality.

After saying goodbye to Juls and her sister, I spend the rest of the day keeping myself busy with a massive amount of baking. Seven dozen muffins, six batches of cookies, and an assortment of pastries later, I finally slip upstairs and crash, passing out immediately.

I WAKE UP CRANKY AND miserable on Sunday morning, having experienced one of the shittiest nights of sleep I've ever had. I tossed and turned all night, my usual dreams of Reese and I together replaced with him and a string of women with red hair who he's fucking relentlessly. I wake up constantly, drenched in sweat and when I pass back out, another redhead replaces the previous one. I chalk it up to the fact that I haven't seen or heard from him since

Friday afternoon and I'm in desperate need of my fix. But he hasn't called me or texted and I have no fucking clue how to interpret that. Coming from a man who pursued the shit out of me, sending me sweet notes and packages, and texting me daily. And now, nothing. Panic runs through me that I've actually royally fucked this up by telling him I needed time to think. But time to think doesn't mean leave me alone. It just means what it means. That I've been thinking, which I have, and I'm done.

I've decided I'm done being pissy over the photos I received Friday because it's not doing me any good. It wasn't his fault and knowing him, I'm sure he's dealt with that spiteful bitch to prevent any future deliveries from her. I have no right to be mad or jealous about his previous hook ups, especially since we're not serious. And I've also decided I'm okay with that. This is what Reese wants, the only thing he does, and I'm having fun doing it with him. I refuse to let my emotions screw this up because this, what we're doing, is the best thing I've ever done with a man. He's sweet and fun and hot as hell. And he chose me. Of all the girls lining up, he chose me. What we're doing is enough for him and it can be enough for me. I don't need to be in a serious relationship to be happy; I've never been this happy before in my life. The sound of my phone ringing sends me sprinting up the stairs where I plugged it in before I decided to organize my pantry. Disappointment runs through me as Juls' names flashes across my screen.

"Hey, what's up?"

"Can you meet me, like right now, sweets? I really need to talk to someone and I want it to be you." She sounds upset. Juls never sounds upset.

"Yeah, of course. Where?"

"The coffee shop on West Elm okay? I'm only five minutes away."

"Okay, I'm leaving now."

I hang up and dress quickly, grabbing my keys and locking up behind me as I dash around the corner where I keep Sam parked. Juls' voice is really worrying me and I want to get to her as fast as I can. She's never upset. Her two favorite emotions are elated happiness, which is frequent lately after Ian came into her life, and pissed off hurricane Juls mode. The drive to Brocks Coffee Shop is a short distant from the bakery and I park behind her black Escalade, hopping out quickly and dashing into the building. I spot her at a table in the corner, her dainty hands wrapped around a coffee cup.

"Hey. Sorry if you've been waiting long. Fucking traffic."

"No, I just sat down. Do you want something to drink?" Typical Juls, always concerned about other people and not what's bothering her. God, love her for it.

"No, I'm fine. What's wrong? You sounded upset on the phone."

She glances down into her mug. "I don't know what's wrong with me. Ian and I went out yesterday after I dropped you off and checked out some wedding venues and reception halls, and I just didn't care. Like at all. I mean, what the fuck? I've been dreaming about my wedding day since I was six." Her eyes fill up with tears as she turns them up to me. I reach over and cover her hand with mine. "I love weddings, everything about them. That's why I became a wedding planner. But when it comes to my own wedding, it's like I have zero opinion about anything. I don't care whether or not we get married in a church or if it's an outdoor ceremony. I don't care what music I walk down the aisle to or what favors the guests will receive or what my cake looks like, no offense."

My lips curl up into a smile. "None taken."

"I don't even care who the hell is invited. All I care about is marrying him. As long as Ian's there, that's *all* I care about." She blinks and her tears fall down her cheek. "Dylan, honestly, do you think there's something wrong with me?"

I laugh softly and shake my head. "No, not at all. I think you're focusing on the *only* thing that matters. Who cares about everything else?" My hand squeezes hers and she smiles. "I kind of love how marrying Ian is the only thing that matters to you, because it's the only thing that *should* matter. You're going to spend the rest of your life with this man who clearly worships the ground your pretty little feet walk on, so who gives a shit what the fucking centerpieces look like or what the dinner options are for the guests. Fuck the guests." She bursts out laughing and shakes her head at me and most likely herself for thinking this way. Although, I am a little shocked she doesn't have a few things she's dead set on.

"I love you, Dylan. You really are the only person who understands me."

Leaning back, I cross my legs under the table. "Well, and Ian, I'm sure. So what does he say about all this?"

She takes a quick sip of her coffee. "He keeps saying 'whatever you want, babe,' which would be perfect if I had any opinions at all. I kind of wish he would just take over and make all the decisions, because if he leaves it up to me, nothing's going to get done. Except my dress choice, of course."

"Of course, and what a dress. Does that thing even need to be altered, because it fit you perfectly?"

"Hmmm, so did yours, both of them." She pulls out her phone and swipes the screen a few times before handing it over.

I glance down at the picture of me staring at my reflection in the lace halter dress. *Jesus, it looks good.* "I should make you delete this in front of me." I hand her back her phone.

"Not a chance in hell." She slips it back away, quickly so I don't grab it and delete it myself, I'm sure. "What's new with Reese? You heard from him since the picture incident?"

My stomach knots up and I sigh loudly, rubbing my hands down my face. "No, not a peep. But I guess the distance is good right now. We really shouldn't be attached at the hip."

"Dylan."

I glance up at her serious face. "Julianna." I never call her by her full name and can barely say it without smiling.

She rolls her eyes. "Are you in love with him?"

I lean my elbows onto the table and cover my face with my hands. After a slow exhale, I reply honestly, "I don't know. I feel like I'm putting a lot of energy into *not* falling in love with him, but it's the hardest thing I've ever done." I glance over at her. "For a guy who normally doesn't do the relationship thing, I think he'd be damn good at it. But how stupid would I be to fall in love with someone who doesn't do anything serious? I'd just be setting myself up for a major heartbreak, right?" I begin to rub my temples as she fights a smile. "I've never loved any man before. Definitely not Justin. But with Reese? Fuck, I don't know."

She leans forward and rubs my arm. "Just because he's never

done relationships before or anything besides casual fucking, doesn't mean he isn't capable of doing it. Dylan, for Christ's sake. The man is crazy about you. Everyone can see that."

"He's crazy about fucking me." I glance around quickly to make sure my heightened voice didn't draw any unwanted attention. "That's all this is."

"You're really fucking stupid if you think that's true. Just grow a pair and tell him how you feel already."

I shake my head at her and purse my lips as she sips her coffee. Of course Juls doesn't understand where I'm coming from here. She and Ian have been more than serious since they started dating. A thought that's been running through my mind since Friday comes streaming back. Why *did* Reese end it with that red headed pyscho? Was it because she wanted more, that she was in love with him and he didn't or couldn't feel the same way? I can't help but think the same fate is lined up for me if I were to let myself fall, so I won't. I'm going to keep those unwanted feelings buried deep inside me for now, until maybe he eventually decides he wants more. *Please, God, let him want more.*

I CRAWL INTO BED SUNDAY night after getting a bite to eat with Juls. We both wanted more than just coffee in our system and ate at a local Thai place that we frequent often. I wrap myself up in my comforter and the University of Chicago T-shirt that Reese lent me and stare at my alarm clock. It's only a little after eight p.m., and I know I won't pass out anytime soon, but I'm at least going to try. Closing my eyes, I picture his face, the face I catch him having when he's watching me, studying me. Crease in his brow, jaw set, eyes narrowed in on whatever it is I'm doing. Always so studious.

A loud, deafening crash sends them flying back open. *What the hell was that?* I shoot out of bed and dash down the stairs, skidding to a stop behind my worktop when I see a hooded figure standing outside my now shattered glass store front through the doorway. "Oh, shit." Panic, sheer panic runs through me and I dash back upstairs, grab my phone off my nightstand, and begin dialing the only person I can think of.

"Pick up, pick up, pick up." I dart into my bathroom and close and lock the door behind me. *Jesus Christ! Someone's broken into my bakery! Who the fuck breaks into a bakery?* After three long rings, I hear his voice.

"Dylan?"

"Reese! Someone's in my shop! I heard a loud crash and ran downstairs and—"

"Where are you? Are you safe?" His voice is filled with worry and I can tell he's on the move. *Oh, God, please be at your place and not far from me.*

"I'm in my bathroom. They broke the window and I saw someone." I hear commotion, a lot of commotion through the phone as I crawl into my bathtub and close the shower curtain. *Like that's going to do any good if they decide to break into the bathroom. This is so horror movie cliché; I almost roll my eyes at myself.* "Please, I need you," I cry, dropping my head between my knees and letting myself sob.

"Stay in there. Don't come out no matter what you hear. GODDAMN IT. SHIT." Echoes of footsteps ring through the phone and he's out of breath, but his curse words keep flying. "I'm on my way. Call the police."

"NO. Please don't make me hang up." I'm crying, shaking with fear and my words are broken and strained. I hear the sound of a car starting.

"Fuck. Move the fuck out of the way!" Car horns and another string of cuss words come through the phone as I clutch it tightly. "Love, you have to call the police. I'm almost there. I won't let anything happen to you, I promise. Just hang up and call them and then call me back, okay?"

"Okay, okay. Please hurry."

"I am."

I quickly hang up and dial 911, rapidly telling them the situation and giving them my location. They tell me the police are on their way and to stay where I am. That's not going to be a problem. I have zero intention of moving from this spot until I hear Reese on the other side of the door, even though I haven't heard a noise coming from below me since the sound of the window breaking. I hang up and dial him again.

"I'm here. Don't open the door until I get up there, okay?"

"Okay, but stay on the phone with me." I hear his heavy breathing and the sound of glass crunching and cracking. *God, please don't let that person still be here*. If I hear Reese getting into a struggle with someone, there's no way in hell I'm staying in this bathroom. I don't care what the consequences are. I will claw the fucker's eyes out if he puts his hands on Reese. I hear footsteps outside the door and hold my breath.

"Dylan?"

I drop my phone and crawl out of the tub, scrambling for the lock and swinging the door open. I don't even register his appearance before I jump into his arms and cling to him. "Oh, my God, I was so scared." I'm holding onto him like I haven't seen him in years, my body completely glued to his. "Is he still here?"

His arms wrap me up and he breathes into my hair, his chest heaving against mine. "Dylan." I moan softly at the sound of my name. "It's okay; I've got you. I didn't see anyone, but your front window is completely smashed to shit." He carries me away from the bathroom and into my bedroom area.

I'm shaking against his body and tighten my grip. "Jesus Christ. Why would someone break into my bakery? Do you think they wanted treats?" I hear a small muffled laugh escape his lips, which are pressed into my hair. My tears are streaming down my face as he places me on my feet in front of my dresser. I look him over and take in his appearance. Hair a right mess, no doubt from the rough treatment of his hands as he drove over here, clenched jaw, and prominent crease in his brow. His green eyes are burning into mine, and even though they're filled with worry, they still carry the same intensity as always.

"Here, you need to put on pants before the police get here. They're going to want to ask you questions." He starts rifling through my drawers and I see him taking out several pairs of pants, tops, and panties.

"Umm, do I need to put on layers?" I wipe underneath my eyes and finally stop my tears. Now that Reese is here, I'm no longer scared, and the only emotion running through me right now is elated joy from the sheer sight of him.

"No, but you're not staying here tonight, so you need to pack some clothes. I'm taking you home with me." He glances over at me as he closes my drawers.

"Okay," I reply, picking up a pair of jeans and sliding them up my legs.

"Really? You're not going to try and tell me you could just stay at Juls' house, or how you're not breaking the 'no sleepover' rule again? You're just going to say okay?" He looks utterly shocked and I almost laugh. *Jesus, am I that defiant?*

"Yes, I'm not always so argumentative." The sound of police sirens flow up the stairs and I quickly grab a bra and put it on, keeping his T-shirt on in the process.

He notices it and smiles a bit as he places my things in a nearby duffle bag. "Do you need anything else?"

I take a quick look around the room. "Umm, I guess just my bathroom stuff." I scurry in there and grab my toothbrush, hairbrush, face wash, moisturizer, phone off the shower floor, and conditioner because I'm more than happy to use his shampoo and body wash. Spinning, I see him standing in the doorway. He's studying me, eyes narrowed in on the collection in my hands. "What? I'm a girl and I can't take another shower at your place without conditioner. We can't all have gorgeous, no-product-necessary hair like you." His lips curl up as I drop the goodies into my duffle and follow him down the stairs.

After talking to the police and giving them my very vague description of the hooded figure standing outside my shop, they ask me if I know of anyone who might possibly want to hurt my business or me personally. My eyes quickly flick to Reese who clenches his jaw before giving them his ex-receptionist name and information. He tells them about the package I received and claims she became unstable after he stopped seeing her. I had assumed the figure I saw standing outside was a man because of the dark hoodie covering their face, but I guess it could have just as easily been a woman. I'm assured my insurance will cover the damage, which luckily is only to one of my windows. No damage was done to the inside of the shop, which I am extremely grateful for. The police found a brick that was used to break the glass, which had slid underneath my consultation table, and are going to dust it for prints. I will only have to remain closed for one day for the window to get repaired, so that isn't too bad. It could have been a lot worse. Way worse.

As we drive in silence to his building, the night I just endured is the last thing on my mind. Right now, with my duffle bag packed full of clothes sitting behind me in the back seat, the *only* thing on my mind is how I'll be having another sleepover with Reese. And I can't help but tense in my seat at the anticipation of it.

Chapter Eighteen

HE'S QUIET, TOO QUIET AS he walks into his condo and places my bag on the floor next to the couch. He hasn't said two words to me since we left the bakery and it's making my skin crawl. I plop down onto the couch and kick my shoes off, bringing my feet underneath my body as I hear him banging around in the kitchen.

"Here." He hands me a bottled water and I take it, seeing him walk around the couch and sit on the far end, way the hell away from me. He begins flipping through the channels and stops on some basketball game that I couldn't care less about. *What the fuck is this? He comes to my rescue, and I know damn well I heard him call me love, which means he can't hate me, asks me, no, tells me I'm coming to spend the night with him, and now he's barely acknowledging that I'm even here.* I turn my head and stare at him and his perfect profile as it remains impassive but interested in the game he's watching. He's in running shorts and a navy blue T-shirt that has some emblem on the front that I can't make out. Several long minutes go by as his eyes remain on the television, not once flicking toward me. *Jesus, is this how it's going to be all night? Fine then. If I'm sleeping over, I'm at least going to get comfortable.* I stand up and quickly shimmy out of my jeans, tossing them on top of my duffle and reach up and slip my T-shirt off. Turning around so I know he can see me, I drop it on the couch and remove my bra. I make quick eye contact with him as I slip my bra down my arms, his eyes lingering briefly, really fucking briefly on my chest before flicking back toward the game. I grunt and grab his T-shirt and slip it back on before I snatch the remote out of his hands and turn the television off.

"What the fuck?"

"What the fuck is right. What's wrong with you? You're acting weird."

He reaches forward and plucks the remote out of my hand, turning the game back on. "How am I supposed to be acting?" His eyes go back to the game and I no longer want to be here. Picking up my duffle, I quickly put my pants back on and throw my bra inside as I slip on my shoes and turn toward the door. "Where the hell are you going?"

"Like you give a shit. Thanks for making sure I didn't get murdered." I'm almost out the door when his arms grab my waist and pull me back inside, locking the door behind us.

"You're not going anywhere." I'm picked up, carried in his usual caveman style manner and taken back over toward the couch. My duffle is dropped by the edge and I'm dropped on the cushion.

"You don't want me here, obviously, so why should I stay?" I yell up into his stare. His hands come around me, bracing himself on the cushion behind me and bringing his face inches from mine.

"What the fuck makes you think I don't want you here? I always want you here."

"You haven't called or texted me since Friday afternoon, I get topless in front of you and you barely react, and you're not looking at me the way *you* look at me. You don't even want me anymore. You just want your stupid game." Tears fill my eyes and I'm not sure if it's from the night I've endured or the Reese style rejection that's knocking the wind out of me. His hand drops and grabs mine, forcing it against the massive bulge in his pants that I hadn't noticed. *Oh, wow.*

His face inches closer. "I *always* want you." And then it happens. His mouth, his hands, his everything is on me in seconds, ripping my remaining clothes off as I frantically try and keep up with the removal of his.

"Tell me *you* still want me," he grunts as he flips me onto my hands and knees and positions himself behind me. Before I can answer the obvious response, he rams into me and I cry out at the force.

"REESE." I grip the leather with my fingers, scratching into it with my nails as he pounds hard, then harder, into me.

"Answer me, Dylan," he grunts and I yell out between cries.

"Yes. Yes, I'll always want you." He's fucking me harder than he ever has and I know it's because I challenged him and he's proving himself to me. That or he's making damn sure I don't question it again. Either way, I'm letting him handle it. His hands grip my hips, pulling me back to meet him, and if I wasn't so turned on, so hot for him all the time, I might not be able to handle his power. I'm moaning, crying out with each thrust and he's right there with me. "Oh, God. Harder."

"Shit. You want harder?" His thighs crash against mine and my elbows give out. "This hard enough for you, love?"

"Yes!" I scream, needing him to give me this right now. I push back against him and feel his one hand grip my shoulder while the other digs into my hip the way I like.

He groans loudly, his sounds filling the condo. "You drive me fucking crazy. Fuck, Dylan."

"Touch me." His hand wraps around my stomach and drops between my legs. I whimper as his fingers rub my clit while his other hand grips harder on my shoulder. He's so forceful that he's knocking the air out of my lungs. "I'm gonna come." I manage to get out through a faint breath.

"Not yet. Wait for me."

I reach down to remove his fingers but he tightens against me, moving them in his perfect rhythm. "I can't. Please."

He rams into me harder and I cry out, hearing his loud throaty growl. "Now, love." And I let it go, all of it. The pain of the past several days without him, the anger from the pictures, the terror of the hooded figure. I let it go and feel him, just him. I'm panting, barely able to take in a full breath as my upper body collapses down onto my forearms and I feel his head drop to my back.

Hot breath warms my spine and I loosen my grip on the leather. "Hold on." He pulls out of me and I wince a bit in pain, which has never happened with him before. Of course, I've never been fucked like that before, so hard that my teeth chatter with each push. I roll onto my side, facing the cushions and curl into a ball. That was intense, really intense and I'm actually a bit sore after that Reese style fucking. He returns moments later holding a washcloth. "Lie on your back." I obey and keep my eyes on him as he wipes me clean, gently after he notices my scrunched up face. "I hurt you."

"I'm okay, it doesn't hurt that much." He bends down, planting a gentle kiss between my legs before he scoops me up into his arms. I quickly bury my face in his neck and nuzzle the shit out of him. "Mmm, this is my favorite spot, right here." I inhale deeply and let out a soft moan.

"I know; you seek it out often." He carries me into his bedroom and places me gently on the bed. I pull the covers around me and scoot over to allow him some space.

"Now that I've fucked some sense into you, let me be perfectly clear about something." I've already settled on his chest, my leg draped over his and my hand wrapped around his waist as my eyes slowly glance up at him. "I haven't called or texted you since Friday because *you* told me you needed time to think. And I don't know what the fuck that means because no woman has ever told me that before, but I assumed it meant you didn't want to hear from me." His fingers gently stroke my back, trailing across my skin and I moan softly.

"Okay."

"And just because I don't jump on your breasts the moment you whip them out doesn't fucking mean I don't want to. I didn't know where we stood, so I wasn't going to push my luck." I bite my lip to hold in my smile. He looks rightly irritated with having to explain himself, but the explanation is needed. "Dylan, I'm really sorry about those photos."

"I don't want to talk about it. I'm done talking and thinking about it. Between Friday night with Joey and Juls and all day yesterday and today, I'm done." My arm wraps tighter around him. "Nothing's changed between us. It didn't change anything."

He lifts my chin up to meet his face and I see the tension in his jaw. He looks unsure and that look sends a panic through me. *Nothing's changed for me, but has it for him?* I sit up quickly and move to lie next to him when his hands grab my waist and pull me back down, only this time I'm flipped around, straddling him. The movement's so quick I barely have time to register it. "Don't," he states.

I take a second to study his features in my new position, given the fact that we're now eye to eye. Crazy mess of hair that I'm noticing makes him look younger than he is, green eyes that are narrowed in on mine, and stubble? A lot of stubble. I reach out, brush my hand along his chin, and can't contain my smile. *Oh, man. Reese with a day or two worth of facial hair is sexy beyond belief.* "Why did you just try to move away from me?"

I shake my head quickly.

"Dylan." *Oh, Mr. Persistent.*

"Nothing's changed for me, but has it changed for you?" I ask quickly, getting out the question I fear the answer to before I can think myself out of it.

"No," he answers firmly.

"So you still want this?"

He drops his head and it hits the headboard with a loud thump. "Yes, whatever the fuck this is, I still want it. You're in control here, Dylan. You have all the fucking control." His eyes are burning into mine with the same intensity they've always shown for me. *I'm in control? Of what? Of us?* I decide not to probe because I'm not sure I want to know the answer. He lets out a forceful breath that warms my face. "If something would have happened to you tonight…" His eyes close tight and the crease in his brow appears. *Oh, Reese.* The man's mood swings are enough to give me permanent whiplash.

"Nothing happened. I'm okay. I called you and you came for me." I reach out and stroke his face as his eyes pop back open, green and blazing. His tenseness softens a bit.

"I tried locating Heather and sorting this shit out with her, but I didn't find her. All fucking weekend I've been looking." He grits his teeth. "She wasn't at her house and she's not answering my calls." I swallow loudly and he shakes his head. "I'm fucking dealing with it. I just want you to be prepared. Fred didn't deliver that package, so just don't open any that aren't from him. Okay?" I nod. *Jesus. I really don't want to have to deal with this again.* But if Reese is dealing with it, then I'm sure it will be dealt with, in a very Reese like manner no less. "But after tonight, Dylan, I don't want you there by yourself." His hands grip my waist and pull me closer to him, our foreheads falling together.

"I don't want to be there by myself either, but I want to keep an eye on my shop. It's important to me. It's mine and I've worked hard for it." His hand reaches up and pulls my bun loose, letting my hair fall down my back. "I'm going to have a door installed at the top of the stairs. I'll call about getting it done along with the window repair and a security system tomorrow. I can't believe I never thought about having some type of system in place already." He nods at me, but I know that isn't what he wants to hear. I lean in and kiss him gently. "I'll be fine. I've lived there on my own for three years. Plus, I have you and you're only five minutes away if something happens."

His hands brush lightly down my back, playing with the ends of my hair. "It will never take me five minutes to get to you. I think I made it there in two tonight." I giggle slightly and see his lips curl up. "I might be getting a few red light camera notifications in the mail."

"Worth it?" I ask, running my hands through his hair.

"Worth it. You hungry?"

I nod frantically and he laughs, the infectious sound pulling me in with him. "Sit tight." I'm slid off as he hops out of bed, disappearing down the hallway as I watch his glorious backside stride away. Laughing quietly at the realization that he *always* asks me if I'm hungry after sex, I grab one of his pillows and press it to my face, inhaling deeply as his voice comes down the hallway.

"Do you like your pizza cold or heated up?

"Cold." *Yum. Cold pizza and a sleepover with Reese? Yes please*. Glancing around the room, I spot his iPad on his dresser. I scramble out of bed and grab it, flipping it open and turning it on. I have some googling of a certain CPA to do. The screen comes to life. *Oh. Oh my.* The wallpaper is a picture of me, in this bed. I'm sleeping, curled up on my side with the sheets covering me up to show only a tiny bit of cleavage. My hair is a mess of blonde waves that are spilling down my right shoulder and my lips are parted. The camera is mainly focused on my face and I look to be in a deep sleep. I look up and see Reese staring at me, stopped in the doorway carrying our food.

"Umm, you found my iPad I see." He moves toward the bed and puts the plates down on his nightstand, his eyes only momentarily leaving mine. "Nobody sees that. I would never show that to anybody."

Placing it down on the bed, I get up on my knees and crawl to the edge where he's standing, pulling him toward me and wrapping my arms around his neck. After a moment's hesitation, he wraps his arms around me and relaxes against my body. "You're not mad? I can take it off."

I reach around and place my hand over his mouth, silencing him. "I'm not mad. It can stay on there." Dropping my hands, I scoot back over and reach out for my plate playfully as his smile returns.

"Cold pizza, huh? I thought I was the only other person who still preferred it cold to heated."

I take a bite and shake my head. "I hate heated leftover pizza. The cheese gets all rubbery and gross." He drops a chilled bottled water in my lap and I yelp. "So, why did you take that picture of me?"

He stops chewing briefly, looking over at the iPad on the bed. "I don't know. I think I just wanted a reminder of you in my bed, just in case you refused to get back in it." I laugh and he winks at me. "I watched you for hours before I took it. Do you know you make little noises while you sleep?"

I swallow my bite and arch my brow at him. "Little noises? Like what?"

"Like moans. Tiny little whimpers."

"What? No, I don't." I unscrew my bottle and take a big sip while he nods at me. "I do not make any noises when I sleep."

He turns and places his empty plate on his nightstand. *Jesus, the man devours his food in a matter of seconds.* "Yes, you do. You even said my name a few times." My mouth drops open.

I place my plate down on the nightstand before I trample him. "No, I did not. Take that back, Carroll." I'm poking him everywhere, trying to find a weak ticklish spot on his body and he's only laughing at me in amusement.

"Reese. Oh, Reese. Right there."

I feel my face redden. "You're evil," I scoff before I roll off him and lie back on my pillow, pulling the covers up over my head. *Good Lord, I hope he's joking because if he isn't, how embarrassing is this?*

His laugh shakes the bed and I feel the covers slowly slide down to reveal his face hovering over mine. "Love."

"What?" I try to pull the covers back up, but he holds them down. I've never been told I talk in my sleep before or make any weird noises, and I've had plenty of sleepovers with Juls and Joey. Of course, I doubt *they* watch me for hours after I pass out. *Humph.* He climbs under the covers with me and pulls me close to him so we're nose to nose.

"So, I hear we're going to be paired up at the wedding." His hand trails down my shoulder to my waist and holds me there as I try to keep my smile at bay. "You okay with that? It will be like a date you know. Rather intimate." His lip curls up and I give in to it.

"I'm okay with that. I *have* been on a few dates before. Have you?"

"No, well, not in a really long time." *A really long time? What classifies a really long time? Why is he so against dating now?* I push these questions out of my head and focus on another.

"Have you always been monogamously casual with girls?" This has definitely been on my mind recently. I had initially pegged him as a total player with multiple women at all times, but had never dared to ask.

His eyes flick to mine quickly before he drops them. "No." I reach up and run my hand down his arm, rubbing his shoulder the way he likes and seeing his eyes close slowly. "I've never really wanted to be before you." I stop breathing at his admission. *Holy shit. Was Joey right? Am I a game changer?* My hand stills on his bicep and his eyes shoot open, locking onto mine. "You make me want different things, things I've never wanted before."

"Why?" I force out and continue rubbing his arm. I need to know the answer to this. I want to know if his reasons are the same as mine. I've experienced more before, but not in the way I want with Reese. I want everything with him.

He keeps his eyes on me and sighs softly. "I don't know, but I can't stand the idea of *not* being monogamously casual with you. I have no desire to be with anyone else and the thought of you with another man," his hand comes flying up through his hair, stopping my massage, "it fucking *infuriates* me."

Well, that settles that. Like there's any other man on the planet I want to ever be with now that I've experienced this one. I scoot in closer and continue working his arm, reaching around toward his back. "I know the feeling," I reply as his eyes close shut again, his lips quivering into a smile. Silence falls between us and I let my mind wander while I work his back and shoulder. I feel like I'm making progress with Reese, progress out of the casual zone and toward something more serious, which I am dying to sprint to. But I know I can't rush him and he'll have to do this at his own pace if he even wants to. If I've learned anything from the past few weeks with him, it's that he does *everything* at his own pace. He likes to be in control, even though he told me I have it all, which completely threw me for a loop. I'm chalking that up to him just worrying about my safety. He was obviously scared for me, and when you're scared, you say crazy shit. He likes to show how much power he has and his authority over situations, as he clearly displayed when he destroyed my dress. So I'll let him control this, control us, because I like the pace he's taking. As long as he takes me with him.

Chapter Nineteen

AFTER GIVING HIM A DECENT one handed massage and enjoying all of his tiny little moans of pleasure, Reese flips on his back and pulls me on top of him. He scoots up so his back is against the headboard and we're chest to chest. All the tension in his face is gone and the only thing bothering *me* anymore is my now stiff hand from his drawn out rub down. His hands wrap around my waist, tightening their grip and I feel him, his desire for me growing against my backside.

"Missed your face," I whisper and see his lip curl up in the corner.

"Just my face?"

"Never." I move in slowly and capture his mouth with mine, licking along the seam of his lips until he opens up for me, which only takes half a second. I relish his minty flavor and moan into his mouth. His tongue strokes mine in a way that sets my skin on fire, and I'm desperate for him. Tangling my hands in his hair, I pull him closer to me and rub my chest against his. His hands run up my back, tickling along my spine and grazing around toward my front. I'm not sure what he's better at, touching or kissing. Both send me into a frenzy where I feel like I'm going to combust at any moment. His callused hands expertly squeeze my breasts. "Mmm, right there." I kiss him along his stubbled jaw and toward his ear. "I need you."

His mouth runs down my body between my breasts, kissing and licking every inch of me. "Dylan, I want to do something."

My lips pull at his ear and I release it enough to reply, "Anything." Because I would do anything with this man. It's obvious to everyone at this point. I feel his hot breath on my chest and he hesitates, causing me to lean back. He lifts his face up to mine. "Anything," I repeat.

His Adam's apple rolls in his neck and his lips part. "I want to make love to you."

I gasp, completely shocked and unprepared for this request. I was honestly expecting something along the lines of anal play, which I'm totally up for with him, even though I've never done it before. The thought of anal sex terrified me once, but this, this request that he's just thrown out between us? I'm not sure there's anything *more* terrifying. But I want to, and I can at least try, right? For him, for Reese Carroll, for the look he's giving me right now, yes. I can at least try.

My heart constricts so much that I reach up and place my hand on it, making sure it didn't just beat for the last time. He wants to make love to me. Love. Not fucking. My mind is scrambling for words. He's studying me, waiting for my response. I know I've been silent for at least several minutes and I'm sure it's killing him inside, but he's not showing it. His face is soft and pleading, eyes searching mine and conveying that we can do this. That I can do this.

"Okay," I say finally, and I think we're both shocked that I actually spoke. "I just need to use the bathroom first." He grins wide, my favorite lines appearing, and kisses me quickly on the lips as he lifts me off him. Without a glance back, I scurry into the bathroom and close the door behind me.

Shit. I'm about to make love to a man who I'm struggling to not fall in love with? What am I insane? I stare at myself in the bathroom mirror and quickly comb my fingers through my hair. My cheeks are flushed, my nipples are hard, and I'm beyond ready for him between my legs. Everything about me is ready for this right now, everything except for what's burning inside my chest cavity. I can't even begin to imagine what making love to him consists of. Fucking him is intense and borderline intimate as it is. And that's definitely all we've done so far. If I didn't know it before, his request just confirmed it. So what exactly am I in for? Have I ever even made love before? I think long and hard about that as I quickly use the toilet. No, no way. Not with Justin. I'm not even sure he's capable of making love to anyone. He was always so distant when we were having sex that he barely kept eye contact with me. And making love consists of eye contact I'm sure. I hurriedly wash my hands and try to mentally prepare myself for what's about to happen as I exit the bathroom and return to his bedroom. I'm halted in my tracks. *Oh, God.*

I'm stopped in the doorway by the sight of candles lit and covering both nightstands, providing an amber glow throughout the room. Reese is messing with his phone as he places it on the docking station on his dresser when he turns to me, seeing my expression and straightening instantly. "Too much?"

I bite my lip and shake my head. *It's perfect; he's perfect.* "No, I like it." I settle on the bed, kneeling and resting back on my heels as I watch him continue playing with his phone. He's looking for a song and I'm almost one hundred percent sure I know what song he's looking for. *Damn it, I need to look up those lyrics.* But that's not what starts playing as he walks over toward me. "Look After You" by The Fray pours through the speakers. I'm familiar with this song and its lyrics, which will surely rip my heart out if he's not trying to tell me something with this selection. "This isn't cliché is it? Candles and music?" he asks as he runs his hands through his hair and down his face.

I smile playfully at his nervousness. "No, there's nothing about you that's cliché." This is completely true. I've never met a man like him before and I doubt I ever will. Reaching out to him, he slips his hand in mine and allows me to pull him toward me. "Make love to me, handsome."

I see it, the layer of anxiety drop in front of me as he crawls onto the bed and pushes me onto my back. Settling between my legs, he begins kissing me in the gentlest way possible. There's tongue, because with him there's always at least *some* tongue, but it's different. I'm used to the rough, quick strokes of his against mine, against my lips, but these strokes are much more unhurried and tender. Groaning softly into his mouth, I'm quickly melting around him and I'm suddenly not sure what kind of Reese kissing I prefer. His hard *I want you now* kisses are insanely hot, but this, the *let me make love to you* kisses are radiating through my body, sparking something untouched. He slowly works his way down, kissing every part of me with the same gentle mouth I just personally got very acquainted with. The song begins to play again. *He's put it on repeat?* I feel his hot breath between my legs and arch up into him.

"Yes, God, yes." The first long lick causes me to fist the sheets tightly between my fingers. I pull my bottom lip into my mouth and bite it hard as he works me.

"Look at me," he pleads and I immediately drop my gaze, meeting his green eyes. He's watching me, capturing my every response to his movements and I'm not holding anything back. His tongue laps in and out, around and between every fold and dip. He's even somehow making *this* more intimate with his unrelenting stare. His strokes are soft but carry the perfect amount of pressure. I don't want to come yet so I concentrate on the lyrics of the song to give me a distraction. *Like that's possible. The man's mouth is a machine.*

There now, steady love, so few come and don't go
Will you won't you, be the one I'll always know
When I'm losing my control, the city spins around
You're the only one who knows, you slow it down

Damn these lyrics. I'm not sure about him, but they are definitely pushing every emotional button in my body. He moans against me and my eyes roll back into my head, the sensation moving through me like a current. His lips pull my clit into his mouth and I cry out, unable to hold back any longer. "Reese." I'm panting and moving my hips against his mouth as I come, long and hard. His tongue laps up every ounce of my arousal, slowly and tentatively, keeping me on the brink of another orgasm. Gradually releasing me, he places sweet kisses on the insides of my thighs as I stare down at him.

"Come up here."

He crawls up my body and settles between my legs, gazing

down at me as he positions himself at my entrance. I feel him right there, and know the slightest movement will plunge him into me. But he doesn't move. His hands hold my face and I stare up at him, hearing the beginning of the song and smiling.

"I like this song."

"Me, too," he whispers, bending and trailing kisses to my ear. With a slow push, he's in me and I grip his back tightly, gasping and clinging myself to him. "Fuck," he says into my ear before he leans up and holds himself above me. Keeping my gaze, he begins moving slowly, his hips thrusting gently into mine. I stare at his chest as it tightens with each push, the muscles in his abdomen rippling with his movements. He's never been this unhurried with me. This is different, way different from what we've done before. The intimacy is pouring straight out of him into me and I feel him everywhere. His eyes are soft and warm, penetrating mine and conveying unspoken words that I pray I'm not misreading. I want to tell him so many things in this moment as he lovingly strokes me, in and out, but I don't. I wrap my legs around him and let myself feel it.

"Tell me you've never done this before," I whisper, seeing his eyes dilate above me. "That you've never made love to anyone but me."

There's no hesitation in his reply. "Never. It's only you, Dylan. Just you." I grab his face and bring his lips to mine. Our moans are silenced by each other's mouths and the music that is playing all around us. His panting increases and my hands are gripped as he brings them on either side of my face and laces his fingers through them. I love it when he does that to my hands. It's such a boyfriend move. My breathing quickens as his tongue works against mine. Slow and steady thrusts, I'm pulsing around him and trying not to end this too soon. Making love to this man has gone way above any expectation I could have conjured. He increases his pace, thrusting deeper and harder, and I'm close, so close, but I want him to unravel with me. I need it like a drug.

"Come with me," I beg and he drops his forehead to mine and grunts loudly. I'm there instantly with the look he gives me and fall out around him, trembling against him and feeling his warmth run through me.

"Dylan," he whispers my name instead of his usual climatic scream, pumps into me and stills, collapsing down on top of me as I soak him and what we just did in. Our breathing is uneven and loud, his blowing across the skin of my neck and mine pushing out above us. I don't care that his is making me hot, I don't care that his hip is digging into mine and causing a shooting pain across my pelvis. I don't want to move. Ever.

"That was..." I start to say but can't finish because there are no words.

"Yeah, that was." He kisses my lips quickly before sliding off the bed and muting the music. "Are you sore?" I flick my eyes up to meet his stare, his serious expression also containing a bit of hesitation.

"No, I'm perfect. That was perfect." *It was beyond perfect.* I reach up and stretch above my head, as he crawls back over top of me, settling on his side and pulling me close to him.

"Hi," I whisper.

"Hi, yourself." His sweet smile pulls at his lips.

"So, tell me all about how you called Joey *after* I fell asleep Thursday night and not Friday morning."

His eyes widen and his grin spreads. "I was wondering how long he'd keep that from you. Did he even make it twenty-four hours?" His hand reaches up and brushes my hair out of my face, tucking it softly behind my ear.

"No way. Once the wine started flowing Friday night, he blabbed everything." I reach out and run my hand along his jaw. "I like this, a lot. You should go all scruffy more often."

"So should you." His hand brushes between my legs and my eyes widen.

"What? Seriously?" I reply through a shocked grin.

"No, I like you like this. I can see every part of you without anything in my way." I wiggle my brows at him and his infectious laugh pulls me in. "You know how much I hate anything getting in my way when it comes to you."

"Is *that* why you steal my panties? To prevent me from putting a barrier in between us?"

He shrugs playfully, his lips curling up into a smile. "You wax it, right?" I nod. "Doesn't that hurt?"

Yes. "Nah, Will is really gentle." *Oh, I'm devious.*

"Excuse me?"

My smile cracks through and his face releases some of its tension, but not much. *He's too easy.* "He is. He's been doing me for years."

I'm quickly being pressed into the mattress by his tall frame. "I hope you're fucking joking. I am *not* okay with a guy waxing you there." My arms are pinned to my side by his knees and I'm now face-to-face with his erection. *Whoa. He's hard again, already?*

"What if I told you he was gay?"

"Doesn't fucking matter." He inches forward and brushes the tip against my mouth.

"Oh, please, are you going to discipline me by making me suck you off? That's hardly a punishment." I dart my tongue out and lick the tip, seeing him shudder a bit as he stares down at me.

"It will be once I withhold *your* orgasm, which you know damn well I'm good at doing." *Oh, shit.* The memory of my worktop flashes through my mind. *That was horrible.*

"All right! No, it's not a guy named Will. It's a girl named Lacey."

"Really, Lacey, huh?" I roll my eyes at his sexual tone. *Men.*

"You're perverted."

"I am and so are you. Now, open that pretty mouth of yours and make me come."

"Say please." Another quick flick of my tongue pulls a groan out of his throat.

"Fuck that. Not after what you just put me through. Open." *Yum. Hello, dominant Reese.* I smile and open my mouth as he inches forward, granting me full access to his member.

"Fuck yes," he grunts through gritted teeth as he fucks my face. Bringing one hand down, he holds the back of my head and plummets deeply into me, his quick thrusts causing my eyes to water. I glance up and see his other hand gripping the headboard until his knuckles are white. "So fucking good."

I moan around him, my lips vibrating against his skin as he shifts his knee and pulls my right arm out. "Wrap around me." I grip the base with my hand and begin sliding up and down his length as he stills, keeping just the tip of him in my mouth. I'm gliding easily, the saliva from my mouth completely drenching him. Working him hard and fast, my tongue flicks against him and my lips tease his head. He pulses inside me and I see the tension in his jaw. I love doing this to him and get just as much pleasure out of it as he does. Dropping his head back, his Adam's apple slides and his veins protrude in his neck as he moans deeply. His body is vibrating with his sounds, moving against my tongue. I keep my eyes on him, watching his chest heave with each thrust and his stomach clench as I work him. Sucking and teasing him, my hand grips harder and I see his shoulders hunch forward. "I'm close, love. Don't stop."

"Do you want to come in my mouth?" I ask, as I lick the tip.

His eyes widen. "Yes, unless I have options?" His voice is strained and I know he's on the brink.

"You could come on me if you want. I think I'd like that."

He swallows and quickly backs down my body, angling himself at my breasts. "Here?" he asks and I nod, pumping him hard and seeing his lip pull into his mouth. We both stare at the spectacle of him coming on my breasts, the white warmth rolling between my mounds and a few drops landing close to my neck. "Holy shit. That's so fucking hot."

I nod in agreement and stare down at myself, letting go of his cock and seeing him shiver a bit. "You marked me again." I swirl a bit of it on the softened red mark on my left breast and see him watch me, studying me.

"I think you like it when I mark you."

I dip my finger into my mouth. "I love it when you mark me." He climbs off the bed and disappears into the hallway as I gaze down at my sticky mess. It really is hot, seeing what I've pulled out of him. Having him label me with it. *I wonder if he's done that before. Nope, stop it, Dylan.* He comes back in moments later with a small hand towel and begins wiping me off.

"That was amazing, you know," he says through a smile.

"I know. I want to mark you now."

His eyebrow arches as he tosses the towel onto the floor,

planting quick kisses to both my nipples. "Do you? With what?" My eyes search around the room and land on a notebook that's sitting on his dresser with a pen marking a page in it. I quickly hop off and grab it, scurrying back over to the bed and pushing him down onto his back. "Are you going to draw on me?"

"No, not draw. I'm going to write on you, but where?" My eyes rake all over his beautiful body as I suck on the pen cap. "I mean really, your body is almost too pretty for tattoos. Would you ever get one?"

He shrugs. "I don't know. I'm not opposed to it entirely. What are you going to write?"

"Patience, professor." He muffles his laugh under me as I drop his arm open and begin writing on the inside of his bicep. The ink is dark, a deep blue as I scroll in overly girly handwriting and smile at myself.

"You seem to be enjoying yourself. Why are you putting it there?"

"Because I love your arms and it's hidden. I like thinking that I'm the only one who knows it's there. Just for me."

"You say that like it's permanent."

I shrug. "I can rewrite it daily if I have to." I retrace the letters to darken them and feel his eyes on me. "Do you study everything the way you study me?"

"No. Unfortunately, not everything in my life is as fascinating as you are."

"I'm a twenty-six-year-old baker who's lived in South Side her entire life. How is that fascinating?"

"I don't know, just is. And you study me just as much, so I should ask you the same question."

I recap my pen. "Well, that answer should be obvious. I'm looking for a new tax guy." Leaning down, I blow gently across his arm and dry the ink. "There, all done."

His head raises and he glances at his arm, the words **Do I Wanna Know?** printed on him in my script. He studies it for a moment, pulling his bottom lip into his mouth and I watch his long lashes flutter before his eyes flick to mine.

"I like your mark."

"Me, too." I chuck the pen onto the dresser and settle in next to him, pulling the covers up around us. He wraps his arm around my waist and closes his eyes, his breathing slowing down to a soft rhythm as I observe him. It doesn't take long before I know he's sleeping. Chest rising and falling slowly, eyes fluttering as if he's mid-dream, and lips slightly parted to allow for his breath to escape. I study him for minutes and then minutes become hours. I'm so ridiculously happy in this moment that when I begin to silently cry next to him, I don't know what to think besides what I'm now willing to admit to myself. I'm crazy in love with this man. I love everything about him. From the tiniest detail like the little lines next to his eyes and the slit that runs down his bottom lip, to the way I can only seem to be able to take a full breath when he's near me. I love the words he says to me and the look he reserves only for me; even if that look is one that's a preamble to a Reese style flip out. I love the way I can sense his presence and the way my heart beats in my chest when I finally lock eyes with him. I love him. Just him. And the tears I let myself cry are both of worry that he's not going to reciprocate these feelings, and because I'm finally willing to let myself feel them. So
I'll let my tears fall, because I've been denying my feelings for him since the moment I fell into his lap, and because I'm a silly girl who is going to turn into a brave woman tomorrow and finally tell him how I feel. Fuck being casual. I'm so over that bullshit.

Chapter Twenty

I WAKE UP MONDAY MORNING, my eyes fluttering open slowly to adjust to the sunlight pouring through the window, and I notice immediately that I'm alone and not in my bed. Glancing over at the clock, I note the time is nine forty-two a.m. and realize he's probably gone to work after trying to wake me countless times. I really need to figure out a way to be woken up out of my slumber. What if we eventually have kids and they try to wake me up to make them breakfast or some shit and I'm dead to the world? *Jesus, did I just say if we eventually have kids?* When have I ever thought about having children before? *Never.* I've *never* thought about having children. I picture a miniature Reese meandering around the house, trying to keep his siblings in line and raking his hands through his wild hair when they don't listen. I giggle silently at the thought and quickly push it out of my mind. *Crazy, Dylan. Utter craziness.*

I crawl out of bed and duck into the bathroom briefly before finding my clothes scattered all around the couch. The memory of their quick removal sends a shiver through me. *That was fun. I should challenge his desire for me more often.* Slipping on my panties and his University of Chicago T-shirt, I find my phone and quickly dial Joey, feeling like a complete idiot and shitty friend for not having called him last night after the break in.

"Cupcake. What the fuck, girlie? Can you believe that psycho broke our window out?"

I plop down onto a dining room chair and begin rubbing my head. "Well, at least we think it was probably her. I'm so sorry I didn't call you last night, my mind was all over the place." I sigh heavily as the image of the hooded figure creeps into my mind.

"No worries, your casual fuck buddy called me when he was on his way over to rescue you. I'm sure he figured you had other things on your mind than reminding your assistant *not* to show up to work today." I grunt at the casual fuck buddy reference and spot a piece of paper hanging off the edge of the kitchen counter. I reach over and grab it, noticing my favorite handwriting.

Dylan,

I have no fucking clue how I ever survived not waking up to you. And before you say anything, yes, I did try to wake you up to go for a run with me. You were adorably out cold, as usual. Enjoy your day off.

X Reese

P.S. Here's a spare key if you go out today. Keep it.

Swoon.

"Hey, so listen, I have some phone calls to make to the insurance company and to find someone to put in a security system and a door above the stairs, but when I'm done, any chance you could pick me up and take me to Reese's office?"

"Yeah, sure. I'm pretty bored myself over here since Billy's gone to work. What's going on at the office?"

I smile. "Oh, you know, the usual. Just me going to finally tell our favorite numbers guy that I'm madly in love with him." I hear the phone drop and Joey's insanely high pitched screams.

"DYLAN. Oh, my fucking God. Yes, girl, yes. Hurry up and make those stupid phone calls and then text me when you're ready. Ooohhh, I'm bursting over here."

"And don't say anything to Juls. I'd hate for her to leak it to Ian who would most likely blab. I feel like those men talk just as much as we do sometimes."

"Mmmm mmm. Don't you worry; my lips are sealed on this one. Take care of your shit, and then let's get to the important matters at hand."

I CALL THE INSURANCE COMPANY and make sure I won't be responsible for any of the damage from the break in. They assure me the window is in fact being repaired during our phone call, and I will be up and running by tomorrow. Grabbing Reese's iPad off the bed, I look up the number to a security system company and get an estimate on a top of the line alarm system to install. Using the commission from Justin's stupid wedding, I go ahead and arrange for the men to come today and set it up. That way, it will also be ready by tomorrow. I'm not sure who the hell to call about getting a door put in, so I dial my parents and hold my breath knowing I'm about to get a huge ear full for not having called them last night.

"Oh, for Christ's sake, Dylan. Something horrible could have happened to you. You could have been raped, murdered, Jesus Christ. I can't believe you're just now calling us." My mother's tirade goes on for a good ten minutes before I'm able to get a word in.

"I know, I know. I'm sorry I didn't call. But I'm fine. Nothing happened and we're pretty sure we know who it was and the police are looking for her." *Stupid red headed bitch.*

"Her? It was a woman? What kind of a woman throws a brick through a store window? Good grief, what is the world coming to?"

"Just some ex-girlfriend of Reese's, Mom. Look, everything is fine. The window is being repaired right now and a security system is being installed today as well. I just need to talk to Dad about putting a door in to separate my living space from the bakery." Which, really, I should have done years ago. I just didn't feel the need to do so until now. That or I could get a guard dog. No, that has to be unsanitary around all those baked goods.

"Ex-girlfriend? Humph, a woman scorned no less. Well, at least you're safe and this finally makes you put in a well overdue alarm system." She exhales forcefully. "Here's your father. Bill, go easy on her, she's fine."

"Dylan, sweetheart, you're all right then?" My dad's voice is incredibly calm compared to my mother's, but that's always been his personality. I definitely get my short fuse from the women in my family.

"Yes, Dad, I'm fine. But I need to get a door installed at the top of the stairs leading from the kitchen. How do I go about doing that?" He immediately goes into daddy-mode and tells me not to worry about it, he will head to a local hardware store today and purchase a door for me. When I tell him I can handle it, he shuts me up quickly and I let him. I don't think there is anything my father enjoys more than doing something for me that keeps me safe. After I am reassured it will be taken care of today, I hang up, text Joey to head on over, and hop in the shower.

I relish in Reese's shampoo and body wash, letting the steam create a cloud of his yumminess all around me as I clean up. I'm surprisingly not nervous at all about telling him I love him. After last night, the love making, him telling me I make him want things he's never wanted before, I feel empowered to do this. I quickly slip into a pair of jeans and a cute top as a knock on the door sends me dashing through the condo. I fling it open and beam at my assistant.

"AH! I'm soooo excited. *Please* let me be there when you tell him."

"What? No way. This is a private moment. You may wait outside." I slip into my shoes and grab my cell and the spare key Reese left for me, slipping it onto my key ring and locking up behind us. "Okay, let's do this shit before I lose my nerve."

WE STOP BY THE BAKERY on the way to his office. The men who are in charge of replacing the window are just finishing up and have me sign a few pieces of paper before they give it a final wipe down and leave. Joey and I both watch the security guys go over how to arm and disarm the system, giving us both the code and a few forms to sign as well before they too hit the road. My mom sent me a text informing me that my father has purchased a door with an insane amount of locks and he will be stopping by later on today to install it. I won't have to stick around, because other than Joey and myself, my parents also have a key to the bakery. So, after piling back into the Civic, we finish the short drive to the Walker & Associates building.

"How nervous *are* you right now?" he asks me as I sit in the car, and trying to find out where the fuck all my bravery has disappeared to. We've been parked outside the building for at least ten minutes and I haven't budged.

"Uh, a lot. Maybe this is a bad idea?"

"Fuck that." My seatbelt is unbuckled for me as he reaches across my body and opens my door, giving me a quick, but gentle, shove out of the car. "Go do it, Dylan. That man in there loves you fiercely. It's written all over his beautiful face. But I'm afraid you might be the one to have to say it first. Damn it, I had my money on Reese being the one to crack before you did, but oh, well." I quickly run my fingers through my hair and give him a weak smile. I'm certain he means what he says, no doubt a small wager having gone on between him and Juls. She'll never let him hear the end of losing to this one.

"Okay, thanks, Joey." He winks at me as I close the door and walk into the building and toward the back of the lobby where the elevators are lined up. My hands are clenched into fists and I'm shaking a bit, but I'm here and I'm fucking doing this.

Stepping off the elevators and onto the twelfth floor, I walk straight past the first reception area and toward Reese's office. I haven't even thought about the fact that I'll be seeing a new face sitting behind his reception desk until I see it. And it is a lot manlier.

"Good afternoon. How may I help you?" The young man, dressed sharply in a dark suit greets me with a crooked smile. His dark brown hair is slicked to the side with some sort of product. *Hmm. I like him already.*

"Hello. I was wondering if Mr. Carroll is available."

"Oh, actually he is in Mr. Thomas' office right now with a few more associates having lunch. Would you like me to call him?" He reaches for his phone but I shoot my hand up to halt him.

"Oh, no, that's okay. I know where Mr. Thomas' office is."

He gives me a warm smile and places the phone back down. "Wonderful. Well, go right on and knock since his receptionist is out at lunch. Have a nice day."

"Thanks, you too."

Man, he is cheery. I can't help but giggle at the fact that Reese hired a man to be his receptionist instead of a woman. I walk quickly toward Ian's office, seeing the door already a few inches open, and go to knock when my favorite voice halts me.

"She's fucking psychotic. I've never had a girl go that nuts on me after I tell her I'm done fucking her," he says through a partially full mouth. *The man does love to talk with his mouth full.* I smile slightly and shake my head.

"Yeah, well, I'm pretty sure most women you stop fucking usually flip out on you in some way or another. But that's really fucked up that she targeted Dylan like that." I recognize Ian's voice and cross my arms over my chest, leaning against the wall as I listen in. "She obviously hasn't had the pleasure of seeing Dylan's pissed off side. Pretty dumb move on her part."

A third voice chimes in that I'm not familiar with. "Who is this Dylan chick anyway? She hot?" *Ahhh, yes, so glad I arrived here at this exact moment. Nothing like a little ego boost to brighten a Monday.*

I hear chip bags ruffle. "Hot doesn't even begin to describe her. She's fucking beautiful," Reese answers and I bite my lip.

"He met her at Mr. Walter's daughter's wedding a few weekends ago. She's Juls' best friend and one hell of a baker. She owns Dylan's Sweet Tooth on Fayette. That's the store that got the brick thrown through the window," Ian says through a mouthful.

"Shit. So, you like this girl or is she just another one of the many women that Reese Carroll destroys in his path?" The third voice asks and I brace myself. *Jesus Christ, that sounds horrible. Although, I can totally see how it applies. He is a force of nature.*

Silence fills the room, several long seconds of silence. I hear a few throats clear and then his voice.

"It's not serious if that's what you're asking me. You know I don't do that shit. I like fucking her, so I do." My mouth and my heart drop at the same time as I hear Ian's voice say something in response to his description of our situation, but I don't register it. Instead, I run quickly for the elevators and slip in the first one that opens.

"Oh, God. Oh, God. Oh, shit." I'm gripping the wall in the empty elevator as it takes me down to the first floor, my head spinning and my heart no longer with me, having left it on the floor outside of Ian's office. *I can't believe he said that. After everything. After last night and after his birthday. I'm still just someone he likes to fuck. That's it?* The doors open and I run through the lobby and toward the red Civic that is still parked on the curb. Joey is leaning against the passenger door with his phone up to his ear. My appearance makes him end his call.

"What happened?"

"Take me to his place, now. I need to get my shit." My face is covered in tears and he moves quickly, not asking any more questions as we both pile into his car.

The drive doesn't take long and Joey remains silent as I burst into the condo and grab my duffle, aimlessly throwing my belongings into it and triple checking that I don't leave anything behind. Because I'm never coming back here to get it. I grab my items out of the bathroom and break down when I spot his body wash, wanting to take a final whiff of it, but managing to pull myself away from the shower before I can let that happen. I run to his bedroom and grab the notebook that I got the pen out of last night and bring it out to the dining room, opening up to a blank page and grabbing the pen. I feel Joey's hand on my back as he comes to stand next to me.

"Dylan, what happened?"

My hands are shaking as I hover the pen above the paper, not sure what exactly I want to write for him to see. There's so much I want to say. I want to tell him how badly he's fucked up, how much I love him, and how angry I am at him for *making* me fall in love with him. Because that's exactly what he did. He pulled that love that I had buried down deep inside me right up to the surface, and now I'm drowning in it. I wipe under my eyes and look up at Joey.

"He doesn't love me. He's just fucking me. He doesn't do serious." I take in a deep shaky breath. "I'm done." My hand begins to move as he brings his over my shoulder and holds me while I write. It's a sloppy mess, but it's legible. I leave it open on the table for him to read.

Reese,

I can't do this anymore. I'm sure you'll have no trouble finding someone who can give you what you want, but it's not me. Please let me go.

Dylan

Turning, I drop my head against Joey's chest and cry harder than I've ever cried before. His arms envelope me and he whispers reassuring words into my ear as I sob, drenching his navy blue polo shirt.

"Sweetie, did he really say that?"

I nod. "Yes. He said he doesn't do serious and he's just fucking me because he likes to."

"Shit, Dylan, I've seen him with you. He's not going to let you go without a fight and you know it."

I shake against him and grip him closer to me. "Joey, I can't do this with him. Please make sure he understands that I can't see him. I fucking can't."

I back away from him and see him nod weakly, most likely

fearing the Reese tirade that he will certainly be up against as I grab my keys and remove the spare one he gave me, placing it on the note I just scribbled. I look up at him. "I really hate to ask this, but would you and Billy mind if—"

"Fuck no. I already decided that you're moving in with us until this shit blows over. Reese will break through that new window of yours if he knows you're upstairs in your loft." I give him half a smile and pick up my duffle, swinging it over my shoulder as the tears begin to fall again.

"Come on, cupcake. You'll be okay." And with one final look, I lock up behind us and let Joey move my body down the hallway and toward the elevators, because I have no control of it myself anymore.

AFTER A QUICK STOP AT the bakery to pick up some things, Joey takes us back to Billy's condo and quickly pours us two massive glasses of wine. He offers me the guest room, which I place my stuff down in before zoning out on the couch, staring down at my glass. I'm still crying, but not as heavily, only a few tears streaming down my face in between blinks. I've rubbed and cried off all my makeup and haven't dared to look at myself in a mirror for fear as to what I might see. My heart physically aches, like it's slowly being pulled apart by some unseen force and it's taken its ever loving time doing it, too. I just wish it would speed up the process and rip it to shreds already. After several minutes alone with my thoughts, Joey joins me on the couch with a heavy sigh.

"I'm so fucking confused right now. Dylan, I really thought, shit we *all* thought Reese wanted more than just some casual bullshit." He grabs my hand as I keep my head turned down toward my glass. "I'm so sorry, cupcake. Do you want to call Juls?"

I take a massive sip, hoping to dull some of the pain because alcohol is the poster child for broken heart syndrome. "I will, although I probably don't have to. Once my note is discovered and he can't find or talk to me, he'll be calling Ian who will in turn inform Juls." I swallow another gulp. "I feel so stupid. Everyone warned me about him, you especially. Telling me what Billy said about how he doesn't and will never do a relationship." I shake with my cries and have to put my glass down, covering my face as it all comes back again. "I hate him." Joey wraps me up and hushes me as I convulse with intense sobs against his body.

This is it. This is what being broken feels like. And a man that I wasn't even in a relationship with did it to me. *Fucking hell.*

Chapter Twenty-One

TWO DAYS BEFORE THE WEDDING

"OH, FOR CHRIST'S SAKE, JULS. You need to decide on a cake flavor now or you're not getting a fucking cake." *Good Lord.* I get that the girl only cares about her sweet husband-to-be, but shit. I'm in charge of providing something decadent and she's only given me the type of flowers she wants on it. Juls just laughs at me as she flips through my design book in my kitchen bakery.

It's been close to three months since I ended things with Reese. After he came home and found my note, my phone didn't stop ringing for a week straight. I ignored all of his calls and texts, and I also ignored everything Juls would try to tell me about him. I didn't want to know how upset he was or how bad he wanted to talk to me about things. I moved back into my loft after only spending a few days at Billy and Joey's condo. They were very sweet to me and overly hands on with my healing process, but I knew if I was going to move the fuck on, I needed to do it in my own place. The texts and calls from Reese stopped after a month, and a part of me wishes I hadn't deleted every text without reading it or every voicemail without listening to it. I miss his voice, and I hate myself for it. I miss his words even more, and that makes me want to punch someone. But he got the hint, and I haven't seen my phone light up with his name in exactly fifty-four days. Juls got the hint also and stopped bringing him up, but I think that is mainly because her wedding is quickly approaching and she's had a lot of shit to take care of. And Ian knows better than to talk about him around me. He's been a witness to some of my verbal attacks on men.

I've seen her and Ian a lot in the past two months, helping them plan the wedding that my best friend basically put into her husband-to-be's hands. He's been amazing, like really amazing, at handling everything except for the goddamned cake selection. *That* he decided to leave up to Juls, and I'm about to hit her upside her pretty little head with my design book if she doesn't pick something out already. The fact that I have her cake to make isn't the only thing stressing me out. Tomorrow night is the rehearsal dinner, and I will be stuck in the same room with the man who broke me eighty-three days ago. I've been reassured that we won't be sitting anywhere near each other, but that doesn't help much. I still have to rehearse the ceremony with him, which means I'll be standing directly across from him up on that stupid altar and my arm will be looped through his when we walk down the aisle. *God, I hate weddings.*

"All right, here's the deal," Juls says after thirty minutes of me tapping my fingers on my worktop at her. "I want a three-tiered, almond lemon cake with lemon filling and a cream cheese frosting. There, that wasn't so hard, now was it?" *Oh, she's gone mad.* She slams the book shut and pushes it toward me, her glowing bride-to-be smile chipping away at my remaining patience. "Now, onto more pressing matters, the bachelorette party. I want to go dancing."

I roll my eyes and laugh as I write down her wedding cake selection. *About damned time too.* "Sounds good to me. As long as the booze is flowing, I'm all in. I plan on staying highly intoxicated for the next two days anyways." I begin pulling the ingredients I need off the shelves to start her cake.

"Well, you better not be drunk at the wedding. You are in charge of making sure everything runs smoothly, and how the hell are you going to do that if your head is stuck in a toilet?"

"Oh, relax, of course I won't be plastered at the wedding. Just tipsy enough to tolerate the situation." I pull out my mixer and set it aside. "Where do you want to go tonight anyway? I'm going to have to meet you there since I have a shit load of baking to do." I glare at her at the end of my sentence and she gives me her goofy grin.

"I was thinking Clancy's since we haven't been there in forever. Oh, shit. Remember the last time you, me, and Joey went there? Didn't he end up hooking up with three different guys in one night?"

"Of course, in true Joey fashion. *That* definitely won't be happening tonight considering he's practically engaged as it is." My face drops at the fact that I'm the only single friend in our circle. I shake my head at myself. *No sulking. You don't need a man. Men are dickheads.*

"Dylan." She reaches over and grabs my hand that's on my mixer, pulling me close to her and gripping both of my shoulders. I brace myself for what's coming. "I know the next two days are going to be hard for you, but you're the strongest woman I know, and have bigger balls than *any* man I know." I let out a weak laugh. "If anyone can get through this, it's you." She pulls me in for a hug and I let her. At least she didn't mention he-who-shall-not-be-named. "He's just as miserable as you are." *Damn it. So close.*

"Juls, don't."

"Well, at least he was. I haven't heard anything for a while. Apparently, he's slammed at work."

"I don't give a shit!" I push away from her and begin ripping open my bags of flour. "He's miserable? Doubt it. I'm sure he's sticking his dick into every whore in the South Side zip code as we speak." My voice breaks at the end and I struggle to hold back my tears, but they've been on reserve lately and are never far away. Her arms wrap around my back and she sighs heavily.

"I'm sorry, sweets. I'm gonna head out, but will see you tonight at Clancy's, right?" I nod and sniff loudly as she plants a quick kiss on my back before she exits the shop.

I take a minute to dry my tears before I start mixing up the ingredients for the almond lemon cake. God, I can't wait to start drinking tonight. If I don't show up hung-over to the rehearsal tomorrow, it will surely be a wedding miracle.

CLANCY'S IS PACKED, BUT I manage to spot Joey, Juls, and Brooke propped up at a round table by the bar. I shimmy my way through the crowd and receive very alcohol induced greetings from all three of them.

"Dylan. Fuck yes! I'm heading to the bar. What do you want?" Brooke asks as she stumbles off her stool. "I'm good, I'm good. Good," she turns and says to whoever is watching her. *Well, drunken Brooke didn't take long to come out and play.*

I try to muffle my laugh. "Whatever you're having sounds good."

"No," Joey and Juls say together quickly.

"Oh. Uh, okay, glass of Pinot then?"

Brooke spins toward the bar as I eye up the other two. "Why don't I want to drink what she's having?"

"Because I'm pretty sure she's drinking straight jet fuel," Joey barks around his beer. "She's completely out of control and *I'm* in charge of babysitting her for some stupid reason." He narrows his eyes at Juls. "I'm letting it slide this one time since you're getting married in two days."

"Love you," she replies as she blows him a kiss. "After you get your drink, Dyl, we're hitting the dance floor." I nod and glance down at her phone, which is lighting up on the table.

"Hey, husband-to-be. Oh, just drinking and dancing. What are you boys doing? If you say strip club I'm finding myself another groom while I'm here." She takes a sip of her drink and smiles around her straw as Brooke returns, miraculously without spilling anything.

"Here you go, Dylan. By the way, the bartender asked for your number." I glance around her as Joey whips his head in the same direction. The big, bald bartender sends a wink my way.

"Uh, no thanks." I take a generous sip of my wine.

"Seriously, like he'd ever stand a chance with you. He's more your type isn't he, Brooke?"

"Fuck you, Joey. You've been on my ass all night. What's your problem? Billy holding out on you?"

"Please. I get laid *way* more than you do. Tell me, has your virginity grown back yet?"

"Jesus Christ, Joey," I bark and try not to crack up laughing at poor Brooke's expense. She isn't the only person at this table not getting laid. He merely shrugs and glances toward the dance floor.

"So, Dylan, isn't tomorrow going to be insanely awkward for you?" I glare directly at her and suddenly wish I wouldn't have just come to her defense. Brooke Wicks and alcohol do *not* mix well. She talks a lot of shit and then ends up passing out or throwing up all over the place. Not a good look for anybody.

I brush my hair off my shoulders. "No, Brooke, I'm not expecting it to be awkward at all. In fact, I can't fucking wait to have a reunion with my ex-fling. It's not like things ended badly between us or anything." My voice is thick with sarcasm, but given her current state, she probably won't pick it up. *How much has she had to drink?*

"Christ, Brooke. Don't be so fucking rude," Joey says as Juls turns her back away from the table and continues her phone call. She's in blissful bride mode and I don't blame her for avoiding this conversation.

"What? I'm just saying, I would feel awkward if I had to play nice with my ex. You should just hook up with someone else in the wedding party."

"Jesus Christ, like that's the answer to all the world's problems. Just hook up with someone in the wedding party. For your information, the only two other men *in* the wedding party are gay or married, and even if they weren't, no. I'm not hooking up with anyone at the rehearsal dinner and definitely *not* at the wedding. That's how this whole fucked up situation got started in the first place." I glance over at Joey who is staring at me, wide-mouthed and stunned. "You remember right, Joey? 'Go ahead, Dylan. You know you want to slip off into some dark corner and do something else in that lap of his.' This is all your fault."

His eyebrows raise and he leans across the table toward me. "*My* fault? How is this my fault? I didn't push you into his lap. I didn't make you run off to the bathroom with him and tell him to fuck you. And I sure as hell didn't put a gun to your head to continue being his casual fuck buddy." His finger darts across the table and points directly at me. "That was all you, cupcake."

Juls spins around and glares at both of us, phone still up to her ear. "Jesus Christ, you two. Keep it down before we get thrown out of here."

I reach over and grab his finger, bending it a bit as he screeches and pulls it away from me. "All me? Are you fucking serious? *You* were the one who said to be his sexy little mistress when we thought he was married. And *you* were the one who kept trying to convince me that it was more than just casual sex. 'Oh, Dylan, the man sends you love letters and he's so romantic.' Remember *that* bullshit?" I point right back at him and he jerks back in his stool. "Don't you *dare* tell me you didn't have a part in this. I had you yapping in my ear all day about how what we were doing meant more to both of us when *clearly*, it only meant more to me." I slam my hand down on the table and grab my drink, downing it quickly. My sparring partner's face softens and he shakes his head.

"Fuck, Dylan. You're right." He throws his hands up in the air dramatically. "You're right. I'm sorry. I really hate fighting with you. You scare the shit out of me." We both burst out laughing and I feel a pair of eyes on me as I turn quickly to Brooke who looks confused.

"You two are fucking weird. And I don't care if the other two groomsmen are gay, married, or pre-female to male transformation; I'm getting laid by someone."

"Bitch, you better stay the hell away from Billy," Joey says sternly. Juls quickly spins around and all arguments come to a halt at the sight of her beaming face. We all regain our composure and she's none the wiser.

"Okay, baby, I love you, too. Have fun." She hangs up her phone and hops off her stool. "All right, bitches, I believe it's time for me to show your sorry asses up on the dance floor." She does a quick spin and her black dress fans out around her knees.

"Ha!" I yell playfully as I get down and run over to her, putting her hand in mine. A clumsy Brooke follows while Joey quickly downs his beer.

"Let's do this!" he yells.

We dance all night into the early morning hours, finally leaving

Clancy's at two a.m. and all piling into the same cab. None of us drove, which was a good thing because we are all rightly smashed and in zero condition to do anything but go to bed. We're giggling like idiots in the backseat of the cab, throwing out our addresses and confusing the hell out of the driver.

"Christ, already. Who am I taking home first? I can't understand four directions at once," the driver yells back as we all fall into a fit of tearful chuckles.

"Brooke, oh, my fucking God. That guy you were dancing with looked like Mr. T." I laugh and she searches her brain for the image. "He even had all the gold chains."

"But he could move. Whew."

"Yeah, he could. I'm pretty sure he had better moves than me, which says a whole fucking lot," Joey adds as Juls wipes the tears under her eyes.

The driver spins around to face us. "Ladies. Oh, and gentleman, sorry. Where the hell am I going?"

"I'm closest. Dylan's Sweet Tooth on Fayette please." I fall back against Joey. "Oh, man, this was so fun. Juls, seriously, thanks for this."

She winks at me as we pull away from the club. "*So* fun. I love you three. AND I'M GETTING MARRIED TOMORROW!" We all laugh and cheer as we drive off down the road, the petty arguments of the night left behind along with Brooke's vomit that came shortly after we started out onto the dance floor. I called it though. The girl should really not be around hard liquor.

I'm dropped off a mere fifteen minutes later and say my quick goodbyes before I stumble inside and lock up behind me. After peeling out of my dress and removing my makeup, I open my dresser drawer and spot the University of Chicago T-shirt that I had stuffed into my duffle bag when I was packing up my stuff the day I ended things with Reese. I should have sent it back to him through Ian when I realized I took it, but a part of me, a part of me that nobody knows about, likes wearing it to bed some nights when I want to smell him. I don't wear it often for fear that my scent will overpower his. But I do decide on wearing it tonight. I slip it on and climb into bed, grabbing my phone and opening up my internet search.

While on the dance floor tonight, the Arctic Monkeys song pumped through the speakers and I let myself dance to it, not wanting to give away how badly it killed me to hear it. And as I moved my body to it, I remembered how I never looked up the lyrics and it's been on my mind the entire evening. So now in the privacy of my dark bedroom, I'm finally looking up the lyrics to the song that reminded him of me.

"Oh, God." I read the lyrics again, and again, letting them sink into me and cursing myself for even looking them up in the first place, and for the stupid club for playing this stupid song. "Fuck." I shut down my phone and roll over, burying my head into the pillow to soften the cries that are coming from me now. *Jesus, that song? Really? It's a song about wanting to be with someone so badly, thinking about them all the time, wanting more with them. Dreaming about them. That song? How could that song remind him of me?* I bury my face into his T-shirt and cry harder, trying to push the lyrics out of my head to give myself some relief. I inhale his scent, the scent that is slowly fading, and I finally calm myself down enough to fall asleep. And sleep I am definitely going to need if I'm going to survive the next forty-eight hours.

Chapter Twenty-Two

I WAKE UP A LITTLE after eleven a.m. on Friday and prepare myself for the day ahead. I decide to go on a run by myself today, only wanting my own thoughts to occupy my head and not Joey's relentless ranting. After my five miles, I lock up shop and head upstairs to shower and get dressed to finish Juls and Ian's wedding cake. The shop is closed and will be until Monday since we've had her wedding to prepare for, and I'm grateful for the quiet. I slip on my apron and whip up the cream cheese icing she requested, admiring the sugared dahlias I've already created to cascade down the cake. I curse myself for thinking of Reese at the sight of them and whip faster. *Damn it. What guy pays attention to details like that? I'd put money on Ian not giving two shits about the flowers that took me hours to create.*

After icing the cake and cleaning up my mess, I glance at the time on the oven. It's three thirty p.m. and I need to be at the church in an hour, and definitely need another shower. I untie my apron and throw it on the worktop before I dart up the stairs. I've picked a black sleeveless dress and pumps to wear tonight, pinning half of my hair up and leaving the rest in loose waves down my back. My makeup looks elegant, but not too done up, and I smile weakly into the mirror as I gaze at my reflection. My dress is hanging off my body more than it used to, and I know it's because I haven't been eating much. Besides my daily taste tests, I'm having to choke down my meals that Joey has been bringing me, or at least parts of my meals. But at least I *am* eating. After one last look, I grab my clutch and head toward the night I've been dreading.

St. Stephen's church was Ian's pick, as was the reception and mostly every other detail for that matter. I park along the side of the beautiful building and straighten my dress out as I make my way to the front steps. Stopping at the bottom and glancing up at the double doors, my nerves hit me in one hard rush and I want to turn right around and get back into the comfort of Sam, but I can't. I close my eyes and grip the handrail. "Come on, Dylan." I pick up my feet and move up the stairs, clearing my throat before I open one of the doors.

The church is beautiful, with dark wood furnishings and stained glass windows allowing the sunlight to shine through in all different colors. Even if you aren't religious, try stepping into a catholic church and not feeling the presence of something way the hell bigger than you. I glance up at the massive cathedral ceiling and admire the painted murals when I hear Juls screeching my name.

"There you are. Now if Brooke would just hurry the hell up, we can get started." She's at my side instantly and looks beautiful. Dressed in a deep plum dress and her hair pulled up sleekly, she's practically glowing. She leans in and hugs me as my eyes glance up toward the bodies at the front of the church. But of course, I don't need to look to know he is here already. I felt him the moment I stepped inside this stupid building. My eyes find his instantly as he stands with Ian and the other men. His lips part slightly and I watch his chest rise with a deep intake of breath. Before I can rake my eyes down his body, I pull back from Juls and break the contact.

"You look beautiful and ready to be married."

"Thanks. You don't look so bad yourself. Come on, my parents have been asking when you'd get here." She grabs my hand and pulls me up front as I keep my eyes fixed on anyone but him. Luckily, we stop a few pews short of the men where all the parents are congregating.

"Dylan, there you are. Wow, you look stunning, dear. How's the bakery business going?" Mrs. Wicks wraps me up in a hug. She was always like a second mother to me.

"It's great and thank you. You look amazing yourself. And how are you doing, Mr. Wicks? Ready to give your oldest daughter away?"

He pulls me into his arms and I'm immediately hit with the smell of cigars. "Fat chance. She'll never get rid of her old man. It's good to see you, Dylan."

"You too." At that moment, the front doors swing open and Brooke comes barreling through, looking like she just woke up and most likely feeling a lot worse. I hear Juls gasp behind me. "Excuse me," I say politely before I begin quickly making my way down the aisle toward a very stupid looking bridesmaid.

"Dylan. Remember that guy last night?" I grab her wrist and pull her behind a pillar as she tries to get out of my grasp. "Jeez. What's the big deal?"

"What the fuck? Are you still drunk?" I ask as Joey comes rushing up to us with Juls on his heels. I notice quickly that all talking has stopped at the front of the church and can feel a million pairs of eyes on us.

"No, I'm not drunk. I'm just hung-over. Ooohhh, which one is Reese?" I grip her harder and she yelps.

"Oh, for Christ's sake. Way to keep it classy, Brooke," Joey whispers harshly as the preacher walks over toward us. We all straighten up a few inches.

"Are we ready to begin, Miss. Wicks?" he asks and she smiles quickly and nods, glancing back at me with her panicky eyes.

"We're ready," I confirm, keeping my hand on Brooke's arm as we all follow the preacher toward the front. I glare over at her and she cowers beside me as we walk up to the front. "Pull your shit together. And if you act like this tomorrow, I will personally make sure you don't get laid. I will vagina block the shit out of you." Her mouth drops open and I hear Joey laugh behind us.

"What? You better stay the hell away from my vagina," she grunts and my grip tightens.

"Ha! I bet you've never uttered *those* words before, Brooke," Joey laughs.

We stop as the preacher turns and faces everyone, and I quickly glance up and over to my right, finding Reese's eyes on me and quickly dropping my stare back down. I let go of Brooke and she sighs in relief, massaging her reddened arm.

"Okay, everyone, we're going to do a quick run through of the ceremony, just to make sure everyone knows their places. So, if I can have the groomsmen, best man, and the groom all standing to my left right here," he motions down at the stairs below him. "And, ladies, and gentleman, if you would line up at the front doors and we'll get started." *Oh, good. I'll only have to walk with Reese at the end of the ceremony down the aisle. That's not too bad. What is it? Twenty-five, thirty feet of contact? I can handle that.* We quickly form a line at the back of the room as I stand in front of Juls, Joey in front of me, and Brooke, hopefully, leading the way. God, help her if she can't make it up to the altar.

"You ready for this?" Joey leans back and whispers.

"Yup. You?"

"Oh, please, have you seen my baby up there? Gorgeous." I giggle at his response and hear the preacher announce for Brooke to start walking, which she does after Joey gives her a right shove. "Asshole. She's going to be such a pain tomorrow," he says before he begins walking and I can't help but smile. My assistant as a bridesmaid. Of course.

"I love you," Juls says behind me and I feel my eyes water a bit.

"Love you," I say as I begin making my walk up the aisle. I don't want to. I really don't want to, but my eyes find his immediately and I finally get my first real look at him in eighty-four days. He's wearing a black suit, perfectly tailored to that body with a green striped tie and white dress shirt. His hair looks like it's been cut a bit, but still has its perfectly tousled look to it, and his eyes are piercing into mine, the green beaming out of them thanks to his tie color choice. I see them quickly drop and run down my dress before he flicks back up to meet mine, jaw set and tense. I take my spot on the same step as him and finally look away toward Juls who is with her father at the back of the church. She begins her walk up and

I keep my eyes on her even though I can feel him looking at me. Studying me.

The preacher runs through the ceremony, going over the vows that Ian and Juls' picked out for tomorrow. I smile and laugh as they recite them and keep turning around to make sure Brooke is still upright and awake. Joey gives me a reassuring wink with each turn and I know he's got her covered. *Thank God.* After the mock exchanging of the rings and pronouncement of their marriage, the two of them begin filing down the aisle and I quickly clamp my eyes shut, knowing what's coming next. *Shit. He's going to touch me. He's going to touch me and I'm going to lose it.*

"Okay, now Dylan and Reese, you may walk down together. Billy and Joey, you can follow when they are about halfway down the rows." I open my eyes and step forward after the preacher finishes and see Reese already waiting for me, elbow out so I can easily slip my hand through it. I swallow loudly and grip the inside of his elbow as we begin walking silently down the aisle. I can hear his breathing, slow and steady as if he's unaffected by this entirely. *Figures. I wasn't sure what I was expecting here. The sight of me causing him to faint possibly?* But no, not even uneven, nervous breathing.

"You look beautiful," he says, low and throaty, and I gasp slightly, but don't respond. We reach the end of the aisle and I quickly drop my hand from his arm and move to stand next to Juls and as far away from him as possible. *Shit. Don't be affected by that, Dylan.* After the rest of the wedding party comes down the aisle, we all say our momentary goodbyes as we file out toward our vehicles. I quickly walk to Sam and scramble in, wanting to avoid any alone time with Reese as I see him walking out with Ian and the other men. His eyes fall on my delivery van fleetingly before he hops in his Range Rover and pulls away from the church. I drop my head on the wheel. "Okay. Half of the night is over. Now, you just need to get through the dinner and you'll only have to worry about tomorrow." After my little pep talk, I start up Sam and make my way toward Casa Mia's.

The rehearsal dinner is booked at a quaint Italian restaurant and a long rectangular table has been set aside for us in the very back.

My place is next to Juls and three seats down from Reese who is sitting next to Ian. I'm immensely grateful that he isn't seated on the opposite side because I've done enough looking for one evening. Joey plops down next to me and let's out an exhaustive sigh.

"Problems with our favorite bridesmaid?" I ask, noticing she hasn't graced us with her presence at the table yet. I pick up my water and take a few sips.

"I'm going to kill her. She insisted on riding with me and then tried to feel me up in the car." Water shoots out of my mouth and covers the, thankfully, empty place setting across from me as I quickly bring a napkin up to my face.

"Jesus, Dylan. Are you all right?" Juls asks as I continue coughing. I glance over at her and see everyone is staring at me, and I mean everyone, as I quickly shake off my choke fest.

I turn quickly toward Joey. "Are you serious?"

"Do I *look* serious? I feel like I've been molested. She almost made me cause an accident on highway eleven."

My coughing turns into giggling as I lean my head onto his shoulder and we both crack up at the situation. "Oh, my God. That's amazing. I so needed to hear that right now." I laugh as he shakes his head at me, picking up his water.

"What's going on?" Juls asks softly as our dinner is brought out to us. I'm suddenly starving and the dish that's in front of me is about to be destroyed.

I eye her up mischievously. "Your lovely sister has been putting the moves on JoJo." Her fork drops.

"What? Oh, great. That's just great." On cue, Brooke appears and quickly claims her seat next to Joey who stiffens next to me. Juls leans across and snaps her fingers at her sister. "You're an asshole."

"Yeah, I'm sorry, Joey. That was a bit embarrassing. Although, was it just me or did something move?" She giggles and orders something alcoholic from the waiter, which Joey quickly cancels for her.

"Did something move? Are you fucking insane? And no booze for you. I can only imagine what would happen if you started drinking."

I shake my head and take a bite of my chicken picatta, moaning around my fork as a familiar face moves toward our table and stands across from me.

"Hey, Dylan. How's it going?" Juls' cousin Tony eyes me up and I quickly smile and wave at him from my seat. We've known each other for years and go way back, but never anything more than friendship.

"Hey, Tony. How are you?"

"I'm great. Get your sweet ass out of that chair and come give me a hug." I laugh and scramble out of my seat, walking down the side of the table that does not contain my ex-fling, and get quickly lifted into the air. "You look good, girl," he says into my hair as he gives me his usual bear hug.

"Thanks. Jesus, put me down already." He sets me on my feet and I shake my head at him, straightening out his tie. "So, what's new in the world of computer programming?" My eyes quickly flick toward Reese who is staring at me with daggers. *Oh, please. Like you have any right anymore.*

"Nailed it. Nice memory. It's good. How about you? Juls told me something about your bakery getting broken into or some shit a few months back? That's fucked up."

"Yeah, well, it's fine now. They caught the psycho who did it and there wasn't any permanent damage." Heather was apprehended by the police a few weeks after the break in. Her prints matched the ones on the brick and she admitted to everything, getting charged with breaking and entering and also getting moved out of the city by her parents. Juls had relayed the information from Ian when he found out about it.

"So, any man in your life or have I finally caught up with you when you're single?" I smile sweetly at Tony, but shake my head. He is definitely not my type and even if he was, I have no interest in dating anybody right now. Especially when the man who broke me is sitting no more than ten feet away from me, continually staring at my profile.

"Oh, please, like you could even handle me," I playfully respond and he nods in agreement. "It's good to see you. I'll catch up with you later, okay?" I turn to go back around the table, but see a major pile up of bodies at the end I want to walk down and grunt as

I have to make my way toward the other end. I walk behind Trent and Billy's chairs, giving them both smiles, as I quickly move past Reese's and feel his hand grip my elbow, halting me at his side.

"What the fuck was that?" he growls up at me.

I snatch my arm out of his hand and scowl back down at him. "What the fuck was what?"

"You know what. Are you seriously going to blatantly flirt in front of me? Is that how this shit is going to play out?" *Is he serious? I am in no mood for any Reese style tirade and this is definitely not the place for it.*

I bend lower to get my face nice and close to his and see him back up a bit. "You think *that* was flirting? I've known Tony for ten years; he's like a brother to me. But if I *did* want to flirt with him, it wouldn't be any of your goddamned business, now would it?" My tone is clipped and I'm fuming, feeling Ian move quickly out of his seat.

"Okay. Wow, that didn't take long. Umm, Dylan, why don't you go over to your seat, and, Reese, just calm the fuck down, man." Ian ushers me past Juls. I quickly pull out my chair and plant myself down in it, glaring over in his direction as Reese narrows his eyes at me.

"Jesus, what the hell was that?" Juls asks as Joey leans in.

"Actually, I'm surprised it didn't happen sooner. I had money on you kicking him in the nuts at the church," he adds. I wave my hands at both of them to back them off me.

"Nothing. He accused me of flirting with Tony. Fucking prick," I say through clenched teeth. I was definitely not flirting with him. I've never seen Tony as anything other than an acquaintance, even though he's asked me out more times than I can count. My eyes glance down the table and I see Ian leaning in and talking to a tense looking Reese. *Ugh. Stupid men.*

"You and Tony? That's fucking hilarious," Juls says and continues cutting up her chicken. "And even if you were, he has no right to act like that."

"I know," I agree loudly and get quickly shushed. "Acting all holier than thou. I'm sure he waited a whole five seconds before he threw another girl into his bed after I left it." I shove a piece of chicken in my mouth and start chewing as Brooke leans across Joey's lap.

"I heard him tell you that you looked beautiful. That was really sweet," she whispers and earns herself the evil eye from all three of us.

"Shut up, Brooke," we all say in unison as we continue eating our meals. I don't look down the table again for the rest of the night and keep my conversations with anyone other than Juls and Joey to a minimum. This evening has been exhausting. I'm emotionally drained and unsure how the hell I'm going to handle tomorrow. I'm reassured that I'll only really have to deal with Reese during the ceremony, and once we're at the reception, I can stay as far away from him as I'd like. But it's the mere fact that we'll once again be at a wedding together, where this whole fucked up situation started that is going to have me in knots. I need to focus on making sure everything runs smoothly for Juls, so that's what I'll do. It's my job as her maid of honor and it will keep my mind off unwanted memories of falling into laps and bathroom sex romps. Speaking of bathrooms, I plan on avoiding the ones tomorrow at all costs.

Chapter Twenty-Three

JULS AND IAN'S BIG DAY has finally arrived and miraculously, everything is running smoothly. I got up early and delivered the cake with Joey to the reception hall before we headed over to the bridal suite where we are all currently getting ready. Juls is glowing, Joey is routinely sneaking out to get a peek at the men who are dressing at the other end of the church, and Brooke is completely sober and has her wits about her. After slipping into my stunning chocolate brown floor length strapless dress, I help Juls into hers, along with her mother.

"Oh, sweetheart. This dress," Mrs. Wicks says, tears filling her freshly painted eyes as I try to hold mine back. My makeup is looking pristine and fabulous and I have no desire to ruin it with unwanted tears. We finish buttoning her up and step back. She's stunning, absolutely gorgeous in her wedding gown and I bite my lip to hold my emotions in.

"Damn, Juls. I have money on Ian losing his mind when he sees you at the end of the aisle," Brooke says as she smoothes out her dress. Joey comes bustling back into the suite and drops his jaw on the floor.

"Holy fuck. You look amazing."

"Joseph! You're in a church," Mrs. Wicks sternly informs him, both hands flying up to her hips. "Easy on the language today please, and that goes for all four of you. Especially you, Dylan." She flicks her daggers at me.

"Me? Please, I'm such a lady." I shrug and catch a wink from Juls in the mirror as the suite door swings open again, this time revealing a very handsome and slightly nervous looking Mr. Wicks.

"Oh my. Darling, you look so beautiful." He moves and stands in front of Juls, grabbing both of her hands in his and pulling her off her stool. "That's it, wedding's off. You're too pretty for that man."

"Daddy," she says through a huge smile and he softens in front of her. I move up to the mirror and take a good look at myself as they exchange a private father-daughter moment, Joey joining me at my side. My hair is pinned up into an elegant twist, a few pieces pulled out and tucked behind my ears, which are adorned with the amber stud earrings Juls gifted us with this morning. My makeup is sophisticated but subtle, a light dusting of rose lip-gloss that I'm somehow managing to pull off without looking like I belong on a street corner, and my dress is perfect, hugging me across my chest and showing a classy amount of cleavage if there ever was such a thing. I feel Joey's hand on my lower back.

"Look at us. We almost look *too* good for this wedding. I'm afraid we might just upstage the bride," he whispers as we both glance over at Juls who is hugging her father.

"Not a chance," I say and he nods in agreement. Mr. Wicks backs away from his daughter and turns toward all of us.

"It's time people. Let's move this along before I lock my daughter in this room and refuse to let Ian have her." We all giggle at his comment, hearing the hint of seriousness in his tone as we file out of the bridal suite and down the back staircase that leads toward a hidden area where we're supposed to line up. I haven't seen the inside of the church since we arrived here hours ago and I'm a bit nervous at the number of people in attendance who will be watching me walk up the aisle. My heels are insanely high, dark brown sling backs that I've scuffed the bottoms of to prevent any major slip up. But I'm still nervous about walking in them. Karma could easily give me a right shove in the back and send me falling flat on my face, given the amount of hate she's shown me lately. *All this animosity. And for what? Because I fell in love with a man who only cared about fucking me? Nice, Karma. Way to stick with your fellow woman.*

We line up in order behind the double mahogany doors and wait patiently for them to open, the soft sound of violins streaming through the air. Another decision on Ian's part. The man apparently loves classical music. I clutch my beautiful bouquet in my hands, grateful to have something to hold on to as the doors slowly open in front of Brooke. My view is blocked entirely by Joey's massive frame, but I feel him. I always feel him. And I know as soon as I start walking, my eyes are going to lock on to his and I'm going to give in to it. *Whatever.* I just have one more day to endure and then I can go back to my shitty life. I turn around and spot Juls who is smiling at me, eyes gleaming and hand tightly looped through her father's arm. I give her a quick wink before I turn slowly and step forward, seeing Joey make his way toward the middle pews. It's now my cue to start walking, but I can't. My eyes have locked on to the most glorious sight I've ever seen and he's standing, waiting for me at the front of the altar in a tux. *Holy fucking shit.*

I know I'm supposed to be moving; I've walked up this aisle before. I just accomplished the feat last night. But I'm stuck. My two feet won't budge an inch and I hear the muffled voices of people around me wondering what the hell is going on. Joey is up at the front, motioning for me to start moving and Brooke is trying desperately not to crack up laughing. Meanwhile, Reese is staring at me, eyes burning into mine and I'm melting on the spot. I've never seen him look this handsome before and I'm suddenly regretting everything. The break up, the fact I agreed to be a part of this wedding, the shirt I kept. Everything. I force out a shaky breath and glance quickly back at Juls who is trying to remain calm but coming apart slowly. Her father is staring at me and looks unsure what to do as I clutch my bouquet tightly and shut my eyes. *Jesus Christ, Dylan. You need to move. Just start walking and you'll be up there before you know it.* I shake my head and open my eyes, and if I was unable to breathe before I closed them, I've completely forgotten how to work my lungs now.

Reese is making his way down the aisle toward me, purpose in each step and eyes glued on mine as everyone watches him and who he's walking toward. My lips part and I shift on my feet as he reaches my side, grabbing my hand and looping it through his arm. And without saying a word, he begins walking me up the aisle, earning a few sounds of amusement from the crowd, and smiling politely at them. I'm deposited on my step and he drops my hand, leaving an emptiness inside me as he returns to his place across from me. Our eyes meet briefly and I smile weakly at him, seeing his lip curl up slightly as the wedding march song begins to play.

The rest of the ceremony plays out the way it's supposed to. Rings and vows are exchanged, and I keep my eyes on the bride and groom who haven't broken contact since Juls hurriedly reached Ian at the front of the altar. I manage to only shed a few tears but quickly wipe them away before my makeup is affected. And as the preacher announces to the congregation Juls' official title as Mrs. Ian Thomas, they kiss and everyone stands and cheers. Ian showers her with affection as they begin their walk toward the back of the church, and I move to stand next to Reese who is already waiting and watching me. Always watching. We follow the bride and groom to the doors, not exchanging any words this time, even though I wanted to at least thank him for what he did earlier. I'm not sure I would have made it up to my place on the altar had he not come and gotten me. I quickly release my hand from his arm when we reach the bride and groom and wrap Juls up into a massive hug.

"You're married," I squeal. Joey and Brooke come scurrying up behind us and wrap their arms around me and Juls.

"I know. And now, we get to go parrttaaayyy." I release her with a giggle and turn around, walking over to Ian and giving him a big hug.

"You hurt her and I'll cut you up into tiny pieces and bury you throughout the city." He lifts me up and spins me around, a muffled laugh escaping his lips. Trent, Billy, and Reese are all watching and I hear laughs coming from them after my declaration.

He sets me down gently. "Oh, don't I know it. I'm well aware of your capabilities, Dylan. Even though you sometimes manage to forget how to walk." He smirks at me and I roll my eyes. I don't linger with him since Reese is at his side, chatting it up with the other groomsmen. And after Ian and Juls walk down the church steps through a cloud of tiny bubbles, we all pile into a stretch limo and head over toward the reception hall.

THE HALL IS BEAUTIFUL, IMMACULATELY decked out in fall colors and everything to Juls' liking. It's also massive and probably close to the size of the Whitmore Mansion, which pulls at my heart strings a bit. But it's somehow classier because if Julianna Thomas is anything, it's classy. I'm doing my best to keep some distance between Reese and myself as we all stand cramped inside a small room, waiting for the guests to make their way into the hall so we can all be introduced together. And that part, I fear is what I've been dreading the most. Reese and I will be publicly announced together as best man and maid of honor in front of everyone, and we'll have to make our way through the crowd and onto the dance floor, all eyes on us. This just might kill me.

"All right, everyone, line up. The DJ is about to make your introductions so pair up with your person and let's get this party started," the chipper older woman who had ushered us into the room says. I mumble a curse under my breath as we make our way toward the double doors, taking my place behind Billy and Joey who are all over each other.

"You two make me want to vomit," I say as Reese steps up beside me, grabbing my attention immediately. His scent is intoxicating, and I almost stumble as it fills the air around me. I shake my head quickly and regroup.

"Don't hate, Dylan. It's not a good look on you," Billy says through a teasing smile.

"And why the fuck can't you be single? Damn it, Trent," Brooke grunts ahead of us and I buckle over in giggles. She's been hitting on poor Trent all night and he hasn't paid her any mind. It's really perfect considering the way she's behaved the past several days. "Ugh. Reese, switch with Trent." She turns back toward us and my body stiffens, but Reese doesn't react at all. Billy and Joey make wide eyes at me.

"Brooke, turn your fucking ass around right now before I cut you," I growl at her and feel Reese's jacket shake against my arm as he tries to muffle his laughs. Billy and Joey crack up in front of me and Trent shakes his head in amusement.

"God, I've missed you." The voice next to me makes me go completely rigid, as do Billy and Joey who turn around quickly. "Oh, um, sorry I didn't… fuck." My eyes meet his briefly, and before I can even think of a reaction to that, the doors swing open and the DJ begins announcing the wedding party. Brooke and Trent, followed by Joey and Billy are sent through as Reese and I move up and he slips my hand through his arm. My breathing is irregular, I'm nervous as hell, and he can sense it. "Dylan, relax. I've got you." I open my mouth to tell him to *stop* getting me when the DJ comes through the speaker system.

"And now please give a warm welcome to our lovely maid of honor, Dylan Sparks, and her handsome escort, the best man, Reese Carroll."

Cheers and whistles fill the room as I'm practically dragged behind Reese. We pass a table of women who hoot and holler at him and he gives them his perfect smile as we walk toward the dance floor. "Jesus Christ," I mutter under my breath at them and feel his soft laugh shake against my body. We stand next to Joey and Billy and watch as Ian and Juls are announced, my hand removed from his arm to allow me to clap along with the crowd of people as they walk joyously into the hall. They stop in the center of the dance floor and begin their first dance as husband and wife. The wedding party moves about, talking amongst themselves, and I glance over and see Reese make his way toward a table where a dark-headed woman is sitting, her eyes beaming at him. She stands and practically hurls herself up into his arms and he wraps her up, planting kisses into her hair. I immediately turn away. *Shit. Are you serious right now? He brought a fucking date?* The sound of the song is blurred out around me as I move toward Joey and yank him away from Billy, pulling him toward the opposite end of the dance floor.

"Jesus, what?" he asks as I finally let go of his jacket. I'm shaking and he eyes up my appearance, his hand coming up to grab my bare shoulder. "What's wrong?"

"He brought a date. A fucking date, Joey. I was *not* expecting that." My chest is rising and falling rapidly and I feel like I might just pass out right here in the middle of this thing. I see his eyes search across the dance floor and spot Reese, who is talking closely with the young and very attractive woman.

"Fuck. That's so not cool. Want me to say something? I can throw his ass out of here. Or hers if you want."

"Oh, please, like you would stand a chance against Reese. But her, maybe." He narrows his eyes at me and makes a face. "Fuck, this is awful. He's all over her. I figured Brooke would be the only bitch I'd be fighting today." The soft song dies down and everyone is told to take their seats so the meal can be served. I make an obscene gesture in the direction of Reese who is none the wiser as I walk up to the bridal party table and take my seat next to Juls.

I'm quiet during the meal, my only words to Juls being I'm so happy for her and she looks radiant. I pick at the food on my plate and keep finding myself glancing over at the table that Reese had been hovering over during the first dance. The woman is young, probably close to my age, and has dark brown curly hair that falls just above her shoulders. She's talking amongst the other guests at her table and having a blast, while my mind is eyeing up my utensils and deciding which weapon of choice I'd like to use on her if I get the chance. But really, is it her fault he asked her here as his date? She probably doesn't know about me, let alone the history we share. She's an innocent bystander who he's dragged into this mess like a complete fucking asshole. I'm gripping my knife tightly in my fist and feel Joey pry it out of my grasp, quickly putting it far away from me.

"Relax, please. I'd really rather not have the cops called at Juls' wedding reception," he says under his breath as I let out a forceful one. The DJ softens the music and talks through the speakers as I try and calm down.

"And now I will ask the wedding party make their way out onto the dance floor for a special number."

"Oh, great. Give me my knife back," I growl at Joey as we all stand up and he shoves it farther down the table. He grabs my waist and directs me down the stairs, the rest of the wedding party meeting us out on the dance floor, and finally letting go of me when he plants me directly in front of Reese. I cross my arms over my chest and refuse to look up and into his eyes. *Bastard.* I hear a small sound of amusement from above me as he steps into me and pries them down, wrapping his hand around my back, while his other holds mine against his chest. A song that guts me begins playing overhead and I flick my eyes up to his and see his soft smile. Of all songs the DJ could have picked for this stupid moment, he picks "Look After You"? *Perfect.*

"What the fuck is this? Did you ask for him to play this song?" I ask angrily as I try to wiggle free. His grip around me tightens.

"So what if I did? It doesn't mean anything to you anyway, so what's the problem?"

"Oh, you're so right, Reese. It means nothing to me. You're a fucking asshole, you know that? I can't believe you brought a date to this thing and had the nerve to accuse me of flirting with Juls' cousin." I glare up at him as he moves me around the dance floor, my anger level rising at the realization that he's also good at slow dancing. Really fucking good at it.

"What date? What the fuck are you talking about?"

I tilt my head in the direction of the pretty brunette who is staring at us, smiling for some weird ass reason. "That date. I saw you with her. Kissing her and talking all close and intimate. Fuck you. I would never do that in front of you."

He shakes his head at me. "*That* is my fucking sister, Dylan. Ian invited her *and* her husband who couldn't make it because he's away on business and I haven't seen her for months. That's why she got such a warm welcoming from me. But it doesn't really fucking matter if it's my sister or not, now does it? You ended things, remember? You fucking *destroyed* me."

I push away from him and take a step back. Staring, shocked at his admission. "I destroyed you? Fuck you. You completely broke me, you stupid shit." I slap him hard across the face because it's what I do and storm off the dance floor, pushing my way through the crowd of people who, I'm sure, have been focused on us since our heated argument started. I'm out the double doors and make my way down the long empty hallway, unsure of where I'm headed when I hear the doors swing open in the distance behind me.

"Dylan!"

I keep moving, picking up my pace but stumble forward once my heel catches on my dress, landing hard on my knees, my hands breaking my fall and hitting the marble floor. Falling back onto my heels, I drop my head into my hands and try to muffle my cries. I don't want him to see me like this, but it's too late. His body drops down and I'm lifted off the floor and onto my feet as he tries to pull me against his chest. I push away and pry his hands off my waist.

"Let go of me. I hate you. I fucking hate what you did to me." I wipe under my eyes and mentally curse myself for the mascara that appears on my fingertips.

His eyes widen. "What did I do? Dylan, goddamn it. What the fuck did I do besides everything you wanted?"

"Everything *I* wanted? How was what we did what I wanted? You're the one who wanted a casual hook up. You're the one who never did anything serious and only wanted it to be about sex. I *never* wanted that."

He steps closer and I back up, but I'm pressed against the wall, unable to put anymore distance between us. "What the fuck are you talking about?" His eyes search my face for an explanation. "*You* were the one who said this was just fun and nothing serious. You labeled it that when we were at The Tavern that night. *You* were the one who refused to let me get close to you, never wanting things to get too intimate between us. That was *all* you, Dylan. I fucking told you that you had all the control." He roughly rakes his hands through his hair and down his face. "This shit was never casual for me. Never. You've owned me since that fucking wedding."

"I fucking heard you with Ian. I came to your office the day I ended things to tell you I loved you, and I fucking heard you. You said you didn't do serious and you were just fucking me because you liked to. How could you say that about me? After everything. After your birthday and," my face falls apart in tears and I push against his chest, "and after you made love to me. How could you say that?"

His hands grip mine, holding them to his chest, his eyes widening and pupils dilating. "*That's* why you ended things? Fuck, love, if you would have just stayed and listened."

I pull my hands away from his. "Don't call me that. And listened to what? I heard everything I needed to hear. I meant nothing to you and you meant *everything* to me."

He shakes his head and grabs me by the waist, pulling me against him so our chests are touching. He sighs heavily. "Christ, Dylan, if you would have just stayed and listened for a few more seconds, you would have heard Ian call me out on my bullshit." His hand comes up and he pushes my hair behind my ears, his thumb lingering on my cheek. "I only said those things because I'd been desperately trying to convince myself that it was only about sex between us, because I knew that was what you wanted. I was certain that was what you wanted and the only way I could have you. But it was never just about sex. Not for me. After Ian called me out, I admitted how crazy I was for you. How you were the only woman who ever got to me and that drove me completely insane, and not just because you like to challenge me. Which you do so *fucking* well."

My breathing becomes labored as I stand pressed against him, unable to move or blink. His eyes are burning into mine and his hands are now softly squeezing my hips. I open my mouth to speak but he silences me with his words.

"I was so in love with you and I couldn't admit it, because admitting it meant dragging you out of your casual fucking comfort zone and into it with me. And I was scared you would pull away. And you pulled away from me anyway without me ever getting the chance to say it."

I'm shaking against him and don't know what to say, or if I can even speak anymore. He's admitted everything I've ever wanted to hear and I can only stare up at him through a tear stained face.

"I called you, every day and sent you messages. Begging, pleading for an answer from you and you ignored me." His hand comes up and strokes my cheek and I lean into it. "Why? Why wouldn't you talk to me? We could have fixed this, but now…"

My eyes widen in panic as he drops his hand and shakes his head. I'm frozen against the wall, unable to move as his body turns and he begins walking back toward the reception hall. *No. He loves me. And I love him. This shit can't end like this. Fuck that.*

"Seriously?" I yell and he halts, his hand on the door and his face down so I can't see his expression. I march over to him and rip his hand off the doorknob, pulling him away from it, and slamming his back against the wall. "You're really going to leave it like that? You said you loved me, do you not anymore?" My rapid breathing fills the air between us as he gazes down at me, clenched jaw and furrowed brow. But he doesn't speak.

I grip his tux jacket with both hands and stare up into his soft eyes. *Fuck this. He's here. I'm here, and I'm saying it.* "I love you. I want you, Reese. Just you, and not at all in the stupid casual bullshit way. I want everything. Sleepovers and sex in beds. All kinds of beds. Yours, mine, whoever's. I want to introduce you to my parents and I want to bake your birthday cake every year while you sit and look at me the way only *you* look at me." I take in a shaky breath while he stands, watching me, studying me. "It fucking *killed me* to pull away from you."

I step in close to him and bury my face into his neck, not knowing or caring if this is appropriate. I need to be here right now, and as his arms slowly wrap around me and pull me close to him, I finally exhale.

He moans softly, his hand stroking my hair as I feel his lips curl up against my forehead. "You know, this shit could have been avoided entirely if you would have just stormed in and slapped the piss out of me after you overheard that bullshit." I pull my head back and see his perfect smile gleaming down at me and I tightly wrap my arms around his back. "I mean really, the one time I would actually *want* you to slap me, you don't. I would have scooped you up right then and told you how much I loved you. Where the hell was my hot-headed girl *that* day?"

I shake my head at the memory. "Broken on the floor. You're right though, that was very uncharacteristic of me."

He plants several kisses to my forehead. "Well, I've been a miserable piece of shit without you. Apparently, unbearable to be around, if you ask Ian. How have you been, love?"

I laugh my first real laugh in months and wipe under my eyes. "Bitchy and more hostile than usual. Poor Joey, he really has taken the brunt of our breakup."

"That sounds about right. Now, you have two options here." I smile big at his words.

"They better both involve your hands and mouth on me or I'm finding myself another groomsman."

He issues me a warning stare and I smirk. "Obviously, I've gone eighty-five days without touching you, and it's taken every ounce of strength in my body to not rip you right out of this dress, which you look absolutely beautiful in by the way." He plants a quick kiss to my lips as I back up and wait for my options.

"Option one, we can go back inside and you can let me dance with you some more, enjoy your company that I have greatly missed over the past grueling months, and, hopefully, witness you getting into it with Brooke again because that shit was fucking hilarious." I laugh at him as he pushes off from the wall and grabs my face between his hands, his thumb slowly tracing my bottom lip. The pull between us is stronger than ever and I'm about to say fuck option one without even hearing my other choice. But I let him give it to me anyway. "Or, we can go off somewhere and I can fuck you until you scream my name in that sexy way that you do, all throaty and raspy." His tongue sweeps across my lips and I pull him in, firmly stroking mine against his. I moan softly into his mouth, tasting and relishing in his flavor. "Christ, I'm so in love with you, Dylan. Insanely in love. Do you have any idea how much I've missed your face?" His finger slowly trails over my lips and along my jaw while he studies me.

I lean in and plant quick kisses on his lips. "Just my face?" My hand runs down the front of him and cups his length. His eyes widen.

"Option two then? Thank fuck, because if you would have picked one I would have taken you in front of everyone on that dance floor and not given a shit about who watched us." He bends down and I'm quickly hauled up onto his shoulder. I'm issued a firm slap on my backside as he takes me down the hallway. I squeal and laugh against him, admiring my own view of his perfect behind. I'm quickly slid down his front as we stand just outside the men's bathroom, his brow arched at me as his hand grips the handle.

"It is rather fitting, picking up where this whole thing began."

He opens the door and peers inside as I jump around on my heels.

"Well, hopefully, this time you won't get all weird on me afterwards. I'm sure you're used to sex with me by now." I'm pulled into the restroom and the door is locked behind me as I'm lifted off my feet, legs firmly wrapping around his waist.

"Oh, I don't know, love, you always surprise me. Fuck, I don't ever want to leave this bathroom. Any issue with not returning to the reception?" His mouth latches onto mine and I'm quickly silenced, my answer not worth a damn anyway when I can be kissed like this. *The man can kiss better than anyone; I'm sure of it.* I'm pressed against the wall, my bare back stinging on the cold tile as his tongue roams freely inside my mouth. He licks along my lips, pulling my tongue into his mouth and softly sucking on it before he releases it and moves down my neck.

"I've missed you," I say as his mouth kisses and sucks on the top of my breasts, his hands gripping my ass and hiking up my dress. "Oh, God, I'm so wet for you."

He growls against my chest as his hand slides up between us, running up my inner thigh and meeting the fabric of my panties. "Shit. I need to taste you before I fuck you. I'm dying here." I'm carried over to a small leather bench that's on the opposite side of the restroom and laid out on it, my dress quickly hiked up to reveal my white lacy panties and matching garter. "Holy fuck," he says as he drops down to his knees and moves between my legs. The bathroom door rattles with someone's knocking. "Go away!" he yells and I laugh at his completely flustered state. He tucks my panties into his pocket with a smirk before he delivers his first lick. "Damn, I've missed this. So sweet." He hums against me, moving his face rapidly between my thighs.

"OH!" I cry out, my hands gripping his hair and holding him between my legs as he devours me like I'm his last meal. His tongue is all over me, his movements ranging from quick flicks to my clit to slow savory laps of my length. I'm not holding in my moans, my voice is echoing throughout the bathroom, but I don't care. I want everyone to hear me. I love this man and his mouth and everything he does with it. He teases my clit and sucks on it slowly, pulling it into his mouth as he slips two fingers inside of me. I arch into him.

"I fucking love this pussy. Tell me it's mine, Dylan."

"It's yours. Oh, God, Reese, I'm so close." His fingers move in and out of me, the pace quickening as my hands tangle in his hair and I pull it hard. My back arches off the leather as he grabs my hips, his tongue rolling in my favorite rhythm. I'm whispering, pleading with him to lick me, harder, deeper, right there and he grabs my orgasm that's his to command and pulls it out of me.

I come and scream his name, over and over until my voice is strained and my throat aches. He takes his time sucking up all of my arousal, lingering on my clit the way I like as I tremble against him. The tight grip he has on my hips is slowly lessened as he plants the softest, gentlest Reese kiss to my pussy. My breathing slows and I cover my eyes with my arm as he stands on his feet.

"Well then, that didn't take long. How have your orgasms been without me?" His smug voice makes me giggle and I gaze up at him, hair sticking out every which way as he licks his lips.

"What orgasms?" I reply and quickly get up and switch spots with him, pushing him onto his back and making quick work of his belt. "I'm going to fuck you so hard; you're not going to be able to walk out of here." He smiles wickedly at me, the lines that I've missed so much appearing on either side of his eyes. "That okay with you?"

His pants are quickly pushed down along with his boxers and I marvel at his erection. *Now, that I definitely missed.* "Fine with me, love." His hands grip my waist as I straddle him, reaching under my dress and positioning himself below me. I lock eyes with him, waiting to lower myself down.

"I love you," I say as his hands pull down my top and reveal my breasts.

"I love you," he replies without hesitation, his eyes flicking up from my chest and holding my stare. I quickly crash down, pulling a throaty grunt out of his throat.

"Fuck. Dylan."

Oh, God. This. I forgot how perfect he feels in me. The way my body forms around him, molds to him like he's made for me. Just me. I can't move yet. I'm too caught up in the way he feels just like this and the look he's giving me. Green eyes burning into mine with that intensity, his intensity that I've missed so much. He's looking at me the way only he looks at me, the way I only ever want to be looked at by the man I've chosen. I chose him.

I pull my lip into my mouth as I rock against him, sliding up and down his length. His hips move beneath me as his hands firmly cup my breasts. He moans, grunts, and growls as I move, and I know he's not holding anything back. He's letting everyone know what I'm doing to him as my hands grip his jacket. I can't stop staring at him. The way his head falls back when I slide out of him and the way his neck rolls when I take him in. His tense jaw and slightly swollen lips with my favorite slit running down the middle. The way his body looks in his tux, broad, built, and fucking powerful. *Christ, has anyone ever looked this good in a tux before? Doubt it. Seriously, it's ridiculous.* Our sounds fill the room and it's the hottest thing I've ever heard. I'm soaked, completely drenched from his expert mouth and the sheer sight of him. I feel him tense under me as I slide him all the way out before I slowly move back down. I know he loves that, the feel of entering me over and over again. Arching into him and throwing my head back, I grip his thighs and begin to move fast, then faster.

"Just like that, love. Christ, I'm not going to last long. You're so fucking good." He sits up and wraps his arms around my back, pulling my chest to his face and latching onto my left nipple.

"Reese."

He sucks it hard, flicking it with his tongue before releasing it and moving beside it to where his mark has completely faded off me. His mouth sucks the tender skin there and I moan against him, my hands grabbing his head and pulling him closer to me. "I hate how they faded. I cried for days when I couldn't see them anymore." He moves to my other breast and gives my other nipple equal attention before freshening up the mark next to that one as I rock slowly. Strong hands grip my back and move down to my hips, moving me at the speed he wants and needs. Our eyes are locked and I let him control me because I've missed it and he needs it. My orgasm isn't far, the familiar pull building between my legs and slowly spreading out in every direction.

"Yours didn't fade on me. It's still there," he says as I drop my forehead to his, our breath warming each other's faces. *My mark on him? What mark? The writing?* His bottom lip gets pulled into his mouth and I know he's close.

"How could it not fade? Have you gone without showering for three months?" He slows down my movements, letting me glide along his length and linger where I want. I shudder against him at the speed change, feeling him rub me the way only he does.

"Do I smell like I haven't showered in three months?" His hands come between us and he begins unbuttoning his tux jacket, pulling it off while I balance myself on my knees. I'm anxious, giddy as hell to see his naked body and watch in amazement as he quickly makes work of his dress shirt.

"No, you smell amazing like you always do." I lean forward, drop my head into his neck and feel him laugh. I inhale deeply as his shirt is removed, and my eyes go to his right arm where my handwriting is visible in dark blue ink.

"What the… you got it tattooed?" My fingers run over the words that clearly won't rub off as he studies me. Always watching me. "Holy shit. That's so hot." I lean in and trail kisses over the words, my words that I wrote on him, as he lovingly strokes my arm. "Oh, my God. I love that you did that." My mouth makes its way up his shoulder to the curve of his neck. Grabbing his face with both hands, I kiss and lick up to his face and latch onto his mouth, pulling his bottom lip and sucking on it. He groans loudly as I slowly release it.

"I took a shower the day you," he shakes his head at the memory, "and it was starting to wash away even though I tried to avoid any soap getting on it. I was so fucking pissed that it was fading, like it was pulling away from me too. Christ, I was mad. I went out the next day and got it made permanent." *He tattooed himself with a reminder of me.* "I love that it's in your handwriting and that you put it there, just for you." His eyes study mine as I blink rapidly, sending tears down my face. He quickly reaches up and wipes them away, and I bend forward and kiss him sweetly.

"Just for me," I echo and push him back down on his back and start moving again. His hands grip my hips and pull me up and down, quickening my pace as I roam over his bare chest. Trailing over every inch of exposed skin, my hands become reacquainted with the feel of him, his muscles, and his softness, just him. I run down his shoulders, his arms, his chest, and linger on his stomach, which clenches as I ride him. His gaze is locked on my breasts, driving me to bring my hands up and touch myself. Molding them, I watch his eyes widen as I play with and pinch my nipples.

"Fuck, yes. That's so sexy, love." His hips come up to meet me and I drop my eyes down, locking onto his. Harder and faster, I feel him moving through me and pulling my orgasm to the surface as his thumbs press into my hipbones. I tell him to press harder, to bruise me because I want his marks on me, all over me. My hands drop to his chest and I pant against him, feeling him pulse against my walls. "Come for me, Dylan." I obey, quickly coming apart on top of him and rocking my hips to pull out his orgasm.

I droop forward and sprawl out onto his bare chest, feeling his arms wrap around me as we gasp against each other. "I love slutty wedding sex with you," I force out through my ragged breath, feeling his body shake slightly.

"Same here. We should really make a habit of this."

We let ourselves stay like that for several minutes, holding each other and coming down slowly before Reese sets me to the side and grabs some toilet paper to clean me up with. After resituating ourselves in the mirror and making out against the door for several, totally worth it, minutes, he reaches up and unlocks it, allowing for a mad rush of young boys to come into the bathroom.

"Uh oh," one says through a crooked grin as Reese quickly brushes past him, my hand in his with his fingers laced through mine the way I love. *Total boyfriend move.* We stop at the door leading to the reception and he turns toward me, bringing my hand up to his lips for a quick kiss.

"You ready for this, Sparks? You're officially mine now and I plan on being very intimate with you, and often. Lots of sex in beds and sleepovers." He smiles behind my hand quickly before his face turns serious. "But just so you know, when I say you're mine, I fucking mean it. I will personally remove anyone and anything that stands in my way of you. Including your panties."

My grin bursts through my face and he laughs with me as I

place my hand on the doorknob with him. "Please, Carroll, bring on the intimacy because I'm not taking you any other way. And just so *you* know," my eyes narrow in on his and I spy his wicked grin behind my hand, "*you* are *mine* and I will dismember any chick who looks at you twice. And I fucking mean it."

We walk hand in hand through the crowd of people and spot the wedding party on the dance floor who all begin to cheer and whistle at the sight of us. Juls and Joey move quickly and pull us into the group.

"Fuck, yes. Who had the reception?" Joey asks and Billy and Ian both raise their hands. Juls, Brooke, and Trent all start clapping as Reese pulls me against his chest and kisses my hair.

"Damn it, Dylan. I really thought you two would fix your shit at the rehearsal. You just lost me a hundred bucks," Juls scoffs as Joey shakes his head at her. Reese grins widely at the lot of them and Ian moves in and slaps him firmly on the back, issuing me a quick wink.

"I was way off. I pegged your rekindled romance to happen tomorrow after you two went home and sulked over one another all night. Oh, well, at least my baby won." Joey beams, giving me a quick kiss on the cheek and rolling his eyes at Reese.

"Thank fuck, Dylan. This man has been so miserable. I've barely been able to stand him around the office. He's fired three receptionists in less than three months. No one wants to work for him."

Reese glares at Ian and I gasp. "Three? Why? What happened to that one guy? I liked him."

"He annoyed the hell out of me, so fucking cheery all the time. Then the one girl didn't know how to work the phones properly and lasted about twenty minutes before I made her cry. And the last one used your shampoo. Shit drove me crazy." Ian bursts out laughing and walks away from us as I fling my arms around my boyfriend's neck. *Yup, that's right. My boyfriend.*

"Awww. I'm sorry, handsome. I do hope you'll lighten up on your staff now that you have me back. I plan on making frequent visits to your office and would hate to see you giving your poor receptionists a hard time." I kiss his lips quickly as he smiles against me, his arms wrapping tightly around my waist.

"Frequent office visits? Mmmm, I can't wait, love. Any chance we can substitute frequent for daily?" He spins me around as a song begins to play and we pick up where we left off with our slow dance.

"Could you even handle me on a daily basis? I would insist on multiple orgasms and get rather hostile when I don't get my way," I whisper against his mouth, relishing in the combination of his minty flavor and me.

"Hostile with a dirty mouth?"

I arch my brow at him and nod slowly, his grin spreading across his face.

"Fuck, yes. I love that girl."

His hand firmly grips my ass and pulls me against him as we move slowly between the other couples. Our eyes are locked, bodies pressed together, and my head is tucked in my favorite spot in his neck. This is where I want to be, with the person I want to be with, and now that I have him, there's not a chance in hell I'm letting him go. And I'd love to see anyone try and stop me. Seriously, I know exactly where Joey hid my butter knife.

Epilogue

"CUPCAKE, YOU HAVE A SPECIAL delivery," Joey sings, emerging in the doorway with the familiar white box.

I wipe the flour off my hands and set my measuring cup on the worktop. "Do I need to sign for it?" I try and look past Joey to spot Fred in the main shop, but Joey's massive frame blocks my view.

"Nope. I signed for it. Here you go." He places it on the worktop and steps back.

Sliding it across the wood, I pull the white ribbon and lift the edges, opening the top of the box. *Hmm.* I'm rewarded with the same white box, only a bit smaller, with the same white ribbon. "That's strange." I pull the ribbon and lift the top, only to reveal yet another white box. I chuckle and shake my head. *My boyfriend is crazy.* Going through the motions once more, I lift the top of the significantly smaller box, and gasp loudly. Sitting in the middle of the smaller box is a brown card, but that's not what makes my heart flutter. What's making my pulse race faster than it ever has is the tiny black box that's peeking out from underneath it. "Oh, my God. Joey, look." I turn and if I wasn't already hyperventilating, I'm definitely losing my shit now. Standing next to my sobbing assistant is

Reese, decked out in a dark gray suit, and making it look better than any man every could. "Hi," I manage to choke out, but it's barely audible.

"Hi, love. Read your note."

I force my fingers to move and pick up the brown card, opening it slowly.

Dylan,

One hundred and thirty-two days. That's how long I've loved you. That's how long I've wanted to protect you, take care of you, and cherish you. I've known for one hundred and thirty-two days that you are it for me, that you are my forever. You've completely captivated me. My heart, my soul, my entire being. I can't imagine my life without you in it, and as long as I have you, I don't need anything else. Just you and me. Forever.

I love every single part of you, and I always will.

X, Reese

"Oh, my God," I cry, my tears dropping down on the card. I glance to my right and have to drop my gaze. Because my gloriously handsome boyfriend is now on his knee, holding the little black box that he delivered to me himself. Joey wails behind him, naturally, and I reach up and wipe underneath my eyes. "What are you doing?" I'm not sure anyone will make out my words through my shaky, sob filled voice, but I say them anyway.

"I'm doing what I've wanted to do since you fell into my lap." He smiles that killer smile, the one that melts me every time I see it, and opens the box. My jaw hits the floor. I've never seen a more beautiful ring, and he chose it just for me. "Dylan, I never knew I wanted this, until I met you. All of the love I have in me has been yours and it always will be." My hands cover my nose and mouth as I stare down at him, the tears rapidly falling onto my fingers. "You've given me everything, love. Will you marry me?"

I drop down to my knees and throw my arms around him. "Yes. Yes. Yes." He wraps me up, pinning me to his body and buries his face into my neck. "Yes." I look up, seeing Joey, holding his phone out in front of him, and crying like a baby above us.

"Mmm, I can't wait to make you Mrs. Carroll," Reese says against the sensitive skin of my neck. "Here, let me put this on you." I lean back and drop back to my heels, holding my trembling left hand in front of me. He takes the ring out and slides it on my finger, pressing his lips to the top of my hand. "Do you like it?"

"Are you fucking kidding me?" Joey squeals behind him. "She loves it. I love it. Goddamn it, Billy."

Reese and I both laugh as I stare down at my hand. "I do love it. It's perfect, just like you." I hold his face in my hands, bringing our lips together. And I don't let go.

Acknowledgements

THANK YOU TO FAMILY FOR being so incredibly supportive. To my mom for reading my dirty little thoughts and not slapping me across the face. And to Jess for not looking at me differently after you read some of my smut. I know it was hard. :)

To my favorite little X-Ray bestie, Farin. I think you were just as excited about Reese and Dylan's story as I was. Thank you for carrying the pages of my book around and reading it at red lights. Your encouragement got me here.

To R.J. Lewis for being too badass for words. I'm so grateful for you and your countless emails. You've been the biggest inspiration to me, and my filthy soul found its match in yours.

Last and certainly not least, thank you to everyone who read Sweet Addiction. I hope I made you chuckle and gave you other tingly feelings. (You know what I'm getting at.) I loved writing this story and I sincerely hope you enjoyed it.

If you have a second, please leave me a review on amazon.com or goodreads.com. I'd LOVE to hear from you, so feel free to follow me on Facebook.

Thank you again,

J

J. DANIELS

To my readers, for all the love you have shown me. This is for you.

WHY DO PEOPLE EVEN BOTHER with weddings?

I know, that sounds insane coming from a person who makes a living off creating decadent wedding cakes for the happy couples. The crazy-in-love future Mr. and Mrs. are what keeps Dylan's Sweet Tooth afloat, and without weddings, I wouldn't be able to afford my rent. Not to mention the fact that if it weren't for dumbass ex-boyfriend weddings, there's a chance I would've never have met Reese and I honestly can't imagine not having him in my life. But in my defense, I've never had to sit and listen to hours of debating whether cotton-blend or silk napkins are the best choice for my big day.

Until now.

Joey lets out an irritated sigh and gestures toward the direction of my mother and soon-to-be mother-in-law who are loudly arguing at my consultation table. "This shit makes me want to drink at 9:00 a.m. How many times have I suggested to you that we keep hard liquor in the back? We could totally make a drinking game out of this mess."

I tilt my head up to meet his eyes. "What, and take a shot every time one of them utters the phrase, 'this will be the wedding I've always dreamed of'? We'd be tanked before the lunch rush."

He nods, smiling over his coffee cup. "Exactly, and we'd be completely oblivious to this annoying discussion that you couldn't care less about anyway."

Joey's right. I really didn't care what type of fabric the napkins were; I really didn't care about much of anything. I've pretty much left everything in the hands of my trusted best friend who could plan a wedding wearing a blindfold. I only had a few stipulations: the cake and my dress. That's it. Napkins? Who the fuck cares about napkins?

He slides closer to me, dropping his voice to a hushed whisper although, with the noise level currently booming through the bakery, I'll definitely be the only one hearing him. "I knew your mother was a little nutty when it came to marrying you off, planning this shit since you were nineteen and all, but Reese's mother is bat-shit crazy. Did you hear her say she wanted to come out with us for your bachelorette party? Can you imagine?"

I shrug once before leaning against the counter. "I don't even know what I want to do for that. Maybe we'll just have like a spa day or something and if that's the case, who cares if she tags along?"

His mouth drops open, letting escape a loud, dramatic gasp. "Um, no. We will be going to a strip club if I have to throw you over my shoulder and pull a Reese on you myself. That's what you do for bachelorette parties. Why the hell do my two best friends not know that?"

"Excuse you. Juls' bachelorette party didn't involve any naked men, and we still had a great time. Who says we have to go to a strip club?"

"I do," he says through a tense jaw. "The only reason I let that shit slide for Juls was because I was in charge of babysitting her dumbass sister, and I knew I'd be distracted if I had a bunch of dicks in my face."

I arch my brow at him. "Isn't that a typical Saturday night for you?" We both chuckle together, and my attention is suddenly drawn to my mother who is throwing napkins into the air.

"Dylan, sweetheart, silk or cotton-blend?" she asks, tapping her foot on the hard tile.

I flick my gaze between the two mothers who are both silently pleading with me to pick their choice. If I had to guess, I'd say my mother wants the silk, but Maggie Carroll is giving off a bit of a fancy vibe right now. She's head to toe in designer clothing, which is screaming silk at the moment. *Shit. I really don't care one way or the other, but who the hell do I side with on this one?* I grimace and nervously tap on the glass display case. "Um, does it matter? They're napkins. People are going to be wiping their mouths with them."

"It matters a great deal," Maggie says, picking up two napkin swatches and carrying them over to me. "The silk is much more sophisticated. And given the location you've chosen for the reception, I think that's the one you should go for."

"But the cotton blend comes in this antique-white color that would go beautifully with the pale-gray bridesmaids dresses," my mother adds, joining Maggie's side.

Jesus. Since when does it matter if the napkins match the bridesmaid dresses?

I look back and forth between the two of them before turning toward Joey. "Thoughts?"

"Nope. I'm afraid you're on your own there, cupcake." He backs away and sips his coffee, leaving me alone in my misery.

I reach out and feel both choices between my fingers. "Um, well, I guess the cotton is most likely cheaper? So, why don't we go with that?"

Maggie gently lays her hand on top of mine. "Oh, sweetie, money is not an issue. If you want the silk napkins…"

"She just said she wants the cotton blend," my mother states with a firm tone. "Which I agree with, sweetheart. Beautiful choice."

"But, Helen, the silk would be so much more… elegant."

I drop my forehead to my hands and groan my irritation while the two of them continue to hash it out. *Who cares about napkins!* Am I completely crazy for not giving a shit about this tiny, insignificant detail? The guests could wipe their mouths on their coat sleeves for all I care.

This is how it's been for the past six months. Ever since Reese and I got engaged, our mothers have been in a battle of who can plan the better wedding, and poor Juls and I have been stuck in the middle, trying to rein in the madness. They've been so crazy about this whole thing, I've found myself contemplating the benefits of a Vegas wedding. Unfortunately, my soon-to-be husband is dead-set on marrying me in front of all our families and is having no part of that discussion. Every time I suggest he steal me away for a quickie wedding, he just shuts me up with his mouth, or his cock. And because I'm weak with lust around that man, and given the fact my head is sure to explode soon from all this momma drama, I bring it up. Often.

The front door chimes and I look up, smiling as my best friend strolls into the bakery. She takes one look at the mothers waving napkin swatches into the air and immediately goes into wedding-planner mode.

"Ohhhh, no. There will not be any changes made. Give me those." She snatches the napkin samples from the two mothers who both stare at her with shocked expressions. This is the Juls I know and love, the one who knows how to run shit. "This wedding is happening in ten days, and all decisions are final. And really, the napkin issue? Again?" She motions toward me with a crumpled-up napkin in her hand. "The bride-to-be doesn't care about the napkins. In fact, you two are the only people I know who have *ever* cared about the napkins. And I've planned over one hundred weddings. For the love of God, let it go."

My mother crosses her arms over her chest and sneers at Juls. "You know what, Julianna? One of these days, when you're planning *your* daughter's wedding, you'll care about the napkins."

"I seriously doubt that. Besides, I'm planning on having all boys."

Maggie and my mother grab their purses off the consultation table while Juls smiles in her minor victory over the two of them. The moms both walk around the counter and smother me with affection.

"We're going to go swing by the venue to take another look around," Maggie says as she releases me from a hug. "Now, don't forget to let me know about the bachelorette party. I'm all in."

"Ha!" Joey yells from the kitchen.

I smile and clear my throat loudly, hoping to cover up the end of my dear assistant's crack-up. "Tell Mr. Carroll I said hello."

My mother kisses my cheek and smiles. "I'm sure the napkins you originally picked out will suffice."

"Mom," I say in a warning tone. "There's still a chance I'll convince Reese to cancel this whole thing and get hitched in Vegas." Her eyes widen, along with Maggie's who swivels in place to gawk at me. "Don't push it."

"That's not even funny," she retorts, swatting at me with her clutch.

Once the two wedding-obsessed mothers exit the shop, Juls lets out an 'I'm glad I'm not in your shoes' chuckle and Joey reemerges from the back. I slouch back against the counter top, feeling a Vegas wedding now more than ever. "I cannot wait until all this is over with. How I've managed to survive the last six months without being heavily-medicated or drunk off my ass twenty-four hours a day is beyond me."

"Reese's mother, though she has impeccable fashion sense, is out of her mind. I am not having a fucking chaperone at your bachelorette party," Joey states with a shake of his head. Apparently, keeping my future mother in-law away from whatever I decide to do for my last night of freedom is his only concern.

Juls tosses the napkin swatches into the trashcan, which will hopefully be the last time I ever lay eyes on them. She returns to her spot on the other side of the display case. "Speaking of which, what are we doing for that, anyway? You wanna go to Clancy's like we did for mine? That was fun."

Joey slams his hand down on the counter, gaining our attention immediately. "For fuck's sake. What the hell is wrong with you two? Spa days? Clubs that have been played out? I wanna do things that I'll be ashamed to tell people about. Let me live, damn it."

"I'm sorry, but is this *your* bachelorette party? Did Billy pop the question and you've decided to keep that information from us?" Juls asks, biting back her smile. It cracks through and she winks at Joey whose mood has suddenly waned, no doubt in response to the reminder that he isn't engaged yet.

He shrugs dismissively. "Whatever. You bitches can celebrate with watered-down drinks and facials. Just don't be surprised if I bail on it."

I slide closer to him and wrap my arms around his waist, pressing my face into his shirt. Tilting my head up, I see him smiling down at me. "I'll choose something fun. You have to be there; it wouldn't be the same without you."

"She's right." Juls rounds the counter and mimics my position against Joey's back. "We'd miss you terribly, JoJo."

He grunts above us. "You're lucky I'd do anything for either one of you." Juls and I both unlock our death grips from him and stand side by side. "But I swear to Christ, there better at least be a cake shaped like a penis at this thing."

"Chocolate or vanilla?" I ask teasingly.

He smiles, bending down and removing a half-empty tray of pastries from the display case. "Chocolate. I've never had black dick."

Juls and I both chuckle as he walks toward the kitchen, giving us a scandalous eyebrow raise over his shoulder.

"So, I have a favor to ask you." Juls pulls me into the far corner behind the bakery counter, clearly wanting to put distance between this favor and Joey. *Oh, Lord.* My best friend doesn't ask me for many favors but when she does, they're usually whoppers. A certain wedding dress she made me try on months ago comes to mind. I motion for her to spill it, and she eyes me up nervously. "Umm… so, Brooke got fired from her job at that bank. Apparently, she was caught blowing one of the other tellers during work hours."

"Good Lord." That sounds about right, though. Brooke Wicks was in the running for horniest bitch in Chicago, competing solely with Joey.

"Yeah, she *needs* a job and fast; otherwise, she'll lose her apartment." My eyes widen, the realization of her favor hitting me. "And since you're so busy at the shop…"

"No fucking way."

She fists both hands at her side. "Oh, come on, Dyl. She's having trouble finding something, and she's been looking for over a month." Her face softens and she reaches out to me, pulling my hand into hers. "Please? If she loses her apartment, she has to move in with Ian and me. And that shit can't happen. I love my sister, but I can't live with her."

"What about moving back in with your parents?"

"Not an option. She and my mom would kill each other." She pauses and squeezes my hand gently. "I really want to help her out."

Damn it. This has bad news written all over it, but I have trouble saying no to Juls. She's always been there for me. Always. I groan and her eyes light up. "Fine. She can start Monday. But don't think I won't fire her just because she's your sister." She pulls me into a hug with an excited squeal. I cringe as Joey strolls through the doorway, coming from the kitchen. He grins, adorably oblivious to the information that will surely send him into a shit-fit. "I should really make you drop this bomb on him," I mumble under my breath.

"Oh, relax. It's not that big of a deal."

"Yeah, okay. We'll see about that."

We both release each other and Juls spins on her heels, walking over toward Joey and placing her hand on his shoulder. "Don't freak out."

His eyes widen with a curious fear. "If I don't get my penis cake, I'll disown both of you. Nobody comes between me and my dick-shaped sweets."

I walk up to him and brace myself for the reaction that is sure to blow the roof off this building. "Joey. JoJo. Bestest friend." He rolls his eyes as I play with the string on my apron, wrapping it around my finger. "You know how busy we've been lately with custom orders and all the spring weddings coming up? It's getting pretty crazy in here, and I think maybe it's time I hired another employee."

"That's fantastic." His body relaxes and he glances between Juls and myself. His brows set into a hard line. "Why the hell do I have a feeling I'm about to regret those words?"

"Just remember how much you love us," Juls says. "And this… addition will allow you and Dylan to spend more time together. The benefits are sure to outweigh any concern you might have."

I pause, waiting to see if he'll pick up on the clues that are obvious to me. It only takes him a few seconds; the reaction spreads through him like a wild fire.

He squeezes his eyes closed tightly, reaching up and rubbing his temples with his fingers. "Please tell me this addition is a blind monkey, because they would surely get more accomplished than who I fear you're about to say."

"Brooke could be a good addition, Joey," I state with a mild assurance.

"Are you insane? Why the fuck would you hire that mess?"

Juls shoves his arm. "Hey! She's my sister, and she's been through a lot."

"A lot of what? Dick? Dylan, this is not a good idea."

I limply shrug. I'm not at all surprised he's reacting this way; in fact, I predicted it. But, unlike Joey, I'm willing to give Brooke the benefit of the doubt. And as long as she doesn't try to molest him like the day before Juls' wedding, things shouldn't get too hostile. I gotta give the girl a chance. "She needs a job or she'll lose her apartment."

He throws his hands into the air. "Oh, I'm sorry. How is that *our* problem?"

"Joey," Juls scolds. "Don't be so rude."

"She's on a probationary period. If she messes up, I'll fire her without thinking twice about it. Right, Juls?"

She nods in my direction before turning back toward my heated assistant. "Right. So, calm the fuck down, JoJo." She makes a face at him and he issues her his smile, softening her expression. "And a lot of dick? Like you're one to talk."

The three of us start laughing, letting go of the stress of knowing Brooke Wicks will soon be gracing us with her presence. This could actually be a good thing. We are extremely busy, and having another employee means being able to spend more time in my kitchen instead of ringing up customers. So, I'm not going to let this worry me; I have enough stress with my upcoming wedding to last me a lifetime.

Juls gives us both hugs before she exits the shop to go tackle a bride. Just as a customer slips inside and makes her way up to the counter, my phone beeps in my pocket. Joey gives me a smile, indicating he's got things handled and allows me to slip into the back.

Reese: What are you wearing?

I giggle as I hop onto a stool.

Me: Are you spanking it right now, handsome?

Reese: That depends on your answer.

I'm definitely not wearing anything worthy of a wank session. My ripped skinny jeans and flour-covered apron have seen better days, so I let my imagination take over.

Me: A skin-tight, pale-pink dress that stops just below my panty line. Or, it would, if I was wearing panties.

Reese: You are such a tease. Do you have any idea how hard my dick is for you right now? I could probably fuck you through a wall.

Jesus.

Me: It's a shame you'll have to handle that situation on your own. I'm locked in consultations the rest of the day. Otherwise, I'd give you a hand. Or a mouth.

Reese: You can handle my situation as soon as you get home. I want that pussy wet and ready for me.

I smile, loving that dominant edge in every word he types.

Me: Always is.

No imagination needed there.

AFTER LISTENING TO JOEY RANT about all the possible ways Brooke could screw my business over, six o'clock finally came and I was able to wave goodbye to him and his negativity. Reese and I split our time between my place and his, usually only staying at mine if I have to wake up early to get started on some baking. Reese has affirmed his desire to move me into his condo permanently after the wedding, but I've been dragging my feet on preparing for that. I like having my loft above the bakery. It was the first place I ever owned all by myself, containing many Joey and Juls memories I don't want to let go of. But I understand his reasoning; it wouldn't make sense to make payments on both places. So, even though it saddens me, I'll be saying goodbye to my loft in ten days.

I park Sam, my delivery van, in my usual spot next to Reese's vehicle in his parking garage. The contrast between my cupcake-covered van and his pristine Range Rover still makes me giggle, especially when Reese expresses his concern over my choice of transportation. But I let all that Sam-hate roll off my back; he's reliable and very hip, in my opinion.

I step off the elevators onto the tenth floor and stop at Reese's door, fumbling with my keys. Once I'm inside, I lock the door behind me and toss my purse and keys onto the table. I glance around at the immaculate space, noting my fiancé has been very busy cleaning today. Everything is in order and the entire place smells like something Italian. I'm starving, but not just for food, and the meal waiting for me on the stovetop will have to wait.

"Reese?"

I walk down the hallway, stopping at the bathroom door when I hear the shower running. Swinging the door open, I'm hit in the face with a cloud of citrus and have to grip the doorframe to steady myself. *Good Lord, he's delicious. His smell alone riles me up like nothing else.* The curtain is pulled back and our eyes lock, his mouth curling up in the corner as he breaks our contact and slowly rakes over my body. His lip twitches into a smile.

"Liar. I was expecting a dress with no panties."

I lean against the doorframe, admiring my amazing view of the gorgeous man in front of me. "If I said I was wearing this—" I sweep my hand in front of my body, "—would you have appreciated it as much?"

"I appreciate you in everything you wear." His tone is low and thick, and it still has the same effect on me as the first time I heard him speak. Like he could command me to do anything. It's not just his body that leaves me pooling at his feet. That voice of his is my undoing. He shoots me a smile, opening the curtain farther. "Get your sweet ass in here."

I strip hastily, swiftly stepping into the shower with him. Inhaling deeply, I wrap my arms around his neck and relish in the glorious sight and smell of him. His arms scoop me up and pull me against him, his forehead dropping to mine. I close my eyes and let the water cascade off his body, running down my front that is pressed to his. His warm, minty breath heats my face as his hands lightly stroke my back, slowly trailing lower and lower. I open my eyes and meet his, the greenest eyes I've ever seen burning into mine with that same intensity. His intensity.

"You know, it's literally impossible to not want to fuck you every time I see you naked. Or clothed, for that matter." He cocks an eyebrow at me, and I run my tongue along my bottom lip. "You have me perpetually wound-up here."

"I know the feeling." I tilt my head up and press my lips to his jaw, slowly trailing kisses down his neck and onto his chest. He moans softly, his body vibrating the tiniest bit against my mouth as I work my way lower. His stomach tenses, the way it always does as my lips brush against his taut skin. I'm almost to my destination when his hands grip under my arms tightly, lifting me up and pressing my back firmly against the cold tiles.

"Oh! Hey, I wasn't finished." My legs wrap around his waist, his hands firmly gripping my hips the way I like. His chest heaves rapidly, pushing up against mine with his quick, forceful breaths. I feel him there, right there, and the anticipation is killing me. "Come on, do it," my raspy voice taunts him, daring him to give me what I know we both want.

"Do what, love?" His lips meet mine and his kisses are gentle, the sweet kisses he gives me when he wants to take his time. I fucking love this kind of Reese-kissing and he knows it, but in all honesty, I'll take his mouth any way I can get it. I open for him, allowing his tongue to stroke softly against mine. He delivers the perfect amount of pressure and I moan into him, firmly tangling my hands in his wild mess of hair. He moves down, tilting my head up for access. "I love you," he whispers against my neck.

Those words send me into hyper drive like they always do, ever since he first said them to me the day of Juls' wedding; a day I started off dreading and now am immensely grateful for. I'm panting, clawing down his back and I know what he needs to hear to get him where I want him. "Please, I need you. Please, Reese." I beg him because he likes it and because it's true. I do need him; I'll always need him. How I ever managed to convince myself otherwise is beyond me. I was a complete fool for ever denying my feelings for him. He's always been it for me, ever since I fell into his lap.

He tilts his head up and locks eyes with me, slowly easing forward as his breath comes out in a quick burst. "Christ, Dylan." He begins to move, sliding in and out of me easily due to my fully-aroused state. I'm certain I'm permanently wet around him and am totally fine with that; he owns my body. "Jesus. So fucking good. Every damn time."

"Oh, God, yes." I grip onto his neck with one hand and his

bicep with my other, squeezing tightly and feeling his muscles contract. His hips pound against my pelvis, pushing me farther and farther up the tiled wall. I don't think I'll ever get used to his power during sex, the way he moves in me and with me, commanding my body that willingly obeys without any hesitation. Groans and grunts echo around us as he moves fluidly inside me, hitting the end of my channel. "Reese." His hands grip my hips harder and he becomes more forceful with his thrusts, my back slapping hard against the wall.

"You're almost there. Let go, love," he says against my lips.

He always knows when I'm close, and it never takes me long to get there. I'm extremely responsive to everything this man does, and he loves it. With one quick movement, he unhooks my legs and places me on the shower floor, dropping down to his knees in front of me. His mouth is on me instantly, sucking my clit as he grabs my thighs and hooks them both over his shoulders.

"Come for me, Dylan."

"Shit. Oh, God, right there." I come hard and fast, reaching down and gripping his hair with both hands. He's so unbelievably good at this, and he knows it. Moving his head rapidly between my legs, he moans softly against my clit, lapping between my folds. I'm trembling against him like I always do, seeing his eyes flick up to mine as he gently places me down on my feet. My legs are wobbly, and it takes a lot of effort to remain upright. "Jesus. How do you keep getting better at that?" I rake through his hair as he gazes up at me, giving me the slightest shrug as his answer. "My turn," I declare, seeing his eyes light up as he stretches out above me. I excitedly push him against the wall, practically bouncing on my post-orgasm feet as he watches me in amusement. "Hands or mouth?"

He arches his brows at my question, his sweet smile pulling at the corner of his lips. "Both."

I enthusiastically rub my hands together and lean in, pressing my lips against his mouth for a quick kiss, which turns into an intense make-out session the moment he grips my neck. His tongue tangles with mine, swallowing my tiny whimpers and sending a shock wave through my body.

"See how good you taste? Like fucking candy."

I shudder against him like I always do when he talks to me that way. The man is an expert in dirty talking, dirty texting, and dirty love-letter writing. Yes, I've decided all his little notes to me during our *casual bullshit* phase were love letters. I know, I was a fucking idiot to think they weren't.

I reach down and grip him in my hand, his body jerking at the contact as he drops his head against mine. My hand doesn't slide as easily as I'd like and I get an idea, a very naughty idea. Stepping back, our eyes meet as I pull my bottom lip into my mouth and slip two fingers inside me. His penetrating green eyes broaden as I moan and swipe my wetness onto his cock, repeating the action until I've gotten him well lubricated.

"Holy shit. That's so fucking hot."

"I just thought I'd share what you do to me," I reply playfully, stepping into him and stroking his length. "You make me so wet." I lick his stubble and hear him moan softly. "Just by being in the same room with me." My free hand grips his arm as his breath warms the side of my face. I'm sliding up and down, fast then faster, my grip tightening as his hands wrap around my waist. "No man has ever done that to me before." He groans deeply against me, and I know it's because of what I'm doing to him and what I've just confessed. He loves that he's the only man who's ever affected me; the only man who ever will.

His bottom lip is pulled into his mouth, indicating he's close. It's his tell; that and when he rakes his hands through his hair, signifying he's either anxious, nervous, or really fucking pissed. "I love how wet I make you. That pussy belongs to me." His breathing hitches in my hair. "Fuck, I'm gonna come."

Dropping to my knees, I wrap my lips around him and stroke him with my hand, pumping him into my mouth. He grunts loudly above me, his thighs tensing and his hands holding my head, tangling in my hair. I swallow every ounce of him, moaning against his skin and feeling him twitch. His breathing steadies above me and I glance up, seeing a very-amused grin on his gorgeous face.

"I love you," I say softly, planting a quick kiss to his cock before I stand up. His arms wrap around me and I immediately shove my face into his neck, claiming my spot.

"Me or my dick?"

I giggle against him and feel his laugh shake my body. "Your dick." He pulls me away from him, issuing me his *don't fucking push it, Dylan* look, and I crack. "You *and* your dick. I'm mad for both of you. Can't live without either one of you, actually."

Reaching up, I grab my shampoo and turn to see his hand held out for me, waiting for me to squirt it into his palm. I do it and grab his body wash, squirting it into my hand before I put it back on the shelf. I wash his body as he washes my hair, my hands roaming freely over his skin. I linger on his shoulders and upper back, giving him a rubdown as his eyes close. He loves this, me touching him this way, pulling and kneading his muscles until they loosen. His tiny moans of gratification make me smile as I move down his body and spread the lather around. He massages my scalp the way he always does, building up the suds with his hands until they begin to trickle down my face. I'm rinsed off quickly, and my body wash is grabbed.

"Hey, use yours," I demand, trying to snatch it from his grasp but remembering instantly just how quick he is, and how I don't stand a chance in taking *anything* from him. We've been down that road.

"No. I want you to smell like you."

I grumble unconvincingly, loving how he prefers the way I smell to anything else, even though I'd be much happier smelling like him. I watch as I'm thoroughly cleaned as only Reese Carroll would do. The man is meticulous about everything, concentrating on covering every inch of my skin in the soapy bubbles. He lingers on my breasts, kneading them for several minutes before he rinses them clean. His marks are on me, permanently branded onto my skin due to his daily freshening-up sessions. I moan softly as he latches onto the left one, pulling the skin into his mouth and planting a soft kiss to it after it's darkened.

"So, how bad was today?" he asks, licking the mark on my right breast before sucking on it.

I grab his head and hold him against me. "Tolerable." He narrows his eyes at me, not buying my elusiveness. I sigh, dropping my head down. "I mean, if you *really* loved me, you wouldn't want to wait ten more days to make this official. You'd whisk me away to

Vegas and make me yours right now."

He stands up, pressing his lips to my forehead. "Do you need my dick in your mouth again?" I nod quickly and he laughs. "If I could arrange it, I'd have the entire world witness you becoming mine." He smirks. "Officially."

"Officially," I echo, reaching behind me and shutting off the water. For all intents and purposes, we both know I've been his since that first wedding, but until his last name becomes mine, it won't feel real to either one of us.

After securing a towel around his waist and blocking my amazing view, he wraps a towel around me and follows behind me into his bedroom. I don't bother getting dressed because he prefers me naked in bed; anything I put on my body right now would be ripped off and discarded.

No barriers.

Nothing getting in his way of me.

That's his thing.

"You hungry?" he asks after stepping into a pair of boxers.

"Aren't I always after you ravage me?"

He disappears down the hallway, returning moments later with two bowls. He hands me mine with a smile and I lean back against the headboard, lifting the bowl to my nose. "Mmm, this smells amazing. I might just keep you."

He laughs softly next to me before he begins inhaling his food. "So, there's this last-minute account Ian and I are taking on that requires some traveling this weekend. And we were talking and thought it'd be cool if everyone came with us."

"Where are you going?"

He stretches his legs out next to mine, my feet stopping at his calf. "New Orleans. We have to be there really early on Friday, so you'll have to take a separate flight." He pauses, exhaling roughly. "I need to talk to you about something." I cock my head and see his jaw twitch slightly just before he rakes his hand through his hair.

Uh oh.

"This account, it's a business Bryce is investing in. He hired us to show them how to make better use of their resources and increase profitability. The only reason why I agreed to do it is because…" he clenches his eyes tightly, swallowing loudly. His eyes refocus on mine after he takes in a calming breath. "It's just important. I need this account, and I need you to understand that."

Bryce Roberts has been flying under the radar since Reese and I got engaged but before that, he made it very clear he was interested in me. The last time I saw him was when I delivered treats to Reese's building for a business meeting. I had no idea they knew each other, but there that little shit sat, staring at me like I was one of the pastries I had made. They don't work together and apparently, hardly ever have to deal with each other, which is a good thing. Reese isn't shy when it comes to how he feels about guys hitting on me or making me feel uncomfortable, and Bryce did both.

I see the pent-up irritation on his face that he's failing miserably at hiding. Humor works best in situations like this. "Well, it sucks he's still breathing. I was hoping he had gotten mauled by a bear." My jokester smile fades when Reese remains in serious, concerned-fiancé mode. I dip my head, forcing his eyes that are burning a hole into the sheet to focus on mine. "I get it; it's an important account. I told you before, I can handle assholes like Bryce."

In fact, I'd very much like to handle Bryce. I haven't slapped anyone in months, and my hand is beginning to twitch.

He aggressively stabs his noodles, taking out his anger on the delicious dinner he's made us. "And I told *you* before, if he makes you uncomfortable in any way, I'll break his fucking neck. That doesn't just include him coming into your shop. If he so much as looks at you in a way you don't like…"

I place my hand on his arm, halting his threat. "Relax. He won't." *Unless he's dumber than I think, which is entirely possible.* I swallow my mouthful and twirl some noodles onto my fork. Time to get the subject off Bryce before my fiancé has a coronary. "I've never been to New Orleans. I'm kinda excited." I shove my forkful into my mouth and bob my head to the side, chewing animatedly. Reese laughs softly next to me, finally relaxing. "So, what do I need to do?"

He sits his empty bowl on his nightstand, sliding down in the bed and settling on his side facing me. "Just book your flight. I already rented the house for all of us to stay."

I arch my brow at him. "And what if I would've said no?"

He pinches my side and I yelp, prompting him to pull me closer so our bodies are touching. Constant contact. "I knew you'd say yes. You don't have a wedding to bake for this weekend, so you're all mine."

I smile wide. "Look at you knowing my schedule. Oooo! We can do our bachelor and bachelorette parties this weekend! In the Big Easy!" I kick the covers off and scramble out of bed, setting my half-eaten bowl of spaghetti on my nightstand.

"Where are you going?"

"To call Joey! He's going to freak out!"

I hear his faint laugh as I grab my phone from my clutch and dial Joey's number. Returning to the bedroom, Joey answers as Reese pulls me back into bed.

"If you're calling to tell me Reese's mother is in charge of making my penis cake, I'm hanging up."

I giggle and settle back down on my side, staring at a very sleepy-looking Reese. He's been working long hours lately, plus some weekends, leaving him exhausted most nights by the time I get to him. Especially if he decides I need a good dicking as soon as he sees me, which is what usually happens. He lets his eyes fall closed, keeping his one arm wrapped around my waist.

"What would you say to a weekend in New Orleans with your two best friends and our men?"

"I'd say count me the fuck in. When?"

"This weekend. It's perfect. We don't have any weddings to bake for, and Reese and Ian have to go anyway. Plus—" I pause for dramatic effect, prompting Joey to give me an impatient grunt, "—we can go all-out for my bachelorette party, Mardi Gras-style."

"Oh, fuck yes! Do you know how many gay bars they have there? Oooo, cupcake, I'm busting. This is going to be fantastic."

I listen to my easily-excitable best friend and smile at the man I love who has completely passed out next to me. Reese's breathing is slow and steady in my ear as I press my forehead against his, feeling the dampness of his hair against my skin.

"Billy's in, too, right?"

"Of course. As soon as he heard me say 'gay bar' he was in. Do

I need to do anything besides buy our plane tickets?"

"Nope. The place we're staying at has already been booked. Oooo, maybe it's in the French Quarter."

"Babe, I want a window seat. A *window*." I hear Billy's muffled response in the background, prompting Joey to let out a cross grumble. "Oh, for Christ's sake. Cupcake, I gotta go handle this. You better book your flight now if you want a decent seat."

I roll over and sit up, grabbing Reese's iPad off the nightstand. "Yeah, I'm on it. I'll see you tomorrow."

Just as I hang up from Joey, my phone beeps with an incoming text message.

> *Juls: NEW ORLEANS, SWEETS! Booking my flight now. There's just the one leaving late afternoon on Friday, so you'll have to close up early. Hope that's doable.*

> *Me: Totally doable. I'm so excited!*

> *Juls: Me, too! I may have mentioned it to Brooke.*

I slam my head back against the headboard. *Seriously? Has she gone completely mental?*

> *Me: You are out of your fucking mind.*

> *Juls: It'll be fun. And don't worry about JoJo. I'll handle him.*

> *Me: Good. Cause I'm not.*

I place my phone down and power on the iPad, letting go of *that* stress and grinning at the image that appears on the screen. It's still the one of me, passed out after my first-ever sleepover in this bed.

I can't believe I ever fought it.

Him.

Sleepovers.

Him.

Intimacy.

HIM.

Even though I acted like a complete idiot and tried to ignore every screaming thought in my head that said what we were doing was more than I was prepared to admit, I wouldn't take it back. I will never regret the way I fell in love with Reese; I can't. Every single second of it was worth it because it led us to this. And I'd go through eighty-five more days of complete torture to have him next to me, because he's always been mine. And in ten more days, I'll officially be his.

"ARE YOU SURE YOU WANNA send that bag through security? What with all the sex toys you have tucked away in there?" Juls teases as Joey puts his suitcase on the conveyor belt. Billy conceals his smile behind his hand, turning a slight shade of pink.

Joey turns his eyes up to the monitor, watching as his delicates are scanned. "I doubt National Security gives two shits that I like to use a spreader bar."

"Baby, really? Is that public knowledge?" Billy asks, grabbing his and Joey's suitcases.

I bite back my laugh and join the three of them after retrieving my luggage. "There's nothing sacred between the three of us, Billy. You should know that by now."

"Especially when it pertains to sex," Juls adds.

We all begin the walk through the terminal toward our gate. Reese and Ian left early this morning on their flight, so we'll be catching up with them later on tonight. And, by some miracle, Brooke is late and keeping Joey blissfully ignorant at the moment; it might actually be in her benefit to miss the flight entirely. Juls thought it best to let the news of her crashing our weekend getaway 'unravel organically', as she so innocently put it. *Organically?* I'm not sure how organic it's going to be watching Joey freak the fuck out in the middle of an airport. Because other than Maggie Carroll showing up and boarding our flight, Brooke Wicks is the only other person who could send my dear assistant into a shit-fit.

"This is going to be ahhhmazing," Joey sings as he puts his luggage into the overhead compartment. Juls and I have settled into our seats behind the boys and my eyes keep darting to the front of the plane, even though I'm sure I'll hear Brooke before I see her. "I hope you're all aware we will be having separate bachelor and bachelorette parties." Joey shifts his eyes between the three of us. "Baby, you're with the boys."

Juls and I both laugh as he sits down next to Billy. Then I sense it: the shift in the atmosphere, causing my back to go rigid in my seat. Juls must feel it, too, because she leans forward into the crack between the seats at that exact moment.

"JoJo, please don't do anything that could get you kicked off this flight."

He turns his head, gazing back at us with suspicion. "What? I'm not *that* inappropriate."

"Hey, bitches. Who's ready to party in the Big Easy?"

I see Brooke in my peripheral vision, not able to turn away from Joey's face, which has tensed up considerably. He doesn't even look in her direction. "You have got to be fucking kidding me," he snarls between the seats before finally whipping his head around and greeting Brooke with what I can only assume to be anything but a smile. "Who the hell invited you?"

"Joey!" Juls snaps.

Brooke's lip twitches into a conniving grin. "Will the three of us be sharing a bed? I've been told I'm an excellent little spoon." She tucks her luggage away and ruffles Joey's hair before taking her seat next to me. He grumbles under his breath, prompting Billy to reach up and fix his coifed do. "Who bottoms of the two of you, anyway?"

"Jesus, Brooke," I say, just as Billy and Joey turn around in their seats. "There are other people on this airplane."

"I hope your dildos got through airport security, since they're going to be the only thing entering that mess of a vagina this weekend." Joey points to Brooke's lap, smiling after delivering his dig.

She flips him off, moving her finger closer to his face and prompting him to lean back. "If you want to enter a competition with me to see who can get the most dick over the next two days, bring it, bitch."

"Battery operated doesn't count, Brooke. Remember that," Joey retorts.

I put my hands between them, breaking up the verbal battle. I glance to my left and lock eyes with Brooke. "It better not be like this between the two of you every day in the shop. I'm telling you right now, I'm not putting up with it. I'll have enough stress on me next week as it is."

"I can be civil," Brooke states, feigning affection toward Joey. He rolls his eyes and turns around, entering quiet conversation with Billy, which I'm sure is revolving around the hot mess sitting next to me. Brooke offers me a genuine smile. "Thank you, by the way. You're really helping me out here."

"You're welcome, but be warned. I don't care that you're my best friend's sister; I will fire you if you and Joey can't get along."

She nods her understanding, buckling her seatbelt and prompting me to do the same. The flight attendants begin their safety demonstrations in the aisle as Joey continues to animatedly gesture to Billy.

Juls leans over me and taps her sister's knee. "Do us all a favor and try not to torment him too much this weekend. Don't make me regret inviting you to this."

Brooke huffs and scowls in the direction of her sister. "Everyone needs to relax. Jesus Christ, you all act like I'm incapable of handing myself in public."

Thankfully, at that exact moment, the flight attendant stops in front of our row with the cart of beverages, preventing a rebuttal from Juls and myself. "Would anyone like anything?"

"Liquor," we all answer simultaneously. The flight attendant smiles and hands out mini-bottles of vodka which none of us waste any time in downing.

"All cell phones off, please. We're about to take off."

Everyone reaches into their pockets and messes with their phones. I notice the text message on my screen and open it with the same nervous excitement I always have when I see his name.

Reese: Eight more days, love. Get your ass here already.

Me: Hurrying. And you can do better than eight more days. Put that brain to work, handsome.

I power off my phone and tuck it away, relaxing against my seat. Eight more days that can't get here soon enough.

"HOLY HELL. THIS PLACE IS fabulous."

I hear Joey's voice register somewhere in the house as I make my way upstairs toward the bedrooms. He isn't lying, though; this place *is* fabulous. My man did well. It looks like a civil war-era mansion from the outside, and the inside is very rustic and warm. The kitchen and living area are downstairs, both spacious and lovely, and the house is equipped with three bedrooms. I open the first door I come to and notice the brown, worn-leather luggage on the bed that screams Ian in every way.

"Juls, your room is the one on the right," I yell over my shoulder toward the stairs. She's probably too busy moderating downstairs to even hear me at the moment, but I give her a heads-up anyway.

I open the room across the hall and am immediately hit in the face with my favorite smell in the world. Reese has probably only spent a limited amount of time in here, considering he and Ian had to meet with the client shortly after arriving earlier today, but his scent is already saturating the space we'll share for the next two days. And I couldn't be happier about that.

I drop my suitcase next to his on the floor by the dresser and spot his iPod laying on one of the pillows on the bed. A tiny brown card is next to it. I crawl up the length of the bed and grab the iPod, setting it on my stomach as I open the familiar card.

Dylan,

64,863 seconds. (Give or take a few depending on when you read this note.)

X, Reese

P.S. Listen.

I can't help the ridiculous smile that spreads across my face; I never can. It's always been like this, and I know it'll always be like this. No matter how many notes he leaves me or deliveries he sends me, I'll never lose that wild excitement I feel at even the smallest gesture. I grab the ear buds and pop them into my ears. After turning on the iPod, I scroll to the songs, expecting to find a huge playlist because I know this is the iPod Reese takes with him when he goes to the gym. But there's only one song on it, so I conclude he must have erased all his other music specifically for this moment. I close my eyes and let the music fill my ears, concentrating on the lyrics just like I did the first time he played this song for me. I think every time Reese and I have sex, it's always some form of making love, even when it's rough and urgent. But he only reserved this song for that first time.

The bed dips by my feet, prompting me to peek one eye open as I listen to "Look After You" for the second time. Joey joins me by my side and steals one of my ear buds and the card I'm holding to my chest.

I study his face as he places the bud in his ear and reads my note. He frowns, hands the note back over, and lets his head fall on the pillow next to me. "That man of yours makes every other guy in Chicago look bad. Especially mine."

I elbow his side, seeing him smile through a silent 'ouch', and turn the song down so it's playing softly for both of us. "Billy does a ton of romantic stuff for you. He asked you to move in with him after only knowing you a little over a week, and he worships the ground your pretty feet walk on. He'd do anything for you; you know that."

"Then why hasn't he asked me to marry him?"

I open my mouth to speak but shut it almost instantly. I honestly don't know the answer to that question. I've wondered it myself, especially lately with all my wedding planning going on. Billy is perfect for Joey. He keeps him grounded but also brings out the playful side in him that I completely adore. I love seeing them together; I've never seen my dear assistant this happy before with anyone. But maybe Billy isn't the marrying type.

"Have you two talked about it? Getting married?"

He plucks the ear bud out, seemingly done with the love song that is probably fueling his irritation. I do the same and wrap them around Reese's iPod before turning on my side and facing Joey.

"Sort of. He said he could see himself getting married someday, but he didn't name drop and say with me."

"Well, maybe he's waiting for you to ask him."

Joey snaps his head toward me and raises his eyebrows. "Are you insane? I'm not proposing; that's his job. He can at least give me one fucking grand gesture."

My bedroom door pushes open and Billy fills the doorway, looking apprehensive. He rolls his eyes and grimaces in our direction, keeping one hand on the door while the other pinches the top of his nose. "Baby, Brooke wants to know if she can share our room."

"Ha!"

I chuckle at Joey's outburst before turning my attention back to Billy.

"There are only three bedrooms. It really doesn't bother me if you don't mind."

Billy's face is filled with a softness I only ever see him use with Joey. Though I'm not sure he knows what exactly he's in for by agreeing to this sleeping arrangement; he's barely had to spend any amount of time with Brooke.

Joey sits up, bracing himself on his elbows. "Oh, I do mind. There's no way in Hell I'm sharing a bed with her. I believe I saw a couch downstairs she can plant her ass on when it comes time to sleep."

"Well, do you want to go tell her? I think she is already starting to unpack in our room."

"Of course she is." Joey swings his long, muscular legs off the bed and walks toward the door, passing Billy after planting a brief kiss to his lips. "Brooke. You're out of your fucking mind if you think I'm sharing a room with you." I hear her muffled response, followed by Joey's dramatic rebuttal, which causes both Billy and me to laugh.

He turns to me and smiles. "You ready for next weekend? Tying down the unattainable bachelor of Chicago and all is a pretty big deal."

"Ha ha. Speaking of bachelors—" I scoot off the bed and walk over to him, "—can I ask you something?" He closes the door and leans against it, waiting for my question with a welcoming expression. I put my hand on his shoulder. "You wouldn't hurt Joey, would you?"

He tilts his head with a frown, seemingly thrown off by my question. His eyes dart to my hand that's resting on his shoulder before flicking back to me. "Dylan, I'm well aware of your capabilities when it comes to bitch-slapping somebody, but even if I wasn't, I'd never hurt Joey."

I squeeze his shoulder before dropping my hand to my side. "Okay. I'm just looking out for him."

"I know. You and Juls are crazy-protective over my baby. One of these days I'll be married to all three of you." He notices my quiet enthusiasm and puts a finger to his lips. "Not a word."

I nod eagerly. "That's so exciting," I whisper.

He opens the door and peeks his head out into the hallway, glancing in both directions. "All's quiet. Think they killed each other?"

My phone begins to ring in my pocket. I slip it out as I reply, "It's possible. You might want to go check."

Billy gives me a wink before he walks out of the bedroom, closing the door behind him. I answer the call as I walk back over to the bed.

"Hi, handsome."

"Hi, love. Are you here?"

"Yup. Just got in about an hour ago. When will I see you? It's already almost eight o'clock." I fall back onto my pillow, rolling over and placing the note he left me next to his iPod. "I need my Reese fix."

He laughs softly. "Are the two orgasms I gave you last night not keeping you satisfied?"

"No way. I'm greedy when it comes to that mouth of yours."

"Just my mouth?" I can practically hear his smile through the phone. Playful Reese is one of my favorites.

He probably could keep me satisfied with just his mouth if he wanted to. But I've had the rest of him, and I'm not giving that up for anything. "You know I'm addicted to all of you," I reply before my grin breaks into a yawn. I'm suddenly not wanting to leave this bed at all, especially after Reese does get here.

"You better be. Tired?"

"Very. Long day. Even longer flight." I reach up behind me and pile my hair on top of my head so the coolness of the pillow touches my skin. "Brooke and Joey are already going at it."

I hear Ian's voice in the background. "All right," Reese directs away from the phone. "I gotta go. We should be getting out of here in a few hours, though."

I yawn again. "Mmm, okay. Miss your face."

"Miss yours."

I hang up the call and get out of bed, picking up my suitcase and plopping it down in my place. Grabbing the University of Chicago T-shirt Reese gave me months ago, which, besides a garter and stockings, is the only thing he willingly allows me to wear to bed, I strip quickly and slip it over my head. Our bedroom has its own private bath, which I'm grateful for; sharing a bathroom with two gay guys and two other girls would be a nightmare, I'm sure. Joey alone has more hair care products than I do. After I remove my makeup and brush my teeth, I climb back into bed just as someone knocks on my door.

"Come in."

Juls pops her head in with a smile. "Hey. The guys should be here in a couple of hours."

"Yeah, I just talked to Reese. I'm exhausted. I'm just gonna turn in for the night."

"Good idea," she says through a mischievous grin. "You'll need your energy for tomorrow." She closes the door after giving me a quick wink, and I pull the covers up around me.

Tomorrow.

My bachelorette party.

Juls and Joey have been whispering all over the shop the past two days, secretly planning my last hoorah. I know I'm going to be dragged to some strip club against my will. Joey is insistent on male nudity happening, that I know for sure. In all honestly, I'd much rather just go dancing at a club like Juls did for hers. I don't need to celebrate my remaining days as a single woman with greased-up men grinding on a stage. I'm dick-set for life. I don't need to look at other options.

Goddamn it, Billy. Propose to your boy already so he can worry about his own bachelorette party.

I FEEL HIM, HIS MOUTH, his hands, his everything on me and I'm immediately pulled from my dream. Slowly opening my eyes, I see Reese on top of me, trailing kisses below my breasts and running his hands up my thighs. His wild hair is perfectly disheveled, sticking out every which way and brushing softly against my skin. He quickly removes my T-shirt and panties and tosses them off the bed.

"Mmm. I love waking up like this." I feel his lips curl up against me as he trails lower. Nibbling at my hip bones, his teeth graze along my skin and I squirm underneath him. I glance to my right, seeing the time on the alarm clock. "Did you just get here?"

"Yeah." His lips brush along my ribs while his hands mold over my breasts. "I know it's late. And if you're too tired…"

Yeah, right. Like I would ever object to this.

Reaching down, I grip his shoulders and pull him up to me, bringing his face to mine. "I don't care what time it is; you always have my permission to wake me up." I lift my head and brush my lips softly against his, tasting his minty flavor. "Thank you for my note and my song. Let's go get married right now."

He laughs against my mouth, the gentle pressure turning urgent. I'm silenced, as I always am when he kisses me this way, and

I really couldn't care less. Opening for him, we move our tongues against each other's, stroking and savoring as my fingers tangle in his hair. His hands move all over my body, touching and caressing every inch of me with his calloused palms. I moan softly as he teases my breasts, pulling and pinching my nipples in the way I like. My need for him builds quickly, and I reach down between us and grip his length in my hand. "Hard day?" I ask playfully.

He groans deeply before he answers. "Hardest. I hate being away from you."

"We're always apart on Fridays for work." I slowly stroke his length, feeling him thicken even more in my hand.

"I know. This just felt different."

My heart constricts at his words, knowing exactly how he feels. Even though we're used to some distance, this did feel different somehow. Maybe it's because he's so close to becoming officially mine, or maybe it's because I've been stressed to the max lately. Either way, I'm not a fan of being away from this man; where he goes, I go.

"Reese," I whisper across his lips, hearing his breath hitch at the sound of his name.

"I need you," he proclaims, thrusting forward and entering me in one quick push. I gasp with him, pulling my legs up and wrapping them firmly around his hips. He moves fast and hard, plunging deep then deeper into me. My eyes are locked onto his as he holds himself above me, lunging forward in his perfect rhythm. He whispers his sweet words to me between each drive.

"It's like Heaven being in you. Tell me you're mine, Dylan."

"I'm yours. I always have been."

"Fucking right."

I arch my back and press my chest against his, needing the contact. Needing every part of him touching me. I can never get close enough to this man. I want him on me at all times; I crave it. I love the way our bodies fit together, so perfectly and so in tune with each other's. He drops his head and latches onto my right breast, flicking against my nipple before sucking on it. I groan loudly, loving the way his mouth feels against every part of my body. My eyes go to the inside of his right arm, seeing the words I scrolled on him all those months ago. The fact that he got it tattooed still blows my mind, and every time I look at it, my heart swells. I lean up and press my lips against the words, my words I marked him with. Trailing my tongue across my script, his thrusts pick up, as he slams harder into me. Hearing his loud grunts ring out above me, I glance up and see him pull his bottom lip in and bite it.

"Make me come, Reese."

Dropping his hand between us, he picks up his movements and brushes against my clit, in the way only he does. He knows exactly what to do with my body, and he does it better than anyone ever could. Not that I have any desire to test that theory; this is the only man I'll ever want. I'm falling fast, clenching around him and softly chanting his name.

"Dylan," he growls, crashing his mouth down on mine. I pull his tongue into my mouth and suck on it slowly, swallowing his moans as he gives me his release. Our lips brush against each other's, tasting and teasing as we both come down from our high. He lifts his head toward the direction of the nightstand.

"Seven days," he says before looking back down at me. "You know this is hard for me, right? To be this damn close to having the whole world know you're officially mine."

I slide along his cheekbone with my fingers, studying his face. "I thought I was the only one struggling out of the two of us. You're always so quick to silence my quickie-wedding suggestions."

He shakes his head slightly, leaning into my palm that's resting flat against his cheek. And then I see it: the shift in his eyes, the possessive, hungry glare he does so well. "It fucking kills me to wait, but I want this to be perfect for you. I don't ever want you to regret the way you gave yourself to me, and I'll have no problem moving that preacher along. That ceremony will be brief."

I laugh softly before planting a kiss on his jaw. "I love you," I murmur against his skin.

He drops his forehead to mine and closes his eyes. "I love you."

He always says it like that when I say it first. It's never *I love you, too*. Never. It's as if he's stating it as a fact, not giving me an automated response to my declaration. The way Reese says 'I love you', I feel it more than I hear it.

He lets his weight press me firmly into the mattress as he collapses down on top of me, tucking his head next to mine. "Seven days," he whispers, and I barely make it out. It's as if those words are just for him, the reassurance he gives himself.

I kiss his shoulder and hold him against me, not wanting him to move. I could wake up with the worst cramp in the morning, but this closeness would be worth it. I press my lips to his ear. "We got this. Seven days is nothing."

And with those final words, I feel his body relax.

I FEEL THE BED MOVE and hear the soft creaking sound of the mattress. Peeking one eye open, I see the back of Reese as he sits on the end of the bed, facing the bathroom. He's shirtless, his broad back covered in tiny water droplets. His hair is wet and fuckably messy and his scent is overwhelming me, blanketing me and causing me to purr as I stretch. At the sound of my noise, he turns his head and lets his eyes roam freely over my body, which is barely covered in the white sheet.

"You are impossibly beautiful. Do you know that?"

I hold my hands out, reaching for him. He drops the towel he is holding and crawls toward me in a pair of shorts, settling on his side and pulling me against his chest.

"You showered without me," I state as I press soft kisses to his chest.

"I had to. Ian and I went for a run."

I lean back to look into his face. "You're that disciplined to work out on vacation?" My eyes take in his hard body, and I realize the absurdity of that question. "Never mind. Look at you. The term 'rest day' is not a part of your vocabulary." A knock on the door prompts Reese to grab the sheet and cover me up to my neck.

"Hold on," he yells over his shoulder.

He shifts quickly and straddles my waist, moving his hands along the side of my body and tucking me in burrito style. I squirm underneath him. "Reese, I could've just grabbed a T-shirt."

He smirks at me before turning toward the door. "All right, you can come in."

The door opens and Joey pops his head through. He smiles at the sight of the two of us on the bed. "Well, look who's finally awake."

Finally awake? I quickly turn toward the alarm clock. "Oh, my God. It's after twelve o'clock already?" I gaze up at Reese. "You tried to wake me, didn't you?"

"Of course I did. Multiple times."

I shake my head at myself with a grimace; I'm in New Orleans, and I'm spending my time here in bed. Of course, if Reese promised to stay with me, I'd never leave this bed. What girl would?

"The party bus is leaving at three o'clock. And no boys allowed," Joey says with a smile. He looks almost devious in my doorway, no doubt thinking of everything he and Juls have planned for the evening. "And I have two rules for you, cupcake: wear the sexiest outfit you have in that suitcase, and hand over the cell phone."

"What? No way. I'm not giving you my phone." Reese shifts above me and grabs my phone off the nightstand before getting out of bed. "What are you doing?"

"He took my phone, too. Let him have it; I don't need a phone to get to you."

I watch him hand my cell over and Joey takes it with a smile. "Thank you. And don't even think about *getting to her*."

I don't see Reese's reaction to what Joey's just said, but I do see Joey's reaction to the look he is getting from Reese, and that look makes my dear assistant straighten up in the doorway. I hide my giggle underneath the sheet as Joey exhales loudly.

"If I see your gorgeous face at any of the places we go to tonight, you and I will be having words."

"Joey," Reese says, placing one hand on the doorframe and gripping the edge of the door with the other. Even though he and Joey are roughly the same height, Reese seems to tower over any opponent with his body language alone. "Nothing stands in my way of Dylan. Not even you."

Joey sighs heavily and glances in my direction. "Three o'clock, cupcake."

"Got it."

The door closes and I immediately flail my arms and legs, breaking free of the cocoon I've been wrapped in. I slide off the bed and grab my T-shirt, pulling it over my head. When I brush my wild bed-hair out of my eyes, I see Reese staring at me in the way only he does, like he's committing me to memory. I sit on the edge of the bed and tap the spot next to me. He smiles, sitting down and placing his hand on my thigh.

"So, what are your plans for tonight? Naked girls? Lap dances?" I ask as I twirl my engagement ring around my finger.

His forehead creases with concern. "Do you think I have any desire to see another naked woman when I have this waiting for me?" He tugs at my T-shirt, exposing my bare hip. His finger trails along my skin. "I love this spot right here. Do you know why?" I watch as his finger glides over my hipbone toward the taut skin of my inner thigh. When he turns his head up and locks onto my eyes, I shake my head. The corner of his mouth curls up into a smile. "When I kiss you here, you shake against my lips. You always have." His finger trails lower, dipping between my legs. I gasp when he feels how wet his words have made me. "Mine."

"Yours," I answer breathlessly. I let my head fall against his shoulder. "I need to start getting ready. Joey will freak out if I make us late to wherever the hell we're going."

He kisses the corner of my mouth before sliding his hand out and sucking on his finger. "I need to get ready, too. But you will be sitting on my face later."

"Promise?" I tease, standing and making my way to the bathroom. I turn when I don't get a response just in time to see him drop his shorts, displaying his massive erection. I stumble a bit. "Wow. I mean, we have a little time, right?"

He arches his brow. "Get in there before I pin you against the wall. You know I hate rushing when it comes to you." I pull my shirt over my head, flashing him and pairing it with my best flirtatious smile. He shakes his head. "Go, love."

"Yes, Mr. Carroll."

BY THE TIME I REEMERGE from the bathroom, ready to get this night over with, Reese has already dressed and left the room. I walk over to my suitcase and grab the black high heels I packed. They are dangerously high, buckle around my ankle, and scream sex kitten. I might actually kill myself wearing these tonight, but when the hell else am I going to wear them? Besides to bed with Reese, which will definitely be happening very soon. I strap them on and walk over to the floor-length mirror hanging on the wall. My blonde hair is falling over my bare shoulders. My makeup is looking on point and very sexy, thanks to my false eyelashes, and my dress is short, black, and practically a second skin. It's probably a good thing Reese has left the room already because I seriously doubt he'd let me walk out of here in this. He took it upon himself months ago to categorize the majority of my wardrobe as *for his eyes only*, leaving me with only a few dresses deemed fit for public outings, according to his standards. And none of those dresses would do tonight. This *is* my bachelorette party; I'm supposed to look sinful. Besides, he can rip this off my body later and do whatever the hell he wants with it. And by it, I mean my dress *and* my body.

"Holy shit," Joey practically squeals as I walk very carefully down the stairs. Juls and Brooke are standing by the doorway, both in tight dresses themselves, and Joey is looking exceptional in a dress shirt and khakis. "Thank Christ the guys left already. There's no way in Hell Reese would approve of that dress, which you look amazing in."

I smile widely. "Thanks. You don't look so bad yourself."

"You look incredible, sweets," Juls adds as I come to a stop at the last step. She points at my feet with her perfectly manicured finger. "I need to borrow those shoes immediately. *They* are fabulous."

"The limo's here!" Brooke chirps, swinging the door open. "Let's get this party started."

I hold my clutch with one hand as Joey takes my other, looping it through his arm. "Are you ready to get down and dirty, cupcake?"

I smile at him, concealing my apprehension. "As ready as I'll ever be."

"I CAN'T BELIEVE YOU GOT a limo for this. Did the boys leave in one, as well?" I ask, climbing into the back of the stretch-Hummer-style limo that could easily fit twenty people. The last time I was in a limousine was prom, and it was nowhere near as nice as this one. The cool leather of the seats chills my legs as I slide over to the bench seat.

"No. They aren't fabulous like we are. They all left in a cab," Joey answers as he settles into the seat to my right. Juls slides in next to him and smiles at me, pulling the hem of her dress down on her bare thighs.

Brooke opens one of the cabinets and grabs a bottle of champagne and several flutes. "Let's make a toast."

"Should you be pouring that? Didn't you pre-game it at the house with a few of the minis from the fridge?" Joey asks, scooting closer to Brooke.

Brooke glares at him. "Shut up, you queen. I'm perfectly capable of pouring under tipsy conditions." She fills the glasses, handing them out to the three of us. Joey takes his with a disapproving look before dropping it to give me his winning smile. "Who wants to do the honors?" Brooke asks.

"Me. I have to practice for Saturday anyway." Juls holds her glass in front of her, prompting the rest of us to do the same. She beams at me sweetly. "To my very best friend, Dylan, who deserves all the happiness in the world. We all love you very much, sweets." Her lip quivers a bit and she looks down, hiding her teary eyes. She wipes her finger across her cheek. "Sorry. I'm just so happy for you."

Joey sniffles next to her and squeezes her knee.

"You guys are lame. Is this how it's going to be all night?" Brooke asks. She tips her glass back when no one responds and downs the contents. I smile over at my two best friends, motioning to them for us to do the same. Brooke collects our empty glasses before reaching up and rubbing the back of her neck. "That stupid couch was not meant to be slept on. I'm getting a bed tonight."

"Not mine," Joey informs her. He looks out the window as the limo begins to slow down. "Oooo, we're here!"

My nerves hit me in one big rush, not knowing what to expect when I step out of the vehicle. I try to look out the window, but Brooke blocks my view as she stands and smoothes her dress. *Shit. I really don't want to go to some seedy strip club where you're most likely to catch an STD just from breathing the air. But I can't bail, not when we're already here.*

Juls places her hand on the door, looking back in my direction. "You ready, sweets?"

I nod and force my most convincing smile. Juls and Joey file out of the limo, followed by Brooke. I scoot myself along the bench seat and take Joey's offered hand that's held out for me, mentally preparing myself for what I'm about to endure. And then, I step out of the limo.

I am expecting neon lights and loud music pumping from a building.

I am expecting drunk patrons stumbling along the street and the smell of booze and cigarettes.

But I am not expecting this.

The limo has dropped us off outside a very ritzy establishment, the words 'Bella Donna Day Spa' scrolled in fancy script above the doorway. I turn toward my two best friends who are smiling at me.

"We're having a spa day?"

"This is what you wanted, isn't it?" Juls asks.

The tenseness in my shoulders has disappeared completely. I reach for Juls' hand and she places hers in mine, squeezing it gently.

Joey wraps his arm around my shoulder. "Did you really think I'd make your bachelorette party all about me? What kind of friend would I be if I did that?"

"But you told me to dress sexy."

He runs his eyes up and down my body. "And you knocked it out of the park. Don't worry, we'll put that dress to use when we go dancing after this."

I lay my head on his shoulder as he directs me to the door, following behind Juls and Brooke. "Thank you, Joey."

He kisses the top of my head. "Come on, cupcake. Let's enjoy some massages."

I REALLY HAVE THE TWO best friends in the world.

Juls and Joey set me up with a two-hour hot stone massage, which worked every single knot from my back that had begun to set in due to wedding-planning stress. Juls, Joey, and Brooke all received massages themselves while I passed out during my session. If I had my phone with me, I would've informed Reese that my masseuse had amazing fingers. Very feminine, amazing fingers. I'd never let him think another man had his hands on me. I'm very aware of his views on that, even if it is in a spa setting.

After that, the four of us drank wine while we got manicures and pedicures. Brooke even seemed happy about the festivities, not once complaining she wasn't getting her rocks off somewhere. Once we were all relaxed and buzzing from the wine, we were served a fancy lunch in the private bridal room: tiny cucumber and chicken salad sandwiches, assorted fruits and cheeses, and of course, more wine. Thank God for the food because I would've needed carrying out of there if I didn't have something to absorb the alcohol that seemed to be free flowing.

Feeling full and borderline-tipsy after my relaxing afternoon,

I can barely keep my eyes open as we make our way to our next stop. Juls and Brooke are talking quietly as I lean my head on Joey's shoulder.

"What do you think the boys are doing right now?"

He sighs. "Well, if it were a different bunch of men, I'd say they were getting panties thrown at them. But Reese only desires your panties, and Ian is so whipped it's almost laughable." Juls overhears this and flips Joey off as she continues to giggle with Brooke. "And Billy…" Joey's voice trails off as he reaches up and fixes the collar of his shirt.

I lean up and kiss his stubbly jaw. "He loves you. You know that, right?"

He nods, dropping his worried façade. "I know. I'm just in a funk. Once you're hitched, I'll be the only single girl left at the party." I swat at his leg and he laughs just as the limo comes to a stop. He peers down at me. "You ready to work that outfit at the hottest club in the Big Easy, cupcake?"

Dancing with my two best friends... and Brooke? I glance around at the three smiling faces. "Hell yes, I am. Let's do this."

Joey leads the way past the bouncer and into the Raging Rhino. The dance floor is packed with people, and the music is bumping through the speakers. This place is massive and a serious step up from the clubs we've been to in Chicago, and I always considered Clancy's to be on the fancy side. It's two floors, the bottom one containing a bar that stretches the length of the dance floor. The top level is roped off and a security guard is standing at the bottom of the stairs, granting access to certain individuals. Brooke squeals excitedly behind me as Juls turns her head and leans close to Joey and me.

"I say we dance first then hit up the bar," she yells over the music. Joey and I both nod in agreement, making our way toward the middle of the dance floor.

By some miracle, I'm able to dance without any problem in my sky-high heels, and I do just that with Joey, Juls, and Brooke dancing next to me. Even though there are tons of people around us, the dance floor is so large we all have plenty of room to move. Joey uses that to his advantage and spins around in a way only he does.

I hold my hair off my neck and move my body to some remixed version of "Sexy Back" by Justin Timberlake. It becomes a competition, the three of us all trying to out-dance the other for what feels like hours. My feet at one point become numb, and I don't care in the least that I'll probably have blisters; I'm having too much fun to care. As one song blends in to another, I glance around and realize Brooke is missing.

I wave my hands out in front of me, getting the attention of Juls and Joey. "Where's Brooke?"

They both glance around, Juls spinning in a circle and looking over the heads of the other dancers. She shrugs when she turns back to both of us. "Bathroom, maybe?"

"Who cares where she is? Ooooo, this is my jam!" Joey squeals.

"Single Ladies" by Beyoncé comes on, and Joey begins to do the entire dance routine from memory, probably better than Mrs. Carter herself, and that's saying a lot. Juls and I buckle over in laughter as he nails it, not caring what the hell anyone thinks of him. Because it's Joey we're talking about; the man has zero shame and I love him for it.

Not wanting to interrupt my best friend's dance number, I wait 'til after the song is over to demand a break. I grab his arm, motioning to Juls, and give them the universal hand gesture for 'let's go get a drink'. They both nod, Joey reaching up and wiping the sweat off his forehead and Juls resituating her dress, which shifted on her body.

We all walk up to the bar, and Joey motions for one of the four bartenders. "Hellooooo. Seriously? How can you ignore this?" Juls and I chuckle as he frantically waves his hand out, desperately trying to get someone's attention. Just then, Brooke comes stumbling up to the group, rubbing her left eye.

"Does anyone have any Visine?" she asks, dropping her hand down and blinking rapidly.

"Where have you been?" Juls asks. "And why the hell do you need Visine?"

She rolls her one eye that isn't being rubbed. "I got semen in my eye."

I don't know what the hell I was expecting her to say, but it definitely wasn't that. And given Juls' and Joey's reaction, they weren't expecting it either. I slap my hand over my mouth to contain my hysteria while Juls throws her head back, unashamedly laughing her ass off. Joey covers his face with his hands, his shoulders shaking with his laughter.

Brooke's face turns bright red as she rubs her eye with the heel of her hand. "Oh, like none of you have ever had a face shot go wrong. This really fucking burns. I've been flushing it out for the past hour."

"Oh, my God, Brooke," I barely get out through my chuckles. "Why did you let him shoot it on your face?"

She stares at me like I've just asked her the most ridiculous question. "I'm not swallowing a stranger's load. It was either that or on my dress, and this shit was expensive." She takes note of the laughter around her and huffs loudly. "It was an executive decision I'm seriously regretting. Someone Google whether or not it's possible to get permanent damage from this." The three of us are too busy roaring with laughter to be able to Google anything. Brooke surveys us with annoyance. "Asses. Next time you get cum in your eye, you're on your own."

"Finally," Joey says through a giggle as one of the bartenders walk up to where we're standing. He's holding a bright pink cocktail and places it on the table in front of us. "Uh, I didn't order yet. Although, that looks delicious."

"It's for her." The bartender motions at me with his head. "From the guy at the end of the bar."

The four of us all turn toward where he has directed, the laughter fading out as we all seemingly focus on the same individual.

Fucking motherfucker.

Bryce is staring at me with that same smug smirk, which is apparently a permanent fixture on his face. He's as eerie looking as I remember, with those yellow eyes that seem to glow in the bar, like a stalking reptile.

"What is that fucker doing here?" Joey asks, moving closer to me. I register his question but can't seem to find the words. I'm too busy coming up with ways to lay this asshole out.

"Damn. He's hot. Who is that guy?"

The three of us all turn to see a very horny-looking, one-eyed Brooke.

"Really, Brooke? You just gave some stranger head and you're patrolling for more ass? Maybe you should pace yourself," Joey says before returning his gaze back to Bryce. Brooke simply shrugs her response as he continues. "He must have a death wish to be in the same building as you. Reese is going to freak out."

"Is that Bryce?" Juls asks. I nod and see her eyes widen. "Shit. You were right, sweets; he is creepy looking."

Creepy seems to downplay it. The man makes my skin crawl, and this is only the third time I'm seeing him. I step up to the bar and grab the drink off the counter. There's a possibility that what I'm about to do will get me kicked out of this pristine club, but right now, I don't care. I've had an amazing time with my friends and if it ends now, I'm fine with that.

"Dylan! Hold up!"

I hear Joey's voice behind me as I move between the patrons. Bryce keeps his chilling smile on me as I inch closer, either not knowing or not caring how his gesture is being received. In fact, if anything, his stupid face seems to break into an even-bigger grin as I step next to him.

"Dylan, it's been too damn long since I laid my eyes on that tight body of yours. Remind me to thank your fiancé for bringing you along on this little trip," he spews through his venomous grin. His eyes slowly rake over my body, giving extra attention to my breasts. "Damn, girl, that dress belongs on my bedroom floor. Wanna get out of here and make that happen?"

I waste no time in drenching his face in my bright-pink cocktail, placing my now-empty glass down on the bar and gaining the attention of everyone around us. "Go fuck yourself, Bryce. Even if I wasn't with Reese, I would never go anywhere with you. The dickhead vibe you got going on doesn't really do anything for me. Nor do your lame-as-shit pick-up lines." I feel movement at my back as Juls, Joey, and a stunned-looking Brooke flank my side.

Bryce wipes the drink from his eyes, not dropping his smile even the slightest. "I heard you had a bit of a temper. Does Reese like that? Do you fuck him angry?"

"Oh, no, you did not just say that," Joey spits, stepping closer to Bryce.

I hold my arm out and stop him from getting in Bryce's face. "Don't, Joey. He isn't worth getting arrested over." Because that's exactly what would happen. Bryce is such a punk, he'd press charges instead of manning up and actually fighting back.

Joey looks down at me, nostrils flaring. "He's not going to talk to you like that. Let me handle this."

"Oh, but I'd much rather Dylan handle me, Joey." Bryce leans against the bar, his white polo shirt now stained light pink. "You want that, don't you, baby? You want to handle me?"

"Fuck you, asshole. I really hope we're all around to see you get your ass beat," Juls says, grabbing mine and Joey's elbows and tugging us back. Bryce's smile touches his eyes, making them practically twinkle at the sentiment. "Come on. Let's go."

"Just for the record: up close, you're not hot," Brooke adds behind us. I turn and see her flip him off over her shoulder.

I place my hand on Joey's back, making sure he's moving with me as we both follow Juls away from the bar and toward the entrance. "Goddamn it," I utter to myself. Nothing would've pleased me more than to slap the snot out of that jerk. Well, except for maybe throwing my first punch. But I couldn't do that. I couldn't do anything.

We all pile into the limo and as soon as we get situated, Brooke opens the liquor cabinet. "I don't know about you three, but I need to get trashed."

A collective "yeah" fills the inside of the limo. *Alcohol after that encounter? Yes. Absolutely.* I find the button that lowers the window dividing us and the driver, dropping it down. I meet the man's eyes in the rear view mirror.

"Would you mind driving around for a while before you take us back to the house?" I ask him.

"Not at all, Miss."

"I cannot wait until Reese finds out about this. That prick is going to get the ass-beating of the century," Joey says, taking a champagne bottle from Brooke. She hands Juls and me ours after opening them.

"Reese isn't finding out about his," I inform him after taking a swig. I glance between the three pairs of eyes on me, all filled with concern. "I mean it. This account he and Ian have with Bryce is important enough for Reese to put aside his hate for that asshole and actually work with him. If we say anything, he'll drop the account for sure, and most likely go to prison for murder. He doesn't need to know. Nothing happened."

Juls taps her free hand nervously on her knee. "Shit. That account is huge. Ian said it's the biggest one their company has taken on. They're going to make an insane amount of money off it."

"Who gives a shit about the money?" Joey asks with a clipped tone. "That prick seriously crossed the line, and Reese needs to know about it."

"Joey, please, let it go." My voice is firm and final. I can't have Reese finding out about this; he will surely go homicidal on Bryce's ass. And it really wasn't that big a deal, so there's no reason to involve him. Nothing happened.

"Fine. Whatever." Joey tips his bottle back, taking several loud chugs. He wipes his mouth with the back of his hand when he finishes. "How many bottles are in there, Brooke?"

Brooke opens the cabinet and ducks her head inside. "A lot. It's fully stocked."

"Good," he says.

"Good," Juls echoes.

"Fucking great," Brooke adds.

I take a massive drink, letting the alcohol burn away the memory of those sinister, yellow eyes.

Each and every bottle that the limo came stocked with is emptied, and the mood inside the vehicle elevates with each sip taken. There's dancing, laughing, and Brooke, who cracks us up with her recount of the face shot heard round the world. When we're all fully tipsy, giggling loudly in the back and falling all over each other, the limo comes to a stop.

"Oh, my God. This was so much fun," I choke out, wiping underneath my eyes. I am way past the point of tipsy, as is everyone else in the vehicle.

"Brooke, you are fabulous. Any time you want to come out

with us, feel free," Joey slurs out. "That cum-shot story won me over."

She smiles up at him, pushing her curly brown hair out of her face. "Even though my eye is still slightly blurry, that guy can come at me any time. He was smoking hot." Slapping her hand over her mouth, she spits out a laugh. "Psst! Get it? *Come* at me!"

Hysterical laughter fills the limo as the door opens, prompting Brooke and Juls to climb off the floor they had slid onto sometime during our joy ride.

"If you still want a bed, Brooke, you can share ours," Joey says as he crawls along the seat to the open door. "But I'm sleeping in the middle. Nobody touches my baby."

Brooke's mouth drops open. "Really? We get to snuggle?"

Juls and I both gawk at each other in complete shock. Joey must be out-of-his-mind drunk to have offered that. I smile at Juls and motion for her to let this one play out. The morning after should be quite interesting to say the least.

We all file out, everyone's laughter fading into the air as they step out of the car. I steady myself on my feet, grabbing Joey's arm for stability, and lift my head toward the front door of our house. Ian and Billy are both sitting on the stairs, grinning amusingly in the direction of the four of us. But I don't linger on them. I can't, because Reese's frame is filling the doorway; his very tense frame. As my eyes focus on his face, the hard lines, the tight jaw, and those eyes of his that are heavy with disapproval, I'm quickly reminded of my wardrobe selection for the evening and the reaction I knew I'd get. What were my thoughts earlier? *This is my bachelorette party. I'm supposed to look sinful.*

Dylan Sparks. You asked for it.

"UH OH," I WHISPER, HEARING Juls' and Joey's muffled laughs next to me. My eyes widen as Reese makes his way down the stairs, walking between Ian and Billy who both stand. I step to my left and slide behind my very tall assistant, concealing my inappropriate outfit. Like that will do me any good. One, he's already seen it, and two, it's Reese; nothing stands in his way of me.

Joey steps aside and looks over at me with raised eyebrows. "Are you nuts? He'll chuck me across the street to get to you."

I open my mouth to argue but close it when I realize he's probably right.

"You four look like you've had a nice time. I think Brooke wins for most drunk," Ian says with a teasing tone, crooking his finger and motioning for Juls to come to him. Juls immediately begins walking as Brooke moves past her and practically trips up the stairs, laughing in the process.

Joey leans over and kisses the top of my head. "Good luck, cupcake." He moves away from me and grabs Billy's hand. Billy winks at me over his shoulder before leaning in and kissing Joey.

"Oh, thanks a lot. Way to stick with your fellow woman," I yell out, seeing everyone turn and laugh at me as Reese stops inches away. I can practically feel the irritation boiling off him, radiating in waves directly onto me. I customarily tug the hem of my dress down, knowing full well it won't do me any good now, and then I look at him, all 6 foot 3 inches of him. He's so hot when he's angry that I momentarily consider wearing dresses like this daily, consequences be damned. This look is worth it. I'm certain there is no other man who can command attention the way Reese does, especially when he's pissed. I glance up at him from underneath my lashes, connecting briefly with his eyes before dropping my gaze and letting it take in his casual-yet-ridiculously-sexy polo shirt and khakis. "Hi. You look nice."

Understatement of the century. Reese has probably never looked *nice* a day in his life.

He steps into me, flattening my body against the limo and letting me know that even though he's about to freak the hell out on me for my dress selection, because that's what he does, he can't deny the way I affect him. I let out a soft gasp as he presses his lips to my temple. "What the fuck are you wearing, Dylan?"

"Uh, a dress. You never labeled this one."

"That's because I never fucking saw it," he growls. "Did you really think I'd be okay with you wearing this out tonight? This shit barely covers you."

I wrap my arms around his waist and pull him against me tighter. Harder. Wanting to feel the desire that is betraying his anger right now. It really is the only thing saving me from a Reese-style flip-out. Besides, I'd much rather get fucked in the traditional sense as opposed to verbally. If I can get my hands on an advantage here, I'm taking it.

I tilt my head up, my drunken smile spreading across my face. "I think you're *very* okay with me wearing this right now, handsome. Your massive and very-loved boner is giving you away. And just so you know, I'm not attached to this dress, so feel free to rip it apart." I slide my hand down between us, stroking him through his pants.

He grabs my hand and halts me, pinning it against my body. "No playing for you tonight, love. Not after this stunt." He bends down and lifts me, throwing me over his shoulder while keeping one hand on my ass; no doubt to make sure it remains covered.

"Reese! I'm going to throw up." The ground beneath me begins to spin as he carries me up the stairs and into the house. I bring one hand up and cover my eyes. "I'm serious. Can you not go all caveman on me right now? Drunk Dylan is getting dizzy."

He shifts me in his arms, bringing me down and cradling me against his chest. I immediately stick my face in his neck and inhale, wrapping my arms around him as we begin the climb up the second set of stairs. I feel his lips on my forehead. "Must you always challenge me? You know it makes me crazy."

"Mmm. I love you, too." I press kisses to his neck, feeling the vibration of his growl against my lips. "Do you like my shoes?" I ask, kicking my feet in the air as he pushes the door to our bedroom open. I tilt my head up and see his eyes darken, feeling his intensity hit me like a bullet.

"Very. I want them digging into my back while I fuck the breath out of you."

Holy Hell. Yes. Tonight. Please.

He drops me on my feet at the foot of the bed, keeping his arms wrapped around my back. I drop my head against his chest with a soft thump.

"How much did you have to drink?"

"Not sure. A few bottles, maybe," I reply, keeping my head down. *Definitely a few bottles.* I hear his gruff exhale, prompting me to raise my head. "Relax, Mr. Sassypants. I was only slightly tipsy shaking my ass at the club." I cover my mouth with my hand, muffling my giggle. *Mr. Sassypants. Good one.*

"That gives me no comfort, Dylan."

I drop my hand and wrap it around his waist. "Well, what did you guys do tonight? I'm sure you weren't angels."

Keeping me in his arms, he turns us so the back of my legs hit the bed. "We went out to dinner and then came back here."

I turn my head up to him. "That's it? What kind of a bachelor party is that?"

"I didn't care about having a bachelor party; you know that. Now, stop talking and get on the bed."

Oh, hello, bossy Reese.

I bite my lip to contain my smile, doing as I'm told and

stretching out on my back. "Are you going to fuck me now?"

He leans over me, grabbing the hem of my dress with both hands. "No," he sternly replies as he tugs my dress in separate directions, ripping it up the middle.

"No?"

His hands move higher underneath the material, brushing against my upper thigh. His eyes lock onto mine. "No," he repeats, pulling again and splitting my dress even higher. My garter and panties are revealed to him in the process. His eyes appreciate the sight with an endearing caress while his lips remain in a hard line.

"What do you mean 'no'? You said you wanted me digging into you with my shoes." Bending my knee back, I press the sole of my heeled foot against his crotch and apply the tiniest bit of pressure. Keeping one hand on my dress, his other grabs my ankle and he gives me a warning look. I shoot him one back, my tipsy state giving me the courage I need. "I want to get fucked. By you." In case clarification is needed.

He pushes my foot down and grabs the two halves of my dress, locking eyes with me as he yanks the remaining material apart, exposing me completely. I lay underneath him, practically naked, and I see the struggle in his eyes to stay angry with me. But he manages. "You're not coming tonight, Dylan. Not after going out in public in this shit." He pulls the shredded material out from underneath me and tosses it onto the floor. "And don't even think about trying to handle that situation on your own. If I hear one moan or sexy little whimper out of you, I'll spend the rest of the night withholding your orgasm."

My eyes widen at his threat. *Shit. That sucks. He's crazy-good at that.* I cross my arms over my chest, blocking his undeserved view as he brings my foot in front of him, his fingers working the strap around my ankle. "Whatever. If I don't get off, then you don't get off either. You'll be suffering as much as I will."

He drops my shoe onto the floor and arches his brow at me. "Is that right?"

"Yes," I state with a clipped tone. My other shoe gets tossed over his shoulder, but I don't care where because all my attention is drawn down to his hands as he works his cock free and begins stroking it. I gasp and reach out for it, my mouth watering at the sight. "Oh, my God. Let me do that."

"No." He lets his khakis slide down to mid-thigh as he stares at my body, his hand working his glorious cock. I've never seen Reese jerk off before, and I'm kicking myself for never requesting that he do it in front of me. This is insanely hot, probably one of the hottest things to witness. His upper body is flexed completely, every muscle bulging out at me, screaming for my hands. And then there's his cock.

That. Cock.

So desperately hard and making my pussy ache with a stark need, because it belongs there. He strokes it leisurely, letting this moment last as his breathing becomes irregular. *Sweet Jesus*. I begin to pant right along with him.

I sit up, putting my face at the perfect height. "Fuck my mouth."

He pushes me back down and continues pulling his cock. "No."

"What? Why?"

"Because you get off on that. And I told you, you're not coming tonight."

Goddamn it. Why do I have to enjoy sucking him off so much?

Because it's awesome.

I grunt my irritation, slipping a hand between my legs. He grabs my wrist with his free hand and pins it against my body, angling himself over me. "I told you no," he grates out through clenched teeth, his lips curling back and revealing them to me. "You knew I wouldn't approve of that dress, so why did you wear it?"

My eyes stay glued to the hand around his cock, ignoring everything else around me. I see the veins in his arms jut out as he gives me the biggest tease of my life.

"Dylan."

"Huh?" I croak, reaching up and placing my hand to my chest. It's heaving, forcefully pushing against my palm. He slows his stroking, prompting me to look into his eyes. "I wanted you to rip it."

His eyes widen, sparkling with curiosity.

I swallow the uncomfortable lump that's lodged itself in my throat before explaining myself. "I… I think it's really hot when you get all crazy over what I wear. You like showing me who has control, but I see you struggling with it when you see me in outfits like that. I like knowing I can do that to you. You're not easily unraveled."

He releases my wrist and grips my hip, digging into my skin as he slides me closer to him. He's hovering above me, close enough to touch, but he won't let me. His face relaxes slightly. "Your body belongs to me. When you wear shit like that and I'm not around, other men think they have a shot at what's mine. They don't. And I'm half-tempted to go to that club and kill every motherfucker in there who looked at you."

I place my hand on his chest, lightly applying pressure. "Hey. It was just a stupid dress. Are you going to act like this on Saturday and go on a killing spree at the Whitmore? The bride gets a lot of attention on her big day."

One eyebrow raises. "Are you planning on wearing something like that?" I smile sweetly and shake my head, my eyes dropping to watch him return to his task. "You want to see me lose control?"

"Yes," I answer breathlessly.

His eyes roll closed and he starts stroking faster, gripping tighter, breathing heavier. I can only lie back and watch, completely fascinated and way the hell turned on. "Fuck," he pants, eyes flashing open. "You unravel me every second, love. Every time I look at you." He groans loudly, finding his release and shooting it onto my stomach. His nostrils flare as his eyes slowly reach my face. "My eyes only. Remember that."

I nod, unable to form a verbal response. My mouth is too dry for words at the moment.

He straightens up and lets his pants and boxers fall to the floor, stepping out of them. His shirt is removed next and I watch in complete awe as he walks toward the bathroom, his glorious, bare ass tempting me to give my clit the attention it's screaming for. "Don't even think about it."

His voice cuts into my lustful thoughts and I stop myself from responding with a lie. Because that's exactly what it would be. I was thinking about it; it's hard not to at the moment. He returns with a small towel and proceeds to wipe me clean.

"Reese?"

"Yeah?" He chucks the towel across the room, returning his

eyes to mine. And there it is, that endearing look he seems to reserve just for me. The look that makes my heart swell against my ribs. No tension in his face, no tight lips or creased brow, just him. The man I'm going to marry.

I turn and glance at the alarm clock. I was originally going to threaten to withhold his orgasm someday, but that look of his totally gets to me. Like it always does. "Six days."

His eyes flick quickly to his left, verifying what I've just told him. A light smile touches his lips as he climbs onto the bed, sitting with his back against the headboard. He taps his lap, eyes soft and no longer laced with anything besides affection. I can't resist that look. And I want my spot. Crawling into his lap, I lay my cheek against his chest and nuzzle away. His arms wrap around me, pulling me closer before he bunches the covers around my waist. My favorite smell in the world fills me, intoxicating me further, and I feel my body relax into his as my sexual frustrations slip away.

"So, Juls said this account with Bryce was worth a lot of money. Is that why you're doing it?"

I feel his fingers play with the ends of my hair as it falls down my back. "No. I'd never work with somebody who made you uncomfortable because I want to get paid. It's just really important, that's all."

I lean back, not feeling satisfied with his cryptic answer. "Why?"

We stare at each other for several seconds before he speaks. "Do you trust me?" My back stiffens and he notices, prompting him to grab my hips and pull me closer. "Do you?"

"Yes."

"Then trust me when I say it's important. I can't talk to you about it; not yet, anyway. But I will. I promise I'll tell you everything when it's all said and done."

I don't understand how any part of Reese's job can be secretive; he's an accountant, not in the mob. But I do trust him. Completely. So I'm not going to question this. "Promise me something?"

He smiles cunningly. "Depends on what it is."

I grab his face and lean in, brushing my lips against his. "Don't do anything that would keep you from marrying me. I will be a very angry bride if you spend our wedding day in jail."

He laughs against my mouth. "Nothing could keep me away, love."

I drop my head back down and close my eyes.

Nothing could keep me away either.

I'M NEVER DRINKING AGAIN.

My head is pounding, my stomach is rolling, and my face is plastered to the cold tile of the bathroom floor.

This is not a good look for me. Nor is it one I wear often.

I've puked most of the night, the wave of nausea hitting me hard sometime after I passed out on Reese's chest and sending me barreling head-first toward the toilet. But miraculously, I'm a quiet puker, so my well-rested fiancé was kept blissfully unaware about my nightly vomit-fest. That is, until he caught me praying to the porcelain God this morning, which is where I've spent most of my time while he packs for both of us. I'm dressed now, so at least progress has been made.

I feel his hand on my hip as I stay in my permanent fetal position. "Here, love. I brought you some water and two Advils. Have you thrown up recently?"

I shake my head, keeping my eyes closed.

"Do you think you're going to throw up any more?"

I shake my head again. I haven't thrown up in a least an hour, but I also haven't tried moving either. I hear the soft clink of a glass and then feel his arms wrap me up as he lifts me off the floor, effortlessly as usual. I lay my head against his chest until he shifts me in his arms. I feel the bathroom countertop underneath my thighs as he sets me down on it and settles between my legs.

He picks up the glass of water and holds it out to me with the two pills in his other hand. "Take these. It'll help. And we'll get you some ginger ale on the plane for your stomach."

I swallow the pills and drink close to half the glass before setting it down next to me. My head drops forward and my shoulders slouch. "I hate having you see me like this."

He laughs quietly. "Like what?

I tuck my hair behind my ear and groan, keeping my eyes on my legs. "Like a train wreck. This isn't like me; I can usually hold my alcohol. I don't think I've gotten sick since the singing-telegram tequila incident." My stomach churns at the word tequila. That hateful bitch and I can't be in the same room together. I bring my fingers up to my face and begin massaging my temples. "What time do we have to leave?"

"Soon. The cabs will be here in thirty minutes." His hands run down my bare arms, gently applying pressure. "Can I do anything else? Do you need anything?"

I shake my head before dropping it against his chest. "Just you."

He presses a kiss to my hair. "You got me."

The sound of our bedroom door opening alerts us both, and Ian emerges in the bathroom doorway. He surveys my pathetic condition as he leans against the doorframe, crossing his arms and his ankles. "What the hell did you and Juls drink last night? She's been throwing up since 3:00 a.m."

I shrug, barely moving my shoulders an inch. All my strength seems to have left me. "Just champagne. We had some wine at the spa, but not enough to make us sick." I grab onto Reese and slide off the countertop. "Let me go see her."

I pull my hair into a messy bun as I walk through our bedroom and into the hallway. My head still feels like it's in a vise, but my stomach seems to have settled. I see the suitcases lined up outside the rooms, ready to be taken out. Four suitcases. Reese, Ian, Juls, me. *Where are the others?* Joey's door is still closed and I panic that he and Billy might oversleep and miss the flight. Without knocking, or thinking, I open his door and barge in like I own the damn place.

Three heads pop up in the bed. Three very startled heads. And one of those heads becomes very alarmed being sandwiched between the other two.

"Brooke! What in the fuck are you doing in here?" Joey grabs the covers and pulls them up into his lap, covering him and Billy.

"Relax, baby. You invited her," Billy says, before lying back on his pillow.

Joey looms over him. "I sure as shit didn't. Did you?"

Billy grimaces before rolling over, pulling the covers over his head.

Brooke rubs her eyes and smiles. "You invited me, Joey. You also called me fabulous, I think, and said I'm welcome to join you guys anytime you go out." She slips out of bed, revealing herself in a man's T-shirt that barely covers the line of her panties. She flattens her palm against her forehead, frowning. "Oh, hello, hangover."

"I would never invite you to share a bed with us. And get the hell out of my T-shirt. That's one of my favorites."

"Calm down, JoJo. You most certainly did ask her to share your bed. Drunk Joey is a major fan of Brooke," Juls' voice comes from behind me. I spin around a bit too quickly and have to steady myself with a hand on the wall. And then I look at her. She's dressed in skinny jeans and a blouse, her hair pulled back into a bun and her makeup looking fresh. Even if she has been throwing up since 3:00 a.m., she doesn't look it. Julianna Thomas has never looked anything less than chic a day in her life. She grins at me. "Sweets, can I talk to you?"

I nod, turning back around. "Cabs will be here in thirty minutes. You guys better get moving." All three bodies scramble out and around the bed while Joey quietly grunts his disapproval of the situation. I follow Juls out of the bedroom, down the hallway, and down the flight of stairs.

"What's up? And why don't you look like shit? I know I do," I say as we make our way into the kitchen. She holds a cup of coffee out to me, and I take it with an appreciating moan.

"I think I'm pregnant."

I inhale the biggest, hottest mouthful of coffee known to

mankind when I hear her statement. The scalding beverage slides down my throat, searing my tissue as I cough it up and hang my head over the sink. Mouth open, I let it run out down my chin and into the deep basin. "Owwwahhhhhh."

Her hand touches my shoulder. "Oh, shit. Are you okay? Do you want some water or milk or something?"

I wave her off, wiping my chin with the nearby hand towel. "No. But maybe next time wait 'til after I've put my coffee down before you say something like that." I let my mouth hang open, inhaling the cool air that fills the kitchen while my mind processes her words to me. I feel my slightly-sore lips curl up. "You think you're pregnant? I didn't even know you guys were talking about that yet."

She hesitates slightly before nodding with quick drops of her head. "Well, Ian wants babies yesterday. I always thought I'd wait until I was in my thirties, but it's all he talks about. And the more he talks about it, the more I think about it." She plays with the buttons on her blouse, looking over my shoulder in the direction of the stairs. I turn and see Ian and Reese walking down the stairs with our suitcases, both of them smiling in our direction before they walk out the door. I return my attention back to Juls as she begins twisting the diamond stud in her ear. "My doctor told me it can sometimes take a while for birth control to get out of your system completely. Years for some women. So I stopped taking the pill a few months ago and didn't tell Ian."

I step closer to her, the excitement building in my gut. "Are you late?"

"My periods are irregular. I really haven't had one since I stopped taking the pill. But, my boobs are really sensitive and there's no way the amount of champagne I drank last night could've made me that sick. I can usually handle way more than that and not have my head stuck in a toilet."

My thoughts begin to scramble as I lean back against the counter and stare at the floor. I can usually handle way more than that, too. I was pretty tipsy last night, but I wasn't *that* drunk. Not to the point of it warranting the dry-heaving session I endured for several hours; at least I don't think. And my periods are so damn sporadic I never know when to expect them. But I got my shot a few months ago, so

I should be covered. There's no way I could be…

"Sweets, are you okay?"

Juls' voice cuts into my thoughts. I twist the towel around my one hand, making it look like something a boxer might wrap his punching hand with. "Huh? Uh, yeah. I just—" I look up at her, "—are you going to tell Ian?"

She shakes her head. "Not until I take a test first. You know how he is. He'll tell everyone on that damn plane he's going to be a daddy if I say anything to him now. And I'd hate to get his hopes up."

I chuckle. Ian would do something like that. That man is crazy when it comes to Juls. I smile at the idea of my very best friend driving a minivan full of little black-haired Ian lookalikes. She'll have no trouble balancing her wedding planner business with soccer practice and PTA meetings. She's amazing at everything and makes it look effortless. And then another image fills my mind: me, working in the kitchen of my bakery while tiny little feet run circles around my worktop. I can see the wild mess of brown hair just above the counter height and little grubby hands reaching for a taste of whatever it is I'm making. And that image makes my eyes suddenly misty.

Juls grabs my hand, squeezing it gently. "Hey, what's wrong? No crying during your wedding week."

I reach up and wipe underneath my eyes, turning my body toward her. "I want to take a test, too. Do you think we could do it together?"

Her eyes go wild with excitement and then instantly water over. She wraps her arms around me. "Oh, my God. Yes, of course. Have you talked to Reese about having kids yet?"

"No, not yet. But it's weird. I got sick too."

She leans away from me and frowns. "That is weird. Although, it could just be nerves. You have been stressed out to the max lately." Her eyes glance over my shoulder and she immediately shakes off any trace of baby emotion on her face. "We'll keep this between us until we know for sure," she whispers.

I nod, spinning around and seeing Brooke pull her luggage down the stairs, followed by Joey and Billy who are arguing. Once they reach the bottom, Joey hands Billy his suitcase and makes his way over toward us with distinct annoyance. Billy and Brooke walk outside, leaving the three of us alone in the kitchen.

"Any chance your sister can ride with the luggage? I'm in no mood for another plane ride with her."

Juls steps into him and pokes her finger at his chest. "Buck up, JoJo. And drop the attitude. Poor Billy doesn't deserve to put up with your moodiness because you're on your man period." She stalks away from him like she's just delivered an epic blow, swaying her hips and letting her heels click loudly on the marble floor.

Joey huffs dramatically. "My 'man period'? What the hell has gotten into her?"

Hormones.

Reese walks through the front door, grabbing the last suitcase Brooke apparently left for whomever to pick up for her. My eyes narrow in on his perfectly-messed-up hair, and I can't hide the smile that will most likely blind anyone who looks at it.

Mini-Reese's running around my shop. How crazy cute would that be?

He raises his head and locks eyes with me, shifting the suitcase into his left hand and holding his right out for me to take. "Cabs are here. Are you two ready?"

I'm ready. To go back to Chicago. To take a test and find out if I'm simply losing my edge when it comes to my drinking ability. To be one day closer to marrying the only man I've ever pictured having tiny lookalikes with.

I could be pregnant right now. There could be a tiny peanut inside me, pissed the hell off that I chose to drag him to my bachelorette party. I flatten my hand against my stomach as I move toward Reese, holding out my other hand for him to take.

His brow furrows. "Is your stomach still upset? I can ask the driver to stop on the way to the airport to get you something for it."

I shake my head, patting my stomach before dropping my hand down. "No. I'm okay."

You hear that, peanut? If you're in there, I'm definitely okay.

"YOU WANT THE WINDOW SEAT, love? Is doesn't matter to me."

I glance up at Reese, bringing my attention away from my belly. He secures my carry-on in the overhead compartment above our row before turning his eyes to me. I smile and press a kiss to his stubbly jaw before I move between the seats, feeling his hand smack my ass. "Thanks, handsome. Juls hogged it on the way here," I say with a teasing tone, loud enough for her to hear.

She scrunches her face at me in the row ahead of us.

"I'm going to use the bathroom before we take off," Brooke says, getting out of her seat in front of me and proceeding toward the back of the plane.

Joey stands from his seat across the aisle from us and claims Brooke's, kneeling so he's facing me. He motions for me to come closer, grabbing Juls' attention in the process. "So, what happened with the dress? Did it survive the night?" he asks in a hushed whisper.

I glance over my shoulder at Reese, making sure he's unaware of Joey's questioning which apparently can't wait 'til we land in Chicago. His head is tilted down as he glances at his phone, completely focused. I scoot to the edge of my seat. "No, it was destroyed in a very Reese-like manner."

"Hot." Joey wiggles his brows playfully at me. "I bet you got laid hard, didn't you?"

Juls slaps his arm. "Shouldn't we be asking you that, Mister Threesome?"

"That did not happen. I'm gayer than gay, and so is Billy. We just snuggled."

"Oh?" I ask, teasingly. "You snuggled with Brooke?"

He looks from me to Juls and then back to me. "Yes. In my drunken stupor, I snuggled with a girl. Now, if you both don't mind, I'd like to hear about someone getting laid last night because I sure as shit didn't."

Juls rolls her eyes as I scoot closer to both of them. Frowning, I shake my head before I reply. "No one got laid in my bedroom. I wasn't allowed any relief and was forced to watch Reese jerk himself off. It was hot and frustrating. And hot. Did I mention hot?"

Joey and Juls' both stare at me, mouths gaped open. Ian turns his head and glares over the seat. "What did you just say?"

Oh, shit.

I sit back quickly, glaring at Juls and Joey with panicked eyes. Juls turns and plants her butt down in her seat while Joey stands and excuses himself across the aisle.

Reese places his hand on my leg. "Everything okay?"

"Hmm mmm." I slide my hand underneath his, interlocking our fingers. "Do you want to have kids?" The words cascade out of my mouth like the scalding coffee did earlier, surprising us both in the process. *Shit, Dylan. Way to just blurt it out.* I drop my head against the seat, feeling my hand tighten against his and my breathing become slightly restricted.

He tilts his head, leaning closer to me. "With you? I've thought about it."

"Yeah?"

He nods, his lip twitching in the corner. "Yeah." Before I can pry anymore, he brings his free hand across his body and places it flat against my stomach. I stop breathing all together as I watch his eyes go to my belly. "I want to mark this, too." I feel his palm slide across my shirt, applying the tiniest amount of pressure. He's studying his hand on my belly like he always studies me, with pronounced focus. Like nothing could pull him out of his moment.

"Shit. He couldn't stay here," Juls grumbles in front of us.

My eyes lift and land on Bryce as he walks down the middle aisle. I immediately tense and Reese feels it. The hand on my belly is removed, and he brings our conjoined hands to his lap. I take my eyes off Bryce and watch as Reese sits back in his seat, his chest rising with a deep inhale. He's radiating with an unspoken threat, and I know Bryce feels it. I can see the apprehension in his eyes as he approaches our row. He tries to hide it, but it's there. And it should be; Reese could easily snap this asshole in half.

He doesn't say anything to us, but I see the shift in his expression, the moment he grows balls as he walks up to our row. All uneasiness fades and I immediately recognize the Bryce who came into my shop that day. The one who stared at me as I kissed Reese goodbye outside the conference meeting. The one who bought me the drink last night.

The fucker who thinks he actually has a shot.

"I'm sorry," Reese says to me as Bryce moves past our row to the back of the plane. I look at him with confusion and he shakes his head with a heavy sigh. "I didn't know he was going to be on this flight. I thought he was staying here for a few more days."

"It's okay."

"It's not. I don't like him around you."

I place my free hand on his forearm. "Reese, it's fine. Really." My voice is full of conviction, and I see it working on his suddenly-geared-up state. He brings my hand to his lips and kisses it just as Brooke walks past him and stops in front of Ian.

"That guy is a total douche-canoe." Her eyes meet mine as I hold my breath.

Don't say it. Please, God, don't say it.

"Seriously, Dylan. Good on you for throwing your drink in his face last night."

Fuuccckkkkkk.

"Sit your ass down," Juls growls, reaching out for her sister and yanking her into the row. Brooke yelps as she tumbles over Ian, claiming her seat next to Juls.

I clamp my eyes shut, preparing myself for what could quite possibly ground this airplane. I don't need to look at Reese to know that he is fuming right now. I can sense it in the air.

"Dylan, what the fuck is she talking about?"

Maybe if I jump out the emergency exit, he won't follow me. That might be my best option here. Or I could punch myself in the face and pray for unconsciousness.

"Dylan, answer me."

His voice is so commanding, my body submits without a fight. I'm immediately turned toward him and grabbing both his hands, pulling them into my lap. "He was at the club we went to last night. We didn't know he was there until he bought me a drink and when that happened, I threw it in his face. He ran his mouth a little and then we left. That's all that happened, I swear."

His chest rises several times, heaving with fury. "He saw you in that dress." He pulls his hands out of mine and settles back into his seat. He's rigid, every muscle flexed as he struggles to keep himself seated. I know he wants to run to the back of the plane. I know he wants to beat the shit out of Bryce. And I know, by the way he isn't touching me, that I'm in deep shit for keeping this information from him.

Goddamn that dress. It's really screwing me left and right.

THE TWO-AND-A-HALF-HOUR PLANE RIDE HOME was the longest of my life. I'm not sure why I complained about the one to New Orleans. I would much rather listen to Joey and Brooke banter endlessly as opposed to complete silence from my fiancé, the man who is never quiet with me. Juls kept giving me sympathetic looks over the seat, while Brooke kept mouthing 'I'm sorry' throughout the eerily quiet flight. But even though he was pissed, even though he was angrier than he's ever been with me, he was still my Reese.

He got me a ginger ale from the flight attendant without me asking for it. He carried my luggage with his as we walked from the terminal to his Range Rover. And he opened every door for me. I knew he wasn't purposely trying to make me feel even worse about keeping information from him, but that's definitely what ended up happening.

I hear the TV turn on in the living room as I plop myself down on the edge of his bed. I feel drained, mentally and emotionally. We've been home for nineteen minutes, not that I'm counting, and he still hasn't said one word to me.

I hate this.

Reese's words mean more to me than a lot of things. It was what I missed the most when we were apart for eighty-five days, and I could give him space right now and let him talk to me when he's ready, but I don't want space from Reese. I never will. If he doesn't want to talk to me in the traditional sense, maybe I can coax a few written words from him. I grab my phone out of the suitcase I haven't bothered unpacking yet and sit back down on the bed, folding my legs underneath me.

Me: Do you know the exact moment I knew I loved you?

I press send and hear the alert on his phone go off in the distance. I can't see if he's reading it and typing a response, reading it and deciding I don't deserve a response, or ignoring me completely. I go with option two. I'm not sure I deserve much of anything right now.

Me: It was on your birthday. Do you remember what we did?

I'm typing the answer for him when my phone beeps.

Reese: How could I forget? I never thought I'd get you in my bed.

I blink and send the tears down my cheeks, sniffing loudly. Loud enough to possibly alert him of my crying. But it's hard not to cry when he's given me his words. I've only been deprived of them for a little over three hours, but it felt like longer. Much longer. As I type my response, movement in the doorway catches my attention.

I'm in his arms before I can speak, before I can tell him I'm sorry, before I can wipe the tears from my face. I'm so drawn to him that even if I wanted to remain on the bed, there's not a chance in Hell I could. Not when I've fucked up and I need him to *feel* how sorry I am. My body trembles as he lifts me off the ground and holds me against him. He moans into my hair, and I cling to him like I'm desperate. Like I've been deprived for years of his contact. Like it could be taken away from me at any minute. And that's exactly how he holds me.

It kills me.

I cry harder, grip him tighter, bury my face so far into his neck it becomes borderline painful. I don't register that he's carried me throughout his condo until he crouches down and sits on the couch with me in his arms. I scoot closer until I'm practically in his skin. Until it's hard to determine where he ends and I begin. He keeps one arm on my legs while the other stays wrapped around my upper body.

I brush my lips against his neck, fisting his shirt in my hands. "I'm so sorry, Reese. Please talk to me. Yell, scream, I don't care. Just give me something. I can't stand not hearing your voice."

His breath warms the side of my face as he tilts his head down. "I wanted you on that trip with me because I can't stand being away from you. I'm selfish when it comes to you, Dylan. I always will be. I knew there was a possibility you would have to see Bryce. I knew he made you uncomfortable, but I took that risk and asked you to come with me anyway." He shifts me in his lap so we're face to face. "And then when I saw how you reacted to him on the plane, it killed me. I put you there. I made you feel that way. He saw you in that dress because of me. He stared at you, thinking the same thing I thought when I saw you in it. Because. Of. Me. I didn't put you first, and I should have. I don't deserve to know when you fell in love with me. I don't deserve to hear *your* voice."

My heart thunders in my chest as I absorb his words, words I wasn't expecting to hear. I had prepared myself for a Reese-style flip-out, but not this. How can this man think I wouldn't follow him anywhere? That any of this is his fault?

"No." I grab his face with my hands, brushing along the stubble on his jaw. "I wanted to be with you just as much as you wanted me there. Even if you wouldn't have asked me to go, I would've snuck in your suitcase or booked a flight without you knowing. I can't stand to be away from you either, so don't you dare act like this addiction is one-sided. I'm just as obsessed and selfish as you are."

Did I mention how much I hate to lose at anything? The competitive streak in me is fully engaged right now and if Reese thinks he's got me beat on this, he's dead wrong. In a battle of who loves who more, I'm taking the prize on this one.

I turn my body completely, straddling his lap and dropping my hands to his shoulders. "Now you listen to me, Carroll. I'm the one who should be feeling like shit here. Me. Not you. I'm the one who's constantly challenging you with outfits and my incessant need to push your buttons. And I'll always be like that. You're marrying someone who will most likely drive you crazy for the rest of your life. Why?"

Why? Shit. Why the hell did I ask that? Good job, Dylan. Let's make the man you love question the biggest decision of his life.

He opens his mouth to speak but I quickly slap my hand over it. "Ignore that. We're getting off topic." I feel his laugh against my hand before dropping it to my lap, allowing the slightest smile to touch my lips. "I should've told you I saw Bryce at the club last night. I didn't because I was afraid of what you would do to him. And I also didn't want anything to mess up that account."

"What happened?" The sorrowed look he had moments ago has completely vanished, replaced with a look I'd never want to go up against. He seems to grow in size as he waits for me to recount my evening; that, or I'm suddenly cowering down. Could be a bit of both. "Dylan, do I need to call Brooke and ask her to tell me?"

I narrow my eyes at him and pout. "No. You don't." I exhale loudly, grabbing his hands and moving them to my breasts.

He frowns, looking at his hands. "What are you doing?"

"I'm using what I have to my advantage. You need to stay calm, and keeping your hands on my body is like a mild sedative for you."

"Not for my cock," he grunts. "And don't try to distract me. I want to know right now what happened last night. Every fucking detail."

I slide my hands to his wrists, lightly holding him. He doesn't make an attempt to move, so I decide to continue. "None of us knew Bryce was at that club until we went to the bar. The bartender gave me a drink and told me Bryce had bought it for me, which really pissed me the hell off. I mean, really. The nerve of that asshole. Like I would ever accept a drink from him."

"Dylan… focus."

"Right. Sorry." I clear my throat and think back to last night. "I went over to him with it and he opened his big stupid mouth, saying it's been too long since he's seen me and my dress belonged on his floor." Reese clenches his teeth and tries to drop his hands but I keep them on me. "I threw my drink in his face and he acted like he liked it, which pissed me off even more. Then he said something about me having a temper and asked if I fuck you angry. Joey tried to step in but I told him to drop it. Juls cussed him out. Brooke did, too. We left right after that."

Reese closes his eyes, keeping his hands on my breasts. I see his nostrils flare, and the veins in his neck become taut like tight coils. He takes five deep, calming breaths and I move my hands to his chest, flattening them out. His heart hammers against my palm as he slides his hands down and grips my hips tightly. "You should've slapped the shit out of him for saying that to you."

I lift my gaze off his chest and see his eyes beaming at me. "Your eyes are so green right now." I hold his face, studying the brightness. I've never seen anything like the color of Reese's eyes. Close to emerald, but not quite. "And you're right, I should've. But I couldn't because he's a little bitch who would either like it or call the cops on me. Bryce isn't a man, and he'd never take a slap like one."

"He won't be taking a slap from me."

And this is what I was worried about. "Reese, you can't. What about the account? And if you hit him, he could have you arrested."

He grabs my wrists, pulling my hands off his face. "I'm going to hurt him, Dylan. It's going to happen." He pauses, blinking heavily. "This shit better work," he all but whispers, dropping his gaze away from mine.

"Please," I beg through a strained voice, ignoring his last comment and only focusing on his threat. "Please, don't do anything. Beating the shit out of him isn't worth losing your job or going to jail over." My lip begins to tremble and the tears come again. "Please, Reese. I can't have anything happen to you." *We can't have anything happen to you.* I drop my head to his shoulder, feeling his arms wrap around me as I place a protective hand over my belly. Something *would* happen. This gut feeling I have isn't going away.

"Shhh. I don't want you to worry about this, okay? Dylan, I'm a smart guy. You need to trust me. I'm not going to do anything that's going to get me put in jail. Hey, look at me."

I keep my head down. "No. I'm ugly-crying right now."

He laughs into my hair before forcing my head back, tucking my hair behind my ears. "You don't ugly anything." I see his eyes drop down to my stomach. My hand is still there and he places his on top of mine and studies it for several seconds. I hear my breathing quicken as his brows furrow. And then he looks back up at me, lips partying slightly, and I see it. The moment it hits him. His free hand cups my face. "Love, are you…"

I place a finger to his lips and smile. "I don't know. I was thinking maybe I could be. It would explain why I got so sick this morning. Juls put the thought into my head. She thinks she's pregnant, too." He shifts me off his lap and gets to his feet, stepping into his shoes. "What are you doing?"

"I'm going to the store to get you a test. You're taking one tonight."

I sit on my knees and stare up at him. "What? No, I'm not. I'm taking one with Juls. We made a pact."

He glares at me. "Fuck that. I'm not going to be able to fall asleep tonight unless I know." He places a kiss to the top of my head. "I'll be back." He goes to walk toward the door but halts mid-step. Turning around, he bends down and places a kiss to my belly.

I giggle. "Reese. You could just be kissing the pretzels I ate on the plane."

He hits me with a wink before grabbing his keys off the counter and walking out the door.

"HOW MANY DID YOU BUY?" I hover my finger over the boxes Reese has just dumped onto the bed, counting them out. All my Bryce anxieties vanished the moment Reese assured me he'd be smart about things. And now the only thing I'm concerned with is how much money my fiancé just spent at the local drug store. "Fifteen, sixteen, seventeen? You bought seventeen pregnancy tests? These things are like twenty bucks a piece."

He looks over at me curiously. "How the hell do you know?"

I wave him off. "Please. Every girl knows how much these

things cost." I pick up the one that has a smiling mother-to-be on the front. "Well, I guess this one looks good." I take the box with me out of his bedroom and step into the hallway bath. Turning around, I see him at the door. "Um, what are you doing?"

He shakes his head, seemingly in a trance. "I don't know. Should I come in with you?"

I scrunch up my face. "You want to watch me pee?"

"No, I guess not."

I lean into him and kiss his cheek. "Relax. I'll be out in a second."

Closing the door behind me, I begin to open the box and hear a faint whooshing sound. I place my ear to the door. "Reese?"

"Yeah?" he answers immediately.

"Are you sitting outside the door?" I hear movement and smile, followed by a faint "no" in the distance a few seconds later. I pull out the instructions and read them over quickly, trying to calm the anxiousness building rapidly within me.

He's pacing in front of the bed, hands raking through his hair and down his face in a continual pattern. He looks up just as I step into the room. "Well?"

"Three minutes."

He sighs heavily, gripping the back of his neck with one hand. I sit on the edge of the bed and watch him burn a hole into the carpet. Back and forth, each step more purposeful than the last. His hair is a right mess and he's chewing nervously on his bottom lip. I see his eyes routinely go to the clock on the nightstand. I'm not even taking note of the time. I know he'll let me know when the three minutes are up. He glances once more at the clock and stops, turning toward me.

"Ready?" I ask, holding my hand out to him. He hesitates before forcing a nod and grabbing my hand. I stop at the doorway to the bathroom and look up into his glazed-over eyes. I've never seen Reese nervous before but right now, he's definitely nervous. I'm trying to keep my apprehension hidden, but it's there. "Can you check? I'd rather you tell me."

He drops all hint of uneasiness and steps into the bathroom, placing one hand on either side of the test and hovering over it. He leans in closer, studying it before grabbing the instructions I left out on the counter. I watch him for what feels like hours, his eyes going from the test to the instructions and back again. I see his shoulders sag, and my stomach drops. He places the test down and walks over to me, grabbing both my hands.

He shakes his head. "It's negative. Two lines mean you're pregnant, right?"

I nod, swallowing the huge lump that formed at hearing the results.

"There's only one line." I drop my head against his chest, and he immediately picks me up and carries me down the hallway. "I'm sorry, love. Are you sad?"

I nod as he places me down on the bed. He settles on top of me as I lay back on the pillow. "I really thought I was pregnant, but I guess I'm just losing my edge when it comes to drinking. How depressing is that?" I look up at him and run my fingers through his hair, taming the wild mess. "Are *you* sad?"

He shrugs once, his finger tracing my jaw. "A little. But I think I'd be really fucking worried if you were pregnant and went out drinking like that last night. Did you stop taking your birth control?"

I shake my head and bring my hands down to his shoulders. "I got my last shot almost three months ago. If you wanted to start trying now, I just wouldn't get it again."

He smiles, dropping his head and kissing my lips. His tongue trails along my bottom one before he nips it. I whimper and he moans softly. "I want to start trying. Right now." He sits back between my legs and removes his shirt. "How effective is that shot?"

I furrow my brows, confused by his questioning. "Umm, like 98% I think. Why?" He sits me up and pulls at the hem of my tank top, his boastful smile growing. "Oh, you think your super sperm can get through my defenses, huh? Is that it?"

He tosses my shirt and crawls on top of me, pressing his lips to my stomach. "Nothing stands in my way, love. Modern medicine included." His fingers work at my jeans, unbuttoning and unzipping them. "And I'm always up for a challenge. Fuck that 98%."

I giggle as he slides my jeans and panties off. "Reese?"

"Yeah?" He keeps his head down as he unbuttons his shorts.

When I don't answer immediately, he lifts his gaze to me and his smile fades.

I bite the inside of my cheek, straining to keep the serious face I have on. "You know we can't have sex when I'm pregnant, right?"

Oh, I'm devious.

He freezes after dropping his shorts and boxers. "I can't fuck you for nine months? Are you serious?"

"Yeah. It's not good for the baby. You could poke it and stuff."

He strokes his jaw, dropping his gaze to the floor. "Why haven't I heard about this?" he asks himself. He drops his hand, slapping his thigh and lifts his head. "Well, can we do other stuff during that time? There's no way in hell I'm going to be able to keep my hands off you for that long. Not happening. We'd have to live separately."

My body begins to shake with my silent laughter as I cover my face with my hands. I feel the bed dip and slide my hands down, seeing his curious expression above me. I smile wide and continue laughing. "I'm sorry. That was too easy. You should've seen your face."

He looms over top of me, dark and dangerous, and my laughter quickly fades out. "Oh, you're going to pay for that one, Sparks."

I reach up and grab his face, bringing his lips to mine. "Bring it on, Carroll."

He totally brings it.

REESE WASN'T KIDDING WHEN HE said he was up for a challenge. I'm pretty sure some orgasm-giving record was broken last night by him. Every time I came, it seemed to drive his need to do it again and again. He was relentless, fucking me until he didn't have anything left to give me. Literally. I'm fairly certain the man is out of viable baby-makers today. And he didn't need time to re-charge between sessions, either. While I was panting on the bed, the couch, and in the shower, trying to catch my breath and needing a moment to regroup, he was bouncing on his feet like a boxer, amped and ready for the next round. I've never seen him so geared-up for sex before, so I gotta give it to the man. When he sets his mind on something, he definitely goes for it.

Hard.

My vagina is screaming for an ice pack as I make my way down Fayette Street and toward the bakery to meet Joey for our daily run. Running always helps me keep my sanity, and I'm going to need it with the week I have prepared. Not only is my wedding in five days, but Brooke is also starting today, and besides that, I'm feeling bloated and terrified of the possibility of not squeezing into my lace masterpiece of a dress tonight at my final fitting. I'm not even sure alterations can be made this close to the big day. And it has to fit. I'm wearing that dress. It's *the* dress. The one Juls made me try on all those months ago when we were shopping for her wedding gown. The one I desperately tried to not picture myself walking down the aisle toward Reese in. The one I was always meant to wear. So my injured vagina can hate me all she wants, but I'm pushing myself during this run.

After parking Sam behind Joey's Civic, I round the corner and see my dear assistant bouncing around on his feet in front of the bakery. He turns his head, smiling when he sees me, and flattens his palm against the glass window as he stretches his hamstrings.

"Morning, cupcake. You look freshly-fucked."

I wince at his sentiment, mimicking his position and grabbing my ankle behind my back. "That's an understatement. I think Reese broke my vaj."

He switches legs, raising an eyebrow. "I just pictured the weirdest image." He seems to picture it again, blinking several times as he stares off past me. I laugh, prompting him to bring his focus back to me as he bends at the waist and reaches for his toes.

"So, I'm going to assume he isn't still pissed at you for keeping the whole Bryce incident from him?"

I grab my other ankle, stretching out my sore muscle. My vagina isn't the only thing recovering from my marathon sex.

"Actually, he was more mad at himself than anything. He hates that he put me in that position in the first place, which is ridiculous. Like there isn't a possibility of me running into that massive dickhead here. I'm actually surprised he hasn't come into the shop since the last time."

Joey straightens quickly, averting his gaze toward the busy street. I notice his shifty behavior and drop my leg, stepping sideways and forcing him to look at me.

"Joey, Bryce hasn't set foot in my shop since his initial creepy visit, right?"

He drops his head from side to side, stretching out his neck. "He may have stopped in a few times while you were in the back or on a delivery. I dealt with it."

Oh, that piece of shit. "What? Why didn't you tell me?"

He motions with his head for us to start running, setting the pace as we make our way down the sidewalk. "Because I dealt with it. The last time was weeks ago, and I told him to stay the hell away from you. He hasn't been back since."

I jump over the jagged part of the sidewalk I'm sure to trip over one of these days. "I want to know if he comes in again, Joey. I'm not putting up with this." That jerk has another thing coming if he thinks I'm okay with him coming into my shop. I don't care if it's for treats or not. He can get his baked goods elsewhere. He probably wouldn't even eat my decadent creations anyway. He'd probably just use them to taunt children or something; lure them into his creepy van with cookies and non-existent puppies.

I'm not sure when Bryce became a pedophile in my mind, but right now, that's how I'm picturing him.

Joey huffs loudly as we make our way up the hill. "Can you get a restraining order on somebody for just being a creeper? My cousin tried to get one a few years ago on this guy who kept asking her out but the cops said because he hadn't threatened her in any way, she couldn't get one."

I shake my head and push myself harder, picking up speed. "I don't know. Slapping that asshead with a restraining order isn't exactly the kind of violence I have in mind. I was thinking more along the lines of shoving his dumb ass into oncoming traffic."

"Preach," Joey says through a laugh. He turns around, jogging backwards as I slow down a bit. "Let's talk about something else. You're getting all worked up, and this week needs to be relaxing for you." He spins back around and blows out a loud breath. "What time is the fitting tonight?"

I smile over at him, letting go of the anger causing me to clench my teeth. "6:30 p.m. Are you coming?"

"Of course. The Man of Honor wouldn't miss it for anything."

We both chuckle at the title I gave Joey when I asked him to be in my wedding six months ago. I couldn't pick between him and Juls for the highly-coveted Maid of Honor spot. They are both so special to me, so I decided to make Juls my Matron, since she's married, and Joey my Man. It works out perfectly, and Joey couldn't be happier about it. He even tossed around the idea of getting it sequined on the back of his tux for the big day. I wouldn't expect anything less.

"I can't wait to see you in that dress. You're going to look fabulous."

I take off running, hearing him yelp behind me. He catches up and gives me a flustered look. "If I'm going to look fabulous, I need to burn off the booze we drank this weekend." I nudge against him and he laughs. "Come on. I'll race ya around the block."

AFTER MY FIVE-MILE RUN, WHICH leaves my legs feeling like over-cooked noodles, I dash upstairs and hop into my shower. Another reason why I love keeping the loft above my bakery is for this very reason; I don't have to go back to the condo to get ready for my day after my daily runs. The space still looks the same, seeing as the only thing I moved out of here was half my wardrobe. I actually wouldn't mind it if Reese agreed to just move in here after the wedding. I know it's a small space, but I don't need much. Of course, if we are to have kids, I'm not sure a one-bedroom loft will cut it. Especially if we have a lot of kids, which is what I'm leaning toward. I want a bakery filled with mini-Reeses'. Tons of green-eyed, messy-haired cuties who can taste test my creations all day. And if last night was any inclination as to how he feels about the subject, I'm thinking he won't be disagreeing to that idea.

I hear my cell phone ring as I wrap a towel around my chest, prompting me to dart out of the bathroom and grab it off my bed before I miss the call. I don't even register the name on my screen before I answer.

"Hello?"

"Hello, sweetheart. And how is my bride-to-be?"

My mom's voice has me falling backwards onto the bed with an exhaustive grunt. *Damn it to Hell.* I should've looked at the name on the screen, or let this call go to voicemail entirely. There's only one reason why she's calling me. One topic she wants to discuss. I hear the sound of papers ruffling and know she's got her trusted notepad ready, full of last-minute changes she's about to suggest or insist I make. Because with five days until my wedding, we have all the time in the world to change shit around.

I rub my free hand down the side of my face, bracing myself for this phone call that will surely end in her throwing that same notepad across the room.

"I'm good, Mom. How are you?"

"I'm wonderful, dear. Listen, I swung by this quaint little Italian restaurant yesterday in Printer's Row, and it would be the perfect venue for the rehearsal dinner. And I already checked to make sure they're available."

I feel my frustration level quickly rising. "Mom, Reese and I don't want a rehearsal dinner. I've told you this already. We want to run through the ceremony and go out afterwards with our friends."

My mother gasps as if she's just now hearing this information for the first time, which is definitely not the case. "Dylan, every wedding has an actual sit-down rehearsal dinner. You can't skip that detail. It's crucial."

"Crucial? You make it sound as important as our wedding vows."

"It is," she insists with a firm tone.

I grumble and roll over, rubbing my face into the comforter. The faint smell of citrus calms me down a bit, but not enough to agree to this absurdity. "Mom, this is what Reese and I want. It's *our* wedding. I'm sorry if you don't agree with our decision, but it's final. No dinner. If people get hungry, they can go hit up a drive-thru."

"Oh, that's just ridiculous, Dylan. A drive-thru? How tacky is that." The sound of her exhaling loudly fills my ear, followed by the crinkling of paper. "Fine. No dinner. I suppose I'll have to pack some snacks for your father to munch on during the actual rehearsal. You know how he gets when he goes without a meal."

I chuckle into the comforter just as the sound of my loft door opening catches my attention. I roll over quickly, keeping the phone against my ear as Reese emerges behind the door. He closes it and I hold my hand out, palm up, silently asking him what he's doing here. It's almost six o'clock and he's usually at the office by now. He smiles his response before he walks toward me. He's dressed in his usual work attire, a dress shirt, tie, and khakis, and it gets me like it always does. The man does office-wear like no other.

"Hey, Mom, I gotta go. I'll see you tonight at the fitting, right?"

More papers rustling comes through the phone before she answers, prompting me to roll my eyes. "Of course. I'd never miss it. Maggie and I will meet you there at 6:30 p.m. Goodbye, sweetheart."

"Bye, Mom."

I press end and drop the phone onto the bed before lifting my gaze to Reese. "Handsome, what are you doing here? Don't you have numbers to crunch?"

He steps around my screen that divides my one large room into two and stops just in front of me. "I do. But I couldn't stop thinking about something."

"Oh? My sparkling personality?"

He laughs, reaching out and opening my towel. His eyes linger on my breasts for several seconds before he lifts his gaze to meet mine. "Do you think one of the times last night took?"

I watch his eyes shift back down and trail lower. "Um, I don't know. Maybe. You definitely gave it your all. Is that really what you can't stop thinking about?" '*Cause your body language is screaming something else entirely.* Of course, Reese always looks at me like this. I'm certain that even if we were in church, he'd be able to melt the panties off me right in front of Jesus.

He nods, keeping his eyes on my body. "I want that so bad. I've never wanted that, Dylan. You don't understand. I've never thought about having kids before. Hell, I've never thought about getting married before." He leans into me, forcing me to lie back onto the bed. I reach for his tie, wrapping it around my hand as he holds himself above me. "But when I look at you, it's all I can think about. Marriage. Kids. Everything. I want it all with you. And I don't want to wait."

Oh, Reese. I raise my eyebrows, loosening my grip on his tie. "To marry me or to have kids?"

"To have kids. I'm dealing with the other thing." He leans down and kisses the corner of my mouth, once and then once again before slowly moving down my body. "Don't make me wait, love. I need to see you like that."

I moan as he brushes his lips against my rib cage. "Like what?"

I know what. I just want to hear him say it. Because what the hell is hotter than the man you love wanting you to carry his child? Nothing. Especially coming from this man.

"With my baby inside you."

I reach down and thread my fingers through his hair. "Are you going to be late for work so you can make that happen right now? Because I'm all for another round of baby-making sex with you if that's where this is headed." *Suck it up, vagina. You can be sore tomorrow.*

"No, that's not exactly why I'm here. Close, though." He drops to his knees and drapes my legs over his shoulders. His hands grip my hips and he slides me closer to the edge of the bed, his lip curling up into a sly grin. "I'm going to be late for work because on top of not being able to stop thinking about last night, I also can't stop thinking about the taste of your pussy. And I was too busy yesterday fucking you all over the condo to get any of it. So lie back, keep your legs open, and give me what's mine."

"Jesus. I love when you order me around like that. Seriously, please do that all the time. Just not like to do your laundry or anything." He swipes up my length with his tongue, prompting me to fist the comforter. "Oh, God." His fingers dig into my hips as he flicks against my clit in a pulsing rhythm. At the feel of his teeth on my swollen spot, I arch off the bed and dig my heels into his back. "Reese. Jesus Christ."

"Mmm. You like that. You want it rough?"

I push his head down to silence him. I'm shaking, my thighs convulsing against his cheeks as he ravages me like it's his first time tasting me. Of course, he always goes at me like this, like he'll never get enough of me. He alternates between my clit and my pussy, stroking and sucking until he begins to fuck me with his tongue. I can't take it. I'm begging him to stop, to keep going, to do whatever the hell he wants. I'm a blubbering idiot right now because that's what his mouth does to me; it wipes all coherent thoughts from my head. And when I feel his finger dip into me briefly before trailing my wetness down to my backside, I lose my mind completely.

"Yes. Oh, God, please. Right there. Right fucking there."

He buries his face between my legs, humming against me while he presses his finger against my ass. This move of his, one I never thought I'd be into until he was the man doing it, this move makes me see fucking stars when I'm coming. He doesn't do it all the time, but when he does surprise me with this stellar addition to his orgasm-taking routine, my body vibrates for hours afterwards.

"Goddamn, you're beautiful when you come. Did that feel as good as it looked?"

"Hmm," I reply, unable to form a proper response as I slowly come down. My lifeless body hangs limp on the bed and over his shoulders as he plants gentle kisses to the inside of my thigh. I look down the length of my body and catch his smile. "Anytime you want to be late for work to do that, please, go for it."

He stands, licking his lips and holding his hands out to me. "I need to get going. Thanks for my fix." He pulls me to my feet, the towel covering me falling to the floor.

"You stole my line," I say against his mouth as he kisses me sweetly. "You good? No hand or mouth action required?"

He reaches down and adjusts himself in his khakis with a wince. "Actually, I think I need some recovery time after last night. Ask me again in eight hours."

I giggle as I bend over and grab my towel, securing it underneath my arms. "Don't forget, I have my fitting tonight so I won't be home until late."

He eyes me up suspiciously. "Do you really think you need to remind me about anything involving you?" Grabbing the back of my neck, he pulls me into him and plants a kiss to my forehead. "Bye, love." He releases me, turning and walking toward the door.

I enjoy my spectacular view, nodding in appreciation. The man's ass is a thing of wonder. Muscle upon muscle; it's insane, even through his pants. I don't know what exercises he does to work that perfectly-sculpted entity, but it's working.

I'm brought out of my fantasy when he opens the door. Lifting my gaze, I see he's caught me in my obsessive gawking. I'm not ashamed, not in the slightest. I smile the biggest, cheesiest grin I can muster and he laughs. "Bye, handsome. Five days."

He shakes his head, turning back around. I don't miss the smile on his face as he disappears behind the door, my words no doubt playing on loop in his mind.

Because they definitely are in mine.

Five days.

AFTER STEPPING INTO SOME JEANS and one of my favorite tees I left behind, I slip into my ballet flats and head back into my bathroom. I yawn as I pull my hair up into a messy bun, tugging a few stray pieces out and tucking them behind my ears. After the all-nighter marathon sex, my five-mile run, and the orgasm that just rocked my body, I'm suddenly feeling ready for a nap instead of the day that's ahead of me. I apply the usual minimal makeup I wear daily and walk back into my living space, grabbing my phone off my bed. It's almost time for the shop to open and I have a massive amount of baking to do, considering I didn't get any done this weekend. And if I don't get started on it now, we're sure to run out of treats by lunch time.

As I pull out my mixer and set it on my worktop, the doorbell dings and seconds later, Joey comes rushing into the back.

"Extra-large, double shot of caramel for my favorite cupcake," he sings, depositing my piping-hot cup of coffee on the wood and pulling up a stool to watch me. He's dressed in one of his favorite baby-blue polo shirts that brings out the color in his eyes, his blond hair still damp from his shower.

"Oh, man, I seriously love you." I grab it and immediately take a sip, moaning as the hot liquid coats my throat. "Brooke's supposed to be here any minute and I've got a shit-load of baking to do, so unfortunately, you're going to be in charge of showing her the ropes."

He keeps all grumbles to himself, taking a sip of his coffee. "Whatever. As long as she doesn't try to grope me, I'm sure I can tolerate her for eight hours."

The doorbell dings and we both glance up, seeing Juls emerge in the doorway. She's chicly dressed in a tight, black dress with sky-high heels, her hair wrapped in an elegant twist. "Morning, lovies." She glances around the kitchen and her smile disappears. "Where the hell is Brooke?" Joey and I both shrug as I open my bags of flour, pouring a generous amount into my mixing bowl. "Oh, for Christ's sake. I'm going to kill her." She pulls her phone out of her purse and stalks out into the main bakery, leaving Joey and me alone with our amused expressions. A flustered Julianna Thomas is not something we're used to seeing.

"Ten bucks says she's late," Joey says confidently.

I cock my head and turn on my mixer, wiping my brow with the back of my hand. "Ten bucks says you'll snuggle with her again if the moment arises."

He narrows his eyes at me as Juls reemerges moments later.

"It went straight to voicemail. I'm sure she's on her way."

I start throwing the ingredients for my banana nut muffins together into my mixing bowl, feeling Juls' eyes on me. I glance up. "What?"

She pouts and moves closer to me, placing her hand on my arm. "I'm sorry. I know we agreed to wait to take a test together, but I slipped up last night and blurted out to Ian I thought I might be pregnant. As soon as I said it, he rushed out and bought me a test. There was no stopping him. I'll still take one with you, though."

"Umm, excuse me?" Joey asks, tapping the counter top impatiently with his fingers. "What the hell are you talking about?"

I turn the mixer off and smile at Juls, ignoring Joey's comment. "I took one, too. I'm sorry. The same thing happened with Reese. He was dead-set on me taking one last night. Mine was negative."

"Mine wasn't."

My mouth drops open as Joey squeals next to Juls. "What?

You're pregnant?" There is no hint of sadness or jealousy in my voice. Even though I was disappointed last night in my test results, the news my best friend just dropped on us fills me with the same excitement I felt at the possibility of being pregnant myself.

She nods her response, putting her hands up to her face and covering her crimson cheeks. Joey and I both engulf her in a giant hug, and she wraps an arm around each of us. "I took several just to make sure. I thought Ian was going to make some sort of public service announcement last night. He's beyond excited."

"Oh, my God. Juls, this is amazing," I blink and send the tears down my face. "You're going to be such a kick-ass mommy."

"Helloooo," Joey interjects, stepping between the two of us and dropping his enthusiasm. "Both of you cock whores thought you were pregnant and didn't tell me? What the fuck? I thought we were besties."

I shove him off with my hand. "We are. We just didn't want you to get all excited for nothing."

Juls turns her attention to me and grabs my hands, her smile fading and replaced with a look of concern. "I'm sorry you're not pregnant, sweets. I know you were excited about the possibility."

Of course Juls would think about me when she should be jumping up and down like a maniac. She always puts others before herself. And she probably thinks I'm sensitive to this topic, but I'm not. I couldn't be happier for her.

I squeeze her hands gently and smile. "It's okay. Reese is in full-on 'get me pregnant' mode, so I'm sure it'll happen soon enough."

"Oh, shit," Joey mumbles, gaining mine and Juls' attention. His eyes widen and he grabs his coffee cup off the worktop before elaborating. "Reese is going to be crazy when you get pregnant. I can't imagine him being any more possessive over you than he already is, and you're not carrying his baby yet. He's nuts when it comes to you. Unreasonably nuts at times." He pauses, glancing around the kitchen. "Mmm. Do we have any cashews back here?"

"Over on the shelf," I scoff, dropping Juls' hands and turning around to grab my muffin tins. "And he's not *that* possessive over me."

"Yeah, right," Joey says at the same time as Juls' "yeah, okay."

Joey chuckles softly, popping a few cashews into his mouth as I place my tins onto the worktop. “Face it, cupcake. That gorgeous man is going to put you on lock-down when he knocks you up. And when that time comes, your wardrobe won’t be the only thing he dictates.”

I restart my mixer, licking the splash of batter off my finger. “I like possessive Reese. It’s hot.”

“It’ll be real hot when he gives you a food list you have to eat from. Or when he asks you to stop working.”

I snap my head up at Joey. “I’m not quitting my job. Reese would never ask me to do that. He knows how important my business is to me.” Juls reaches over and stops the mixer, dipping her finger into the bowl. I swat her hand away. “Raw egg, prego. Back up.”

She grunts and retracts her hand. “Damn it.”

I shake my head, walking over to the racks and pulling out the container of muffins I made before closing on Friday. Grabbing a banana nut one, I hold it out to Juls and she excitedly takes it. “And it’s not like I do manual labor. With Brooke starting, hopefully sometime today, I’ll be able to plant my butt on a stool and bake away back here. I won’t even have to be on my feet that much when I’m pregnant.”

Juls bites into the top of her muffin, leaning her body against Joey who has reclaimed his stool. “She’s right, JoJo. It’s totally doable. And Reese may be possessive over her, which I agree is mad hot, but he’d never ask Dylan to give up working. This is her love.” She glances down at her watch, straightening up. “I gotta get going. I’m meeting with the caterers this morning to make sure the menu is finalized. Text me when Brooke arrives.” She plants a kiss to the top of Joey’s head and blows me one before turning on her killer heels and heading for the door.

“If she arrives,” Joey murmurs, winking at me before he heads up front.

I KNOCK OUT SEVERAL DOZEN cookies, cupcakes, and pastries, which helps keep my mind mostly off all things wedding.

But not entirely. One, I am crazy excited about it and two, my mother calls three times in a forty-five-minute time period. I let her rant in my ear while I baked, ignoring her last-minute suggestions, because these aren't tiny, doable suggestions. These are major. Like why in the world aren't we having a full-blown Catholic service in the middle of our ceremony. Why? Because a Catholic wedding ceremony is anything but brief. I sat through one of those a few years ago and almost fell asleep. And there is no way in Hell Reese will wait that long to give me his last name; she should know that. He's going to have a hard enough time as it is waiting the thirty-five minutes it should take us to run through everything. In fact, I'm predicting his hair will look a right mess by the time the preacher pronounces us man and wife.

And I can't wait to see that.

Joey occasionally pops his head into the back while I bake to see if I need help, and to remind me that Brooke still hasn't shown up. I'm all about giving the girl a chance, but I am not the type of boss who tolerates lateness well. An occasional few-minute slip-up? Fine. But not a few hours, and definitely not on your first day.

As I'm cleaning off the worktop, having finally finished all the baking I'm planning on doing for the day, the shop door opens and Joey's voice comes booming from the front.

"Well, look who finally decided to show up."

I move quickly through the doorway, stopping at the sight of Brooke's nervous expression. "Oh, my God, Dylan. I'm so sorry. I swear to God…"

I hold up my hand and cut her off midsentence. "If you're late again, you're fired. This is serious, Brooke. And you could've at least called me." Stepping behind the counter, I grab the new employee paperwork I'd set out for her to fill out two hours ago. "Here, go in the back and fill this out."

She eagerly reaches for the paperwork and rounds the counter, wrapping me up in a massive hug. "I forgot to set my alarm. And I forgot to plug my phone in to charge. I'm so sorry. It won't happen again."

"Good," I reply.

Stepping back, she holds onto my arms and smiles warmly at

me. "I do have one question though." I tilt my head and wait patiently, hearing Joey's soft grunt of disapproval from behind her. "Any wiggle room on the pay?"

"Ha!" Joey squawks.

Her eyes widen at my stern look. "Get your ass in the back and fill these out before I change my mind."

"Right. Sorry." She turns and brushes past Joey, earning herself an evil look.

"Fucking disaster. Seriously, let's keep her in the back away from the customers. Lord knows she'll probably only drive away all the business." He reaches into the display case and pulls out two muffins, offering me one. I take it and begin peeling off the wrapper.

"Give her a chance, will you? I can remember you being late, on occasion. For example, last week when Billy refused to untie you from your bedpost."

Joey wiggles his brows at me as he tosses his wrapper into the trashcan. "That lateness was totally worth it. As were the rope burns on my wrists."

I roll my eyes at him just as the front door dings open. A young woman, probably close to my age, comes barreling through the doors, eyes reddened and misty. She walks up to the counter, tucking her clutch under her arm.

I smile, setting my muffin down on the counter. "Good morning. How can we help you?"

She lets out a shaky breath, looking around the bakery quickly before meeting my eyes. "I don't know if you can help me. I know this is terribly last minute, but you're my only hope at this point."

Joey steps up next to me. "Are you okay? Would you like a glass of water or something?"

She shakes her head and offers him a weak smile. "Oh, no, thank you." She flicks her stare back to me. "You make wedding cakes, right?"

"She makes kick-ass wedding cakes," Joey corrects, motioning toward me. "Not only do they turn out looking fabulous, but they taste amazing. Trust me. I've eaten my fair share."

The young woman's face seems to relax a bit but not completely. "I'm getting married, and the bakery I had originally lined up to make my wedding cake closed down. They didn't even tell me. I went there this morning to make my final payment and the place is boarded up."

A sickening feeling rumbles in my gut. I can't imagine having that happen to me. "Jesus. That's awful. When is the wedding?" I ask.

She winces. "Saturday. Like I said, I know this is last minute. I've been to every other bakery in town and you're my last option." She looks down at her feet. "I'm sorry. I'm not trying to put any pressure on you. It's just... I don't know what else to do. I need to have a cake. I'll pay you extra. Double if I have to."

I reach my hand out and place it on her shoulder, prompting her to lift her gaze. "You don't have to pay me double. I'd love to make your wedding cake."

"Really?" Her soft voice is filled with a cautious hope.

Joey loops his hand through my elbow and pulls me back, dropping his lips to my ear. "Are you crazy? You'll have enough to do on Saturday getting ready for your *own* wedding. How will you have time for this?"

"You're getting married on Saturday, too?" the woman asks. Her excitement seems to fade as she glances between Joey and me. "Maybe he's right. You'll be so busy that day. It's okay if you can't do it."

I shrug off Joey and smile at her. "I won't be that busy. And besides, your cake will be done the night before. I'll just need to add the finishing touches to it that morning." I step closer to the counter. "But I probably won't have time to deliver it. Would it be a problem if someone stopped by here that morning to pick it up?"

Her eyes widen as she fidgets with the clutch under her arm. "No. Not at all. Thank you so much. You have no idea how much this means to me."

I smile and point to my consultation table. "Why don't you have a seat over there and you can tell me all about what kind of cake you want for your big day."

The sorrowed mood she entered the shop with has completely vanished, replaced with that typical bride-to-be joy I love seeing. As she makes her way toward the table, I turn and see Joey shaking his head at me.

"What?" I ask quietly.

His lip curls up in the corner as he crosses his arms over his broad chest, his muffin still in his hand. "You. You'd be late to your own wedding if it meant making some stranger's day perfect. Not many people would do that."

I reach underneath the counter and grab my design binder. "You'd do it, too, Joey Holt. I know you would."

"Not for just anybody. You or Juls? Yes. But you, cupcake, you'd do it for somebody you don't even know. And that's what makes you amazing."

I straighten up and blink heavily, feeling the tears well up in my eyes. "That's what you should say."

His brow furrows in confusion. "Huh?"

I walk up to him and shift my binder to one side of my body so I can wrap my free arm around his waist. I lay the side of my face against his chest. "On Saturday. I know you're worried about giving your Man of Honor speech. It doesn't have to be long. You should just say that." I let go of him and see his glowing smile.

"Oh, I'm going to rock that speech. Don't you worry. Now, while you do your bride thing, is there anything you'd like me to do?" I don't say a word. I simply grin at him and shift my eyes toward the kitchen. He closes his eyes tightly while reaching up and pinching the top of his nose. "Of course. You're lucky I love you."

"I am," I reply, rounding the counter and taking my seat at the table. I lay my book out and open it up, turning it so the excited young woman practically bouncing in her seat can look at my portfolio. "Here you go. This is some of what I can do, but I'm not limited to this. Take a look, see if there's anything you like. I can modify just about anything in there. And the cake and icing flavor choices are listed in the back."

She smiles wide and slides the book closer to her, her eyes shifting between each picture.

Joey's right. I would do this for anybody. Because the look on her face right now, the blissful glow radiating from her, this look is totally worth it. It's what makes my job so rewarding. The long hours. The late nights of baking. The sometimes overly-picky clients. I love my job because I get to see this look. And even if I am a few minutes late to my own wedding, it won't matter.

Nothing will ruin that day.

"TRY AND SUCK IN A little more," the woman says behind me as she struggles to zip and button my dress.

If I suck in anymore, I might actually crack a rib. *Thanks a lot, five-mile run. You obviously were pointless.* I shift on my feet and brace myself against the mirror with my hands while I take in shallow breaths. "I am sucked in. How close is it to fastening?" She pulls the material taut and I gasp, dropping a hand down to my diaphragm.

"There. Have you been eating a lot?"

"No," I barely manage to get out. "Jesus Christ. I can't have it be this tight for Saturday. I'll pass out before the ceremony starts." I spin around and see five pairs of eyes on me. Two amused sets, courtesy of my best friends, two motherly pairs full of anxiety, and the distraught-looking set belonging to the seamstress. My mother's jaw is tight, her face full of discontentment. "I swear to God, Mom. I haven't been eating a lot."

"Did you have a lot to drink lately? Like in the past week?" the seamstress asks, stepping forward and grabbing onto sections of my train.

I don't reply right away, and my mother decides to cut in. "Oh, for Christ's sake, Dylan. Don't you know not to drink alcohol at least a week before your final fitting? That's common sense."

"To who? And it was my bachelorette party. Of course there was drinking." I look down at the hands tugging the side of my dress. "Can't you take it out a little?"

She sighs, flattening her hand against the material and smoothing it down the front. "I could. But if it's just tight from drinking, I wouldn't alter it. As long as you don't drink anymore this week and stick with a low-carb diet, it should fit perfectly on Saturday."

Well, fuck me.

I grimace at the seamstress. "But I love carbs. And I'm a baker. I taste-test all my stuff."

"I'll take that burden off your hands," Joey offers, stepping up and putting his hands on his hips. His gaze trails up my dress to my face. "I must say, it does look seriously hot on you skin-tight. Fashion before comfort, cupcake."

"It's too tight. She can barely breathe in it," Juls states. She smiles up at me. "But you do look amazing. I'll never forget when you tried this on for me the first time."

I shake my head at her, playing over the memory of that day in my head. "Only you can get me to try on a wedding dress when I'm not even engaged."

She reaches out and squeezes my hand lovingly. "I think we both knew Reese was going to be seeing you in this dress."

I blush, putting my other hand on top of hers. *Yup. I definitely knew.*

"I must say, I absolutely love this dress, Dylan." Mrs. Carroll walks up to stand in front of the pedestal I'm on. She motions with her hand for me to twirl around and I humor her. "You look stunning in it. I love all this lace and the pearls on the back. And this train. My goodness. Absolutely gorgeous." She moves around me and grabs the train of my dress, fanning it out in front of me. "My son is going to lose his mind when he sees you in this."

"And his sperm count," Joey snickers under his breath. I glare down at him and he clears his throat as Juls elbows him in the side. "Well, it looks like I'll be the only one partying Friday night at The Tavern. Fine by me. And just in case this needs to be said, I'm retired from Brooke babysitting duty."

My mother steps up next to Maggie and looks at Joey critically. "Joseph, I will not have anyone showing up to this thing Saturday hung over, so keep that in mind, please. This will be a classy event."

"Of course it will be. I'll be there," Joey retorts. "Nothing screams class like the sight of me in a tux."

I spin around on my pedestal and look at myself in the mirror while the four of them talk amongst themselves. Even though my dress is uncomfortably tight right now, it still looks just as amazing as it did the first time I stepped into it. Lace upon lace, it's so elegant I feel almost undeserving of wearing it. But no other dress is worthy of Reese. This has always been the one he was meant to rip off me. So, even though my love affair with carbs has been my longest and second-most-satisfying relationship, it will have to be sacrificed. Because there is no way in Hell I am not wearing this dress in five days. Maggie says her son will surely lose his mind on Saturday at the sight of me in this.

And that's exactly the reaction I'm going for.

AFTER PEELING OFF MY DRESS and being reminded what foods and beverages to avoid for the next five days, I say goodbye to everyone and make my way out to Sam. Reese and I will be staying at the loft every night this week, which I'm grateful for. I want to have as much time there as possible since I'll be moving out this weekend. Juls, Joey, and I will be having our last sleepover together on Friday night there while the boys all stay at Ian's condo. That took some major convincing on my part; Reese doesn't like being away from me, not even for one night. But I begged, telling him it'll be sweeter if we go a little bit without seeing each other before the wedding. He was still reluctant until I told him I didn't want him seeing our wedding cake beforehand. That got him to agree to it. He appreciates my work more than any other person and knows I want him to be surprised. And now I'll have two wedding cakes to tackle on Friday night after the rehearsal, so he might as well hang out with the guys and have some fun.

As I walk up to the driver's side of my trusted delivery van, I notice something red on the windshield. A stand on my toes and reach my hand across the glass, grabbing the single red rose tucked underneath my windshield wiper. I study it curiously and smile. Roses are definitely not Reese's style. Nor is any flower. He's way more original when it comes to sweet gestures. But even though this isn't his typical way of showing me he's thinking of me, or that he loves me, it still warms my heart.

The sound of a car slowing down next to me catches my attention. Turning, I see Joey's red Civic come to a stop and the passenger window rolling down. He lowers his head to see me. "What's up, cupcake? Everything okay?" I hold out the flower in front of me and see Joey's face contort into a snarl. "Goddamn it, Billy. One fucking gesture would be nice. I'm a major fan of flowers."

I try to contain my laughter but fail at the sight of his irritated face. "So not like Reese, though. Maybe Billy put it there for me." I grab my door handle and duck my head down, winking at my assistant. "I'll see you in the morning."

He speeds off down the street, no doubt on his way to give Billy an earful as I hop up into Sam. After placing my rose on the passenger seat, I buckle up and pull away from the curb. It's late, already after 8:00 p.m., and I know as soon as I put my head on my pillow, I'm going to pass out.

Once I enter the security code, setting the alarm for the front door of the shop, I grab a small glass off one of the back racks in my kitchen work area. I fill it with water and place the rose in it, putting it in the middle of my worktop. Taking the steps two at a time, I make my way up the stairs and swing the door open.

There are boxes everywhere. On my bed. On the floor. On the kitchen counter. Way too many boxes for the amount of stuff I have. I close the door behind me and peek around my screen, seeing more boxes filling the space around my bed. "Jesus."

The bathroom door swings open and Reese emerges, a cloud of steam surrounding him. He's dressed in only his boxers with a towel draped over his shoulder. I moan softly at his appearance. The man could seriously rock a shampoo commercial.

He rubs the towel over this head. "Hi. Did you just get here?"

I nod, glancing around the space and motioning with my hand around the room. "Where did all the boxes come from?"

"A guy at work brought them in for me when I told him we were moving you this week. I've gotten a lot of stuff packed away already." He places his towel on the counter, the crease in his brow becoming prominent as he surveys my expression. "Are you okay?"

I move over to the bed and sit down, kicking my shoes off. "Yeah. I'm just tired." I pull my knees up to my chest and rest my chin on top, staring at one of the boxes Reese has labeled 'miscellaneous'. *I'm not ready to pack. Not yet. But I get it. It makes sense to start.*

I feel the bed dip behind me and hear the soft creak of the mattress.

"Come up here."

I turn, seeing him sitting with his back against my headboard. Letting go of my knees, I crawl toward him and straddle his lap. His hands run up my thighs, stopping on my hips. I let my eyes wander over his face, admiring his features before settling on his eyes that are studying me. Always watching. "Hi."

His lip twitches. "Hi, yourself. What are you thinking about?"

I trace the muscles of his arm with my finger, trailing up toward his shoulder. "That I'm not ready to say goodbye to this place." I see his smile fade and shift closer, feeling his hands wrap around my waist. I drop my forehead so it's resting against his, my fingers interlocking behind his neck. "It's not because I don't want to live with you. Please, don't think that."

He licks his lips before exhaling roughly. "I don't. I wish we could live here. I know how important this space is to you. But with us trying to start a family now, I don't see how it would work. We're going to need more than one bedroom." I nod against him, feeling his fingers trace along the exposed skin of my back where my tank top has ridden up. "Dylan, I'll pay for you to keep this place if it'll make you happy. You can use it as storage or for whatever you want. Do you want me to do that?"

"No. It wouldn't make sense to pay for a space we really wouldn't use anymore. It's fine. I guess I just wasn't prepared to see the boxes yet."

He frowns. "I'm sorry. I knew this would be hard for you so I figured I would do the packing. I'll do it all, I don't care."

I run my finger along his jaw, feeling the day-old stubble tickle my skin. "You're too sweet to me. How much did you get done?"

"About half. I found your yearbooks."

I drop my head and cover my eyes with my hand. "Oh, God. Please tell me you didn't." *Why the hell did I keep those?* I know everyone goes through an awkward stage, but something tells me the man I'm currently straddling never went through such a thing. And I definitely did.

He laughs, grabbing my hand and pulling it away from my face. His fingers tilt my chin up to meet his stare. "I did. You were fucking hot at sixteen."

Relief washes over me. *Thank God. My high school years were good to me.* I arch my brow playfully, licking the corner of my mouth as I make a mental note to burn all my middle school yearbooks. "Oh? Would you have liked sixteen-year-old, virginal, Dylan?"

"I would've gone to jail if I touched you. But I definitely would've thought about it."

Christ, that's crazy-hot to think about.

I slide my hands along his bare chest, feeling his chiseled body tense against my palms. "Mmm. I would've thought about you touching me, too." I glance up at him from underneath my lashes, seeing his green eyes blazing. "At night. When I was alone in my bedroom." I lean in closer, pressing my lips to his ear. "I would've thought about it a lot," I whisper.

He growls, moving his hands underneath my tank top and rubbing along the skin of my back. "Would you have gotten yourself off thinking about me and what I'd do to you?"

I nod against his cheek, grinding my hips into him. "Every night. I masturbated a lot back then. I was the horniest teenager."

"Shit," he grunts, grabbing my hips and directing the tempo. I hear his breath hitch as he tilts his pelvis up, his length rubbing against me in the most delicious way possible. "I don't know if I would've been able to keep myself from you. I can't now. I would've done anything to touch you. To taste you. Jail would've been worth it if I got to watch you come apart in my arms."

"Reese," I moan, rocking my hips faster against him. "This feels… oh, God, this feels so good." *Who would've thought a little grinding with clothes on would feel this spectacular?* Of course, the dirty-talking man underneath me doesn't hurt.

"I would've made you come like this. Rubbing my cock against you. Letting you feel how fucking hard I am for you." His fingers unbutton my jeans and tug at the zipper. "Take these off. It'll feel better."

I quickly discard my jeans onto the floor and am pulled back into his lap. His rough hands grab my ass, pulling me closer so we're chest to chest. "Now, where were we?" I ask, as he rocks me against him, putting us back into that erotic rhythm.

"You were about to come."

"Was not," I reply, dropping my head to his shoulder as he rubs his cock against my clit. *Wow. If he keeps this up, I definitely will be coming. A lot.* I moan loudly, digging my nails into his shoulders. "Why are we still wearing underwear?"

He turns his head and presses his lips to my temple as a groan rumbles in his throat. "Because I'm pretending I've just snuck into sixteen-year-old Dylan's bedroom. This is how I'd get you off. I don't need you naked to make you come."

I moan again, tilting my head up and locking on to his eyes. "I've never done this before."

His breathing becomes labored as he grips my hips harder. "You've never done what? Dry-humped?"

"No," I reply through a gasp. I lean back and see him take in what I've just confessed. A smirk forms on his lips. "You like that, don't you? You like knowing you're the first guy to do this to me."

"No, I don't like it," he answers, his jaw clenching. "I fucking love it. You want me to make you come, love? Just like this?" I nod, closing my eyes as the slow burn in my gut becomes almost unbearable. "Look at me. You know I have to see you."

I obey and open my eyes, bringing my gaze down to his mouth. That mouth that drives me completely wild with his words and the way he uses it. I brace my hands on his shoulders as he begins thrusting his hips up to meet each grind. Each pulse against my clit sends me into a frenzy. "I'm so close. Please, tell me you're close."

"Fuck. I'm right there," he grunts out through gritted teeth. He digs into my hips to the point of it being painful as I feel him shudder underneath me. "Holy fuck. Now, Dylan."

I take over, moving against him as if he was inside me and we aren't just fooling around like horny teenagers. And then it hits me, the orgasm racing through my body like the blood rushing in my veins. I arch my back and shout his name, riding out my climax. I'm panting, barely able to take in a deep breath as I drop my head down and see the sexiest grin on the man who's just snuck into my bedroom. I bite my lip playfully. "Holy shit. I'm kinda crushing on the twenty-two-year-old version of you."

His amused smile spreads to his eyes, softening them as he drops his head back against the headboard. His slightly-tanned chest heaves with two deep breaths. "Next time I sneak into your room, you'll be grinding that pussy against my face."

Sweet Lord. I clench my thighs against his, feeling like I could come again just from that declaration. "Did you love going down on girls back then, too?" I ask, shifting off his lap. I know he hates these types of questions, but I ask anyway. I can't help that I'm curious with everything involving Reese.

He stands and slips off his boxers, bunching them up in his hand and wiping himself off. He shakes his head before replying. "I would've loved going down on *you*. It's the way you react to me, Dylan. The way you taste. That's why I love doing it." He tosses his boxers into the hamper, looking back at me. "Good answer?"

I nod and reach out for him. "Great answer. Come back to bed."

"Hungry. You want some Chinese? I got those egg rolls you like."

I grunt and plop down sideways onto the bed, resting my head on my hand. "Can't. I'm on a strict no-good-food diet until Saturday. I can't even taste-test my treats."

"What? Why?"

I watch his bare ass walk into the kitchen, appreciating the angle I'm currently in that's giving me this amazing view. I sigh before responding. "Because my dress was a little snug on me tonight. The seamstress said it's probably because of the booze over the weekend." I tug at the hem of my tank top, covering my hip.

"That goddamn champagne is ruining my life. I'm never drinking that stuff again." I glance up as he returns to the bed, carrying a bowl and munching on an egg roll. "You suck. Guys can eat whatever they want and not have to worry about buttoning a lace bodice."

He shrugs before sitting down on the bed and leaning back against the headboard. "I don't know why you have to worry about it. That dress isn't going to be on you long."

I sit up and leer at him. "It'll be on me long enough. I can't have it gaped open in the back. Everyone will see my present to you."

His eyes fill with curious wonder. "Your present to me? And what would that be?"

I roll off the bed and pull my tank top off. "Not telling. It's a wedding day surprise." I toss it into the hamper and walk to the bathroom to take care of my nightly routine. After washing my face and brushing my teeth, I reemerge and find Reese putting his dish in the sink. "You ready for bed?" I ask.

"Yeah. I'm fucking beat." He rounds the counter and brushes past me, slapping me on the ass before he steps into the bathroom.

I crawl under the covers, laying on the side I always occupy and facing my one and only window. I'll never forget the first night Reese slept in this bed with me. It was the night of Juls and Ian's wedding. The night that is permanently branded into my memory.

The night that will always mean more to me than he'll ever know.

SEVEN MONTHS AGO

"WHERE DO YOU WANT ME, love?" Reese asks, backing up the stairs that lead up to my loft.

This is it. The moment I've been dreaming about, thinking about constantly. We've only been official for two-and-a-half hours, but getting him in my bed has been the only thing on my mind. I wanted to leave Juls and Ian's wedding reception early, but I didn't. I held out. I do have some willpower; not much, but some. And having any willpower around this man is an extremely difficult task, trust me. If he hadn't fucked me in the bathroom two-and-a-half hours ago, I definitely wouldn't have made it, but he did. So we stayed. And now, he's mine. He's had me in his bed, and I'd be damned if I was going to go another second without having him in mine.

"My bed. Now." I push against his heaving chest, feeling his heart beating rapidly against my palm. He's still deliciously decked-out in his tux and it's killing me. He's killing me. The look he's giving me right now, the way his body towers over mine, his intoxicating citrus scent. It's fucking killing me. I've never been this turned on before, I'm sure of it. My panties are still in his pants pocket and right now, I could probably use them. I can feel my wetness pooling

between my legs. I lick my lips, biting down on the bottom one as the back of his long legs hit my bed. With one tiny push, he falls back and I'm on him.

"Mmm, my girl is impatient," he says, smiling up at me as I straddle his waist. "You can take your time, you know. I'm not going anywhere." Take my time? Nonsense. His hands tug at the hem of my dress and with one quick motion, it's pulled over my head and discarded somewhere. Anywhere. Who the fuck cares where my dress is because right now, the only thing I care about is him.

"Fuck taking my time." My fingers frantically rip open his dress shirt, the tiny white buttons flying out in every direction. "You can take your time with me, after I fuck you."

He was just inside me a few hours ago, but the anticipation of having him again in my bed is enough to make me loopy. But, that's what happens when you stupidly decide that beds are off-limits during your casual bullshit phase. What the hell was I even thinking? I mean, yes I was trying to not fall in love with this man, which was inevitable. I convinced myself that beds were too intimate and it would be best if we didn't go there. Seriously the worst idea of my life. I've paid the price severely for that horrible judgment call, having spent the last eighty-five days wallowing in my bed which didn't contain any memories of him. But, that bullshit is all in the past and gazing down at him right now, I can't believe I ever initiated the no-bed rule. His body belongs in my bed.

I stare down at him and take in the perfection beneath me. Hair a mess and green eyes wild with lust. My hands run up his chest, feeling every inch of him as he slides further up the bed. I lean down and trail my tongue over the lines of his muscles, every cut and every dip. He moans against my lips as I trail higher, kissing and licking his neck. I close my eyes as his hands run up my thighs, stopping and playing with the clips of my garter. His thumb runs over my aching clit and dips in my wetness.

"God, you're so fucking wet. Is this killing you? Not having my cock in you right now?"

Oh, the dirty talking. Reese is a master at everything dirty, and he knows it. I bring my mouth down against his, rough and needy as I whimper against his lips. He pulls my bottom lip into his mouth and sucks on it as my hands find his belt. It's hard to concentrate, especially when he's doing that thing I love with his tongue. You know, the thing he does really fucking well when his head's between my legs. Yeah, that thing. Except he's doing it to my mouth, and I'm panting, moaning, stroking my tongue against his as his belt is finally removed. I work his zipper and slide his pants down, gripping his length in my hand. He tenses and throws his head back.

"Christ, I need you. You're right. Fuck taking our time."

In one quick motion, he's on top of me and I'm being pressed into the mattress.

My mattress.

My fucking bed.

Fuck, this is Heaven.

His mouth is on my neck, licking and kissing as my eyes roll back into my head. His warm, minty breath blows across my skin, goose bumps immediately forming on the surface. I open my eyes and lock onto his, deep-green pools of emerald burning into mine with that intensity. His intensity. My hands grip his shoulders as he positions himself there. Right there. Christ, I'm so horny I might actually combust before he enters me.

"Reese, please. Get in me already."

He laughs softly and hovers there, running his length up and down my slick pussy. "Tell me what you want, Dylan. I wanna hear you say it."

I moan loudly as he presses against my clit. But I don't talk; no, I'll let him ask me again. Because I know he will.

"Dylan." He drops his head, pressing his forehead against mine. His neck rolls with a deep swallow. "Fucking say it."

I close my eyes and tilt my head up, bringing our lips together. "Just you," I whisper. "I never stopped thinking about you. Not for one second." I open my eyes and see him studying my face as if he hasn't seen it in years. He's caressing me with his sight, delicately memorizing every inch of me. My hands grab his face, my thumbs lightly stroking his cheeks. We've been apart for eighty-five days.

"Eighty-five days. Did you..." I stop talking and see his eyes read what I was going to say. But I can't say it. Because even though he had every right to be with other women, I suddenly realize I don't

want to picture it.

"No." His hand brushes my hair off my forehead, tucking it behind my ear. "I tried, though. I wanted to forget you, because it was fucking killing me. Images of you, in my mind. They were constant." His Adam's apple rolls in his throat and he lets out a shaky breath, still holding himself at my entrance. "I went out a few times to pick up someone, but I'd end up leaving almost immediately after I got there. And then I'd just go home and give in to it. I'd let myself think of you. Or I'd go for a really long run, which only made me think of you even more."

My eyes rake over his sculpted upper body, looking even leaner than it had a little over two months ago. His muscles are even more defined, the edges more rigid. "Have you been running a lot?"

He nods and swallows again. "Yeah. You have, too. You've lost weight."

I shake my head. "No, I just haven't really been eating. My appetite usually disappears when I'm an emotional wreck." I run my hands down his neck to his shoulders, feeling his muscles flex under my touch. "What did you think about?"

He smiles the tiniest bit and eases forward, entering me slowly. I moan quietly and arch off the bed, my chest brushing against his. "That, right there. The sounds you make when I'm moving in you." He begins thrusting in a slow rhythm, taking his time while he watches me below him. "The way you arch into me." His hand brushes down my face and onto my chest. "Like you need to be touching me with every part of you." His hand moves lower and grabs my leg, pinning it in front of him. "How fucking beautiful you look when you come. I couldn't get you out of my head. You were always there. Every look you gave me, every moment I held you. I couldn't let go of it." He stops moving and runs his finger along my lower lip. "I could be without you for the rest of my life and I'd never want anyone else."

I blink heavily, sending a tear down the side of my face. When I reopen my eyes, I see the pain in his, the memory of those eighty-five days and how it affected him. I reach up, laying my hand against his cheek. "You'll never be without me again. I'm yours. I always have been. Even when we were apart."

"So, you didn't..."

I shake my head, seeing the tension that set in his features when he started to ask that question slowly release. "I could never be with anyone else. Not after you."

He drops his head and kisses me like he needs my air to breathe. It's urgent. Hungry. And I feel that kiss throughout my entire body, reigniting my ache for him. "I need you to move," I whisper against his mouth.

He bends my knee and pushes it against my chest as he starts thrusting into me again. His eyes stay glued to mine, capturing my gaze, daring me to look away. I can't. Even if I want to. I missed this look of his. The look I know he only reserves for me. The look that could make me do anything.

"You know what else I thought about?" he asks.

"What?" I reach above me and search for something to grab, wrapping my hands around my bed post. His slow thrusts are hitting every nerve ending in my body. The heavy drag of his cock as it fills me, pulsing against that spot only he has ever been able to find. I'm coming apart below him, and he doesn't seem to be anywhere near done with me. "Reese, please."

He growls through a moan. "That. How you beg me, over and over again. Like I'd ever deny you." His hands grip the sheet next to my head as his thrusts become more forceful but still slow. I tilt my pelvis, bringing my hips up to meet him and giving him deeper entry. "I'm so fucking lost in you, Dylan. I always have been."

"Fuck, Reese." My orgasm rips through me, burning in my core and spreading out quickly. I'm clenching around him, my hands raking down his back and clawing at his skin. I'm sure I'm drawing blood but I don't care, and he doesn't seem to either. He lunges deeper, deeper again and continues the sweet torture. "I want you to come."

"Not yet. Give me another, love." His hands run down my sides and grip my hips as he thrusts hard, then harder into me. His eyes are locked onto mine, holding me, keeping me with him. "Too damn long. I've been without you and it nearly killed me."

"Me, too. I... holy shit." Bracing myself with my hands over my head, I feel my second orgasm building in my gut.

Again? Already? Of course, look who's above me right now. Why the hell do I question this man's skill level?

His grunts ring out around us, filling my loft. His forehead is creased and the sweat is building just below his hairline. A drop hits my chest and rolls between my breasts. I arch off the bed, pushing against him, needing the contact. Needing every inch of him touching me. I can't get him close enough, not after eighty-five days, not ever. And then it happens. That second orgasm spreads through my body and I'm clinging to him, rocking against him as he pounds into me.

"That's it. Christ, I love watching you like this."

I'm shaking, trembling as I come down. And then I'm quickly flipped onto my knees, Reese bracing himself behind me. The movement's so fast, I don't have time to think before he enters me again. "Reese, I don't know if I..."

"You will. You know I can do this to you all night."

Oh, God. Death by orgasm. Is it possible to have three orgasms back to back like this and actually be able to function afterwards? Shit, who the hell cares? This is Reese Carroll we're talking about. Plus, how sweet would it be to die this way? Screaming his name in ecstasy. Falling to a slow, post-climatic death. Absolutely. I'll take that.

I bow my back and push into him, dropping to my elbows as his hands wrap around my waist. I feel his breath on my back, quick bursts of air. His lips kiss the skin there, trailing lower to my hips. He's pounding into me, giving me every bit of him and I'm taking it. He's so deep this way, his hips crashing against mine as I grip the sheets. My knuckles are stark white as I desperately try not to collapse under his power. I can feel him tense against my body, knowing he's close and I'm right there with him. "I need you to come with me. Please. I don't want to come again without you."

"You need it, love?" he questions as he fucks me relentlessly.

"Yes. Please. Let me feel you."

He hammers into me at rapid speed as I stretch my hands out above me. "Fuck. Get there, Dylan."

"Touch me."

His hand snakes around my body and drops to my clit, two

fingers working me. Sliding against me. Pulsing, pulsing, until my orgasm surges through me. I grab his wrist and stop him, throwing my head back. "Now. Coming," I say breathlessly, barely able to speak.

Both hands tighten against my hips and pull me back to meet his thrusts. He groans his release as I'm rocked to the point of being delirious. I collapse on my belly, pulling him down with me. He rolls to his back and shifts my weight for me so I'm lying on his chest. We lie there in silence, my head resting on him as we steady our breathing. And then my emotions hit me in one big rush. The fact that he's here with me, when I never thought I'd be with him like this. In my bed. Me in his arms. It's overwhelming.

"I can't be without you again," I say, so low I'm not sure if he'll hear it. But I needed to say it, if only for myself, because there is no way in Hell I'd survive being apart from this man again. I'd do anything to avoid feeling that pain, the agony that ripped me apart for eighty-five days and left me a shell of the woman he fell in love with. I wrap my arm tighter around his body. "I don't care if this is all we ever are. I don't need anything besides this. But I'll always need it."

His hand is on my chin, tilting my head up to meet his gaze. That stare of his causes me to stop breathing as he studies me. Always watching. It's so extreme, full of unspoken words as he remains silent. I take the opportunity to admire his features, the features I've missed so much. Soft eyes. Full, slightly-chapped lips with my favorite slit running down the middle. Smile lines that wreck me. Mild stubble that I reach up and run my finger across. He shifts to his side, pulling me even closer so we're chest to chest, my body completely flattened against his. His lips meet my forehead and he holds them there, humming softly against my skin. I feel my body completely relax next to his. All the stress, all the tension, all the sadness and misery of the past eighty-five days dissolves instantly as he wraps himself around my body. I'm completely smothered, completely cocooned in his long limbs, wild mess of hair, and hot breath.

He's in my bed. In my fucking bed. And I never want him to leave it.

"Hey. Are you okay?"

Reese's voice cuts into my thoughts, causing me to roll over.

He pulls me against his body so we're lying just like we were in my memory. I smile, wrapping my arms around him and pressing my lips against his chest.

"I'm more than okay. I have you in my bed." A low laugh rumbles in his throat as I dig into the muscles in his back with my fingers. "Do you remember the first night you were in it?"

"Yes," he answers without hesitation. "Do you remember what you said to me before we fell asleep?"

I glance up at him, momentarily stunned he remembers, and nod once. "That I couldn't be without you again."

His eyes focus on my mouth as he brushes my hair off my shoulder. "That. And you said you didn't care if that was all we ever were. That you didn't need anything else." He pauses, his eyes reaching mine. "I almost asked you to marry me right then."

My heart thunders in my chest. "Really?"

"Really." He leans forward and captures my mouth in a tender kiss, his tongue lightly brushing against my lips, seeking entry. I give it to him and moan softly into his mouth. He pulls back after several seconds, blinking heavily before locking onto my eyes. "I knew then, Dylan. I knew way before then you were it for me. And I would've never let that be all we ever were." He kisses my cheek, my jaw, and the side of my mouth. "You were always meant to be mine. Even before I knew it."

I kiss his jaw before tucking my face underneath his head and relishing in his scent. "Damn straight."

He wraps me against him, pressing his mouth to my hair. "You're so romantic, love."

I chuckle, feeling his body shake with laughter as he holds me. "You're hard to compete with. Shall I try?"

"If you want."

I nuzzle closer. "Will you marry me?"

He laughs, dropping a kiss to the top of my head. "Hell yes, I will."

And for some reason, hearing his answer does something to me. Even though I said yes to him six months ago, it does something to me. "I was yours when I was sixteen."

I feel his reaction to what I've just said. The way his grip on me tightens. The pause in his breathing and the shuddering exhale that follows. “Damn straight,” he finally replies after several seconds of silence.

And I smile as I’m pulled closer. Never close enough.

TUESDAY IN THE SHOP WENT by without a glitch. Brooke showed up on time, surprisingly, and was proving herself to be a good addition to Dylan's Sweet Tooth. She was great with customers, her bubbly personality winning over several of our regulars, and she and Joey were even getting along. For the most part. They were by no means besties, but they were at least tolerating each other and keeping their bickering to a minimum.

I stayed in the back all day, whipping up two special orders getting picked up on Wednesday. One was for Mr. and Mrs. Crisp who were celebrating their anniversary this week. They were my longest-standing customers, stopping in practically every morning for two of my famous banana nut muffins. I adored them and insisted on not charging for their cake. They've given me so much business over the last three and a half years, and this is my way of thanking them. Of course, the two of them argued with me until they were blue in the face about it, but I refused to take their money. I wanted to do this for them. Sixty-five years of marriage was definitely something to celebrate, and I felt honored to be a part of that.

Staying away from the foods I was told to avoid was becoming increasingly difficult. I'm sure there is no baker in the history of bakers who has gone on this strict of a diet before. I've never deprived myself of food; I'm not one of those girls. I eat. A lot. And this low-carb shit was seriously getting to me by mid-day on Wednesday. Not only did I not taste-test the German chocolate cake with extra coconut in the frosting I made yesterday, but I also steered clear of the red velvet cupcakes I whipped up for the other special order. And I don't say 'no' to cupcakes. Ever. They are my go-to treat, the thing I'd request as my last meal if I were on death row. The one dessert I'd cut a bitch for, and they were off-limits. I was eating like a damn rabbit and hating every second of it. I've never been on a diet a day in my life and for the first time in the three-and-a-half years of owning my bakery, I was finding myself wishing I would've picked a different career path.

I'm pushing the pieces of lettuce around in my to-go container, hungry but not hungry enough to swallow another bite of this garbage while my dear assistant scarfs down a cheesesteak sub next to me. I've been giving him dirty looks since he returned with our lunches fifteen minutes ago, and he's been doing his best to avoid my judging stare.

"I should fire you for eating that shit in front of me. As my Man of Honor, you should be suffering right along with me." I shove my container away down the counter and flick my disapproving stare between his sub and his face. "Give me a bite of that."

"Hell, no." He turns his body so his back is to me, keeping his sandwich out of my reach. "You only have three more days and if you don't fit into that dress, you'll be pissed at me for giving you a bite." Spinning around, he holds up his empty hands and chews animatedly. "This is so disgusting. You'd hate it," he says through tight lips, his voice thick with sarcasm.

I scowl at his obvious lie as the shop door dings, gaining mine and Joey's attention. Freddy comes walking into the bakery, the familiar white box in his hands. My chest tightens at the sight of it.

"Freddy! Perfect timing. This one is in a mood and could use something from her man." Joey nudges me with his shoulder and steps up to the counter.

I pout at him playfully before I reach out for the white box Fred has placed on the counter. "Pick something out from the display case, Fred. You know the drill." He bends down, his eyes lighting up as he surveys his choices. I quickly sign the clipboard as Joey pulls out a chocolate cupcake, slipping it into a bag and handing it to Fred.

Fucking cupcakes. I should just give him the whole tray and get them out of my sight.

"Thanks, Ms. Dylan. Enjoy your delivery," he says cheerfully, taking his clipboard and his cupcake before exiting the shop.

I pull the white ribbon, lifting the sides of the box and flipping the lid. Joey moves closer to me as I pick out the dark brown card, opening it and feeling that same nervous energy I always get when I'm about to read one of Reese's notes.

Dylan,

Don't give me a hard time about this. This is long overdue.

X, Reese

Confusion sets in as I place the card next to the box and begin sifting through the tissue paper. I'm digging, looking for whatever he's placed in here that weighs close to nothing.

"Where is it?" Joey asks as he hovers at my shoulder.

I continue moving the paper around. "I don't know. Maybe he forgot… holy shit." I reach in and lift out a set of car keys, letting them dangle in the air below my fingers. "Oh, my God, Joey." Turning toward him, I see his shocked expression as his jaw hits the floor.

"Holy shit is right." He snatches the keys away from me, turning them over in his palm. A dramatic squeal escapes his lips as he points to the emblem on the key. "A BMW? He bought you a BMW?" His eyes look past my shoulder, widening even further before he grabs my hand and drags me around the counter.

I'm in a state of shock as he opens the bakery door and pulls me outside onto the pavement. And then I really lose my shit all together. Parked right in front of the bakery is my gift from Reese. A brand new, insanely-shiny, highly-underserved, white BMW.

Joey hits the unlock button on the keys and opens the passenger door. He ducks his head inside while I stay completely frozen in place a few feet behind him.

He bought me a car. A really expensive car. Probably more expensive than the one he drives.

Joey straightens up and motions for me to join him. It takes great effort to move from my spot on the sidewalk, but I manage and step up next to him, ducking my head down to look inside the vehicle.

"Leather interior, sunroof, and you have a built-in navigation system. Please, for the love of Christ, let me borrow this sometime."

I reach inside and run my hand along the leather seat. "This is crazy. I can't believe he bought me a car."

"I can. That man outdoes himself every time Freddy steps inside the shop. I'd only be shocked if *I* was the one getting a brand new vehicle." We both stand and he shakes his head at my car. "Remind me to tell Reese he needs to give Billy tips on how to be an amazing boyfriend."

"Poor Billy." I nudge him and he laughs against me. "He has to put up with your moody ass and what does he get out of it?"

Joey grins wickedly at me and we both chuckle. He doesn't need to say what Billy gets out of it, because I'm sure the entire population of Chicago knows full well the elaborate workings of my lovely assistant's sex life. He isn't shy about that information and will tell just about anybody.

I close the car door and take the keys from Joey. "I need to go see him. Do you think you could man the shop for me?"

He smiles giddily. "Hell, yes I…" he stops midsentence as Brooke comes hustling down the sidewalk, department store bags in her hands. Joey turns and leans his body against the car, crossing his arms over his chest. "Seriously, Brooke? When I say you can take a lunch break, it doesn't mean a fucking two-hour shopping spree."

She sneers in his direction, coming to a stop in front of us. "Relax, bitch. You're getting premature wrinkles."

Joey immediately turns, dropping down to examine his face in my side-view mirror. "That's not even funny," he growls.

She places her bags at her feet, flipping her car keys in her hand. "You're just jealous because I've got a hot date tonight and *you* don't."

"I've got a hot date *every* night, and one I don't have to pay for," he snarls, straightening up and spinning back around. "What do you charge for your company these days?"

Brooke's jaw tightens, her nostrils flaring with rage. "You know what? Now you're not getting the shirt I bought for you!"

"Brooke, knock it… wait, what?" I look down at the bags at her feet.

"What? Did you say you bought me a shirt?" Joey asks with genuine curiosity, stepping closer to her.

She shrugs, averting her gaze. "It's not that big a deal." She reaches into her Macy's bag and pulls out a light blue T-shirt, holding it against her chest. "It was on sale, and I thought it would look nice on you. You look good in blue."

I smile at her thoughtfulness, watching as Joey takes another step closer to Brooke. She holds the shirt out to him and he takes it with an astonished expression. She looks at me and grins. "Anyway, I'm sorry I took so long. It won't happen again." And before Joey can give her a thank you or react in any way to her gift, she picks up her bags and walks into the shop.

"Damn. This shirt is fucking fabulous. I kind of feel bad for the boyfriend comment," Joey says.

"You should. That was really nice of her."

He shoots me a challenging look, but it's short lived. Brooke did well and Joey knows it. And the smile he tries to hide as he folds the shirt against his chest isn't missed. Once he's done, he smoothes out his skin once more in the mirror behind him, tucking the shirt underneath his arm. "Do you think I have wrinkles?" *Oh, Lord.*

"Don't be ridiculous. Your skin is flawless."

He grins. "You know why, don't you?"

I immediately hold up my hand to stop him from talking. "Please, spare me the 'semen is the fountain of youth' conversation. I find it hard to believe that mine and Juls' swallowing habits are directly related to the number of crow's feet we end up getting." I shake my head at the memory of that discussion a few years ago. Joey really is a piece of work, trying to convince us to up our blow-job game to ward off any fine lines.

"You good?" I ask. I need to go get ready for my visit with Reese, knowing full well his lunch break is the best time to get him alone.

He smiles. "I'm great. Go properly thank that man before I do it for you." He arches his brow, the wicked gleam in his eyes beaming at me.

I chuckle at his comment as we both walk back into the shop. Practically sprinting up the stairs, I run straight for my lingerie drawer with only one thought in mind. Naughty Dylan is about to come out to play, and she's not going to hold anything back either. *Reese Carroll, you have no idea what you're in for.*

THIS IS CRAZY. SERIOUSLY, COMPLETELY insane. I'm riding the elevators of the Walker & Associates building, my knees shaking against each other under my oversized trench coat. Glancing down at myself, I tighten the belt around my waist and bite the inside of my cheek. I've never done anything like this before or even remotely close to this. I mean sure, I've shown up to Reese's work multiple times and given him an office quickie, but I'm always dressed appropriately when I do it. Never, and I mean never, have I pulled a stunt like what I'm about to do. I try to shake off my nervousness as the doors ping open. Stepping out onto the twelfth floor, I begin the stroll toward his reception area.

I need motivation, so I think of the delivery he sent me as I walk down the long hallway. *A brand new car definitely deserves this type of a thank you.* A brand new car that drives like a fucking dream.

Sorry, Sam.

I spot Dave, my favorite receptionist who Reese re-hired. After firing him for being 'too cheery', I convinced Reese to give him another chance, which he didn't fight me on. And since I've spent a considerable amount of time in this office over the past eight months, Dave and I have become fast friends. His crooked smile lights up his face as I point toward Reese's door, silently asking if he's available. He nods and, like he always does, motions for me to walk right in. Glancing down one last time to make sure I'm covered, I swing open the door and step into his massive office.

He looks completely focused, eyes on his computer screen and pen stuck in his mouth. *Lucky pen.* With the sound of my entrance, he glances up slowly, his eyes locking onto mine as I close and lock the door behind me. All my nervousness is left in the hallway, and before I can give him the chance to speak, move, or even breathe, I open my coat and drop it to the floor. And that's not the only thing that drops. His pen falls out of his mouth as his eyes slowly take in my attire.

I've chosen a matching red lacy bra and panties, garter, stockings, and my black stilettos I wore the night of my bachelorette party. My bra and panties are insanely see-through, barely even classifying as underwear, and when I say red, I mean fire-engine red. I'm standing in his office, screaming at him in this outfit like a siren. My skin is flushed from the sheer contact of this ensemble. This is has to be the craziest thing I've ever done and by the way Reese is looking at me right now, it's totally worth it.

He leans back in his chair, his eyes staying glued to my body as he rakes both hands through his hair. "Jesus fucking Christ." His eyes meet mine briefly before he drops them to my chest. "I can see right through that."

"You don't like it?" I ask playfully, seeing his tongue dart out and lick my favorite slit that runs down his bottom lip. *Oh, yes, my tongue will be doing that in just a minute.* "I've come to thank you for your gift."

"I'm not gonna last long," he replies quickly, his hands firmly gripping the arms of his chair. "I'm telling you right now, whatever you've planned," his Adam's apple rolls in his throat, "I'm not gonna last with you wearing that."

"That might be the best compliment you've ever given me." My smile busts my face open, and I can practically feel his erection from where I stand. With the heated look he's giving me right now,

I'm positive I won't last long either. *Please, like I ever do with this man's skill level.* I place my hands on my hips and stand up straight, ready to start my fun.

"Now, there are two rules you must follow in order for this to play out in your favor." I bend down and grab my coat, placing it on the chair after I retrieve my cell phone out of it.

"And what would these rules be?"

I can feel his penetrating stare as I scroll to my playlist. After finding my selection, I stride over to his desk and walk behind it. "Rule number one," I place my phone down next to his computer, "you're not allowed to touch me at all during the song."

"Fuck that," he states firmly, crossing his arms over his broad chest. At the sheer sight of him behind his massive desk, I'm almost tempted to agree with him and say fuck rule number one. He's magnificently dressed in his work attire, which never ceases to have the same effect on me as the first day I saw him in it. His hair is fuckably messy, his deep emerald eyes are piercing into mine and continually raking over my body, and his lips are wet and ready for me.

I lean forward, giving him a better view of my cleavage and seeing him notice it instantly. "You touch me, and I leave. *And* I'll do it without my coat on." *Yeah, right.* I'm praying he doesn't call my bluff on this one, because there's no way in Hell I would walk outta here without being covered up.

His eyebrow arches. "How long is this song?"

"Four minutes and thirty three seconds."

"No fucking way. I'll give you two minutes and then I'm touching every part of you." He reaches out and runs his hand up my thigh, playing with the clips on my garter. I tremble at the contact. "What's the second rule?"

I smile slyly and stand up, seeing his body tense as I reach for him. "You only get to feel me." His expression shifts quickly to confusion as I loosen his tie, pulling it out from underneath his collar and walking behind him. "And if you take your blindfold off, I'll be withholding *your* orgasm."

"I can't touch you *or* look at you? Not happening." I'm quickly grabbed and pulled into his lap, his mouth firmly pressing against mine. "Nothing stands in my way of you." He kisses me brutally, his tongue invading my mouth with firm strokes. "Nothing."

I pull back, which is an extremely difficult task, and grip his shoulders tightly. "Let me do this." He starts to shake his head when I grab it, holding it in place. I drop my forehead to his and exhale softly. "Please. I love that you hate the idea of not being able to touch me or look at me, but I swear I'll make it worth it." His minty breath warms my face and I feel his muscles relax beneath me. "Let me properly thank you."

After several seconds of him contemplating my offer, he places the tie back in my hand, giving me the okay to follow through with this. Leaning closer to me, he presses his lips to my hair. "Make it count."

I shudder against him and bite my lip. *Come on, Dylan. Focus.*

"Two minutes." He pulls out his phone and sets his timer as I move behind him, draping the tie across his eyes.

After securing it, I move around him, making sure to brush against his body as I reach for my phone and cue up the song. Leaning down, I brush my lips against his ear. "Are you ready, Mr. Carroll?" I whisper, hearing him inhale sharply at my words. The song starts playing and I watch him to gauge his reaction, seeing him smile immediately at my selection.

"Two minutes," he repeats, and I'm with him on this one. There's no way I'm making it four minutes and thirty three seconds without begging him to touch me. No fucking way.

"Two minutes," I echo softly, feeling my skin flush at the thought of his hands on me.

Two fucking minutes that, I'm sure, will feel like an eternity.

"DO I WANNA KNOW?" BEGINS playing throughout the office, the erotic tempo pulsing through the air. The bass is pumping through my body, slow and steady as I close my eyes and feel the music. It really is an insanely hot song, one that carries the perfect rhythm for fucking, or dancing. And in this case, the dancing comes first. This song holds so much history for us, and when I had decided this was going to be my response to his delivery, this song was the only song I thought of. I press the start timer on his phone and turn away from him, gripping his strong thighs with my hands. Spreading them open, I lower myself down and firmly brush my backside against his crotch along with the tempo. I repeat the motion several times, rubbing into his erection and feeling it twitch against me. He is already hard, no doubt from the sight of me in this lingerie he's never seen before, but with each movement, he gets stiffer.

"Shit, Dylan," he pants, his voice strained and fragile.

I've never heard him say my name like that. So delicately. Helpless even. I'm making him weak. Doing this to him, rubbing against his body with my own and not allowing him to touch me or see me is slowly pulling him apart. I sway my hips, continually brushing against the massive hard-on straining at the zipper of his khakis. I can see the outline of his cock, the heaviness of it and its perfect length tempting me. *Take me out, Dylan. You know you wanna touch me.* It's insanely difficult to ignore, but I can handle two minutes. Leaning back against his chest, I feel his hot, panting breath on my bare shoulder as I grind to the music.

"Mmm, you're so hard for me."

"I'm always hard for you. Let me see you."

I groan softly, gripping his thighs and dipping my body between them. "Not yet."

He moans, lifting his pelvis to meet my movements. His hands are holding tightly to the arms of his chair, his knuckles stark-white. Low, rumbling groans escape his slightly parted lips as I press my body against his. I feel him shake against me with each breath he takes, straining to stay still and keep his hands off me. My body glides against him, swaying and pushing against his with a teasing pressure.

"If I come in my pants, it's your own damn fault."

I giggle, shaking it off instantly because I need to stay focused. I've never given a lap dance before and was actually worried walking in here that I wouldn't be capable of pulling it off. But apparently, according to the reaction I'm getting from my sexy-as-fuck fiancé, I'm more than capable. I slide against his clothing, feeling him tremble slightly from the contact.

"You're doing so well, Mr. Carroll. Only one more minute."

Spinning around, I straddle one of his legs and lean in close. I hear his deep inhale as I brush my breasts against his face, letting him linger between them for several long seconds. His breath warms my chest, tickling between my breasts and instantly heating the area. He moans softly against my skin, his lips vibrating as he plants a gentle kiss to my breast before I pull back. I'll allow that one touch, considering how good he's being. I run my hands through his hair as I move to the beat, pulling on it slightly before I move down. Roaming over his broad shoulders, I squeeze gently and rub my hands down his heaving chest. His muscles contract beneath my touch, his torso pushing roughly into my palms. Aching for more. Begging for me to touch every inch of him. I'm insanely aroused right now, having gotten instantly wet when I stepped into this office. I'm certain my panties are drenched and I hardly care. I'm not stopping for anything.

His face is tense, jaw locked tight and twitching ever so slightly. This is killing him and I know it. He hates not being able to touch me, and the reality of just how much he hates it fuels my actions. That and the fact he's actually allowing this torture to happen, giving me the control which I'm sure isn't easy for him. I begin to move faster, my hips gyrating with purpose against his thigh as my leg brushes against his cock. Reaching down, I palm the front of him and he grunts loudly, his head falling back against his chair and the veins in his neck pulsing. His breathing becomes more strained, blowing sharply across my face as I lean into him. Our lips are close, so close that if I moved in we'd be kissing, but I don't. I drag my body against his instead, rubbing my breasts against his face and down to his chest. My hand cups around his length and he jerks against my touch. I want his hands on me, I want him all over me, but I can wait. Being this close to him, seeing what I can do to make him come apart is making this agony worth it. He flexes his hands and pounds his fists on the arm rest.

"I'm fucking dying," he grunts, dropping his head and brushing his face against my skin. "As soon as that alarm goes off, I'm bending you over my desk and fucking you harder than I ever have. Good luck walking out of here."

Jesus. I stumble a bit at his words. "Do you want to see what you're doing to me?" I ask in my best seductive voice.

He nods his answer, licking his lips.

Dipping my hand down the front of my panties, I slide along my wetness and moan softly against my touch. I swipe my finger across his bottom lip and he opens immediately, pulling my finger into his mouth and sucking softly.

"Kiss me," he demands, his tongue running along his bottom lip. *Fuck it.* I lean forward and brush my lips against his, my soft kiss quickly getting overpowered by his rough one. He assaults my mouth with his, and we're all tongues, lips, and sharp breaths in this moment. I wouldn't even classify this as kissing; this is primal and borderline dangerous. My lips hurt from the contact but I don't care. Nothing could pry me off this man. I bite down on his bottom lip and he groans into my mouth, the metallic taste of blood mixing with our saliva. It's hot, really fucking hot, and I'm praying for the two minutes to hurry the hell up already. The alarm on his phone beeps and my stomach tightens, a soft gasp escaping my lips. *This is it.*

"Touch me," I whisper.

"About fucking time." His hands immediately rip his tie off and spin me in his lap, bending me forward. "Grab my desk and don't let go."

I do as I'm told, quickly pushing to my feet as he stands behind me. My arms are shaking and my legs are struggling to keep myself still and upright. "God, I'm so wet for you," I whimper, hearing the sound of his belt being loosened behind me. I'm more than ready for this and I want it hard. He can make love to me later. Right now, I want dominant Reese and I know I'm about to get it.

He slides my panties down my legs, tapping each ankle for me to lift them. I look over my shoulder and see him slipping them into his pocket, a lustful smirk forming on his lips.

"I wanna make you scream so bad, but I fucking can't. You had to pull this shit at my work instead of waiting 'til I got home to tease me?"

"I couldn't wait."

"Neither can I." He enters me forcefully, the impact knocking the air out of my lungs and causing my body to collapse on his desk. His arm wraps around my waist and pulls me back up. "I said don't let go," he commands, and my hands grip firmly onto the edge of the desk. Slamming into me, he rocks my body forward with each thrust.

"Oh, God," I yell, causing his hand to wrap around my face and muffle my sounds. Each push is more powerful than the next and I'm crying out, unable to control my response to him. My body bends forward as he picks up his pace. His free hand grips my hip tightly, pulling my body back to meet his every push. I close my eyes and feel him, just him. His hand digging into the skin of my hip, hopefully marking me where only he has touched me. His cock and the way it barrels into me. His warm breath, short quick bursts of air on my back.

"If I move my hand, will you be quiet?" he asks and I quickly shake my head. *No way.* "Good girl. I love that you can't control yourself when I'm fucking you." His hips crash against me and I moan into his hand. "My girl likes it rough, doesn't she?" I nod quickly and he drives harder, my body slamming against the desk. My thighs sting from the contact but I don't care. My body is so primed for him and whatever he has to offer, I'll fucking take.

I don't know how he does it, but he manages to keep his sounds to a minimum, the loudest noise coming from the impact of our bodies striking against each other's. The slapping sound fills the office, mixing with my muffled whimpers and Reese's breathing. It really is hot, the sound of our bodies coming together in this heated moment. My core constricts and I feel a tightness forming between my legs.

"Turn around." He pulls out of me and turns me before I can even think to move. Lifting me slightly, he sets me on the edge of the desk and grabs my legs, wrapping them around his waist. He grabs my face and commands my attention. "You remember what I said about these shoes?" he asks, his voice gritty and urgent. I nod, unable to speak due to my ragged breathing, but I definitely remember. He enters me to the hilt and I brace myself on his desk, flattening my hands on the wood. "Do it."

As soon as he begins fucking me, I arch my back to give myself leverage and bear down with my legs, digging my heels into his back. He growls his response, throwing his head back as he barrels into me.

"I'm so close." Reaching up, I grab onto his bicep and dig my nails in as I anchor my heels into him.

His hand grips my neck, pulling my face into his and crashing our mouths together. "Come on my cock. Let me feel it." And at those words and the commanding tone behind them, I lose control.

He thrusts into me harder, gripping my neck with one hand and my hip with the other. I'm biting my tongue to keep myself from screaming, certain he's going to either snap me in half or the desk he's fucking me against. But considering the car currently parked outside, I'm sure he can afford another desk.

"Fuck, yes. I love this pussy," Reese pants, the veins in his neck protruding and his forehead beading with sweat. He keeps his eyes on me, allowing me to watch him unravel as he plunges into me once, twice, and then a third time before he drops his head against mine. I let my legs fall limp around his side, not having the strength to dig them into anything anymore.

"Thank you for my car," I say softly, not missing the way his lip curls up into a half-smile. I reach over and hit the stop button on my phone.

He slowly pulls out of me, holding up a finger for me not to move as he tucks himself away. Opening his desk drawer, he grabs a few tissues and wipes me clean. "I was half-expecting you to refuse it."

I laugh subtly. "Have you *seen* the car? Sam will completely understand my reasoning for not driving him everywhere now." I hop off the desk as he tosses the tissues into the waste basket. "You didn't take out a massive loan to afford that, did you?"

He sits down in his high-back leather chair and pulls my panties from his pocket. "Come here." I stand in front of him and he allows me to step back into them, keeping his eyes on me as he slides them up my legs. "Only because you have to walk out of here. Otherwise, these would be mine."

"You know, one of these days I'm going to find your hidden stash of my lingerie. And I will be getting every single pair back."

"Good luck with that." He taps his lap and I scramble onto it, wrapping my arms around his neck. "And to answer your question, no, I did not take out a massive loan. We got paid from that account with Bryce."

My stomach knots up temporarily at the sound of that asshole's name. "So, you saw him?" I twist in his lap, glancing down at his hands wrapped around me and checking for any visible bruises or cuts. This is a justified inspection and he allows it, laughing quietly while I do it. When I've thoroughly examined both, I turn my attention back to him. "And you didn't hit him?"

"I didn't see him. Ian met with him. I had some other stuff I was trying to take care of."

"What other stuff?" He gives me the same look he gave me on the couch when he wouldn't elaborate on why this account was so important. Before I took his vague *trust me* reasoning without question. Now I can't hide the slight irritation bubbling inside me. *Why is this such a secret? Is it really that crucial I not find out about anything?*

I shake off these questions, grabbing his face and planting a kiss to his lips. "I should go before Joey and Brooke kill each other."

I stand and round his desk, grabbing my coat and slipping it on. I push the questions filling my head about this account aside, not needing any additional stress. And I do trust Reese. I know he'll tell me when he can, so I'm not going to worry about this.

As I'm securing the belt around my waist, his arms wrap around me and pull me back against his chest. He roughly exhales into my hair before pressing his lips to the shell of my ear. "Three days," he whispers before kissing down my neck as he slips my phone into my pocket.

"Mmm. You keep doing that and I'm never going to leave here."

"Don't give me any ideas." His arms release their hold on me, allowing me to walk toward the door. I grab the handle, glancing once more over my shoulder and seeing him perched on his desk. Hands gripping the edge. Feet crossed in front of him. Cocky, sexy-as-fuck smile growing on his face. It's the same position he was in all those months ago when I came storming into this very office to confront him on being married. I slapped the shit out of him, found out he wasn't married, and then proceeded to blow him behind the very desk I was just fucked against.

So many memories in this office. Mostly sex-filled, but I'm not complaining.

"I'm glad you weren't married," I say, seeing the confusion wash over him momentarily before he realizes the meaning of my words. He doesn't respond, but he doesn't need to because the look he's giving me right now is speaking for him. It's the look I always find him giving me when I catch him watching me. Like he's just now seeing me for the first time. It's a look I don't know if I'll ever get used to, because it still has the same effect on me as the first time I saw it at Justin's wedding. When I stood up from his lap and spun around, getting my first real look at the man who would completely change my life. My bones seem to vibrate while my heart beat fills my ears. I would do anything for this look. For this man. And it takes every ounce of effort I can muster to leave this room. But I manage, giving him a wink and seeing my favorite smile lines appear next to his eyes before I close the door behind me.

I pull myself together enough to give Dave a wave and a smile, getting a very enthusiastic one in return.

"Can't wait for Saturday," he excitedly declares, holding up the wedding invitation he's kept on his desk since I delivered it to him months ago.

"Me either," I reply with a smile that literally makes my cheeks ache. But it's hard to not react that way when someone mentions Saturday.

I step into the empty elevator, hitting the lobby button before I lean back against the wall. Glancing down at my left hand, I study my engagement ring, which I find myself doing a lot lately. I never take it off: not before bed, not while I bake, never. I think it's common for girls to imagine what their ideal engagement ring would look like. To have a specific diamond cut in mind or at least know whether they want platinum or gold. But I never thought about it. I never once had a preference until Reese slipped this ring on my finger in the middle of my bakery kitchen. This elegant, princess-cut diamond is the ring I was always meant to wear. It's the ring I would've picked out myself, but the fact that Reese designed this specifically for me is the main reason I adore it. I can picture him sitting down with the jeweler, having an exact idea in mind and not settling for anything less. I can also imagine how messy his hair looked during that design process.

The elevator stops a few floors down and even though I'm already leaning against the wall and giving plenty of room to whoever is about to enter, I move closer to the corner anyway. As the doors slide open, I'm too busy admiring my ring to register who steps on. But I sense it. I feel the tightness forming in my gut and slowly lift my eyes and lock on to the reasoning behind it.

"Well, isn't this a sweet surprise."

"Fuck," I utter under my breath through gritted teeth, keeping my eyes down and making sure I'm still completely covered. The last thing I need is this grade-A asshole to get a look at what's underneath my trench coat. Out of my peripheral vision, I see him move to the opposite side of the elevator, keeping his full attention on me.

"Is it raining outside?" he asks, and even though I'm not looking at him, I can tell he's wearing that eerie smile that makes my skin crawl. "Because when I arrived here, it was sunny and close to seventy-five degrees out. You must be burning up in that, baby."

Baby. God, this creeper makes me nauseous.

When I don't acknowledge him, he moves closer to me and I instinctively back further into the corner. "Are you hot, Dylan? 'Cause you look hot to me. Need a hand slipping that off?"

At that absurd question, I turn my head and glare at him. "If you step any closer to me, I'll be the only one leaving this elevator with a set of balls." He either doesn't have a pair, or he doesn't value them, because my threat doesn't stop him from moving quickly and bracing himself with a hand on either side of my face. His body is pressed against mine and if this intrusion isn't enough to make me sick, his erection digging into my stomach pushes me over the edge. I clench my teeth and flatten myself further against the wall. "Back the fuck up."

"And if I don't? Removing my balls would require touching them, so by all means." He lifts a finger, trailing it down the side of my face to my neck. "Did you like my flower?"

My breathing was already labored, but now I'm borderline-hyperventilating. *That fucking flower.* I stare up into his eyes, my fists shaking at my sides.

"I was planning on stopping by your shop this week. My father has been craving your tarts and I've been craving something, as well. Think you could fill both our orders?"

"Stay the fuck away from my shop," I hiss as my nails cut into the skin of my palms.

"Or what?" he asks, leaning closer and bracing himself on the wall next to my head. "Nothing stands in the way of what I want, Dylan. Not even your boyfriend."

"What is it? What is your weird-ass obsession with me? I don't want you. I never will. So get the fuck over yourself and find someone else to creep the hell out."

I push against him but he pushes back harder, flattening me against the wall. He tilts his head down, brushing his nose against my forehead. "You want to know what it is about you?"

"I *want* you to get the fuck off me."

"Then do something about it," he snarls in my face.

I could slap this asshole, but I'm suddenly flooded with the urge to do something that'll hurt a hell of a lot worse. Grabbing his shoulders, his eyes enlarge and he drops his finger from my neck as I fist his dress shirt and swiftly bring my knee up, striking him right where I need to with enough force to bring him to his knees.

"Awhhhh, fuckkkkk." He's on his side, rolling in a fetal position with his hands clutching the balls I just crushed.

The elevator comes to a stop at that exact moment, allowing me to step over him and move toward the opening doors. When I hear laughter, I look back at him over my shoulder, seeing his face contorted into a mix of agony and mischief.

"That," he says through a faint voice before blowing out forcefully through pursed lips. "Fuck, yes. That's what it is." He laughs again, but it's snuffed out by more groans as he clutches his groin.

I slam my hand on the elevator door, holding it open. "Stay the fuck away from my shop. And if I were you, I'd get the hell out of Chicago before Reese, my *fiancé*, does a lot worse than what I just did." I glance down at his crotch. "Good luck having kids, douchebag."

I step out of the elevator, hearing the doors ding close behind me. *Hmm. Kneeing assholes in the balls is just as satisfying as slapping them across the face. Maybe a bit more.*

Thanks a lot, Bryce. You've just given me a new favorite go-to move.

I'M PUTTING EVERY SAFETY FEATURE of my new car to the test as I drive back to my bakery. I'm fuming, more mad than I can remember ever being as I weave in and out of traffic and keep the pedal pressed against the floorboard. Thank God this car has those sensors that alert you when you're too close to a vehicle in front of you, because I'm definitely not paying attention to prevent that on my own. My mind is elsewhere, the vision of Bryce cornering me in the elevator and the feel of his finger against my neck overwhelming my thoughts. I've never felt invaded like that before. Not even when Justin put his hands on me. And his hands left bruises. But this? How Bryce touched me? This was different.

I kept my cool for the most part in the moment, but now I'm feeling the aftershock of the encounter. My nerves are completely shot, my chest is so tight I'm finding it difficult to take in a deep breath, and the urge to consume the one thing I've been told to avoid until Saturday is stronger than ever. I know I have to tell Reese about this, and that's making my anxiety level rocket off the charts. It's one thing if Bryce verbally creeps me out; that I can handle. But he put his hands on me. Well, a finger, but still, he *touched* me. And I'm no longer worried that Reese might do something that could get him into trouble, because I know he'll be smart about it and he deserves to know what just happened. I'd sure as hell want to know if some bitch laid a finger on Reese. And I'd be pissed if he kept that information from me, so I'm going to tell him.

After I park my car behind Sam, I storm down the sidewalk and swing the bakery door open, nearly ripping it off the hinges. Joey and Brooke are behind the counter, both of them focusing on me immediately and halting their conversation that, for once, looks pleasant.

"What's wrong? You look pissed," Joey correctly observes. "Did your thank you not get received well?"

"That's not why I'm pissed." Storming into the back, I feel Brooke and Joey on my heels as I grab the glass that's been sitting in the middle of my worktop. Not even bothering to pick the flower out of it, I chuck the glass and its disturbing contents into the trashcan, the sound of it breaking echoing around me.

"Jesus. What the hell happened?" Joey asks.

"Yeah, Dylan. You look ready to murder somebody," Brooke adds.

I ignore both of them and make my way up the stairs, knowing Joey will be following me. I swing the door open and step behind my decorative screen, ripping my coat off and throwing it onto the bed.

"Dylan, what's going on?" Joey asks from behind the screen, genuine concern in his voice. "You're kind of starting to freak me out a little."

I grab some clothes from my dresser and throw them on the bed. "Reese didn't leave that flower on Sam the other night. Bryce did."

"What? Are you fucking serious?" Joey grunts out.

"That asshole from the club?" Brooke's voice fills the room, and I'm momentarily shocked she was concerned enough to follow me up the stairs. But she is Juls' sister, after all, and Juls would definitely follow me.

"Yeah, the asshole from the club. He cornered me in the elevator after I thanked Reese for my car. God, I fucking hate that guy." I button my jeans and grab my shirt just as Joey walks out from behind the screen.

"What do you mean he cornered you? What happened?" Joey asks.

I clench my eyes shut at the memory of it. "He pushed up against me." I open them, turning my head and seeing Joey's alarmed expression. "Right in my face, Joey. I kneed him in the balls, but I should've done worse than that. He put his fucking finger on my neck." I shiver, reaching up and rubbing my skin raw with my hand. "Jesus, I'm so grossed out right now."

"He touched you? Oh, fuck that. I don't care what you say, cupcake. I'm telling Reese about this. And if I ever see that motherfucker again, I'll risk jail time."

"Yeah, me, too," Brooke says, stepping up beside Joey. She flips her dark hair off her shoulder before crossing her arms over her chest. "He seems worthy of a good beat-down. One I'd personally like to deliver."

Reaching for my coat, I grab my phone from the pocket. "You won't have to tell Reese. I already decided he needs to know about this. I was just waiting until I wasn't putting myself and others in danger to tell him. He'd flip out if he knew I was talking on the phone while driving." I sit on the edge of my bed, dialing Reese's office number and placing the phone to my ear. I look up and notice that neither one of my employees have moved from their spot. "Would one of you like to go downstairs in case someone comes in to buy something? We can't all be up here." Joey turns to Brooke who gives him a look like she shouldn't be the one leaving. "Or both of you could go. I don't really need an audience."

Joey snaps his head in my direction, his eyes narrowing on mine. "I take offense to that, but fine." He grabs Brooke's arm. "Come on. I'll show you what to do when someone comes in with a special request. Dylan has a specific way of doing things."

Just as my loft door closes, the phone picks up.

"Reese Carroll's office. Dave speaking. How can I help you?"

"Hi, Dave. It's Dylan. Can I speak to Reese, please?"

"Absolutely. He just went to Mr. Thomas' office, so I'll transfer you to his line. Hold on one second."

Speaking of Mr. Thomas', Juls will definitely be filled in on what I just went through as soon as I hang up from this phone call.

"Ian Thomas."

"Hey, Ian. It's Dylan. Is Reese with you?"

"Yeah, he just walked in. Hold on." I hear shuffling through the phone followed by a muffled "it's your girl."

The tenseness that has set into my shoulders seems to release a bit at the sound of my title. I love being 'his girl', and that's always how Ian labels me. Even during mine and Reese's casual bullshit phase.

"Love. Are you missing me already?"

I smile, my first smile in twenty minutes. "Always. But that's not why I'm calling."

After several seconds, he asks, "Are you going to tell me or am I supposed to be guessing?"

I sigh heavily, mentally preparing myself for the reaction that will surely ruin the amazing, post-orgasmic mood he's floating around with. Mine sure as hell has been ruined. "No. But before I tell you this, I'd like to start off by saying I think I handled this very well and am quite proud of myself."

"Is this wedding shit? Because you know I back you up one hundred percent. Whatever you decide is fine with me."

I let out a small laugh. "No, it isn't wedding shit. I'd actually prefer a discussion with both our mothers' over the one I just had with Bryce."

I don't need to be in Ian's office right now to know Reese's free hand is in his hair. "What do you mean the discussion you just had with Bryce? You saw him?"

I hear Ian's voice in the background, saying something I can't make out before I respond. "He got on the elevator with me when I was leaving your building."

His breathing fills my ear. "Did he? And what did you two *discuss*?"

I can sense the irritation in his voice and suddenly feel like it's being directed toward me. "What's with the attitude? I didn't ask him to get on the elevator with me."

"No, but you picked out that fucking outfit you had on."

I'm on my feet, rage coursing through my body as I begin

pacing alongside my bed. "Are you serious right now? I don't remember you complaining about my wardrobe when you had your dick in me. And how the hell was I supposed to know he was in your building? I thought Ian closed the account with him."

"He did. Don't fucking yell at me because you, once again, decided to wear something that could draw you undesirable attention. You could've stripped all your clothes off once you got in my office, or waited until I fucking got home to pull that stunt."

"Yeah, well, that's not my style."

"No shit. What did he say to you?"

My free hand fists at my side as I burn a hole into my carpet with the strides I'm taking. "You know what, Reese? Don't worry about it. I don't need you to fight my battles for me. I fucking handled it like I said I would."

"Tell me what happened."

"No. And if you want to yell at somebody, yell at yourself. *You're* the one who decided to work with that asshole after I told you months ago he creeped me out. Thanks a lot for thinking of me."

"Dylan!"

I hang up my phone before tossing it onto the bed. *What in the actual fuck?* I actually do the right thing here and before I can even tell him what happened, he's blaming me for it? How is this in any way my fault? I'm not the one who agreed to work with that prick. I wouldn't care how *important* this account was or how much money was involved. I would never work with someone who made my fiancé uncomfortable. If anyone has the right to be angry in this situation, it's me. Reese got paid, laid, and has the nerve to take this out on me?

No. Fuck that.

My phone rings on my bed but I ignore it, making my way downstairs. I have no desire to talk to him right now or anytime soon, for that matter. And I'm in desperate need of a cupcake. Nothing else will do right now.

I march through my kitchen with purpose, through the doorway and behind the counter. Brooke and Joey are sitting at my consultation table as I slide the panel on the display case open and reach for one of my chocolate mousse cupcakes with a ganache-filled center.

"What are you doing?" Joey asks, the sound of the chair scraping on the floor following his voice. "Dylan, no sweets."

I straighten up and leer at him. "If you come between me and this cupcake right now, I will end you." Removing the wrapper as quickly as I can, I shove the whole thing into my mouth as Joey rounds the counter, disapproval on his face. "I mhey have anonther," I say through a mouthful, closing my eyes and moaning at the chocolaty goodness. *Fuck yes, cupcakes.*

"What the hell is going on?" he asks, snatching the wrapper from my hand and tossing it into the trashcan. "Did you tell Reese?" I reach once again for the display case, but my hand is batted away by Joey before he blocks me with his massive frame. "No more until you talk to me. What happened?"

I open my mouth to give him the rundown of my phone call when the shop phone decides to ring at that exact moment. There's no doubt in my mind it's Reese, and I have no intention of answering. Leaning against the counter, I stare at the phone on the wall as Joey moves toward it.

"It's Reese," I say with a clipped voice after swallowing my mouthful.

Joey ignores me and grabs the phone, putting it up to his ear. He frowns at me before saying, "Dylan's Sweet Tooth." I tap my fingers against my arm, seeing his expression change to indicate I was correct in my assumption. "I'm not sure this is the best time to talk to her. She just inhaled a cupcake and is staring at me like she's going to eat me next."

I roll my eyes as Brooke comes to stand next to me. "What's going on?" she asks softly, her eyes flicking between Joey and myself.

"Boys are idiots. If I were you, I'd go lesbian."

She shrugs slightly. "I've dabbled. It's not really my thing. If there isn't at least one dick involved, I can't get into it."

I slide closer to her, my interest in Brooke's sex life suddenly blanketing all my Reese concerns at the moment. "At least one dick? Have you done multiple?"

"Once. But they were bi and seemed to like dick more than me. I felt like a third wheel."

"Someone actually liked dick more than you? I'm shocked," I reply before laughing under my breath and seeing her eyes light up with mischief. Joey's elevated voice grabs both of our attention.

"Listen here. I don't have to do anything. Dylan clearly doesn't want to talk to you right now and as her best friend, I back her up one hundred percent. Hoes before bros." He leans his shoulder against the wall, bringing his free hand up to his hip. "And another thing, I think it's really shitty that you and Ian agreed to work with that asshole. He's clearly psychotic, given the fact he put his hands on Dylan when he knows you… what?" Joey looks over in my direction, his agitated expression softening. "Uh, she didn't tell you that? Well, yeah, he… hello?" He brings the phone away from his ear briefly before returning it. "Helloooo?" Hanging it up, he spins and tilts his head to the side as he strokes his chin. "Funny thing. Reese apparently didn't know about the elevator incident. Care to explain that to me before he comes barreling through the shop door and hauls you out of here over his shoulder?"

I take the elastic band off my wrist and secure my hair into a pony. "I was going to tell him until he opened his stupid mouth and blamed me for drawing undesirable attention with my outfit. Like wearing snow gear would've prevented that jerk-off from touching me. And for Christ's sake, I had a coat on. It's not like I was strutting around half-naked." I run my hands down my face before stepping up to Joey and poking a finger at his chest. "I'm eating another cupcake. You can either join me or step into the back, but it's happening."

"Well I'm sure as hell going to eat one," Brooke says behind me. "I've been practically eye-fucking them all morning."

Joey's eyes dart over my shoulder, dropping to the display case. He sighs before nodding sharply. "Right. This situation definitely calls for massive sugar consumption." He drops his eyes down to look at me. "But fair warning, I will be pushing you during our run tomorrow to make up for this moment of weakness. And no faking shin splints like today. I was so onto you."

I smile up at him sheepishly. "I have no idea what you're talking about."

Brooke hands us both a cupcake, taking one for herself before sliding the panel closed. She gestures toward the clock on the wall with her free hand. "Wanna take bets as to what time Reese arrives? I'd put money on 2:37 p.m.."

Joey shoves half the cupcake into his mouth before responding. "No way. He'll be here within the next few minutes. I'm saying 2:26 p.m.. What do you think?" he asks, nudging against me.

I take a bite out of my cupcake, glancing up at the clock. "Knowing Reese, he's going to hunt down Bryce before he deals with me. And I'd give him an hour for kill time and dumping the body." I swallow my bite, hearing Joey and Brooke's muted laughs next to me. "I'm going to say 3:32 p.m.."

The shop door dings open, causing us all to spin around quickly. I'm sure we're all anticipating Reese to walk through the doorway, but Mr. and Mrs. Crisp step inside the bakery wearing their brightest smiles and carrying a large, elegantly-wrapped present.

"Happy anniversary," I direct at them, setting my half-eaten cupcake on the counter. I glance over at Brooke who is finishing hers. "Can you grab their cake for me? It's the German chocolate one."

She gives me a thumbs-up, chewing animatedly before she walks into the back. Mr. Crisp places the gift he's carrying next to my cupcake, sliding it closer to me as his wife flanks his side. "And happy wedding week to our favorite baker. This is for you, dear," she says as she straightens out the white and gold ribbon on the top.

"For me? You didn't have to get me anything."

"Oh, it's nothing much. Just something small off your registry," Mrs. Crisp says with a smile. "Don't open it until we leave, though."

Joey brushes his hands off before sliding the gift down the counter so it's in front of him. "What a wrapping job. I can never get my corners straight."

"You can't get anything straight," I counter through a teasing smile. He arches his brow playfully at me.

Brooke comes walking from the back, carrying the anniversary cake I made. She hands it off to me and I hold it over the counter, letting my two favorite customers examine it. Mrs. Crisp gasps softly, putting her hand up to her chest. "Oh, my. Dylan, this is so lovely," she says, lifting her eyes to me. "Thank you so much."

"German chocolate. My favorite." Mr. Crisp grabs the cake and licks his lips. "I might just dive into this on the way home."

"There's extra coconut in the frosting just for you," I direct toward him. His eyes enlarge as his grin spreads across his face. "And thank you for the gift. You really didn't have to do that."

Mrs. Crisp waves me off with her hand, her other tucking into the crook of her husband's elbow. "We're so happy for you, dear, and we hate that we can't make it. Make sure you bring in lots of pictures when you get them developed." She waves goodbye, Mr. Crisp winking at me before they slip out of the shop.

Joey slides the gift back over in front of me. "Go on. You know you want to."

I look at him, then at the gift and decide that yes, I definitely want to. After tearing the paper and handing it off to Brooke who deposits it into the trashcan, I pop open the top of the box. Joey helps me shift the tissue paper around until I feel the smooth edge of something. I grab it with both hands and lift it out, smiling so big my cheeks begin to ache.

I place the hot-pink, brand new, industrial-size mixer on the counter. "Oh, wow. This wasn't on my registry."

"No, but you definitely needed this. I always said you should have more than one mixer," Joey says, running his finger along the top of the handle.

"And it's pink. I love that," Brooke adds. "Every girl needs a pink mixer."

I nod in agreement, lifting it off the counter and carrying it into the back. I slide it onto my shelf next to my beaten-down, ten-year-old mixer I still love as much as the first day I got it. Of course, it pales in comparison to this brand new one, but it will always be special to me.

Brooke comes walking into the back and steps up next to me. "Would it be okay if I watched you bake sometime? I'm really interested in learning how you whip up these incredible creations. That cupcake I just ate was insane."

I grin boastfully at the compliment. "Sure. If you want, I could use some help tomorrow when I start the two wedding cakes. Joey can manage up front without you if you want to give me a hand."

She places her hand on my arm, her face falling in surprise. "You'd let me help make *your* wedding cake? What if I mess it up?"

"Are you planning on messing it up?" I ask.

"No. But I can be a bit clumsy."

I grip onto both her shoulders, gaining her full attention. "I'll let you help out on the *other* wedding cake. How's that sound?" She laughs, giving me half a smile. "Come on, let's go finish those insane cupcakes."

We did just that, Joey grabbing two more and polishing off the rest of the chocolate mousse ones. My eyes kept darting between the clock on the wall and the front door, especially when the bell would alert us of someone walking in. But Reese never came. He never stormed into the shop. He never hauled me over his shoulder in typical Reese fashion. He didn't even call the shop number again. By the time 6:00 p.m. rolled around, I was no longer agitated with my quick-tempered fiancé or fuming over what happened with Bryce. After saying goodbye to Joey and Brooke, I took to the stairs with an emotion I didn't plan on feeling the week of my wedding.

Disappointment.

AFTER KICKING OFF MY SHOES, I plop down on the bed and grab my cell phone I had discarded hours ago. Seventeen missed calls from Reese, all stopping around the time he called the shop phone. I scroll through his text messages, noting the time on them, as well. His last one to me was at 2:13 p.m. and it wasn't the usual sweet and dirty text messages I'm used to receiving from him. I roll over onto my back, holding my phone out above me as I re-read it.

Reese: Ignoring my phone calls is really mature.

Yeah, well… okay, fine. It wasn't my most mature moment. But him jumping down my throat about an outfit he thoroughly enjoyed was a bullshit move, especially after he got his rocks off on it. I get that this situation is irritating and making us both homicidal, but I was not at fault here. And right now, I'd really like hearing that from someone other than my inner self.

I close out Reese's text message and pull up Juls' contact info.

"Hey, sweets. It's so weird you called. I was just thinking about you."

I grab a pillow and stuff it underneath my head. "Oh, yeah? Let me guess. Ian filled you in on my afternoon of fun?"

The sound of chips crunching enters the phone. "Hmm? No. What afternoon of fun? Ian's working late tonight, and I haven't talked to him since before lunch."

"I had a run-in with Bryce after giving Reese a lap dance in his office."

The loud, crinkling sound of the chip bag fills my ear. "Chips aren't cutting it. I need real food. Have you eaten yet?"

"Um, no. But did you hear what I just said?"

"Yes, and you can fill me in on every single detail when you meet me at Fletchers. I'm dying for a burger the size of my head."

My mouth waters instantly. *Carbs? Hell yes. Fuck you, salad. Nobody wants you.* I sit up and swing my legs over the side of the bed, stepping into my ballet flats. "Okay. I'll meet you in twenty."

Standing up, I grab my keys off my kitchen counter, freezing in place when the BMW emblem catches my attention. I should tell Reese where I'm going. Even if I was avoiding him earlier, I'm not anymore. And coming home to an empty loft and not knowing where I am would surely make things worse. I open a text message as I lock my door behind me.

Me: Going out to dinner with Juls. Be home later.

AFTER PARKING BEHIND JULS' BLACK Escalade, I walk into Fletchers and spot her at a table in the back. She waves at me with one hand, her other popping a few fries into her mouth.

"Sorry. I hope you don't mind that I already ordered for us. I'm crazy hungry," she says, chewing behind her hand.

"Not at all. You know what I like." I grab a seat, taking a quick sip of my water and watching in amusement as my best friend inhales her plate of fries. "Pregnancy cravings kicking in?"

"Nah. I've just been busy all day with wedding stuff. This is my first actual meal today." She pushes the plate of fries to the middle of the table and wipes her mouth with a napkin. "All right. Spill it." She tosses her napkin onto the table before leaning back in her chair.

"Do you promise not to go into hurricane-mode in the middle

of this restaurant?"

"Depends," she replies, motioning with her hand for me to continue.

I take in a deep breath, filling my lungs to capacity. "Reese bought me a car and had it delivered to the shop this morning. But not just any car. A BMW." A knowing smile spreads across her face, prompting me to lean forward with interest. "Did you know anything about that?"

She shrugs dismissively. "I may have given my opinion on car color. He was going mental trying to decide on his own."

I picture his frustrated state and it brings a smile to my lips. "I can imagine. Anyway, I wanted to really wow him with a thank you for such an undeserving gift."

She holds up her hand, halting my speech. "Dylan, you deserve the world and that man will give it to you. Don't sell yourself short."

I feel my cheeks flush at the compliment. Grinning, I issue her a wink and she gives me one in return. "So, I put on my sluttiest lingerie, covered myself with a trench coat, and went to his office." I pause, crossing one leg over the other and seeing a small smile play at the corner of her mouth. "I gave him a lap dance, which he appreciated greatly at the time, and when I was leaving, Bryce got in the elevator with me. I would've been creeped out had he not touched me, but he did. He got right up against me and made crude comments about my outfit. And then he slid his finger down my neck." I mimic his move and Juls shakes her head, her face taut and her fingers tapping on the table.

"What did you do?"

"Kneed him in the balls."

"Good. Continue."

"I knew I had to tell Reese about it, so I called him as soon as I got back to the bakery. And you know what he said? That I shouldn't have been wearing that outfit and that I once again drew attention to myself. I didn't even get to tell him what happened. Once he put the blame on me, I hung up on him. And then when he couldn't get a hold of me on my cell, he called the shop phone and Joey told him Bryce touched me." I glance down at the table cloth, rubbing my fingertip along the seam. "I was so pissed off at him for blaming me for it, but now that I haven't seen or talked to him in over four hours, I'm not pissed. I'm hurt more than anything."

"Because he made it seem like it was your fault for what happened?" I nod in response to her question. "I can see why you feel that way. It wasn't your fault and Reese knows that. But he's extremely protective of you; he always has been. And hearing that you were put into another situation with Bryce when he once again wasn't around to protect you I'm sure infuriates him. And when guys get angry, they say shit they don't mean. Ian does it all the time." She takes a sip of her water, prompting me to do the same. "I can't even begin to tell you how many petty arguments the two of us get into because he says stuff without thinking. I swear to God, I think testosterone has some sort of negative effect on all rational thought." I laugh, grabbing a fry and popping it into my mouth. "I can't believe that fucker touched you. Reese didn't come to the shop after finding out that information from Joey?"

I shake my head. "No. And he stopped trying to get a hold of me. I'm actually considering calling the local jail to see if he's been locked up." I grab the small vase sitting on our table and place it on the empty table next to us. Juls gives me a questionable look and I remember she doesn't know about the flower on my van. "After my fitting the other night, I found a rose on my windshield. I had this gut feeling it wasn't from Reese. That's so not something he would do. He's way more romantic than that."

Juls crosses her arms over her chest and purses her lips. "That asshole put a flower on your van? That's fucking disturbing, Dylan. You better call the police if he comes into your shop."

"I will." I had already decided that. There is no way I am going to let him into my bakery again. That prick has officially crossed the line.

"I was ready to kill that tool at the club when he was running his mouth. But now? I will seriously take pleasure in dismembering him. I'm not just stellar at planning weddings. I'm resourceful, too. I can make a shiv out of practically anything."

I giggle at my heated best friend as the waiter arrives at the table with our meals. And then my laughter fades immediately as I survey the Cobb salad placed in front of me.

Goddamn it.

I grit my teeth, glancing up at Juls who is smiling widely at me, obviously finding my order humorous. "What the hell is this? I thought we were destroying burgers."

"I never said we." She points her manicured finger at me. "You have a dress to fit into, sweets. And as your Matron of Honor and wedding planner, it is my job to make sure everything goes as planned for Saturday." She picks up her giant, heavenly-looking burger and brings it to her lips. "Besides, Joey told me you had three cupcakes today."

I scowl at her as she takes a massive bite. "Seriously? He told you that?"

"Yup," she says through a mouthful.

I grimace, poking my lettuce with my fork. "I don't know how people eat this stuff all the time."

She moans softly, catching an evil look from me. "Sorry," she murmurs.

And I can't help but laugh at the sight of her, thoroughly enjoying her burger and not caring in the least that she's eating it like a caveman. All of her table manners have been left at the door as she takes bites that would rival Reese's. I eventually dig into my salad after my stomach starts growling at me, but I don't enjoy myself nearly as much as Juls. I do however enjoy her company and the conversation that stays far away from eerie elevator encounters. We talk about her upcoming doctor's appointment and how excited she is to possibly hear the baby's heartbeat. We talk about my wedding and the fact that my mother has also been harassing her with phone calls about last-minute alterations, and we wrap up our meal with talk of my honeymoon to the Cayman Islands. Two weeks with Reese in a bathing suit is the second thing I'm most excited about in terms of upcoming events. The fact that it'll be my husband I'll be staring at for those fourteen days is still strongly holding the lead.

As it should.

AFTER SAYING GOODBYE TO JULS, I head back to the loft,

expecting to have it out with Reese as soon as I arrive. I mentally prepare myself for our discussion as I set the alarm at the front door before walking through the bakery and up the stairs. But when I step through the door, a dark, empty space greets me instead of his expectant scowl. And then I remember what Juls' said about Ian working late. Reese is probably still stuck at the office, and when he does work late, he usually isn't home until after 9:00 p.m., which gives me another hour before I could be expecting him.

I grab an empty box off the floor and sit it on the bed. Packing should help me pass the time, and even though Reese wanted to do this for me, he shouldn't have to. This is my stuff, and I've accumulated a lot over the past three and a half years. I'm not a hoarder by any means, but I also am not one to throw away anything that holds even the tiniest bit of sentimental value. I've kept every movie stub, concert ticket, and playbill holding a Juls and Joey memory. I've kept every thank you note I've ever received from a customer. But probably my most prized possession is the tin I keep on my dresser that holds all of Reese's love notes to me. I grab it, sitting down next to the box and popping off the lid on the tin. I thrum through the contents with my fingers, scraping along the tops of the cards. Every now and then, I'll blindly reach in and grab one, reading it and reliving every emotion I felt when I first opened the tiny brown card. I have every single note in here, even the first one he sent me that I thought I'd thrown away. But Joey had grabbed it for me while I was delivering my apologetic blow job in Reese's office after slapping him for thinking he was married. I had no idea he kept it until he gave it to me at my bridal shower last month as part of my gift. I cried when I read it that day, which I suppose was funny considering how I reacted to it the first time. But that note started everything. If Reese hadn't sent it to me with the bag of flour, I'm not sure what would've happened between us. Maybe we would've eventually seen each other again at some function involving our two best friends, but maybe not. So even though his first note to me is an apology for fucking up and not one that spells out how much he loves me, it's still my favorite.

Next to the one he gave me with my engagement ring.

After packing up a good amount of clothes and what I won't

be using the next three days, I stack the boxes in the corner behind my decorative screen and get ready for bed. It's almost 9:00 p.m., and even though I'd like to stay up and wait for Reese to get home, I know he'll wake me up if he wants to talk about it tonight. And I'm too tired not to crash hard right now. This day has been exhausting, both mentally and emotionally, and as I cuddle up on my side of the bed, I find myself missing not only the wedding stress that was once my only concern, but also the man who blankets me better than any down comforter.

A LOUD, PIERCING NOISE JOLTS me awake and upright, and my body immediately goes rigid. I clamp my hands over my ears, muffling the noise as my eyes adjust to the dark room around me. I'm alone, Reese's side of the bed is completely untouched, and it takes me several seconds to realize what's happening. That noise. I haven't heard it before but I know what it is. My shop alarm is going off, and I need to enter the code to stop it. I slide off the bed and run toward the stairs but freeze when my mind draws a conclusion to the reasoning behind the alarm.

Someone's trying to break in.

I drop to my knees beside the bed and grab the baseball bat I've kept there since that psycho bitch threw a brick at my window last summer. Nobody messes with my business, and I am seriously prepared to do damage with this thing.

I run downstairs, keeping a tight grip on the bat as the noise becomes even louder. I go along the far side of the worktop, trying to see through the doorway as my heart rate jumps to a rapid pace. I can't make out anything and I need to stop the alarm before my ears begin to bleed. Mustering up every ounce of courage I have and keeping the bat at a ready position, I run through the doorway leading into the main bakery.

And then I see him.

He's punching in numbers on the keypad, his legs staggering underneath his tall frame, struggling to keep him upright. He stumbles, leaning into the glass window before straightening up again. I drop the bat and step closer, keeping my focus on him.

"Reese?"

He doesn't hear me over the screeching alarm as his fingers continue to enter incorrect codes. I move quickly, putting my hand on his shoulder and stepping next to him. As I press the correct pattern of numbers, the smell of alcohol permeates my senses. The alarm stops abruptly and silence fills the space between us. I turn my head up, seeing unfamiliar eyes staring back at me. Glassy and dilated, they no longer hold the intensity I'm accustomed to. Even the shade of green seems dulled out, lifeless even. Besides that obvious difference, he's clearly intoxicated, which is not a look I ever imagined seeing on this man. Reese doesn't get drunk. He'll have two, three drinks maybe and then cut himself off. I've never even seen him tipsy before. And as he slouches against the wall, his heavy eyelids closing and his head hanging low, I'm finding myself questioning if I was the only one hurting earlier.

"HEY. ARE YOU OKAY?" I ask, reaching up with a gentle hand. I stroke the side of his face and see him turn into me, pressing his lips against my palm. His breath warms my skin and I feel the uneven rhythm of it, the quick burst and then the shuddering inhale he takes before he drops his head again.

"Need you," he says through a broken voice.

My heart wrenches in my chest cavity as I stare up at this man who looks defeated and beaten down. And also way too drunk to get behind the wheel. "You didn't drive here, did you?"

"Cab. My car's at The Tavern."

Relief runs through me before I'm startled once again by the sound of the shop phone ringing. I dash over to it to answer, double backing when I think Reese is going to topple over. After he seems steady, I run to the phone.

"Hello?"

"Miss Sparks? This is Lenox Security calling to check to make sure everything is okay. We received an alert that your security system was triggered."

"Yes. Yes, it was, but it was an accident. Everything's okay."

"Okay, ma'am, we just wanted to make sure. Have a great

night."

"You, too."

I hang up the phone, rounding the counter and stepping next to Reese. I lift his arm, draping it around my neck and keeping a firm grip on his wrist. My other arm wraps around his waist and pulls him off the wall. "Come on. Let's go upstairs."

Normally when I'm this close to him, I'm relishing in his fresh, citrus scent and setting up camp in the crook of his neck. But right now, he smells like he's hit up every bar in South Side and for the first time since I met him; the urge to nuzzle him is absent. He maneuvers himself with me across the bakery, but I'm doing most of the work as we make it inch by inch. It's a slow effort and when I finally lift my head and size up the stairs we'll have to tackle, my grip on him tightens and a feeling of determination fuels me. I look over at him as I position us at the first step. "You need to help me, okay? It's not that many steps."

His lips twitch into a smile before he drops his head to the side, bumping it against mine. "You're so pretty."

I chuckle, lurching forward and trying to bring him with me. "Thanks. Come on. Lift your feet."

"I stare at you sometimes when you don't see me. I like doing that."

"Oh, yeah?" I sound surprised, but I'm not. I know Reese stares at me. I always feel his eyes on me when he does it. And I like that game we play, where I pretend I don't notice and let him watch me. He does the same when I partake in my own obsessive gazing. I know he sees me. His lip will twitch or he'll coincidentally adjust himself as I'm studying him, drawing my attention off his face.

I'm on to his tactics.

He lifts his left, then his right foot, putting us both on the first step. "I stared at you on my phone tonight. I didn't really like it."

We make it a few more steps as he leans further into me, causing me to let go of his wrist and grip the handrail instead. "Yeah? Let's get you upstairs and then you can tell me why you didn't like it."

"I didn't like it, Dylan."

"I know. Come on. Just a little more. We're almost there." We get two steps away from the door when Reese suddenly drops to his knees, pulling me down with him. "Reese! Hold… what are you doing?"

He turns awkwardly until he's sitting on the step. His head drops between slouched shoulders, and I see the slight shake of his hands as they hang over his knees. I slide next to him, placing a hand on his thigh. He lifts his head and turns to me, the worry in his eyes evident. "I can't just stare at pictures of you. It's not enough."

"Well, I'm right here. You don't have to stare at pictures. Let's go upstairs and you can look at me all you want." I go to stand when his hand grabs my wrist, halting me.

"I watch you all the time." I lower myself back down as he drops his gaze, staring off at nothing. "If I'm not touching you, I want to be."

"I know the feeling," I interject, gaining his attention immediately.

His face hardens. "No. You don't." I open my mouth to argue but stop myself when I see the conviction in his eyes. "It's constant, Dylan. You invade every thought I have even when they have nothing to do with you. I'm not just in love with you. I'm kind of obsessed. And the thought of somebody else watching you the way I do, or needing to touch you like I do…" He pauses, squeezing his eyes shut. "I'm terrified."

I scoot closer, crawling into this lap. His eyes open and refocus on mine as I cradle his face in my hands. "He barely touched me. I'd never let him or anyone else put their hands on me the way you do." He tries to shake his head but I stop him. "You don't need to be scared. I got him good. And I'll do worse if he tries it again."

His hands grab my wrists and pull down, removing my grip. "I'm not scared he'll touch you. I'm scared of what I'll do when I find him."

I'm familiar with that feeling. It consumed me until Reese took it away. Now it's my turn to comfort him.

I look down at his hand resting in my lap. "I used to be scared of what you would do to him. It's why I didn't tell you about seeing him at the club. But then you told me something that took away that worry. Do you remember?" He registers my questions with a slight shake of his head. I shift in his lap, placing my hands on his shoulders and apply gentle pressure. "You said you were a smart guy, and you would never do anything that could get you into trouble. And I knew that was true. I also knew you would never do anything to hurt me. And getting yourself taken away from me because of what you want to do to Bryce would hurt me. You're not the only one who couldn't survive on just pictures to stare at." He rakes a quick hand through his hair, leaving it a right mess. "Is this why you went out drinking?"

He frowns. "I hated what you said to me. About me working with Bryce after knowing how he made you feel. It killed me to hear you say that. Because I know how it looks. I fucking know. And I just wanted to stop thinking about everything." He squints, flattening his hand against his temple. "It didn't help."

"I didn't mean it. I was just angry because I thought you were blaming me for what happened."

He grabs my face with both hands and forces me closer, putting us inches apart. "I'm sorry I yelled at you. I didn't mean to say that. I'm just so fucking frustrated that this shit is taking so long. But I'm close. I'm so fucking close, Dylan. It's almost over, okay?"

I don't question what he's saying to me. I know he won't tell me anyway, and I don't want to focus on this anymore. I slide off his lap, standing and reaching for him. "Come on. Let's go lie down."

We make it up the stairs, me still supporting a good amount of his weight. I shuffle him toward the bed, dropping his arm from around my neck and giving him a light shove. "Go ahead and get on the bed. I'll be right there."

He grabs my waist with both hands, pulling me against his chest. "Come with me."

I laugh against his dress shirt before turning my gaze up to him. Tender eyes meet mine. "I am. I just need to get you some water."

He grumbles incoherently before letting me go. Grabbing a glass from the cabinet, I fill it with some tap water and toss a few ice cubes in. As I round the counter, I spot Reese's long legs hanging off the edge, the rest of him face-planted in the middle of bed. I set the glass on my nightstand and pull his shoes off, dropping them on the floor.

"Roll over, handsome," I say, kneeling next to him and nudging his side. He moans but doesn't move. Not in the slightest. He's dead weight, and I can't help but recognize the fact that even a passed-out, face-down Reese is better-looking than any other guy put in this scenario. I shove my hands underneath his body and push as hard as I can, rolling him onto his back. Eyes closed. Hair a right, sexy mess. I take a moment to appreciate the sweet look on his face, which will most likely be nowhere in sight tomorrow if the hangover I'm predicting decides to show up.

His heavy, even breathing fills the air as I tug off his khakis and socks. I loosen his tie, unbuttoning his dress shirt and placing them with his pants. I grab the pillows and tuck one under his head, knowing full well there is no way I'll be able to shift his body up the bed to lie how we usually do. So we're going with this arrangement tonight.

Placing my pillow next to his, I get settled on my side and tuck my hands under my chin. I stare at his profile until my eyelids become too heavy to hold open anymore.

NORMALLY WHEN I WAKE UP after having passed out next to Reese, I'm used to seeing an empty side of the bed next to me. He's always up before me during the week, getting in his own workout at the gym before he heads into the office. And even though he came home drunk last night, I still expected to wake up alone. He's so dedicated, it wouldn't surprise me in the least if he pushed through it with the worst hangover in the history of hangovers. But before I even open my eyes when my alarm goes off, I know he's next to me.

I'll always feel his presence before I see him.

I sit up after turning off my alarm, spotting him lying on his side. That's also different. Reese is usually sprawled on top of me when I wake up, his head pressed against my chest and his long legs tangled with mine. I decide to let him sleep while I run with Joey. If Reese is sleeping in, he must need it.

After putting on my workout clothes and stepping into my

Nike's, I press my lips to his forehead, hearing him moan softly into his pillow. I make my way downstairs and see Joey's tall frame stretching on the other side of the glass.

"You are not going to believe who I ran into last night," he says as he pulls his arm across his chest.

I lock the door behind me and tuck my key into the pocket on the inside of my shorts. "Who?"

"Your loser ex-boyfriend."

I pull my knee up to my chest, feeling my muscle tighten. "Get the hell out of here. Where?" I haven't seen Justin since he made the mistake of coming to my bakery to apologize for putting his hands on me last summer. I was in no mood for him or his apology, and Reese just so happened to be there. I've never seen my stupid ex look so terrified before.

It was a good look on him.

"The market. He seemed to be shopping for one, so you know I had to pry. And upon further inspection, I noticed he wasn't wearing a wedding ring."

I shrug impassively, switching legs. I'm not surprised if his cheating marriage failed. Nor do I give a shit. "Did you say anything to him?"

He pops his gum before smiling cunningly. "Nah. The little chicken-shit practically sprinted down the frozen food aisle when he spotted me. I'm sure he saw your engagement announcement in the paper, though. That advertisement took up the entire page."

I laugh as I roll my ankle on the pavement, loosening it up. Reese made sure to send in the biggest photo he had of the two of us to the local newspaper several months ago. When I insisted on something a bit smaller out of sheer modesty, he distracted me the way he usually does and I forgot all about it until it was published. Well, until he had it framed and delivered to me.

I stretch my neck from side to side as Joey moves down the sidewalk, motioning for me that he's ready to start running. I jog up to his side and we take off at our usual pace. The fact that Joey gave me a warning yesterday about pushing me during this run stays locked away inside my head. If he doesn't remember it, I'm not reminding him.

"So, what happened with Reese last night after he got home? Was he pissed about Bryce?"

"Oh, you're not going to believe this. He showed up drunk and woke me in the middle of the night with the shop alarm going off. He couldn't even enter the code, he was so plastered."

Joey flicks his head toward me, his mouth dropping open and the wad of gum nearly falling from his mouth. "Shit." He pushes it back in before responding. "Reese was drunk? Are you serious?" I nod and he continues. "What kind of a drunk was he? Sloppy? Horny? I looove when Billy gets drunk. He's extra frisky."

I nudge him hard in his side and he flinches. "No, he wasn't horny. He was actually kind of sad."

"Ughhhh. I hate depressing drunks. My mother's like that."

We round the corner and start up the big hill, causing us both to grumble our exhaustion until we make it to the top. I steady my breathing after taking in three deep breaths. "What do you think Reese could be doing with Bryce that would make working with him so important? He keeps telling me to trust him and that it's almost over, but I don't understand why he can't just tell me."

Joey thinks silently for several seconds, the sound of our feet striking the pavement becoming more prominent. "I don't know. I feel like we're in a fucking episode of The Sopranos, only with accountants instead of Mob bosses." He ducks his chin into his T-shirt, wiping the sweat off his nose. "Maybe he doesn't want you to be involved if things don't work out the way he's hoping. Like maybe he thinks Bryce will retaliate by hurting you if he finds out Reese is up to something."

"But what could he be doing? Like you said, he's an accountant."

"I don't fucking know. Tax shit? Whatever it is, it must be worth it to Reese. I don't think I could work with some guy who hit on Billy. I'd go crazy. I can't imagine how hard that must be for him."

"I think that's why he got drunk." I picture those desperate eyes he had last night while sitting on the steps, stripped down and raw. I never want to see him like that again. And I suppose Joey's right. Reese could be keeping me in the dark to keep me protected. Bryce does seem like the type to lash out, and if he wanted to get back at Reese, he could do it by getting to me. But I'll never let that happen. I'll never let that douchebag anywhere near me. And God help him if he decides to take it out on Reese. If he lays one finger on my fiancé, I'll be the one spending my honeymoon in jail.

A sharp slap on my ass breaks me out of my mind set. "Ahh! What the hell?" I shriek, rubbing my left cheek.

"Cupcakes, cupcake. I told you I'd be pushing you today. Think I forgot?" He drops back and gets directly behind me. Another slap and I'm arching away from him, hissing in pain. "Move it. Or you'll get to explain to Reese why you let me spank you. I'm sure that'll go over well."

Laughing, I pick up speed and put some distance between us, but it's fleeting. Joey catches up within a few seconds and we continue our run with him on my heels. I'm rewarded with a few more slaps when I absentmindedly slow down, but I'm not used to this pace. This is the speed which renders you unable to speak to your running buddy. My legs are burning, as are my lungs, and I'm sweating more than I ever have in my entire life. And it isn't even sixty degrees out yet.

But I don't complain.

I don't quit on Joey and give up even though my body is screaming at me to do just that.

I have a dress to fit into, so I muster up every ounce of willpower in my body and push through my run. Because let's be honest, the chance of me sneaking another cupcake before I walk down that aisle is looking pretty good right now.

I'M DRIPPING SWEAT AFTER WHAT feels like the hardest run of my life. After saying goodbye to Joey, I head upstairs and expect to see Reese still passed out in bed, but it's empty. I see the light creeping from under the bathroom door and kick off my shoes before I make my way into the kitchen. As I'm pulling a bottled water out of the fridge, I hear the reason behind Reese being out of bed. The unmistakable sound of him throwing up has me rushing to the door, twisting the locked doorknob.

"Reese?"

The toilet flushes and then I hear his gravelly voice, barely above the noise. "Yeah?"

I jar the knob again, tossing my bottled water onto the floor. "Open the door."

"No. I don't want you in here."

"Well, that's too bad," I scoff, grabbing one of my kitchen chairs. I climb up on it, skimming my hand along the top of the door jam and feeling for the key I keep up there. Once I grab it, I jump down and move the chair out of the way. "I'm coming in. I can handle vomit."

"Dylan, please don't come in here," his raspy voice begs me.

I wiggle the key around until I feel it unlatch the door. I turn the handle freely this time and swing it open, spotting Reese on his knees. He's slouched over the toilet, shirtless and only in a pair of boxers. His head is resting on his forearm and he doesn't bother to lift it when I enter the room. I place the key on the bathroom counter and crouch down behind him, placing my hand on his back.

"Are you okay?" I ask as I begin rubbing my hand along his clammy skin.

He coughs a few times, dropping his head and spitting into the toilet. "I asked you not to come in here. Why would I want you to see me like this?"

"In two days, I'll be vowing to be with you for better or for worse. Or did you forget about that?" He tilts his head to the side so our eyes meet. "You took care of me when I was like this. Now it's my turn."

He's either too weak to give me a rebuttal, or the fact that I've reminded him of how many days we have left is soothing him. I run my fingers through his hair, which is sticking out every which way, feeling the dampness of his sweat on my hand. He looks thoroughly exhausted, with bags under his eyes and his complexion looking paler than I've ever seen it, but somehow, he pulls it off. Not that I'm the least bit surprised.

I place my lips to his shoulder. "You're beautiful even when you're hung-over."

He drops his chin, smiling. "You're beautiful even when you ugly-cry."

His words have me wanting to feel his mouth against mine, even if he has been puking his guts up. But I bite back the urge and settle for a wink instead, which prompts his smile to grow the tiniest bit. I stand and grab a washcloth from the cabinet, wetting it at the sink. "I'm going to get you some water," I say as I lay the cool rag on the back of his neck. He acknowledges me with a subtle nod before closing his eyes.

I grab the bottled water I had discarded and return to the bathroom just as a wave of nausea hits Reese. He arches over the toilet, gripping the seat with his hands. His back goes rigid, every muscle flexing as he proceeds to vomit and dry heave. I kneel behind him and hold the rag against his neck, rubbing his upper arm with my other hand. This round lasts several minutes, and when he slouches down, seemingly finished, I pick up the water bottle and unscrew the cap.

"Here."

He looks over his shoulder at me and takes the bottle. After swishing the water around in his mouth, he spits it into the toilet and repeats the action several times. He tries to stand, but I stop him with a firm hand on his shoulder.

"Are you done?"

He nods, pushing to his feet. "I think so. That shit sucked. I haven't thrown up since I was little." I follow him over to the sink, watching as he splashes some cold water onto his face. He grabs his tooth brush and slicks some toothpaste on it, connecting with my eyes in the mirror. I see his rake down my body. "How was your run?"

"Difficult. I had cupcakes yesterday and paid for it greatly." I begin stripping out of my sweaty clothes while Reese continues brushing his teeth. "Are you going into work today?"

"No. I took a sick day. I need to go get my car and then I thought maybe I'd watch you bake." He spits into the sink and rinses off his tooth brush. "If that's okay with you."

I smile, tossing my clothes into my hamper. "That's definitely okay with me. You haven't watched me bake in a while." I reach into the shower and turn it on, testing the temperature. "But you'll have to disappear when I start working on our wedding cake. That is off-limits."

He steps up behind me, wrapping his arms around my body and pulling me against him. His hands splay across my lower abdomen, protectively caressing it. Like he knows without a doubt there's something in there worth protecting. When I look down to watch, I see the sweat pooling between my breasts. Suddenly grossed out, I try to slip away but his grip tightens. "What are you doing?"

"I'm all sweaty." I continue to squirm in his arms but freeze when his lips touch my neck.

"I like you sweaty."

"You like me sweaty when *you're* the reason for it."

"Hmm. Let's explore that."

I turn in his arms, staring up at him with disbelief. "Don't you feel like death? How can you even think about sex right now?"

He shoots me a baffled look. "You're naked and I'm touching you. But honestly, you could be on the other side of the room in a fucking parka and I'd be thinking about it. I'm always thinking about it. Hangover or not."

I flatten my hands against his chest and push. "Rain check, handsome."

"With frosting?"

His request has my insides burning as much as my legs were on that run. We haven't played around with frosting in a few weeks. Usually, the urge to lick it off me hits him in the middle of us fooling around, sending him sprinting into the kitchen for the ready-made tub I keep on hand for such occasions. He's too impatient to wait for me to whip up a batch, which he proved when he bent me over my worktop and fucked me while the neglected, half-put-together icing went untouched. That happened a few days after we reconciled. And now, you'll always find a tub of it in both our fridges.

I shoot him a cheeky grin and nod. At my promise, he drops his arms and returns to the sink, allowing me to finally step into the shower.

The loft is empty when I step out of the bathroom with a towel wrapped around me. I slip into a sundress, one that cinches at my waist, and step into my favorite pair of strappy sandals. After applying some tinted moisturizer and mascara, I blow-dry my hair partially and clip half of it back.

Reese is sitting on a stool pulled up to my worktop, dressed in a pair of running shorts and a T-shirt. He lifts his head at the sound of me coming down the stairs, the apple turnover he's about to bite into stopping inches from his mouth. I grab my apron off the hook by my shelving unit and slip it over my neck. I know he's still looking at me. Even though I'm pulling out the racks of pastries, muffins, and cupcakes with my back to him, I feel it burning into the back of me, no doubt appreciating my outfit. I glance at him over my shoulder, prompting him to lift his gaze.

"I love you in dresses," he says before finally taking a bite of his turnover.

"I know," I reply. "Wait 'til you see the one I'm marrying you in."

His eyes lose focus momentarily as he drops his hand to his lap. Clearing his throat, he adjusts himself discreetly and I feel my face heat up as I place the racks on the worktop. I love that the very idea of me in my wedding dress gets that kind of reaction from him, even though he has no idea what the dress looks like.

"Do you need any help?" he asks after regaining his composure.

"Sure."

He shoves the rest of the turnover into his mouth, standing up and wiping his hands on his shorts. We each carry a rack up front and fill the display case. As Reese meticulously arranges the cupcakes in a way only he would do, the shop door dings open and Joey walks in, followed by Brooke.

"Well, isn't this a nice surprise," Joey says as he steps up to the counter. I see the side of Reese's mouth twitch into a smile as he straightens up and greets both of my employees with a tilt of his head.

Brooke places my cup of coffee on the counter. "Sorry, Reese. I would've gotten you one if I knew you'd be here this morning."

He shrugs before grabbing my cup. "That's okay." I watch as he takes a sip of my usual order, which is entirely too sugary for his taste. Reese is a black coffee kind of guy, and the look on his face is priceless as he swallows his mouthful. He holds the cup out to me with a frown. "Jesus Christ. That tastes like ice cream."

"Mmmm. Just the way I like it." I place the cup to my lips and take a sip. "So, Brooke. How was your date last night?"

Her smile fades instantly, hardening as the memory of it washes over her. "Painful," she grits out. "I swear to God, I'm done with dating sites. The guy last night, Dustin, was a major let-down in the package department. One look and I was like," she brushes her hands off in front of her, holding them out with her palms facing us as she steps back. "I'm out." The three of us burst out laughing as she moves toward the kitchen, smiling over her shoulder before she slips into the back.

I take another sip of my drink, moaning against the brim. The caffeine perks me up instantly, and the caramel might just be enough to curb my sweet tooth for the remainder of the day.

Maybe.

Doubt it.

Joey drums his fingers on the counter, his eyes flicking between me and Reese while his lips stay curled up into a sly smile. "And how is my favorite soon-to-be-married couple this morning? Anyone getting cold feet?"

I lift my eyes to Reese, catching the look he gives as his response.

"Right. What a ridiculous question," Joey says through a laugh.

I reach behind my back and untie my apron. "Reese and I need to go get his car this morning. Can you handle things? We shouldn't be long."

Joey nods, running a hand through his hair. "Yeah, no problem. Just don't forget about the other wedding cake you need to start on. Besides your own." He adds that last part with a playful smile.

"I haven't." Spinning around, I take another sip of my coffee and place a hand on Reese's arm. "Come on. You ready?"

"Yeah, let me run upstairs and get my keys."

I slip my apron off and toss it under the counter as he disappears into the back. Brooke walks back up front, wearing her biggest smile.

"This is adorable. I love that he's here."

"Me, too," I reply. I *really* love that he's here. In fact, I'm tempted to ask him to take another sick day tomorrow. I smile at her, remembering what I promised yesterday. "When I get back, it's you, me, and a wedding cake."

She claps her hands excitingly in front of her. "Oooo, yes! This is going to be awesome! What kind of cake are we making?"

Joey holds his hand up, halting my response. "One that doesn't sound appetizing at all. Banana cake with caramel cheesecake mousse." He grimaces, sticking a finger in his throat to mimic throwing up.

I shove his shoulder. "It's going to be a beautiful cake. The bride wants sugared orchids cascading down one side. I love that.

And those flavors work really well together." Reese walks back through the doorway, twirling his keys on his finger. I walk around the display case to join him. "We'll be back soon. Play nice, you two."

Joey wraps his arm around Brooke's shoulder. "Who? Us? There's nothing but love here."

I stop at the door, eyeing him suspiciously over my shoulder. Brooke is staring up at him with her own, as he wears the biggest teasing grin I've ever seen. "Did you get laid last night?" I ask. His playful eyebrow wiggle answers for him. Brooke pushes away from him, scoffing in the process as I roll my eyes. "Later, bitches."

"SO, WHAT EXACTLY DID YOU drink last night? Do you remember?" I ask as I weave in and out of traffic.

"I remember everything."

I glance over at him, seeing his set profile. "You do?"

He runs his hands down his face, dropping them to his lap before responding. "Yeah. I know I drank whiskey. A lot of it."

"Do you remember getting home?" I steal another glance and see him drop his head against the seat.

"I remember everything, Dylan. The way you looked at me after you stopped the alarm. The conversation on the stairs. Everything. I promise you'll never see me like that again."

I pull over in front of The Tavern and put the car in park before I grab his hand. He immediately threads his fingers through mine, keeping his eyes focused on them. "I didn't mind taking care of you. Not last night and not this morning either. It's my job."

His eyes meet mine, flashing with assurance. "It won't happen again. The only thing that makes me lose control is you. Nothing else. Okay?"

I give his hand a gentle squeeze while his other grabs the door handle. "Okay. I'll meet you back at the shop?"

He leans over, pressing his lips against mine. What starts off as the lightest touch quickly dissolves into a searing connection. I fist his shirt with both hands, holding him to me as he devours my mouth. His lips tease my jaw, my neck, the delicate skin below my ear. He has me worked into a wild frenzy in a matter of seconds. Breaking away, he pants loudly against my mouth before licking his bottom lip.

"You taste like your coffee."

"Sorry."

He smiles. "Don't be. I love how everything tastes on your tongue." His lips meet mine once more, briefly, before he opens the car door. "I'll follow you."

"Good luck keeping up," I tease, earning myself a warning look before he steps out. He closes the door, and I watch him walk to the driver's side of his car through my rear-view mirror. I lick my lips, tasting the combination of sugar and coffee.

Apple turnover, caramel macchiato, and Reese Carroll.

I'm doubting anything has tasted better.

"WHY DO YOU USE EGGS at room temperature? I never got that."

I register Brooke's question over the sound of my brand new mixer, which is an absolute dream. Not only does it have all these settings my old mixer failed to come with, but it's also whipping my ingredients in record timing. After depositing the bags of flour and sugar onto the worktop, I answer. "Because they mix better into the batter. And it makes the finished product fluffier. I can always tell when someone doesn't use room temperature eggs."

"It's a tragedy when cold eggs are used," Joey adds, sticking his head through the doorway. "Brooke, grab me the container of blueberry muffins. We're almost out up here."

I measure out my dry ingredients as Brooke hands off the Tupperware container. She returns to my side, brushing the flour along the wood with her finger. "Do you always make wedding cakes a few days in advance?"

"I like to. Especially if I have more than one to make. We'll knock out the cake layers today, and I'll freeze them overnight. That will help lock in the moisture. And tomorrow afternoon, we'll focus solely on assembling the cakes and all the intricate detail work." I look over at her with a playful expression. "The fun stuff."

"This is so cool. I can't wait to see the finished products."

I see that familiar excitement beaming off Brooke that I always have when I make wedding cakes. Maybe this will be her niche. Maybe she was always meant to be a baker. I step to the other side of the worktop, motioning toward the measuring cups I've readied for her. "Can you add those in after the batter turns a light, golden color? That's when you know the caramel is fully mixed."

"You're not going somewhere, are you?" she asks with wide, startled eyes.

I laugh, grabbing the bowl of bananas in front of Reese. He lifts his eyes off his phone screen to give me a quick wink before returning to his task. Whatever he's looking at, it's kept his attention for the past hour.

Looking over at Brooke, I shake my head and begin peeling the twenty-five bananas I made Joey run out and get this morning. "No, I'm not going anywhere. We're doing this together."

She opens her mouth to respond when the sound of Reese's cell phone ringing halts her.

He stands abruptly, nearly knocking his stool over but grabbing it before it crashes to the ground. He frantically brings the phone up to his ear. "Reese Carroll." His eyes drift from the stool to my face, and I see his chest rise with a deep inhale. He mouths "I'll be right back" and takes quick strides across the kitchen, taking the stairs at a rapid pace.

"Jeez. Must've been important," Brooke jokes, but at her word usage my mind begins to wonder if this urgent matter has anything to do with Bryce. I feel my pulse quicken at the thought but quickly focus on my task. I have two cakes to make, and one can't even be started until Reese disappears. He can't see the ingredients I'm using for our wedding cake. It will definitely give away my surprise to him.

I'm slicing the bananas and depositing them into a big mixing bowl when Reese comes running back down the stairs. His heavy footsteps gain my attention, spinning me around. He's dressed in his work clothes now, wearing one of my favorite gray-plaid ties of his.

Hands grab my face and he plants the sweetest, gentlest Reese kiss to my lips, melting me like the caramel sauce I used in the batter.

He pulls away, and I see the sheer thrill pouring out of him, like he's just won the damn lottery or something. He smiles and I melt further at the sight of my favorite lines next to his eyes. "I need to run to the office."

"You seem very happy about that."

He laughs, kissing the corner of my mouth. "I am," he whispers against me. "Two days, love. Two days and you are *mine*."

His words send a chill through me. I'm his already but God, the way he says *mine* like I'm not even close to being his yet makes my mouth go dry. I watch him walk away with the biggest smile I've ever seen on his face.

And I know it has nothing to do with going to the office.

LUCKILY WITH REESE'S SWIFT DEPARTURE, Brooke and I were able to throw together not only the cake layers for the other wedding but for mine, as well. I had a great time cooking with Brooke, and she seemed to pick up on things like a natural.

I've never seen any bit of my best friend in her sister, and I've known them both for over ten years. Brooke always seemed so brash and extroverted. She never let you get a word in usually, especially if it contradicted what she was trying to get across. And even though she seemed popular in school, she never had any friends who stuck around. Joey, Juls, and I have been together for as long as I can remember. Yes, there were others who floated in and out of our lives, but the three of us always stayed true to each other. Brooke didn't seem to have that, not even now. Her closest friend was Juls from what I observed. She and I were always friendly, but this is the most I've ever talked to her. And as we spent the afternoon with just the two of us in the kitchen, laughing and talking like we've done it for years, I find myself forgetting who I'm with.

I see glimpses of her sister shining through. The way she focuses on her task but still keeps the conversation going, not allowing for a dull moment. The way she reaches over and brushes the flour off my cheek I had absentmindedly smudged on. But most of all, I see it in the way she tears up when she asks me to recount how Reese proposed to me. Juls always has the waterworks on reserve, especially for romantic moments. And Reese's proposal can never be topped, in my opinion. So even though I spend the afternoon with Brooke Wicks, it feels like Julianna Thomas is standing next to me.

I'm wiping off my worktop after putting away all my baking supplies. Joey and Brooke left a little while ago, and the shop is quiet.

Too quiet for me right now.

I'm antsy, and the anticipation of Reese getting back and hopefully returning with that same smile plastered on his face is making me fidget. I'm trying to stay busy, but I'm certain I've wiped down my worktop at least five times now. If it isn't disinfected at this point, it never will be.

At the sound of the shop door opening, I lift my head and glance through the doorway. Reese comes walking into the kitchen, his tie loosened and his sleeves rolled up to mid-forearm.

I drop the rag on the worktop, spinning around and greeting him with a smile. He's storming toward me with purpose, determination in each step. I grip the edge of the wood, recognizing the feverish look in his eyes. My lips part, but not to speak because I can't. Not when I know he's about to kiss me, and I know that's what he's about to do. My mouth becomes parched as he presses his body against mine, his hands flattening on the wood behind me. Boxing me in. Keeping me right where he wants me.

His mouth molds to mine with desperation, rendering me speechless. I tremble against him as his tongue invades my mouth, easily gaining entry. I lift my hands to hold him to me but only get halfway up my body before he grabs my wrists and slams my hands back down on the worktop.

"No, love. It's your turn not to touch me."

"What? No, let me touch."

He shakes his head, releasing my wrists. I keep my hands where he's put them and watch as he reaches up and undoes his tie.

I know what's coming. I know I'm about to get my last look before he does whatever the hell he wants with me.

God, how fucking lucky am I?

"Wait," I plead as he holds his tie between both hands, ready to take away my sight. He tilts his head, waiting for me to speak. I hit him with a smile first, loosening the tightness that's set in his face. "Tell me what's going on? What was the phone call about earlier?"

He keeps the tie in one hand and brings the other up to my face. I lean into it, blinking heavily as he moves closer. "Do you remember when you asked me if I worked with Bryce? Because you didn't want to have to see him if you came to visit me?" I nod, thinking back to that day on Reese's couch. "The thought of some guy making you uncomfortable drove me insane. Even then, I was so possessive over you I would've killed him if he so much as looked at you again. I shot him down every time he wanted to hire me after that. I didn't want to be near him. But then I found something." He takes his hand off my face and rakes it through his hair. "I was looking through the file I had on him and something caught my attention. Bryce is a smart guy. He's successful with his investments, but some of his figures weren't adding up. He told us the last time Ian and I worked with him that people donate to his company. Anonymously. Which can happen but he had a lot of donations and the figures weren't small. I showed it to Ian and told him if Bryce asked to hire us again, I wanted that account."

"You thought he was doing something illegal?" I ask.

"I *knew* he was doing something illegal. But I needed access to all of his monies to prove it. So I've just been biding my time, hoping he would pursue our company to work with him again. I didn't know if it was going to happen. I turned him down a lot after I met you, but he finally came to us." He reaches out and tucks my hair behind my ear. "I took a major risk in working with him. I knew he'd try to get to you once he got around me again. Bryce likes to push people's buttons, and he's good at it. Every fucking time I met with him, he brought you up, but I couldn't react. I couldn't lose that account when I didn't have what I needed yet. Ian got this guy, some private investigator, to work with us. I was supplying him with what I thought could bring Bryce down, but he was taking forever with it. He kept needing more documents or telling me what I gave him couldn't be deemed illegal. I was getting impatient. I couldn't have something happen to you." Both hands grab my shoulders. "It killed me to work with him, Dylan. You have to know that."

"I know. It's okay."

"It's not okay." His hands slide down so that he's gripping my elbows. "I saw what he did to you in that elevator. After Joey told me he touched you, I called security and asked to see the surveillance footage. I saw how you reacted to him. And I fucking saw him touch you." His eyes close tight momentarily. I reach up and touch his cheek, seeing them flash open. "I lost it. I searched that entire building for him. I didn't know if he was still there but I knew if I found him, I'd kill him. Ian tried to calm me down but I didn't want to hear it. He *touched* you. He touched what was mine. And it was my fault. I brought him back around. I put my need to get to him before you. And I hated myself for it."

"It wasn't your fault. You didn't bring him back around. Joey told me the other day that Bryce had stopped in the shop a few times before you took on that account with him. He was always there. You were trying to protect me. Don't ever hate yourself for that."

He sighs heavily and rubs his eyes. "I'm honestly glad I didn't know he's been in here. Thank you for not telling me about that."

"You're welcome," I say, biting back my smile. "I hate keeping stuff from you, too."

"Well, it doesn't matter anymore. That phone call I got earlier was from the PI. He discovered that Bryce has been embezzling funds from clients' accounts. That's what all those anonymous donations were. I had to go into the office to give him everything I had on Bryce. He's done. I fucking got him."

I feel a lightness take over my body, like the biggest weight has been lifted off my shoulders. "He's getting arrested?"

He nods. "He's looking at twenty-five years." He presses himself against me again, wrapping his arms around my waist. "I'm sorry I couldn't tell you. The PI told us we couldn't say anything to anybody. It fucking killed me to keep that from you, but I needed this to work. I needed to do something that would keep him away from you permanently, and killing him wasn't an option."

"Thank you for what you did."

He brings our foreheads together. "I will always protect you,

Dylan. We might not be married yet, but I said my vows to you a long time ago."

I reach around and slide the tie out of his hand, holding it between us. "And I will always trust you. With everything. Including what you're about to do to me."

He takes the tie from me as all the softness fades from his features. I see the transformation happen immediately, like a switch has been flipped inside him. The predatory shift in his eyes. The way his nostrils flare and his jaw twitches just below his temple. This is dominant Reese. This is the man who takes what he wants and right now, I'm his target.

"Close your eyes."

I obey instantly. There is zero thought involved. Nor is there any part of me that wants to fight him. I want this; I want everything from his man. He's never taken away my senses before, leaving me vulnerable, but I trust him completely. He could do anything to me right now and I wouldn't object.

The silk material of the tie slides over my eyes. I turn my head and press my lips to his arm as he secures it behind me with a knot. I feel his hands on my waist as he lifts me off the ground and plants me on the edge of the worktop.

"Lie back. I want you to keep your hands flat on the table, and I don't want you to remove them. Do you understand?"

"Yes," I answer, lying back on the wood. I flatten my palms out next to me and wait for my next instruction. I feel his body settle between my legs as his hands slide up my thighs, teasing the bottom of my dress.

"Do you know the exact moment I knew I loved you?"

I gasp softly, not expecting him to go there right now. Not at all anticipating him using my question to him on me. My body and mind are prepared for sex, completely primed and ready, even if it is in a way I've never experienced before. But this? His words I cherish more than anything he could possibly give me? I'm not at all prepared for this admission.

I don't answer; I'm not sure I can right now. Every muscle in my body is taut and I keep finding myself holding my breath, not wanting my suddenly erratic breathing to muffle what he's about to tell me. This might very well top the vows we're going to be saying to each other in two days. And we picked out some pretty emotional ones. I cry every time I read through them.

"You're nervous," he states. "Is this something you don't want to know?"

I smile, releasing my bottom lip from between my teeth. "No, I do. Of course I do. I just wasn't expecting you to get all sweet on me right now."

"It'll be brief," he replies. "You told me when you knew, so it's only fair you know how long it's been for me." His hands move up my body on top of my dress, skimming over my breasts. The weight of his touch feels different now that I can't watch him. All my energy is focused on his hands and where they might go. One palm flattens on my chest, resting there.

"What are you doing?" I ask when he doesn't move his hand.

"I want to feel you react to what I'm about to tell you."

I shudder underneath him. "Okay."

He gives me a few seconds to calm down a bit. I need it. If he wants to feel my reaction, then my heart rate needs to slow the hell down. I take in several calming breaths, feeling everything settle.

And then, he speaks.

"I knew I loved you when you sent me that text, asking if I would stop whatever I was doing to come to you and I didn't have to think about it. At all. Dylan, before I even finished reading your question, I was grabbing my keys and heading to the door."

I feel my tears being absorbed into the material of the tie. Not being able to see him while he tells me this is doing things to me. I'm purely focused on his voice and the raw honesty in it, not his eyes that usually hold onto me. I feel like my entire body is quivering beneath him while I try to anticipate his words. And I know he's feeling my reaction to him. My heart is slamming so hard against my sternum my bones feel like they're vibrating.

"Love," he continues in a much softer voice, "I could've been on the other side of the country and I would've found a way to get to you if you asked me. Nothing was more important to me than you. And nothing ever will be. You said you knew you loved me on my birthday, right?"

"Mmm hmm." I reach up and wipe the tear that's escaping from underneath the blindfold. "Why?"

"Because I think you loved me that night, too."

There's no stopping the tears now. It's a useless act. I nod repeatedly as I reach up and cover my face with my hands. I'm crying because he's right. I did love him then. I knew it when I had to see him that night after being so damn adamant about not seeing that much of each other. But I was determined to fight those feelings, and I buried them deep. But he knew. He always knew.

"When I opened my door and saw you standing there, I knew it wasn't just me. Even though you would've never admitted it, you loved me then, too."

My entire body shakes with my cries, and I feel his palm slide up my chest and around my neck. He grips me there, pulling me to a sitting position. I drop my hands to bury my face in his neck but stop when I feel the tie being pulled down. My eyes slowly flutter open, adjusting to the light as his thumbs wipe away my tears.

"I did love you then," I whisper, fisting his dress shirt as he cradles my face in his hands. I sniffle loudly, slowly calming myself and staring into his bright green eyes. "I was so scared to love you, but I did. You're kind of impossible not to fall in love with, damn it."

He laughs, running his finger along the tie, which is now around my neck. "I love how you reacted to that. Your heartbeat sped up like crazy."

"Well, that's nothing new. If you're in the same room as me, it goes haywire." I strain my neck to steal a kiss. "Thank you for telling me that."

"You're welcome. Now," his hands trail down my side, stopping at my waist. "We need to go upstairs and get a new tie. You soaked this one."

I cock my head to the side, arching my brow and going to the dirtiest place in my head because he's easily set me up for it.

He notices my reaction and smiles. "Go ahead. Say it."

"Say what?"

"You know what."

"Nope. Sorry. I have no idea what you're talking about."

"Really? I find it hard to believe that right now, you're not dying to say something involving the word 'soaked'."

I giggle, dropping my gaze to the buttons on his dress shirt. I tease them with my fingers. "It sounds to me like *you're* the one with the perverted mind right now. Not me."

"Is that right?"

"Yup."

"Okay." He quickly slips a hand between my legs and presses against the front panel of my panties.

"Oh, God." My head rolls to the side as I grip onto his arms. *Holy shit.* I shudder when he moves along the lace material, teasing me with the tiniest bit of contact.

"Don't say it then," his deep voice taunts me. "Don't tell me you're not completely soaked for me right now. That I couldn't make you come all over my hand if I wanted to."

"If I don't say it, are you… Reese… shit… are you going to stop?"

"Yes."

I shift my eyes up to meet his. "Okay. Say your line again."

"We need a new tie. You soaked this one."

"That's not the only thing that's soaked!" I reply animatedly. "I'm soaked. Really soaked. My panties are pretty much useless at the moment. You should probably just remove them. They're not doing me any good right now, and they are definitely in your way. Did I mention the word 'soaked'?"

He smirks before his face breaks into a smile. "Pervert. I knew you couldn't resist going there." He slides his hand out and grabs the back of my thighs.

"Can we get back to getting a new tie? You've teased the hell out of me and if you don't finish what you've started, I'll take matters into my own hands. Or more specifically, fingers."

His brow furrows. "Nobody finishes what I start when it comes to that pussy. Not even you. You come when I make you. And it will be happening on my cock and in my mouth, not on your fingers."

"Fine by me," I reply, scooting to the edge of the wood. "As long as it happens in the next five minutes. Otherwise…" I pause, shooting him a teasing look.

He grabs me off the worktop and flings me over his shoulder. I squeal, wrapping my arms around his waist as we move toward the stairs. "Otherwise nothing. You hurry me along in any way or threaten to handle your own orgasms and you won't be coming at all. I'll tie you to the bed and make you watch me handle my own situation all over your tits this time."

"All I heard was bed. Your ass is distracting me." I give it one good smack as he starts up the stairs.

"Speaking of asses, I plan on fucking yours tonight."

My eyes widen as my body becomes instantly rigid. *Fuuccckkk. Anal? Am I ready for that?*

He senses my apprehensiveness and rubs his hand on my bare thigh, soothing me. "Relax, love. Trust me with your body. I'll always make it good for you."

"Oh, God," I nervously mumble, dropping my head against his back.

"You'll be screaming that a lot in a minute."

I laugh against his shirt, instantly relaxing and leaving my nervousness on the stairs.

I'M NAKED, LYING IN THE middle of the bed with my hands above my head. I was given three instructions after Reese set me on my feet and removed my dress and panties. Three instructions I eagerly obeyed.

"Get on the bed, grab onto the bed posts, and don't let go."

My hands are wrapped around two wooden spindles as I watch him standing at the foot of the bed. He hasn't taken away my sight yet and right now, I'm extremely grateful for that as I watch him slowly remove his dress shirt button by button. He's taking his time and he knows what it's doing to me. He also knows that if he hadn't told me to keep my hands where they are, I would be ripping that shirt off him in record timing.

I take in the sight of him shirtless. The leanness of his body which is sculpted with that perfect amount of muscle. Broad shoulders and slightly-tanned skin. The hard lines of his abs which my hands are yearning to roam over.

My grip tightens around the wood.

His fingers loosen his belt as his eyes roam my body, slowly taking in every inch of me. Lower, lower, until he suddenly flicks them up to meet mine.

"Bend your knees and spread your legs." I do as I'm told. "Wider."

I drop my knees to the side as far as they can go, leaving myself completely open. My pussy is throbbing for him, aching to the point of being agonizing as he studies me. His eyes are locked between my legs, and the view seems to speed up his movements. Bending at the waist, he drops his pants and boxers and steps out of them. As he takes a few steps toward my dresser, I close my legs a few inches.

"I didn't tell you to do that," he says, looking at me over his shoulder as he opens my top drawer. "Open them."

I submit to his command and lower my knees so they are inches from the mattress. I see him slip out one of his ties before he walks to the side of the bed, authority in each step. There is zero trace of the man who told me minutes ago when he knew he loved me. That tenderness is gone. He's exuding control right now, and I've never seen anything hotter.

Looming over me with the tie in one hand, he slides his other hand up my arm and wraps it around one of mine, gripping me and the post. "Keep them here. If you move them before I tell you to, I'll tie them in place. Do you understand?"

"Yes."

"Good." He presses his lips against mine, searing me with a brutal kiss. "These will be the last words I say to you before I take you in the way I've been dying to take you. You won't be able to see or hear me until I want you to. Understand?"

"Yes." My voice comes out steady, devoid of any apprehension.

He leans back and drapes the tie across my eyes, blinding me. "Right now, I want you to concentrate on feeling everything I give you. Nothing else."

I lift my head, allowing him to secure it behind me. And then the bed dips as his weight is removed, leaving me alone with only the sound of my breathing filling my ears. But it's not uneven, nervous breathing. The pace of my lungs taking in air is quickened due to the eagerness I'm feeling. I want to experience this with him, everything he's about to give me in a way I've never had. I'm not tense. I'm ready.

So fucking ready.

The sound of movement in the kitchen has me turning my head in that direction.

A cabinet closes.

The soft clink of ice hitting the bottom of an empty glass.

I expect to hear the tap water running next, but I don't.

I gasp as my ankles are grabbed. My legs are straightened on the bed and then his hands are gone. I strain to listen, looking down the length of my body even though I can't see anything. I imagine him standing at the foot of the bed, glass in hand as he stares at me. He's hard. Painfully hard. Stroking himself to ease some of the ache. My grip tightens further as I clench the muscles in my core.

Is it possible to orgasm from anticipation alone? Because I might just be the first.

"Oh, shit." I jerk when I feel the stark chill of ice on my skin, trailing up the inside of my leg. My legs are spread wider and then his body fills the space between them. I think I know where the ice cube is going. I'm positive actually, but just when I think he's going to dip it between my legs, he avoids the area entirely.

I feel his free hand wrap around my hip, holding me in place. The ice cube glides over my stomach and up to the crease between my breasts. The heat of his mouth follows the path, warming my skin. I tilt my head up as he moves along my collar bone before circling my nipple.

"Reese."

I bite my lip to contain myself. I want to squirm. To thrash about because this is almost intolerable.

But I don't.

I whimper as the ice cube moves over my nipple. The bite of it is severe, but it feels too good for me to protest, especially when his mouth latches on and takes away the chill. He doesn't moan into my skin like he usually does. He doesn't give me any sign that he is enjoying this. But I knew he wouldn't. He warned me I wouldn't hear him, and apparently, sounds are included.

He moves slightly and I know he's marking me. I'm familiar with the pull of that spot. Alternating breasts, the pattern is repeated. Cold then warmth, and then the chill is gone, as is the heat of his body over mine. I feel the hair on his legs brush against mine as he shifts, and then his hands are wrapped around my thighs, spreading me open. I figure the ice has been discarded, no longer needed. I wait for the heat of his mouth to press against me. His warm breath. The scorch of his tongue.

"Fuck!" I arch off the bed, almost letting go of the posts when he runs up my length. His tongue is frigid, mimicking the sensation of the ice cube and melting into me just like one. The feeling is overwhelming as he dips inside me, tasting ever inch. His mouth never warms, and I know it's because the ice is in his mouth, which is confirmed when I feel the sharp edge of the cube press against my clit.

"Holy shit, Reese."

He dips lower, pressing the ice cube inside me with his tongue. In and out. He's fucking me with it, driving me toward my climax with this new sensation. I'm barely keeping my composure as my insides become liquid. My thighs are shaking against his head as I try to control my trembling. I'm close, moaning his name and gripping so tightly onto the wooden posts I'm certain they're about to snap off. Then the chill is gone, followed by the sound of him crunching on the ice. Seconds go by and I think maybe he isn't going to allow me to come. I take in several deep breaths, feeling my orgasm slip away from me until he buries his face between my legs.

His mouth still has the slightest chill, but his warmth is taking over. He fucks me with his tongue until I'm begging and incoherently pleading with him to make me come. He runs up and down my length, spreading me open with his fingers. His tongue swirls around my clit, flattening against it then flicking it in that rhythm I like. I'm once again right at the brink of orgasm and he knows it. He must, because that's the moment he chooses to prop my ass up with his hands and lick along my rim.

"Oh, shit! Wait, wait, don't...oh, God, just... Reese, I don't... unghhhh."

He's never done this to me. The only time he's ever gone anywhere near my ass is with his finger. I clench out of reflex; it's automatic. He shouldn't be there with this tongue, and it definitely shouldn't feel this amazing.

Right?

Wrong. So fucking wrong.

He's licking me like he works my pussy, and it feels unlike anything I've ever felt. My heart is thundering in my chest as I replay his words to me over in my head.

"Right now, I want you to concentrate on feeling everything I give you. Nothing else."

So I do. I concentrate on this new sensation, blocking out my instincts and not letting any anxiety overpower me. I feel his hands shift, one elevating me while the other moves around my waist. At the brush of his fingers against my clit, I lose it. I throw my head back, screaming his name until my voice breaks. And then I feel him press against me with his tongue, slipping inside, and my orgasm stretches out, rocking me with a blinding intensity. Paralyzing me. I feel shattered. Stripped of all coherence.

And it's incredible.

I don't even realize he's lowered my body back down until my blindfold is removed. I open my eyes, meeting his. There's apprehension in them. Not much, but I see it. The uncertainty of what he's just done to me. But when I smile at him, one that I'm sure looks completely dopey because that's how I feel, his insecurity vanishes.

"You can let go of the bed," he says as he kneels between my legs.

I do and shake my hands out, bringing them down to my sides. He reaches across the comforter and picks up a bottle I hadn't known he put on there. One I've never seen before. I really don't want to be nervous right now, because I do trust him, completely, but I know what that bottle is. I know what he needs it for. And I do a shit job at concealing my worry because he sees it, prompting him to drop the bottle and lean over me. His hand conforms to my cheek.

"I would never hurt you, Dylan. You liked what I just did, right?"

I nod and lean into his palm. "Yes. I didn't think I would, but I definitely did."

He gives me half a smile. "Trust me. I'd never lie to you. This will feel a little uncomfortable at first, just in the beginning, but it won't hurt. And then it's going to feel really fucking good. Okay?"

"You've done this before?" I ask, hearing the slight hurt in my voice. *Jesus, Dylan. Don't go there right now. Who cares what he's done before you.*

"I haven't done it with you. You are the only woman who matters. And the only one I want to experience this with." He picks up the bottle and flips the cap open. "I'll tell you what to do. Just listen to my voice and keep your eyes on me. If you have to close them you can, but when I'm all the way in you I need you to look at me."

"Okay," I reply, watching as he spreads the lube on his cock. "Did you like what you just did to me? I mean, you were… you know."

He squirts a bit of the liquid onto his finger before tossing the bottle to the other side of the bed. "I like everything I do to you." I flinch as he spreads the cold liquid along my entrance, applying the tiniest bit of pressure. He watches me as he slips one finger inside, flattening his other hand on my pelvis. His thumb begins rubbing my clit as he moves his finger in and out of me.

"Mmm." I close my eyes and take in the sensation, trying to stay relaxed.

"Two fingers, love."

He pulls out of me and then I feel the slight sting as he stretches me. But he enters without restriction and begins moving his fingers around in slow circles. "Feel good?" he asks.

I open my eyes. "Yes," I answer honestly. "So good. Can you do another?"

His thumb rubs against my clit as he slides his fingers out. I scrunch my face when he re-enters me, clamping my eyes shut. He stills inside me, letting me adjust to the foreign size. And it doesn't take long until I'm begging him to move. He stretches me further as my eyes shoot open, immediately seeking out his cock.

I want it.

There.

"Reese, please."

His eyes flash with a new desire. Maybe he wasn't expecting me to beg for this. Maybe he just assumed I'd go with it and then hopefully enjoy myself. But here I am, begging because I need to have him in this way.

He slides his fingers out and grips the base of his cock. "Hold your knees back for me." I do as requested as he positions himself.

His eyes trail up my body, landing on mine. "You want this. You just begged for it. Focus on that." He presses against my opening, meeting the tight ring of muscle, and I suddenly feel like my insides are burning up. "This is the uncomfortable part."

"No shit," I respond, letting go of my legs and clawing the comforter at my sides. I can't relax.

I'm no longer finding the urge to beg.

This fucking sucks.

"Dylan, you need to push against me."

"What?"

He grips my hips, steadying himself. "Push against me. Like you don't want me in."

Well, that's not hard to imagine.

I swallow loudly, trying to loosen up. "Okay, okay. Just… fucking hell, just wait a second."

He muffles a laugh above me but I don't respond to it the way I normally would, by telling him to fuck off unless he wants to switch positions. Instead, I do as he asks and push, feeling him slip further in. Inch by inch. I watch as his face contorts into one of immense pleasure, and that drives me. To want it more. To pull my knees back so my thighs are against my chest, opening up to him.

"Fuck, yes." He growls, deep and guttural as he slides in to the hilt. "Christ, you're so fucking perfect."

I wasn't sure what I was expecting to feel, but it wasn't this. A wave of heat washes over me at the sensation of him all the way in me. "Oh, my… Godddd."

And then he starts to move in and out as he works my clit with his thumb. I keep my eyes on him even though the intensity of the pleasure I'm feeling is urging me to close them. It's too much. I need to take away some of this stimulation before I break so I close them, but it's brief.

"Dylan, look at me." I do, and he takes over holding my legs back as he thrusts into me. "Feel it. Feel how I make every part of you feel good. You want this. You want me here."

"Yes," I answer, but it comes out as a plea. To keep fucking me. To never stop. To love every part of me, because that's what he's doing.

His breath comes out uneven, ragged. He's gasping above me, struggling to not lose control yet. And seeing him like that gets me right there with him.

"Reese."

"Fuck, I can't… Dylan, I can't stop."

"Don't stop. I'm so close."

His movements become urgent, slamming into me with a crucial force. Pushing me up over the edge. And he's right there with me.

"Coming," I barely choke out as my orgasm moves through me like a tidal wave. I need to see him. I need to watch him lose it even though my eyes are straining to remain open while I ride this out.

"Holy fuck. Oh, my God, Dylan. Fuuckkk!"

He keeps his eyes on me, giving me the satisfaction of seeing him unravel. And it's unlike anything he's ever done. He's wild. Screaming out my name between moans. Throwing his head back and flexing every muscle in his upper body. He gives me everything in a way I've never seen. It's chaotic almost, the way he lets go, but it's beautiful.

When his orgasm subsides, he drops my legs and pulls out of me. Arms wrap around me as he sits back and pulls me against his chest, burying his head between my breasts. I feel him tremble against me and thread my fingers through his hair.

"Thank you, love. Thank you for giving me that."

Dropping my head, I press kisses into his hair. "See, that wasn't so bad. I told you you'd like it," I tease.

He lifts his eyes to me, stunning me with that sweet face. "I love you."

"Love you, too." I brush my nose against his. "Now what? Should we box up more of my stuff? I feel like we still have a lot to do."

He cocks an eyebrow, looking around the room. "Anal sex and getting you ready to move in with me permanently? Fuck yes. That's my kind of Thursday night."

I throw my head back, falling into a laughing fit as his arms tighten around me, pinning our bodies together.

Close, but never close enough.

I'M GETTING MARRIED TOMORROW.

I'm finally becoming Dylan Carroll.

Holy shit.

Okay. Focus, Dylan.

I'm chopping up the bars of semisweet chocolate I'll need for my wedding cake frosting while Brooke watches the mixer with keen interest. She completely lost her shit this morning when I told her she would be in charge of making the caramel buttercream frosting for the other wedding cake. I've been right beside her, supervising everything, but this really is her baby and she's studying it with a mix of pride and restlessness.

"Can you grab the peppermint extract off the shelf for me?" I ask, breaking into her trance. She gives her frosting one last glance before she grabs the bottle I've requested and places it next to my cutting board. "Thanks. How's it looking?"

She begins to twirl a strand of her hair, a nervous habit I've picked up on today. "Umm, I don't know. Like frosting? It might taste like ass, though."

"Oooo, I love ass," Joey rejoices as he carries in a gift bag. I blush instantly and he notices. "Hmm. Care to elaborate?"

"Nope," I state firmly, shaking off my reaction to the word ass. *Really, Dylan?*

He places the bag in front of Brooke and she surveys it peculiarly. "Here. This is my thank you for the shirt you got me. Which I look amazing in, by the way."

I roll my eyes at his astounding modesty.

"Oh. You didn't have to get me anything." She stops the mixer, sliding the bag closer to her and peeking inside. I've placed my knife down, not wanting to miss the reaction to what I already know is in the bag. Her mouth drops open as she pulls out the apron Joey special-ordered for her. "You got me my own apron?" She holds it out, and I see the moment she notices her name on it. Her eyes well up with tears at the sentiment, just like any Wicks girl. "Thank you so much!" She flings her arms around Joey's neck, clutching onto her apron.

Joey looks over at me and smiles as he returns the hug. "I was the last person who thought you should be working here, Brooke. But you've actually done really well. And you're a natural back here with my cupcake."

She spins around and slips her apron on, tying it around her neck. "Look, Dylan! It matches yours!"

"Apron sistas," I sing, seeing Joey grimace behind Brooke.

"Goddamn it. I knew I should've ordered me one," he mumbles as he turns around and disappears up front.

I stifle my laugh, dumping my chopped-up chocolate pieces into a mixing bowl. I brush my hands clean on my apron and walk over to examine Brooke's frosting. Dipping a teaspoon into the bowl, I pop a small amount in my mouth.

"Well?" she asks fretfully. "Oh, God. Please, tell me we have time to make another batch of this?" She slaps a hand over her eyes. "I will never forgive myself if I've ruined some girl's wedding cake."

I grab her arm and pull her hand down. "It's delicious, Brooke. Really. Try some." I hold out a spoon and she takes it after studying it for several seconds, the obvious shock pouring out of her.

She dips it into the bowl and tests her creation. Her eyes flutter closed. "Mmm. Holy shitballs." They pop back open, full of wonder. "I made that?"

I hold out my hand and she high-fives me. "Told you you could do it. Don't doubt yourself back here." I walk to the fridge, grabbing the heavy cream and catch her taking a picture of her frosting with her phone.

I love that: her excitement, her pride over what she's created.

I'm so glad I hired Brooke Wicks.

After setting a large saucepan on the stovetop, I pour in the heavy cream and turn on the heat. Once I get it to a boil, I can add the peppermint extract and strain the mixture into the chocolate. Then it has to cool before I can frost my cake.

My wedding cake.

Both cakes are already assembled and ready to be iced. I've timed everything perfectly, allowing us to frost the other bride's cake while my icing cools. The sugared orchids are already assembled for her cake. I tackled those bright and early this morning, knowing they would take me several hours. They turned out amazing, incredibly life-like, and I sent a picture to Reese so he could see what had me skipping my run today. His response was just as sweet as the flowers.

Reese: You amaze me, love. You always have.

And then he sent me one more a few seconds later.

Reese: One more day.

I turn the heat off for the cream and carry the saucepan over to the worktop. I slowly pour the mixture into my mixing bowl, whisking the contents as they melt together. As soon as the cream touches the chocolate, that familiar smell permeates my senses, filling me with the memory of this frosting. The only one I have besides the time I made it for Mrs. Frey's anniversary cake. Reese hasn't had this frosting since he ate it off my body on this very worktop, and when I was deciding on what to do for my own wedding cake, I knew I had to incorporate this flavor somehow. However, it's not going to be hot pink this time. At least, not on the outside of the cake. I've tweaked the recipe to leave out the shaved peppermint sticks, opting for the flavor from the extract instead. And with a little help from some food coloring, I'll have a beautiful white-mint chocolate wedding cake, as opposed to a pink one.

The shop door dings open as I set my empty saucepan back on the stovetop. Juls comes walking into the kitchen, carrying a small envelope with Ian right behind her. She's dressed chicly as usual, while Ian is wearing the same attire I'm used to seeing Reese in.

"Is someone getting married tomorrow?" Juls asks, walking toward me. She stops when she sees Brooke's apron. "Aww, I love that."

"Joey got it for me," Brooke states, smiling over at my thoughtful assistant as he walks into the back.

Juls darts over to him and wraps her arms around his waist. "You're the sweetest, JoJo."

"Christ, it's just an apron. I didn't propose or anything," he counters.

"Babe, hurry up and show Dylan what we came here for. I need to get back to the office." Ian walks over to the assembled cakes and studies them, leaning in closely. "These will get frosted, right?"

"Yes," all four of us answer in unison, the obvious implication evident in our voices.

He straightens and stares at us like he hasn't just asked a ridiculous question.

Who the hell wouldn't ice a wedding cake?

"Okay, are you ready?" Juls asks, opening her envelope and waving over Joey and Brooke. We all three huddle around her as she pulls out the tiny black and white photo and holds it out for us to see. "Look at my little nugget."

"Oh, my God!" I snatch the photo out of her hand and run my finger over the image. Tracing over the tiny splotch, because that's exactly what it looks like, I can't contain the magnitude of emotions beginning to course through me.

My best friend is having a baby.

When I glance back at her, it's through teary eyes. "Juls! I love your little nugget!"

"Give me that." Joey grabs the picture and studies it with Brooke. He gasps, looking from the picture to her stomach. "Can you feel anything yet?"

She shakes her head, wiping underneath her eyes. "No, not yet. But we heard the heartbeat today. That was amazing." Ian comes up behind her and wraps his arms around her waist. "Wasn't it amazing, babe?"

He kisses her neck. "It was. I wish I could've recorded it." He removes one hand from around Juls and takes the picture away from Joey. "Let me see my baby again."

I watch as the proud father-to-be looks at the sonogram with his wife. He whispers something into her ear and she nods, tearing up again. It's a private moment and I let them have it, turning around and busying myself.

At the sound of the shop door, Joey disappears up front, returning moments later and carrying the familiar white box. He sets it down on the worktop in front of me. "Not sure how he's going to top a set of car keys," he says jokingly, tugging at the white ribbon.

I open the box and pull out the card, not bothering to contain my excitement. I can't. I'm marrying this amazing man tomorrow, my best friend just showed me a picture of her little nugget, and I have the two best employees a girl could ask for.

I know tomorrow is going to be the best day of my life, but I'm finding it hard to imagine topping this moment.

I open the card as Joey sifts through the tissue paper, stopping to read over my shoulder.

Dylan,

You asked me to keep my eyes on you before when you danced to this song, and I've never taken them off. Dance for me now.

X, Reese

Joey pulls out Reese's iPod and darts up front with it as I tuck the note into my apron pocket. He returns moments later with the docking station, plugging it in and setting everything on the worktop. "I love how he knows we dance on Fridays. Could he seriously be any more perfect?"

"No," I answer, earning myself an annoyed look from him.

He cues the song up and seconds later, Beyoncé's "Naughty Girl" fills the kitchen. Juls, Brooke, Joey, and I all begin dancing around the space and when I glance over at Ian, he's holding his phone out with it focused on me.

"What are you doing?" I yell over the music, moving in between Juls and Brooke.

"What I've been instructed to do." He smiles and motions for me to keep going.

Oh. Well then.

My man wants me to dance for him? Okay. I can do that.

I playfully spin around, bringing my eyes back to Ian's phone every few seconds, pretending I'm looking right at Reese. Imagining him sitting behind his desk and watching me with that focused stare of his. I don't dance sexy at all, because I'm still kind of dancing for Ian and that would be entirely too weird, so I keep it fun, letting Joey spin me around and dip me. Grabbing onto Brooke and waltzing her around the kitchen. It's the best Friday dance party I've ever had with the most amazing people I've ever known.

After Ian and Juls leave, Brooke and I get started on icing the wedding cake for the other bride. That part itself is relatively easy, considering the bride didn't request any intricate piping work or anything besides the sugared orchids. And those won't be added until tomorrow morning. My cake, however, contains a ton of complex detailing that will take me the rest of the day to create. I wanted my cake to be very romantic, yet still traditional in a sense. Nothing modern or edgy. I was inspired by my dress when I came up with this design, wanting to mimic the lacework I instantly fell in love with. And sticking with the theme, which made my mother overly-ecstatic, I decided on a pale-gray lace pattern which will adorn my five-tiered cake, tying it into the bridesmaid dresses.

It takes me five-and-a-half hours to finish my cake, leaving me with just enough time to take a quick shower and get ready for my rehearsal. Reese is driving straight to the Whitmore from his office so I'll be meeting him there, which is perfect because I wanted to surprise him tonight with my outfit. I actually had something else picked out to wear tonight: a deep plum-colored halter I picked up a few weeks ago. But when he surprised me earlier today with my dance party song, the memory of that day inspired me.

Apart from the engagement ring on my finger, I look exactly like I did the day I met Reese. My black strapless dress still looks brand new, considering I haven't worn it since that day. My hair is falling in soft curls over my shoulders, and my makeup is fresh and elegant. After grabbing my clutch, I walk toward the door but stop, taking a look around my living space.

It doesn't look like my loft anymore.

The only thing left in it that hasn't changed yet is my bed, which I'll be sharing with Juls and Joey tonight at our last sleepover. Everything else is packed away in boxes, except for what I'll need to get ready tomorrow. All my pictures are gone, my kitchen counters are bare, even my decorative screen is folded up and leaning against the wall. Reese is having all my stuff delivered to his condo tomorrow while we get married, that way we don't have to worry about it. Then my landlord will be making some changes to the loft so the future tenant doesn't have to go through the bakery to get to it, which I'm extremely grateful for. For security reasons alone, I wouldn't want someone walking through my shop all the time who doesn't work for me. I suppose until it gets rented out, I could still come up here if I wanted to, but I'm not sure I will. My new life starts tomorrow, the one I've been counting down toward, and I'm excited to move in with Reese and put my single life behind me. So tonight, with my two very best friends, I'll soak in my last night in my loft and every memory it holds.

I can always take those memories with me.

Chapter Twenty-Two

WHEN REESE AND I FIRST sat down to talk about where we wanted to get married, I never thought the Whitmore could be an option. I knew how expensive it was, at least from what Juls told me after planning Justin's wedding here. And I'd never hit my parents up for that kind of money. To be honest, I could get married to Reese in his condo and it would be perfect. I don't need a fancy venue to make tomorrow the best day of my life. So I threw out other options, such as the church Juls and Ian got married in and a small reception hall down the street from it. And while I did this, Reese just sat back with a smile on his face, letting me list off any and every idea I could come up with. When I asked what he had in mind, he told me he wanted to marry me where he first saw me, and that money wasn't an issue; he wanted to pay for it. I almost argued, but seeing how much marrying me there would mean to him, silenced me. I couldn't argue with that look; I never can. It's this perfect blend of honesty and love. And it's a look that I would do anything for, including letting him pay for everything.

I park my car next to Joey's Civic and lock it up. Joey and Juls are waiting for me by the doors, and as I get closer to them, I see their reaction to my outfit.

It's emotional.

Really emotional.

"He's going to lose it," Joey says after dabbing his eyes with a tissue.

"Seriously, sweets. I'm not sure Reese is going to agree to stay with the guys tonight at my place after seeing you in this." Juls brushes my hair off my shoulder, letting out a few sniffles.

"Well, staying with us isn't an option. My bed isn't big enough for four."

Joey holds the door open for us and Juls and I step inside. I glance over my shoulder at him. "Did you pick up the dresses and your suit? And the ring? You have his ring, right?"

He frowns. "Please. Like I'd drop the ball on something like that." He looks past me and practically starts to glow. And I don't need to follow his gaze to know who he's looking at. Joey only reserves that look for one man. Even though he likes to complain that Billy doesn't shower him with Reese-style gestures, there's no mistaking the effect he has on my dear assistant.

I watch as Billy walks up to us, giving Juls and me a smile before grabbing Joey's face. They share a kiss, one which causes my skin to flush. One which causes Juls to sigh. And one which seems different from the other kisses I've seen them share.

"I'm pretty sure people have had sex in this building. In fact, I know they have. In case you two need a minute," Juls cracks, causing us both to laugh.

Yup. I've definitely had sex in this building.

Billy and Joey turn to us, breaking their kiss. "A minute? I'm not a fucking virgin," Joey snaps.

Billy laughs, releasing Joey and walking to me. He leans in, dropping his voice. "Can I talk to you for a minute?"

"Sure," I answer, looking over at Joey and Juls. "I'll meet you in there. Tell Reese to give me a minute."

Joey looks strangely between Billy and me. "Umm, okay."

"It's something Reese wanted me to tell Dylan," Billy says.

Joey nods, wrapping his arm around Juls and ushering her toward the back room where the ceremony will be held.

I look up at Billy. "It doesn't have anything to do with Reese, does it?"

He smiles. "No. I wanted to ask your permission to do something at the reception tomorrow. For Joey. It's your day and I completely understand if you don't want me to do it." He reaches up and straightens his tie, looking over at the door Juls and Joey walked through moments ago. "This is the grandest gesture I can think of," he says in a low, guarded voice.

I almost fall apart in tears but I manage to hold it in, saving my makeup in the process. When he looks back at me, I answer. "You never have to ask my permission to do anything that will make that man smile. Do you need my help?"

His shoulders seem to relax as he shakes his head. "No, I got it. Thanks, Dylan." He grabs my hand and loops it through his arm. "Come on. I'm sure that man of yours is waiting." I glance up at him and see his eyes trail down my dress. "Have I seen you in this before?"

"Mmm hmm."

"At the wedding. Right? Your ex-boyfriend's?"

"Mmm hmm."

He opens the door and lets me walk ahead of him. "Oh, shit. Reese is going to lose it." I chuckle at the very words Joey used minutes ago as we step inside The Great Hall.

Rows upon rows of chairs line both sides of the aisle, the end ones adorned with mini versions of the white gardenia bouquet I will be holding tomorrow. The lights are dimmed and all around the room, candles are lit, and giving off a warm glow. I let my eyes wander, taking in all my best friend's hard work. It's perfect. Every little detail. And then I give in to the temptation waiting for me in the group gathered up front.

Everyone is watching me, stopping all conversation when I stepped into the room with Billy. I'm just now registering that he has left my side when I see him standing by Joey. My parents and Reese's mom and dad are together, along with Reese's sister and her husband, who I met a few months ago at a family dinner. Juls is with Ian and they're all over each other, as usual. But I don't linger on them, or anyone else besides the man who is standing out amongst them. Dressed in a dark-gray suit, Reese seems to be the one unable to move as he takes in my outfit.

The very outfit I fell into his lap in.

I save him the trouble of coming to me and begin walking up the aisle, tucking my clutch under my arm. I'm ready to get through this as quickly as possible. I want this night to be over. I want it to be tomorrow already. But as I try and get past the cluster of people to get to who I really want to talk to, my mother grabs me.

"Sweetheart! You look stunning," she says, kissing me on my cheek.

Shit. So close.

I'm passed around like a damn baby, getting showered in affection while my eyes strain to stay on Reese. I have to pull them away from him to talk to his sister and brother in-law, exchanging pleasantries and trying not to seem rushed about it. I don't want to be rude, but Jesus Christ, I'll see everyone tomorrow. Maggie and Phillip, Reese's dad, steal me next, gushing over me in the sweetest way possible. And then by some miracle, the preacher decides to cut in just when I think I'm going to be stuck in this conversation forever.

"Miss Sparks, are you ready to begin?"

"Yes!" I yell excitingly, hearing everyone react to my enthusiasm. I get within a foot of Reese and take his hand, positioning myself directly in front of him while the preacher moves around us. "Hi," I whisper.

He smiles. "Hi, yourself. Nice dress."

I feign humility. "This old thing? I wasn't sure if you'd like it or not."

"Shall we begin?" the preacher asks.

Reese looks at him. "One second." He pulls me in and presses his lips to my ear. "You're driving me crazy. I'd prefer not to get hard in front of my parents."

"Well, then you shouldn't have invited me."

He releases me with a smirk before nodding at the preacher. "All right. Let's go."

We run through the ceremony and even though I don't want to, I bawl my eyes out when I recite my vows to Reese. When I promise to cherish him forever, to love every part of him with every ounce of myself, I cry harder. Juls and Joey's sobs behind me blend into mine, while I hear the faint sound of everyone else's emotions getting to them as they watch from their seats. And then I really become a wreck when he repeats them. But unlike me, Reese doesn't cry. His voice isn't a quivering mess. He doesn't have to pause to try and pull himself together. But even though he doesn't react the way I do when he recites them, his words seem to hold more sentiment than mine. As if this is the only time I'll hear them from him. As if he isn't going to be reciting them again to me tomorrow.

He vows to always be mine, to honor me and stand by my side through everything life throws at us. To make me laugh and to hold me when I cry, prompting him to pull me against him since I am, indeed, crying. He finishes his vows into my hair while I cling to him like he's my life line. His scent soothes me as I nuzzle him long after he finishes talking, relishing in the way my body fits perfectly against his. And everyone gives us that moment. No one asks if we'd like to continue with the mock ceremony. No one clears their throat to speed things along. We don't break contact until we're both ready, which feels like hours instead of minutes.

After finally separating, we finish the ceremony and share a brief kiss, one I know will be much longer tomorrow. Everyone pairs up and walks back down the aisle, Reese and I leading the way. We say goodbye to my parents and Reese's family before he and I walk through the parking lot, our friends a few feet behind us.

"So, did I surprise you with my dress?" I ask as we stop in front of my driver's side door. I lean my back against it and tug at his suit jacket, bringing him closer to me.

"You always surprise me, love. Especially when you're in *that* dress."

"Oh? I surprised you in this before?"

He puts a hand on either side of me, bringing our foreheads together. "Well, I wasn't suspecting to get knocked on my ass by a wedding hookup. So, yes, you surprised me."

"See you two at The Tavern!" Juls yells, gaining our attention. We wave to her and the rest of the group as they all walk to their vehicles.

"I was just as affected, you know," I say, bringing his attention back to my face. "I couldn't stop thinking about you, which annoyed me because I thought you were married. But don't think you were the only one who got knocked on their ass," I repeat his words to me with a playful tone. "Thank you for my delivery today. Did you see the video?"

He presses his lips against mine. "I did. I watched it at least ten times before I left the office. You looked so happy."

"I am so happy."

"So am I," he replies against my mouth.

I bite at his bottom lip. "We should probably get married then. Since we're both *so happy.*"

"Makes sense."

"I think so."

Joey beeps his car horn as he drives by us, waving out his window. Reese shifts me so he can open my door. "Come on. They're going to be waiting for us."

I slide into my seat and start my car. The time on my dash catches my eye. "This time tomorrow night we'll be married." He ducks down and reaches across my body with my seatbelt, buckling me in. I give him a quirky look. "Really? I'm capable of buckling myself in, you know."

"You were too slow about it." He kisses my temple. "Don't speed this time."

"Yes, Mr. Sparks."

He goes to close my door but the title I've just given him stops him. "Mr. what?"

"Sparks. I like the sound of that. Reese Sparks. Some men take their bride's name."

"I'm not one of them," he says with authority in his tone. One that's saying this is in no way negotiable. He closes my door and walks toward his vehicle. And I could pull away, but I wait because I know he's going to give it to me. Even though I can't see his face, I know he's smiling at what I've just said despite the seriousness in his voice. And as he grabs his door handle, I see the slight shake of his head before he gives me that smile over his shoulder, the smile I'll always wait for. Satisfied, I finally pull away from the Whitmore with a very happy man behind me.

"JESUS. THIS PLACE IS PACKED," I yell over the music as Reese leads me through the crowd of people.

Friday nights at The Tavern do tend to be a bit busier, but I don't think I've ever seen it this mobbed before. I stay close to Reese, my hand in his as he weaves me in and out of the mass of bodies toward one of the tall tables surrounding the dance floor. I spot our friends once we get close enough. Juls is sitting on Ian's lap, Joey is talking intimately with Billy, and Brooke is looking between the two couples, rolling her eyes.

"Why I agreed to show up here dateless is beyond me," she snaps before taking a sip of her drink. Her eyes widen when they focus on Reese and me. "Ahhh! You're here!" She moves past Billy and Joey, wrapping her arms around me. "Thank you for inviting me out tonight. I'm so fucking excited about tomorrow." She glances up at Reese. "Wait until you see your wedding cake. It's unreal."

"I can't wait," he answers, dropping my hand. "You want anything from the bar?"

"Just a water." I turn to Juls once Reese leaves the group. "Is that what you're having?"

She holds up her glass. "Nothing but water for me for the next eight months. I need it tonight anyway after bawling my eyes out at the rehearsal. I can't imagine how emotional this is going to be tomorrow."

"Am I the only one who didn't cry?" Billy asks, reaching up and fixing Joey's collar.

"I didn't," Ian says, glancing over at Juls who shoots him a disbelieving look. "What? I wasn't crying. My allergies were acting up."

"Sure they were," Brooke teases. "Because you didn't shed a few tears during your own wedding, or when you heard your baby's heartbeat. You're practically a chick, Ian. Whereas Reese exudes manliness."

"Easy, hornball," I direct at her. She wiggles her brows at me as a response.

Reese returns to the table carrying a beer and a glass of water for me. Ian points at him. "You think he won't be emotional tomorrow? Are you fucking kidding? I'll bet a hundred bucks he cries before any of us. Including you." He motions toward me and smiles. "Shall we make it interesting?"

"Fuck you. I haven't cried since I was a kid. I'll take that bet," Reese says. He looks down at me as he slides his arm around my waist. "Honeymoon money."

I laugh as Joey slides off his stool. "I'm in."

"Me, too," Billy adds.

"Yup. I say you're going to weep like a baby the minute you see her," Juls says behind her glass, smiling at Reese. "I've seen the dress. Good luck getting any money from us."

"I want in. I don't have a hundred bucks yet cause I'm waiting to get paid," Brooke pauses, shooting me a look which I give right back to her. "But, I'm betting Reese holds his ground. I think Dylan will cry before he does."

Reese presses his lips to my hair. "You want in on this, love?"

Demi Lovato's "Really Don't Care" begins blaring overheard, and I put my glass down and shimmy out of his grasp. "Nope!" I yell over the music, moving toward the dance floor. I connect with him from the other side of the table. "But if I were, I'd be betting against you, handsome." I grab Joey by the shirt and pull Juls off Ian's lap. I wave over Brooke and the four of us move into the crowd of people on the dance floor.

The guys stay at the table, watching, amused as we all twirl around each other and sing at the top of our lungs. I keep meeting Reese's eyes, motioning for him to join me, but he stays put and occasionally shakes his head in disapproval when I begin dancing way more flirtatiously than I did today in the shop. Billy joins us after a few songs and takes turns dancing with all four of us, giving Joey extra attention. The dance floor is mobbed and we get moved farther and farther away from the table when more people try to pack in. Juls motions she needs a drink after a while, and I do, too. I'm sweaty and definitely parched, but I need to use the restroom first.

"I'll be right there!" I yell over the music, seeing all four of them indicate they've heard me as they walk back toward the guys.

I push my way through the crowd toward the back hallway which leads to the bathrooms. There are entirely too many people in the bar tonight. There must be some sort of crowd cap that is definitely being ignored. But as long as there isn't a line for the ladies room, I'm fine with the mob.

I follow a group of girls into the women's room, who luckily only want to check out their makeup situation, leaving me an empty stall. Once I'm finished, I wash my hands and clean up my face a bit, forgetting all about the tears I shed earlier and what it ended up doing to my eye makeup. But luckily, it's so dark in the bar I doubt anyone noticed. Once I'm satisfied with my appearance and so thirsty I contemplate drinking straight from the tap, I exit the bathroom.

I'm stopped by a hand on my upper arm, big enough to wrap around my bicep. It tightens and pulls me out of the bathroom doorway while another hand grabs my hip, pinning me against the wall. Everything happens so quickly, I don't have time to register any of it. The hard body is pressing against me, preventing me from moving and keeping me boxed in. I look up at a man invading my space and meet those eerie yellow eyes I never thought I'd see again.

"Get the hell…"

My words are cut off when his hand covers my mouth, He moves closer, flattening his body against mine. I clench every muscle as I try to squirm from his hold. I know the hallway is packed with people, but the way Bryce is pressing against me and given his size compared to mine and his ability to shield me completely, it probably looks like two people making out. I try to shake my head to remove his hand but he stays with me. He pins my arms together in front of me when I try to push him away. Panic sets in. Blood fills my ears and I want to scream, but I can't.

And then he leans in and I squeeze my eyes shut. I don't know what he's about to do. I don't know if he's just going to run his mouth like usual. Given the fact he probably knows he's going to prison, I'm thinking he isn't going to hold anything back.

"Hey, baby. Miss me?"

I gag at the alcohol and cigarette cocktail filling my nasal cavity with each word he spews. It's nauseating, as is everything about this guy. I feel his nose rub against my forehead and hear him inhale.

"Your bastard boyfriend messed with the wrong guy. And he was really fucking stupid to let you out of his sight."

"I didn't."

Reese's voice and the closeness of it has me shooting my eyes open. He's over Bryce's shoulder, grabbing him and pulling him off me before he slams him against the other wall. Bryce protests with flailing limbs and some incoherent words which are broken apart when Reese punches him in the jaw. Repeatedly. His arm flies back, fist clenched, and he delivers blow after blow while his other hand pins Bryce in place. Blood starts pouring from Bryce's nose and mouth, and that creepy grin of his is nowhere in sight.

"Fight!" someone yells.

I'm glued to the wall, unable to move as I watch the crowd form around us, which includes our group of friends. Juls and Brooke both gasp, covering their mouths as they watch Reese pummel this loser, while the guys all react differently.

Billy pulls his phone out of his pocket and quickly dials what I assume to be the police.

Ian pushes his way back toward the bar, yelling over the commotion for someone to get security.

And Joey comes straight over to me. "Are you okay?" he asks, alarm in his voice.

I nod my response, keeping my eyes on Reese. No one stops him and I know someone has to. He could kill this prick.

He should kill him.

Just when I'm about to open my mouth, Reese grabs Bryce by his shirt and drags him off the wall, moving across the hallway to where I'm standing. Juls and Brooke both dart out of the way and Joey flanks my side. Bryce looks like shit run over. His nose has to be broken by the looks of it, his left eye is swollen shut, and he seems to be having trouble standing.

Aww. Poor baby.

Reese holds him up in front of me. "You see her? Do you?" Bryce moans. "Fucking look at her, you piece of shit!" Bryce peeks his good eye open while the blood pours from his nose. "Get a good fucking look, because this is the last one you're ever going to get. If you so much as think about her again, I will hunt your ass down and fucking kill you. Do you hear me?" Bryce moans again as Ian comes rushing back over to the group.

"All right. Cops are here. I don't know where the fuck security is, but it looks like you don't need them." He looks at Juls and then at me. "You okay?"

"Yes," we both answer.

"Dylan," Reese says, gaining my attention. "If you want to hit him, you better do it now."

He holds Bryce by his shirt in front of me and I step closer, tilting my head down so his one eye focuses on me. "I've been wanting to do this for a really long time." I bring my hand back and strike him hard across the face, the loud cracking sound filling the hallway.

"Damn!" someone yells through a laugh.

I smile at the crowd. I don't think I've ever felt this satisfied with slapping someone before.

Brooke steps up next to me. "Ooo! Can we all take turns? I want a go at him."

Just then, Billy pushes through the crowd, signaling for the police to follow him. "Oh, damn it," Brooke utters, moving back and falling in next to Joey. One officer grabs Bryce from Reese and moves him away from the group while the other walks over to us.

"Someone want to tell me what happened here?" the officer

asks, looking at each of us.

I give him the rundown of the situation, making sure to point out that this isn't the first time Bryce put his hands on me. I tell the cop about the time in the elevator and mention he's kind of been stalking me, using the flower on my van as an example. When I get a stern look from Reese, I realize I forgot to tell him about that and mouth "I'm sorry", seeing his face soften instantly. Reese tells the officer about the investigation on Bryce and how he thought he should've been arrested by now. The officer tells us they have been looking for him, but he hasn't been at his condo and also hasn't shown up to work for the past two days. But now that they have him, he'll be in custody until his trial. After everyone gives their statements about what they saw happen, we are told we can leave.

"Well, this has been interesting to say the least. I'll see you crazy kids tomorrow," Brooke says as we all walk outside. She heads down the sidewalk, glancing over her shoulder. "And I got dibs on every single guy there!" she yells.

"All right, boys. Say your goodbyes," Juls says. Ian grabs her and kisses her sweetly while Billy and Joey share their own private moment a few feet away on the sidewalk.

I glance up at Reese. "Hi."

His eyes meet mine after scanning my face. "I don't want to say goodbye."

I predicted this, especially after what just happened. But it's over now. Reese has nothing to be worried about.

I wrap my arms around him and tilt my head up, pressing my chin against his chest. "I tell you what. I'll text you as soon as I get home, and then every fifteen minutes until I fall asleep."

"Every five minutes," he counters, pressing his lips to my forehead. His arms envelop me and hold me against him.

I'm about to argue but let it go and agree to it. "Okay. Every five minutes. How is your hand?"

"Fine."

"Let me see it."

"It's fine, Dylan."

"Reese."

He sighs heavily and lets go of me, holding up his right hand for me to examine.

"Fine, my ass. See how banged-up it looks?" I run my fingers over his fourth and fifth knuckle where most of the damage seems to be. The skin is cut up and a bit swollen, and he flinches at my touch. "You might need an x-ray, Reese. It could be broken."

He flexes it several times before grabbing my hip with his other hand and pulling me against his chest. "It's not broken. I'll ice it when I get to Ian's."

As if he hears his name, Ian comes up to us and slaps Reese on the back. "Come on, man. She'll be all yours tomorrow."

Reese looks at him and then back down at me. He tilts my chin up. "Every five minutes."

I press my lips against his. "You got it."

Juls and Joey flank my side and we watch our men walk toward their vehicles. They both grab one of my hands.

"You ready for your last sleepover as a single woman?" Juls asks.

I smile at Reese as he looks back at me one last time before getting into his car.

Yup. Absolutely. "I'm so fucking ready."

WHEN WE GET BACK TO the bakery, Juls and I help Joey carry the dresses inside and up the stairs to my practically empty loft. After changing into our pajamas, I hang my dress up and unzip the bag, smiling as the white lace slowly comes into view. I run my hand over the material while Juls and Joey laugh on the bed behind me.

"It's been five minutes, cupcake," Joey reminds me.

I zip up the bag and grab my phone before falling back onto the bed between the two of them.

"Thank God all this shit with Bryce is over," Juls says as I type my message to Reese. "I can't believe Ian didn't tell me the real reason for working with him."

I press send and look over at her. "They couldn't. You know Ian wouldn't keep anything from you unless he absolutely had to."

"Fo' reals. I'm sure he'd tell you the nuclear codes if he had them," Joey jokes. "I'm actually surprised he didn't spill it. That man likes to gossip more than me."

Juls reaches over me and slaps his arm. "No one likes to gossip more than you."

My phone beeps as I laugh at the two of them. I hold it above my head and quickly scan Reese's message.

Reese: I told you. My hand is fine.

"So, are you ready to move out of here permanently, sweets?" Juls asks.

I look down my body and around the empty space surrounding my bed, tucking my hands behind my head after placing my phone on my chest. All the sadness I felt just last week at the very thought of moving is absent. The boxes stacked against the wall and on the kitchen counter no longer depress me. This is my last night in my loft, and although I once never imagined leaving it, I can no longer picture myself living here. The majority of the memories I have of this space are missing one vital element. And I want all my memories to include him.

I look over at her and smile. "What's your favorite memory of being here?"

"Hmm. I don't know. We've had so many good ones," she replies, grabbing the pillows and handing them out to us. She takes one for herself and places it under her head. "You?"

I open my mouth to tell her I have no idea when Joey cuts me off.

"Well, I'll tell you what mine wasn't. Fucking tequila drinking games." Juls and I both make noises of agreement as Joey rolls on his side facing us. He smiles that winning smile of his. "You're getting married tomorrow, cupcake. And I think you need to let everyone on this fucking block know."

I glance between the two of them before quickly scrambling to my feet on the bed, placing a hand on either side of my mouth, and yelling at the top of my lungs, "I'M GETTING MARRIED TOMORROW!"

Juls and Joey both hoot and holler at me as I drop to my knees and fall back between them. And we don't move from our spots for the rest of the night.

There's laughing and talking more about the wedding, a few more text messages between Reese and myself, and a ton of discussion revolving around Juls' pregnancy. It's my last night in my loft, and it's one of the best ones I've ever had.

With two of the most important people in my life.

TODAY, I MARRY MY WEDDING hookup.

Not that I'm an expert on this sort of thing, but I'm pretty sure most people never see their flings again after sharing that one moment together. That's the whole point of wedding sex, isn't it? You're watching two people vow to love each other for the rest of their lives while you wallow in your own single self-misery. Then you see an opportunity in the form of another hopefully-not-married wedding guest and proceed to get it on to help ease your loneliness. Or I suppose in my case, experience something you never have that your overly-knowledgeable best friend brags about. Either way, I'm certain in most cases of slutty wedding sex, no one expects to fall in love with the guy who romantically takes you against a bathroom sink at your ex-boyfriend's wedding reception. It's supposed to be a one-and-done deal. A shake of hands and saying how nice it was to make each other come before walking away. You're not supposed to continually think about that person after you've gone your separate ways. You're not supposed to lose sleep and briefly contemplate pursuing anything further with a man who you've been told is married. And you're definitely not supposed to begin a casually-monogamous relationship with that same man, especially when you're incapable of not falling in love with him.

But like I said, I'm not an expert at this sort of thing. And it's a good thing, too; otherwise, I probably wouldn't be standing in front of my mirror while my mother and fabulous wedding planner/best friend button me into my wedding gown. Without any difficulty, I might add.

"I knew you could do it, sweetheart. This dress fits you perfectly now," my mother says behind me.

It does fit perfectly, thanks to the diet I'll never be adhering to again. My low-carb days are way the hell behind me.

"Yeah, well, I plan on tearing into that wedding cake later, so I better have plenty of room." I connect with Juls in the mirror, smiling at the sight of her in the floor-length, pale-gray bridesmaid dress she looks amazing in. "What time are you heading over?"

She looks over at the stove and quickly spins around, grabbing her stuff. "Shit. Right now. I'll have your bridal suite set up for you, so go straight there when you get to the Whitmore. And use the side entrance. If Reese sees you beforehand, I'll kill him."

I laugh and hear my mom's agreeing noise behind me as Juls walks to the door. It swings open just as she gets to it, Joey emerging from the stairs and decked out in his tux.

"Wow. Look at you," he says to Juls, earning himself a kiss on the cheek.

"Right back atcha. I'll see you guys there." She disappears down the stairs as Joey comes to stand beside me.

"Everything go okay?" I ask as my mother steps back, seemingly done with her task. I spin around and face Joey, seeing his awestruck expression.

His eyes twinkle with adoration as he takes in the sight of me. "You look fucking fabulous."

"Joseph," my mother scolds.

He glances over at her. "Well, she does! Seriously, I don't think anyone has looked this good in a wedding gown before. Aside from Juls." He shakes his head with an exhaustive sigh. "Single gal, party of one over here."

I smack his shoulder. "Whatever. No problems with the cake?"

He steps up to the mirror, straightening his tie. "Of course not.

I gave it the Joey treatment. It's waiting for you at the Whitmore, as is your anxious groom."

"You saw him?" I grab his shoulder and spin him around. "How does he look?"

His eyebrows raise. "Like he might pass out if he doesn't see you soon."

I frown. "Really?"

He nods before the crease in his brow sets in. "Billy, on the other hand, is acting all weird. It's like he purposely avoided me while I was there. And let me tell you, if this is how it's going to be today, Brooke might have some competition on her hands. I don't need this shit from a guy who obviously has zero plans of one day giving me the wedding of my dreams."

"Dylan, sweetheart, we need to get going," my mother says as she grabs the stuff I'll be taking with me to the bridal suite.

I grab Joey's chin and lower it, narrowing my eyes at him. "Don't count Billy out just yet."

His eyes widen. "What does that mean? Do you know something?"

I put on my best poker face and loop my arm through his. "I *know* he loves you. Now stop making this day all about you. I seem to be the one in the fancy dress."

He gives me a smile as we collect the rest of my things. Standing at the door, I look around my loft one final time. The movers will be coming sometime during the ceremony and taking everything out for me. The next time I come to work, my loft will be an empty space above my bakery. And I'm okay with that.

"Let's go, cupcake."

I take one last mental shot before heading down the stairs behind Joey. I beam at the beautiful white lilies sitting in the center of the worktop, a gift from the other bride. I assumed someone else in the wedding party was going to stop in this morning to pick up her cake, but she wanted to personally thank me for fitting her in on such short notice. And she also wanted to give me the flowers herself.

Joey holds the front door open for me as my mom walks close behind, holding my train off the ground. Cool air lifts my hair off my shoulder. The driver smiles and opens the back door of the limo, allowing the three of us to file inside. The excitement I feel rushing through me as we make our way to the Whitmore is unlike anything I've ever felt. But I know it won't top the moment I see Reese.

WE'RE ALL HUDDLED IN THE bridal suite as I check my hair and makeup in the mirror for the thousandth time in the past half hour. I twirl a few curls of my hair around my fingers before fluffing the waves falling past my shoulders. My makeup is looking better than it ever has; elegant yet simple. One of the girls from Chicago Bridal worked her magic on me early this morning while her partner styled my hair. Juls has been in and out of the room, keeping everyone in line while Joey slipped out minutes ago to take care of something he wouldn't elaborate on. My mother has been trying to keep herself from crying, but every time I make eye contact with her, she loses it. And then there's my dad. The calmest of the bunch without a doubt. He's sitting in a high-back leather chair, looking out the window between stealing a few glances at me I've caught in the mirror. He really is the yin to my mother's yang. Complete opposites, the two of them. She's barely holding herself together while he looks like it's just another Saturday. Nothing major happening today or anything.

The door to the suite swings open and Joey darts through, slamming it shut behind him. "He's trying to see you! Is he nuts? That's bad luck!"

I step off my pedestal, letting my dress fall out around me. "What? Who is?"

"Reese!"

My heart flutters at the sound of his name. I move closer to the door just as the knob begins to rattle.

"Dylan?"

Joey spins around and presses his mouth to the door. "You are out of your mind if you think I'm letting you in here."

"Joey, it's okay."

"It most certainly is not," my mother adds. "Dylan, you can't see each other before the ceremony. This isn't like *not* having a rehearsal dinner." She moves between me and the door, pulling Joey off it. "Reese Carroll. You are not allowed in here."

"I don't need to come in. I just want to hear her."

Joey looks back at me and then his eyes lose focus. "Goddamn it, Billy."

I chuckle, stepping up next to my mom. She looks over at me and sighs before waving her hand and giving me the go-ahead. I move up to the door and flatten my hand against it.

"Reese?"

A soft thump knocks against my hand. "Please, tell me you're almost ready. I'm fucking dying."

I giggle. "I'm ready. I've been ready. I'm just waiting for Juls."

I hear a faint growl. "Go get your wife and tell her we're starting. Now." The sound of footsteps leading away from the door makes me smile as I picture Ian as a man on a mission. "Love, can I… I don't know, can you just give me something? Crack the door open a little?"

I glance over my shoulder, seeing my mother and father in quiet conversation. Joey hears the request and immediately spins around and blocks my parents' view of me. I turn the doorknob and pull, opening the door a few inches and peering around, making sure to keep my body completely hidden. His eyes meet mine, and I see the desperation in them.

I keep all focus on his face, not letting my eyes wander down his body. I want to save that for the ceremony. I smile behind the door. "You okay now?" I whisper, not wanting to alert my mother.

He leans his head against the doorframe, blinking heavily. "I'm not spending another night away from you. I barely got any sleep last night."

"What, is Ian not a good snuggle buddy? I've heard otherwise."

He smirks. "You're hilarious. Give me a kiss."

"No way."

"Why?"

"Because the next time I kiss you will be when you're officially my husband."

I hear the clicking sound of heels as Reese argues my reasoning with a scowl. Juls grabs his shoulder. "Get the hell out of here! Are you insane?"

"You're the one who's making us wait. She's ready. I'm ready. Let's fucking go."

Juls shoves him in the direction of The Great Hall. "Go. We'll be there in a minute."

He looks past her, connecting with me. "If you make me wait, I'll be hauling you down that aisle over my shoulder."

"I'm right behind you," I reply as Juls pushes her way into the room.

My mother walks over to us, disapproval stamped on her features. "I'm not saying a word."

I shrug before turning to Juls. "Can I *please* get married now?"

Juls waves my dad over who has remained in his chair. "Are you ready to give your daughter away, Mr. Sparks?"

He looks at her then at me before standing and tugging at his suit jacket. Reserved and poised, he walks over and takes my hand, looping it through his arm. He tilts his head down, giving me an endearing look. "I will never be ready to give my daughter away. But if I had to pick one man to take care of her in my place, it would be Reese."

I blink rapidly, trying to stop the tears from forming. Juls sniffs and wipes underneath my eyes, keeping my makeup intact while Joey fans his face and my mom pulls out a handkerchief, blowing her nose into it.

My dad leads me toward the door. "Come on. You heard the man. He isn't going to wait much longer for you."

We walk down the side hallway which dumps into the main room of the Whitmore. It's empty, all the guests already inside The Great Hall. I hear the soft music playing behind the closed giant double doors. My mother comes up to me and kisses my cheek before doing the same to my father. Joey moves me to the side, shielding me while Juls opens the door and allows my mother to enter the room and take her seat.

"Okay," Juls says in a soft voice. "Let's line up." She walks over to the side table and grabs my bouquet, handing it to me and taking hers. Joey stands at the front of the line, Juls right behind him. He grabs the door handles, glancing back over his shoulder.

"Ready, cupcake?"

Juls gives me a quick wink and I nod, shifting my weight on my feet.

God, yes. Come on already.

The doors open and the music becomes noticeably louder. I move forward once Joey begins his walk, gripping my bouquet tightly. As Juls makes her way between the rows of chairs, my father takes a few more steps with me. I look around the room, smiling at the familiar faces of family and friends who have joined us today. And then I can't stand it any longer. I give into the biggest temptation of my life and let my eyes find Reese.

I see his reaction to me immediately. And even though I know this ceremony is being videoed, I won't need any help remembering the look on his face right now. I know without a doubt I will never forget this moment and the mix of emotion in his eyes.

My dad turns me toward him. "Are you sure I can't walk you down the aisle, sweetheart? It's my only job today."

I smile and look back up at Reese, because it physically pains me to not look at him at this point. "No," I reply, letting go of his arm. "He'll come get me."

My father makes his way down the aisle alone, gaining muffled reactions from the guests. No one knows why I'm standing back here by myself. No one but Reese. And as my father takes his seat next to my mom, Reese begins his walk toward me.

Actually, it's more like a sprint.

I hear the familiar laughs of our friends from the front of the room as Reese gets to me in record timing. He cradles my face in his hands and drops his forehead to touch mine.

"Thanks for coming to get me," I whisper for his ears only.

"I'll always come to get you, you know that." He leans back and looks down my body. "You have never looked this beautiful, and you always stun me, Dylan. This dress…"

"Wait 'til you see what's under it." My tease gets the reaction I was hoping for out of him. I'm quickly being escorted down the aisle, almost at the same pace with which he reached me moments ago with. The hall becomes filled with everyone's laughter as they take in my flustered fiancé. Once we reach the front of the room, I hand my bouquet to Juls who can't seem to stop giggling. Reese positions me across from him, steadying me with his hands on my upper arms before releasing me.

He looks up at the preacher. "Hurry up."

We run through the majority of the ceremony without any glitches. When it comes to our vow exchange, I turn around and grab a few tissues from Juls. If last night was any indication to how I'm going to react to this, and given the fact Reese has never looked sexier than he does right this moment, I'm going to need these.

I go first, with the steadiest voice I can muster, repeating after the preacher. I only shed a few tears but quickly wipe them away before my makeup is affected. Reese keeps his eyes on me the entire time, giving me the sweetest smile I've ever seen as I promise to love him forever.

And then I prepare myself for his turn.

The preacher doesn't ask him to repeat anything. In fact, he doesn't say anything after I finish reciting mine. I look up at him and then to Reese with what I can only assume to be my most perplexed expression. Reese reaches into his inner jacket pocket and pulls out the familiar brown card he's always sending me notes on.

I crush the tissues in my hand as my breath lodges in my throat.

He steps closer to me, holding it out for me to take. "Did you really think I'd ever use someone else's words on you?"

"Oh, my God," Juls chokes out behind me.

I hear Joey's annoyed reaction, too, but can't respond to it. I have to put all my focus into taking the card from him. It's a difficult task. My hands are shaking so bad I'm not sure I'll be able to stop them enough to read the card. I go to unfold it when his hands cover mine.

"No, love. That's for you to never forget the words I'm about to say. Right now, just listen."

I bring the card against my chest, holding it there while he barely leaves an inch of space between us.

"Dylan, until today, the day you fell into my lap, the day you came back to me, the day I knew I was going to marry you, those were the best days of my life. I promise to always look at you this way. To give you every part of me, and to cherish every second I share with you. Because you have always been mine, ever since I first saw you in this room. And I will spend the rest of my life being yours." He looks down, breaking our contact briefly as I wipe underneath my eyes. "I feel like I've been waiting for this day forever. I still can't believe I'm the one who gets to marry you." He finally lifts his eyes and I see the tears in them. "I want you in every way, Dylan. I want the woman who fell into my lap, and the one who's slapped me across the face more times than I care to remember."

I laugh through a cry, hearing everyone's chuckles around me.

Reese's lips curls into a smile. "I want the woman who dances around her bakery every Friday, and the one who lets me watch her from across the room and acts like she doesn't know I'm doing it." His hand tucks my hair behind my ear, and my throat suddenly feels too dry to swallow as he holds my face. "I want the woman who protected her heart when she had to. The one who gave it to me when she was ready. And the one who is now giving me the best day of my life."

I can't control myself now, nor can any other woman in the room, I'm sure. Even Joey is blubbering behind me as I reach up and wipe the tear that's trickled down Reese's cheek.

"I promise to always love you. To send you deliveries when I want or when I think you need them. Even if it's every day. To hold your hand and your hair when you're hung-over. And to let you take care of me when I'm at my worst. I promise to give you every day of my life. To always protect you, even if it means breaking my hand in the process."

My eyes widen. "What?"

He gives me a half smile. "Yeah, I… it might be broken."

"Oh, my God," I grab his hand and hold it out in front of me. I barely glance at it before he puts it back on my hip. "I wasn't finished."

"Neither am I." He pulls my body against his, wrapping his arms completely around me. "I promise to laugh with you and comfort you. To love you when life is easy and when it's hard. And to be the man you deserve." He sighs, his face breaking into a smile. "Okay. I'm finished."

"That was the best note you've ever given me." Instinctively, I tilt my head up to kiss him but am stopped when the preacher clears his throat. Reese and I both turn our heads.

"Not at that part yet, folks. We still need to exchange rings."

"Oh! The rings!" I spin around and hold out the card for Juls to take, swapping it for the ring. Turning back, I look over at the preacher. "All right, start talking. I need to kiss him."

The bridal party and congregation all share a laugh before the preacher instructs us to slip the rings on the other person's finger. I study the way the platinum band stands out on Reese's skin.

My man looks good wearing a wedding band.

And then finally, after what feels like an eternity, we get to the best part.

"And now, by the power invested in me by the State of Illinois, I now pronounce you husband and wife." He looks at Reese and I follow suit, bouncing up and down on my feet. I'm so ready for this fucking kiss, I might just burst before I get it. "You may now finally kiss your bride."

"About time," Reese grunts before pressing his lips against mine. This kiss wipes my memory of anything besides him, leaving me breathless as he cradles my face. I hear everyone clapping and cheering around us, but Reese doesn't pull back. Not until he's ready. "You're mine, Mrs. Carroll," he says against my lips, finally ending our kiss.

"Always have been," I reply.

We walk down the aisle, my hand in his while everyone claps around us. Once we get through the doorway, Reese leads me to the room where the bridal party has to wait until it's time to be announced upstairs. He pushes the door open and immediately pins me against the wall, his lips crashing against mine.

"Reese." His name comes out as a plea. To stop because the bridal party will be in here any minute. To keep going because I'm dying to be with my husband this way.

"I need to get you out of this dress." He kisses down my neck, nipping at my skin. His hands roam my body like he hasn't touched me in years. There's an urgency to it, a drive to touch every part of me. He grips my waist and spins me so I'm facing the wall. "How the fuck do I take this off?"

I flatten my palms against the wall as his fingers pop the buttons of my dress. I should be telling him we don't have time for this, and we're definitely about to be interrupted, but all words have escaped me.

"What the hell… Jesus Christ, Dylan. What are you wearing?"

The door swings open just as I'm about to answer and Reese quickly spins me around, closing in on me and shielding me with his body. I glance over his shoulder and see our friends walk in, all wearing the familiar 'busted' look on their faces.

"Mmm hmm," Joey teases, pointing a finger at us. "You may have won the crying bet, but we just all won one hundred bucks from both of you for trying to stick it in before the reception."

"I never agreed to that," Reese scowls over his shoulder. "And will you all give us a fucking minute?" His fingers are trying to secure my dress blindly as I laugh against him, dropping my head against his chest. And then I feel him relax into me, his laugh echoing around us as we both enjoy the humor of this situation. The fact that we can't make it through a few-hours-long reception before we need to have each other.

"You have two minutes before we need to line up," Juls voice fills my ears as I keep myself completely submerged against Reese. Embedded almost. And then the sound of the door closing and the fading voices in the hallway are the only thing I hear besides our breathing

I glance up and take him in. All of him. Maybe I didn't get a good look when we were standing in front of the congregation. Maybe I was too distracted by the heaviness of the situation and his vows to me, so honest and real, so Reese in every word. Because now as he looms over me, hands stilled on my back, I take my first real look at the man I've just given my life to.

Hair that's been pulled by my fingers. Eyes wide and wild. Lips parted to speak, or ready to clamp down on my skin. His tongue teases the slit in his lip, and I know he *knows* exactly what he's doing. I'd be doing the same thing if I didn't think Juls would drag me from this room by my hair. But we don't have time to tease or touch. Not yet.

I drop my head back as his finger runs along my jaw. "You need to button me up, husband."

He stops all movement at the sentiment. All breathing ceases as he closes his eyes. I watch his neck roll with a heavy swallow. "Say that again."

God, I love him. I love how he needs to hear me call him that. Not only to be mine, but to own the title.

"Husband," I repeat before turning around. "I need some help."

I feel his lips form to my shoulder. My neck. The shell of my ear. And now I'm the one closing my eyes and silently begging to hear him speak. To say the word he hasn't spoken yet. "Wife," he says against my ear. The material of my dress shifts as he buttons me up. "Can you please explain to me what you're wearing under this? It looks like a torture device."

I blush at my naughty secret. "It's a corset. I figured I'd up my game a little for my wedding night. It's uncomfortable as hell, so you're welcome."

He grabs my waist and spins me. "I better not have any trouble getting that off you. It looks complicated."

"You can always rip it."

His eyes turn feverish as he contemplates that solution while he leads me to the door. "Done. Let's get this over with. I need my wife alone."

I smile, feeling my body spark with anticipation, and can't agree more.

ALL THE GUESTS ARE WAITING for us inside the reception area while Reese and I stand at the back of the bridal party line in front of the double doors. Juls and Ian are directly in front of us, stealing kisses every few seconds while Ian doesn't try to keep his hands off her belly. And Joey and Billy are in front of them. I hear a few words of their not-so-lovey conversation over the music pumping underneath the door. Straining to hear more, I lean to the side and see Joey shove Billy before storming back toward Reese and me.

"Joey!" Billy yells.

My fuming assistant stops next to me, connecting with Billy over Juls' head. "I'm not walking in with you. Why should I? You've barely spoken to me all goddamn day! Fuck you. Walk in by yourself."

I grab his arm and yank him forcefully. "What the hell is going on?"

He opens his mouth to answer me when the doors are opened and the voice of the DJ spills out into the hallway.

"The wedding party is ready to make their grand entrance! And starting us off, we have Groomsman Billy McDermott and Man of

Honor, Joey Holt!"

"Joey, get up here," Billy harshly orders over the cheers of the guests.

Joey crosses his arms, firmly holding his ground next to me. "Fuck. You."

Juls tries to pull him in the direction of the room. "What are you doing? Are you not going to walk in?"

"Not with him I'm not."

We all look over at Billy who gives his forehead a quick rub. "Fine. Whatever." He walks into the room by himself, disappearing into the crowd.

I smack Joey on the arm. "That was really mean. Now who the hell are you going to walk in with?"

He thinks silently for a moment before pulling out his phone.

I ignore him and turn to Reese. "Do you know what's going on with them?"

He looks at me, shaking his head impassively. "Why the hell would I know what's going on?"

Before I can answer him, the DJ interrupts me.

"And now please give a warm welcome to our Best Man, Ian Thomas, and his beautiful wife, Matron of Honor, Julianna Thomas!"

Reese and I step forward as Juls and Ian enter the room. Brooke slides past them and waves at us.

"Hey. I told the DJ. Now what?" she asks, pulling down the hem of her dress. She looks from Joey to Reese and me. "That ceremony was so beautiful. I cried my eyes out. Well played, Reese."

Joey grabs her arm and slips it through his. "Come here. You're being introduced with me."

"What? But I'm not in the bridal party." She tries to pull her hand from his grasp but doesn't get anywhere. "No way! I'm not being introduced!" The DJ's voice comes overhead again.

"And now our Man of Honor is ready to grace us with his presence. Everyone please show him some love. Mr. Joey Holt!"

"Joey!" Brooke protests as Joey moves her with him into the room.

"Billy wasn't acting weird or anything when you were with him earlier?" I ask Reese as we step up to the entrance. "Joey said he was avoiding him or something."

He places his hand over mine. "Dylan, Billy and Ian could've been fucking each other in front of me and I wouldn't have noticed. I was too busy pacing the room."

Billy and Ian? Shit. I'd pay to see that.

I give him a cheeky grin. "Oh, man. You just gave me the hottest image. Would you ever watch gay porn with me?"

Not that I have, but let's be real here. I've read some crazy hot M/M books recently, and I'd be lying if I said I haven't gotten heated over Logan and Tate's sex scenes. In fact, Reese has benefited greatly from my extracurricular reading habits.

He glares down at me as the DJ's voice comes booming out into the entryway.

"All right, folks. The moment you've all been waiting for. Everyone please go crazy for the couple of the hour, MR. AND MRS. REESE CARROLL!"

"Ready?" he asks, but he doesn't give me time to answer before he bends down and hauls me over his shoulder.

"Reese!"

I wrap my arms around his waist as he carries me into the reception hall. A mixture of cheers, laughs, and whistles greet us and I lift my head, smiling at everyone the best I can as my hair falls into my face. Once Reese stops walking, he slides me down the front of his body, depositing me on my feet. I look around and see we're in the middle of the dance floor, the crowd fanning out around us.

I smile up at him, watching as he lifts his gaze off my face and connects with something or someone over my shoulder. His lips part slightly, and a look of admiration washes over him as he studies whatever or whoever it is with deep concentration. I turn, looking through a gap in the crowd and instantly narrow in on what he's looking at.

Our cake.

He takes my hand, moving me with him across the dance floor. He holds a finger up to the DJ before we slip through the mass of people and step in front of the dessert table. He leans down and studies my creation with great interest as he tightens his grip on my hand.

"Do you like it?" I ask, expecting him to glance over at me. But he doesn't. He doesn't take his eyes off our cake.

"It looks like your dress," he says, moving around to the side and back to the front, making sure he takes it all in.

"And it's all mint chocolate. The icing. The filling. Pretty much the whole cake."

That makes him straighten up and turn to me. He brings our conjoined hands up to his mouth and kisses the back of mine. "The perfect union of flavors."

I nod, motioning with my head toward the center of the room. "Dance with me, handsome."

After he escorts me out into the middle of the dance floor, he wraps one arm around my waist, taking my hand and holding it against his chest. '"Look After You'" begins playing overhead and I smile up at him as we share our first dance, letting him lead me all around the floor. When we get close to the bridal party, I notice Joey standing as far away from Billy as possible. And I also notice Billy's anxious eyes and the fact that they are glued to his heated boyfriend. As the song comes to an end, I steal a kiss from Reese before we're instructed to take our seats at the bridal table.

I snap my fingers at Joey, gaining his attention once he sits two seats down from me. "What the hell is wrong with you?"

He leans back, seemingly insulted by my question. "Me? Nothing. I'm not the one acting like I want nothing to do with my boyfriend. I'm so sick of this shit."

I look over my shoulder at Billy who is seated at the opposite end of the table next to Ian. He seems to be lost in thought, fidgeting nervously with his napkin and tearing it into tiny pieces.

Shit. My mother better not see that. It'll be the cloth-napkin debacle all over again.

The sound of a woman's throat clearing overhead gets my attention and I turn back around, seeing Juls standing behind me and holding a microphone. She smiles at me before looking out over the crowd.

"Can I have everyone's attention for a moment, please?" The sound of shushing fills the room before the silence. "I don't think there's a person in this room who knows Dylan better than I do. Well, except for Joey." She places a hand on his shoulder and he smiles up at her. "We've been best friends for as long as I can remember, and I have seen every side of her. Her pissed-off, slap-happy side. Her tipsy, nickname-giving side. Even her focused, career-driven side. I've seen every emotion. Every personality trait. Except one." She focuses on me. "I've never seen my best friend in love. Not until she met Reese."

His hand squeezes mine and I look over at him, smiling before Juls continues.

"She fought it. She was scared, but there was no denying what that man did to her. Or what she did to him. And I loved watching it. I loved seeing them completely blissed out on each other. I also loved seeing them both lose their shit over the other person."

"Julianna," my mother scolds from her seat. She shakes her head disapprovingly, glaring at me like I'm the one who just used profanity.

Juls laughs into the microphone, and we all join in. "Sorry." She clears her throat, dropping all humor. "Anyway, I love you both very much and I couldn't be happier for you. To the bride and groom."

Everyone cheers as I stand and wrap Juls in a hug. She kisses Reese on the cheek as I take my seat again.

"And now, the Man of Honor has a few words," she says, handing the microphone over to Joey as he stands out of his seat.

"Actually, the Man of Honor isn't saying anything." He looks over at me as he walks off the platform. "I, uh, put together a little video instead. I hope that's okay, cupcake."

I nod, bracing myself for what I'm hoping isn't some slideshow of my awkward years. I was at a wedding once where the Maid of Honor did that to the bride. But I'm sure Joey knows better. I'm not afraid to use any of the utensils in front of me if a picture of me with braces pops up. And he knows that.

He steps in front of the DJ booth, leaning close and exchanging some words with the man. Everyone turns in their seats as the video is cued up, projecting on one of the walls. Soft music begins playing and I glance over at Reese who is watching intently, completely focused. And then I see a baffled expression set into his profile and look up at the wall, following his gaze.

Pictures of Joey and Billy begin filtering onto the wall. Selfie shots of the two of them together, and others of just Joey when he isn't looking at the camera. I glance over at the DJ booth and see the puzzled expression on my Man of Honor's face.

"Uh, this isn't… what the hell?" He turns around and begins talking to the DJ, motioning over his shoulder at the wall. "Where's the video I gave you? Where did you get this?"

I turn to look back at the strange collage when Billy begins walking off the platform and over toward Joey. I squeeze Reese's hand as tightly as I can, remembering Billy's words to me before my rehearsal last night. *"This is the grandest gesture I can think of."*

Oh, shit.

Billy steps up next to Joey and takes the microphone, moving into the center of the dance floor. Joey remains glued to his spot, mouth gaped open and eyes full of panic and curiosity.

Billy brings the microphone up to his mouth while his eyes scan the room. "Umm, so this obviously isn't the video Joey put together for Reese and Dylan. I watched him put that video together and it's really sweet, and I guess he kind of inspired me. I don't know. I'm not really good at this sort of thing. I'm really private, and I'm kind of freaking out right now." He rubs the back of his neck with his free hand before looking up at the wall. "Reese isn't the only guy who met the love of his life at a wedding. I did, too. But unlike Reese, I'm not the kind of guy who sends deliveries or writes his own wedding vows." He looks up at the platform, connecting with my husband. "Seriously. You kind of make us all look bad." He ignores the laughs he's just earned and turns around, focusing on Joey. "I know I've been a complete shit today, and I'm sorry. I've just been really nervous about this, but not because I'm not sure about what I want. I am. I'm very sure." He pauses in thought briefly before continuing. "I'm sorry I'm not the kind of guy who does these romantic, grand gestures like Reese. I might not ever be. But I am the kind of guy who will risk a major rejection in front of hundreds of people if you don't agree to marry me."

My free hand slaps over my mouth as I gasp, hearing Juls' dramatic reaction next to me. I glance down at movement on my lap and see Reese's other hand, holding out a bunch of tissues for the two of us.

I look at him. "Did you know about this?"

He simply smiles his response as Juls and I both take the tissues, readying them for use.

"Joey," Billy says, his voice much softer now but somehow steadier. "Can you come over here, please?"

Everyone's eyes are on my dear assistant as he falls apart, head down, shoulders shaking with his cries. I want to get up and console him, but I know these are happy tears. So I stay put next to my severely emotional, pregnant, best friend, and my husband who apparently knew about this all along.

Joey makes it to the center of the dance floor, slowly, but he gets there. And when he does, Billy drops to his knee in front of him. I'm a mess. Makeup be damned; there is no stopping my tears right now. Billy holds the microphone to his mouth, ready to ask the most important question of his life. Until suddenly, he brings it down and sets it next to him on the floor. He reaches into his jacket pocket and pulls out a ring box, holding it open for Joey as his lips begin to move. Juls and I lean in, wanting to hear Billy's words, until we both realize this moment is for the two of them. His words are only for Joey. And we must sense it at the same time because we both sit back together.

Billy's face breaks into the biggest smile I've ever seen him have before he stands up and grabs Joey's face, kissing him passionately in front of everyone. I stand, along with everyone else, and cheer for them at the top of my lungs. Once they break away from each other, which seriously takes a good several minutes, we all join them on the dance floor to congratulate them.

"Oh, my God! I'm so happy for you!" I scream, wrapping my arms around Joey. Juls does the same and when she pulls back, he holds his left hand out for us to see.

"Look how good my baby did!" he squeals. A platinum band with diamonds set into it adorns his finger, and we marvel over the beauty of it. "God, I'm so fucking happy right now. I'm engaged!"

"And now we can plan your bachelorette party. Naked men galore!" I yell, earning a curious expression from Ian who is congratulating Billy. Juls and Joey both laugh as the man who surprised us all walks over to us.

"Thank you for giving me that moment, Dylan. I can stop the slideshow and play your video now," Billy says into my hair as I hug him.

I lean back. "No. Leave yours on. It's the sweetest thing." I reach up and ruffle his hair. "I'm so excited for you."

"Holy shit! This wedding is insane," Brooke declares with her drink in her hand as she comes up to the group. She motions with her free hand toward the rest of the crowd that are all mingling and dancing. "Side note. There is zero play for me at this shindig. You all seriously need to find some more single friends." She winks before grabbing Joey and Billy, congratulating them. Juls and Ian begin dancing and I look around for my groom, only scanning half the room before I feel him behind me.

His lips press against my hair as his arms wrap around my waist. "I love you, Mrs. Carroll."

I spin around and link my fingers behind his neck. "I love you. Feel like taking a bathroom break? I've heard the amenities here are prime for fucking."

He shakes his head, laughing at me. I think he's going to respond with some filthy comment, but he kisses me instead. And when that happens, I no longer hear the hysterical excitement of our friends. I no longer hear the song playing overhead or the noises of the crowd around us. I'm purely focused on Reese and the way he kisses me.

The way my husband kisses me.

And nothing could pull me out of this moment with him. Not even a vacant men's bathroom.

"WHY ARE WE STOPPING AT the bakery?" I ask as the limo pulls in front of my shop and comes to a stop. Reese and I left The Whitmore underneath a cloud of bubbles before getting into our getaway vehicle. It was supposed to drive us straight to his condo. Or so I thought.

I don't get an answer from my groom before he opens the door and steps out, offering me his hand. I take it and exit the limo, looking up at him.

"Umm, did you not get enough of that cake? Is that why we're here? For treats? Because I thought I saw you eat, like, four pieces."

He opens the shop door, keeping my hand in his as he enters the alarm code. "That was the best cake I've ever had. And I meant what I said about you making that every year on our anniversary."

"Not to scale, I hope," I reply with a smile.

He pulls me through the back and toward the stairs. I stop him, firmly holding my place by the worktop.

"Wait. What are you doing?"

Did he completely forget that all of my stuff was moved out today?

He smiles sweetly. "Come upstairs with me."

I can feel the wrinkles setting into my skin as I put on my most baffled expression. Before I have time to ask any more questions, he steps into me, lifting me off the floor and cradling me in his arms. I hold onto his neck as he carries me up the stairs, swings the door open, and steps out into my old loft.

Because that's what it is.

What I'm looking at now is definitely not the loft I'm familiar with.

Some of my stuff is here, but it's been moved around. Blended with his. A perfect mix of his furniture and mine. The screen that separates the bedroom area from the living room space is now moved to the far corner of the room, separating a smaller area from everything else. The arrangement is different, making the space seem bigger somehow. My bed has been moved against the wall, leaving more room around it. After taking in my surroundings, I turn my head to meet his anxious eyes.

"I'm confused."

He smiles, setting me down on my feet and taking my hand in his. His other hand works at loosening his tie. "Why are you confused? This is your wedding present." He pulls me toward the bed and spins me around to face it while he stays at my back. I feel his fingers tug at the buttons on my dress. "Dylan, I don't need things. I don't need a big condo, or extra room, or all this shit I've accumulated over the years. This place is tiny, but we can make it work. I had the rest of our stuff put into storage until we figure out what to do with it."

"But what about when we have a baby? We agreed we'd be cramped in here."

His finger points over my shoulder, and I follow it to the decorative screen. "The baby can be right there. That way he's right next to us."

"He?" I ask, biting back my smile. I feel his fingers unsnap the clasp behind my neck holding my halter up and seconds later, my dress drops to the floor. Turning around, I watch his gaze slowly move up my body, taking in my wedding present to him. His chest rises with a deep inhale as his eyes seems to lose focus somewhere between my stomach and my neck. I let him look for a few more seconds before I coax an answer from him. "Reese?"

"Hmm?"

"You said 'he'. We're not having any daughters?"

With that question, his eyes quickly meet mine as he grabs my waist and tosses me onto the bed. He lowers himself onto me. Blanketing me. "I don't know if I can handle more than one of you. I'm shooting for all boys." I throw my head back and laugh as he straddles my waist. "Now, what the fuck am I supposed to do with this thing?"

I look down my body, seeing his hands physically tremble as they hover over my corset. "There's ties in the back that…ahh!" I'm quickly flipped over on my stomach as his knees brace him on either side of my body. I feel the strings being loosened as I rest my head on my cheek, looking out at our loft.

Our loft. No longer mine. Every memory I make here will now contain my husband and the family we create.

"Thank you for what you did. I really love my wedding present."

His lips press between my shoulder blades. Then lower, as my corset is loosened completely. Once my back is completely exposed, I'm flipped over so I can see him. He sits back on his knees between my legs, taking in the sight of me, and I see his chest shudder with his inhale. As if it's the first breath he's taken in hours.

"Are you okay?"

"It'll always be like this with you." His eyes hold mine with a gentleness I don't remember ever seeing from him. And I want to ask him what he means, but I wait, because I know he's going to give it to me. I see his throat roll with a swallow, his lips parting slightly as his eyes commit me to memory with the most profound look he's ever given me. "After 323 days, I should know the effect you have on me. But I don't. I'm never prepared for it. Every time I see you, it's like I'm at that wedding all over again."

The air leaves my lungs in a trembling rush, and I'm suddenly not concerned with breathing at all. Nothing gets to me like the words he chooses for me. And I know nothing ever will.

"How do you do that? How do you make me love you more than I ever dreamed possible?" I ask as the tears pool in my eyes. I reach my hand out, needing to feel him. Needing that constant contact now more than ever.

His hand touches mine and he laces our fingers together. "I should ask you that."

I blink, sending the tears down the side of my face. He releases my hand and grabs my foot, resting my heel against his chest. One shoe is removed then the other. I watch him run his fingers up the inside of my leg along my stocking until he reaches the metal clips of my garter. And after his declaration to me seconds ago, I think this is going to be gentle. I think his next moves with be unhurried and tender.

Until I see the tremor in his hand as he brings it up to rake through his hair.

He pushes off the bed and starts ripping his clothes off, not giving a shit about buttons or zippers. He's frantic, like a man deprived, watching me frozen on the bed.

Hungry.

Greedy.

He's normally so controlled, so calculated with everything he does. Especially sex. His movements are precise. Well-orchestrated. Practiced. And I love that side of him. But when he's chaotic like this, when he can't seem to settle himself enough to remove clothing properly, when he appears human, faulted like the rest of us, this is the side of Reese which drives me insane.

"I don't think I've ever needed to be inside you so badly before. I'm fucking shaking," he pants as he drags his rigid cock up my leg. He puts a hand on each of my thighs, digs his fingers into my skin, and shreds my stockings away from my body. My garter and panties are removed, tossed off the bed and disregarded like everything else that isn't him and me in this moment. His hands anchor into the skin of my hips as he lifts them off the mattress and, in the same motion, drives into me.

"Reese," I cry out, digging my nails into his shoulders.

He pushes my knees against my chest, lunging so hard into me my teeth chatter. "You're finally mine. I've waited so long for this."

I nod through a moan, closing my eyes and silently chanting. *Yes. Yes. Yes.*

His hands massage my breasts as his thrusts become frenzied. Fingers pinch my nipples and my eyes flash open when I feel the slide of his tongue over one hardened peak.

I thread my fingers into his hair, fisting it when he bites down. "Oh, God," I cry as he buries his face between my breasts.

"Say it, Dylan." He lifts his head, capturing my mouth and stealing the words from me. "Beg me like you do."

I don't hesitate. I never will. "Please, Reese," I say against his lips, hearing him react with a soft moan. "I need you. Please."

His arms brace himself on either side of me, flexed and fully extended as he begins thrusting forward in a slow, steady rhythm. We keep our eyes on each other, never breaking contact. He runs his hands over every inch of me. His lips follow. Then his tongue. He drags his cock on my skin each time he pulls out, the heaviness of it slicked with my desire for him. He gives me his words, sweet and filthy, as he moves in me. He's wild one minute and tender the next, sliding between my tits while he tells me how hot my tight, little pussy is and then whispering against my ear how he'll need me forever while he finger-fucks me. I'm clawing at his skin, wanting to somehow embed myself beneath his surface as he brings me to orgasm over and over, denying himself his own release to focus on me. He grinds into me from behind, his deft fingers rooting themselves into my hip bones as he bottoms out with punishing thrusts.

My body breaks, bowing in submission as a wave of pleasure surges through me. He tastes the skin of my neck. My breasts. Between my legs. My fingers tangle in his mess of hair as my body arches off the bed into another rolling climax. I don't think I can take anymore as he crawls up my body, chin and lips wet, prowling over me like a lion.

I grab his face, making our foreheads touch as he slides his cock between my legs.

He enters me, brushes against my mouth with his, and says, "Mine."

"Yes."

"My wife." He lunges forward, then back.

"Yes." My response is softer, barely above a whisper, and I feel his body tense against mine. Ready to break.

"Dylan." My name escapes his lips the moment he loses all control. Sweat drips from his forehead to my chest before he collapses on top of me, sealing our bodies together.

And we stay like that, long after our breathing steadies.

Long after the dull ache of his hipbone against mine becomes familiar.

Reese gives me the contact we both need. The intimacy we both crave.

His life.

His love.

He gives me everything.

And I know he always will.

I CAN'T CONCENTRATE.

I haven't been able to concentrate for over a week.

I know I'm supposed to be contributing to this meeting, but all my attention is on the phone weighing down my pocket. And the conference room doors. Any second now, any fucking second I could get the call.

Papers shuffle. Ian's voice fills the room again, followed by collective murmurs. All distractions I need right now, but don't give in to. I can't. But it's been like this. I've been a walking zombie, present in the office but not functioning at the level I'm used to. Or that my colleagues are used to seeing from me.

It's pathetic, really. I haven't felt this unhinged since I first met Dylan.

I twist the band around my finger as my eyes lose focus.

I've been told this kind of anxiety is normal for this situation, but constant? Is it possible to have a coronary at thirty-three? The problem is I have zero control over this situation. None. And I need fucking control.

The conference door swings open, grabbing my attention immediately, and I'm on my feet before I even register who steps through because there are two things I know for sure right now.

Everyone who is supposed to be in this meeting is here.

And no one's stupid enough to barge into this room without knocking first. Unless the reason behind the intrusion is too important for pleasantries, such as knocking.

Dave sees me walking straight at him. "Mr. Carroll, it's time. You need to go."

My hand is in my pocket, pulling out my phone. "Why didn't she call me?" But before he can answer my irritated question, I see the missed calls. One from the bakery number and one from Joey. "Fucking piece of shit phone." I look around at the stunned faces of my colleagues, giving them an apologetic nod.

Ian's at my back, hand halting me on my shoulder. He pulls me into a hug. "This is it, man. You ready?"

"Yeah. Yeah, I…" I stammer on my words, suddenly not feeling prepared for the moment I've been more than prepared for.

He slaps me on the back, ending our hug. "You're ready. You'll be fine."

I think I say goodbye to him, to Dave, to every person I pass in the hallway. It's all a blur of distractions. Fucking distractions I no longer want to be aware of. I go over what I'm supposed to do, replaying my role over and over again in my head. The classes, the books I've read, marking pages, highlighting shit that freaked me the fuck out. Internet searches and YouTube videos I ignored the warnings of.

"Don't watch those. It won't be like that," she said to me.

But I did. I watched them all. Trying to somehow retain enough knowledge of every possible scenario that could play out when the time came. Needing to know more information than the damn doctors who have studied this for years. I've smothered her with my overbearing, overprotective side that's way the hell surpassed anything she's ever seen from me. And anything I've ever felt. I will always be possessive over my wife, but the domineering drive which took over my body two hundred and eighty seven days ago is borderline psychotic. Luckily, she seemed to have been expecting my behavior.

I don't know where to go, so I stop at the information desk. The young woman looks up at me, expectantly waiting for me to speak with raised eyebrows. *Speak. Speak, asshole!*

"Dylan Carroll."

Her fingers press the keys like a fucking child would, one at a time. I close my hands into fists, clamping my eyes shut because I can't watch her do this to me right now. Twelve keys. That's all she needs to press. Twelve. *Come fucking on.*

"Take the elevators to the second floor. She's in room two fifteen."

I see the line of people waiting in front of the row of elevators. Too many people. I opt for the stairs, taking them two, three at a time and exploding onto the second floor.

Two fifteen. Two fifteen.

I push the door open, stepping into the room filled with people in turquoise-colored scrubs. Joey and Juls are standing on either side of the large hospital bed, each of them holding a delicate hand. My delicate hand. I think I hear the doctor say something to me but can't comprehend it as I step up and connect with who I'm here for.

Dylan lifts her eyes to me, those big brown eyes that dilate every time she sees me. Her hair is sticking to the side of her face, cheeks flushed bright red, and lips pursed as she squeezes her eyes shut and lets out a sound that has me shoving Joey nearly clear across the room to get to her.

"Jesus Christ, Reese!"

I give him the quickest once-over, making sure I haven't drawn blood, and then all my attention is on her.

I can concentrate on this.

"We'll be out in the waiting room. I'll let your parents know you're here," Juls says, letting go of Dylan's hand. I hear the door close and the movement of the nurses, but I don't look up.

I touch her cheek and she leans into it as the contraction lessens. When she rolls her head back onto the bed, I flatten my hand on her extended belly. "Can I do anything?" I ask, feeling the jabs against my palm I've become addicted to ever since I first felt them. Before she can answer, I press my lips to her hospital gown, just above my hand. "Don't hurt your Mommy."

She laughs but it's short-lived as her hands grip the rails of the bed. "Fuuuckkkking shit!" Her body arches, head thrown back as her belly begins to jerk against me.

"Mrs. Carroll, I need to check you," the doctor says, sliding his hand into a glove.

I know what that means and I can't watch him. Him. Why the fuck Dylan insisted on a male doctor is beyond me. The only reason why I agreed to it was because he's apparently the best in the state. But that doesn't ease the throbbing tension which sets into my body whenever he's examined her.

Especially now.

I brush her slick hair off her forehead as she moans in discomfort. Eyes clamped tight, face contorted in pain.

I hate this.

"You look so beautiful right now."

Her eyes flash open, and the magnitude of her stare and what it does to me is profound. I'd do crazy shit for that stare.

"Reese, shut up."

Especially when it's paired with that mouth.

"You do," I affirm, kissing her sticky forehead.

She frowns. "I'm massive, sweaty, and will seriously injure someone if I'm not told I can push in five seconds." Her eyes narrow in on the doctor between her legs. "Well?"

He reaches into a compartment on either side of the bed and removes two metal arms with brown straps on the end. "You're ready. Baby's head is down and in position. Put your feet in these and scoot all the way down."

I feel my body surge with panic as Dylan slides down the bed. Legs in the air, spread wide. Body flattened out on the bed. She grabs my shirt and tugs me down. "Hey, look at me."

I do. I can't not look at her. If Dylan is anywhere within my line of sight, she has my full attention. And for six hundred and sixteen days, my eyes have strained to stay on her because nothing else matters to me.

I hear her breathing quicken as she breaks our contact to look down her body. "When do I push?"

"As soon as you feel the next contraction. Push for ten full seconds, Dylan. Don't stop until you get to ten."

"Love, please, I…" I feel my legs shake underneath me. The strength in my body seems to evaporate as I lean over her. Everything I've read. Every pamphlet, book, internet site. Every instruction from our labor and delivery coach, everything leaves me. My mind draws a blank as I stare down at my wife, looking up at me for support. For me to do my job. For help through this. "Fuck… what do I do?"

She grabs my hand and squeezes it as she takes in quick, short breathes. "You're doing it."

Everything clicks, and it's just her and I in that room. Doing this together.

Ten seconds. Come on, love. You're almost there. Push. Push. Good. Okay, take a breath. You're doing so well. I love you. I love you so much. Look at you. Look how amazing you're doing. Here comes another one. Don't stop, Dylan. Push. Six. Seven. Eight. Squeeze my hand. You want to meet our daughter. Come on, you're almost there.

"Arrggghhhhhhhh!"

Everyone has moments in their lives, which are superior to others. They become an obsession, your reason for living, and all my moments involve Dylan. The moment I saw her, standing at the end of my row next to Ian. Our wedding day, when she officially became mine. And now this.

She's so tiny in my arms. I've held babies before. My nieces and nephews. Even Juls' and Ian's son. But none of them seemed this delicate. I've counted her fingers and toes several times. I've memorized the feel of her skin and every detail of her face. She looks like Dylan, except her hair is darker and apparently resembles mine after I've run my hands through it, whatever the hell that means. She waited forty-one weeks to meet us, but she still seems so small. I've been told seven pounds is a very healthy weight, but that information isn't comforting me. I was a nervous wreck before she arrived and now, maybe I'm worse off.

"You're going to stress me out like your mother, aren't you?"

She coos against me, a reaction I've picked up on since I started whispering softly to her.

I never want to put her down. Ever. That crib I spent hours

putting together weeks ago isn't going to be used any time soon. I hold her closer to me, running my nose along her cheek, when I feel a hand in my hair.

I look up and meet my wife's sleepy eyes. "Hi, handsome."

Standing from my chair, I carry our daughter over to her. "Do you want to hold her?" *Please, say no. Let me keep her for a few more hours.*

She shakes her head slowly. "She'll want me when she wakes up hungry." She slides away from me, patting the bed. "Come here."

I climb into bed, cradling Ryan against my chest. Dylan leans over and kisses the top of her head.

"Mmm. She might have you beat on smell." She reaches for the birth certificate on the tray next to her and grabs a pen. "I thought of a middle name."

I pull my eyes off the only other girl who commands my attention and look over at my wife. "Yeah?"

She looks at Ryan, then at me. "Love. Ryan Love Carroll. Whatcha think?"

I smile and her face lights up before she begins filling out the blank box on the birth certificate. We picked Ryan months ago, something I threw out as an idea. But we couldn't settle on a middle name. And Dylan refused to pass hers down.

She caps the pen and pushes the tray away, just as her phone beeps on her lap. Grabbing it, she looks at the screen before smiling over at me. "They want to meet her."

I pull Ryan away from my chest when she begins to stir. Her body goes rigid in my arms as her lips part with a yawn. I relax when she stills, looking over at Dylan. "Five more minutes?"

"You can't keep them out forever. Your mother is probably going crazy." She rolls onto her side and runs her hand over Ryan's head. "This hair," she says with snarky disapproval.

"She's perfect." I look up. "She's just like you. She's already hit me in the face twice with her tiny fists."

We both laugh as I shift onto my right hip, turning my body toward her and lying on my side. I hold Ryan between us as Dylan drapes her arm over my body.

"Do you have everything you want?" she asks through a yawn,

her eyes struggling to stay open.

"Not yet."

My answer puzzles her. I smile at her confusion and lean in, pressing my lips against hers. "I want to do this again."

She leans back. "You know we have to wait six weeks before we do *anything* again, right?"

"What?"

She laughs, lying her head on her pillow. "No sex for six weeks, handsome. Doctor's orders."

I feel my jaw twitch as my hand pulls her hip so she's closer to me. She's never close enough. I could crawl inside her skin and bury myself there and I'd still need more.

"I'll be speaking to him about that."

Nobody gives me the go-ahead to touch my wife. I'm certain rules can be stretched. In fact, I think I read it somewhere. *As long as she's comfortable. Shit. What did that article say?*

"You're thinking very loudly over there."

Her voice cuts into my thoughts, bringing my attention back to her. I press my lips to Ryan's head, inhaling the second-best thing I've ever smelled. "Thank you for giving me this."

She smiles, closing her eyes and humming softly. My eyes drift from her face to the one who fiercely entered this world with a scream, which rivaled a damn war cry.

I do have everything I want. Everything I never imagined wanting, but now, I'd do anything for.

Dylan Sparks came into my life, grabbed onto me, and rooted herself so deep she practically became a part of my genetic makeup. She challenges me, she pushes every button I have, and she loves me more than I could ever deserve. I vowed to give her my entire life, but I didn't need to. She took it the moment she fell into my lap.

I'm a better man for knowing her.

A father because of her.

And I have everything I will ever need as long as I have her.

The End

Acknowledgements

SWEET JESUS! I DON'T EVEN know where to begin with these Thank yous. So many people have helped me on this journey. Family, friends, bloggers, authors, readers… the list is endless. But first and foremost, I'm going to start off by thanking my main man. The man I fell in love with when I was eighteen years old. The man I married a year later. And the one who will always be my favorite person in the entire world. I love you hard, Mr. Daniels, and I always will.

My beautiful bloggers!!! Oh, I just want to squeeze every single one of you. My girls over at Give Me Books, thank you so much for all you have done for me. Kylie McDermott, I'm tackling you in Vegas. You've been warned. Thank you to A Book Whore's Obsession, BestSellers & BestStellars, Dirty Girl Romance, Romance Room, Blushing Reader Michelle, and all the other blogs I know I'm forgetting for helping me reach more readers.

To my lovely betas! Beth Cranford, Erin Thompson, Lisa Jayne and Heather Peiffer. You girls rock! Thank you for reading Sweet Possession when it still had massive typos and strange word usages. You made it better. You make me better. And I heart all four of you.

And, lastly, to my readers. Thank you all so much for waiting for this story. Reese and Dylan will always be my favorite couple, and it makes me so happy to see your enthusiasm over them, not to mention all the Juls, Ian, Joey, Billy, and Brooke love. You all have embraced them and me, and I can't thank you enough for that. Goddamn it, Billy.

Thank you all again,

J

Sweet
OBSESSION

J. DANIELS

This book is dedicated to my amazing street team,

T's Sweeties.

You ladies rock my socks off.

Author's Note

Sweet Obsession is a standalone novel in the Sweet Addiction series, and crosses over with the Alabama Summer series. Chronologically, it is set after Sweet Possession and between All I Want and When I Fall.

Chapter One

Brooke

"FUCK YEAH, BABY. YOU READY? Huh? You ready to come all over this cock?"

I dig my nails into Paul's shoulders, arching my back off the bed. My breath hitches. "Yes, God . . . fuck, don't stop."

"Fuuuck." He squeezes my hips while he pounds into me. Sweat beads up on his brow, on the dusting of hair coating his chest as he throws his head back, filling the condom with a groan, the cords in his neck straining.

My own orgasm follows seconds later.

"Coming!" I yell, closing my eyes as that sweet heat burns down my spine, exploding into a thousand stars between my hips. I lock my ankles behind his back, keeping his firm body pinned between my legs, his cock exactly where I need it while I ride this out. My body hums, my thighs shake against his skin.

God, I love sex. I mean really, who doesn't love this right here?

I'd consider giving up cupcakes for this.

I grind my hips against his pelvis as a life without salted caramel icing flashes in front of my eyes.

Chocolate chip cheesecake. Red velvet. White chocolate raspberry.

Okay, maybe not cupcakes, and maybe not this sex. I've had to tag myself in a few times.

"Greedy girl," Paul murmurs, sliding his hand between my tits. He pinches my nipple.

"Mm," I purr, slowly peeking up at him as that perfect ache settles, leaving me sated.

A lazy smile beams down at me, but blurs into something indiscernible as Paul's spent body suddenly collapses on top of mine.

"Lord, move off." I rock my hips, shoving against his shoulders. "Asshole. You're going to kill me."

He laughs, rolling onto his back and pulling off the condom with a satisfied groan. He ties it off. "Goddamn, I don't think I've ever filled one of these this much before. My dick might need a week to recover."

Mm. I guess I'll take that as a compliment.

Go, Brooke. Wreck those penises.

I stand from the bed and grab my clothes off the floor, dressing hastily as Paul treads to the bathroom. Slipping into my heels, I spin to grab my clutch off the nightstand and run straight into a bare chest.

"Oh, hey, sorry," I mumble, shifting my weight on my feet. "Just grabbing my stuff."

He squeezes my hips, bunching the material of my dress in his hands. "Where are you going? Stay for a little while."

"Can't. I need to get home."

"We can order take-out or something. Are you hungry?"

"I already ate."

His brow furrows as his grip on me loosens, then vanishes completely. His shoulders drop. "Why do I feel like I was just used?"

A laugh rumbles in the back of my throat. I move past him, picking up my clutch. "I had a nice time tonight. Maybe I'll see you around."

"And do what? Is this going to happen again if I do see you? 'Cause if I'm being honest, Brooke, I'm not really feeling the love right now."

I lift my head to look at him. His dark eyes are suddenly unsure. He looks wounded.

Wow, really? Didn't peg you as a clinger, Paul.

Securing my clutch under my arm, I plant a brief kiss on his cheek, whispering, "don't act like you didn't know what this was."

As I pad toward the door, my heels tapping against the hardwood, I wait for that moment to hit me where I feel remorse, or regret. Anything to make me turn around and reassure this man, but it never comes.

I don't feel bad for this. I never feel bad after having an orgasm, even if some of them are brought on by my own efforts. And really? Why should I feel bad? He came. A lot, apparently. Enough to make him gaze at that condom like a proud father cradling a newborn. We're both walking away from this experience satisfied, even if I am technically the only one walking.

Regret? Remorse? Fuck that noise. I'm Brooke Wicks, and I love sex. A lot of it. I don't see any problem with my hit it and quit it philosophy. I'm doing what I want with the men I want to do it with.

Period.

Hand on the doorknob, I turn and give Paul one last look; a sweet one. "Good night."

His eyes, lost in focus, slowly lift to meet mine. "Yeah . . . yeah, good night."

With little resistance, I slam the door shut, smiling at the sound.

A hard, satisfying bang.

Nope. No regrets here.

I STEP INSIDE THE CONDO, shutting the door behind me and setting my keys and clutch down. Two sets of eyes peer curiously at me over the back of the couch.

Let the interrogation begin.

"Yes?" I ask, pulling my heels off and setting them by the door.

Billy turns around, throwing his arm behind Joey. "Well?"

I limply shrug. "Five."

"That's it?" Joey's back goes rigid. His eyebrows meet his blonde hairline. "On a scale of one to ten, he was a five in bed? Are you fucking serious?"

"Oh, I thought you were asking me how big he was."

Billy clears his throat, his wide eyes roaming the condo uncomfortably.

I look between the two of them. "Seven. Extra point for the dirty talking."

Joey grimaces, waving me over. "A seven with a dick smaller than your vibrator? God . . . you poor, poor baby."

"I know. I was going to bail when I saw it, but then I thought I'd see what he could do. You know me . . . always the team player. Plus, it was pierced."

I round the couch and sit on the end next to Joey, who by the look on his face, is visualizing a pierced dick. Billy mouths the word "no" when he's given an inquisitive stare, prompting a low laugh to push past Joey's lips.

I twirl a chunk of hair around my fingers.

Mm. Out of the two of them, I'd peg Joey to be the one with the barbell through his junk. Billy wears too many suits, and don't lawyers go through metal detectors when they go to court?

I can't see him wanting to explain his Prince Albert every day to security.

My body forms to the soft leather as I relax, head tilted back, my gaze on the ceiling. "He got all clingy on me when I was leaving. Full-on puppy-dog eyes and everything. I wasn't expecting that."

"Humph. Are you sure he didn't have a vagina?"

I scoff at Joey. "I think I would've noticed. I was all up in it."

Billy stands and grabs the large, half-empty bowl of popcorn off the coffee table as Joey and I share a laugh.

"You want to watch a movie with us? We just started *The Best Of Me*."

I smile up at Billy. "Nicholas Sparks? How very gay of you."

He feigns a laugh, hand flattening on his chest. "Hilarious,

Brooke."

"Oh!" I shift onto my knees so that I can look between the two of them as Billy moves into the kitchen.

I almost forgot!

"You are both about to be so, so proud of me. I went to Agent Provocateur today, and didn't spend a dime. Not one cent! Do you have any idea how difficult that was? I started shaking like a crack addict when I saw the new spring line." I hold my hand up, beaming when Joey high-fives me. "I even tried on stuff. What I did today, the restraint I showed, is seriously unheard of for me. I should actually go back to the store now and buy something to celebrate the fact that I didn't buy anything earlier."

I go to get up and Joey grabs my wrist, tugging me down. We share a teasing look.

"Kidding, they're closed, obviously, but seriously, how great am I doing with my spending? My bank account is looking awesome lately. Give me a few weeks, and I should be out of here."

Getting evicted from my apartment two months ago was probably the lowest moment in my life. Well, that and the cum-shot gone wrong in New Orleans.

I swear my eye twitches occasionally because of that mishap.

After I found the notice taped to my door, I flipped off my landlord and weighed my options.

My overbearing parents—God, no, I'd rather get my teeth drilled, or Juls.

I love my sister, I do, but I can't live with her. Besides, her and Ian are in tiny-tot land. She's popping out a kid every nine months it seems. They need their family space. I need to not have to explain to my four year old nephew why Aunt Brooke has things that vibrate in her bedroom.

My landlord gave me one week to get out. I thought I was screwed. I was ready to deal with the ramifications of living under my father's roof again. I'm sure he would've tried to tag me with a curfew, even though I'm twenty-five, haven't had a curfew since I was seventeen, and mastered the art of sneaking through my bedroom window when I used to live there. However, these two amazing men saved the day and offered me a place to crash. The three of us have gotten close since I started working at the bakery, me and Joey especially.

Who would've thought me and Joey would become besties? I hated that bitch growing up.

Billy hands me a daiquiri. His eyes, warm and kind, stay glued to mine as he moves to his seat. "You know we don't mind you living here, right? We're not kicking you out, Brooke. There's no rush."

"Ha!" Joey smirks, his eyebrow arching playfully as he settles against Billy's side. "No, we're not, but I would like to fuck loud eventually. I'm all for you kicking your shopping addiction if it means we can go back to trying to break the sound barrier."

I swallow my mouthful of daiquiri quickly before I spit it out. A quick chill runs through me. "Please. I have to wear those giant noise-canceling headphones when you two go at it, and I can still hear you begging, Joey. You don't know how to be quiet."

"Oh, and you do?" Joey rolls his eyes, lifting his own glass. "You're loud even by yourself, Brooke."

"It's not my fault I'm amazing. Ask Paul. He can confirm that."

Billy grabs the remote, a tense wave passing over his features. "Can we start up the movie and get off this topic? I had no idea you could hear us."

"Everyone can hear you." I point at the wall behind me when he turns his head and eyes me cautiously. "Mrs. Kessler caught me in the elevator last week and asked me if you two were remodeling in here. Something about you yelling 'give me a hammer.' You should've seen her face when I told her you were actually saying hummer."

Billy closes his eyes, groaning. "Jesus Christ."

"No wonder that old bitch has been giving me strange looks lately." Joey waves a dismissive hand in front of his face. He shifts about on the couch. "Fuck her and her moss covered vagina. My sex life is fantastic, and I don't care if the entire state hears my baby asking me to suck him off. We quiet down for no one."

I pull my glass away from my lips, laughing as Billy rakes a hand down his face, noticeably uncomfortable.

He's so different from Joey. The complete opposite, actually, but they complement each other perfectly.

Especially in the bedroom. I hear a lot.

"I told you both I would only stay here until I had enough money saved up to move out. I love you guys, but I need to get my own place again. Our combined hair-care products are overtaking the condo." I cock my head with a pout, shifting my gaze between them. "But I will miss the sleepovers. You're such a sweet little spoon, Billy. All soft and cuddly."

He frowns. "There's nothing about me that's little, Brooke. Or soft," he pauses, grinning. "Haven't you heard?"

Warmth floods my cheeks.

Sweet Lord. Did Billy just insinuate . . .

"No, there is definitely not," Joey proudly affirms, cutting into my thoughts of R-rated antonyms. He squeezes Billy's thigh. "Was that a hard 'no' on the dick jewelry? Any wiggle room on that?"

The movie begins playing. Apparently, Billy's answer was final.

Joey's lips brush against my hair as I swallow another mouthful of my daiquiri. "How was it with the piercing? Honestly," he whispers.

Typical Joey. Needing to know all the tricks of the trade. I am shocked he hasn't been down this road himself, though.

"The one spot that's hard for some guys to hit," I begin softly, bending my finger in a rhythmic motion. Our eyes lock. "He didn't have any problem."

Joey slowly leans back. "Damn it. Am I seriously missing out?"

"Shh."

We both glance at Billy, then resume whispering closely.

"I know for a fact he hits all your spots just fine. As do the neighbors across the street."

"True. But I love trying new things with him. Maybe I could get it done." Joey looks down at his lap, the corner of his mouth pulling tight. "That shit could go south, though. Really fuck up my perfect form. Not to mention it probably hurts like a motherfucker."

I press my lips to the edge of my glass, murmuring my next words when Billy tilts his head down and glares in my direction. "Want me to call Paul and ask? He's probably staring at his phone expectantly."

Joey smiles. "He loved you, Brooke. How could you walk out on what you two shared?"

Oh, my God.

"Please."

"I'm sure he was seconds away from proposing. Or at least suggesting you move in with him."

I shake my head. "He was oddly fascinated with his own semen. That living arrangement would never work."

Seriously. Did he even flush that condom? Is there a chance he set it aside to frame it instead?

Gross, Paul. You'll never get a girl to stay that way.

Joey bumps his shoulder against mine, pressing his weight into me. "That's kind of hot, actually. But . . . okay, I have to know. Was it a barbell? Or one of those stud things? Oo! Did he have it going down the shaft?"

The noise from the TV abruptly cuts off. Silence fills the condo.

Billy leans forward, elbows resting on his knees, the look he reserves for moments when Joey and I go off on dick tangents at the dinner table ghosting across his face.

I clear my throat, lowering my glass. "Hi, hey there, little spoon. Sorry, we'll be quiet."

His eyes, steady with doubt, shift to Joey and soften marginally.

There it is. Sweet Billy. No one else looks at Joey like that.

Mindful to the fact that the only way to keep his husband on the couch with us and not locked in his office, going over documents that can surely wait until tomorrow is to shut up and watch the movie, Joey slides over and plucks the remote out of Billy's hand.

The movie resumes playing.

I tuck my knees against my chest as the two men at the other end of the couch dissolve into each other, recommencing the intimate embrace they always share. The closeness that stills the two of them, even Joey, who is nearly impossible to silence.

I sip leisurely on my daiquiri, my thoughts on piercings and poor, poor Paul, struggling to find the perfect spot to display that condom.

THE SIDEWALK IS ALREADY BUSY at a quarter after eight Monday morning as I make my usual trek down Fayette street, carefully juggling four coffee orders, my over-sized Coach bag, which just so happens to be the purchase that sent me over my spending limit two months ago, *worth it, it's fabulous*, and the design binder I took home on Friday of Dylan's.

I wanted to organize some of the notes she had penciled in over the past several years and make things more legible, pretty even. I used textured paper and script font. The letters and thank you cards she received since opening the bakery that had been stuffed into the back pocket for keepsakes are now laminated and on display for clients to read in a section titled 'Sweet Testimonials.'

I'm honestly not sure how Dylan will take my modifications to the only thing she seems to study more than her husband. The thought of her hating what I've done, the one thing I haven't cleared with her beforehand that involves her business, causes me to miss the giant crack in the pavement I'm usually careful to step over.

"Ow, shit!"

The binder goes down first, followed quickly by my Coach bag.

But the coffee? Ha! Not today, city of Chicago.

As I bend down, securing the leather strap on my shoulder, the binder pinched between my fingers, a car horn sounds and I lift my gaze to the street. Traffic clears. My eyes roam the row of shops on the west side of Fayette, until landing on one I haven't seen before, or maybe, I just haven't noticed.

No, this has to be new. I would've noticed this.

Sandwiched between a florist and a family-owned candle shop, the words Hot Yoga scream against the brick front in burnt-orange lettering. A simple logo swirls in the corner below the 'a'.

Yoga?

"Yoga?"

I straighten and stare a little longer at the new business, which just so happens to be in direct line-of-sight from the bakery.

That's almost laughable. Here, sweat your ass off, then skip across the street and stuff your face. Maybe we could go in with the owner and have some sort of a coupon-deal worked out.

Five sessions and you get a free cupcake?

I swallow down a giggle.

Look at me, all business savvy, trolling for ways to pull in new customers while helping to promote other local enterprises.

I should seriously run for president.

The door chimes as I step inside the bakery, the scent of sugar now mingling with the aromatics wafting from the four coffees in my hand. With an exhaustive sigh, I set the cardboard carrier on the glass display case, followed by my bag and the design binder.

Dylan perks up from behind the counter when she sees the latter.

"There it is! You know I tore this place apart this weekend looking for that? What the hell, Brooke?"

I flatten my hands on the glass, then hesitantly nudge the binder. "I, uh, did some reorganizing. I hope that's okay."

Her face remains expressionless. I take in a shallow breath.

Rule number one of life: Don't piss off your employer, especially if that employer happens to be Dylan Carroll. She's been known to go a little slap happy.

Moving closer, she flips back the cover, then a few more pages, running her finger along the edge of the new font. Silently judging, meticulously studying every alteration I've made. She halts at the back where the testimonial section begins.

I wipe a hand across my brow, relieved when I don't feel the sweat I fear I'm releasing.

"Mm."

I lean closer, staring at her mouth, the small crinkle in her nose. "Mm?"

God, why the hell didn't I ask permission first? Could she fire me over this?

After what feels like the longest seconds of my life, she looks up at me, narrows her eyes, then smiles. "I love it. Brooke, this is . . . surprisingly thoughtful of you."

My mouth falls open. *Surprisingly?* "Hey, I'm thoughtful! I do stuff for other people all the time. Take last week when Ryan wanted that Elsa dress and Reese was on the brink of losing his ever-loving mind looking for it. Who stepped in and saved the day? Huh? Who almost got arrested at Target? You?"

She laughs, tucking her long blonde hair behind her ear. "I know. I'm just kidding."

My spine straightens with pride as I pluck my coffee out of the carrier. "Well, you're welcome. I'll take that raise whenever you're ready."

She cocks her head with a glare. I take a step back. *Easy, Rocky.*

The door chimes, followed immediately by Joey's booming morning voice.

One volume. The man has one volume.

He hooks his thumb over his cashmere covered shoulder in the direction of the window. "Did you see the yoga studio across the street? What is that mess about?"

"Not just yoga," I correct him. "*Hot* yoga. Lots of sweaty women with camel toe, being forced into ungodly positions."

Joey makes an amused sound in the back of his throat. "Sounds like somebody's high school years."

"Yours?" Dylan throws out, resting her hands on her swollen belly. "Didn't you wear an alarming amount of spandex back then?"

Joey spins the carrier on the display case, tugging out the cup with his name scrolled on the side. "I'll ignore that jab, since you're carrying Joey Jr."

"His name isn't Joey Jr."

"What?" Alarmed eyes flick between myself and Dylan. "Okay . . . Joseph? I'm fine with that."

"I'm afraid not."

I smile against my cup. "Excellent. We've settled on Brookes then? Suck on that, McDermott."

Joey glares at me over the top of his cup. I glare right back, laughing a little.

Dylan gently sighs. "Sorry. We're going with Blake. That's the name we both like."

"Who's we?" Joey squawks, his face suddenly two shades redder. "I don't remember that name being on the table for discussion.

And I definitely don't remember receiving a phone call, asking my opinion before you started getting shit engraved."

"Why do I need to call you? And engraved? Really, Joey? Who got anything engraved?"

A soft noise comes from the kitchen, followed by the familiar quick tapping of tiny feet on tile.

Joey sweeps his free hand around the shop. "I'm sure there's something around here with that name already on it. Is it possible to fill out the birth certificate before the birth? Has Reese figured out how to do that?"

"Joey." Dylan exhales exhaustively. "Fucking relax, all right? You haven't heard the middle name yet."

"Momma!"

Ryan comes barreling into the shop, her dirty blonde hair pulled up into two little sprouts on top of her head. Wearing a polka-dot dress and rainbow tights, she bounces up and down behind the counter, her hands grasping at the air.

"Momma, wook! Wook at my pwetty dwess."

Dylan laughs, leaning down to kiss the top of her head. "You look so pretty, baby. Did Daddy let you pick out your clothes?"

"Uh, huh. Wook. My shoes, Momma. I wove dem."

I risk a glance at Joey, catching the quick work of his finger along his cheek, no doubt catching a tear.

"You okay?" I ask quietly, stepping closer as the tiny voice continues to shout up at her mother.

He hesitates, then gives me a sly smile, mischief dancing in his crystal blue eyes. "Middle name. Did you hear? Suck on that, Wicks."

"Whatever." I shove against his shoulder, moving him a few inches away.

Not that it matters much to me. I was only tossing my name into the ring to rile up Joey.

Success.

"Aunt Bwooke!"

I turn around, set my coffee on the glass case and rest my hands on my knees. "Hey, girlfriend. I love your dress."

Ryan spins, fanning the material out around her.

"Daddy says I'm his pwincess. He's wetting me dwive to Nana's today." She dances away, twirling in circles around the shop.

"Is that so?" Dylan puts her hand on her hip just as Reese steps into the room, diaper bag on his arm, baby carrier in his hand, guilty as shit grin on his face.

Mm. Busted.

"What's that?" he asks, his voice catching. Looking between his two girls, a cooing sound from the carrier draws his attention down. He smiles at Drew, *Lord, the man is whipped*, then focuses back on Dylan. "I never said that."

"Sure you didn't." She lifts her head up, welcoming his kiss. "Brooke got your coffee."

"Mm. Might not need it. I'm wide awake after that little shower session this morning," he mumbles all too loudly against her mouth.

"Good Lord," Joey says, almost groans, from my right.

I turn my head, expecting to see him still standing next to me, engaged in this conversation since I'm positive he just reacted to it, but instead I find him staring out the glass window, intently fixated on something.

"What's up?" I ask, joining his side, sucking the warm mocha off my lips.

My eyes follow his across the street, widen, then nearly pop out of my skull and roll around on the floor.

The door chimes, and I think I hear Reese's faint goodbye, Ryan's more animated one, and something Dylan says, but honestly, a fucking meteor could strike the earth right now and I wouldn't notice.

I inhale sharply. Maybe a little too sharp. My hand flattens on the window pane, steadying myself when I start seeing double of the man standing outside the yoga studio. I blink once, then once more, hard, waiting for him to suddenly up and vanish into a cloud of smoke.

He can't be real.

He seriously can't be real.

A mirage, that's what this is. I'm not standing in the bakery, on the verge of licking the window like some mental patient. I'm in the desert, dying of thirst, my throat raw as I struggle to stay alive. I look up and this man, my hallucination in the distance, is beckoning me closer with promises of clean water and wild sex.

Two resources I'd be a damn fool to pass up. It's all about survival in these elements.

I bite my lip through a groan when the man places his hands on the back of his head and gazes up at the yoga sign on the building.

My God, he's the owner, he has to be. With that body? He's practically a walking advertisement for Abercrombie and multiple orgasms.

My eyes sweep over the length of him, slowly, before settling on the ass to beat all asses. Even from this distance, that thing would stop traffic in Times Square.

"I, for one, am suddenly very interested in hot yoga," Joey remarks under his breath.

I whip my head to my right. "You're married, and I'm calling dibs."

"Dibs? What are you, ten?"

"What are you two looking at?" Dylan asks from somewhere behind us. "Can one of you lazy asses finish filling the display case, or am I the only person working today?"

What am I looking at?

Sex. That's what I'm looking at.

I look down, giving a quick once-over of my outfit before I make my move.

Black v-neck tee, skinny jeans, and . . . *fuck!*

Sneakers? Why am I wearing sneakers today? There is nothing sexy about the Nike swoosh. And my thoughtless choice of footwear definitely isn't doing anything for my legs.

I spin around and march past Dylan toward the kitchen. "I need to borrow some shoes."

"What?" she asks.

"What?" Joey echoes in the distance, but I'm already halfway up the stairs, too focused on my mission to answer either one of them.

Pumps. I need pumps. Something with a heel.

Shoes are flying everywhere as I rummage through Dylan's small closet. How she manages to fit her and Reese's clothes in this thing, along with her gorgeous selection of handbags and other accessories is beyond me. They are in serious need of a bigger space, but I get it. She likes living above her bakery, and Reese will do anything to make her happy.

With this third baby coming though, one of them might have to start sleeping in the bathtub. No way is another crib fitting in this loft.

"Oh, hello pink." My hands close around a delicious pair of Steve Maddens. I toe off my sneakers and remove my socks.

Maneuvering carefully down the stairs, I re-enter the bakery, now three inches taller. Dylan and Joey take notice immediately.

"Help yourself to my wardrobe, Brooke."

Her sarcasm isn't lost on me.

"Will do."

I grab an empty bakery box and slide the display case open, reaching inside.

Joey nudges against me. "Do you really think he's going to be staring at your feet, Miss Cleavage?" His words are muffled by the mouthful of danish he's devouring.

"I always feel more confident in heels."

"And the cupcakes?"

"It's a gesture. Welcome to the neighborhood, now let's go get naked and eat these off each other."

Dylan laughs quietly. "I think it's sweet. What's that saying? The fastest way to a man's cock is through his stomach?"

"Mm, I don't think that's right," Joey says, laughing. "Although, how many apple turnovers did Reese consume when you two were dating, but not dating, but totally dating?"

"Shut up."

I straighten and close the box, rounding the counter and heading for the door. "Right. I'd say wish me luck, but we all know I don't need it."

Their remarks, if they have any, are lost amongst the traffic from the street as I step outside. I wait not so patiently for a break to cross, shifting on my feet, taking quick bursts of air into my lungs.

Why am I suddenly nervous?

Because you're about to suggest a night of scandalous indecency to a man who looks like the definition of the word 'orgasm.'

Ridiculous. He can't be *that* hot. I'm sure some of his attractiveness will soften the closer I get.

Like a mirage. He'll vanish before I can touch him.

Steadying the box in my hands, I quickly pad across the street.

Determined.

Mildly apprehensive.

One hundred percent turned-on.

Chapter Two

Mason

I DID IT.

Holy fuck, I actually did it.

Linking my hands behind my head, I gaze up at the sign I had installed yesterday. The morning sun strikes against the sharp edge of the letters, deepening the richness of the color.

My chest swells with pride. My stomach flips wildly, reminding me of my nerves and the giant risk I'm taking doing this.

Contradicting reactions battling for dominance. Equal in strength, I'm the perfect blend of fearless and frozen.

This is official, scary as hell, and quite possibly the biggest thing I'll ever do. I've dreamed of owning my own studio for years, since I first started instructing. The passion I have for this, the drive, it's there, but bloody hell, so is the worry I'm in way over my head. Never did I imagine I'd actually get this opportunity. And here I am, starting this new venture in a city completely foreign to me.

I pinch my eyes shut through a slow inhale.

This has the potential to be amazing, my greatest accomplishment, maybe the only fucking thing I'll ever do that'll mean something.

I have the potential to completely fuck it all up.

Right, mate. Way to stay positive.

"Admiring the view?"

My arms fall heavy to my sides. My eyes fly open.

"I gotta say," the low, velvety voice behind me continues. "I really don't blame you. I've been doing my own fair share of staring this morning."

I turn my head, intrigued.

A woman, obviously, I knew before I turned around I'd be coming face-to-face with a woman. Only not *this* woman. Never in my wildest imagination could I conjure up this vision as she steps up to join me on the footpath, then stumbles forward the second our eyes lock.

"Oomph!"

I reach out, gripping her elbows and taking her weight. Her skin feels electric. "All right there, sweetheart?"

Steadying herself, she slowly lifts her head, her lips parting as she stares at my mouth with the strangest look. A mixture of intrigue and disbelief.

"You've got to be shitting me."

I exhale a laugh. "I never quite understood that expression. What exactly does 'shitting me' mean? Seems like a bad thing, yeah?"

"Bad?" She smiles, just the slightest, dangerously slow pull of her lips, as if she's already planned out this interaction and is ten steps ahead, waiting for me to catch up. "No, not bad, just didn't think it was possible you could get any hotter. Then, boom, you have to go and open your hot Australian mouth and completely blow my mind. 'Shitting me,' in this case, is a very, very good thing."

"But, it could also be used negatively."

"Of course. If you dropped your shorts and I discovered you were in the process of going through gender reassignment surgery. In that unfortunate scenario, my 'you've got to be shitting me' would carry a whole new connotation."

"Ah, well, I assure you," I begin, leaning closer. "That wouldn't be the case."

Her eyebrow arches. "Prove it."

"You're serious."

She tips her chin up, waiting.

Jesus Christ. This little thing could destroy me.

Drop my shorts, right here? No, obviously I wouldn't, but fuck if I don't want to maybe pull her inside and shock her a little. Show off my cock to a woman who looks like she's ready to eat me alive.

A soft laugh erupts from her. She's amused. I feel like I'm watching a wolf circle an innocent flock of sheep.

Eyeing up one very tempted sheep in particular.

Dimples, possibly the only cute thing about her, draw my attention from one side of her face to the other, and then my eyes can't seem to stop roaming over her features, drinking her in. Dark, soft curls. Large hazel eyes. Her skin, olive and pink in the cheeks.

Now I'm the one doing my own fair share of staring. I clear my head and look down, realizing then I still have my hold on her.

"Sorry." I let my hands fall away. "I'm Mason, by the way."

"Brooke. And no need to apologize. I'd never complain if your hands were on me."

I almost step back, if only to keep myself from pulling her into my arms and testing that theory. Groping a woman I just met in broad daylight isn't normally a desire I find myself battling against.

But it's never been *this* woman challenging me.

"Is that so?" I ask, smiling. "You'd never complain? No matter what I was doing?"

"Mm. Only one way to find out."

I grip the base of my neck. "Christ. I fear I've just met the devil. Figures she's a woman."

"Ah, but does the devil come bearing gifts of delicious treats?" Brooke flips back the lid on the box in her hands. She holds them away from her. "I made them myself."

The pride in her voice is unmistakable. A sweet warmth coating her words, giving me a glimpse of the woman behind the shameless exterior. Possibly the real, true version of herself.

I see you, Brooke.

I look down at the four cupcakes, sliding my hand over hers so we're both now holding the box.

Maybe she needs help holding it.

Maybe I just want to feel her skin against mine again.

I stare into her eyes. "If they're laced with poison, then sure. I imagine not many men being able to resist a beautiful woman with baked goods. The devil is notoriously both dangerous and alluring, is she not?"

"So I've been told."

"From previous victims?"

"Victims?" She laughs, throwing her head back and revealing the graceful line of her neck. "You make me sound like a man-eater. I'm not *that* bad. Here." Her finger dips into the frosting, then slides into her mouth.

Her eyes close through a moan.

Jesus fuck.

I press a hand to the front of my shorts.

When was the last time I got hard in a matter of seconds? When I was eleven and I saw my first pair of tits? I'm normally way more disciplined than this juvenile display I'm exhibiting, but shit if that isn't the sexiest noise I've ever heard in my life.

She pulls her finger from her mouth. Our eyes lock. Saliva pools on my tongue, and I force a swallow before I actually start to drool.

"See? Can't be poisoned now, can it?"

I smile, and her eyes quickly dart to my mouth. "I suppose not."

She allows me to take the box. I close the lid and study the logo. "Thank you. I'll enjoy these later."

"I'd like to enjoy you now."

My eyes widen. I nod in the direction behind her. "Don't you need to be getting back to work?"

She shrugs. "I can spare a few minutes."

"A few minutes? You wound me, Brooke. Give a guy a little credit, yeah?"

A grin twists across her mouth. *Christ, that mouth is wicked.*

"Okay. How long do you need?"

"With you?" I slowly move my eyes over her body.

This is the first time I'm really appreciating every gorgeous inch of her. The swell of her breasts, the black material of her top stretching, barely confining, and in the end, making me ache with a need I'm not sure I've ever felt. The gentle curve of her hips I want to splay my hands across, then move over, grip, and dig my fingers into. She's shapely and soft. Delicate and dangerous.

How long do I need? I could look at her for a lifetime.

"Mason."

My eyes re-focus on her face, the amusement in her eyes. "Mm?"

Shit, how long was I staring? Who's the wolf now?

"Hey, Brooke!"

A voice cutting across the street jolts my attention off her. Brooke turns her head. I lift mine to see a man holding the bakery door open, leaning his head out. He doesn't look too pleased.

"Hurry up already. You've got that birthday cake to work on today, remember? It's getting picked up at ten and Dylan is swamped."

"Shit," Brooke mutters. She spins back around. "Sorry. My few minutes are up."

Damn. She needs to get back. I have a ton of shit to do myself, but I'm not done with this one. Not by a long shot.

"What are you doing tomorrow night?" I ask.

"Why?"

"I have my first class at seven. I'd love to see you."

Her arms cross over her chest. She tilts her head with a smirk. "Private class?"

I frown, then glance back at the sign. "Honestly, I hope not. If this is going to work out for me, I'm going to need a good amount of interest. I handed out a bunch of fliers this weekend." I turn back to her. "Do you think it's too much to expect at least a handful of bodies on my first go?"

Not that I wouldn't mind having a one-on-one session with Brooke, but I do have a lot riding on this. There is no back-up plan.

"You personally handed out these fliers to women in Chicago?"

I nod. "And men."

I spent my entire Saturday going in and out of shops at the mall, standing outside of the local market like a bum seeking a hand-out.

The women I talked to seemed at least partially intrigued. The men, not so much.

I had several papers crumpled up and tossed into the rubbish bin directly beside me, while I watched.

She runs her gaze down my body, then slowly back up. Her eyes, dark and mischievous. "I don't think you're going to have much of a problem packing the house."

"Brooke!" the urgent voice calls out again.

She whips her head around. "Jesus! All right! Go eat another danish!"

The man glares at her, then mumbles something I can't make out over a car-horn in the distance before fleeing into the shop.

Brooke turns back around, her curls bouncing against her top as she shakes her head.

I shift the box to my left hand, holding out my right. She takes it immediately. "Tomorrow night then?"

Her hand gently squeezes mine. "Maybe."

She stares up at me. I stare right back, running my thumb along her skin.

"Are you going to let me go?" she asks.

A strange pressure tightens around my chest.

I keep my hold on her, maybe even securing my grip a little firmer.

Try and run, little sheep.

My lip twitches. "Do I have a choice?"

"No."

"No?" I release her hand, but only to pinch her chin between my thumb and finger. I lean down, slowly inching closer. "But what if I don't want to let you go?" I ask quietly. "What if I can't?"

Her eyes focus on my mouth, an inch away from hers. "Too bad. I'm not giving you an option."

"Do you always decide how this works?"

"Yes," she says, her voice now a whisper.

I know she's expecting me to kiss her. The way she's wetting her lips, tilting her head up to meet mine. The urgency of her breath.

I could kiss her, God knows I want to, only . . .

I'll want more. More than just a kiss. More than she's been

offering me since she made her existence known.

I force her face to turn left and slide my mouth to her cheek. "Tomorrow night. Seven o'clock. Don't make me come looking for you." I press a chaste kiss to her skin.

She looks up at me as I lean back and drop my hand. Her eyes narrow. "You better deliver."

"I always do."

I watch in a daze as she crosses the street. Her ass, this perfect heart-shaped entity, makes me rethink my decision to go a day without tasting her. I imagine peeling her out of those jeans and pressing my lips against her skin. The quiet slap of her body against mine as I bounce her on my . . .

Jesus. Again with the hard-on?

I carry the bakery box inside and upstairs to my loft, adjusting my cock in the process.

Juvenile. If she bent over, you probably would've busted a nut right there on the street.

Standing in front of the rubbish bin, I hesitate, look down at the box in my hands, then glance over at the fridge.

Brooke made these. And fuck, how sexy was she when she made that declaration? Her voice vibrating with pride, then melting to something softer.

I don't eat stuff like this anymore. I don't even keep it in the house. My lifestyle transformation seven years ago included a major re-haul of my eating habits. Out of sight, out of mind has always worked best for me. I haven't eaten a cupcake in . . . actually, I can't even remember the last time I ate a cupcake.

But she made these. She was so proud showing them off.

Decision made, I stick the box on the shelf in the fridge, concealed by condiments.

I palm my phone and send Tessa, my closest friend from where I just moved from, a quick text.

Me: Just met a woman who might have bigger balls than you.

She responds within seconds.

Tessa: Doubt it.

I chuckle in the silence of my loft. Seeing the three missed calls from my mum, I dial her number as I slump down on the corner of my bed.

"Hello, sweetheart. How are things?"

"Great. You know, settling in. The studio is beautiful, Mum. You'd love it."

"I'm sure. No issues with anything? It's okay if there is. You know, a lot of major corporations fail in the beginning, or at least have little mishaps. Doesn't mean they aren't meant for greatness."

My mum worries. Especially when her youngest child lives nearly sixteen thousand miles away.

"No catastrophes yet. Give me a day or two."

"Oh, Mason." She sighs heavily.

I smile, resting my elbows on my knees. "How's Dad and Ellie?"

"Good. Ellie just got a new job at one of the markets near her home. She seems to like it."

"Yeah? That's great. Tell her to call her little brother when she gets a minute. I miss her."

Two quick beeps of a car horn sound somewhere outside the building. I pad to the only window in my loft and spot a delivery truck parked below.

The equipment I ordered.

"Hey, Mum, I need to get off here. I'll talk to you soon though, yeah?"

"I love you, sweetheart."

"Love you."

I disconnect the call and slide my phone back into my pocket.

The mats, towels, and wedges I ordered all arrive within a few hours of each other. I sign the slips the drivers provide and set about organizing everything, then re-organizing.

Having seven sisters has made me meticulous with arrangement.

The studio itself is gorgeous, with bamboo flooring I had installed before the move. The hardwood that was originally in here never would've worked for the humid conditions I'm anticipating. The wood would've swelled and cracked. I probably would be out a couple thousand replacing it.

Not an option for me at the moment. Between my lease and the rent I'm paying for the loft above the studio, the flooring, the equipment for class, the sign . . .

It's fucking ridiculous how expensive an aluminum sign costs. Highway robbery at its best.

I take to the footpath after grabbing a quick bite to eat.

Apple slices and some almond butter. The last of my stash of what I brought from Alabama. I jot down a note to pick up another jar, along with a few other items.

The sky is warm and clear. The street noisy, a steady line of traffic obstructing my view of the bakery. Of the window I want to peer inside, once, just one glance to see Brooke in her element.

Joggers move past me on the path, ignoring the hand I hold up to stop them, my other clutching the stack of fliers. Everyone seems tuned into their own world, the music pumping through their headphones, and ignoring everyone around them. I'm not sure how many fliers I ended up handing out over the weekend, but I drew up two hundred.

My stack feels light.

Good sign. Possible bad sign if they all ended up in the rubbish.

I step inside a small bookstore a few businesses down from mine. Old editions are propped up on display in the window. *Wuthering Heights. To Kill A Mockingbird. Moby Dick.* The woman behind the counter lifts her head at the sound of the bell.

"Good afternoon."

"G'day, Miss. How are you?"

She slides her glasses back on her nose, grinning. Her silver hair is cut shorter than mine and spiked on the top. "I'm terrific. What can I help you with today?"

I pass a flier across the counter. "I just opened up a studio just down the way there. First class is free, if you're interested. It's tomorrow night. Have you ever tried yoga?"

She shakes her head, laughing as she sets the flier down in front of her. "Oh, Lord no. I don't think I can make my body move like that anymore. I'm nearing sixty."

"It's really easy. God's honest truth. It's more about the breathing than anything."

I hear her pick up the flier again as my eyes fall to a photo aside the computer.

"Is this your daughter?" I ask, picking up the frame.

"Yes, that's my Amber. She's beautiful, isn't she?"

My mouth twitches as I study the picture. I look up at the woman. "She is. Would she be interested in attending a class?"

"Oh, um, maybe. I could ask her. She's busy tomorrow night though."

"That's all right." I set the frame down and grab a pen, turning the flier over. The ink saturates the paper. "Here's my number, and email. I check that daily. Stop in and see me or give me a call. We'll work something out, yeah? I'd love to have her."

The woman takes the flier and the pen, then shakes my hand. "Okay. That sounds great. I'm Trish. Welcome to the neighborhood."

"Mason, and thanks. Everyone seems . . ." I pause, my mind racing to Brooke.

Those eyes, hungry and calculating as she circled me, sizing me up.

After a hard swallow, I continue. "Friendly. Very friendly."

Trish chuckles softly, dropping her hand. "That we are."

I wave on my way out, tucking the remaining fliers against my body.

Chapter Three

Brooke

"I'M GOING TO RUN OUT for lunch today," I announce as I secure the lid on a container of icing and slide it on the shelf in the fridge. I close the door. "Is it okay if I take forty-five minutes instead of thirty?"

Dylan glances up from the worktop. "You're buying lunch? What happened to packing every day to save money?"

"I did pack." I grab my bag off one of the stools and pull out a can of soup. *Progresso, Italian Style Wedding.* "See? I'll heat this up when I get back. I need to get something to wear to yoga tonight." I set the soup on the wood.

Me, buying work-out clothes. Seems ridiculous. My idea of cardio has never involved clothes.

"You can borrow something of mine if you want."

"No, thanks," I reply, sliding off my apron and hanging it on the hook by the fridge. I grab my bag and slide the strap up my arm.

Dylan sticks her hand on her hip, the fingers of her other hand drumming the wood. "What exactly are you planning on buying? I have a ton of running shorts and T-shirts. And we're the same size, practically. Save your money and just borrow something."

"I've seen the clothes you wear when you go running. Your tops barely give the illusion of breasts, and I plan on highlighting mine tonight."

I also plan on leaving the tags on whatever I end up buying. Wearing an outfit for an hour, or less, depending on how long it takes Mason to kick everyone else out and strip me naked hardly classifies as a non-refundable purchase.

"Oh." Dylan smiles. "I see. Really, Brooke. Why don't you just save yourself the hassle and walk over there naked? I'm sure what's his name won't mind."

"Walk over where naked?" Joey steps into the back, eyeing up the bag on my arm curiously.

Shit.

He raises an eyebrow. "Going somewhere?"

"No," I lie to the man who for the past two months has taken it upon himself to monitor my spending. "Just . . . putting this up front."

"She's going to buy an outfit to wear to yoga. Something that gives the illusion of breasts."

I whip my head around and glare at Dylan. "You have a big mouth, you know that? And I hardly need an illusion."

Please. My biggest asset has never failed to get me the attention I want, when it's showcased properly. Dylan's baggy T-shirts are a tragedy to the female race. She has always had a killer body, but she looks like a potato with legs in those things.

Joey takes a step back and blocks my exit. Dylan chuckles off to my left.

"Really? What happened to saving up so you can move out?"

"I'm planning on returning it tomorrow," I explain, stepping closer to him. "This is a necessary purchase in the name of sex. Sacrifices have to be made. Besides, I read somewhere that if you don't use your credit card at least once every few weeks, the banks assume you've died and will close down all your accounts. I'll lose my savings if I don't go through with this."

My eyes evade his, roaming casually around the shop.

I don't understand why I have to explain one freaking purchase to either one of them. I'm an adult, for Christ's sake. I've been extremely disciplined the past two months. The only thing I still buy is our morning coffees, and I never hear either one of them riding my ass about that. One calculated credit card charge isn't going to kill me. And hello! Are they both not hearing the plan I have to return this shit tomorrow?

A throat clearing grabs my attention. Joey stares at me for a long second, his thick shoulder wedged against the door frame. "You don't read."

I throw my head back. "Ugh. Whatever, I'm going. I'll be back in forty-five."

"Thirty."

I look over at Dylan. She smiles around the spoon in her mouth.

I roll my eyes. "Fine. Thirty."

Damn it. It's going to take me at least ten minutes to get to the mall. A girl who has never once shopped for a sports bra needs ample time to peruse. Do they even come in cup sizes? Is it a one size fits all deal?

Joey moves toward the worktop, freeing up my exit. "I'm going with you tonight."

My feet skid to a halt in the doorway. I crane my neck to look at him. "Excuse me? What's that now?"

"Going with you," he repeats dryly, grabbing a spoon and dipping it into the vat of frosting Dylan just whipped up. He tastes it, makes an appreciative noise in the back of his throat, then looks over at me. "Billy will be at the office until God knows when. I'll be bored sitting at home. Plus, I'm intrigued. Hot yoga. Even hotter instructor. *You*, trying to get his attention while working out for the first time in your life. Sounds like a good time for Joey."

My teeth clench.

Oh, great. Like I need more people to shove out the door tonight for some much needed privacy.

I stare at the side of his big, nosy head. "You know, when you talk in third person, you sound like an idiot. Especially during sex.

Joey's so close. Joey's going to come."

Dylan gasps, her mouth stretching into a ball-busting grin. She shoves against Joey's chest. "Oh my God. Please tell me you don't do that. That's fucking awful, Joey. Jesus!"

"I do not do that!"

"*You make Joey feel so good. God, suck Joey's . . .*"

I purse my lips when his eyes flash with the threat of revenge.

Shit. Tonight. Yoga. He could seriously derail my plans to get some if he refuses to leave.

"Kidding. Totally made that up." I curl my fingers around my shoulder strap. "I'm out. See you in forty."

"Thirty!"

I smile at the two voices behind me.

"My time starts when I get to the mall. Later, bitches!"

The shop door chimes, drowning out their protests.

I GRAB MY THINGS OUT of the dressing room and move past the racks of clothes in the direction of the registers.

My left hand holds the items I'll be purchasing.

Light gray fitted pants, white tank, and pink sports bra.

My right, the items this store needs to just go ahead and burn. There's no way in hell any woman looks good in these obnoxious patterns. And the one pair of pants made me itch so bad, my thighs are flushed in streaks of pink from my nails.

Who works out in a wool blend? Why is that material even an option?

I keep the clothes separated as I drop them on the counter.

"I'm keeping these. Can you put the rest back for me? I'm on a time crunch."

"Sure thing."

The woman behind the counter begins scanning the tags. I glance at my phone, noting the time.

1:16 P.M. I might just make it in thirty.

A paper taped to the back of the computer monitor grabs my

attention as I'm slipping my phone away.

Hot Yoga with Mason King.

I quickly read the information, my eyes focusing, locking in on certain key words.

Deep healing.

Deep stretching.

Deep breathing.

Deep. Deep. Deep.

A throat clears. The woman behind the counter points at the flier. "You should've seen the guy who dropped that off. He had this accent," she pauses, mouthing the word "wow." I quietly laugh as she grabs a bag and drops my purchases to the bottom.

Wow is right.

The memory of Mason's accent sends a pulsing current through my body, warming my blood with a delicious heat that pools between my hips. His voice was deep and rich, a bit husky.

Especially when he lowered it and moved his lips against my cheek.

"Don't make me come looking for you."

My pulse thrums below my ear. Again, I focus on certain words, maybe the only words I want him to say.

Make me come.

"I'd shove my husband in front of a bus for a man with an accent."

I startle at the woman, my mouth falling open. Blush creeps up her face.

"Easy, Barb." I squint at her name-tag. She laughs with a hand to her mouth. "When I hear on the news about some poor man who met his untimely death getting run over by a Greyhound, I'm going to know exactly where to point the cops."

I hold out my credit card and she takes it.

She shakes her head through a grin. "I'm just saying. You should've seen him. Heard him. If I didn't think I'd break a hip, I'd take his class."

She swipes my card and hands it back to me with a receipt to sign. I slide my card back into my wallet. After scribbling my name, I glance once more at the flier.

The handwriting is surprisingly neat. All capital letters, evenly spaced. Most men I've noticed have atrocious handwriting. Joey's penmanship looks like a person in the midst of a seizure taking a pen to paper. But not Mason's. Even his attempt to replicate his sign on the top of the page is more than an attempt. It's spot on in design. The letters perfectly bolded, the lines sharp.

"Here you go."

I look up and take the bag Barb is holding out for me. "Thank you. I'll tell your future husband you said hello at his class tonight."

Her face burns a deep red. Stuttering, she responds with, "O-Oh, I was just kidding. Really. I would never leave my husband, let alone kill the poor man. He's lovely. We've been married for seventeen wonderful years. Sure, he doesn't always remember to take out the trash, but Lord knows he makes up for that with his grilling skills. The man could give Bobby Flay a run for his money. Have you watched his TV show? It's very entertaining."

I smile at how flustered poor Barb has become. Her words flying past her lips a mile a minute.

Like you're any better. You nearly face-planted at the sight of Mason.

"Relax," I chuckle, stepping back and ignoring my ridiculous inner thoughts.

Clearly, it was the heels, not his stellar physique that made me stumble. I was in a hurry and trying to avoid getting hit by traffic. He just happened to look back at me the exact second I lost my footing.

Coincidence. That's all it was. Not directly related to his perfect, fuck-me face.

"Your secret is safe with me. I won't say a word," I reassure her.

Turning, I move past the next woman in line and make for the exit.

An animated voice calls out behind me.

"Look! This is the class I was telling you about. God, that guy. I almost vomited all over him when he spoke."

Stopping next to a rack of water bottles, I look over my shoulder in the direction I just came from. The other chirpy blonde chimes in next.

"I've never been this excited to work out before. We need to get there early so we get a good spot. I want front row. Prime viewing seats."

I laugh under my breath.

Jesus. Okay, so Mason has an effect on *every* woman. At least all the ones within the Chicago city limits.

Get there early? Fight other bitches off for prime viewing seats? I'm not worried about either one of those.

I'll have the best view of Mason *after* class is over.

JOEY APPROVES MY PURCHASE AS soon as I get back to the shop. Not that I needed him to, but it is always a nice ego boost when your fashion savvy friend announces how flawless you're going to look in an outfit that leaves very little to the imagination. He then lamely suggests I go back to the store and return the items before they get torn from my body after he gets a look at the receipt I forgot about.

I stow the items away and pretend not to hear his rantings. Talk of creditors, addictions, and something about his car payment costing less than my yoga pants go on around me as I busy myself with work.

Dylan leaves after we close up for the night to eat dinner with Reese's parents. I think I'm in the clear when Joey slips out of the shop and heads in the direction of his car.

Good. One less person to get rid of later.

Grabbing my bag, I head upstairs to get changed.

A nervous energy buzzes through me. My skin feels hot at the thought of Mason's hands on my body, his lips moving over mine. Questions swirl in my head as I hastily get dressed.

Is his touch gentle? Will he use my body like he has a right to it? I'm sure he's a disciplined guy, his physique gives that away, but does he always maintain a level of control when he fucks? Or is that the only time he allows himself to be reckless and unrestrained.

Do I want him that way? Rough and wild? His hands moving

me how he wants. Taking what he needs.

As I'm securing my hair back with an elastic band, the loft door swings open, snapping my attention off the wall mirror.

Joey appears in the doorway, now dressed in workout clothes and sneakers.

I'm quickly annoyed at the sight of him, until he whistles appreciatively at my outfit and motions for me to spin.

"Well, you look ready for sex."

I give him a sly smile. "That's what I was going for."

Joey moves to stand beside me. He smiles at my reflection. "There's a line half-way down the block for his class."

I meet his gaze in the mirror, my hands frozen in my hair. "What?"

"Yup."

"Half-way down the block? Seriously?"

"Yup."

Scowling, I grab his hand and head for the door. "Let's go."

Fuck! What if the class is already full? I knew Mason would have a crowd at this thing, but *that* many people? If I have to wait another fucking day to bang this guy . . .

I don't even allow myself to finish that thought as we walk outside. I refuse to entertain that possibility.

Joey locks up and joins me on the sidewalk.

"See?" He gestures across the street at the parade of women, his palm outstretched in the air. "I almost ran over three of them when I went to park."

"Maybe you should've."

That would've been ideal. At this rate, if I go to the end of the line I'll be lucky to get in on a class next week.

Joey grabs my elbow and pulls me off the sidewalk after a truck passes. "Nervous?" he murmurs, dropping his head.

I slowly look over at him. "Of?"

"I saw how flustered you were after talking to him yesterday."

"What? No I wasn't."

I think back to the minutes in the shop which immediately followed that interaction.

My quick consumption of a cupcake. Hardly the breakfast of

champions.

I shake my head. "You're delusional if you think I was affected in any way by a kiss on the cheek."

"Or an accent."

I nod. "Right."

"Or the body of a Greek God. No way would you have reacted to a combination of the three."

I glare up at him. "Why are you here again?"

He smiles.

Excited chatter fills the air around us as we step up onto the sidewalk. The line forms just outside the door and continues in front of the large studio window, completely obstructing my view of the inside.

"Excuse me?" A woman at the front of the line points behind her. "The line begins back there, around the corner."

"That's nice," I reply, pairing my sarcasm with my fakest smile. I look up at Joey. "I'm good right here. You?"

He stretches his arms above his head. "Fantastic."

The woman scowls, then turns to her friend. Behind her, the door opens and Mason steps outside.

Hushed "oh, my God's" and "that's him" are spoken. People further down the line step out to get a better view of the man captivating everyone's attention.

God, he's practically edible.

Dressed in loose shorts that hang low on his hips and a sleeveless tee, Mason surveys the crowd with wide, stunned eyes.

Did he really not think he'd have much of a turn-out? Does the man not own a mirror?

He steps further out onto the sidewalk. A hand flies through his blonde hair. "Evening, ladies. This is quite a shock."

Joey obnoxiously clears his throat.

Mason acknowledges him with a quick, apologetic nod, then our eyes meet. The air leaves my lungs. He looks like he wants to say something, possibly walk over to me, *please, God, walk over to me*, but he shows restrain and instead, levels me a stare that has me contemplating public sex.

I gather a shaky breath. Joey chuckles next to me.

"Shut up," I whisper.

Mason turns back to the crowd. "Right. Unfortunately, due to building capacity, I won't be able to squeeze all of you in tonight. But, I'm a man of my word. You will all get your free lesson. Check out the class times on the door, yeah? First twenty-five in line get to attend tonight. I hope to see the rest of you at another class." He motions for me and Joey to come forward.

"Hey, they aren't even in line," someone calls out from the crowd.

"They signed up yesterday," Mason explains, keeping his eyes on me as I move closer. He holds his hand out to Joey. "Sorry, mate. Didn't see ya standing over there. Good on you for coming."

Joey shakes his hand. "I usually don't go unnoticed. You're clearly straight."

Mason smiles, shifting his eyes to mine as he drops his hand. "Hello, gorgeous. How are you?"

"Ready to collect." I grab Joey's arm and lead him inside, looking back at Mason over my shoulder.

He pulls his gaze off my ass when two women walk over to him.

I claim a mat in the center of the room and toe off my shoes and socks.

Joey does the same next to me. "Christ, it's hot in here. I'm about to take off my shirt."

Mason steps into the room, closing the door behind him.

"Me too," I murmur.

That should help get things moving in the right direction.

After adjusting the thermostat on the wall, Mason moves to the front of the class. The room goes silent.

"Right. Everyone ready to get started?" he pauses, smiling at everyone's enthusiasm. "The most important thing to remember in my class is I want you to take your time. Understand that you have the rest of your life to make this perfect, yeah? Yoga is a great way to improve flexibility and strength, but also, it benefits the mind and the spirit. I want you to concentrate on your breathing. Breathe through every pose. You might not get everything today, and that's all right. I'm here to help you. If you need to step away and get a quick drink, or if you're feeling like you need a break, take it. It's going to get very warm in here . . ."

"It already is," Joey announces, fanning his face. "Any objections if I start stripping?"

A few women giggle. Others make similar comments about the temperature in the room.

"By all means." Mason reaches behind him, grabs his shirt, and pulls it off with one hand. He tosses it aside. "I hope nobody minds. I normally don't wear a lot of clothes when I do this."

"Oh, dear God," someone behind me murmurs.

I stare at the hard lines of Mason's body. The thick cuts of muscle in his arms. His broad, lightly-tanned chest.

He wants me to concentrate on breathing while he looks like this? What is he fucking crazy?

The man has an eight pack. Eight. Pack.

He looks directly at me. "Ready?" he asks, tilting his head with a coy grin.

I nod, a lot. Joey elbows me and I finally get myself under control.

Mason leads the class through a few basic breathing exercises. Thank God. I can't seem to remember how to properly work my lungs anymore. With the slowly rising temperature in the room, Mason's glorious body, and the knowledge of my impending orgasm minutes away, it's a wonder I'm not getting rushed to the hospital by ambulance for lack of oxygen to the brain.

"Now, release the hands and come out onto all fours," Mason instructs.

"Hello," Joey whispers. "All fours, yes please. I should've dragged Billy to this."

I lift my head and watch Mason.

"Hands underneath the shoulders. Knees underneath the hips. Inhale, drop the belly, and look upwards."

Our eyes lock.

"Exhale, push the floor away, and look down at your navel."

My spine arches. I close my eyes and hold the position.

Mm. This actually feels really good.

"Inhale, look up."

He smiles. My hand nearly slips out from under me.

"Shit." I wipe my hand on my pants leg, removing the sweat that's built up on my palm.

"Stop distracting him. I'm really into this."

I narrow my eyes at Joey.

"Last time. Exhale, press away."

I drop my head and slowly breathe out.

The next series of poses doesn't allow for eye contact, so I'm able to get through those without any difficulty. Sweat beads up on the base on my neck and down my spine. My muscles are loose and warm.

I feel amazing. I'm actually really enjoying this.

Several women have to step outside to get some air while others gulp water from the cooler in the corner. I don't need a break. I don't want one either.

Mason instructs everyone to lie on their backs. He moves between the mats, his voice growing closer.

"From here, bend the knees, place the feet on the floor. I want you to lift your hips off the mat. Try and reach for your heels with your fingers."

He looks down at me as I struggle to grab my heels. With a huff, my back hits the mat.

"Little help?" I smile up at him.

He drops down to his knees beside me. "You're doing great. Have you done this before?" he asks, grabbing my hips, his fingers pressing into my back.

"Nope. First time. I'm very motivated to please my instructor."

His mouth twitches in the corner.

"Ready?"

"Oh, hold on. Not yet." I grab the hem of my shirt and strip it over my head, leaving me in only my hot pink sports bra.

His lips part with a rushed exhale. He looks beautiful, eyes wide and wild.

"There. That's better. I was burning up in that."

I watch his neck roll with a swallow, the heavy bob of his Adam's apple I want to run my tongue over and taste. His hands shake as they move over my skin to resume their grip.

"Devil," he whispers, leaning down and lifting my hips. "Stay after class."

Yes.

His hands leave me. I hold the pose as he moves around the room, meeting my gaze every few steps.

Twenty minutes later, I'm practically bouncing on my feet as the class dismisses. I wave to Joey as he slips out the door, then take a moment to fix my disheveled pony.

I shouldn't bother. It's about to get a whole lot messier.

Holding my discarded tank, I wait for Mason on my mat as he walks a few stragglers to the door. He closes it and turns the top lock. Taking his shirt, he wipes it across his face, removing the sweat.

"Great class," I tell him as he walks toward me.

An honest observation. I never thought I'd actually enjoy working out, let alone yoga.

His mouth stretches into a proud smile. "Yeah? I thought it was all right. I was a bit nervous."

"Why? You made it easy. Nobody seemed to have trouble keeping up."

"Except you." He stops in front of me, looking between the shirt in my hand and my face. "Or, was that just a ploy to get me to touch you?"

I shrug. "I don't think I need a ploy. I think you want to touch me."

"I do."

"And here I am. Touch away."

His eyes, the color of autumn, do this shift from playful to something else, something darker.

Make me come.

My fist tightens on my tank.

All too soon his smoldering gaze is gone, swiftly darting across the room.

"I need to shower. Will you wait? My room is just upstairs. I'll be quick."

I stare at his profile, a bit confused.

Shower?

Once again, the 'why bother' question fills my head. We're about to mount each other. I, for one, plan on utilizing every hard surface in this studio. It's 90 degrees in here, and my entire body is coated in a light sheen of sweat.

Everybody has their routines during sex. Maybe Mason likes to start off freshly washed?

"Yeah, okay. Hurry though."

He gives me a curt nod and takes to the stairs.

Mm. He lives here. Strangely, that thought hadn't crossed my mind. Even though Dylan lives above her business, I hadn't considered Mason having the same situation.

I pad about the studio for two, three minutes, maybe.

Curiosity gets the best of me. Or maybe I'm too horny to wait any longer.

I quietly slip upstairs.

I've always loved shower sex.

Chapter Four

Mason

WARM WATER HITS THE BACK of my neck as I drop my head between my shoulders.

With a soapy hand, I stroke my dick. My free hand braces my weight on the wet tile.

Brooke. Brooke. Brooke.

What the fuck am I doing?

I could be feeling her tighten around me right now. Roaming my hands over her soft curves. Licking the sweat off her tits while I palm her arse and lower her onto my cock.

Instead, I'm jerking off to thoughts of her like a desperate juvenile.

Fuck, but if I don't . . .

I've been fighting off an erection since I saw her on the footpath. That struggle intensified when I got a view of the back of her, and then she had to go and strip in the middle of my fucking class.

She has me and she knows it.

I pinch my eyes shut.

She is so incredibly beautiful.

Barely any makeup. The glow of her skin from exertion. Her hair, tousled and slick with sweat.

My hand works faster. I rock my hips.

God, I need to come.

I want to talk to Brooke. I want to know her, and I'd really love to do that without my dick being hard and without the overwhelming desire to bury myself balls deep mudding up my thoughts.

When was the last time I couldn't get through a single conversation with a woman without imagining what she would look like wet and begging beneath me?

I'm not that guy. I sure as hell don't want to be that guy for Brooke. And I won't be . . .

I just need to get this ache out of my body.

My thighs tense beneath me. I take a moment to rub my thumb over the head of my dick, mingling the water and precum. I let myself moan. The quick slapping of skin echoes off the walls of my small bathroom.

I remember what she felt like as I held the slender curve of her hips. She was smooth and warm. Sweat pooled in the dip between her collarbones.

"Holy fuck," I gasp, my hand working furiously now.

If only she knew what I was doing. What I was thinking. How close I was to . . .

"Mm. Need a hand with that?"

My eyes flash open at the sound of a voice at my back. Equal parts wicked and sweet. Stilling my hand, I squeeze the base of my dick and look over my shoulder.

Brooke peers inside the small opening in the shower curtain, smiling, her gaze lingering on my arse.

"Shit." I wrench the handle and cut off the water. *Fuck . . . fuck! I probably look like such a fucking wanker.* Covering myself as best as I can, I turn to look at her. "Brooke, I . . ."

She slides the shower curtain back.

Good fucking Christ.

My mouth falls open. My breathing quickens. Brooke, now

completely naked, stands before me, proudly showing off her insanely sexy body as she leans against the wall. Calculating smirk twisting across those sexy as fuck lips.

I can't pull my eyes away. I knew she would be a fucking sin to look at, but I had no idea . . .

Her full tits sit high on her chest. A faint blush spreading over them. Her nipples, a dusty pink, hardened and ready for my tongue. The soft flare of her hips. Long, shapely legs. Her bare . . .

My cock jumps against my hand.

She lifts her leg to step inside the small shower with me.

"Whoawhoawhoa." I shove the curtain open further and reach for two towels. "Here. Fuck, please put this on. I'm . . ." I struggle to speak, to secure my own towel around my waist while holding one out for her. The cotton brushes against my cock and I moan.

I was so fucking close. Why didn't I lock the door?

She laughs softly, lowering her foot. "Why the hell would I do that? And why are you covering up? Turn the water back on and fuck me."

I step out of the shower. "I think maybe we should talk a little first."

"Talk? Yeah, okay. Were you not just jerking off thinking about me?"

"No, I was. I was, I just . . ."

"Then what is there to talk about?"

I give up on wrapping the towel around my waist and hold it against my cock, offering her the other one. "Please, Brooke."

I need her to cover up. I can't hold a conversation with this woman with her tits out.

Speaking of tits . . .

She crosses her arms underneath them. They bounce a little and I bite back my moan.

"Do you want me or not?"

"I want you," I answer quickly. *God, isn't it obvious?* "Trust me, Brooke, I want you, but maybe we could take this a bit slower, yeah?"

"Slower? Why? I want to fuck you. You clearly want to fuck me, based on your massive erection, which bravo, by the way. He's beautiful." She takes the towel from me and drops it on the floor, inching closer. "You came up here to jerk off to thoughts of me. I know you didn't finish. How close were you?"

"Close." I step back. My hip hits the sharp edge of the sink.

The wolf circles her prey, ready to attack.

"It would be a shame to stop now, don't you think? I hear blue balls are a bitch."

I grab her wrist when she reaches for me. "Brooke." My voice is much softer now. I sound weak. I *feel* weak. I'm so close to saying fuck it and bending her over the sink.

She stares up at me. Her thick lashes flutter closed before she steps back out of my grip. Anger flares to life in her eyes. "What is your problem? What the fuck is this?"

Damn it. She is pissed, clearly, but the way her gaze avoids mine and scatters about the room, she's feeling something else too.

Rejection? Does she not see how difficult this is for me?

"If I were to fuck you right now, then what?" I ask, although, I fear I already know the answer to this. She's moving way too fast to want anything real with me. "What would happen after, Brooke?"

"After?" Her eyes slowly find mine.

"Yeah, after. What would I be to you?"

She breathes a laugh, tucking a piece of hair behind her ear. "If you think it'll be weird for me, you're wrong. I can handle casual sex. I'll even wave to you if I see you out. It won't be awkward." Her gaze lowers to my towel. "You're still hard, by the way."

"I'm aware."

It's bloody painful.

She leans back against the wall. Her calculating smirk returns. "Tell me you don't want to fuck me right now."

"I can't do that," I reply, briefly glancing down at my raging hard-on that's tenting the towel. I lift my head. "Look, I want to fuck you, but I want to know you, Brooke. I can't do a meaningless fuck. That's not me. And I don't want that with you. Why don't we get dressed and go get something to eat. Talk a little. I want to know about you."

She stares at me for several seconds. The silence between us grows deafening.

"You're serious."

"Very." I straighten my spine. My chest suddenly feels tight. "Go out with me."

Blinking several times, she turns away. "You've got to be fucking kidding me." She snatches her clothes off the sink. "You're actually shooting me down right now."

"I'm not . . ."

"This is unbelievable," she mumbles. She pulls on her pants, then slips her top over her head, leaving her bra and panties off.

I don't try and stop her. If I am going to walk around the city with Brooke without an erection, she's going to need to be clothed.

Of course, knowing she's wearing nothing underneath those fucking pants could cause a bit of an issue. And her nipples . . . God, this might be torture.

Her hand turns the doorknob. "Thanks for the class. It was surprisingly fun." She storms out into my living space, leaving me behind.

"Hold up a second. Let me get dressed."

I head for my dresser, still pressing the towel against my cock. Brooke takes to the stairs without looking back at me.

"Brooke!"

She disappears to the first level.

"Fuck." I don't bother drying off. Grabbing a pair of boxers, I tug them on, then pull some shorts out of the drawer. Water drips down my face to my neck. I wipe it from my eyes.

She's not waiting for me. She doesn't want to go for a walk and let me find out about her. She feels rejected, which is entirely my fault. But with Brooke . . . even if I give in and fuck her for the sake of fucking her, I'll feel like the biggest tosser on the planet. Sure, it'll probably be one of the hottest romps of my life, maybe even *the* hottest, but then it'll be over. She clearly won't want anything else to do with me.

"I'll even wave to you if I see you out."

Wave to me? Fuck that. I want a lot more than a bloody wave from her.

My feet beat against the wood as I dash down the stairs, only to step out into an empty studio. I swing the door open and move outside, hoping to catch Brooke, but the footpath is quiet. A street lamp flickers in the distance as I dart my eyes left, then right. The bakery is dark across the narrow street that separates my business from hers.

I push a hand through my wet hair. Frustration burns the back of my throat.

I refused her.

I refused the knockout I can't stop thinking about.

I drop my head back and stare up at the stars. My groin throbs.

Blue balls? Can't be all that bad, can it?

Blue balls are, in fact, the worst fucking thing I've ever felt in my entire life. Brooke might as well have taken a jackhammer to my nuts before she stormed out. I feel ready to explode. My legs barely get me up the stairs before I'm whipping my dick out and squeezing it roughly.

The pain is indescribable. The urge to fuck burns like a wildfire in my veins.

Even as I move my hand over my dick in the silence of my loft, frantically chasing my orgasm, I'm getting no relief. Everything is so sensitive. I squeeze harder, stroke faster. It hurts to do this. It hurts not to. I want to scream.

I need to come. Goddamn, I need to come.

I'm sure I could wait this out. It can't stay like this, can it?

That unnerving fear has me reaching down and cupping my balls with my free hand. I roll them between my palm. My thoughts race to Brooke standing outside my shower, leaning against the wall, pressed *against* the wall. Her tits, her arse, her smooth pussy I want to nuzzle with my mouth.

My breath hitches. *Fuck! Finally!*

With a strangled groan, I come all over my hand and stomach. The ache between my thighs dissipates.

A familiar satisfaction settles over me, but will it last? Will I ever be truly satisfied until I have Brooke in the ways I *want* to have her? Which includes every filthy act of depravity I can think of.

I sag against the mattress as I reach for my discarded towel from earlier and wipe myself clean.

My eyes close. I listen to the beginnings of a storm in the

distance. The low rumble of thunder.

I hope she isn't walking home.

Sleep evades me most of the night as my mind refuses to settle. My body is spent from class, from my orgasm, but I'm restless. My cock slowly grows hard against the sheets. I ignore it and roll over, rubbing it into the mattress.

The morning sun rises too early. Light burns across my eyelids, and I make a mental note to pick up curtains or some shit to keep my room dark when I need it. I hope to God this isn't any indication how every sexual encounter involving Brooke, fantasy or not, leaves me.

I'm not going to be able to teach six classes a day if I'm up half the night.

Coffee. I need a fuckton of coffee.

I get dressed and head outside, pulling on my sunnies. The footpath is wet from last night's rain, and the air is a bit sticky. I avoid the puddles as I head south on Fayette, my eyes glancing back in the direction of the bakery until I can no longer see it clearly. A little shop on the corner across the street grabs my attention, and I jog between cars and step up onto the curb.

I pull the door open and step inside, inhaling a lungful of the delicious scent.

My glasses get pushed back on top of my head. I freeze. A body I'd have to be dead not to recognize stands a few feet ahead of me, leaning against the small counter as she waits for her order.

Her perky arse sways as she moves her hips to the beat of the song playing softly overhead.

I move closer, smiling. "Brooke."

Her head whips around, then the rest of her turns to face me.

My eyes rake over her tiny form.

She's in jeans again, tight on her hips and legs. Her red shirt dips low in the front to reveal a generous amount of cleavage. And on her feet, runners, an old pair of Nike's.

Her hair is up, pulled back into a dark, messy knot, with a few pieces framing her face.

She raises an eyebrow. She looks agitated. "What are you doing here? Did you follow me?"

I almost laugh at her suggestion, but decide against it when she shows no sign of her question being a joke.

"What? No, I like coffee. I'm here for coffee. This was purely a coincidence." I take a step toward her. "You left last night. I wanted to talk to you."

"Talk," she laughs. "There's that word again. Did you have fun *talking* after I left?"

My brow furrows. "Uh . . . to who?"

She eliminates the space between us. Her hand flattens against my chest as she stands on her toes to get as close to my ear as possible. I inhale her perfume. Some sort of berry scent. It's light and sweet.

"Did you finish getting off after I was gone?" she whispers.

My hands form to her hips. I drop my head, brushing my lips against her hair. "Yeah. I had to."

"Mm. So did I. You were amazing in my head. I came all over my fingers."

"Fuck," I groan. Not meaning to, my fingers squeeze her hips, hard enough to possibly bruise her. I move my hands to her back.

God, she feels good against me.

"Me too. I . . ." My words trail off.

Am I really doing this? Am I about to confess to this woman how hard I came last night in the middle of a fucking coffee shop?"

She leans back to look up at me. "It's a shame we couldn't have handled that shit together. A damn shame." She slaps her hand against my chest and spins back around, leaving me reeling.

I grab her elbow. I'm not done with this conversation. "Hey."

"What?" Her voice sounds distant. She barely turns her head to acknowledge me.

The bloke behind the counter carries over four coffees before I can get her attention again.

"Here you go, Brooke. Sorry about the wait."

She steps forward. I move quickly to grab the carrier, being sure not to completely shove her out of the way in the process. Only the side of my arm bumps against hers.

"I got these. Did you pay?" I ask, reaching blindly with my other hand for my wallet.

"What?" Eyebrows pinched together in confusion, she tries to grab the carrier. Her height difference from mine doesn't allow for it. She really is tiny without those heels.

With an exasperated huff, she jumps with her hand in the air. "Yes, I paid. And can you give me that please, you big tree?"

"I said I got it. Come on."

"Come on? I thought you were getting coffee."

I shrug, looking down at her. "I'll come back."

Her hand slaps against her thigh. With a shake of her head, she moves toward the door. "Fine. But there's a crack in the sidewalk and I'm not going to tell you where it is. If you fall, that's on you."

I stifle my laugh, following behind. "Fair enough."

We walk side by side on the busy footpath. People move in a blur around us. Brooke keeps her arms tightly crossed against her chest and her gaze locked ahead of her. Mine wanders between the path ahead and her profile.

"How tall are you?" I ask, breaking up the silence after only standing it for a whole ten seconds.

She looks over at me. "I don't know. 5'2", I think. Why?"

"Just curious. You threw me off with your shoes the other day, when we first met."

"Mm." She turns her head.

My mouth curls up in the corner. "You were right about blue balls. Bloody awful, that was. I thought I was dying."

A small laugh erupts from her. She quickly conceals it with a cough. "Well, that was all your doing."

"Actually, it's yours. I can't stop thinking about you."

"*Thinking* about me," she repeats, tucking a piece of hair behind her ear. "But, you don't want to *do* anything with me. You turned me down."

"I want to do a lot with you."

I wait until she glances in my direction before I continue. Her eyes slowly reach mine.

"A lot, Brooke. You have no idea how much I've thought about doing things with you. I just want to know you first. Spend some time with you. Like this. I like talking to you."

"Crack."

"What's that?"

She points ahead of us. "Crack. Right there. Watch out."

I look down, careful to step over the jagged edge of the concrete that protrudes a good five centimeters from the flat plane.

Fuck. That would've been one hell of a fall.

"I thought you weren't going to warn me," I ask through a grin.

She shrugs. "I don't feel like going back for more coffee. You would've spilled it."

"Ah, okay. I thought maybe it was because you care about my well-being, or something. My mistake."

She stops walking. I look back over my shoulder.

"What is it?"

"Are you married? Is that it?"

Confusion pulls my brows together. "Do you think I'm married?"

When have I given her the impression that I was married?

She hits me with a sturdy glare as she marches directly for me. "I don't know, that's why I'm asking. You aren't wearing a ring, but not all married guys wear their rings, especially ones who like to jerk off to the idea of other women. Is that you?"

I stare at her, long and hard. Is she fucking serious with this? I grab her hand and pull her in the small alleyway between two businesses.

"What are you doing?"

With a hand to her hip, I guide her back against the brick wall. Chest to chest, I look down at her, trying to contain my anger at this bullshit back and forth while I balance these stupid fucking coffees.

"Do you really think I'm married? Is that the kind of man you think I am? One who cheats on his wife?"

She tilts her head up. "I don't know. That's why I'm asking. It wouldn't be the first time some married guy tried something with me. Although, I doubt any of them would've rejected me the way you did. Was that your guilty conscience talking last night?"

What the fuck?

I bend down, inching closer. "I am not married. If I was, I never would've invited you to my class because I wouldn't have been able to keep my eyes off you. Fuck, Brooke, the way we flirted that first day, that wouldn't have happened. I told you I'm not interested in a quick fuck. I don't do that anymore. I'm not some young kid fucking around. I want more than that." My hand slides higher on her waist, fitting to her curves. "Give me more."

She blinks heavily, then looks back up at me with round, doleful eyes. Her head shakes ever so slightly. "Do you have any idea how embarrassed I was last night? How awkward I felt? I was naked, Mason, and you rejected me." A rush of air pushes past her lips, blowing against mine. "You *rejected* me."

Fuck. I hurt her. I hadn't meant to. I would never.

"Brooke."

Her gaze lowers to a spot on my shirt.

The pain in her voice, paired with that wounded look she's trying to hide from me tears through my reserve.

I tilt my head down. She lifts hers at my sudden movement, gasping as our mouths slide together, searing into a kiss. It's hot and wet, almost painful as we both reveal our desperation. My body presses her to the brick. She parts her lips with a groan as her warm hands wrap around my neck, fingers twisting in my hair and tugging. My tongue moves into her mouth, tasting, gliding against hers. I palm her arse, wishing I had use of both hands right now so I could properly do this.

She sucks on my lip, then bites it, smiling when I bend further with a moan.

"You're a good kisser," she says against my mouth. "Really good. Must be the accent."

I laugh, licking along the seam of her lips, swallowing her taste. Savoring it.

"I want you, Brooke. Do you see now?"

"Mm. I think." She tugs the hair at the base of my neck when I try and lean away. "No, wait, don't stop."

I drop my forehead to hers. Her hand relaxes.

"Do you want more?" I whisper, staring at her mouth, her eyes, the cute little wrinkle in her nose.

She nods, biting at her bottom lip.

"Me too. I want more of that, of everything. Try it my way."

"Try it *my* way. It involves nudity." She attempts to wiggle closer.

I press against her hip, keeping her pinned to the wall.

"Mason," she moans as I bend and kiss her cheek. My mouth moves to her ear.

"I could fuck you right now, up against this brick wall while anyone could walk by us. Would you like that? Would you come for me?"

She shudders. Her hands fit to my waist.

"Oh, God," she whispers.

I kiss the skin below her ear before continuing. "It would be amazing, and I want that, I do, but my way, which involves feelings and knowing someone, trust me . . . it's better. It's so much better, Brooke. I want you to really feel me. I don't just want a hard fuck in an alley and then nothing. I can't do that."

I slowly lean back. My hand falls away from her body as I watch the rapid rise and fall of her chest.

Is her heart pounding as much as mine? I fight the temptation to ask.

I gaze at her. Her cheeks are flushed. Her hair is falling out of the hair-tie it was *haphazardly* contained in.

She looks beautifully undone.

"Try it my way," I insist again.

Please. I want this with you.

She sucks at her bottom lip as she thinks it over, her gaze flicking between my eyes and my mouth. With a soft grunt, she pushes off from the brick and snatches the carrier out of my hand. Her feet quickly carry her away from me.

The hell?

"Is that a yes?" I call out, turning my head to watch her.

"I don't know." She gives me a playful smile over her shoulder. "Is it?"

A laugh rumbles in my chest.

Little devil. Do you think that answer will satisfy me?

I sag against the brick after she disappears around the corner. My head falls forward. I look down at the erection pleating the front of my shorts.

"Fucking persistent bastard, aren't ya?"

I adjust my cock and get out of the alley, heading back in the direction of the coffee shop.

Chapter Five

Brooke

OKAY. OKAY OKAY OKAY.

That was just a kiss. A kiss, Brooke. Stop walking like you just had your vagina smashed.

Pushing my shoulders back, I continue down the sidewalk with the coffee carrier, losing the obnoxious spring in my step. It's hard not to bounce a little. My skin feels like it's vibrating. A continuous pulse moving over my flesh, sending a delicious shiver up my spine and down my limbs.

Darting my tongue out, I taste my bottom lip.

It's swollen, sensitive from Mason's assault. Or mine. I wasn't gentle when I kissed him back. I went at him like a woman deprived, which is exactly how I should *still* be feeling, only . . .

That was, hands-down, the best kiss of my life.

It wasn't just the way he worked his mouth, it was the filth spilling out of it. The soft murmurs against my skin about how he *could* fuck me. How he wanted to, only . . .

He wants more than that. More than a hard fuck in an alley.

Feelings and knowing each other.

More.

My head grows heavy. Am I seriously contemplating this request?

After the way things ended last night, I was dead-set on waving bye-bye to the prospect of Mason and jumping on the next willing and available dick. No man has ever turned me down before. Ever. Definitely not one where we're both already naked and his cock is at full mast. But Mason . . . he *refused* me. Straight up, with my tits out and everything. I was angry and confused. Hurt. God, I didn't want to admit that, but I was. I wanted him. He obviously wanted me. I drove home like a mad-woman on a rampage.

A mad, horny woman on a rampage.

That problem was handled immediately.

After experiencing one of the quickest, most satisfying orgasms of my life, go figure, I gave into the enticing idea of sleep, but tossed around most of the night.

Again, I was baffled. Who passes on this kind of opportunity?

It's not as if I've never been pursued by the men I've slept with for the prospect of more. Take clingy Paul, for example. He definitely didn't want me to dine and ditch his ass the other night. But cases like that have always transpired in the aftermath of sex, not before.

Never before.

Who is this guy?

I empty my mind of that question, of the kiss I shouldn't be obsessing over as I step inside the bakery.

The chime rings out through the small space.

Joey and Dylan are talking closely behind the counter. Whispering, in fact. They both glance up at the sound of my entrance.

"Good morning, sunshine," Joey practically sings.

I barely glance in his direction. He's way too cheery for me right now.

"Hey. They've stopped serving that caramel ribbon crunch you like so I got you a macchiato instead. I hope that's okay." I set the carrier on the display case and look up at Dylan.

Please be okay. I don't feel like walking back there.

A soft smile pulls at her mouth as she steps closer. "That's okay. That's okay. I'll drink caramel anything, sweetie. Thank you."

My brow pinches together in response to the strange tone in her voice, to the nickname.

Sweetie?

"Why do you sound like that? Did someone die?" I ask, looking down at her outfit. Shouldn't she be in all black? Who wears pastels when they're in mourning?

Dylan plucks her coffee from the carrier. "No. And how do I sound?"

"Like someone died."

Joey makes an amused sound in the back of his throat as he reaches for his coffee.

"Nobody died. I heard about last night," Dylan confesses, leaning her hip against the counter. She looks tragically sorry for me. "*All* about it. Are you okay? That must've been crazy awkward."

Oh, terrific. That's why they were whispering.

I glare at Joey, who simply blows me a kiss before taking a sip of his coffee.

Bitch.

I take in a deep breath. "I'm fine," I tell her, which isn't necessarily a lie. If she would've asked me that question last night or any time before my interaction with Mason this morning, then I'd be lying.

Joey lifts a skeptical eyebrow. "You're fine? You devoured half a cheesecake last night, Brooke."

I wince at the memory.

God, I seriously need to get a handle on my sweets consumption during moments of distress. Or, at least eat them discreetly. I publicly tore up that cheesecake like it owed me money.

Shrugging off my pathetic behavior, I grab my coffee and take a sip. "I was hungry. I didn't have much for dinner. And really, last night wasn't a big deal. I'm over him."

I was unfortunately never even under him.

"Oh, well that's good to know, since there's a chance he's about to walk right in here."

"What?" My head snaps in Dylan's direction, then toward the front of the shop.

My eyes go round. Mason walks past the large window and reaches for the door. The grip on my coffee tightens.

What the hell is he doing?

"This should be interesting," Joey murmurs as the chime sounds overhead.

I swallow uncomfortably, nearly choking on my own saliva.

Mason steps inside the shop, his hand now carrying the coffee he obviously went back for. He levels me with a perfectly casual smile, as if he didn't just have his tongue in my mouth five minutes ago, then immediately notices the other two bodies in the room.

"Ah, it's good to see ya again, mate. Didn't catch your name yesterday."

Joey takes Mason's hand into a firm shake. "Yeah, you seemed a tad bit distracted with the chick next to me." He shoots me a quick, cheeky glance, then turns back and jerks his chin. "It's Joey."

I smooth down the front of my shirt as the three of them exchange introductions. My cleavage pops out another inch. Completely accidental and not at all done for his benefit.

Mm. Maybe he'll notice *tomorrow* when he stops chatting up my friends.

Mason gestures at Dylan's belly. "When are you due?"

"A month. I'm hoping for sooner though. I'm so sick with this one."

"This one? Don't tell me you have more than one already. You look too young to be a mum."

"Ha!" Dylan's face lights up. Her hands form to her belly. "Oh, my God. You just became my second favorite male."

Joey whips his head to the left, his eyes wide with alarm. "Second favorite? Excuse you?"

I cough into my fist, breaking up the gab fest I'm in no way a part of. Three pairs of eyes train on me as I slowly retreat toward the kitchen.

"I guess I'll just go get to work, since there's apparently no need for me to hang around up here."

Mason's mouth pulls down.

I quickly regret my half-serious remark as his noticeable remorse tenses up his features.

God, why do I even care? And am I seriously irritated that he's taking a moment to be polite? What is wrong with me?

He takes a few steps in my direction. I halt at the corner of the display case.

Dylan pushes against Joey's shoulder, urging him to walk. "Come on. I need your help with something in the back."

"You never need my help," he snaps, then smiles back at her before the two of them slip into the kitchen, leaving Mason and I alone.

I move my coffee to my other hand. I'm suddenly feeling restless and too hot to drink such a warm beverage.

Mason gives me a lazy smile as he slowly advances. "Little devil. You ran off."

My feet shift underneath me.

Jesus, his voice. Like honey coating the back of his throat. Sweet and warm. His words slow to leave his tongue.

I force my mouth to close.

Oh, my God. How long was it gaped open for?

Barrier. I need a barrier.

"Can I help you with something?" I ask, swiftly moving behind the display case. I set my coffee on the back table and fold my hands neatly on the glass. "Your stalker level is quickly rising, you know. First the coffee shop, now you're coming to my place of business. Should I alert the authorities yet?"

Mason cocks his head with a curious smirk, then moves to stand directly across from me. "Wait until I find out where you live."

"What?"

He chuckles. "Relax, gorgeous. I'll keep it professional, yeah? No house calls until you invite me."

"Mm." I cross my arms under my chest. "Don't hold your breath on that happening."

He smiles, then tips his cup back, taking a long swig of his coffee. His eyes never leave mine.

To keep myself from staring back like a hungry little fiend, I grab a bakery box and open the display case. My hand closes around a pastry.

He leans over, head tilting down to watch me. "You look cute back there, ready for work. How long have you been doing this?"

"A few years," I answer, not looking up. "It started out as something temporary. I needed a job after getting fired from my old one and Dylan needed an extra hand during wedding season. I honestly wasn't expecting to like it as much as I did. But almost immediately everything just seemed to click. I love the artistic side of it. The design process. How everything comes together. I don't know. It's not like I'm curing cancer or anything, but cupcakes seem to make people happy. I think happiness is therapeutic."

I straighten with the box and set it on the case. Lifting my head, I lock onto Mason's gentle stare.

"What?" I ask.

After a beat, he softly replies. "Nothing." He leans forward and looks down into the box. "What's this?"

"Um, it's," I shove the box closer to him. "It's pastries I made. Here. And a cupcake for later. Red velvet. The icing is amazing."

He studies the contents as if I've just offered him the greatest gift in the world. I remember him having this same look when I gave him the treats the other day outside his studio.

Maybe he really likes dessert. Maybe it's a delicacy over in Australia.

Setting his coffee down, he fits the box between his hands, then lifts his head. His eyes appear darker under the bakery lights. "You never gave me an answer. I need an answer, Brooke."

"Why?"

"Because I'll go bloody crazy if you don't give me one."

"Bloody crazy? Not just regular crazy? I'm picturing a massacre."

He shrugs. "Say yes and no one gets hurt."

I laugh, reaching up and pushing my hair behind my ear. "Wow. First stalking, now you're threatening murder? You better be careful, pretty boy. I'm not so sure how you'd hold up in prison."

He stares at me. The corner of his mouth lifts. "What are you doing tonight?"

Joey emerges from the back at that exact moment. I'm certain the queen of gossip was listening to every word of this conversation. If it was anyone else, I'd take his timing as purely coincidental.

"She'll be at The Tavern with a bunch of us after we close up here. It's a little bar we like to frequent. You should come. I'm sure they carry Fosters."

I narrow my eyes at Joey as he comes to stand beside me. He gives me his biggest smile.

"Yeah, I don't drink Fosters, mate. Not a lot of us do."

"Really?" Joey turns to Mason with a hand to his chin, scratching along his stubble. He looks deeply perplexed. "Well, don't I feel like the world's biggest ass."

Mason grabs his coffee and the bakery box. "No worries. You can buy me a round tonight to make up for that little blunder." He trains his eyes on me, stepping back. "And you. I'll see you later, yeah?"

Damn it. I try, really, *really* try not to smile, but he throws on that damn 'yeah' at the end of his sentence, and I can't help it. It's cute. I like it.

Luckily, I don't give him the chance to see it.

I duck down behind the counter, looking busy. "Mm. Yeah, all right. See ya," I call out as I stare at the gray speckled tile on the floor.

The door chimes. Joey crouches down beside me.

"What the hell are you doing?" he whispers, searching my face.

"Working."

He glances around the tiny corner I'm tucked into. "Yeah, okay. What was all that talk about giving him an answer? An answer to what? Did you not tell me something last night?"

I straighten and shove past him, moving into the kitchen. "You are lucky I tell you anything, Joey McDermott."

Snatching my apron off the hook, I join Dylan at the worktop.

My mind begins cataloging possible outfits for tonight. I'll definitely be wearing heels, that's for sure. Mason seems strangely intrigued by our height difference.

Maybe he normally dates taller women?

Oh, my God. Why am I even thinking about what kind of women he dates? That damn kiss has left me stupid.

Joey claims one of the stools, pouting. "Brooke is holding out on us, Dylan. Can you please explain to her that there are no secrets within these walls?"

Dylan keeps her eyes on the frosting she is piping, flatly replying, "Brooke, you know the drill."

I secure the apron string around my waist, ignoring them both.

Screw that. I don't need to divulge anything.

Joey slaps the wood, then stands. "Fine. I'll just go ask Mason myself."

I grip his forearm. "Heyyy, that's . . . not necessary. I'm sure he's busy." I press against his shoulder until he's seated again, then I start to pace around the room, suddenly no longer able to stand still. My palms begin to sweat.

Damn it. I'm about to recollect this morning, that goddamn kiss.

"Uh, okay, so, you know everything that happened last night. Nothing new to report there. I was getting our coffees and Mason walked in, looking all . . . whatever. You saw him. He explained to me in a very private alley a few blocks down that he wants more with me. Like talking, and . . . dates, I guess, before all the sex stuff. He wants to know me first. How crazy is that?"

I chuckle awkwardly. Everyone else remains silent.

Crickets. All of a sudden, I'm surrounded by crickets.

I do another lap around the room. "So, that's basically it. He asked me if I can give him that. More. I didn't *really* answer. I mean, I kind of did. Not really. Oh, and he kissed me. On the mouth."

"As opposed to . . ."

I snap my head up to look at Joey, then drop it into a quick nod. "Right. That's it. That's all that happened."

Dylan sets her piping bag down. "I take it the kiss was good? You seem a bit wound up."

Good?

No. It was fucking phenomenal.

I limply shrug as I grab two baking racks off the shelf.

I've confessed enough sins today. They don't need to know how wet I got from fifteen seconds of making out.

"I like him," Joey beams, resting his chin on his hand.

"Me too," Dylan smiles at me. "Brooke?"

I set the racks on the worktop. My next words come as I keep my head down and my hands busy. "You know what I like? Working. Getting a paycheck. Orgasms are also nice, which I doubt come with *liking* this guy, so, no. I don't *like* him. How many special orders do we have today? Three? We need to get started. *I* need to get started. And God, I need to eat something before I collapse."

I shuffle up to the front and murder a cupcake.

Brown sugar praline. It never stands a chance.

I'M THE LAST ONE TO arrive at The Tavern later that night. I decide to blame my lateness on the traffic, not the forty-plus minutes I spend getting ready, or the pacing I do around Billy and Joey's condo.

"Traffic? What traffic? It's not rush-hour."

My sister Juls quickly calls me out on my lie after I explain my tardiness. I pretend I don't hear her as I slowly sip my Long Island and gage the crowd. Imagine Dragons pumps through the speakers overhead. My foot taps along to the beat.

Ian returns with a few beers for the table. "Two dollar beers. I fucking love college night."

Reese reaches for his mug, his other arm permanently fixated around Dylan. "Don't you feel old being here with this crowd? I feel like everyone's looking at me like I'm a chaperone." He tugs at the knot in his tie, loosening it.

Joey chuckles. "Uh, no. They're looking at you 'cause you're a DILF."

Reese frowns. "A what?"

"A DILF." Dylan rests her head on his shoulder, grinning. "Dad I'd like to fuck."

"Get the hell out of here," he mutters, lifting his beer to his mouth.

"You're sexy, Reese. Own it." Joey holds up his mug. "You

know who else is sexy?" He quickly kisses Billy. "Besides my baby."

I swirl my straw around in my glass. A group of women giggle obnoxiously at the next table. One of them nearly falls off her stool.

The drinks must be flowing over there.

"Brooke."

My eyes lift to Joey's. "What?"

"I asked a question."

"So?"

He gapes at me, then sweeps a hand in front of him. "So . . . would you like to let the table know who *you* think is sexy? Everyone is dying to hear what you have to say."

Jesus. He is laying it on thick tonight.

I stand and smooth the hem of my dress down. No need to partake in this conversation.

"Me. I think I'm sexy as hell." I blow Joey a kiss. "Be back. I'm going to hit up the ladies'."

Joey rolls his eyes, mumbling something under his breath before he turns to Billy and engages him in conversation. I move past them, heading for the crowd I need to get through to reach the restrooms.

"Nice shoes, Brooke. Am I going to be getting those back any time soon?" Dylan's voice at my back halts me.

I spin around, glancing down at the pink Steve Madden's I have yet to return. They work amazing with this dress. With my legs. In all honestly, it would've been a tragedy not to wear them.

Lifting my head, I limply shrug. "I figured I'd break them in for you since your feet are too swollen to wear heels right now."

Dylan's face falls. She glances down at the black strappy sandals on her feet, grumbling, "I'm so over being pregnant." She whips her head around. "This is it, Reese. Three and we're done. No more kids."

Reese leans back to look at her, a deep frown line setting in his forehead. "What? I thought we had agreed on four. What happened to that?"

The look that creeps across Dylan's face has my feet firmly planted where they are, willing to stick around for another minute. It also seems to pull everyone else's attention across the table.

Juls with her wide, curious eyes as she slowly brings her drink to her mouth. Joey, grinning enormously, drumming his fingers on the table and practically crawling across it to get a better view. Billy and Ian both take another route and reach into their pockets for their phones, deciding it's best they look busy and uninterested in Reese's potential demise.

I bet everyone seated at this table has had this 'don't fuck with me' look directed at them at one point. I know I'm familiar with it. Back when I first started working at the bakery I saw this look quite a lot.

And Reese? His ass has definitely seen it.

Turning on his stool, Reese gently smiles at Dylan before moving in for a kiss. "Love."

She pushes against his chest. "I'm sorry, are *you* the one carrying a watermelon around twenty-four seven? Are you giving up sushi and fantastic fucking footwear for nine months? Mm? No, you're not. You can eat what you want, you aren't bloated and sweaty all the time, and your downstairs region isn't going to be pushing out a human. I've been pregnant for the last four years. Four years, Reese. Do you have any idea how exhausting this is for me? I got up eleven times last night just to go to the bathroom. Did you know that?"

He caresses her face. "I only counted six."

Through clenched teeth, she leans closer, grunting, "It was a hell of a lot more than six. Maybe I should start waking you up every time, that way you can experience some of this misery with me."

"You can do that."

"Ugh!" She bats his hand away. "Would you stop being *you* for five seconds? It's making me want to have another kid."

Laughing, Reese grabs her face and kisses her. Dylan seems to melt against him, letting go of her anger, maybe even her conviction on the subject. They break away from each other enough to breathe, but keep their foreheads pressed together, Reese's hands cradling Dylan's face and hers holding his wrists. Their eyes remain locked as if they're sharing this silent moment, conveying unspoken words, and I take that as my cue and remember why the hell I got up in the first place.

I melt into the crowd and push my way to the back hallway. The restroom is cramped and smells like a cross between the fragrance department at Macy's and an ashtray. My nose burns as I apply a light sheen of gloss to my lips.

God, I hate cigarette smoke. Can't these bitches here read? There's a no-smoking sign posted every ten feet.

Tugging the material of my dress away from my body in hopes it'll air it out a little, I drift through the bar, making my way back to my friends. A tall figure standing next to the table halts my progression.

Mason has his hand on the back of my chair as he converses with the group. His dirty blond hair is carelessly tousled, maybe a bit wet. I can't tell from this distance. He wears a fitted blue T-shirt and jeans, and as he reaches across the table to extend his hand to Reese, the material stretches over his ass and lean thighs. A hint of flesh peeks out from above his waistband.

Fuck. Okay, he's here. He's here, and he looks like *that.*

Change of plans.

I cut a hard left through the crowd and grab a stool at the bar.

No way am I going to sit at that table with seven pairs of eyes on me like I'm some sort of freak-show exhibit. Joey is clearly already on a mission to embarrass me tonight, and I haven't had nearly enough alcohol to tolerate his obnoxiousness yet.

I wave over the bartender. "Give me something. Not beer. Something . . . girly. Or wine. I don't care. Surprise me."

The older man smiles, then turns and grabs a glass.

I set my clutch on the wood, fiddling with the contents. Phone, cash, keys, license, lip gloss. A warm body presses against my back.

"Little devil. You're hard to find."

A shiver runs through me as his breath moves against my hair. I turn my head, then tilt it back.

Mason moves to stand beside me. I fight the urge to grab his face and molest him.

It's a struggle.

I wet my lips. "Hey, hi. Did you just get here?"

Obviously, I already know the answer to this question. Way to act like you haven't been watching for him, Brooke.

He smiles and slowly sinks onto the stool next to me. "I did.

Class ran over a bit. I had to shower, find the place. Why are you over here and not with your mates?"

I risk a glance in their direction.

Juls waves. Dylan smiles from her seat.

Oh, my God. Is Joey seriously videoing this with his phone?

"It was a bit crowded." I swivel on my stool so that Mason's body completely shields mine. "And I was trying to avoid this guy who has a tendency to stalk. You might know him. He's Australian too."

He pulls his shoulders back and looks around the bar. "Yeah? Point this wanker out. I'll take care of him. Unless he's a big fella. If that's the case, I'll sneak you out the back."

I laugh as the bartender sets my glass down in front of me.

It's a tall, skinny beverage. Something blended, with red and white slush swirling together and a pineapple wedge tucked on the rim.

"That's fancy lookin'."

I nod at Mason's observation as my hand closes around the chilled glass. I take a sip. Very tropical.

"So, was the turn-out for class today as ridiculous as last night?"

"You thought it was ridiculous?" His mouth pulls tight. He looks adorably puzzled.

"Women were lined up outside like you were handing out free orgasms." I give him a cheeky grin. "Clearly, you weren't. Unless that service was offered to everyone *except* me."

His face softens with a smile. "Nah, that's the Brooke special. It comes with dinners and private lessons. Spending time together. Friendship."

"Friendship? You want to be my friend?"

"Yeah."

"And you want to sleep with me?"

"I want everything," he states negligently. "Friendship is a part of it. Why wouldn't it be?"

I shrug. My eyes fixate on the bar.

This glorious specimen of a man also wants a friendship out of this. How . . . strange.

"Are you drinking?" I ask, desperate for a subject change.

Feelings. Friendship. More.

He needs alcohol.

I glance back up to catch the quick shake of his head.

"I'm all right."

"You came to a bar and you're not going to drink?"

He stares at me, his eyes slowly moving over my face, then down the line of my body. "You look lovely, Brooke. Stunning, really. Has any man told you that today?"

"Um . . ." I inhale a shaky breath. "Today? No. Not today."

"Shame. I should've said something earlier. I was thinking it. In the alley . . . when I came to your work. I couldn't stop looking at you. I still can't."

"In the alley." I clear my throat. Hair clings to the base of my neck. I'm burning up. "I liked the alley."

God, I loved the alley.

Mason eyes me for a moment, then reaches out and takes the drink out of my hand. He sets it on the bar and stands, pulling out his wallet. "Go for a ride with me, yeah? I'll bring you back here. I just . . . I want to talk to you and drive around the city. I've been thinking about doing that." He throws some cash down, tucks his wallet back into his pocket, and grabs my hand.

With a gentle tug, I'm on my feet.

"You're taller tonight," he observes, smiling down at my shoes. "I recognize those."

I grab my clutch off the bar. "And you're a bit bossy."

His brow pulls together. He looks charmingly confused.

I fight the urge to smile as I explain. "I never agreed to go for a ride with you. You did that adorable little 'yeah' thing and took my drink away. Were you even going to wait for my answer? Maybe I'm not ready to leave. Maybe I want to finish my very coconuty drink and spend some time with my mates. Ever think about that?"

I think he wants to smile. I believe I see a slight twitch in his mouth, but he covers it immediately, or I'm simply imagining things.

Am I not as funny as I think I am?

"I'm sorry." He drops my hand. His eyes roam the room. "Right. That was a bit bossy of me. Would you rather we stay here? I thought a drive would be nice. I'll be able to hear you better. I'd like to hear you."

A strange tightness pulls at my chest.

Shit. Even in his high-handedness, his intentions are sweet.

"It's fine. We can . . ."

A body bumps against my back. I brace myself with a hand to Mason's chest to keep myself from falling. His grip holds tight on my waist, tighter as I slowly lift my head to look at him. I turn to get a glance at the creep who shoved me into this tall piece of manly deliciousness.

I should thank them.

Paul sways on his feet behind me. He's clearly intoxicated.

Whatever. I don't hold any ill-will toward any of the men I've slept with. I'm sure him knocking into me was purely accidental. No doubt brought on by the alcohol. Look at him. He can barely stand.

He grabs the bar to steady himself, grinning wildly. "Brooke! Funny . . . funny seeing you again, isn't it? God, I really didn't think that was you."

He didn't think that was me? I just saw him a few days ago. How drunk is this guy?

"Uh, yeah, it's me. Small world." I push against Mason's chest. "Come on. Let's go."

Paul keeps going.

"I thought . . . nah, that's not Brooke. No way! She should be hanging on a street corner."

I whip my head around. "*Excuse me*."

"A street corner." Paul leans closer, tilting his head with a sneer. "You know. Like a whore."

My body goes rigid. Mason tenses behind me.

Paul, you stupid fucking idiot. You asked for this.

Chapter Six

Mason

"YOU KNOW. LIKE A WHORE."

Brooke inhales a quick breath. Her eyes go round, taking up the majority of her face.

The fuck did he just say?

I move to get closer to this piece of shit, putting myself in front of Brooke. "Hey, fuck off, mate."

His head jerks up, his eyes rapidly blinking me into focus. He's barely keeping himself upright. One hand is flat on the bar, the other is clutching the stool Brooke was just occupying.

He's so tanked he'll probably end up falling over soon.

"No." Brooke darts a hand out and grabs my arm, halting me. "No, let me." She steps in front of the bastard. "I'm sorry, Paul. What exactly makes me a whore? Was it the fact that I had sex with you the other night, which I'm now suddenly regretting, or was it that you got your pathetic little feelings hurt when I didn't want to cuddle after?" Her hand flies to her hip. "Are you sad because I didn't want to go for round two? Is that it? Is that why you look like shit right now, Paul?"

Jesus. Brooke and this tosser? This is not some shit I want to hear about.

Paul drops his head, shaking with silent laughter. "You fucked like a whore. What chick bails right after gettin' laid like that?"

"What guy turns into a preteen and cries about it? You're lucky I even went home with you. I had plenty of other options that night."

"Yeah . . . I bet you did." He slouches closer, his eyes gleaming. "Whore."

I move without any thought behind it, getting up in his face, jamming his body against the bar.

"Speak to her like that again and I'll put you through a fucking window, yeah?"

A small hand wraps around my elbow. "Mason." Brooke tugs my arm, but I keep the bastard pinned.

Just knowing he's been with Brooke is enough to provoke me. Hearing him speak to her like that . . . I'm not a violent guy, but I'm suddenly feeling like I could be. I could beat the piss out of this wanker and not feel any remorse. Not a shred.

His head rolls left, then right, his eyes slowly drifting closed. "Mm. Hit me. Go ahead. I-I don't give a s-shit."

He's slurring his words now. He can barely stand.

I don't need to hit him.

I swiftly back away. He isn't expecting that. Eyes wide, his feet slide out from under him and he collapses into a drunken heap on the floor, limbs sprawled like a rag doll, head slumped back against the bar. His eyes pinch shut through a groan, then he slowly topples over until he's laid out between the stools.

A big bloke moves through the crowd and steps in front of me, crouching down to grab Paul.

"Let's go, buddy. You've been cut off."

I turn to Brooke, then notice the eyes on us, the crowd that's gathered behind her who I'm certain heard every bit of that conversation, including the cruel words that fucker had to say. Brooke notices them too, her eyes darting quickly around the room, then dropping to a spot between us.

Her shoulders pull forward, and she lowers her head, hiding behind her hair. She suddenly appears smaller.

She's embarrassed. Maybe a bit hurt. It's hard to tell when I can't see her face.

"Hey." I lift her chin with my hand. "You all right?"

She hesitates for a second, just staring up at me through those impossibly thick lashes as she slowly exhales. Her hand gently presses against my hip. I slide a bit closer, moving my fingers along her jaw and just fucking stare at her.

Christ, she is quite possibly the most stunning woman I have ever laid eyes on.

Her hair is falling out around her in dark curls, covering her delicate neck. She's wearing more makeup than I've seen her in up until this point, but fuck, she doesn't need it. The way she looked in my class the other day, her skin glowing from exertion, clean and sweaty, that Brooke has me.

Finally after taking in a deep breath, she nods slightly, just a jerk of her chin. "Yeah . . . yeah, I'm fine, but can we go? I'd really like that ride now."

I grab her hand and we melt into the crowd.

Tipping my head in the direction of the table Brooke's friends are at, I let them know we're getting out of here while she stays close to my side. It's a brief farewell. Brooke tugging on my hand has me getting her out of there before any of them have a chance to ask us what happened. She clearly doesn't want to linger. I'm not interested in making her stay. Besides, I'd rather have her alone.

We're out the door, her small hand in mine as we walk along the footpath. The sky is free of clouds, a clear blue scene speckled with stars and a bold moon hanging low.

Brooke pulls her hand back after a few seconds and wraps her arms around herself.

"Are you cold?" I ask.

The air has a slight chill to it, but I think it's tolerable. She's not wearing much, though. Her arms could be cold.

She shakes her head, keeping her gaze in front of her.

"I'm just up here on the left." I tug my keys from my pocket. "The white Denali."

"Asshole."

"What's that?" I turn my head, staring at her rigid profile.

"That guy. Paul. Calling me a whore because I only wanted to hook-up with him." She breathes a laugh. "Seriously? It's a fucking double standard. Just because I'm a woman who loves sex I'm automatically labeled a whore? What about men?"

I open the passenger door for her and she climbs inside, securing her seatbelt.

"Men can fuck anything with a pulse and women will actually find that attractive. The whole player vibe. It's hot. It gets them so much ass," she continues after I get in on the driver's side. "But if a woman enjoys sex and goes out to get laid, she's a whore. Why? What the hell is the difference?"

I run a hand through my hair after starting up the car. My fingers quickly dial down the volume on the stereo. I only want to hear her.

"Well?" She angles her body in the seat, waiting for my response.

I rub my jaw. "I'm not sure I'm the best person to answer that question, Brooke."

"Why not? You're a man."

"Yeah, but I'm not running around sticking my cock into everything with a pulse." I catch her smile as I glance over before pulling out onto the street. "I think you're right, though. You should be able to do what or who you want."

"Exactly."

"He was wrong . . . saying that to you. I'm sorry that happened."

I'm sorry I didn't knock him on his arse before he said it a second time.

Out of the corner of my eye, I can see Brooke watching me as I drive us into the city.

"Were you going to punch him? You looked ready to punch him."

"I *felt* ready to punch him." My hand curls around the wheel.

"Have you ever hit anyone? You don't really seem like the violent type. Yoga master who uses organic toothpaste. You probably recycle too."

I turn my head. She shrugs impassively, twirling the ends of her hair around her finger.

"Well, I'm usually not threatening to toss people through windows," I chuckle. "But, I did get into a few brawls when I was younger. Nothing major. Some neighborhood kids pissed me off and I went after them."

"Majahhh. I love how you say certain words."

I give her a quick wink.

"Why did you go after those kids?" she asks, her voice lifting to a mischievous pitch.

Even in the dark, I know this little devil is smiling.

"Did they steal your koala?"

I gape at her. Her quiet laugh fills the car. "Is that what you Americans think? That we keep those nasty little buggers as pets? They'll claw your eyes out the second you get close enough."

"Would they? But they're so cuddly looking." She hugs herself. "And so, so cute."

"Cute. Right. Real bloody cute. I had one nearly take my head off when I was trying to pet it at the zoo once. I was only eight. That mangy bastard scarred me for life."

"Oh, so it's just your *opinion* that they'd make horrible pets," Brooke chuckles again. "Look at you. Giving those sweet things a bad name over here. I bet you were just a little wanker and pissed him off."

She smiles, all big and clever, clearly pleased with herself for using that word correctly.

I relax against my seat. It feels good talking to her like this. Easy, unhurried conversation. The delightful sound of her laugh. Her sweet dimpled face against the backdrop of the city.

I want this drive to last all night.

"Was there a bunch of you? Maybe the cute, gentle, completely innocent and non-threatening koala didn't like crowds."

We stop at a red-light. I shrug, looking over at her.

"The zoo was crowded, yeah. It was me and my mates, a few others gathered around. I don't know. I've tried to forget about the day a koala went psychotic on me. I had nightmares for months.

Surprised I didn't need therapy after that."

She slaps at my arm. I grab her hand before she can pull away and lace my fingers through hers, resting our joined hands together on the console. I haven't held her like this yet. I've wanted to all night, in my studio, on the footpath that first day. My hand practically engulfs hers. She feels a bit tense. Her nails, dark as the night, tap restlessly against my skin.

She stares down between us, biting at her bottom lip.

"So . . . I'm guessing you aren't a fan of kangaroos either? Did one chase you down the street or something? Kick you around a little?"

I grin, giving a gentle squeeze to her hand. She's not pulling away.

Bit of a shock. I was expecting some resistance.

I press down on the accelerator and ease through the intersection.

"Nah. I never had a problem with kangaroos. Although, there have been some cases of rogue ones attacking people. The mums can be vicious."

She laughs softly, gazing out the window.

"Have you always lived here?" I ask her, smiling when her fingers relax against the back of my hand. I turn us onto a side street, avoiding the pile up of traffic ahead.

"Mm. Yeah. Born and raised Chicago girl. I thought about moving to the beach a few years back but . . ." Brooke jolts upright, leaning forward in her seat and staring out the window. She tugs her hand free and braces it on the dash. "Uh, Mason. You're going down a one-way street right now."

"What?"

"One-way street. Shit! There's cars coming! Pull over! Quick! Get off the road!"

My eyes sweep the small alley I've turned down.

"Fucking hell."

I was so focused on not crushing Brooke's hand with mine, on the feel of Brooke's hand, on *Brooke*, I hadn't noticed the well-lit street signs posted in warning, indicating that I have indeed turned down a one-way street.

Cars are parked along either side, leaving me with little room to pull off as head-lights loom closer.

I tap the brakes.

"Shit," she whispers, squirming in her seat, her head whipping left, then right, then behind her. "Can you back up or something? Quickly, like floor it?"

I glance in the rear-view mirror, then ahead of me once more. "It's all right. Look up there. I can pull off a bit in front of that motorbike until they get by."

"That's not going to give them enough room to pass you."

"It might."

She groans, covering her face with her hands.

I pull ahead and squeeze as close to the motorbike and the car parked in front of it as I can get without knocking into one.

Damn. This is going to be tight.

I shift into park. "Right. See? It's all good, gorgeous. No worries."

A blaring horn pulls my attention off Brooke.

I roll my window down as the car at the front of the line heading our direction inches past me at a snail's pace. Their side mirror nearly strips my door of paint.

"This is a one-way street, you idiot!" the man yells up at me, shaking his fist as he slows to a stop.

I hold up a hand. "Yeah, sorry about that, mate. New in town. My apologies, yeah?"

His face visibly relaxes. The female passenger, I'm guessing his wife, leans over him to look up at me. She waves a quick hand. "Welcome to Chicago! We visited Sydney a few years ago on our honeymoon. Beautiful city. We had the best time."

"Oh, my God. You have got to be kidding me," Brooke mumbles next to me, her voice breaking with a soft giggle.

I give her a quick smile, then turn back to the couple. "Oh yeah? I'm glad to hear that. And again, I'm terribly sorry about this little blunder. I hope I haven't ruined your night."

The driver waves his hand dismissively. The car behind him lays on his horn.

"All right! Jesus! Are we all in a hurry?" he yells, craning his neck around to look at them. He gives me a sharp nod. "Enjoy Chicago. Watch out for one-way streets."

"Right. Got it."

They pull ahead and continue down the street.

The next car brushes past, this bloke settling on giving me the bird instead of a quick chat. I nod apologetically, waving a hand at his gesture.

Brooke couldn't be more amused sitting next to me, her head back against the seat and her hands covering her face as she laughs into the silence of the car.

"Unbelievable. You could've done anything if it was just that one car! You could've blocked the street entirely and refused to move. Opened fire on them. Acted like a dick. I'm pretty sure that couple was close to offering to name their first born after you. That guy was pissed, and then . . ." she pauses, pointing a finger at me. "As soon as you opened that mouth of yours, dropping those adorable 'yeahs', it was like the second coming for those people. Mason the Messiah."

I flash her a grin as I make it out of the one-way street. "I told you it would be all right. We had plenty of room."

"Plenty of room. Yeah, okay," she snickers. "It was that mouth. I'm telling you. I know what that mouth does to me. Now I'm seeing it work on the general population. You have a gift, Mason. You should probably go into politics."

I don't hear anything after . . .

"What does it do to you, Brooke?"

An ache pinches in the center of my chest.

She slowly turns her head, then drops it back against the seat, staring at me as the city lights move over her face.

I want to continue looking at her. In the daylight, preferably, where I can really see every emotion wash over her face. The heady look in her eyes I'm hoping is there. I don't need my attention being pulled away for the sake of safety right now, but that's exactly what happens before she can answer me.

"Wait. Just hold on. Don't say anything yet."

I pick up speed and take us back in the direction we came.

We drive through the city in silence until Brooke fiddles with the stereo, tuning the station to soft rock. Coldplay and One Republic become the background noise of our night. It mellows my suddenly anxious mind, my restless body, impatient against the seat.

It takes us twenty minutes to get out of the city.

I want to reach out and take her hand again. I want her to finish what she was going to tell me, but I keep my hands firmly planted on the wheel and my questions to myself until I pull us onto a dirt path that leads to an overlook I found when I went exploring my first day here.

It's a secluded spot. I believe there's a few trails that lead to some campsites, and a lake nearby. I made a mental note the other day to come back here. Discover more of it. I hadn't realized at the time I'd be doing it so soon with Brooke.

I park near a lamp post and turn my attention to her.

She smiles warmly at me. She looks like she's glowing under the amber lights provided from above.

"Wet," she whispers, angling her body, her hair spilling over the edge of the seat.

I lean closer, fitting her sweet face between my hands. "What's that, gorgeous?"

She inhales sharply as I slide my mouth against hers. Her perfect fucking lips open for me, inviting me to take her. We both moan, her hands fisting my shirt and mine moving to her neck, tangling in her hair as I tilt her head. Her warm tongue strokes along mine.

"It makes me wet," she says breathlessly between kisses. "I'm . . . so wet, Mason. God, my thong is probably soaked right now. Useless. I can take it off if you'd like."

I groan as my hand falls to her lap, then moves along the smooth, warm skin of her upper thigh underneath her dress. I press against the lace of her g-string.

Soaked.

"Yes," she moans, her head flopping back. "Yes, please, touch me. God, I need this."

I lick up her throat, dragging my teeth along her skin as I slide one finger inside her, then another. She's silky and hot. She trembles when I press against her clit.

"Mason."

"I want to take you out on a proper date," I whisper against her ear, my fingers slowly pumping inside her, slower when she starts to rock into my hand.

"Greedy little devil. You want to come?"

She groans and I suck on her lip.

"This weekend. Dinner. Say yes to me, Brooke."

She growls, chewing on her lip. "Mm, what? Dinner? Why are we discussing dinner? Can't you just . . . focus on one task at a time? This first. Negotiations later . . . *Jesus*."

I bite back a chuckle. Her plea, even though it is humorous, sounds desperate all the same.

She wants this, my fingers fucking her in a vacant field under the stars. My mouth clamping down on every visible, flawless inch of her body. Maybe she's thought about me doing this to her. God knows I have. I've thought about doing everything. Right now, I'm thinking about pulling her over the seat and stripping her of these clothes, tasting the soft skin between her legs. Toying with her clit while I pump my shaft against her heavy tits.

But anything with Brooke is perfect. This right here, my cock throbbing, straining against my zipper, harder than fucking steel, her breathless words against my mouth . . .

"Harder," she whispers.

"More," she begs.

I move my thumb over her clit and she arches away from the seat, gasping.

"Like that?"

She nods frantically, clawing at my arm, my shirt, the hand between her legs. Her hips begin circling, her pussy seeking friction against my palm.

"God, Mason . . . *Mason*."

I twist my wrist and claim her mouth again, swallowing her indecent noises, the sweet way she pants my name. I want to drown in her. I want her taste to linger in my mouth, her smell to cling to the walls of my lungs.

Brooke.

How can I be so lost in this woman already?

"Perfect," I whisper against her jaw. "You are fucking perfect."

She turns her head to capture my mouth, biting and sucking at my tongue. I add another finger and grip the back of her neck, keeping her pinned to me.

"You're close, gorgeous."

"I know that," she growls, her head rolling back, thighs spreading wider. "If you stop right now, I swear to God I will make it so you never have children. I will pin your balls to the seat with my heel."

I laugh quietly. My cock surprisingly doesn't react in an offensive way to that threat.

I'm too hard to care. To stop. To think.

Curling my fingers, I pump them inside her and move my thumb wildly over her clit. It only takes a few more seconds and she's drenching my hand. Writhing against the seat, she gasps into my mouth, the pleasure tearing through her so perfectly, so exquisitely, I break the seal of our lips and lean back to get a better look.

I thought she was beautiful before . . .

"Mason," she pants, eyes heavy-lidded, her hair sticking to her cheek as she tries to steady her breaths.

"Dinner, Brooke. This weekend. What's your answer?"

Her eyes fall closed. "Yes," she says through a heavy exhale. "Okay, fine, I'll go out with you to dinner. You earned it. That was . . . worth a meal."

The light from above catches in the corner of her mouth. It's lifted slightly. A hint of a smile.

Fuck me. I'm so done for.

I'm suddenly grateful she can't see me clearly. My mouth stretches into what has to be the biggest grin of my life.

I want dates with her. Dinners. Conversation. Hours upon hours of what we shared tonight.

And she said yes.

I slide my fingers out of her, anxious for a taste. A little desperate for it. At the sound of my gluttonous moan, Brooke peeks her eyes open, then gasps and leans forward, getting an inch away from my mouth.

"Well?" she asks, an unruly gleam in her eye as her hand circles my wrist.

She wants to know how she tastes. I could describe her for hours.

I slip my fingers out of my mouth, tracing the wetness along her jaw. "I could live with my mouth between your legs, Brooke. I could die there too."

Her eyes fill with curiosity, and something else. Fear, maybe? Have I said too much?

I pull back and grip the wheel with both hands. My head hits the back of the seat.

Fuck, I had to say that, didn't I? I couldn't just say how fucking incredible she is? How I didn't think it was possible for something to be sweet and fiery at the same time? Shit, even admitting I'm a full-blown addict after one bloody lick would've been a better response.

Why don't you just propose right now, you tosser? Really go full-blown pathetic.

"Mason," Brooke murmurs.

I shift my attention off the endless night sky and onto her.

She reaches for her belt. I can't remember her ever taking it off.

"Can we drive some more? Maybe around here? The stars are insane right now." She dials up the volume on the stereo, tilting her head to see out the windscreen. Ed Sheeran fills the car.

On second thought . . .

Maybe I haven't spoken out of line at all?

Relief warms my blood. I melt against the seat as I shift the car into reverse.

We drive for hours, chasing the moonlight all over Chicago. Our conversation couldn't be more random. We talk about everything. Her job, my home-life back in Australia, our favorite movies. Brooke rambles about her family, her sister Juls and her niece and nephew. How she's living with Joey and his husband until she saves up enough for a place of her own. Sometimes we drive in silence, listening to the radio or nothing at all when Brooke grows agitated with the music selections. It's comfortable, and easy. God, it's easy talking to her. There's no awkward pauses, no need to feel like you have to keep the conversation going. She makes a few more cracks about animals native to Australia, and whether or not I kept any of them as pets.

"Yeah," I tell her, containing my amusement. "We kept a few crocs in our backyard. Mum didn't care much for the safety of her children."

She giggles into the night. The wind blows her hair around her and she tries frantically to tame it.

Fuck, she is precious.

I pull up in front of the Tavern after I catch a few yawns out of her. The footpath is quiet. It's nearing 1:00 A.M. .

I feel wide awake. Drunk and high off Brooke. Reveling in this addiction I don't want to fight.

She stares down at her lap after removing her seatbelt.

I fight the urge to drive off with her and bypass the goodbyes.

"I feel like you tricked me into agreeing to dinner," she mumbles, looking over at me with a weak smile. "That seemed very calculated on your part."

I lean across the console and kiss her cheek. "Not sure I know what you're referring to. But calculated or not, you make the best sounds when you come." I pull back, smiling at the heavy look that's in her eyes, the same one she had in the field when I slid my finger over the smooth rise of her clit.

She wets her lips, then pulls the door handle and exits the car in a hurry.

"Yeah . . . okay, well, I guess I'll see you this weekend sometime."

"I'm just across the street, Brooke. You'll see me before this weekend."

She blinks rapidly, then nods once, her hand pushing her hair off her shoulder. "Mm. Right. You need to commit to your stalker status. It would be weird at this point if you didn't follow me to get coffee, or do random drop-ins at my place of business."

I chuckle, resting my elbow on the console. "What are you doing tomorrow morning?"

"Working."

"Before that."

She stares at me with the most curious expression. It's so sweet I want to reach out and tug her back into the car, pull her against me, feel the grin she's fighting against my mouth.

"Sleeping," she answers, her bold eyes searching my face.

God, what I wouldn't give to see her like that. First thing in the morning, sleep-rumpled and soft against my sheets. Her body tucked against mine while I watch the morning light pass over her skin.

With a jerk of my chin, I clear that image out of my head before it renders me incapable of getting my next words out. "Meet me for breakfast? There's this spot I saw the other day when I was driving around. Just down the way a bit from the coffee shop."

"Rosie's," she offers with a soft voice. Her teeth run along her bottom lip. "Yellow umbrellas out front?"

"Yeah, that's the one."

"They have amazing breakfast foods. Like life-changing amazing." She lowers her eyes to a spot between us, gathering her hair over one shoulder and twirling her fingers in it. She seems a bit unsure all of a sudden, like she can't decide whether to bolt or stand here and continue talking to me.

"So, is that a yes?" I ask her, ducking my head a little.

"I don't know."

"It's just breakfast, Brooke. You're going to eat it anyway, yeah?"

Her eyes flick up to mine, but she doesn't respond.

I smile, hoping to get one in return. "Do I need to pull you back in here and ask that question with my hand up your dress?"

She purses her lips, fighting it, fighting me. Her arms cross tightly under her chest as she stands a little taller. "You'd be wasting your time."

"Hardly."

"You would. I'm not a multiple orgasm type of girl. It's nearly impossible to make me come more than once."

"Really?"

"Yup."

"I'll remember to remind you of that when you're begging me for a break." We share a brief laugh, hers a little disbelieving. I look at her straight on and bite back the urge to beg for this. "Come on, Brooke. Meet me for breakfast tomorrow. Let me have you first thing in the morning."

She stares at me long and hard, then finally drops her shoulders with a sigh. "All right."

"Yeah?"

"Yeah," she answers, looking away to hide her smile. "Only because I love Rosie's and I haven't eaten there in forever. Nice going on your part. If you would've suggested any other place, I would've shot you down."

I wait until she looks back at me to give her a smile. "Seven o'clock?"

She doesn't answer, doesn't give me any sign of agreement. With a swift hand she shuts the door and walks to her car, making sure to give me a nice view of her arse as she bends to unlock the driver's side door.

I drop a hand to my cock, staring at her, waiting for an acknowledgement that she's heard my time suggestion.

I never get it.

She pulls away from the curb and blends into the traffic on the street.

Chapter Seven

Brooke

THE LINE AT ROSIE'S CAFÉ is already wrapping around the building when I arrive this morning.

Typical, and why I didn't argue with Mason when he suggested meeting so early last night. I'm used to grabbing something to eat after I arrive at the bakery, which isn't until eight-thirty. Waking up any earlier for any reason isn't something I'll easily agree to, but if you're going to eat breakfast at Rosie's, you need to beat the crowd.

I move past the line and step inside the café, shifting my attention around the crowded room.

"Brooke." Mason stands from his seat at a booth in the corner. He looks almost relieved to see me.

I suppose I could've given him some indication last night that I was planning on showing up at seven o'clock today. But really, where's the fun in that?

He kisses my cheek when I reach the booth. "Morning,

gorgeous. I went ahead and ordered you some coffee and juice. It's fresh-squeezed apparently."

I giggle as I lean away.

"What?" he asks, eyes curious as we both slide into the booth.

I take a moment to stare at him before I respond.

His hair is still damp from a shower, the curls a bit more prominent now than when it's fully dry, but still just as carelessly tousled on top of his head. Light from a nearby window catches on the stubble coating his jaw. It looks coarse, but I know how it feels against the skin of my cheek. A gentle, welcoming scratch. The crisp white T-shirt he's wearing stretches deliciously across his chest and the muscles of his shoulders.

Damn. Even at this hour, he looks amazing. Would it be weird to order *him* for breakfast?

I bring the glass of juice to my lips, swallowing a taste as my eyes slowly take their time reaching his face. "Nothing. I just think it's cute how you bring that to my attention. Like I'd send it back if it wasn't freshly-squeezed. I'm not a snob."

"I wasn't implying that." He eyes me guardedly. "I just appreciate good quality juice."

"Mm. Figures. You probably own a juicer, don't you?"

"No."

I raise an eyebrow. No way does this guy not own every health conscious piece of equipment invented.

He smiles, tasting his own juice. "I may have left it in Alabama. It was rooted. I should pick up a new one, now that you mention it."

"Ah. See." I point a finger at him. "I got you all figured out."

"Yeah? Think you know me, do ya?"

"Yup."

He leans forward, placing his hand on top of mine. "What do you know, Brooke? Do you know I thought about you until I fell asleep last night? That that's quickly becoming a routine of mine, and I'm not ashamed to admit it?"

My breaths grow heavier as I stare back at him.

Shit. What does he mean he thinks about me until he falls asleep? Sexually? Like, is he jerking off to images of me in his head before he passes out, because I'm pretty sure that's a normal response for most men in this zip code, and not necessarily a declaration that should make my heart thunder against my sternum.

"I know you like my sounds. And that you were attacked by a rogue koala when you were a kid, which I'm still having trouble believing," I finally reply after sliding my hand out from under his and grabbing a menu.

If I let him, I think he'd try and hold my hand this entire meal.

He grins, reaching for his own menu. "I more than *like* your sounds," he corrects me, lowering his gaze. "What's good here? Anything you'd recommend?"

"Everything. I told you, this place will change your life. The pancakes are amazing. That's what I'm getting."

Our waitress arrives, placing silverware in front of us and a stack of napkins. "Have we decided?" she asks.

Mason motions for me to order as he continues surveying his options.

I hand my menu to the waitress. I barely even needed to glance at it. "I'll have the bacon and apple pancakes." My mouth stretches into a grin when Mason gives me a wide-eyed look.

Welcome to America. We put bacon on everything.

He glances once more at the back of his menu, then places it into the waitress's hand. "Eggs Benedict. And if it isn't too much trouble, instead of the hash browns, can I get double sausage?"

"Sure," she replies, stepping away with our order.

I grab two sugar packets and empty them into my coffee. When I glance up after stirring in some cream, I catch Mason's eyes on me, and I wonder how long they've been there.

He leans back with a warm smile. "So, Brooke, tell me about working at the bakery."

"What do you want to know?"

"Do you make everything you sell? Or are you strictly in charge of cupcakes?"

I chuckle against the lip of my mug. The steam billowing from my coffee evaporates into the air. "I'm not in charge of anything. Dylan is. I just do some of the baking for her. Everything except the wedding cakes. That's all her."

He looks surprised. "Why don't you do those?"

"Because it's a *wedding* cake. I don't want to be responsible for something people pay hundreds of dollars for. And have you ever seen a pissed off bride? No way am I risking ruining someone's big day." I take a sip of my coffee. "I occasionally help out with the actual assembly of the cake, but all of the big detail work I am nowhere near skilled enough to do, Dylan handles. She's amazing."

"I bet you could do it," he says. "Those cupcakes you gave me looked pretty complex."

Complex? Compared to a wedding cake? This man is crazy.

"Yeah, okay. Have you ever seen a wedding cake? I can't do that. We don't even take requests for them when Dylan goes out on maternity leave. She meets with brides. Not me, and definitely not Joey. He'd end up somehow weaseling his way into the wedding party."

Mason quietly laughs before taking a drink of his coffee. When he lowers his mug back to the table, he keeps his gaze on me, so plainly attentive, as if nothing could pull his eyes away.

My hands tangle together in my lap.

Have I ever been looked at like this before? With such raw interest, and not with some blatant underlying motive to get me naked and beneath whoever is staring at me?

Probably not, unless I'm related to the person.

We talk until our food arrives, and in between my massive bites of the best damn pancakes in Chicago. Mason polishes off his breakfast minutes before I've even made a dent in my tall stack. He drinks his coffee and freshly-squeezed juice while I finish off my plate, and after paying the check, he asks me what my plans are tomorrow morning.

"Sleeping," I answer, smiling behind my glass when I pick up on his meaning. "No way am I waking up early again tomorrow. I don't think you realize how vital my sleep is."

He scratches his jaw. I can practically hear his mind working this out. "Okay. Friday then?"

I shake my head.

"Come on."

"Why?"

"Because I like having you this early. And I think you had a nice time too. Stop fighting me. It's just breakfast."

I stare at him across the booth.

Just breakfast. Somehow, it seems like a lot more to Mason than just sharing a meal at the earliest part of the day. Will this become something regular, a routine we fall into where he orders for me before I even arrive? Not just beverages, but my food? Will he know what I like and how I like it, and on what days I want pancakes with blueberries instead of bacon?

More importantly, do I want him to know it?

I rub a hand down my face. As my eyes scan the table riddled with napkins and half-empty glasses, I spot an advertisement stuck between the salt and pepper shaker. My stomach makes an embarrassing sound as I look at the picture. *How did I forget about this?* I pinch the laminated picture between my fingers and hold it up for Mason to see.

"I'll give you Tuesdays."

He leans forward, taking the picture from me and staring at it. "All you can eat deep-fried stuffed French toast. Wow. Is that . . . Captain Crunch, the cereal? They put cereal on it?"

He looks adorably baffled, like the idea of using crushed up cereal on anything is the strangest suggestion.

"It's out of this world, and extremely popular. You can only order it on Tuesdays and people will actually call ahead to secure their plates." I snatch the picture from him and drop it between us. "You want me this early? You can have me on Tuesdays . . . only. Take it or leave it."

He drops his elbows onto the table and presses his mouth against his hands. "You drive a hard bargain. I was hoping for multiple mornings."

I shrug, studying my nails and the chipped polish on my thumb, looking anywhere but his face until his foot nudges against mine.

Our eyes lock. He shakes his head, then smiles at the frown pulling down my lips.

Fuck.

"Jerk," I mutter. Of course I have to react to his phony rejection. I can't just sit here and feign indifference. Now I look like the one who suggested this.

Well played, you gorgeous bastard. Well played.

He stands and tugs me to my feet, kissing my lips and murmuring, "I'll take anything you give me, Brooke. Anything."

I keep my hands tucked into the pockets of my jeans the entire walk to the bakery.

I HAVEN'T SAT DOWN ONCE today.

I can't.

I'm full of nervous energy. Restless. Buzzing around my room like this is my first rodeo, and it's not. It's so not.

I've been on plenty of dates. Hundreds. Well, okay, maybe not hundreds, but enough where I shouldn't be *this* anxious about one freaking dinner. Guys ask me out all the time, and who am I to turn down a free meal before we get down to business? I love to eat. I *really* love to have sex. Putting two of my favorite things together makes for one very happy Brooke. And hey, if the sex is lousy, at least I get an enjoyable meal out of it.

But that's just it, right there. A meal is guaranteed tonight, but I have no idea if I'm getting laid. Dinner is pretty cut and dry, but after?

What the hell is happening after?

I, for one, feel like Mason and I know each other well enough for sex, based on his guidelines. More than well enough based on mine. We've talked, information has been exchanged. He knows more about me than any other guy I've been interested in recently. But is that enough for him?

He said he wants more. How much more? How much does he want from me?

I've seen Mason practically every day this week, between breakfast, coincidental, but maybe not so coincidental coffee-shop run-ins, to the occasional treats delivery, which I can't seem to stop myself from doing. Christ, it's like a damn compulsion. Even when he pops into the shop for a brief hello I'm shoving a bakery box at him like he's one of those malnourished children you see on the

UNICEF commercials.

Here! Eat this! You poor thing, you're starving!

It's his reaction that gets me. That's why I do it. He takes that box and studies my creations like they should be displayed in a museum somewhere. Like they're some precious gift. Like I'm giving him something amazing.

Call me crazy, but I'm beginning to feel like maybe I am giving him something more than just a pastry or a cupcake. Maybe he looks at my treats as another piece of me? The *more* he's after?

Yeah . . . crazy. That line of thinking right there is completely fucking crazy.

They're treats. Damn good ones. And he's just a man who enjoys his dessert.

Period.

As I'm sliding up the zipper on my black pencil skirt, my bedroom door bursts open.

Joey walks in like he owns the place, which, if we're being technical, he doesn't. The condo belongs to Billy. But this is Joey, and I've learned since moving in here that the concept of knocking before a grand entrance is not something he is privy to.

I'm fully dressed, but it wouldn't matter. I couldn't care less if he sees me naked. But at night, when I'm more than likely to engage in a little *me* time, my door remains locked.

His gaze sweeps over my attire, slow moving and encouraging. He plops down on the bed. "You look hot to trot. What shoes are you wearing with that?"

"Those." I point to the Steve Madden's on the floor by the closet.

Okay, okay, so I seriously need to return them to Dylan. And I will.

Next week.

"Earrings?"

I hold up the silver hoops I've set out for tonight.

"Lip gloss or lipstick?"

I pull the tube of MAC's Vegas Volt out of my makeup bag and wiggle it in the air. Joey nods approvingly.

"What's this?" he asks, plucking the small gift bag off my night table.

Shit.

I move like lightning, snatching it from him before he has a chance to peer inside.

He stares at me, startled. "Jesus. What the hell?"

Clutching the bag against my chest, I hurriedly explain, "It's nothing. It's a joke between me and Mason. You wouldn't get it. Stop snooping around my room and asking me a thousand questions. God."

I toss the bag on top of the dresser.

My breaths come hurried, air moving in and out of my lungs with desperation. I probably look psychotic.

Maybe he won't notice? He's not that perceptive, is he?

"Mm." Joey lays out on the bed, tucking his hands behind his head and crossing his bare feet at the ankles.

He looks positively delighted.

He noticed.

"Interesting. So you and Mason have inside jokes already? After only knowing each other for five days and one earth-shattering orgasm? Seems a bit fast, don't you think?"

I roll my eyes, sliding one earring through my ear and moving on to the next.

Earth-shattering? I never said it was earth-shattering.

It was so fucking earth-shattering.

I could ride that man's long, thick fingers every day and twice on Sundays.

"Do you want to keep him, Brooke?"

My head whips right. *Keep him? Is that what he just said?*

"Are you high right now? Do we have weed in this condo I'm not aware of?" I step closer, my voice lowering as my eyes shift around the room. "No, seriously, do we? I could really use some."

A few hits would surely mellow me out a little.

Of course, if I knew what to expect tonight, I wouldn't be so wound up and wired. Sex doesn't make me nervous. I own that shit. I can work it in my sleep if I have to. But dinner and the unknown with a man who would rather talk than fuck?

What am I supposed to do with that? How am I supposed to

prepare for *that*?

Joey laughs under his breath. "When was your last actual boyfriend, Brooke? College?"

"High school," I answer, picking at my thumb nail. "I played the field in college. Literally. I think I was one defender short of bedding the entire lacrosse team."

Joey punches his fist into the air. "Go Blue Demons."

"Why?" I stick my hand on my hip. Joey trains his eyes on the ceiling, obviously avoiding.

"Mason isn't my boyfriend, Joey. I'm not in a relationship with this guy."

He wiggles his body, settling between two pillows. "Then what are you doing spending time with him?"

"Hello!" I slap my thigh.

What, has he suddenly been living under a rock? He knows exactly why.

"I'm trying to have sex with him! In order to do that, I have to talk to the guy a little. Share some personal shit. Build a friendship. Then, and my God, will this be so worth it, I get to feast on that glorious appendage I'm actually concerned might not fit inside me."

"Shut up," Joey spits, grimacing. "How many dicks have you had? There's no way you aren't well prepared for a third leg."

"Joey."

I hold my hands out, measuring a very, *very* impressive distance between the two.

My mind becomes flooded with flashbacks, images of Mason working that gorgeous piece of flesh behind a curtain of water and steam.

He was so raw in that moment. Stripped down to the point of depravity as he sought his release. As he pursued it with urgency. Beautiful. God, he was beautiful standing there, the muscles of his back and shoulder working simultaneously. His head bowed as he slowly unraveled. The sound of skin moving over skin.

I wanted to watch him come.

I wanted to *feel* him come.

I still do. Now, maybe even more. I'm like a child who has been told they can't have any candy.

Fuck that. I want that candy.

In my mouth.

Joey slowly sits up, mouth falling open, drool pooling on his tongue. He looks from my hands to my face, back to my hands again.

"You're exaggerating."

"I would never."

"He's *that* big? How is he walking?"

My phone beeps on the dresser. I shrug, turning around and padding across the room.

"How the hell do I know how you boys manage to tuck and move?" I ask, swiping the phone and staring at the unknown number glowing on my screen.

"Shit. You might want to pop some Ibuprofen before you go down that road, or sit on an icepack. Numb it up a little. I've heard about cases where you ladies rip something. That can't be pretty."

I chuckle at Joey, storing away his advice because I may seriously need to consider some sort of preparation when that time comes. I've been with my fair-share of well-equipped men. I've had a few surprise me when that zipper comes down. But Mason . . .

He might take the cake on this one.

Oo, cake. I'll definitely be ordering dessert tonight.

I move my thumb over the screen, bringing up the text message.

Unknown: Hello, gorgeous. Do you want me to come up?

I slowly lift my eyes to Joey.

He's sitting on the edge of the bed, giving me a look that tells me exactly who gave Mason my phone number.

Why am I surprised?

He stands, stretching his arms above him. "He was adorable asking for it," he mumbles before exiting the room.

Adorable. I'm sure. Lots of 'yeahs'. Numbahh. Even I would've given it to him once he started talking.

I program Mason's number into my phone and quickly type my response.

Me: Stalker. Do you know my blood type yet?

Mason: Working on it. Give me a few more days.

I chuckle softly.

Mason: What's your condo number? I'll come up. I feel like a tosser waiting for you out here.

Me: I bet you look sexy. A sexy tosser is better than a regular one, right?

Mason: Either way I'm an arsehole.

Me: Why?

Mason: This is a date. I should come to your door. Walk you out.

I step into my heels, typing with one hand.

Me: Relax. I'll be out in a second.

Lord, the manners on this guy. Is he always like this?

The last time I was picked up at my door for a date was prom. Most guys are too busy tuning to their favorite Pandora station to bother getting out of their vehicles. Or, I don't give them the opportunity and insist on meeting them out somewhere.

The end of the night though, that's a different story.

Men will almost always walk a woman to their door. They want that invite inside. The open door offer of sex.

"I had a lovely evening. Would you like to see my mattress? It's a feather-top."

Sticking my phone into my clutch, I grab the gift bag and exit the bedroom.

Joey is standing in the kitchen, watching Billy cook something on the stove-top, his chin resting on Billy's shoulder, his arms tightly curled around his waist.

Cute. They're so domestic.

They both turn their heads at the sound of my entrance.

"You look hot, Brooke. Where are you and Mason going? Do you know?" Billy holds a spatula in one hand. His other arm wraps around Joey's back.

I keep moving toward the door. I feel like I'm on autopilot.

"No idea. Somewhere with food. Hopefully a place that serves up a little under the tablecloth action."

God, wouldn't that be fantastic? A repeat of the other night as an appetizer. Mason's massive cock for dessert.

It's a wonder I'm not sprinting out of the building.

I wave a hand over my head. "Don't wait up!"

The door closes behind me. I take the elevator down to the bottom floor and push through the revolving door.

Mason is parked at the curb, his tall frame leaning against his car. He's dressed in dark jeans and a black fitted shirt with a collar. His hair is wet, a few curls spilling onto his forehead. The rest is haphazardly combed back.

He straightens when he sees me.

As I move closer, I can see that he's shaven. His smooth, chiseled jaw is free of stubble.

He looks younger.

He looks edible.

He closes the distance between us with two long strides.

I want him to grab me and kiss me. I want him to throw me down and man-handle me in front of anyone and everyone.

Tear my clothes. Take me with desperation. Press those dirty words he likes to spill against the soft skin of my thighs.

Instead, with what has to be the sweetest smile I have ever seen, he bends and lightly brushes his lips against my cheek.

"You look beautiful, Brooke."

I inhale a lungful of his cologne before he leans away.

Yum.

With the hand holding my clutch, I motion in front of me. "Thank you. I like this get-up you got going on. You clean up nice."

His smile gentles. "Shall we?"

We move together across the sidewalk, his hand resting lightly on my lower back. He opens the door for me and I climb inside.

"What's that?" he asks, poking a finger at the gift bag in my lap after he settles in his seat.

I look down at the top of the bag. A fuzzy ear peeks out between tissue paper.

Oh, my God. What am I doing? What grown man wants something like this?

I quickly stow it on the floor by my feet. "It's stupid. Sorry. I . . . I was out, and I saw it and I wasn't thinking and bought the damn thing. But now I'm realizing how dumb it is."

"Can I have it?"

"What?" I turn my head. His hand is outstretched. Did he not hear me?

"Really, Mason, it's stupid. You'll think it's stupid."

"Did you buy it for me?"

"Yes."

"Well . . . give it up then. It's mine, isn't it?"

He doesn't drop his hand. It hangs in the air between us as he moves his attention between my face and the bag he could very easily grab if he wanted. It's within his reach.

But he waits for me to pick it up and pass it to him.

I look straight ahead at the busy street. No need to watch this humiliation unfold.

Tissue paper rustles as he digs into the bag.

My hands knot together in my lap. "I saw it and it made me laugh. You don't have to keep it. Really. I think I still have the receipt somewhere in my room."

A muffled, barely audible chuckle comes from my left.

"My nemesis. We meet again."

I turn my head and watch Mason study the small stuffed koala with engrossed curiosity. He probably thinks I'm strange for giving him a children's toy.

I am! He's not a toddler. Why did I think this was a good idea?

I want to look away. I need to before I end up fleeing the vehicle, but I can't stop watching him stare at this thing as if he's actually charmed by it.

He runs his hand over the fur between the ears, chuckles again, then pats it gently on the head.

We lock eyes.

"It's dumb," I tell him.

"It's not."

"You don't have to keep it."

"I'm going to keep it."

He sets the bag and koala on the floor behind my seat, then captures my lips in a fleeting kiss. "Thank you," he murmurs against my mouth before leaning back.

"Mm. Yeah, sure."

My shoulders drop with a heavy sigh as we pull away from the curb. I didn't realize how tense I was during that inspection.

Serves me right.

Mason stares straight ahead while he drives, keeping one hand on the wheel and the other on the console between us. "Do you like Italian food? I saw this spot the other day when I was driving around. Giovanni's. You ever been?"

I search my memory. The name doesn't sound familiar. "No, I don't think so. But I like all food. You really can't screw up here."

He reaches for my hand, confidently holding it between us.

The conversation with Joey in my bedroom from minutes ago plays back in my mind. Him, accusing me of dating Mason. The underlying implication that he's my boyfriend. The ridiculous 'do you want to keep him' question.

My stomach clenches.

I pull my hand away and go for the stereo, turning up the volume. A song I don't recognize fills the car. The guy sings about love and wanting. I hate it immediately. I go through all of Mason's pre-programmed stations, trying to find something I like, but also, keeping my hand busy and not idle in my lap.

"You all right?"

I give him a quick glance. His eyes are serious. "Yeah . . . yeah, I just wanted to listen to something. I like background noise. I always have music playing in my car when I drive. It's comforting."

He seems satisfied with that explanation and turns back to the road ahead.

"Is the restaurant far from here?"

If it's more than a few blocks away, I'm totally screwed. I'll look like I'm having a nervous breakdown if I scroll through stations for more than a minute. Maybe I can adjust his audio settings? The bass does seem a bit overpowering.

"Ten minutes," he replies.

Shit.

I adjust the balance, the treble and base settings. I change the station again when a song by The Fray seeps through the speakers.

I do not need to hear their shit right now.

Mason's hand circles my wrist after a few minutes of this madness. "Why do you keep fading the music to the front or rear speakers only? What are you doing?"

I hesitate responding. I'm a horrible liar.

"Um, just . . . I'm just trying to give you the best listening experience. Relax. I know what I'm doing."

I have no idea what I'm doing.

"Brooke."

We stop at a red light. I look over at Mason, and suddenly feel guilty for pulling away from him. He doesn't look angry, or annoyed, or even like a person who just witnessed an act of insanity.

His eyes are tender, full of understanding.

I feel like I want to crawl under my seat and hide. I can't remember the last time I felt this uneasy.

"I don't have to hold your hand," he tells me, smiling ever so slightly. "I wanted to, but I don't have to. You can go easy on my audio settings. It's okay. Really." He moves my hand back to my lap and releases me, only to rest his hand on my thigh. "But, I do want to touch you somehow while I drive. Just a little." He gazes at my body. "God, you look incredible. I'm trying to be decent and not throw you in the back, but it's bloody torture with you in this skirt." He slides his hand a bit higher, inching it closer to the apex of my thighs.

Throw me in the back? Yes! I want that! Screw decency!

I suppress a moan, trapping it on my tongue. I don't want to sound too anxious, even though I'm close to jerking the wheel and pulling us off the road, which will in turn free him up to focus solely on me.

He gives my thigh a gentle squeeze. My toes curl. Desire

blooms low in my belly.

"Did you wear this so I could slide my hand between your legs? I think you did. I think you wanted to drive me a little mad, yeah?"

I watch the path his hand is taking. "Yeass," I breathe. My mouth falls open.

Yeass? Did I really just combine yeah and yes? *Think before you speak, Brooke!*

He chuckles as the car rolls forward.

I try and spread my legs, grant him access, ease the ache I'm feeling that's now pulsing with a demanding rhythm, but my legs are pinned together, restricted by the form-fitting motherfucking material of my bloody skirt.

I grunt in frustration, until I remember the use of my own hands.

Do I mind sitting bare-assed in Mason's vehicle? Nope. Not one damn bit. And now would be the worst possible time to start feeling shameful about anything.

I grip the hem of my skirt and ease it up my legs. I'm expecting Mason to dive right in, but before I can reveal the fact that I'm going commando under this thing, he slides his hand in the opposite direction it needs to be going and thwarts my progress, smoothing out my skirt and resting his hand back on my thigh, closer to my knee, far, far away from where I need him.

"What? Come on. You can't be serious." I turn my head. His hand goes stiff when I try and pry it off my leg. "Give me your hand. I want to hold it."

His profile lifts as he stares ahead at the road. "Yeah? You want to hold it?"

"Yes."

"With what? That sweet little cunt you were just trying to show me?"

I gape at him. *Good Lord. Did he just say . . .*

That accent, paired with anything even remotely filthy is enough to put me in the record books as the first woman in history to ever have an orgasm without any touching. I am now officially the wettest I have ever been in my entire life. No panties? What a dumbass decision. If I get up and there is a damp spot on this seat,

I'm never showing my face around this man again.

He briefly looks at me. "Well?"

I shoot him a steely look. "You have no proof of that. Maybe I just remembered how much I liked holding your hand . . . with my hand, pervert. Okay? Maybe I miss it."

He squeezes my thigh. "I think I'm going to keep it here. I like it here."

I slump back against the seat like a child on the brink of a tantrum. "Fine. I like it there too, so . . . whatever. Do what you want. I don't care."

I drown out his laugh by cranking up the volume on the stereo again.

BY THE TIME WE PARK and walk to the restaurant, everything south of my waist seems to be back in check. I'm no longer ready or willing to beg for some sort of physical contact. And fuck! I should be the one driving him crazy with lust. Teasing him. Making him so fucking hard he can't see straight.

Well, the night is young, and I plan on regaining some of my feminine power and working him up. If he thinks he's getting through this meal without getting an erection, he's sorely mistaken.

Giovanni's is a dimly lit restaurant in the heart of the city. I was right, I've never been here, and I think that's because it is a lot fancier than any place I'm used to dining at. Mason checks us in under our reservation while I admire a piece of artwork on the wall. My nephew can manipulate a paint brush and create something similar. Three colors congregating in one messy swirl. I'm betting this thing costs more than the rent I couldn't afford in my old apartment.

We're seated at a table draped with a white, crisp linen by a large window. A small vase containing a beautiful arrangement of flowers sits in the center, which Mason quickly slides to the side so that we can see each other better.

I admire the mural painted on the ceiling. The chandelier lighting. The attire of the wait staff.

"This might be the nicest restaurant I've ever been to. Are you trying to get laid?"

Mason glances up from his menu. I immediately lose the smirk when he doesn't mirror my playfulness.

Shit.

A deep frown settles between his brows. He looks put off. "No. I thought it looked nice. I wanted to take you here the moment I saw it." He pauses, leaning back in his chair. "I'm curious, Brooke. Do you always go out to eat with the expectation of sex afterwards? Do you never just sit and talk with someone? Learn about them?"

My face heats. I swear the temperature in the room spikes ten degrees in this moment.

Hello, mouth? Let me introduce you to my foot. Go ahead and eat it. You'll be doing me a solid favor.

I grab my menu and flip it open. My gaze lowers. "No. Of course not. I was just making a joke. I've never been anywhere this nice before. I think the atmosphere is making me nervous or something."

Or, its you. The way you look at me. The things you say. That could be it.

He taps his menu against mine.

Our eyes meet, and the moment he smiles, maybe a bit apologetically, I forget all about my secret agenda to tease him and get him hard underneath this table. The way Mason is looking at me . . . it's sweet, and candid, and maybe I've never had a man take me to dinner without the expectation of sex, but I don't want to admit that, and I'm also bizarrely happy Mason isn't doing this for that same reason. I no longer want to take away from the conversation or anything else this dinner will entail.

And I also don't want to think about how strangely okay I am with that revelation.

He jerks his chin, motioning for me to pick out my dish.

I resume looking at the menu, really focusing in on the words in front of me for the first time since I opened it. Everything is in Italian. Even the drinks.

What the . . .

My gaze travels the length of the menu, right, then back to the left. My eyes narrow. I lean closer. I have no idea what I'm reading. Well, not reading. Reading implies understanding, and that's definitely not what's happening here. It's more of a guessing game, really. Maybe when the waiter arrives I can just point to the cheapest entrée and hope for the best?

Mason must sense my confusion. I'm sure it's obvious, I'm close to flipping this thing upside down and taking a go at it that way. Or pulling up Google translations on my iPhone. But before I have a chance to do any of that, my menu is stripped out of my hands.

"Hey," I protest.

Mason smiles, almost wickedly, folding the menu in front of him. "What do you like? Pasta? Seafood? Do you want a chicken dish?"

I shoot him a puzzled look. "Um . . . yeah, sure, I like pasta and seafood. I like pretty much anything except for eggplant."

The waiter arrives at our table. I sit back in my chair and watch, stunned, as Mason, who up until this moment was already killing me with his accent, fires off our orders in perfect Italian.

Holy. Fuck.

There's no stutter, no uncertain pause as he trips over a word or two. It's beautifully fluent, hot as Hell, and I'm melting in my seat at this surprising man across from me.

Seriously? Is there anything he's not amazing at?

Yoga. Being a decent person. Consuming large quantities of treats and still managing to look like a sex God.

The waiter steps away. I pry my mouth off the floor.

"You're not really playing fair," I say after I collect myself.

Mason looks at me thoughtfully, concealing his possible understanding of what I'm referring to. "What do you mean?"

"You just completely blew me away by speaking Italian. I was not expecting that."

He limply shrugs.

No big deal. Mastering a language is apparently second nature to this guy.

He runs his finger over the edge of his perfectly folded napkin. "I was a bored kid. My oldest sister visited Italy one summer, and I got into her language books she left behind. I spoke it better than she did by the time she got back."

Our drinks arrive, and I gulp two mouthfuls of wine before I can ask my next question.

"You taught yourself another language? How old were you?"

"Fifteen."

"Fifteen? Mason, that's insane," I chuckle.

He snickers, picking his own glass up for a taste. "Is it?"

"Yes. Do you know what I was doing when I was fifteen? My entire world revolved around cheerleading and boys. I hated school. You couldn't pay me to learn a language. That is . . ." I pause, leaning back in my seat.

Who is this guy?

"That's amazing. You are amazing."

He looks across the table, staring at me with an unreadable expression, stretching out the silence between us by holding up his finger when I open my mouth to speak.

My lips pinch together. I fidget with my hands in my lap, counting the seconds. I hate silence. I especially hate it when I have absolutely no idea what the other person is thinking.

And Mason is a vault right now. He's not giving anything away.

Finally, after swallowing a mouthful of wine, he speaks. "Sorry. I have no idea what all you just said. I stopped listening after you mentioned something about you being a cheerleader. And then I spent all that time just now picturing it."

Heat burns across my face. "Ah, you like that, do ya?"

He nods.

"I did it through college. I was an all-star."

"Do you still have the uniform?" he asks above his glass.

Yes.

"Maybe."

"You should wear it for me sometime."

YES.

"Maybe."

Now Mason is the one smirking, but this smirk is dangerous. One hundred percent alluring. A hunter who doesn't need to chase his prey. They come walking right over to him, ready to hand over their destiny without question. Without pause.

I would run at him. I am talking a full-blown sprint. There would be no walking in his direction.

"Do you like to camp?"

His rapid change of subject rips my mind out of the gutter. I had been thinking about sitting on that smirk of his.

I shake my head through a laugh. "Camp? Seriously? As in sleeping outdoors with bugs and wild animals? No showers. No toilets. Just you and nature? Is that what you're talking about?"

He smiles. "That's the textbook definition of camping, yes."

"Then no. Not at all. But you know what I do like? Air conditioning. Civilization. Beds. I love beds."

"Beds are good."

I rest my chin on my hand. "Aren't they? God, they're so good. I'm not restricted to beds though. I can work with anything."

Mason lifts an eyebrow.

I can go into detail, right now, about how I'd like to explore beds and *anything* with Mason, but his line of questioning intrigues me. Of course, he looks like Mr. Nature-lover. I'm sure he is very fond of camping. Hiking. Saving the world one rainforest at a time.

"Let me guess. You're an avid camper."

He takes another sip of his wine, then nods. "I enjoy it. I haven't been since I lived out in Texas, but I would love to spend a weekend outdoors with you."

Well, that's completely unexpected. And insane.

I throw my head back with a laugh. Tears brim my eyes. "Sorry but . . . yeah, there's no way I'm sleeping outside. It's not happening. I don't do bugs, Mason. I don't have any desire to sleep on the ground where a snake can work it's slimy way into my tent and strangle me to death."

His eyes flash with amusement. "How big is this snake?"

Nice. Perfect set up.

I hesitate responding, tilting my head, watching as he catches up to my filthy mind. His eyes train on my lips, move lower down the line of my neck, then snap back up as if he's just been awakened from a trance.

I love these moments when I catch him staring at me like this.

As if he's fighting the biggest temptation of his life by not touching me.

Fuck though, touch me! This doesn't need to be a struggle for you!

He clears his throat. "You'd like it with me," he states confidently. "I'd protect you from bugs and the snakes you *don't* want around. Trust me. You'd have fun, yeah? We'd lay out under the stars. Share a sleeping bag."

"I'm listening."

"That interest you?"

"Sharing a sleeping bag? Tightly pressed together? Yes. Do you sleep naked?"

He doesn't answer that question. Just slowly grins at me. "Do you?"

I match his expression, only, I can't simply teeter the line of flirtation. I jump right over it.

I lean forward, running my hand down my leg, angling my body down the slightest bit until Mason takes notice of my cleavage. I play with the chain hanging around my neck, which just so happens to tickle between my breasts. He doesn't remove his gaze, and my nipples quickly harden under his scrutiny. Then I slowly sit back, crossing my one leg over the other, waiting until he looks up at me before I leisurely raise my glass to my lips and taste my wine. His eyes flare with desire as my tongue licks the residue from the corner of my mouth.

The longer we stare at each other, the wetter I become.

I never realized how sexy silence can be. How hot I could get from unspoken words, or the idea of something as personal as someone's sleeping habits.

Boxers, I decide. He looks like a boxers guy. No shirt. His lean body modestly concealed, stretching against the sheet.

I subtly tug at the bottom of my shirt below the table. My breasts swell. More skin is revealed.

Mason clears his throat.

I have no idea if he is growing hard in his jeans, until he drops a hand to his lap and inhales sharply through his nose.

My smile broadens. His disappears entirely.

But just like that, the aura around him shifts. All signs of a man starving to throw me on top of this table and feast vanishes the second our plates arrive.

I glare at the waiter. *Can you let the chef know his promptness is annoying?*

He merely smiles at my silent instruction, murmurs something in Italian, and steps away.

I look down at the dish placed in front of me. Seafood pasta, with scallops and shrimp over a bed of linguini. Mason's plate has a lobster tail, a generous cut of steak, and some greens on the side.

Everything looks incredible. I was set on climaxing before I dined but I suppose it can wait.

I twirl some pasta onto my fork and bring it up to my mouth.

"I always sleep naked, Brooke," Mason mumbles quietly.

I nearly drop my fork.

Oh, you gorgeous bastard.

He laughs around his bite of steak as our eyes meet. He looks delighted, reveling in my reaction and clearly thinking he's won this round.

Did I mention how much I love a little friendly competition?

I shoot him my sweetest, most innocent smile as my mind begins calculating my next move.

Silly man. You have no idea who you're up against.

Chapter Eight

Mason

DINNER WITH BROOKE IS . . . interesting, to say the least.

I've never watched a woman so completely focused on my undoing before. So casually sexual with every little movement and shift of her body. Fucking brilliant, on her part. I'm finding it hard to concentrate, which I believe is her every intention. She's had to repeat a question or two. My voice has grown a bit thick at times, leading me to tug at my already unbuttoned collar. I've thought about every way I could possibly get her off at this restaurant, how concealed I would be if I were to crawl under this table and feel her orgasm against my tongue. After thorough investigation of the white cloth stopping well off the floor, my horny arse remains planted in my chair.

What she's doing, it's calculated, and fucking torture not to react to. I can hide my erection but I can't keep that bloody thing under control. Even the placement of her hands while I speak of my classes from earlier today is suggestive.

"I think I've established a good client base," I tell her, tossing my napkin on the table. "I'm seeing some familiar faces come around now and pop in again. That's encouraging. I was worried about that."

Her fingers brush against the smooth dip between her collarbones, then trail lower, openly teasing the swell of her tits.

Fuck. What I wouldn't give to bury my face in there.

She grins. "I don't know why you were worried. I hate exercising and enjoyed your class. Not just the view either."

Her voice remains completely neutral, friendly, delightfully engaged in this conversation. That's the only thing about her that isn't screaming for me to bend her over that chair she's sitting in and fuck her senseless.

I discreetly adjust my cock, again. I'm surprised I'm still able to form coherent responses at this point. There can't be much blood flow still heading to my brain.

"You should come to another one," I suggest, keeping my hand in my lap, a smile tugging the corner of my mouth.

Her eyes dance with mischief. She drinks the last of her wine. "That's a fantastic idea. I would love to *come*."

And there's that. So much for innocent banter. I walked her and my throbbing cock right into that one.

Brooke chuckles, arching her back to gather her hair over one shoulder, pressing her chest forward, watching me watch her, because unless this building caught on fire right now I'm not looking anywhere else.

"How old are you?"

My eyes snap up to hers. I almost laugh. She goes from suggesting I get her off to verifying my age? How adorably odd.

"Twenty-nine. You?"

"Guess."

This time, I do laugh, nodding at the waiter as he returns with my credit card and slip to sign. I shake my head. "I have seven sisters, Brooke. I know better than to guess a woman's age, and I rather like my testicles. How about you just tell me."

"Oh, come on," she chides. "Aim low."

"Sixteen."

"What?" She clamps a hand to her mouth, muffling her laughter.

I sit back in my chair after signing the slip, watching the vibrant glow move over her cheeks as she slowly eases her hand away.

"Be serious." She pinches her lips together, fighting the playful smile threatening.

I shrug, standing and offering her my hand. "You said guess. I did. Now, please fill me in on your actual age before I start feeling like a pedo."

She allows me to help her to her feet and we move together through the restaurant. Her elbow gently connects with my side. "Mm. Nah. I rather like you squirmy and nervous like this. Shame on you for taking out a minor and shoving booze in her face."

"Brooke," I press.

"Really, Mason. What will my parents say?"

We step outside and I freeze on the footpath. She spins around to look at me.

I reach for my keys, shrugging. "All right then. I was planning on driving around and finding a dark spot so I could plant my face between your legs. But, I suppose that's off now. I should get you home. It's probably past your curfew and I'm not interested in finding out what prison is like."

"Twenty-five." She grabs my wrist, tugging me closer until we're chest to chest, her breaths suddenly coming hurried. "I'm twenty-five. Legal. Very much a fan of dark spaces and heads between my legs. Yours, specifically. I'm sure it looks lovely down there." Her body vibrates with a quick burst of laughter.

As I slide my hands to her hips, she keeps her head down, staring at my chest, my neck, almost bashfully trying to avoid my eyes while her hands tease the bottom of my shirt.

I like her like this, gentled, and what seems to be a bit unconventional for her. I like imagining that Brooke's only been this way with me, and that maybe I make her feel a bit undone and out of sorts, unsure of what's possibly happening between us.

I bend to kiss her forehead. "Shall we find that spot then? I want your taste in my throat."

She seems to weave a bit on her feet, then mumbles a hoarse, "yes," taking my hand and leading me down the footpath.

I slowly slide my fingers between hers as we pass a few shops, and my Denali. *Interesting.* "Have something in mind?" I ask.

She seems on a mission to get me somewhere specific. Determination leading her, along with desire.

Her shoulder jerks the slightest bit. "Maybe."

She smiles at me. The moonlight slides across her face, a shadow pooling in her dimple.

"I was here a few months ago, down in this part of the city with Dylan and everyone. Juls and her kids were there. Anyway, we took them to this place down the street a bit and I'd like to go there with you."

"Yeah?"

I can't hide the delighted lift in my voice, the overwhelming warmth that seems to spread up my spine.

This seems pretty personal for her. I *want* personal with Brooke. Every tiny detail of her life, bottled up and given to me.

"It's not anything special."

And there goes that glorious feeling. I run a quick hand through my hair.

Right, mate. Just relax on her a bit.

She clears her throat. "It's funny. When I was here before and used this thing I'm about to take you to, my mind was nowhere near the gutter. I mean, gross. There were kids around. That's pushing it even for me. But now?" She shakes her head, making a soft tsk sound as we cross the street. "Full-on filth. I'm almost a little nervous about this."

I straighten with intrigue, pulling her closer so I can slide my hand around her waist, so she can tuck against my side and I can feel the quick flutter of her heart against my ribs.

I press my lips to her hair. She smells like honey and vanilla.

"Sweet Brooke. I like you nervous. You get very honest with me."

Her head tilts up, brows pinched together. "What? When have I ever been nervous with you?"

She thinks I miss it, the way she peels back a layer of that impetuous exterior of hers to take a breath and slow down. The wide eyed look she seems to give herself, not me, confused and a bit cautious when I reach for her hand or get caught simply gazing at her. It's fleeting, yes. These aren't obvious moments with Brooke and she recovers from them quickly, but I see them.

My fingers splay along her hip. "The alley I kissed you in. Your shop practically every time I walk in there, more so the first time though. You seemed a bit flushed, yeah?" I smile at her. "I was too. I felt that kiss the entire day."

Her lips part, her eyes drop to my mouth. "Yeah," she says on a rushed exhale.

Not a question. She isn't asking me if I'm telling the truth, which I sure as fuck am. I'm honestly not sure if I've stopped feeling that kiss, or if I will.

She's agreeing with me. Another layer is exposed, and I want to keep her like this, open and unconcerned with revealing too much, too soon, too fast. I want her letting go and letting me have her secrets, being perfectly unashamed and trusting that I'll not only like every honest moment she gives me, I'll protect them for her.

But before I can ask her to elaborate on that single perfect word, Brooke presses her hand against my chest, halting our progression.

"This is it."

I look up at the building we've stopped in front of. The large sign set off in neon colors and strobe lights. The hordes of children scurrying in and out of the door with tickets and carnival prizes.

This is it? This is what she has in mind? I never would've guessed anything close to this.

I smile at Brooke, my hand circling around her back. "Are we playing skee-ball, gorgeous? I must warn you, I'm a bit competitive. I've never believed in letting a lady win simply because she's a lady. Nothing honest in that."

She stands on her toes, getting as close to my face as she can, her small hand sliding over my elbow to my bicep. "I'm going to let you in on a little secret, Mason," she murmurs, her breath hot and hungry against my jaw.

I smirk, tilting my head down. "Yeah? What's that?"

"I'm not a lady. Not even close. And I'm about to show you why." She grabs my hand and eagerly tugs me inside the arcade.

The large space is dark and noisy, awarding sounds from

machines mixing with the heavily bassed music pumping through the speakers. Children rush past us, alive with laughter and exuberance. Parents are lined up against the wall engaging each other in conversation while keeping an eye out.

I look around the room. I'm betting aside from the staff, Brooke and I are the only adults in this place who aren't here to chaperone.

What the hell does she have in mind bringing me here?

She leads me to the back of the room and down a long hallway. A young bloke wearing a name-tag steps through a doorway and moves in our direction, nodding at me before asking Brooke if she needs help with anything.

"Bathrooms," she more states than asks, alluding to her knowledge of their location. He takes her meaning and keeps moving in the opposite direction we head in.

The room breaks open. I spot the two doors indicating our destination, I veer right. Brooke goes left.

"This way." She curls a finger, beckoning me to follow.

I glance at the signs on the doors. Frowning, I make my way to her. "No toilets? I'm a bit lost here, Brooke. What are we doing?"

She smiles at me over her shoulder, waving her hand floppily in the air. "Bathrooms are a bit played-out, don't you think? Or toilets. Whatever you want to call them. Everyone fools around in bathrooms. I'm sure you have."

"No," I admit, a bit shocked at her suggestion. "Public facilities that probably aren't cleaned often enough? Am I missing the appeal?"

We stop just outside a small, nearly pitch-black room. Her eyes widen as she looks up at me. "Shut up. You've never done anything sexual in a bathroom before?"

I shake my head.

"Not even a little hj between mates?"

"Bloody hell." I lean back, searching her face, which is now alive with amusement. "A good wank between mates? Is that something you've witnessed in a toilet? 'Cause I sure as fuck haven't."

She giggles, dropping her head against my arm. "Well, I do live with two men. There's a lot of wanking going on in that condo. Semen flying everywhere. It's like a minefield getting from my room to the kitchen."

"*Excuse me*?"

What the fuck?

I've met both of Brooke's roommates. Nice blokes. Seem to be very much in love and fully committed to each other, which I assume means they aren't into sharing. But if I am way off here and they walk around whipping their cocks out around her, I'm going to have a major fucking problem with both of them.

Her laugh blooms to something louder, her small body vibrating against mine. She brushes her lips against my neck. "You seem worried. I'm kidding, mostly. Joey is terribly unashamed, much like myself, but Billy locks that bedroom door and keeps his private life very private. I haven't seen anything. Only heard."

"When are you moving out again?" I bend to kiss her. "Tomorrow?"

She rolls her eyes and pulls away, stepping into the room and swiping her hand along the wall. A light turns on in the corner. I follow her inside what appears to be another gaming room. Table games. Foosball, air hockey, pool. I'm shocked there aren't any kids back here. I know this is where I would be if I were their age.

"Apparently you can only rent out this room for birthday parties and stuff. It's not available to the people just here for the arcade. That's why they keep it separate," Brooke answers the silent questions circling in my head as she walks around the tables.

I take a moment to watch her.

Dark hair curling down her back. That tight black skirt, showing off her slim waist and perfect fucking arse. She turns to face me and I slowly lift my eyes, catching her smirk, knowing she's caught me staring at her and hardly caring. I think she rather likes it when I do that.

"Do you know what this is?" With a quick hand, she pushes back the red curtain of the photo booth she's stopped at in the back corner, then sticks that same hand to her hip. "I mean, do they have these in Australia or is this strictly an awesome American thing, like setting off fireworks on July fourth?"

With an intrigued smile, I step forward. "Ah, your pull from those bloody Poms. I'll celebrate that."

She tilts her head adorably. "Poms?"

"English. Brits. And of course we have photo booths. I believe they are quite popular at weddings and parties, yeah? People take pictures with silly props and what not."

"Sometimes."

I reach her, touching the smooth skin of her arm with the back of my fingers. My smile gentles. "What are we doing here, Brooke? Do you want to take photos with me?"

Something sharp gathers in the center of my chest, spreading down my limbs and prickling in my scalp. Is it possible she wants a keepsake from our night together? A piece she can store away and slowly build on?

The evidence of the beginning . . .

Fuck, it's staggering how badly I want it. How affected I am. She isn't the only one feeling out of sorts here.

Brooke steps inside the booth, which seems to be much larger than any of the ones I have ever seen before. I'm guessing you can fit groups of people in here instead of just one or two. Perfect for a large party of kids, I suppose.

Facing me, the corner of her mouth lightly pulls into a smile. "It's a dark spot. I'm hoping there's enough going on out there to keep the staff occupied for a bit." She holds out her hand to me. I don't miss the slight tremble in it. "I need ones. Got any?"

I stare at her, wondering if she's about to do something she's possibly never done before. If maybe this fresh, charmingly sexual woman wants to give me one of her firsts.

I'll take it.

I dig into my wallet and hand her a few bills. When I move to step inside with her, she presses against my chest, keeping me out.

"Watch for your photos. There." She nods at the slot on the outside panel.

I give her a wary look, but ultimately agree to this. Maybe she wants to give me photos of herself first before we take any together.

Too fucking right. I would love photos of Brooke.

I step back with a quick jerk of my chin. "All right."

The curtain is drawn. It stops a short distance from the bottom of the booth, completely obstructing my view of Brooke. I move to the side and press my back against the panel, waiting. A soft shuffling sound comes from behind the curtain, followed by a click, the shutter of the lens. Three more follow between long seconds, and I imagine her changing her pose, going from something innocent and playful to something a bit silly. Brief flashes of white light streak across the tile floor at my feet. I cross my arms over my chest, only to push away from the panel when I hear something slide into the slot behind me.

I pick up the sheet of photos.

Good God. Holy . . .

"*Fuck,*" I groan, my cock quickly lengthening as I stare at the four shots of Brooke; topless, pinching her rose colored nipples, licking and sucking the skin of her tits. Her pretty little arse turned toward the camera in the bottom shots while she fucks her pussy with two fingers. Over her shoulder, her eyes are round with abandon. Feverish and frenzied. Her red lips parted with a sigh or a moan.

She's giving me this. This gorgeous girl is giving me images of her body to not only admire, but to keep and stare at for later, stroke my cock to, do what I want with.

I wrench the curtain open and step inside, dropping the sheet of photos on the bench and grabbing her face after I conceal us.

She's still topless. Her skirt is still gathered at her waist, and she's panting, breathless from her own touch.

I slide my mouth against hers. "Jesus Christ, Brooke. You're trying to kill me, yeah? You sweet fucking thing." She answers with a moan as I kiss her jaw and suck on the skin beneath her ear. Sugar sticks to my tongue. Gripping her arse in my hands, I groan against her neck. "You taste so fucking good. Like one of those bloody cupcakes you make."

"It's my body lotion. Vanilla cake batter. It's edible."

"Fuck. Don't tell me that." My groin throbs against her belly. I pinch my eyes shut.

Stay focused, mate. You don't want to rush with her.

Brooke giggles against my ear. "Why not? I'm wearing it for you. Lick away."

I lean back and bring her hand to my mouth, drawing on the tips of her fingers.

"Mason," she whispers, moving in to kiss me, sucking her taste off my tongue. Pressing, pressing, harder. Her lips are soft yet commanding, and she tastes like her wine from earlier; a warm, ripe fruit. I bite her lip and she gasps, tilting her head back and brushing her heavy breasts against my shirt. She does the same to me, a quick bite of pain, and I groan, slapping her ass and relishing in the quiet shudder that ripples through her body.

Fucking hell, she likes it.

Her warm hands travel under my shirt and across my stomach, nails dragging against skin, fingers squeezing my hips and pulling me closer while her mouth slowly devours me.

"Filthy fucking devil. Sit. I want to kiss you here." I press my hand between her legs, my other palming her breast, roughly squeezing it.

She drops back onto the bench, meeting my eyes as I lower to my knees in front of her, as I spread her thighs open with my hands and settle my body between them.

"Were you wet before you touched yourself?" I ask, bending over her and licking between her breasts. I pull a nipple into my mouth and she arches her back, hands fisting my hair and breaths growing hurried and sharp. A whimpered *yes* catches in her throat when I drag my teeth across the hardened peak.

I know at any second someone could come walking into this room, see the bottoms of my legs, hear Brooke's quiet, aching noises and investigate behind the curtain.

What would Brooke do? Would she stop me? Cover herself up while I continue working her with my mouth? Maybe she wasn't only shaking when she stepped inside here because this is a first for her. Maybe she was thinking about the risk, doing this here when we can easily be somewhere more private, a room with four walls and a lock on the door.

I don't relish in the thought of anyone seeing Brooke, topless and coming against my face, but I want to give her this. Be the person she associates with this memory.

With a thick voice, she begins begging me with quiet words.

More and move and more and yes.

"How wet were you?" I ask her, kissing her ribs, her stomach, licking the skin of her hip. The sweetness from her lotion soaks into my throat, making me dizzy and delirious.

She tastes too good. Smells too good.

"V-very. It was dripping down my leg."

"Fuck, Brooke," I growl, ducking my head, meeting her gaze as I press my lips against the smooth skin of her inner thigh. "Here?" I ask, opening my mouth and sucking.

She nods, her lips parting, fingers digging into my scalp. "Higher too."

I smile against her. "Obviously. But I rather like kissing you here. Can I keep going?"

"Mm." She tugs gently on my hair. "No. Move up. I want you to taste me."

"I am."

I switch legs and slowly drag my tongue closer to her pussy, kissing and licking her skin. She never stops watching me, her hazel eyes wide and hungry, capturing and captivating me.

"Play with your tits," I tell her, blowing against her clit.

With a soft cry, she lifts and squeezes them, rolling her nipples between her fingers as I slide her legs to my shoulders. I press my nose against her clit and inhale, groaning, blinking up and seeing the awe bloom across her face.

She's beautiful; the way she smells, the way she tastes. That heavy look in her eyes as she watches me.

"Say something," she pleads, moving her hands over her breasts.

I take a slow lick, my eyes nearly rolling closed in ecstasy. "Mi stai rovinando."

You're ruining me.

Her eyes widen ever so slightly. "What does that mean?"

I open my mouth to tell her but she silences me with her fingers against my lips.

"Don't," she whispers, slowly removing her hand and bringing it back to her breast. "Don't tell me. I don't want to know."

There it is; that quiet panic lingering, never too far away when she begins to feel something unfamiliar or different. The little protective shield she slides into place until she senses it's okay and safe to let herself just fucking *be* with me.

I'll wait. Stand still or move, I don't care. I'll go where she goes.

Keeping my eyes on hers, I lean forward again and press my mouth between her legs.

Brooke drops her head back with a sigh, quietly crying, "oh, God." Her thighs tense in my hands while she openly gropes her breasts, her fingers twisting and pulling on her nipples.

I stay as unhurried as I can with my tongue, with my lips sucking gently on her clit. Teasing. Slow. Slower. Drawing this out, leisurely building her to the point of madness. I lick up one side and down the other, again and again. Ignoring where she is wettest until I can't fucking think straight, until I need her coating my mouth more than I need to fucking breathe.

I slide my hand up her stomach and over her ribs to palm her breast, rolling her nipple between my fingers. She gasps and lifts her hips against my mouth, rocking into me, seeking out her release with gentle, pleading circles.

"Put money in," I instruct.

Her eyes flash open, dark and cautious, but only for a second. Hurriedly, she grabs a dollar off the bench and leans over me to insert the bill into the slot. With a shaky breath she falls back and grabs my head, guiding me between her legs where I grin against her, moaning at the feel of her heels on my back.

Click.

"Mason," she whispers through the shyest, sweetest smile, knowing what all is probably being captured right now by the lens behind me; my head between her legs, her hands sliding up her body, over her bare breasts where she lifts and squeezes them, blissfully unashamed.

I add my fingers, two inside, stretching and fucking her, my teeth toying with her clit. She bucks against my face, hands pulling my hair and roughly scraping along my scalp.

Click.

I can't stop watching her; the smooth line of her body, her flat stomach quivering every time I dip my tongue inside to fuck her with it. Her perfect breasts, and the rapid heave of them as she slips closer to the edge.

Her whimpers turn into frantic words, begging me for more, for faster, to fuck her with my fingers again. To make her come. To tell her how she tastes and if I like it.

Click.

"So good," I assure her before adding another finger and twisting my wrist.

"I told you I could live here. Die here. I meant it," I don't say, for fear she'll pull back again, but I think it. I whisper it in my head as our eyes lock.

Hers, heavy-lidded and pleading for release.

Mine, so willing to give her this and anything. Everything.

I suck and suck on her skin. Her hands fall away from her body, slapping against the bench, and with a startled cry she falls, sweet and warm and perfectly. Lips parting with a gasp and a beg, one last word.

"Please."

Click.

Her fingers thread through my hair, pacing me while I go on and roughly devour her. I can't help it. Oral sex has never felt this intimate with a woman before, this profoundly carnal and I don't want to let up. I don't want to pull away and risk Brooke regretting any second of this. The haze of desire lifting and revealing how personal this moment was for her, allowing regrets and bloody protective shields to slip in and taint it.

"Mason," Brooke whispers, touching my forehead with two fingers.

With a heavy blink, I press one last kiss between her legs, then lean back enough to rest my head on her thigh.

I ready myself for it, the pull away, but the eyes I meet are tender and content.

She smiles lazily. "Holy shit. That was so much fun."

I suck in a burst of air, trapping it in my throat.

Goddamn. This one is full of surprises.

Tilting her head, Brooke laughs a little; a light, sweet sound.

"You are so fucking pretty." I reach up and touch her cheek, running the back of my fingers over her flush.

"I thought I was beautiful," she says, smirking.

"You are. There's no denying that." I kiss her thigh once more before standing and helping her to her feet, my hands smoothing down her skirt. I cup her face and bend to kiss her. "But after you come, you're softer, Brooke. Sweeter even. I can't explain it well, but I think you're more pretty in those moments. I like seeing you like that with me."

She turns and grabs her shirt and bra. "Make me come more often and you'll see it all the time."

A laugh rumbles in my chest as I help her, insisting on clasping her bra.

"These gorgeous fucking tits needs to be well secured. Here. Let me. I'm better suited for the job."

She giggles against my neck, moving her hands over my waist and under my shirt. "Taken a good number of bras off, have you?"

"Don't you worry about that."

I look around the booth as she slips her shirt on, tucking the photos she took for me into my pocket and glancing behind her to check the bench. "Where are your undies?"

Her eyes widen with amusement. She smiles. "What undies?"

I feel my mouth fall open. *The little minx*. "You mean to tell me you were naked under that bloody skirt all night and didn't tell me?"

Laughing, she draws the curtain back and steps out of the booth, retrieving the photos.

"Maybe."

I scratch my jaw, moving to her. "Fucking hell, Brooke. Had I have known, I wouldn't have shown that much restraint at the table. I probably would've gotten you off before our entrees were brought out. Why didn't you tell me?"

I nearly curse for keeping my wits about myself earlier on the drive to the restaurant. She was trying to show me she wasn't wearing anything underneath, hiking up her skirt like that, seeking my hand. I was too determined to keep her waiting and wanting.

Good on you, mate. Really fucked yourself with that one.

I touch her hip. She doesn't respond, not with a look or a word. With parted lips she studies the photos in her hand for several silent seconds. I can feel the slow drag of air pulling into her lungs and I slide my hand up her back. She releases it quickly and bites her lip.

"Look at you," I say against her temple, bending lower to see. I point at the shot of her coming. "Fucking perfect right there. Did you like it?"

She hesitates, then quietly replies. "Yes. I just . . . I wasn't expecting to look like that."

"Like what?" I can't read her face, the implication she's making. I step in front of her and run my hands down her arms, ducking to see her eyes.

She keeps them lowered for another few seconds, studying. With a flighty laugh, she brings the photo down between us and gazes up at me. "I don't know. Pretty, I guess? You were right. I do look different." She shakes her head, blinking several times, as if she can't believe what she's saying, or admitting. "It's strange."

I smile, wanting to kiss her, to talk to her more about what she's seeing, but I don't. Instead, I step beside her, my hand sliding to her back as I guide us through the room and toward the exit.

"Come on. Let's get you home and into some undies."

She laughs, curling against my side, giving me the okay to pull her closer.

And I do.

Chapter Nine

Brooke

I PRESS THE NUMBER SEVEN on the elevator panel a second before greedy hands tug me backwards and into Mason's arms.

I go willingly with a squeak, tilting my head as his lips suck gently on my neck, as he whispers just beneath my ear how tight I am, "so fucking tight," and how he nearly lost his mind in that photo booth. His fingers squeeze my hips, pinning me to him, to his rock-hard cock that's pressing against my ass.

Fuck, I want to see it. Touch it. Drop to my knees and feel his hands in my hair. This elevator ride is driving me crazy.

I glare at the numbers slowly rising to my floor.

Two. Ridiculously long pause. Three.

I nearly pout. *Could this shit take any longer?*

"What are you doing next weekend?" Mason asks me, breaking my attention off the electronic panel, sliding his hand to my breast and pinching my nipple through my shirt.

I gasp, rolling my head back as he twists my hardened peak. "*Jesus*."

His laugh rumbles against my back, sweet and cruel. He knows what he's doing.

"Are you going to be attending church, Brooke? I honestly can't imagine going to confess my sins and seeing you there. I think I'd end up just dragging you into the confessional with me and saying, 'Here. She's it. Give me my penance'." He releases my breast and slides his hand back to my hip.

I'm his only sin?

Whoa . . . that might be the best compliment of my life.

I resume staring at the numbers above me as the ache in my breast slowly subsides. I bite back a smile, saying, "I haven't attended church since I was a kid. Well, not regularly anyway. I go every Easter to appease my Nana but that's it."

"So, you're free next weekend?"

"I think so. Why?"

"I'd like to steal you away if you'll let me. Weather permitting."

The elevator finally comes to a stop and I pull away, peering back at Mason over my shoulder as I step out onto the floor.

He looks content, and so sure of himself, like he already knows I'm going to say yes to this.

"For the entire weekend? What exactly do you have in mind?"

With a cocky smile, he steps off the elevator. "It's a surprise."

I spin around, staring at the man slowly advancing on me, and it all clicks in an instant as our conversation from the restaurant trips my subconscious.

"Oh, no you don't." I hold my free hand up as I continue my slow retreat backwards. "*Weather permitting*? Busted. I told you. I don't do camping."

He feigns seriousness. "Who said anything about camping?"

"I'm not going! I'm busy anyway."

"No, you're not." Quickening his strides, he reaches out for me and grabs my arm. We both come to a stop inches from my door. "You just said you weren't doing anything."

"I said I *think* I'm free, but now that I really think about it, I remember I have plans. Ones that don't involve nature or mosquitos carrying the West Nile virus."

I wrench my arm away, ignoring his quiet laugh, and open my clutch to rustle out my keys.

Seriously? He is completely insane. You couldn't pay me to go spend the night out in the wilderness. Naked sleeping bag sharing, or not. There is no fucking way I am agreeing to this.

When I look back up to give him more shit, Mason is watching me, his scorching gaze torn between my lips and everything lower.

I forget about camping, or suggestions of camping. I forget about bugs and wild animals as I slowly drink him in, from his unruly hair, still disheveled from my fingers to his hands clenching and unclenching at his sides.

He's holding back.

Why? There's no need. Doesn't he know how badly I want this?

Anticipation plucks in my belly as I stare at the erection pressing hard against his zipper. As I remember what it felt like minutes ago, sliding between the cheeks of my ass.

Well, if he's not going to give it to me, I'll just take it. No problems there.

I drop my keys back into my clutch and fist his shirt, urgently pulling him until my back hits the wall just beside the door and his body has no other choice but to crowd against mine.

He moves willingly with a moan, his hands bracing himself on either side of my head, boxing me in.

I arch my back and press my hips out away from the wall, grinding into his stiff length. "Mm. You know I never got to properly thank you for what you did earlier with that wicked mouth of yours. I'm also very sad to admit I can hardly remember what your cock looks like. Care to whip it out and kill two birds with one very hard stone?"

With shaky hands, he grabs my waist and drops his head beside mine. "Brooke," he whispers, so faintly it's as if he's trying to resist everything at this moment, including words.

"My turn." I slide my hand between us and cup his length.

He hisses a curse against my ear.

"God, I forgot how big you are. You might actually kill me."

Turning my head, I claim his mouth, sucking on his lips, his tongue, pressing gentle kisses between ones that somehow feel more important or greater than any act of desperation. I lose my mind for a second, a stillness takes over and I allow myself to get lost in this kiss, forgetting about everything I want to come after and just giving in and giving up.

How does he do it? How does he make me want to just do *this* for hours and hours and hours? Sweetly surrender myself over to him and everything he makes me feel.

Shit. Snap out of it, Brooke. Remember why you reached for him.

I break away, panting against his mouth, watching him suck my taste off his bottom lip.

"Come inside, Mason, before I drop to my knees right here in this hallway. I want you on my bed while I suck your dick, but I'm not picky. Here is fine too."

I press harder against his jeans and he groans, his fingers digging into my skin, his arms locking up and trembling.

I go in for the kill, planting a kiss to his jaw and whispering, "think how good it'll feel fucking this pretty little mouth."

"Jesus Christ." He pushes against my waist and leans back, blue eyes blazing as he stares at me. His other hand comes around and grabs my wrist. "Baby, stop."

"Why?"

"Because . . ." he trails off, pinching his eyes shut as he gently removes my hand, forcing it against my side. He exhales a rigid breath. "Because, I want this to be about you." His eyes flash open, and there it is again, that struggle so obvious it's as if it's vibrating across his skin or flashing in neon letters above his head.

Please, Brooke. You're killing me.

I stare up at him, confused. *Why are you fighting this? I don't understand.*

His free hand glides up my arm, stopping just above my elbow where his thumb begins moving softly across my skin. "What I did earlier, it wasn't just so you'd return the favor. I would never think like that, Brooke. When I touch you in any way, it's because I *want* to touch you. Or I fucking need to. I'm not trying to get something in return."

I wet my lips, feeling slightly awkward for even insinuating that Mason was fishing for his own release by getting me off. But honestly, what man is that selfless to not even consider his own needs?

His hand forms to my cheek. "Stop thinking so much. Let me enjoy you."

"You can enjoy me but I can't enjoy you? That hardly seems fair."

"Brooke."

"Mason." I try to pull free from his grip, but his fingers wrap around me tighter, keeping my arm pinned where it is. I open my mouth, ready to argue, to ask nicely for the use of my hand when a thought settles over me.

Maybe Mason doesn't want to risk the chance of getting caught by another tenant, and that's why he's keeping me from very publicly groping him. Maybe what we did earlier in the photo booth was all the thrill he can handle for one night.

He wants privacy for everything I'm offering? I'm good with that. I don't need an audience to relish in every thick inch of this man.

I allow my arm to go limp, yielding to his hold. "All right. Fine, I get it. We don't have to do this here. And I was half serious offering it anyway. I'd rather not get rug-burn."

He watches me curiously as I lift my clutch between us.

"Come on. Joey and Billy won't bother us. They're most likely passed out already and they both sleep like the dead."

I go to spin around but Mason slides his hand back to my waist and keeps me facing him.

"I'm going to go."

"What?" I look up into his eyes, my entire body tensing. "You're leaving?"

Is he serious? Why would he leave?

A hint of a smile touches his lips. He bends down, brushing his mouth against mine. "Yeah," he mumbles, gently kissing me, barely even the feel of skin on skin.

It's more like the promise of a kiss, or the idea of one, when you think of something hard enough or for long enough it almost starts to feel real, blurring the lines of reality and fantasy.

He stays that close to me, never pulling away, staring into my eyes for the longest, most intense second of my life. His breath is hot and heavy against my face, quickened, but I have no idea from what, and as I slide my hand to the center of his chest, I startle at the wild beating against my palm.

"Mason." My voice sounds miles away, frantically chasing after him.

A growl rumbles in his throat. Then, as if something breaks inside of him, he cups my face and forces me against the wall, pinning me while his lips roughly take my mouth in a kiss that has me high and breathless and begging in incoherent words.

It's violent and vital, exactly how a kiss should feel, with greedy hands and pounding hearts.

I drop my clutch and hold him against me, tilting my head to deepen this, to give him more as I plead for it through whispered words, but the second my fingers tighten in his hair he breaks away.

His hands slide to my neck as he moves his lips to my cheek and keeps them there. "Goddamn, Brooke. It's really fucking hard not kissing you," he pants through ragged breaths, leaning back to gaze at me.

I give him an odd look as his hands slip away, and an even odder look when he turns around and leaves me lightheaded against the wall.

What the fuck?

With quick strides, Mason takes his sexy ass in the direction of the elevators, a hand disappearing around the front of him to no doubt adjust the stiff dick I just so rightly earned.

"Um . . . where are you going?" I call out, stepping away from the wall to get a better view of him continuing down the long hallway, to watch in complete shock as he puts more and more distance between us.

He was serious about leaving? No . . . no, he's . . . no, that's impossible. He can't just leave.

Hello! Massive erection! Get back here! I'm supposed to be handling you!

He smiles at me over his shoulder as he bypasses the elevators.

"Goodnight."

My mouth falls open. I bring my hands to my hips as I think of a reasonable explanation for his swift departure, and it comes to me at the sound of his keys jingling. "You're just going to move your car, right? Then you're coming back up? You're not actually leaving . . ."

He pushes the door open that leads to the stairwell, making no attempt to tell me I'm correct or to ask me if I'll wait for him here or leave my door unlocked.

He's actually leaving. He's taking his hard dick and he's *actually* leaving.

I take a few steps to follow behind him. "Is this a joke? Is this strictly an Australian thing, because here, in America, we don't kiss the fuck out of someone and then haul ass in the opposite direction."

I hear the faint sounds of a laugh echoing down the hall.

Before I can think to speak again, to yell out something else to possibly change his mind and end this madness, Mason steps out onto the stairwell.

"I'll see you later, gorgeous," he calls out before the door slams closed, and I know, I just fucking know that gorgeous bastard is smiling as he says it.

"What the hell?" I ask myself, God, if he's listening. Maybe he can shine some imperial light on this situation.

I snatch my clutch off the floor and fish out my keys, jamming them all too aggressively into the keyhole while I mumble every curse word I know into the deserted hallway. I shove the door open and toss my things onto the table behind the couch, kicking off my heels and moving like a bat out of hell across the room.

With a closed fist, I pound against the bedroom door until my skin grows hot.

"I need you both to put something on and get out here. Now. You will not believe what . . ." I cut myself off, shaking my head as I try and wrap my own mind around what just happened, but I have absolutely no idea what to think. I can't even begin to make sense of this.

Mason passes on a Brooke style blow-job? NOBODY passes on that. Is he fucking mental?

With a very aggressive grunt, I drop my hand and stare at the door. "Just hurry up and get out here. Please. I need both of you."

Muffled voices and the creak of a mattress sound before I feel satisfied enough to cross the room again.

I step into the kitchen and open the refrigerator, pulling out a bottle of wine and digging the container of ice cream I keep hidden under bags of frozen vegetables out of the freezer.

Joey likes to eat his feelings also. If I don't hide my snacks, they go missing.

I fill a glass and grab a spoon just as the bedroom door swings open.

Joey emerges first, his fingers snapping the waistband of his boxers. He looks half-asleep, digging the heel of his hand into his eye. "What the fuck is it? You interrupted cuddle time."

I shove a spoonful of Neapolitan ice cream into my mouth to prevent myself from stating the obvious response, that every time Joey and Billy are within twenty miles of each other, I run the risk of interrupting cuddle time.

Assholes. Their perfect relationship is a little hard to swallow at the moment. I'm sure neither one of them keep their dicks to themselves.

Billy files out of the bedroom next with his T-shirt in his hand. He eyes me warily once he takes notice of the wine and the container I have a death-grip on.

"Uh oh. What happened?" he asks, slipping his shirt over his head and sliding his arms through. "Bad date?"

I watch him and Joey each grab a stool and sit at the kitchen island across from me. Boosting myself up onto the counter, I place the container on my lap and dip my spoon in, scraping out the rest of the chocolate.

"No. The actual date was fine," I mumble around the spoon.

Joey drops his chin onto his fist. "Just fine?" He looks doubtful.

I roll my eyes before lowering them to the container. "More than fine," I confess, jamming my spoon into the vanilla. "He took me to this really nice restaurant where he had to order in Italian, which he fucking did, so just go ahead and tack on a few more 'how hot can this guy possibly get' points."

"Damn," Billy comments appreciatively. "I bet that sounds amazing with his accent."

"Mm hmm. Boyfriend is full of surprises," Joey adds.

I don't even bother looking up. "Yeah. Tons. So, we had dinner, and he mentioned wanting to stick his head between my legs and taste me in his throat."

I glance up at the sound of the wine bottle being slid across the counter.

Billy brings it to his lips and tips it back, his eyes round as he swallows a mouthful.

It's funny how squeamish he gets around any sort of graphic sex talk, when his husband is basically a walking advertisement for it.

I shift my eyes when Joey motions with a quick hand for me to continue on with my story. He suddenly appears wide awake and eager for conversation.

"You want details?"

"Yes," Joey says at the same time as Billy's, "Not really."

I split the difference. "He did more than just taste me, okay? I took him to this photo booth I found a couple months ago, and that man worked me out like his life depended on it. His mouth is fucking ridiculous."

A shiver runs down my spine as that familiar ache settles between my hips. I press the back of the spoon to my mouth, hoping to conceal the smile I can't seem to control.

"It was hands-down the best sexual experience of my life," I admit against the cold silver. "And that includes all the times I've actually had sex."

Straightening on his stool, Billy scratches his jaw, his other hand still clutching the neck of the bottle. "Photo booth? Did you two actually . . ." he pauses, his eyes searching my face.

Joey slaps the counter with exuberance. He looks practically giddy. "You little slut. Did you get pictures of this?"

I glance across the room at my clutch, remembering how reckless and exciting it felt being in that moment with Mason, not knowing who, if anyone, was on the other side of that curtain and if they were listening and waiting for those photos.

If they would see me, and how I looked at him. *With* him.

I return my gaze to the two men staring intently at me. "I gave Mason his own set of solo's to keep. That seemed to go over smashingly well. Then, while he was down there, going at it, he told me to put money in." I shrug. "I did."

"Where is this photo booth exactly?" Joey grabs the small pad of paper and the pen we keep by the phone, ready to jot down the address.

"Joey," Billy starts, waiting for his husband to look over at him. He jerks his chin. "No."

Joey shoots him a pleading look. "Oh, come on. You know you'd love it." He leans in for a kiss, hovering a breath away from Billy's mouth. "Just think of how cramped it probably is in there. How *tight* it would be. Mm. I bet there's hardly any room for you to move, but you like that, right? You like tight things, don't you, baby?"

Holy shit.

I shove a massive bite of strawberry into my mouth as Billy groans, pinching his eyes shut and dropping a hand to his lap.

"Brat," he murmurs, adjusting himself while he tries to look annoyed but only succeeds at looking immensely turned-on and on the brink of dragging his husband back to the bedroom.

Joey leans away, grinning and tapping his pen on the paper. "See? Do I know my man, or what?"

"You do. But let's get addresses later." Billy covers Joey's hand with his, forcing Joey to release the pen. He then turns his dissecting attention onto me. "Brooke, what are we missing here? Why are you binge-eating and nearly breaking down doors? What else is going on?"

I drop my spoon into the container and set it on the counter, exchanging it for my glass of wine. I lift it in the air, toasting. "Mason is withholding the dick."

"This is news?" Billy raises an eyebrow. "I thought he made it clear when you two first met that he wanted to wait to have sex. Get to know you and all."

"He did. But apparently, he wasn't just referring to sex."

Joey grabs the bottle of wine. "What else was he referring to?"

"Oh, you know." I sweep my hand through the air. "Everything. Touching it. Sucking it. Anything I could possibly do to get him off. The entire thing is a no-go apparently."

The bottle hovers in the air an inch away from Joey's mouth. He leans to the side to see me around it. "I'm sorry. What?"

I bring my glass to my lips, swallowing a generous amount of wine. "You heard me. After kissing my fucking brains out at the door, he walked away, refusing my offer to come inside . . . pun intended, and left, taking his glorious erection with him. He told me he wants this to be about me. That he didn't get me off just so I would return the favor."

"That's actually kind of sweet, Brooke. Unconventional, but sweet," Billy remarks, laughing quietly at Joey as he mirrors my reaction to this discovery and goes immediately for alcohol. Running a hand through his short blonde hair, Billy turns back to me with a gentle smile. "Name one other guy who has ever done that for you."

I let my eyes roam the condo, pretending to think, but I don't need to.

The truth is, I can't name anyone. I can't think of any man who has ever done half of the things Mason has insisted on or offered. If I could, this might not seem so completely baffling to me.

Why is he putting himself through all of this? He's taken every sexual release I have to give him off the table, and yet he's still fixated on me.

Why?

"Okay." Joey sets the bottle down and wipes the back of his hand across his mouth. "First of all, this wine is terrible. Let's never buy it again."

I quietly chuckle as I lift my head.

"Second, I can see this being a problem if you weren't getting off, Brooke, but you are. And although you refuse to admit this, I think you like this guy."

"But I don't understand him."

And for the first time in my life, I feel completely out of my league.

Joey crosses his arms against his chest, sitting up a little straighter, showing off his proud smile.

"What?" I ask, confused by his sudden disposition.

"You didn't argue with me that time. You like him."

"I like a lot of men who get me off. It doesn't mean anything."

Joey loses the smile and levels me with a skeptical glare. I look to Billy, only to find him mirroring his partner's demeanor.

Fuck this. I've had enough girl talk for one night.

With a heavy head and an exhausted mind, I hop off the counter, polishing off the rest of my wine and setting the glass in the sink. "I'm going to take a shower and go to bed. I can't think about this anymore tonight."

I wave a limp hand in the direction of my two roommates as I pad across the condo.

Billy starts to say something but I shake my head, cutting him off before I escape into my room.

MORNING COMES TOO SOON AFTER I close my eyes, and because of the restless night's sleep I'm suffering from, I arrive late to work for the first time in three years. Luckily, having chatty Cathy as my roommate pays off for me and I don't get much of an earful from Dylan when I step inside the bakery.

I'm sure she has been adequately filled in on the night I had.

"Sorry. Sorry. It won't happen again. I promise," I say, re-emerging from the kitchen after setting my purse down. I secure my unruly hair up into a pony and step behind the counter. "I don't think you want me doing any detailed piping work today. I'm running on about five minutes of sleep."

Dylan drops her head into a nod as Joey finishes up with a customer. "That's fine. Man the front with Joey. I need to be off my feet today anyway so I'm going to stay in the back. I can work from a stool."

"Are you feeling okay?" I watch her close her eyes through several slow, deep breaths.

My gaze shifts to the shop phone hanging on the wall.

Even though I've never had a reason to call it, I was forced to memorize Reese's work number when Dylan was first pregnant with Ryan. I wonder how quickly he could get over here if I called him right now.

I imagine before I have the chance to hang up.

The door chimes as the customer exits the bakery, and Joey comes to stand beside Dylan, resting a hand on her shoulder.

"I'm fine. It's not contractions or anything," she reassures, looking back at him and then pressing two fingers to the inside of her wrist. "I'm just feeling anxious for some reason. I think I should take it easy today."

"Then get your pretty little ass in the back, cupcake. I'm not dealing with that man of yours if you go into early labor due to work-related stress. I'm sure he'll somehow blame that shit on me." He guides her in the direction of the kitchen with a gentle push, then comes to stop beside me, dropping his head next to mine.

"Mason missed you at the coffee shop this morning," he murmurs. "I told him you were up late hitting the sauce."

"Did you really?" I glare at him as he leans away.

That's just what I need, Mason thinking he drove me to alcoholism. He's so fucking sweet he'll probably pay for my rehab.

He smiles. "No. I said you had to do an early delivery this morning and skipped the coffee. He seemed to buy it."

I gaze through the shop window. "I know I just got here but . . ."

"But you need to go talk to him."

Our eyes lock. I nod at his spot-on remark, rubbing my hand down my face. "I'm just so fucking confused, and I need sleep, Joey. My skin doesn't do well without it. I'm going to start looking like I'm in my thirties."

"Heaven forbid." Joey steps back and leans his hip against the counter, exaggerating his stare the longer I look at him. "Go, before Dylan comes back up here and discovers you're missing."

"Right."

I slip behind him and grab an empty bakery box, filling it with four cupcakes.

"Shut up," I snap when I hear Joey's breathy laugh behind me.

It's just because I need something to hold when I'm talking to Mason, otherwise I'll reach for him, hold his face, try and slip my fingers through his hair and feel his soft curls.

There will be none of that happening.

I hastily exit the shop and cross the street. Peering through the large studio window, I can see a class is in session, but that doesn't stop me from barging in with baked goods and a pissy attitude.

"We need to talk," I exclaim, stopping just inside the door and glaring at the twenty-plus pairs of eyes on me. I focus in on one set in particular, crystal blue and softened with curiosity.

Mason steps between mats to see me better, his faded, sleeveless tee darkened with sweat. "Can you give me five minutes, Brooke?"

I look at him, at the crowd of women and their irritated expressions. With a quiet sigh, I slip past the elongated table covered in brochures and vitamin supplements and perch myself against the wall. I hold the box against my belly, letting my eyes wander the studio.

"Whatever."

Class resumes. Mason goes through various positions and breathing techniques, offering assistance when some women struggle to hold a pose.

I reach into the box and bite into a strawberry ganache cupcake, smirking when a nosy chick in front of me scowls in my direction.

Fuck off, I think. *You have no idea what that man is putting me through.*

After the last attendee leaves and I swallow my last bite, Mason pulls the door closed behind him and stalks toward me. He tugs his shirt off with one hand and wipes it across his face.

"You wanted to talk?"

I take in his perfectly sculpted torso, from his lean hips to the muscles thickening his shoulders, every inch of him damp with perspiration.

"Yeah." I set the box on the table and lick the frosting off my lip. "What the hell is your problem?"

His steps falter. "My problem?"

"Don't do that." I point a finger at him, advancing closer. "Don't act like you have no idea what I'm talking about. I'm not allowed to touch you? I can't . . . do anything to you? Why not?"

"Brooke." He tosses his shirt on the table, reaching for me.

I step back to avoid his touch. "Answer my question first." He takes in a deep breath, and my next words slip out before I can stop them. "Is it me?"

Other women have touched him. Other women have done *everything* with him. Why can't I?

His eyes widen and he closes the space between us. "No. Fuck no, it's not you. Jesus. How can you think that?" He slides his hand to my hip, his eyes following his finger as he runs it along my jaw. "It's overwhelming how you affect me. Can't you see it? How I look at you? I'm a bloody wreck here, Brooke. I want to take my time with you, but fucking hell if I don't want everything you were offering last night."

"Then take it." I squeeze his hips, pressing us closer.

Take me. Stop torturing yourself.

"I won't be able to stop," he confesses, bending to kiss the corner of my mouth. "I'm not a God, Brooke. I only have so much restraint, and you on your knees sucking my cock would smash it all to shit."

"So you're just going to jerk off alone after you leave me? Come on, Mason. That's ridiculous. You could at least let me watch."

A small laugh erupting past his lips has me pulling away and out of his reach.

"This isn't funny," I snap, turning my body when he tries to grab me again.

I need distance anyway. He's half naked and those loose shorts he's wearing do a piss poor job at concealing every perfect inch of him.

He slowly advances on me with his hands raised between us, with that cocky smirk tugging at his mouth.

"Are you not enjoying what I'm giving you, Brooke? Because if I'm remembering correctly, you seemed pretty fucking happy grinding that sweet pussy against my face last night. There's pictures to prove it."

Warmth surges between my hips. I narrow my eyes and silently curse my lower region for reacting to that reminder. "You know what? I'm going to go."

His eyes snap up to mine. "Why?"

"Because I have work to do and you're making my brain hurt."

He grabs my waist before I can take a step. Pulling my back against his front, he drops his lips to my ear, whispering my name before he asks, "Are we still on for this weekend?"

I turn my head to look at him, biting my cheek to keep myself from reacting to the smug grin staring back at me. "I don't know. Am I going to be allowed to touch you?"

"In a matter of speaking. I'm sure your hands will be in my hair while you beg me to make you come. That counts, yeah?"

With a grunt, I pry myself out of his arms and gesture at the box on the table as I stride past it. "I ate one of your cupcakes because you kept me up all night, and not in the way I wanted to be."

"You kept me up too. Fucking that pretty little mouth was one hell of a visual. I came all over my sheets."

My mouth falls open. I nearly face-plant . . . again. *Bastard.*

"Yeah? Well, it's too bad I wasn't there to lick it all up for you. Good luck getting those stains out."

I push through the door with the biggest smile on my face.

Have fun with that visual.

I STARE INTO THE DARKNESS of my bedroom, pulling the covers up around me when the AC kicks on.

It's almost eleven, and I could be asleep. I should be. God knows I'm exhausted but I can't seem to close my eyes yet.

The condo is quiet. Joey and Billy have no doubt gone off to bed by now. I stretch my legs against the cool sheets before flipping onto my stomach and attempting to shut down in this position. Within a few seconds I'm turning back over and flopping my head against the pillow.

A soft buzzing sound pulls my attention off the window. I throw myself out of bed and grab my phone out of my purse.

Mason . . . facetiming me? How does this even work? Oddly enough, I've had this phone for two years and have never used this feature before.

I accept the call and hold the phone above me as I settle back against the sheet. I glance briefly at the image of myself in the corner.

Good. I don't look too rough. God knows I feel it.

Mason's neck appears first, bathed in the soft light from a nearby source. He tilts the phone and smiles when he sees my face staring back at him.

"Little devil. I didn't wake you, did I?"

I smirk at the nickname. "No. I'm actually having trouble winding down. I blame you for that."

"Yeah? Am I on your mind?" He adjusts the pillow under his head as his eyes shift about ever so slightly. "You look pretty."

I look at the tiny image of myself again. "Thanks."

"Do you know why I'm calling you like this?"

"Because you're a stalker and you needed a way to see my bedroom? You know, since you refuse to step in it."

He laughs, low and deep in his throat. I feel myself smile and the haze of drowsiness slipping away.

"Brooke."

"Mm."

"You wanted to watch me, yeah?"

"Watch you . . ." I pause, my hand tightening around the hard case of my phone as realization shocks my body into full-on alertness. "Yes," I reply through a quiet voice, running my tongue over my bottom lip and sitting up a little higher in bed.

On the screen, I watch desire pass over Mason's face. His heavy breathing spills through the phone and out around me.

My toes curl against the sheet.

"Are you doing it?" I ask, although I already know the answer. I just want to hear him say . . .

"Yeah." He jerks his chin, lips parted and eyes heavy. He shifts the phone away just enough for me to see the muscles rolling in his upper arm.

My breath catches in my throat. "God," I exhale on a shaky breath.

Watching Mason above me, as if he really *is* above me, does wild things to my mind. I imagine our bodies sliding together, the heavy drag of his cock along my skin, trapped between us, throbbing and wet from the heat of my mouth.

"My cock, Brooke," Mason gasps, staring back at me as I quickly kick my feet out and remove the sheets covering my body. I'm suddenly burning up.

"Do you want to see it?"

I nod, rubbing a hand down my neck. My skin feels like it's humming. "Yes."

His eyes darken to that steely shade of blue I'm becoming familiar with. "Spread your legs for me. Touch yourself. I bet you're drenched, aren't you, you filthy fucking girl."

Again, I nod, even before my hand slides into my panties. Arousal coats my fingers as I press lightly against my clit.

"How wet? Tell me. I want to taste you."

I lick my lips. "Mm. Like this?" I suck my finger into my mouth, releasing it with a wet pop. "Too bad you aren't here. I think I taste better off your tongue."

Mason groans through a clenched jaw, his breathing growing louder, exploding into the air as his arm moves furiously against his side.

"Fuck, baby. Let me see. Show me. Put the phone between your legs. God, my dick is so fucking hard."

With a gasp, I drop the phone against my shirt. "Shit! Sorry," I apologize through a nervous giggle, waving at the screen. "I need to get undressed. I'm in panties. Hold on. I'm putting this down."

Holy shit! This is exhilarating and nerve wracking and crazy and CRAZY. But fuck, there is nothing holding me back from giving him everything he's asking for.

I want this. I want him. I've never felt this way about anyone.

I shimmy my panties down my legs and pick up my phone. Holding it above me, I watch Mason's mouth twitch when I appear in the small square.

"Hey. Okay, I'm going to do it now."

He nods, his chest heaving. "Good. Make me come."

Good fucking God.

I prop myself up with two pillows behind my back. Bending my knees, I let my legs fall open and hold the phone between them.

"Fuck. Look at you. So good, baby." His face appears larger on my screen. "Fuck," he whispers. "Closer. Spread your legs more. I want to see everything."

"Okay," I softly reply, my voice breathy and thick as I open wider and slide the phone closer to my body. "Like that? Can you see? I'm so wet. I'm dripping. I don't know if I've ever been this turned on before."

Mason growls my name, "Brooke."

He tells me how hot his dick feels in his hand. How sensitive it is. How he can't stop thinking about my mouth and my tits and how tight I'll feel around him when he finally takes me. He snarls like an animal when I slip a finger into my pussy, and then he tells me to fuck myself, to think about his cock and to beg for it.

"Please," I gasp, writhing against my sheets, sliding further down the bed with my legs pulling higher and spreading wider.

"Look," he orders through a strained voice, and I glance down my body at the phone in my hand and moan at the image on the screen.

His cock.

His long, thick cock, dripping at the head as he strokes it almost brutally.

I bring the phone closer to my face and slide my fingers over my clit, staring, gasping, telling him I'm close and to come and to show me what I do to him.

With a strangled cry, we fall, words and moans blending into the night. It's hot and filthy, and so profoundly intimate, and again I find myself smiling and so strangely happy, and I wonder if what I'm feeling has anything to do with the climax pulling me apart.

My legs fall heavy against the bed and I lift the phone off my chest. A lazy smile fills the screen.

"Well?" I ask, lifting my hair off my neck and falling back onto the pillow. I laugh at the peculiar look Mason gives me. "Don't you have something to ask me, now that I'm sated from orgasm and willing to agree to even the most ridiculous requests?"

He grins, perking up. "Right. This weekend . . . can I have you?"

I blow him a kiss and end the call. My phone buzzes almost immediately with a message.

Mason: I'll take that as a yes.

Chapter Ten

Mason

THE SHRILL SOUND OF A phone ringing jolts me awake, dragging me out of one hell of a dream.

Brooke on her knees, her skilled hands cupping my balls as she laps at my cock.

I groan into the pillow.

God, I love dream Brooke. Who the fuck is calling me this early?

Lifting my head, I glance around the dark room.

The faintest amount of sunlight pushes across the floor by the window, breaking through the small gap in the curtain. Searching for my cell amongst the sheets I'm tangled in, I find the menacing thing halfway down the bed near my left calf.

Last night . . . shit, I don't even remember hanging up after that spectacular conversation. Best solo session of my life. I will never look at that function on my phone the same again.

Facetiming my mum is now out of the question. Maybe I can

convince her to Skype.

I accept the call and place it to my ear, letting my eyes fall closed again.

"You," I mumble, picturing Brooke's face against the backdrop of her lavender pillow. Her hair messy from sleep. "Morning, sweet girl."

A breathy laugh pulls through the phone. "Oh, my God. You're still in bed, aren't you?"

"You wrecked me last night. I slept like the dead." I peek an eye open and spot the clock on the wall. "My alarm doesn't go off for another thirty minutes."

"Really? Mm, that's funny."

A car horn sounds through the phone, followed by the distant noise of a busy street. Light chatter, heels striking the ground. Birds.

Is Brooke outside this early in the day?

"Is it?" I roll to the side and slide my arm beneath the pillow to build my head up. "My alarm set for ten to eight is funny to you?"

"Yes," she chuckles. "Considering how adamant you were about getting me to agree to another breakfast with you. I give you Tuesdays and you stand me up. What the fuck, dude?"

My hand tightens around the phone. The cloud of content encasing me as I listen to Brooke's warm morning voice quickly rips away, along with any ounce of lethargy keeping me pinned to the bed.

It's Tuesday. I'm supposed to meet Brooke for breakfast on Tuesdays.

"Fucking hell." I throw myself out of bed and dart across the room to grab some clothes. "Brooke, fuck, I'm sorry. I was so bloody out of it last night after we talked, I forgot to change my alarm. I'm up now. Just hang on, all right? Did you order?"

I step into a pair of boxers and some running shorts, fisting a shirt as my eyes scan the floor for my shoes.

"No, I gave up our table."

"What?"

She laughs again, and for the second time during this conversation I take notice of the outside world quietly buzzing around her through the line. She's calling me *after* waiting for God knows how long inside that café. It's twenty past seven now. If she didn't arrive early, that's twenty fucking minutes of her sitting alone, wondering where the fuck I am after I practically begged her for this.

Brilliant, mate. You're such a fucking wanker.

"Mason, relax. Jesus. It's not a big deal. I'm just giving you a hard time because it's funny and I can. Go back to sleep."

I step into my runners and pull my shirt on. "Fuck that. I'm on my way out now. I'll meet you there."

"Can't."

"Why the hell not?"

"Wow," she giggles. "Listen to you. You're really pissed about this."

"You gave me a day, Brooke. I want that day."

My hand pushes through my hair as I step inside the bathroom. The light flickers on, pulsing against the white walls. I switch to speaker phone and hurriedly brush my teeth, glaring at my well-rested reflection.

She clears her throat. "I gave you *breakfast*, not a day. And it doesn't matter. Dylan called me while I was waiting for you and asked if I could come in early to help her with something. So, you see? No big deal. I would've ended up cutting our time short anyway."

I spit into the sink, dragging the back of my hand across my mouth.

She sounds fine, teasing me and brushing this fuck-up off as if it's nothing. But I know this woman. I know she likes to hide behind a tough voice. I know you get more honesty from Brooke by slowing down and *watching* her, which is why I'm hesitant to believe her reassurance right now.

"Where are you?"

A quiet chime breaks through the phone. "The bakery."

"Good."

I move through the room and take to the stairs, walking across the empty studio. After unlocking the door, I jog across the street between traffic. Brooke says something, a greeting directed at Dylan, I assume. It sounds muted as if she's moved her mouth away from the phone.

"Hey, Mason. I need to get off here."

"All right," I reply, ending the call and stepping inside the bakery.

"We're not open yet," a voice, not Brooke, yells from the back.

I move across the room and stop in the doorway opening up to the kitchen, leaning my shoulder against the frame.

Dylan notices me first, a coy smile twisting across her mouth. "Oh, hey. It's you."

Brooke raises her head from the large mixing bowl she's staring down into.

She looks beautiful. Her hair is down, a tiny braid gathering some of it back and out of her round hazel eyes.

With parted red lips, she looks at the phone sitting on the large wood surface, then pins her gaze to me again.

"What are you doing, stalker?" she asks, her voice lifting sweetly. She shakes her head slowly through a tight lipped grin.

"I came to apologize, and to see if I can possibly take you to lunch today, instead of breakfast." I straighten in the doorway and take a step closer, halting before I take another. "Is it okay that I'm back here?" I ask Dylan.

I've never stepped foot inside a professional kitchen before. I have no idea what the rules are for commoners here.

Dylan nods, her eyes shifting curiously between Brooke and myself. She smiles. "It's fine."

Brooke focuses on the containers of baking supplies in front of her as I loom closer. "I only get thirty minutes for lunch. That's not enough time to go out anywhere. Sorry."

"You can have an hour today."

I grin at Dylan. "Brilliant."

Brooke's head snaps up. She looks astonished, maybe a bit annoyed. Her one hand closes into a fist against the wood while the other moves to her hip. "Are you kidding me right now? How many times have I asked you for an extended lunch, and never once were you keen on the idea. Just last week I wanted an additional fifteen minutes and you refused to budge."

"So?" Dylan dumps some flour into a bowl and brushes her hands off. She stares evenly at Brooke. "This is my bakery, my fucking name is on it, and I don't have to explain to you why I'm allowing this today."

"Oh, I know exactly why you're allowing it." Brooke points a finger at my face. "That mouth right there. It makes people stupid."

I keep my laugh muffled as I bring my arms across my chest, looking between the two of them.

Dylan removes her apron and lays it on the stool. "I'll give you two a minute." She hits me with a smile before moving across the room and climbing the stairs.

A door closes.

Stepping behind Brooke, I drop my head and kiss her shoulder. Her hands relax against the wood, while mine snake around her trim waist and pull her back against my chest.

"Think she'll notice if I duck under this table and stay between your legs the rest of the day?" I ask, running my nose along her skin.

"Probably. Dylan doesn't miss much."

I smile. "Shame. I know I'd feel a lot better about fucking up this morning if I spend the next eight hours getting you off."

"Mason." Brooke spins around and tilts her head to look at me.

"I'm sorry," I tell her before she can get another word out, my hands gently squeezing her hips as I fight the urge to inch closer and kiss my way through this.

She stares at me, silently absorbing my apology. Her shoulders drop with a quiet sigh, her eyes lowering to a spot on my shirt, and *that*, fuck, that right there is the reason why I'm here and not relying on her casual brush-off.

She isn't fine. She's disappointed, or hurt, or *something*. Definitely not fine.

"Now would be the perfect time to call me a wanker, Brooke. Or a tosser. I know how much you like slipping those words into our conversations. Feel free to let me have it."

Her eyes flick to mine. She narrows them, draws her fingers into a fist, then knocks it gently against my chest. "What the fuck, dude?" she whispers, repeating her words from earlier, fighting back a smile as she stands on her toes to get closer. "You forgot? How could you forget?"

"It was that hot as fuck phone call last night. I think I lost some brain cells with that emission."

"Aw, are you dumb and pretty now?" she chuckles, lifting a hand to my cheek. "It's okay, sweet boy. I'll still play with you. Do you like shiny things? Here. Let me get my keys."

I grab her waist when she tries to dart away.

Fuck, I love her playful like this. Completely unaware of how open she is to me. It's beautiful, her unguarded heart. I like to imagine it's untouched as well.

She laughs against my neck, her hands sliding under my shirt.

"So," she whispers, her lips pressing to my skin.

"So."

"Last night was fun."

I kiss her hair. "Mm. Maybe I'll bring two tents with us this weekend and we can reenact it in the wilderness. I think your moans will sound lovely in an open field."

She leans back to look at me. "Two tents? You're delusional if you think I'm separating from you at any point during this absurd camp-out. I told you I didn't want to do this. Now you're trying to suggest we sleep apart? Fuck that. Haven't you ever seen *Deliverance*? I know that wasn't set in Chicago, but there are freaks everywhere. You're stuck with me. One tent. One sleeping bag. Get ready for stage-five clinger status, buddy. I'm going to be on you like a hobo on a muffin."

My mouth stretches into a smile. I grab her face, bending for a kiss. "I like the sound of that."

"Of course you do." Her hands circle my wrists. She bites at my lip. "The stalker becomes the stalkee."

"Exactly," I say quietly, opening my eyes to watch hers slowly flutter open.

She stares at my mouth like she wants another taste, but she isn't asking, or moving in for it. I think I'll leave her like this.

Waiting. Wanting.

"What time do you want to do lunch?" I ask, letting my hands fall away and moving beside her.

I tap my finger on the large mixing bowl. The white powder vibrates against the steel.

She nudges against me and slides the bowl in front of her, along with several various sized measuring spoons. "One? That's when I usually take it."

"Great. I have a break between classes then." I rest my hand on her back and kiss her cheek. "You know that park with the water fountain about ten minutes from here? Meet me there. I'll take care of the food." I make for the exit, glancing back when I reach the doorway.

I smile.

Brooke looks like she wants to ask questions, maybe protest the location and offer up a private spot where clothes aren't required.

I know my girl.

Instead, she lifts her hand and waves me off. "Okay, but you better show up this time. No epic facetime wanking sessions between now and lunch. I need you focused. Maybe you should grab a banana or something. I hear that's brain food."

A laugh rumbles in my chest.

"I'll be there," I tell her, I promise her, as I back out of the room.

I will fucking be there.

I BEAT BROOKE TO THE park and claim a vacant bench near the large fountain.

Three sprouts of water erupt from the center, fanning close to the flat stone edge and darkening the rocks. A few children drop coins into the water and stand on their toes to watch them sink to the bottom. Dog walkers and mums with prams filter in between one another along the paved footpath.

It's a nice day, the cool spring air smelling of flowers and cut grass. The sun slicing through the clouds.

My ringtone sounds from my pocket.

I'm expecting it to be Brooke, telling me she's on her way, or maybe that I'm still a huge tosser for standing her up earlier and she's paying me back by for it.

Palming my phone, I look at the screen.

It isn't Brooke. The woman calling might've threatened castration if I would've pulled that stunt with her.

I bring the phone to my ear. "Hey. How are ya?"

Tessa grunts. "Finally! Someone answers the damn phone today. Sweet Christ, I'm going batshit crazy listening to these transcripts and I need a reason to not listen to them." A loud crunch comes through the line. "Humor me. What's new? What happened with that one chick who definitely does not have bigger balls than me?"

I chuckle, my eyes searching for Brooke. "You know, I should be offended you're only calling me to get out of working. You're a terrible mate."

"Hey, screw you. *I* should be offended you left the best fucking state in this beautiful country to be all adult and open up your own business, but I'm not, 'cause that would be shitty of me. Even though I still don't understand why you couldn't open up your own studio here. 'Bama girls love yoga."

We share a light laugh. I know of one particular 'bama girl who doesn't care for yoga one bit.

"How's all that going anyway?" she asks.

"Good. Yeah, really good. It's a bit shocking, actually. I might have to consider tacking on another class during the day if interest stays this fortunate."

"Mason, you're a great teacher, and you look like a male model. I'm sure your interest stays plenty fortunate."

"We'll see." I smile, rubbing my mouth. "So, yeah, this woman I mentioned, Brooke." At the mere utterance of her name, something catches in the center of my chest, warming my blood. My mouth twitches. "We've been seeing a bit of each other and it's been great. I'm quite fond of her."

"Yeah?" Tessa takes another bite of whatever it is she's eating. "You two serious?"

"Serious?" I repeat, considering the word.

My answer is simple.

In my mind, we are. I have never been anything less with Brooke, and I don't relish the idea of it. She is quickly becoming a beautiful constant in my life.

Wake up thinking about her.

Go through the day, counting down the minutes until I can pop in her shop for a quick visit.

Pass out and welcome some of the filthiest dreams I've ever had, all featuring her sweet face and sinful body.

But if asked this question, how would Brooke answer? I know how this thing started out, her casual plans for me, but how does she see us now?

I rub at my neck. "I'm serious about her. She's bloody fantastic, and the only woman I care to be around."

"And how does she feel?"

"Lovely."

There's a brief pause. "Jesus," Tessa laughs. "That's not what I meant. Though I'm impressed you went dirty before I did. Not many people beat me to the punch. Bravo."

I look up and spot Brooke walking toward me on the path. Her hand lifts with a cute little wave, and I grin. "She's warming up to me. I'm meeting with her now so I'm sorry to say you'll have to return to work. I'll keep you posted on my developments. Tell everyone I said hi, yeah?"

"Jerk," she mumbles, then giggles quietly. "Yeah, I'll tell them. And let me know when you decide Chicago blows and need some help looking for apartments back here. I'll be all over it."

I stand from the bench. "Goodbye, Tessa."

"Later."

Disconnecting the call, I tuck my phone back into my pocket and continue watching Brooke moving toward me.

Her cream-colored, short-sleeved blouse dips low in the front, courtesy of several unfastened buttons. Dark jeans fit to her curves. And on her feet, a pair of gray flats.

Those pink heels she likes to wear are sexy as fuck, but I might like her in flats better. When I pull her close and fit our bodies together, she's the perfect height for me to rest my chin on top of her head.

"Hey. You made it." She places her hand to my chest, offering me her cheek. She knows that's where I'm heading.

I fucking love that she knows that.

"I almost called to remind you," she adds, smirking.

"I told you I'd be here." I bend for a kiss and then motion for her to have a seat. Sliding the sandwich bag into my lap, I hold out the to-go box for her to take.

She studies the label on the top of the box, then slowly eases it from my hands.

"You went to Rosie's," she states through a soft laugh. "You know I've only ever been there for breakfast? I have no idea what their lunch menu looks like."

It wouldn't matter, I think, smiling to myself.

I dig my sandwich out of my bag, keeping my gaze in my lap. "Lots of sandwiches and soups. A few salads. Typical lunch stuff." I peel away the wrapper to reveal the top piece of rye bread.

A soft gasp perks in my ear, followed by cardboard creasing. "Oh, my God, Mason. This is impossible. How did you get them to make you this? They stop serving breakfast at ten-thirty!"

I glance over at her, watching as she lifts the box to her face and inhales.

She makes a soft, moaning sound in the back of her throat as her eyes fall closed. The wind picks up, blowing her hair off her shoulder.

I stare at neck, her dimple, the adorable wrinkle in her nose as she practically submerges her face in that box.

She turns and bumps our knees together. "Mason."

"What?" I casually ask, taking a bite of my sandwich and finally meeting her eyes. "Oh, do you like that kind of French toast? It's a bit odd, yeah? With the cereal? I wasn't sure you would like it." I pull a set of wrapped plastic silverware out of my pocket and hold it out.

Our fingers slide together as she reaches for it. I feel a jolt of energy pulse under my skin.

Brooke's eyes widen, lowering to my mouth.

With a quick jerk, she leans forward and hovers an inch from my face, her lungs straining for breath. The movement is so abrupt and clearly so startling for her, given her staggered expression, it's as if she is being pushed into me and held there.

"Brooke," I murmur, looking all over her face. I bring my arm behind her and rest it on the bench, angling us together.

She blinks up at me. "Mm?"

"Do you want to kiss me?"

She doesn't answer, but her eyes, those beautiful fucking eyes drop to my mouth and stay there, flickering open a little wider when I wet my lips.

A heaviness gathers in my limbs as I wait, and wait, and *fuck*, wait for her to make a move. A decision.

This is a first.

Every kiss, every sort of affection we've shared has been instigated and carried out by me. Sure, she's been an active participant, minus a few of the times I've tried to hold her hand, but she's never reached for me. She's never forced the seal of our mouths together and shocked the hell out of *me*.

I inch closer, just the smallest shift, enough to feel her breath on my face. It's warm and smells like fruit, something berry.

"Come on," I whisper.

It sounds like I'm begging. I feel like I am.

Her pink tongue darts out and slides across her lips.

I can see the wild hammering of her pulse beneath her ear. I can practically hear her thoughts and the argument she wages with herself over this monumental affirmation.

Come on, Brooke.

I keep reminding myself to breathe and to not move and to just fucking wait another second. Then another. Time becomes a double-edged sword. The longer she considers this, the more shattering or satisfying the end result will become.

I'll look back on this moment and think it was torture and damaging in the end. She wasn't ready. She might not ever be. Or, I'll only remember the feel of her lips and the taste of her warm breath and I'll think, 'I would've waited hours for that'.

A hand touches my thigh. My blood turns to lava, scorching and slow-moving.

Then with a gasping breath she leans in and presses the softest kiss to my mouth.

FUCK.

I've shared a lot of kisses with Brooke. Hot, hungry ones where it feels like I've captured her after a long-winded chase. Ones that seem imperative and essential to my survival. But this kiss, even though it's fleeting and painstakingly faint, feels superior to every other kiss she has or will ever give me.

And in that moment, my life becomes profoundly simple, consisting of only one person.

Brooke.

With a quiet laugh, she pulls away and opens her cutlery. She lifts a brow when our eyes lock. "You are crazy. Did you promise to rock Rosie's world? Is that why she made this for you?"

It takes me a minute to process her question. I'm still reeling from the ghost of a kiss that just knocked me on my arse.

I run a quick hand through my hair, gathering my wits about me. "No. I never saw Rosie, although I'm sure she's lovely and a minx in the sack."

Brooke laughs, reaching up and tucking some hair behind her ear.

"I asked a waitress if they could make an exception and help a poor bloke out. There was some gentle begging. I may have mentioned how badly I fucked up this morning and that I was declaring my adoration for this one particular woman through the weekly meals she's giving me, which I'm hoping will soon convert to days." I take a bite of my sandwich, shrugging when she turns her head. "If you think about it, I'm already creeping in on lunches. Next it will be routine dinners. Minutes in between. I'll claim a day from you soon enough."

"Are you talking about once a week? Like every Tuesday is Brooke and Mason day?"

I smile. "Yeah."

"Oh, okay. In this fantasy world, do either one of us have jobs? Because I need to work." She licks some powdered sugar off her lip. "How am I supposed to give you a day if I'm working?"

"Weekends, obviously. Or I'll forgo your time in between meals and have you after work." I lower my voice, leaning closer as I set my sandwich on the paper wrapping. "Although, fair warning. I might not be so willing to give you up after the sun goes down. I've imagined how perfect you are waking up to and if I have a chance to entertain that idea, I'm taking it."

She stares at me for a moment, her mouth slowly lifting into a mischievous grin. "And what exactly have you imagined? Anything particularly tight and wet?"

My cock stirs beneath my shorts.

I lower my eyes to the white lace peeking out of her blouse. "Mm. And soft. I wake up with my face buried between your spectacular tits and we go from there."

She lowers the box to her lap and shifts closer, her chest pressing against my side. "Tell me," she murmurs.

I lift my gaze to hers.

She wants me to go into detail about what I've imagined more times than I can count? Now? Here?

With heavy eyes, she slowly nods as if she's heard my internal thoughts. Her hand moves back to my thigh.

I swallow, my heart pounding in my chest, my cock quickly lengthening as pornographic thoughts run rampant in my mind. I turn my body more and hold the sandwich bag strategically in my lap, concealing my unwelcome erection.

This is a crowded park. There's bloody kids running around. I can't will my prick not to react to this woman, but I can at least keep it hidden.

"Dirty girl," I whisper against her ear. "You want to know what I think about?"

"Yes," she replies breathlessly. Her hand squeezes my leg.

"I lick and suck your tits until they're wet enough for me to slide between. Will you let me fuck them, Brooke? I want to. God, I've thought about it. Your hot little mouth opening for me, lapping at my head. Your gorgeous eyes going round while I milk my cum onto your nipples."

"Oh, God," she gasps.

"I dream about your tits, Brooke. And your arse."

She blinks rapidly. "My ass?"

"Fuck yeah, your arse. Are you kidding? I want to come on that too."

Her hand moves closer to my cock. "What else? Just . . . keep going. I won't touch you. I just want to drive you a little crazy."

I groan when her fingers brush against my length. "Brooke . . ."

"Oops. Sorry," she says through a giggle, jerking her hand back. "I forgot how much room you take up down there. That was an accident." Her hand tightens on my leg. "Go on. What happens before you come on my ass?"

I bend to kiss her mouth. I can't fucking help it. Sugar coats my tongue, and again, I'm reminded of the way her skin tasted the other night.

My hand forms to her neck and she tilts her head. "I get you face-down on my bed. You ask me to spank you, and I make you beg for it. I bite and lick your skin. I straddle your legs and hold your ass so I can slide my cock between your cheeks. And then," I pause, kissing along her jaw, smiling against her cheek when she lets out a shuddering breath.

"And then?" she asks.

"I found a quarter!" a tiny voice yells, way too fucking close to whatever the hell is happening on this bench.

With a muffled curse, I frantically move the sandwich bag further up my lap.

Brooke yanks her hand away and falls against my side, laughing unashamedly with a hand to her chest.

"Having a good time?" I ask her before addressing this little mood killer.

I pull back and stare between the round face in front of me and the coin that's being held out for me to notice.

"Look!" The young boy turns the quarter in the air. "There's only ever pennies in there. Sometimes nickels. I found an actual quarter!"

"Brilliant. Why don't you run along now?"

"Aw, let me see." Brooke holds her hand out and takes the coin. She studies it for a moment, smiles coyly at me when our eyes meet, then places it back in the boy's hand. "That's so cool. What's your name?"

I gape at her.

Is she bloody serious? Does she not know how uncomfortable this is for me? What's next? Asking the little bugger if he'd like to join us for lunch?

"Willie!" A woman yells, waving her hands in the air and running at me.

Jesus fuck! Can she see my cock from there?

Heart racing, I look down into my adequately concealed lap.

No. Everything's good here. Nothing hanging out.

My pulse steadies. I suddenly remember how to breathe.

When the woman stops beside the boy and places a hand on his shoulder, I realize she was calling out for him, not announcing to everyone here that I was giving shows.

She gives me an apologetic look, then glares at the kid. "What have I told you about walking up to strangers? Come on. It's time to go." She tugs on his hand and leads him down the footpath.

Brooke laughs unapologetically as she settles back against the bench, then stares down at the bag covering my now flaccid cock. "How are things down there? Anything turning a shade of blue yet?"

"You're the devil." I move the bag and pick up my neglected roast beef sandwich. "Let's spend the rest of your lunch-hour eating, shall we? Hands where I can see them."

She picks up her fork and shoves a massive bite into her mouth. Her lips strain to close. "So good," she says, although it sounds more like the noise a dying animal might make.

We laugh and eat under the midday sun, and I slip a little bit further under Brooke's spell.

Chapter Eleven

Brooke

CAMPING . . .

Am I completely insane?

Not only do I have absolutely no idea why I agreed to this absurdity, I also have no clue how to pack for a weekend in the wilderness.

Outdoors. Zero climate control. According to my weather app, I'm looking at temperatures anywhere between forty and eighty-five degrees this weekend.

Say what? That's basically my entire closet. Random Packing 101 right here.

I have jammed my oversized Victoria's Secret duffle bag full of the oddest combination of clothing. Shorts, sweatshirt, bathing suit, a pair of snow pants just in case. I refuse to be unprepared for this. I even break another shopping rule and run out to the local sporting goods store to grab a few camping essentials, or at least what *I* classify as camping essentials.

Is there such a thing as too much bug-spray? Are road flares frowned upon at campsites? The answer is no and I don't really give a fuck.

I have never been camping. I never wanted to be a girl scout. I have absolutely no desire to spend any time outside unless I'm lounging by a pool with a fruity umbrella drink.

There are outdoorsy people, and then there's me.

So, why am I lugging this duffle out of my car and surrendering myself to Mother Nature for two days? Simple.

Orgasms. Mason's mouth in general. That accent? Jesus. I can listen to him talk for hours. And . . . okay, if I'm being honest, it's not terrible hanging out with him and doing things that don't involve safe words.

He makes me laugh. A lot. The only other time men I've been interested in have made me laugh in the past is when they've dropped their pants.

That didn't happen with Mason. That will never happen with Mason. I will take his cock very seriously.

And soon, if I have any say in the matter.

After locking up my car and making sure I have everything I think I'll need, I adjust the strap on my shoulder and wait for a break in traffic.

It's nearly six-thirty and the sky is beginning to warm with the approaching sunset. Reds and deep oranges color the clouds. The air is slowly dropping in temperature.

Thank God for the sweatshirt I packed. I may need it before we get to the campsite.

Across the street, Mason carries a large cooler around to the back of his car. He's been loading up for the past ten minutes, not that I've been watching from the bakery window or anything.

Okay, I have. He's excited, and it's kind of cute to watch him step back and evaluate his packing job. Move things around. Scratch his head when the back door won't latch shut and then pull everything out and start over.

Frustrated Mason King is surprisingly sexy, and I'm guessing not something people get to see very often, being Mr. Zen.

Traffic finally slows and I step off the curb. I get halfway across the street before Mason turns his head and notices me.

He looks fucking edible in dark gray warmups and a yellow graphic tee.

Fucking. Edible.

His hair is a blonde wavy mess, messier when he pushes a hand through it as he watches me. Both of us are in sneakers, which I had to run home for after he sent me a text this afternoon.

> *Mason: Your arse looks amazing in those heels. It also looks amazing in runners. That's what you should be wearing this weekend. Lots of walking, gorgeous.*

How did I forget about shoes? I remember floss and a nail file, but comfortable shoes? Not a priority.

After setting the cooler down on the back of the car, Mason jogs over and takes my duffle.

"Here. I'll take that." He slides the bag off my shoulder and lifts it with one hand, gauging the weight. His brows pull together as we move to the car. "A bit heavy, yeah? You pack for both of us?"

I hook a thumb behind me. "Oh, that's just my lube. My clothes are in my other bag. Can you grab it?"

His face right now? Priceless.

Mouth falling open. Alarmed eyes shifting between the bag in his hand and my face. His lips pinch together after a few seconds of utter shock, and he fights a smile through a shake of his head. "Your lube? Jesus, Brooke. A bit of a wasted purchase, don't you think?"

We stop at the back of the car. Mason moves a few things around to make room for my bag.

"Wasted? How is stocking up on lube a wasted purchase? You should always have some handy, just in case. And they last a while. I don't think they expire for like two years or something."

"Do you have any idea how wet I make you? You don't need lube, sweetheart. Not with me."

I cross my arms, leaning against the side of the car. "Are you sure about that? What about anal?"

He freezes, keeping his hands on the duffle after he stuffs it beside the cooler.

His head is down. Profile tense and body deathly rigid.

There is something extremely satisfying about supplying Mason with another spank-bank image. I like the high it gives me, knowing he'll get off on that later. Picturing my body to seek out his release.

Enjoy that.

Laughing at my own cleverness, I start to move to the sidewalk, but he reaches out and grabs me, pinning my body between him and the bumper. My breath hitches when his hand connects sharply with my ass and stays there, his other roughly roaming over my curves.

His touch is possessive. Indecent.

I mold to his front like warm putty. I suddenly feel drugged.

So much for having the upper hand.

"Don't give me any ideas about this perfect fucking arse, Brooke. Unless you want me to show you why we wouldn't need lube for that either." He sucks on the skin beneath my ear, then drops his hands, moving away as suddenly as this delicious assault came on. "You ready to get going? I want to set up camp before dark," he says, completely casually, grabbing a rolled up sleeping bag off the sidewalk and sliding it next to my duffle.

I blink him into focus, reaching up and wiping my chin. I'm surprised it's not wet with drool.

"Y-Yeah, sure. Just let me use the bathroom first."

Jesus. Pull yourself together, Brooke.

I rush inside the studio before I see or hear his reaction to my obvious discomposure.

Lord, the man's hands are wicked. Paired with that voice? I'm completely defenseless.

"You started it," I mumble to myself as I tie my hair up off my heated neck. I guess it serves me right for trying to get a rise out of Mason.

He got one. I definitely felt it. And now I can very easily confirm his statement about not needing lube.

I push the door open at the top of the stairs and step out into the loft.

The room is exactly how I remember it from my first

embarrassing experience up here. Lots of grays and blues. Massive wood-panel bed. A small kitchen table that looks to also be serving as a desk. It's covered in membership forms and signed contracts. A laptop. A book about franchising.

I walk over to the accent chair in the corner and pick up the stuffed koala. I crush it to my chest.

"Hey, mate," I whisper.

He kept it.

After using the bathroom and washing my hands, I stop at the refrigerator to hopefully grab a bottle of water. Something to hold in the car when my hands become restless. I swing the door open and startle at the contents littering the shelves.

Boxes. Bakery boxes. A lot of them.

Why are there so many?

"What the hell?" I grab the closest one in reach and open the lid. Four cupcakes fill the container. Four cupcakes I made. Completely untouched. I set the box down and reach for another. And another. Each one still exactly how I delivered it. No bites taken. None of the icing sampled. I find the first box I gave to Mason on the sidewalk the morning we met. The only cupcake that has been disturbed is the dolce and banana I tasted for him.

He isn't eating anything I give him. He's not even tasting them.

Why? Does he not like cupcakes? Fuck, if that's the case, why is he allowing me to make it rain desserts every time we see each other?

I put the boxes back on the shelf and grab some water. I can't get back outside fast enough. When I push the studio door open, I charge at Mason with my bottle pointed at his chest.

"Why is your fridge filled with cupcakes? What is going on?"

The smile on his face diminishes the second I get those words out.

I lower the bottle. I almost tell him to forget what I just said.

He looks uncomfortable, maybe a bit anxious. His eyes are shifting about the sidewalk while he rubs the back of his neck.

But damn it, I want to know. I'm too curious to drop this. And I'm not going anywhere until he explains what I've just discovered.

With a sigh, he pushes away from the car and steps forward,

lifting his shoulders. "Because you made them," he quietly states, stopping a foot away. "I don't eat stuff like that, Brooke. I haven't in a long time."

"So tell me and I won't push them on you. Jesus. I can't believe you never said anything."

"I don't eat them. I didn't say I don't like getting them. You're so proud of what you make. I am too."

What . . . did he just say?

I stare at him as something warm bursts open in my chest, spreading from my neck to my navel. My shoulders sag. I chew nervously on the inside of my cheek.

He keeps them because he's proud of me?

How can someone be so straight-up filthy one minute and this sweet the next? He's like this beautiful balance of dark and light, dirty and decent, and he seems to know *exactly* when to be one and when to give me the other.

Keeping one cupcake because I make it is surprising enough. He keeps them all.

Every single one.

Mason watches my reaction, and what does he do? He waits. He waits while I absorb what he's just disclosed. This completely insane, yet incredibly affectionate gesture. He doesn't say anything else. He doesn't move closer and kiss my cheek, or tell me I look pretty while I struggle to comprehend this.

He just simply waits, and it's so him, and so what I need him to do right now.

I lower my gaze to his arms, the same arms that just had me pinned roughly to that hard body without giving me much of a choice about it.

Funny. Now I'm tempted to willingly throw myself into them.

I don't fight it.

"God, Mason." I reach for his shirt and pull us together. My head hits his chest. I barely move but my heart is pounding. "What are you doing?" I whisper, allowing my eyes to close.

He wraps his strong arms around my body, squeezing me. "I don't know. I couldn't throw them out."

I smile against the soft cotton.

We stand there for several minutes. My head never moves. His arms never leave me. It's soothing, the constant pressure of his hold, and somehow it feels strangely familiar. Like he's held me like this for years. Like I've known him my entire life, and in the moments when I've needed someone to be with me like this, it's always been him.

No one else.

Sighing, I snuggle the tiniest bit closer, clutching my water bottle between us. "You're crazy."

"Yeah."

"Promise me you'll toss them when they start to grow mold."

"All right."

I crane my neck and kiss his jaw. "Now, take me camping before I realize I'm just as crazy as you are."

He smiles, kissing my temple. Tipping up my chin to steal my mouth.

Or maybe I just give it to him.

"*THIS* IS WHERE WE'RE CAMPING? Really?" I unbuckle my seat belt and lean forward, looking out the window at our surroundings.

Dirt covered parking lot. One single lamp post lighting the area.

I turn to Mason, smiling. "You fingered me here."

With a sly grin, he winks at me before exiting the car.

Mm. Ready to build on that stellar experience, Mr. King?

I take a sip of my water and meet him around the back to help unload.

Mason insists on carrying the bulk of our stuff as he leads the way down a small narrow path toward the campsites. I follow behind, clutching the sleeping bag against my chest. Tall trees surround us. I can barely see the darkening sky through the branches.

I move closer until I'm practically climbing onto his back.

He talks the entire time, as if he can sense my apprehension behind him. He talks about camping with his dad back in Australia.

How his sisters never had any interest in going until his friends started tagging along. He tells me he came by here the other day to stake out the grounds for our weekend. There's a lake, and a few hiking trails he thinks I'll enjoy checking out. He smiles over his shoulder when I let out a doubtful chuckle, which I play up. I like lakes. I might like hiking.

It's as if the fresh air is drugging me.

When we reach a large clearing in the woods, I watch Mason set everything down by two logs. Tent. Cooler. My bag and his. He kicks some rocks and branches out of the way and immediately goes about setting up the tent.

I drop the sleeping bag and look around.

It's a wide-open space, room enough for at least a handful of other tents, but we're alone. There's a fire pit contained by an ill-defined rock formation. It resembles somewhat of a circle. The wood in the center looks recently burned. A metal grill that seems to be a courtesy for campers to use is located next to a large rectangular picnic table.

Nice. At least we won't have to eat with our asses in the dirt.

Stepping to the edge of the clearing, I stand on my toes and peer through a break in the trees.

"Hey. We're right by the lake," I tell Mason, looking over my shoulder. "Did you know that?"

Literally, right by it. It can't be more than fifty feet away.

His smiling face appears from around the back of the tent. "Yeah. That's one of the reasons why I picked this campsite. The other two are pretty secluded and nowhere near the toilets. Figured you'd do better out here if I kept us in walking distance of those."

"Good thinking. I'd hate you for life if you told me I had to go pee in a bucket or something."

His chuckle is broken up by the sound of my ringtone. I pull my phone out of my back pocket and look at the screen.

"Hey, Juls," I answer, watching Mason disappear again behind the tent.

"Hey, stranger. I feel like I haven't talked to you in forever. Where are you?"

"Camping."

My nephew Jacob yells something in the background. I hear Ian's voice, then the sound of a door closing. "Say that again? It sounded like you said camping." She laughs. "Jesus. Can you imagine? You? Camping? I think there's a better chance of Ian carrying our next child."

I roll my eyes. "I did say camping. And Ian probably *could* carry a baby if he wanted to. He's hormonal as shit."

"What?"

"I said he's hormonal . . ."

"Not that," she brusquely cuts me off. "You're camping right now? With who?"

Mason moves on to the next post, securing it down with a spike. I spin around and face the trees.

"Mason," I murmur, playing with the hem of my shirt.

Juls inhales a sharp breath. "Oh, really? The hot Australian from the bar," she states, her voice lifting with her obvious approval of this development. "Mm. He was really nice. Are you still seeing him? I figured that would be done by now."

I move as far away from the tent as I can get without stepping into the woods. I lower my voice to a stern whisper. "I'm not seeing him like *that*. We're just hanging out, okay? It's not a big deal."

"Just hanging out doing what, Brooke? Dating? Being in a relationship?"

"Shut up," I snap. "And stop grinning like an idiot. I can totally hear it in your voice."

"Look at you," she laughs. "First sign of being in love is denial. Welcome to the club, sis."

"Oh, my God," I groan, rubbing my forehead. "I'm hanging up."

"Wait! Are we still on for dinner next week?"

"Yes."

"Okay, good. Jake and Izzy miss their favorite aunt. You need to come over more."

"Fine. I gotta go."

My shoulders ache with tension. Why did I even answer this call? Juls is always giving me grief.

"All right. But Brooke? Just remember . . ."

There is a long pause. I drum my fingers on my jeans and sigh exhaustively. Her breathy laugh pushes through the line.

"You're my sister. I love you, and I will totally give you a discount when it's time to plan the wedding. Don't think . . ."

I disconnect the call and power off my phone.

God, she is completely insane. How are we even related?

Stepping over a log, I drop the phone onto my bag. I begin to pace in front of our gear, kicking up dirt and cracking my knuckles. I try and sit down on the cooler, but my ass barely touches it before I'm springing to my feet again.

I should've let that call go to voicemail. Now I'm restless and ready to chew my nails off.

I risk a glance at Mason. He's staring at me like I'm in the middle of a psychotic break.

Talking. Talking might settle me. I can talk. I'm fucking awesome at talking.

"So, possible showers tomorrow night. Did you see? Like a ten percent chance. Not much, but still."

He positions a stake in the ground. "I think it'll hold off."

"It was fifteen percent earlier, then they dropped it to ten."

"Yeah."

"If I got naked right now and jumped into the lake, what would you do?"

I look over to where Mason is crouched down beside the tent. His hammer is suspended in the air.

He looks startled. Confused maybe? I can elaborate.

"I mean, obviously, you'd look. Who wouldn't? But would you take off your clothes and follow after me? Or would you continue pitching that tent *and* the one in your shorts?"

"Are you planning on getting naked and jumping into the lake?" he asks, lowering the hammer and resting his elbow on his knee.

I shrug, kicking a rock out of the way. "Maybe. I don't know. I've never been skinny dipping before. Shocking, right? You would think *I've* done that, but no." A nervous laugh bubbles in my throat. "I'm just wondering what you would do if I did it."

"Probably follow you."

"Would you get in?"

He hits the spike once, then looks back up at me. When he tries to answer, I cut him off.

"Have you ever done that before? Gone skinny dipping?"

"No."

"Yeah, me either." I step over the log and continue my pacing. "Mm. We're both virgin skinny dippers. That's cute."

He hits the spike a few more times. The branches under my feet snap.

"How old were you when you lost your virginity?" I ask, chewing on my thumb nail.

"Brooke." Mason catches my gaze and studies it. He slowly rises to his feet. "Are you okay?"

I stop behind the log.

Am I? Fuck. He's looking at me like I'm definitely *not* okay. Like I'm some wild animal he's just encountered out here and he's trying his hardest not to startle me.

I exhale a quick breath. My hand falls away. "I'm fine," I tell him, stepping over the log again. "Just killing time while you . . ." I pause, looking up at the large red and gray *house* Mason has pitched. "Oh, you're finished. Nice."

Holy fuck. This thing is enormous! Not at all what I pictured in my head when he suggested we do this.

Two-man tent. Close quarters. Little room for space between our sweaty naked bodies.

Mm. Maybe I can unpack and spread my clothes out on one side. That should help force the two of us together. This portable condominium is large enough to contain Joey *and* his personality. Not many things are.

Mason drops the small hammer by our bags and comes to stand next to me. His hand circles my back. "Are you cold?" he asks when a shiver chases up my spine. "I can build a fire."

I look from the tent to our surroundings again, my arms hugging my body. Mysterious noises rustle the branches of the trees. Crickets sing into the night. It'll be fully dark soon.

A knot forms in my stomach.

From being out here? From my conversation with Juls? I can't seem to tell.

"Maybe we can just stay in tonight?" I softly suggest, turning back to Mason.

He cocks his head, trying to understand. I'm sure he thinks I mean stay in tonight, in the car.

I might. Give me an hour.

"We have all day tomorrow to be out in this . . . stuff. You know?" I gesture around us, then at the tent. "Honestly, I'm feeling a little anxious, if you didn't notice. This is a lot for me, Mason. Being out here. Roughing it. Could we just stay in the tent the rest of the night? Would that be horrible?"

A gentle smile lifts the corner of his mouth. "You, all to myself in a tent? Nothing horrible about that." He tugs on my pony. "You want a fire or no?"

I shake my head, spinning around to open my bag. "No. I'm really not that cold. Can we walk to the bathrooms though? I want to brush my teeth and stuff."

"Yeah, sure."

He grabs his toothbrush and a flashlight, leading me down another path after he stores our things inside the tent.

I'm one extremely happy girl when it takes us no more than a minute to get to the bath houses. I can easily find this on my own.

We separate and wash up. I scrub my face clean and fix my hair into a sleeker pony.

When we get back to the campsite, it's nearly dark. Mason unzips the flap on the tent and holds it open for me to climb inside.

I toe my shoes off and step in.

"Wow. Swanky," I say, admiring the large dome ceiling and mesh windows. He's left them partially unzipped, allowing for a cool breeze and the moonlight to cut through.

Mason smiles as he ducks to enter and closes us inside. He sets the flashlight down and turns on a lantern, sitting it on top of the cooler. Soft light fills the tent. He kneels and unrolls the sleeping bag in the center of the space.

"Room for two," he murmurs, shooting me a heated look.

Yes, please.

Leaving it zipped up, he stretches out on his back and pats the spot next to him.

I wet my lips and lower to my knees, crawling closer. I let my head fall beside his. "So, I've been meaning to ask you something."

"What's that?"

"What made you leave Australia three years ago? Was it like a yoga thing? Were you wanting to study it here?"

"No, it had nothing to do with yoga."

I stare at his profile when he doesn't elaborate. My foot nudges his calf. "Were you in love with her?"

Shit. I need to get my mouth under control. Do I even want to know his answer? Will it matter to me one way or the other?

He looks at me briefly, just a glance, then resumes staring up at the ceiling. "I don't know. If you had asked me that question three years ago I would've said yeah. I followed a woman to another country. I felt something for her. I said it, more than once."

"I love you," I quietly offer.

His head snaps in my direction and he gives me the strangest look, full of intrigue and stunned disbelief. Questions. So many questions in those bright eyes staring back at me.

I swallow before I continue. My tongue suddenly feels too large for my mouth. "That's what you said. You told her you loved her."

His lips part with a rushed exhale. "Yeah."

"What does it feel like when you say it?" I bite my lip, rolling to my side to look at him. I prop my head up on my fist.

"You've never said it?" he asks, his eyes searching my face. He continues after I shake my head. "What about to your family and stuff? Like a best mate, you say it to them?"

"That's not the same thing. I mean, yeah, I say it to my family. I have to. My mom would punch me in my teeth if I didn't tell her I loved her."

"Your mum a violent woman with everyone? Should I scream my affection for her when we meet?" He smiles when I poke his side. "You say it to your friends, yeah?"

"No."

"Never? Not even growing up?"

"I didn't really have friends growing up."

"Come on." His brow pulls tight. "I don't believe that. I bet you were very popular in school."

"Yeah, with the boys. And they weren't interested in being my friend. Girls were either nasty to me because they were jealous or they had no idea who I was. I never had a best mate." My eyes lower to a spot between us. "I had my sister, Juls, and we were forced to like each other so that doesn't count. And now, yeah, I'm friends with Joey and Billy. I've known Dylan for years, but it's not the same thing."

I flop back over and blink up at the ceiling. My hands tangle together on my stomach.

I think about Mason that night at The Tavern, how he told me all the things he wanted from this, what *more* meant to him, and how I almost laughed at his desire for a friendship on top of everything else.

Would I laugh now?

Clearing my head, I bump my leg against his. "So, I guess you don't know what it's like saying it then. I mean, *really* saying it. Mates don't count."

"No, I guess not," he chuckles. "If we're not counting mates or mums."

"Or Mother Earth. I'm sure you've pledged your undying affection for that bitch."

In a flash, he rolls over and pins me beneath him. I giggle against his neck.

"Jealous?" His hard torso settles between my legs. He tilts my chin and claims my mouth, stealing my ability to answer.

We kiss slowly, a gentle glide of lips and tongues until our breaths grow hurried and our hands no longer hold our bodies together, but roughly explore skin and shape.

My fingers filter through his hair and tug on the ends. I wrap my legs around his waist. When his hips start gently thrusting forward, pressing his erection against my clit, I gasp into his mouth and squirm beneath him. I reach under his shirt and feel the warm skin of his back. My nails pull him closer, my body jutting away from the earth and further into his arms.

He squeezes my breast, taking and taking my mouth until I'm bruised and breathless.

Nothing is hotter than Mason's desperation, and it's evident in everything.

His kiss. His touch. The way his voice breaks when he says my name.

"Brooke."

I grasp at his body like he's slipping away. I'm worried he will.

I want him to want me so badly he can't remember anyone before. I want him to distract me so I'm not completely terrified of what this is or what it's becoming.

I don't want to think. I just want to feel. His hands. His mouth. The wild pace of his heart.

He sucks on my neck and my head rolls to the side.

I spot my duffle. I remember what's in it.

"Wait. I brought you something." I push against his shoulders and he rolls off, growling his protest. I stand and give him a playful look. "You'll like it. Trust me."

"I liked what we were doing." He tucks both hands behind his head. His feet cross at his ankles. "Is it another koala?

"No," I laugh, unzipping the bag. I strip my shirt off and toss it aside. My bra is next. I look up at Mason and find his attention drawn off my face. "Close your eyes," I tell him, my fingers popping the button of my jeans.

He continues to stare, his erection tenting his pants. "I can't."

"Please? It'll be worth it. I promise."

With a disapproving grunt, he pinches his eyes shut. I don't trust him not to peek so I carry my shirt over and toss it onto his face. He chuckles against the material. I take a full minute to appreciate the line of his cock.

Hot damn.

I strip my jeans off but leave on my blue lace thong. After changing into the outfit I packed, I straddle Mason's waist and sink to my knees.

"Okay. You can look."

He tosses the shirt and opens his eyes, wide, wider the longer he stares at my cheerleading outfit from college.

"Jesus Christ, Brooke. *This* is what you brought me?" He runs his hands up my thighs and under my skirt. The light from the lantern flickers in his blue irises.

"Still fits." I wink, cupping my breasts through the tight polyester. "Itchy as fuck, though. I better make this quick."

"Make what quick?"

I shoot down and tug on his warm-ups. His cock springs free, slapping hard and heavy against his stomach.

He hisses through his teeth. "Brooke. Wait."

I put my weight on my knees. I'm prepared for his protest. "You don't want my hands or my mouth, and you don't want to have sex yet. Fine. But you never said anything about dry humping." I blow him a kiss before spinning around and lowering myself onto his pelvis. I move my ass against his cock, rolling my hips in slow circles.

He twitches beneath me and I smile.

"Mm. Remember those dreams you have about me, Mason? When you spank me and come on my ass?"

"Fuck," he groans, pushing up my skirt, holding it at my waist so he can watch.

I grind my pussy against his shaft. My back bowing as I squeeze his thighs. "Do you like this?" I ask, glancing over my shoulder.

His hungry eyes never leave my body. "So good, baby. Look at you."

I reach back and tug on the string of my thong. "You like this? Do you feel how wet I am?"

I gasp when he slides his cock between my cheeks, his hands squeezing my ass to fit around him.

Our eyes lock.

"Fuck, Brooke. Do *you* like it? Knowing how hard you make me. How crazy you make me feel. Tell me."

"I like it."

He slaps my ass.

I drop my head through a groan. My hips pulsing faster, my chest heaving through quiet, quick breaths. The tiny bundle of nerves between my legs begins to throb and swell. My nipples harden against my top.

I watch the shadow of our bodies on the wall of the tent, and I realize the moment Mason sees it too.

Us. Together. His long body stretched beneath mine.

He growls behind me, fingers pulling at flesh. His body tightly wound like a spring ready to jump.

He's on the edge, right there, and I want him to fall. I want to give him pleasure and take my own.

I arch my back and chase my relief, closing my eyes, gasping when his hand connects with my ass again.

"Brooke," he groans. "Tell me. God, fucking *tell* me."

I know what he wants me to say, but I don't just say it. I don't give him an empty echo of a response. I admit my own truth.

"You make me feel crazy too."

When I come, I gasp in shock as my spine and muscles burn.

Mason's release shoots onto my ass, hot spurts sticking to my skin as he moans my name into the night. He wipes me clean with his shirt, I realize, when he pulls me back and holds me against his bare chest, nuzzling my neck and kissing my jaw, his heart racing and his mouth ravenous.

Turning in his arms, I cup his face, staring into his eyes, pushing my hand through his hair. "I like camping with you," I whisper.

He smiles against my mouth. "Yeah? Thought you might."

We strip off each other's clothes. Mason kills the light from the lantern and we slide inside the sleeping bag. He puts his arm around my waist, whispering how he'll protect me from bears and huge snakes I don't want to dry hump.

I laugh against his neck and close my eyes. I might even snuggle closer.

Sleep takes a hold of me before I can tell.

Chapter Twelve

Mason

GETTING BROOKE TO AGREE TO a hike today came easier than I was anticipating.

It probably had something to do with the timing in which I asked, while she was grinding her tight, wet pussy against my hand and wiggling beneath me in the tent, clawing at my back and crying out in pleasure. She moaned my name before whispering a breathy 'yes' against my mouth, then slapped a hand to my chest and shoved me off, claiming her orgasm had nothing to do with her answer.

Apparently, she's a changed woman, loves everything about nature and is eager to explore it with or without me.

On top of everything else that drives me completely crazy about Brooke, she's a beautiful liar. Fully committed and iron-willed.

Her determination really is a thing to appreciate.

It's midday, and we're halfway through our hike. I watch the cute little sway of Brooke's hips as she tentatively walks the narrow trail in front of me.

Her steps are light against the dirt, quiet and cautious, as if she's trying not to draw any attention to herself from the wildlife. When branches from trees or large shrubs encroach our track, she turns her body sideways, pulls her arms in close, and sucks in a breath until she's made it safely past.

So fucking sweet. I can't stop watching her. I don't know what I'm enjoying more, being out here with her in the sun and gorgeous weather, or every honest reaction she's giving me.

After nearly stumbling over a rock sticking out of the dirt, she digs it up, cursing the entire time, and tosses it into the woods with a strangled yell. When a bee flies too close to her face, she gasps and then flips the thing off, threatening to find its hive and burn it to the ground.

I'm waiting for her to break and beg me to take us back. To tell me she's had enough and that she hates this and me for dragging her out here.

She stops abruptly on the path and I ready myself for her dismissal.

This is it. She's gone three hours with no complaints or sour tone. But instead of turning on me and threatening my life if I don't get us out of here, she gathers her hair off her neck and applies another thin coating of bug spray to her exposed limbs.

This is her eighth application.

"I'm starting to get hungry. Do we have any food?" she asks, bending over and spraying the front of her legs.

I groan when the bottom of her arse peeks out from those tiny fucking jean shorts she's wearing. Again.

This is the eighth time I've gotten hard on this trail.

"See something you like?"

Her voice is tempting, sweet and wily. She's caught me every time we've done this.

I scratch my jaw as I resume looking at her, never peeling my eyes away, smiling when she molds her hand to the back of her jeans. "I more than like it, gorgeous," I say, giving her a quick glance. "If I didn't give a shit about other men seeing you out here I'd pull those shorts down and bury my face in that."

"In my ass?" she giggles, spinning around and tucking the

small tube of bug spray into her pocket. She wipes her hands down the front of her shorts. "That's a win/win for me. You can eat that and I'll eat all the actual food."

Laughing, I reach out and grab her face, kissing her soft mouth. "You hungry?"

"Starving."

I step back and pull my bag around to the front of me, tipping my chin at a large boulder.

It's flat and smooth, wide enough to hold several people.

"Want to sit up there and eat? Seems like a nice spot."

Brooke looks at the path between us and the rock I'm asking her to get to, her brows pinching together and her mouth pulling into a frown.

Her anxiety slips on like a veil.

I follow her gaze. It's not a far distance, but the overgrown grass is thick with weeds and wildflowers, some of it reaching up as high as her knees. We've stayed on clear paths up until this point, nothing unkempt like this.

I know how much I'm asking of Brooke. Bull-headed determination or not. She might just tell me to go fuck off for even suggesting this. I don't really care where we eat. I'll sit on the dirt right here, but I'm curious to see how far she'll go to prove her persistence today.

Another first, little devil? Will you give me this?

I step closer and squeeze her hand. "It'll be a nice view up there. We might be able to see the lake."

She slowly turns her head. Her eyes, more green than brown today, narrow in on mine. "Yeah? You know what else has a nice view of the lake? Our campsite. Maybe even the car. Why don't we go check?"

"I can carry you," I offer, attempting not to smile at her quick-witted apprehension. "I wouldn't mind it."

"You are not carrying me," she scoffs, yanking out of my grip. "I'm capable of getting there myself. And you know what?"

"What?"

She leans in, standing on her toes to get closer, her hands curling around her hips, her face so near to mine I can see the freckles she's hiding underneath her makeup. "That's exactly what I'm going to do, Mason, because contrary to what you think, I fucking *love it* out here."

Brooke lets out a tiny squeak, spins around, and sprints through the tall grass like something is chasing her.

My mouth stretches into a grin.

Fuck, baby. Look at you. Always surprising me.

She makes it to the boulder and, with frantic hands, tries to claw her way on top of it, but her footing slips on the smooth rock. "No! Goddamn it, no!"

Laughing, I follow behind and reach the boulder just as she slips again. Even with a running start, she's too short to get up here alone. I toss my bag on top of the rock to free up my hands.

"Here, my little nature lover," I say against her hair, grabbing her waist and hoisting her up onto the rock.

She thanks me through a breathy pant and shifts over to make room.

I climb up with ease and sit on the warm stone. Reaching for my bag, I watch Brooke scoot to the ledge and look out over the tree-line.

She's tousled and winded. Her hair is coming undone, several thick pieces falling beside her face and sticking to her neck, barely any of it still contained in her pony. Her skin is flushed and shiny from the bug spray. A light dusting of dirt clings to her legs.

I want to freeze this moment. I want to be able to sit here and do absolutely nothing, just stare at this woman for hours and hours. Bask in the stunningly unpolished version of the temptress I met on the footpath that first day.

Fuck, how wild she was then. Luring me. Making it so I couldn't remember ever seeing anyone else.

She's still just as brilliantly captivating as she always is in any arrangement. The little wolf or the docile sheep. I'll take every layer of Brooke. Anything and everything.

You're a wreck for her, mate. This is a lot more for you now.

My world seems to slow.

Brooke moves from her perch to sit on the other side of the bag. She tucks some hair behind her ear, looks up at me through those long, dark lashes, and winks. That's it. Nothing more than a bloody wink, and a commanding warmth spreads in my chest like kerosene poured over an open flame.

Yeah, I'm a fucking wreck all right.

I wipe my hand across my mouth, collecting myself before I speak. She grimaces at the dampness beading on her brow when she touches her fingers to her skin.

"You look pretty," I tell her, ducking my head to see her eyes. "Really fucking pretty."

She shrugs, laughing a little as she drops her hand. "Thanks. I'm sweaty."

"Yeah."

"Yeah," she echoes, fighting a smile. Her gaze shifts between my face and the bag as she crosses her legs beneath her. "What did you pack to eat? I could murder some food right now."

I unzip the pouch and pull out what I grabbed from the cooler before we took off this morning.

Bread with some almond butter, apple slices cut and drizzled with lemon to keep from browning, trail mix, two protein bars, and some fruit leather.

I hand Brooke a bottle of water and set the food between us with some napkins.

"Anything edible in there?" she asks through a chuckle, poking at the fruit leather. "This . . . I'm not going to lie. It looks like a shoelace."

I hand her a cookie dough flavored protein bar. "Eat this."

Her eyes flicker with delight as she reads the package. She tears it open with her teeth and takes a bite, her jaw working through one full chew before it locks up. Our eyes meet. Her nose wrinkles in disgust. She drops the bar and grabs her water, tipping it back and swallowing the bite she took.

"That tastes like glue," she mumbles, wiping the back of her hand against her mouth. She shoots me a disapproving look. "You packed glue bars and shoelace, Mason. Congratulations, we're going to starve to death."

I take a bite of my sandwich, grinning. "We can always hunt for food. Have you ever tried squirrel? It tastes like chicken."

"Me? Oh, yeah. I eat squirrel all the time. It's all I usually eat when I camp." She grabs the bag of apples and opens it on her lap, stretching her legs out in front of her. "Can't we hike to a McDonalds or something? Or a Chick-fil-A? I need a six piece nugget to make my life right." She crosses her ankles and snaps into an apple slice.

I'm smiling, amused at her reaction to the lunch I packed, until something small and black on Brooke's calf catches my attention.

I know what it is. I know *exactly* what it is. Ticks are an unfortunate hazard to camping, one I didn't warn her about.

Fuck. She must've picked it up when she ran through the tall grass. I would've noticed it on her before. I've been staring at her legs all morning.

I need to act fast and get it off.

I also need to keep her oblivious to it.

"What would you order at Chick-fil-A, if we hiked there?" I ask, reaching into the outer pouch on my bag and feeling around for the supplies I need. My hand closes around a small metal instrument. I pull it out and search for my lighter and medical kit.

"Mm. A number one, extra pickles. And a cookies and cream milkshake on the side." She takes another bite of apple. "Or a wrap. They have good wraps."

"Sounds good."

"Better than squirrel," she laughs through a shake of her head. "Which I'm sure doesn't taste anything like chicken."

I set out my supplies and put the bag down, pushing the food out of the way. Scooting closer, I wrap my hand around her knee and gently hold it. "Brooke, I need you to stay still, yeah? Don't move."

"What?" Her leg jumps. The apple she's holding falls on top of the bag. "What are you doing? Why do you have tweezers?"

"You have a tick on your leg."

"WHAT? Oh, my God, where?" She sits up and gasps. Her entire body jerks. "Mason! Get it off!"

I squeeze her leg and look up into her round, panicky eyes. "Baby, relax. I'm going to get it off."

"Have you done this before?" she asks, her voice shaking. Tears filling her eyes and those pouty lips quivering.

I nod. I would nod right now even if I didn't know what the

fuck I was doing. I don't want Brooke to be scared. Her face is killing me.

"Yeah. Plenty of times. Trust me. Can you hold still? That's all I need you to do."

"Oh, God," she whispers, blinking hard and sending the tears down her face. Her leg remains tense beneath my hand, but she doesn't resist me. "O-Okay. Just don't mess up."

"I won't."

"Mason." She puts her hand on top of mine, gripping me tight. Our eyes meet. "Please. Don't mess up."

I stare at her as she slowly pulls away. "I won't," I promise, letting her see my conviction, making sure she hears it in my steady voice. "Hold still and you'll be right."

She nods and blinks away.

Looking down at her leg, I grip the tweezers and position them over the tick, slowly advancing. I pinch as close to Brooke's skin as I can get and gently pull the fucker straight up, making sure to remove the mouth. I blow out a quick breath when I see I have all of it.

"All right there, sweetheart?" I ask, picking up the lighter.

"No," she quietly replies, her face turned away. "Just tell me when it's over."

I burn the tick with it still pinched in the tweezers. When I'm certain it's dead, I dispose of it off the rock and open up my kit. I kneel next to Brooke. "Just going to clean the area. I'm finished. It's gone now."

Brooke nods and wipes at her face. She still isn't looking at me. Her tear-filled eyes are fixated on the tree line.

Once I disinfect and bandage the wound, I clean my hands and rub her leg. "There. See? That wasn't so terrible, was it?"

I immediately regret my words when her head drops between her shoulders.

With a quiet sob, she breaks. My strong, determined girl crumbles, crying into her hands, her tiny body drawing in on itself like a wounded animal.

"Hey, come here." I pull her into my arms, crushing her to my chest as she continues to sob. I push her sweaty hair out of her face and kiss her cheek. "Shh. Baby, it's okay. You're okay. It's over, yeah? Does it hurt?"

She shakes her head and clutches onto my shirt. "I hate it here," she cries, rubbing her face into my neck, her body shaking as she draws me closer. "I hate hiking. I hate all of it. Bugs and my smelly bug spray. All those trees you pointed out. The flowers. Fuck, I hate flowers, Mason. I fucking hate them."

She sniffs and cries some more. I hold her tighter, running my fingers through her hair and rubbing her back.

"I was lying when I said I loved it. I don't love it at all. I want to go."

I press a kiss to her temple. "Okay. We can go."

"I'm sorry."

"Don't be sorry. Hey." I tilt her chin up.

Her face is red, streaked with tears. Her eyes swollen and sad. She looks miserable and scared, and the worst part is she wouldn't look this way if it wasn't for me.

I did this.

I brought her out here and made her uncomfortable. I saw her anxiety and kept fucking pushing because I thought she'd enjoy what we were doing. Maybe not all of it, and maybe not right away, but like everything else with Brooke, I was willing to wait for that moment. Guide her to where I wanted her to be with me.

Fucking selfish is what I am. She probably hates me for this, and if she does I don't blame her. I feel like the biggest arsehole on the planet.

"Come on."

I stand, bringing her with me and setting her on her feet. I quickly pack everything away into my bag.

I don't give her the chance to help. She shouldn't have to. This is all my doing. My bloody mess I need to clean up.

Same goes for the campsite.

Once we make it back, Brooke stands off to the side while I pack up the tent and stow our belongings into our separate bags. I load up my arms with the gear and the cooler. She grabs the sleeping bag, squeezing it against her chest just like she did when we arrived yesterday. Her head stays lowered as she stares at the ground.

Fuck. She can't even look at me now.

"I'm sorry, Brooke," I tell her, ready to drop to my knees and beg for this woman's forgiveness.

She lifts her eyes and nods, acknowledging me, then drops her chin against the sleeping bag and hugs it tighter.

With a jerk of my head, I motion for her to walk in front on the path that leads to the parking lot.

She's ready to go. I won't keep her here any longer.

The trip home is different than every other time I've been in the car with Brooke. I'm the one turning up the volume on the stereo, but not because I'm anxious or avoiding conversation.

I hate silence. I hate how quiet we're both being, but somehow I know she prefers music to hearing my voice right now.

She's completely shut off from me. Head turned and eyes engaged out the window. She hasn't looked at me once since we pulled out of the lot. I doubt she wants to talk.

I park in front of the studio and grab Brooke's bag out of the back of the car. I'm ready to carry it for her when she blocks my path with her body and with quick hands, takes the bag away from me.

"It's fine. I got it." She slides it up her arm and over her shoulder, huffing a loud breath after. Her eyes slowly reach mine.

She looks unsure of what to say next, if anything.

I'm unsure too.

I take a step back and gesture at her leg. "Clean that again when you get home, and keep some antibiotic ointment on it. You should be fine, but if it gets infected or you start running a fever, you need to go to the hospital."

Brooke's eyes widen marginally. She glances down at her leg, uttering a soft, "fucker," before shaking her head and looking back up at me. Her shoulders sag. "All right. Anything else?"

I feel my eyebrows draw together. *Anything else? Is she dismissing me?*

Running a quick hand through my hair, I lift the other between us, then lower it with an exhausted sigh. "I don't know, Brooke. Is there?"

My voice sounds tight and hoarse. I feel like something's got a grip around my throat.

She stares at me like I've just asked her the most absurd

question, her eyes hard and searching. Then, as if snapping out of a trance, she blinks away, tilting her head and wiping a hand along the line of her neck.

"Ugh. I need to take about fifty showers. I'm going to go do that and then coat my body in disinfectant."

Spinning around, not giving me another look or word, Brooke clears traffic and hurriedly crosses the street.

I watch her get into her car. I watch her pull away and disappear around the corner.

I stand there, dumbfounded, my mouth slack, my mind reeling with confusion.

What the fuck? Is that it? Is that how this is going to end between us?

Sure, Brooke has every right to be angry with me. Sure, I fucked up dragging her out into the middle of nowhere this weekend and pushing her to try new things, but what about everything else?

The dates. Our talks and the way she opens up to me when it's just us. Last night in the fucking tent. Does none of that matter?

I slump back against the side of my car and scrub both hands down my face. Tension pulls at my muscles. I feel stiff and tight all over.

I need a long run. Hours on the pavement.

I practice yoga daily. It calms my mind, but nothing substitutes the mental and physical workout a hard as fuck run will give you. I want to be too tired to think. Running will do that.

Haphazardly unloading my camping gear into the studio, not even bothering to take it upstairs, I lock up behind me and go through a few stretches to loosen up. I hit the footpath with quick strides, running down and back up Fayette Street, through alleys and behind businesses. I run faster, harder, down streets I've never been down before and ones that are familiar.

The sun lowers in the sky, dipping between buildings. Sweat soaks my shirt and trickles down my face.

My feet beat on the cement, a steady, relentless pace I push myself to keep even after my muscles ache and my lungs burn.

I think about Brooke and our weekend, but not the shit that happened today. I think about holding her last night in the tent. Her soft body curling against mine, pulling me closer in her sleep. Her breath against my neck and the smell of her hair.

Christ, being with her like that was everything. And fuck me, if I don't want it every single night.

My infatuation with her started out as an idea. A glimpse of a woman I wanted to know and understand. A delightful interest. But the more time I spend with her, the more desperate I feel.

To have her. To keep her. I'm completely mad for this woman and I may have cocked it all up.

Three hours later and I'm staring down at the drain in my shower as cold water beats on my back.

My body is fatigued, my muscles aching and worn, but I don't have the clarity I usually feel after a long run. My goddamn head feels heavier somehow.

So much for de-stressing therapeutically. I debate getting dressed and walking to the nearest liquor store.

Cutting the water off, I step out and cinch a towel around my waist, moving out of the bathroom and toward the bed. I unplug my phone from the charger and send out a quick text.

I did promise to keep her informed of developments. This is, unfortunately, my latest development.

Me: I fucked up with Brooke.

The phone barely touches the dark wood of my nightstand before it starts ringing.

"That was fast," I tensely answer, wiping a quick hand over my face to collect the water dripping from my hair. "Please tell me you weren't expecting that message and waiting around for it. I like to think my chances with this woman weren't doomed from the start."

"How the hell should I know about your chances? I've never met her," Tessa replies, her tone helplessly clever. "And last time we talked, *you* said she was warming up to you, and that you've been seeing a lot of each other. Quite a bit, I believe were your exact words. Based on those two facts right there, I'd say you were doing better than a chump who was doomed from the start. I doubt she would've spent any time with you if that were the case."

"Right, well, as lovely as that thought is, our time together may be over. I'm not sure how warm she is to the idea of me anymore after what I've put her through."

"Oh, Christ. What did you do? And please, don't skimp on the information. Reed still likes to leave out important details to stories just to make himself sound better. It never works. If you want my advice, I'm going to need to know exactly how you fucked up. Like you can't tell me Brooke hates you now because you took her for a moonlit walk last night after your date, because I'm going to hear that and think 'what the fuck is this bitch's problem', when really, you're leaving off the part where you ran over some poor old lady with your car, left her to die in the middle of the street, and then ditched your vehicle because it was evidence. Making someone an accessory to murder is a valid reason to hate you."

"I actually think Brooke might've preferred that to what really happened."

"Ha-ha," Tessa dryly replies. "Spill it. What did you do?"

I blankly stare at my comforter. "Took her camping when she expressed a strong aversion for it. I thought maybe I could get her to like it if she just focused on being with me, and not where she was or what we were doing. Last night I saw how anxious she was out there. I should've taken her home then."

I might still have a bloody shot with her if I had.

Exhaling a worried breath, I pinch the bridge of my nose. "She was trying to like it. Christ, she was beautiful out there, Tessa. So determined. Then today I pulled a tick off her leg and she broke down crying. I felt terrible. I still feel terrible. It was fucking awful seeing her upset like that and knowing I was the reason for it. She asked me to get her out of there and I did. When we got back, she barely said anything before she left to go home. It felt like a brush-off."

"Maybe she was just freaking out and needed a moment to deal with it. Did she actually tell you to go fuck yourself and never speak to her again?"

"Not in so many words," I answer.

"Well, I would've," Tessa chuckles. "Fucking gross. A tick? That's just cold."

I feel the muscles in my shoulders tense. "I didn't fucking put it there. I got the bloody thing off, didn't I?"

"Would you relax? I think you're overreacting."

Overreacting? Am I? I don't see Brooke here with me, so I think I'm reacting just fine.

Tessa breathes a laugh. "Mason. Mason. Mason."

"Yeah?"

"Do you love her? It kind of sounds like you do."

I close my eyes, taking in a deep breath and releasing it slowly.

When did my obsession with Brooke become something more?

I have no doubt of my feelings for her. I've never been more certain of anything before, but I can't pinpoint the exact moment it all changed for me.

Would it even do me any good to admit it to someone now? If it's over, what's the point?

"I . . ." My response is interrupted by another call coming through the line. I pull the phone away to look at the screen, and my spine straightens as I blink the caller's name into focus.

I nearly drop the damn device before I press it against my ear again.

"Tessa, it's Brooke. I need to take this."

"Ah, see? All that worrying for nothing. Let me know how it goes."

"Yeah," I reply thickly, my bloody voice bound by my uneasiness again. I clear my throat before clicking over to answer the call. "Brooke?"

"Hey." Her voice is light and lifted. She sounds like she's smiling.

Why would she be smiling?

"What are you doing?"

I look down at my towel, then around the darkened room. "Nothing. Just took a shower."

"God, I took so many showers. I used an entire thing of body wash," she giggles.

I run a hand through my wet hair.

She's giggling? Why the fuck is she giggling? Is she happy right now?

"So, Mason . . ."

"Yeah?"

"That goodbye sucked. It was awkward and really fucking weird. I didn't like it. You need to do better than that, okay?" A slurping sound comes through the phone. "Mm. Are you coming over?"

"What?"

"Billy is making his famous martinis. They're so, so good. I'm on my third one so I can't drive. You have to come to me."

I sit down on the edge of my bed. *Am I dreaming this phone call?*

"You want me to come over there? After what happened today?" I ask hesitantly.

I almost don't want to shatter this illusion. This Brooke still likes me.

"Yes, hello! You wanted me for the whole weekend, right? I mean, that *was* the original plan before that bloody tick showed up and ruined everything. It's Saturday night. Still the weekend, mate," she laughs again. "You're so funny, Mason."

"I am?"

"Yes. So sweet and funny. A little strange, yeah? I like it." She pauses, humming a bit. "Now hurry up and get over here. I want to kiss you before I'm drunk and don't remember it."

The call disconnects. I bring the phone away from my ear and stare at it.

What just happened?

Brooke isn't upset anymore. She isn't mad or acting like we're through and she's done.

She wants me to come over. She hated that goodbye as much as I did.

She wants to kiss me before she's drunk.

Too fucking right. I want that. I hated that bloody goodbye. I didn't even want one.

I dart off the bed and attack my dresser like a man possessed. Clothes are flying. I pull on a pair of jeans and a T-shirt and stumble into my runners, grabbing my keys and my phone.

My mood is jubilant. There's that runner's high I was hoping for earlier. Only this is better. Leave it to Brooke to shock me back into my usual pleasant self. She can't do or be anything predictable. It doesn't suit her.

Traffic is mild and I arrive at her building within a few minutes, pulling underneath and parking in the garage.

I take the elevators to her floor. I knock twice and step back, scowling at the water I collect off my neck. I didn't even bother running a towel over my hair before leaving. My collar is damp.

The door swings open and Brooke's bright face appears. She squeals and lunges at me, wrapping her hands around my neck and tugging me inside.

My back hits the wall. Her full lips form to my mouth.

"Hey. Hi. Your hair is wet, goof." She filters her fingers through my hair and tugs on the ends. She kisses me slowly. Deeply. Pressing her small body against mine. Her tongue swipes across my lip and she moans. "Mm. My face is so warm right now. Feel." Stepping back, she grabs my hand and presses it to her cheek.

I look at her, at that wild, devilish smile twisting across her mouth. The dimple sinking into her cheek and her brilliant eyes, round and eager.

"I'm so glad you're here," she whispers, smiling so goddamn big. Her cheeks lifting and flushing pink.

My heart thunders in my chest.

Christ, I'm so in love with this girl.

A throat clears in the room. I look up and spot our audience, Billy and Joey, hovering a few feet away by the sofa. Both of them looking more than pleased at what they're witnessing.

"Hey. How are ya?" I choke out, straightening off the wall.

"Evening." Joey tips his glass, arching an eyebrow. "She's been pacing around waiting for you. I almost had to sedate her."

"Whatever. I was not," Brooke snaps over her shoulder. She tugs on my hand. "Come on. Do you want a drink? We have beer."

"And martinis," Billy adds, nodding his greeting and then gesturing across the room. "Liquor cabinet is over there if you want something stiff."

Brooke spins around. Her mouth slowly falling open and then spreading into a knowing smile. "Oh, my God. Do you get it?

Something stiff?" She gets up on her toes, hand beside her mouth as she whispers, "like a cock."

Tipsy Brooke doesn't know how to whisper.

Her eyes pop wider when everyone enjoys a good laugh. Joey and Billy remark about only wanting stiff ones as they move about the condo.

I grin down at Brooke, scratching my jaw. "Yeah, sweetheart. I get it. I'm good with a beer, yeah?"

Her little nose twitches. "Yeah," she chuckles, pushing on my chest. "Go sit. I'll grab you one."

I do a quick take of my surroundings as I pad toward the bar.

The condo is spacious and elegantly decorated. Expensive looking art covers the walls.

"Nice place," I comment, sliding out a stool and stretching my arms out on the cool marble. "I'm still working on getting all of my stuff unpacked. It's been a bit of a slow process. Other things have been occupying my time."

Brooke smiles over her shoulder as she grabs me a beer.

"Oh, this is all Billy. I can't decorate to save my life." Joey comes to stand at the bar with his cocktail. "It's strange how fabulous I am with my own fashion sense, yet when it comes to color schemes for a room I'm a hot mess about it."

Billy steps up behind him and kisses his shoulder, laughing a bit. "It's a good thing I love you for other reasons. Remember when you tried to wallpaper the bathroom?"

"Christ, don't remind me," Joey groans in embarrassment. "I have no idea why I thought that was a good idea."

"Because you had just moved in and you wanted to surprise me with something. It was sweet."

Brooke runs her hand across my back and places the beer in front of me. She kisses my cheek.

"I'll be right back."

I watch her disappear behind a door. I fight the urge to follow her in there when I decide on that being her bedroom.

Slow it down, mate. You damn well know what'll happen if you go in there.

"So, camping . . ."

I turn my head and watch Joey's eyes flicker with amusement over the top of his drink. He takes a slow sip.

I look between him and Billy. "Right. How was she when she got back here? Like this?" I hook a thumb over my shoulder in the direction of the bedroom.

"Hardly." Billy drops his chin on Joey's shoulder, his arms wrapping around his waist. "She was freaking out about the tick, which isn't shocking. This is Brooke we're talking about. She once stayed at her sister's house for the weekend because she saw a spider in her bedroom. Wouldn't come home until we promised her we killed it."

"We never found the damn thing," Joey adds with a cheeky grin. "We just missed her crazy ass and wanted her to come home."

I rub at my mouth. "So, when did she start acting like this? She seems fine now, like nothing happened."

"Do you not know the glorious effects of alcohol?" Joey's eyebrow lifts. "Once we distracted her with drinks, she calmed down about it." He looks at Billy, then back at me, smiling like he's in on some secret. "That's also when she started going on and on about you."

"Another thing you need to know about Brooke," Billy pauses, his eyes lifting to something over my shoulder. I hear a door shut and he quietly adds, "She doesn't do that," before turning his head and pulling Joey away from the bar.

My mind soaks in that obscure bit of information.

She doesn't do what? Talk about blokes like she does me? Drink and forget about unfortunate run-ins with insects?

What the fuck? I need clarity on this.

Brooke moves back into the kitchen and waves at me. I watch her as she reaches for a tall cocktail on the counter, one resembling Joey's. It's a pale green color with a cherry floating at the bottom.

She spins around and closes a cabinet. I study her, resting my chin on my hand. Her long hair falls down her back, curling against her black tank top. Loose trackies hang low on her hips with the words Team Pink covering her arse.

She brings the drink to her mouth and takes a sip. Our eyes meet. I smile, and she cutely waves at me again.

A door slides open behind me and draws my attention.

Billy looks up, places his hand on Joey's shoulder, and muscles him outside. He looks to be struggling with it.

"We're . . . go, will you? Jesus! We're going to go sit on the balcony. Give you two a little privacy for a while." He jerks his chin and then steps out onto the terrace, pulling the door closed and drowning out Joey's flippant protest.

"Goddamn it, Billy," I faintly hear through the glass.

Brooke's quiet giggle turns my head as she sits beside me, her bare feet swinging in the air. "This is my fourth apple martini." She takes a small sip, licking her lips. "It's apple."

Laughing, I twist off the cap on my beer and take a swig. "How's your leg?"

"Mm. Good! Look." She sets her drink down and pulls up her pants. "It's not even red anymore. Not that you can tell 'cause of the Band-Aid, but still. I cleaned it like you said and put some Neosporin on it. Billy said it looks fine. He's had tick bites before."

I wrap my hand around her calf and examine her leg, slowly running my thumb along her smooth skin.

Images of Brooke on the rock, scared and trembling corrode my mind. Her broken voice fills my ears.

"You know how sorry I am for this, right?" I quietly ask, looking up into those big, curious eyes. I tug down her pants to her ankle and release her leg. "I'm so fucking sorry, Brooke. I should've never taken you there. I shouldn't have made you do that."

She gives me a lopsided smile. "I liked the swanky tent. Remember what we did in there?"

"Yeah."

"You didn't make me do any of that."

Straightening with a quick breath, I look down as her hand finds mine under the lip of the bar. She squeezes my thumb.

I close my eyes.

Fuck, she's so different with me right now. When has she ever reached for my hand, or displayed any sort of honest affection for me in front of people she knows? Is it the alcohol?

Christ, just enjoy it, will ya? Stop analyzing everything.

"I thought it was over today," I softly admit, brushing my

fingers against hers and staring down into my lap. "I was shocked when you called. I thought I was dreaming."

"Maybe you were."

Our eyes lock, and she breathes a laugh, taking another sip of her drink and then tipping her head down. Her eyes flutter. "Dreaming about me is kind of your thing, isn't it?"

"*You* are kind of my thing."

"And yoga."

"Yeah." I reach up and grab a piece of her hair, tucking it behind her ear. My phone beeps with a text alert, and I pull it free from my pocket and place it on the counter.

Tessa: Well?

I quickly type my response.

Me: Crisis averted.

"Who is that?" Brooke asks, leaning close to see my screen as I set the phone back down. She studies it for a moment. "Tessa?" Our eyes lock. Hers narrow. "Mm."

I turn my head, smiling as she rights herself on her stool and shrugs indifferently.

"She's a mate from Alabama. I've told her about you."

Brooke lifts her glass to her mouth. "Oh, really? And have you seen her vagina? Because I've never seen any of my mates' vaginas. Just saying. Or their penises, before you ask. No penises or vaginas between mates."

I rub at my neck, watching her, uncontrollably smiling at this development.

Now this is quite interesting.

"Are you jealous, Brooke?"

Her head snaps in my direction, eyes heavy with disagreement. She lowers her glass to the marble. "Jealous? Me? Of who? That ugly bitch who just texted you? Why would I be jealous of her if you've never seen her vagina, which you have yet to confirm. Please confirm that before I toss my drink in your face."

I take another swig of my beer, letting her stew a bit next to me before I respond.

"Tell Theresa to find her own Australian."

I nearly choke.

Wiping at my mouth after my coughing fit, I turn to Brooke and set my beer down, reaching for her hand. She fights my hold for a good three seconds before letting me have it, but keeps her gaze fixed behind the bar.

"*Tessa*, not Theresa, and I went out on one date months ago. I never even kissed her, Brooke. She's just a really good mate."

"You don't need to explain your relationship or whatever with her. I really don't care."

"No?"

She shakes her head.

I lean forward to see her face. "Because I would really fucking care if you were texting some bloke and I didn't know who he was to you. I'm not a jealous guy, but I think for you I would be. It's staggering how you make me feel."

She turns her head, watching me press a kiss to her palm.

"And I rather like thinking you might be right there with me, willing to be jealous and crazy for only one person."

Her face relaxes the longer she stares at me. She wets her lips. "You never even kissed her?"

"No."

"Did you want to?"

"Not like I want to kiss you."

Slowly, like she's fighting it, a gentle smile tugs at the corner of her mouth, then pulls across the rest of it. She shakes her head through a quick exhale, giggles quietly, then slides her warm body into my lap, squeezing my neck and pressing soft kisses to my jaw.

"Tell me something in Italian again," she whispers as her fingers slide through my hair. "I liked it so much before."

I drop my head beside hers. My arms tightly coil around her back. "You like not knowing what I'm saying?"

"Mm." She nods and kisses my neck.

"I could say anything, you know? Maybe something you aren't ready to hear."

"I know." She moves back and stares at my mouth. Her eyes

darken, liquid desire swirling in those wild green and brown irises. She wets her lips and grabs my face. "I think I'm drunk."

"Yeah?"

Nodding, she leans in. "Definitely."

Her lips press against mine. I open my mouth and take her tongue, sucking off the bitterness from the alcohol. Letting her taste saturate my soul.

God, what this woman does to me.

She moans and presses her chest closer, kissing me hard and unhurried, stroking her tongue against mine, sucking on my lips and wiggling in my lap.

I both hate and love how Brooke's being with me tonight, so unashamed with her affection. Abandoning all her doubts. Exactly how I want her to be with me all the time. Exactly how *I* am with her, all the time.

It's bloody torture, knowing why she's acting so free with me, but fuck, it's hard to pull away from.

This is what it can be like. And this, goddamn, this is what I'm missing.

"Mason," she groans, digging her nails into my neck, rocking her hips against my erection.

I snap out of my haze and slow us down, moving my lips to her cheek and kissing her dimple.

"Voglio che questo non finisca mai," I whisper against her skin.

I won't ever want this to be over.

She stills in my arms, her breath blowing hot and sharp against my ear. Then, with a quiet sigh, she drops her head to my shoulder and goes limp.

"Yeah," she murmurs. "I won't remember that tomorrow."

Laughing, I lean back and push the hair out of her face.

"Are you spending the night?" she asks, her fingers dancing along the back of my neck. She looks excited for that possibility.

"Better not."

Her lip twitches. "Think I might forget your rules and try and take advantage of you in my drunken stupor?"

I smile, squeezing her hips. "Yeah, and I might forget you're drunk."

Too much temptation. I know how fucking amazing it feels having Brooke next to me at night. I won't be able to keep my hands off her.

"I would," she confesses through a massive grin. "Forget, *and* take advantage of you. But can you at least stay until I fall asleep? I'll let you stare at my tits a little." She shimmies her shoulders and makes her tits bounce and sway.

My cock stirs.

No bra. Fuck, this is going to be a challenge.

"Jesus Christ, Brooke," I groan, leaning in and taking her mouth again, tilting her head and pressing kisses to her jaw. "You're keeping that on, yeah?"

"Nah."

She laughs and I suck on her neck.

"Good," I tell her. "Then I'll stay."

Chapter Thirteen

Brooke

MONDAYS HAVE NEVER BOTHERED ME.

I know most people would rather skip this day entirely, but I've never had a problem with it. I don't mind working on Mondays, or dealing with the general population on this specific day of the week. Traffic is never really an issue because I work so close to where I live. And as long as I'm not drinking my weight in booze the night before, I never have difficulty waking up and getting my ass to the bakery on time.

Mondays have never bothered me. Until today, this particular Monday.

The Monday after my weekend with Mason.

Why the fuck did I think it was a good idea to come into work today?

Because I was nursing a wicked hangover all day yesterday and spent my life in bed with my door locked, Joey missed his opportunity to run off at the mouth and bug the shit out of me about everything that happened this weekend. But now that I'm fully coherent and stuck in this chocolate raspberry scented Hell for eight hours? I not only get to try and ignore Joey's nosy comments, but Dylan is also weighing in with her opinion on everything.

She's my boss. I can't exactly toss her through a window to shut her up now, can I?

Plus, there's the whole pregnancy thing. I'm sure that wouldn't be good for the baby.

"Cupcake, you should've seen her." Joey's broad smile reemerges as he steps into the back for the hundredth time today.

I sigh and keep my head down.

"Talking about how sweet Mason was when he removed the tick. How he held her while she cried with those sexy ass arms of his. She even mentioned something about having a decent time up until that point. Can you believe it? Our little mini muffin actually enjoyed camping."

I place another pastry into the large bakery box in front of me and glare at him from across the worktop. Dylan laughs quietly from her stool. "I was drunk when I said that," I tell him.

I can't believe it. I actually had fun camping. What is happening with the world?

"You were barely into your first martini. Don't even go there with me, Brooke." Joey points a finger at my face. "I am way past the point of trying to get you to admit you have feelings for this guy, because I think you're way past just having feelings. I saw you with him when he came over, and I know how you flirt when you're drunk. That wasn't it, honey."

I close the box and stack it on top of the other two I have already filled. A sharp, unrelenting tension builds behind my eyes. I ignore Dylan's pleased smile and focus all of my annoyance onto Joey.

"Well, I don't remember how I looked when Mason came over, because like I said fifty times already today, I was well on my way to party hour, but I'm sure I looked how any woman would look when sex comes knocking at their door."

"Oh, give me a fucking break." Dylan pushes a sheet pan away from her and crosses her arms under her chest. "Brooke, when was the last time you had sex? How many days ago?"

I open my mouth to answer, then quickly close it.

Fuck. Fuuuck. I can normally count my response to this question on one hand. But today I have no idea . . .

How long has it been?

Paul. That giant asshat was my last regrettable encounter. I met Mason the following week. Am I into double digits territory?

Holy shit. That had to be at least two weeks ago.

"Do you need a calendar, Brooke? There's one right over there."

Ignoring Dylan and her question, I open up a paper bag and begin filling it with banana muffins, keeping my eyes down and focusing on my task.

"So what if it's been longer than usual since I've had sex. Who cares? I'm doing other stuff with Mason. I'm still getting off. I don't see what the big fucking deal is or why both of you are bugging me about it."

Silence.

No wiseass responses. No amusing little noises like I've been listening to all morning.

Have my prayers been answered? Am I suddenly the only employee of Dylan's Sweet Tooth?

I look up and spot two pairs of eyes on me.

Damn.

Joey looks over at Dylan, grinning wildly. "I so wish I would've gotten that adorable speech on camera. You?"

She nods slowly. "Absolutely."

What the fuck are they going on about now?

"What?" I ask, setting the bag down. My hands flatten on the wood as I flick my gaze between the two of them. "What did I say?"

Dylan straightens on her stool and rests her hand on her belly. "You just admitted you don't care anymore that Mason is withholding sex from you. You, Brooke Wicks, don't care about sex because you're spending time with a man who is making you so happy, you're forgetting what you're missing." She tilts her head. "Now, are you ready to admit *why* you don't care?"

"I just told you!" I yell, slapping a hand over my mouth.

Oh, my God. What am I doing?

Dylan and Joey both startle from my outburst. Worried glances are exchanged, and then directed at me.

Shit! Get it together, Brooke. You like having a job. You need a job. No more incidents like that or your ass is going to be out on the street.

"I'm sorry," I say, lowering my hand and looking across the worktop at Dylan. "I didn't mean to yell like that."

She unscrews the cap on her water and brings it to her mouth. "All right."

Reaching back and untying my apron, I calmly continue after I've settled on a more appropriate work-place volume. "As I told you, I'm still getting off with Mason. The orgasms he gives me are some of the best of my life. Maybe even *the* best. It would be different if I was just hanging out with this guy and he wasn't touching me, but he is. It doesn't matter that we haven't had sex yet. Mason's foreplay is on point."

Joey shakes his head, waving a dismissive hand in the air. "What is he to you? Boyfriend? Friend with benefits? What?"

"We've been over this," I sternly reply, tossing my apron onto the table. "Jesus. He's just this guy I'm spending time with. And in five minutes when you ask me that question again, he'll still be just this guy I'm spending time with."

Dylan stands from her stool and reaches for her pink mixer, sliding it in front of her. "Denial doesn't look good on you, Brooke. Stop wearing it."

"Oh, my God," I softly utter, snatching up the muffin bag and setting it on top of the three boxes.

I need to get out of here. Far away from these two. I've never done a delivery by myself before but I've knocked out tons with Joey. It's usually the two of us.

Well, that's not happening today. If I don't get a break from this madness, I'm going to end up burning this place to the ground just to avoid further conversation.

Joey comes to stand beside me. He rubs his hands eagerly together, looking between the boxes and my face.

"Ready to go, Mrs. King?"

My eyes widen. *He did not just fucking go there.*

Did I say burn this place to the ground? I meant slaughter a third of the staff.

Fists clenching at my sides, I step closer to him. Joey leans back when he registers the look on my face.

"Too much?" he meekly asks.

"You think?" I lift the boxes and balance the bag on top, glaring at Joey as I lower them against my chest. "I'm doing this delivery alone. Do yourself a favor and eat a dick for lunch while I'm gone. You sound deprived."

"Ow, kitten." Joey gapes at me. He looks sincerely hurt. "Just because I'm all up in your business, doesn't mean I'm deprived. Retract the claws, please."

I look up at him, trying to stay angry, swallowing down the remorse I feel burning the back of my throat.

I haven't spoken to Joey this cruelly since before I moved in with him. This used to be regular dialogue between the two of us, back when we could hardly stand each other. Then I started working here. The closer we became, him and I, the more playful our banter. We stopped cracking on each other years ago.

Why did I have to go there just now? Why did *he*?

Why are both of them on my case about this?

I brush past him and move toward the doorway. If I stay any longer, I'll either yell or apologize. Neither one seem appealing right now.

"Brooke, do you know where it is?" Dylan calls out as I step into the main bakery.

"Yeah. We delivered there last year."

I turn sideways to push the door open with my elbow. Movement catches my eye. I look up just as Joey walks in from the kitchen, looking like he wants to tell me something.

I don't wait around to hear it. God only knows what other clever little comments he has to say right now.

With a firm shove, I exit the bakery and head for my car.

I TAKE THE ELEVATORS TO the eleventh floor of the Harding and Associates building, a huge venture capitalist firm in the city.

I have definitely been here. More than once in the same day. While Joey and I made our delivery to one of the offices in this building last year, I caught the eye of one of the associates. Our delivery just so happened to be for a breakfast meeting. The associate ended up being my entire lunch.

I hardly remember anything about him. Dark hair maybe? Glasses? The only thing sticking out in my mind is how irritated I was with Dylan's thirty minute lunch rule that day.

I drop my head back against the mirrored wall behind me.

What if that had been Mason, and it was a year later, or several years later. Would I remember little details about him? Or major ones? Anything?

Yes.

My answer is as certain as my desire to keep breathing. It's terrifying and oddly comforting all at once. I don't understand it. I don't understand any of it. My stomach feels like it's being twisted into a perpetual knot.

Balancing the three boxes filled with treats and the bag of muffins, I step off the elevators and walk across the shiny marble floor to the reception area, praying I leave my anxiety behind me. An older woman directs me down the hallway to the conference room by the large window overlooking the city streets. I say a silent thank you when the doors to the room are already propped open. I would hate to place these boxes on the floor to be able to knock.

That's extremely unprofessional, and probably one of the reasons these deliveries are done in pairs.

I step inside the room, lowering the boxes so I can see above the paper bag. Several men in suits are seated at a long rectangular table. All of them look up at my arrival and halt their dissection of whatever document is in front of them.

"Hello. I have a delivery from Dylan's Sweet Tooth. Pastries and muffins."

The older man closest to me stands and takes the boxes. He smiles warmly. "Excellent. We were just about to get started."

He spreads the boxes out in the center of the table. Lids are quickly flipped back and the contents of the paper bag is examined.

The older man straightens and looks back at me. "Please see my secretary Helen for your payment, Miss . . ."

"Brooke."

I look across the room at the sound of my name.

Seated at the other end of the table is the very associate I gave up my lunch for last year.

Blonde. No glasses. Nothing particularly memorable at all about him. In fact, if he hadn't called out my name just now, I would easily pass this guy on the street and not recognize him. It's only in this setting, large board room with baked goods spread out on a conference table that my memory is being triggered. And that might have everything to do with the treats and nothing to do with the sex we had.

He stands and buttons his jacket, grinning in my direction. "I'll walk you out."

I smile at the older man who took the boxes from me and exit the room. Blonde, no glasses guy has to catch up.

"I said I would walk you out. You can't wait a second?" He gently squeezes my elbow, bending down to whisper into my ear. "In a hurry? I can make it quick."

I wrench my arm away. "That's okay. I need to get back to work."

My feet continue to carry me down the hallway. He stays right with me, his quiet chuckle grating on my nerves.

Christ, just go away. This isn't going to happen.

"Come on, Brooke. I'm about to have to sit through this boring as fuck meeting. Make a guy's day a bit brighter, will ya?"

I turn to glare at him. "I don't even remember your name."

"Vince."

"Well, Vince, like I said, I need to get back to work. But even if I didn't, I wouldn't be interested."

His eyebrows meet his hairline. "Why not?"

"Because I have a boyfriend."

My feet skid to a halt in front of the reception desk. I clamp my mouth shut, sucking in a sharp breath through my nose. Vince begins to blur in front of me, followed by all of my surroundings. The walls seem to pulse, throbbing with the beat of my heart as it fills my ears, growing louder and louder. My breaths become shallow and my palms start to sweat.

What . . .

The . . .

Hell . . . did I just say?

I look around for another woman standing nearby whose voice I had to have been hearing.

That wasn't me. I didn't just say that. I didn't just say I have a boyfriend.

Turning my head, I meet the gaze of the older receptionist behind the desk.

Was it you?

"Ah, gotcha."

I look back at Vince after he speaks.

He tugs on his jacket, lifting his one shoulder. "I'm not trying to break up a relationship. That's too much involvement for me. Good luck with your boyfriend. Hope it all works out."

Boyfriend.

"Shut up, Vince!"

He leans back, looking startled. "Excuse me?"

I look around us, gauging the eyes on me and watching them multiply. I bring both hands to my face and mold them to my cheeks.

My skin feels warm. Too warm. I need air.

I spin around and nearly climb onto the reception desk. "Are you Helen? Please, for the love of God, tell me you're Helen. I need a Helen."

She stares up at me from over the top of her glasses. "I'm Helen."

"That guy back there told me to stop here for my check. For the delivery I made. Dylan's Sweet Tooth."

"Oh, yes." She smiles and picks up a check and a small piece of paper, sliding them both in front of me. "Here you go. Just need you to sign for it."

I grab a pen and scribble something onto the receipt. I doubt it's my name. I doubt it's legible.

There's a strong possibility I just signed it 'boyfriend'.

I snatch up the check, fold it up, and shove it into my back pocket. The elevators have a small gathering of people in front of the doors. I can't wait for those. I take the stairs instead and swiftly descend eleven flights, darting across the lobby and pushing through the revolving doors.

The sun hits my face. Oxygen hurriedly enters my lungs with the ragged gasps I take in. I move to a lamppost at the corner of the sidewalk and place my hand against the warm copper, seeking balance. I suddenly feel dizzy.

Boyfriend. I just said I had a boyfriend. I passed up sex because I have a boyfriend.

Segments of my earlier conversations in the bakery filter through my head. The noise from the busy street fades out to silence. Joey and Dylan's voices are all I can hear as I close my eyes and steady my breathing.

"She was pacing around like a love-sick puppy waiting for him to come over."

"You get this little smile on your face every time he comes in here, Brooke. Don't act like you don't more than like this guy."

"Oh, my God, Dylan. She got jealous over this girl he was texting on Saturday night. You know what that means."

"If you didn't care, you wouldn't be jealous, Brooke."

Jealous. I didn't get jealous. I was drunk. Anything I do or say under the influence of Billy's martinis shouldn't be held against me. I don't even remember Mason texting anyone.

I picture his phone and the name highlighted on the screen.

Tessa.

Fuck!

A hand on my shoulder turns my head and pops my eyes open.

Mason's concerned face studies mine, his hands reaching out to grab me. "Hey, are you all right?"

I step back, avoiding his grasp. "What are you doing here?" I ask, looking over at the building I just evacuated like it was going up in flames. I turn back to Mason and take in his attire.

Khakis and a nice button-down shirt. Not what I'm used to seeing him in during the week.

"Why aren't you teaching a class? Did Vince call you?"

"Vince? Who is Vince?"

I rub my hands down my face. *God, I am losing it.*

"Nobody. He's nobody," I utter, letting my arms fall limp at my sides and looking up at him.

His bright eyes are filled with worry. I probably look like I'm having a nervous breakdown.

Clearing my throat, I ask again. "Why are you here, Mason?"

He moves closer, getting out of the way of other pedestrians on the sidewalk. Sunlight catches in his hair and lightens a few strands. "I was meeting with someone about possibly expanding into a chain. Just discussing ideas. I don't really know if it's something I'm serious about."

I wet my lips. "Oh."

Mason's logo on store fronts around the city. I can picture it. Then merchandise. Water bottles and cute little tops.

He should expand. He'd be fantastic with it.

"Why are you here, Brooke? You look a bit . . . out of sorts." He reaches out and squeezes my arm at the elbow. I don't pull away from him like I did when Vince touched me.

After a year, I would still remember how this felt.

Swallowing through a heavy blink, I lower my gaze to a spot on Mason's shirt. "I was making a delivery in that building and this guy I hooked up with last year asked if I wanted to go at it again. You know, have sex." I briefly glance up at him.

He appears engrossed by what I'm saying, watching me with an absorbing look in his eyes. His jaw tight as if he's clenching his teeth. His grip on my arm tensing.

I drop my head. "I told him I didn't want to. That I had a boyfriend."

"Yeah?"

I nod and step back. "I have to go."

"Whoa. Wait a minute." Mason grabs my arm again. His other hand cups my cheek. The corner of his mouth twitches as he stares down at me. "You said you have a boyfriend."

I close my eyes. "I don't know," I whisper.

My heart pounds in my chest. The blood in my veins warms and heats my skin until a fine sheen of sweat builds on the surface.

"Brooke."

I grab his wrist and pull his hand away from my face. "Stop. I need to go. I just . . ." I move back, but Mason seizes my waist and hauls me against him.

"What's going on? Why are you panicking?"

"Because."

I try and turn in his arms. I try and escape, run away from this, from my worry and the emotions I feel coiling around me and suffocating.

I can't breathe. I can't think. I suddenly feel so small and crowded in my own skin.

"Because why? Talk to me," he pleads, bending to get closer. "Brooke."

My name on his lips and the way he says it, like a familiar embrace, unlocks something inside of me. Another level of uncertainty. Something so overwhelming it roots itself deep in my soul and demands to be acknowledged.

Feel this. Do you know what this is, Brooke?

Panic collapses in on me. I gather a full breath into my lungs and push against his chest with every ounce of strength I have left. "Because I don't know men like you!" I yell, my voice breaking and sounding as fragile as I feel.

Mason staggers back, eyes round and enthralling. The look on his face mirroring my own trepidation.

"I don't understand what we're doing and I just need a minute to breathe, okay?" Tears wet my cheeks. More threaten behind my lashes. "I need a minute," I softly utter, wiping at my face and looking up at him.

God, what is happening to me? I'm yelling at everyone today.

He pinches his lips together through a tense nod, studying me with rapt attention. His eyes gentle yet gripping.

I try and compose myself. I manage to at least stop fresh tears from forming, but my chest feels tight and my hands are sweaty. I pray I don't stroke out right here on the sidewalk.

Mason stares at me a moment longer, then looks over my shoulder and rubs at his jaw. "Why don't we go grab some coffee?

Sit down for a bit."

I shake my head. "No. I need to get back to work."

"Come on." He reaches out for me, but pulls his hand back before he can touch my arm. He tilts his head with a tender grin. "Just a few minutes, yeah? I won't keep you long. Just one cup of coffee."

"I've already given you coffee today," I reply, wrapping my arms around myself.

He seems to fight a much broader smile as he moves closer. "I know, sweet Brooke. But it's either this or lunch, and I figured you'd be more agreeable to a quick beverage." He sticks his hands in his pockets and jerks his chin in the direction behind me. "One more cup. If Dylan gives you grief about it I'll say it was all my doing. That I kidnapped you and ignored your urgent pleas to return to work. You'll look like the model employee, I promise."

I bite the inside of my cheek and contemplate his request.

Coffee, then I can return to work. Do I even want to return to work? I'm beginning to think that maybe leaving the sanctity of my bedroom at all today was the biggest mistake of my life.

Everything seemed so simple this weekend. I was in my perfect little Mason bubble and everyone left me alone about it. I didn't have to explain myself to anyone. I wasn't being asked to define anything. Even though Billy and Joey were around Saturday night, they left the two of us alone and from what I can remember, I enjoyed myself. I usually do with Mason. But now the weekend is over. I'm being forced to analyze what I'm doing and what all happens in my perfect little bubble, and I don't want to. I don't even know if I can.

How am I supposed to explain this to people when I don't know what's happening myself?

I clear that question from my head and look up into Mason's eyes.

He's offering me a chance to delay further abuse from my co-workers. I'd be crazy not to take it right now.

On the other hand, agreeing to this means spending more time with the man I just stuck a label on.

My mind itches with hesitancy.

God, I seriously hate Mondays. I am never partaking in one again.

Wiping away another tear with the back of my fingers, I drop my arms and make my decision.

"Fine. Okay. One more cup."

Chapter Fourteen

Mason

BROOKE STARES DOWN AT HER fingers knotted together in front of her as I wait for our coffee.

She isn't crying anymore, but she doesn't look like my Brooke. No sweet-dimpled smile. No luminous spark in her eyes.

She looks unsettled. Caught up in some worrying thought she's allowing to consume her. A stark contrast from the warm, gregarious woman I openly kissed and touched Saturday night.

The one who very openly kissed and touched me.

I allow my mind to go there for a moment. Be present with *that* Brooke. Feel her hands around my neck and her breath against my cheek. Remember her quiet words, the ones I'm not sure she even realized she was saying as I held her on the couch and enjoyed our time together.

With the softest voice, with her lips moving against my ear, she asked if I could stay a little longer, if I could hold her until her heart stopped racing. If mine was racing too, and if that was normal for me, because it wasn't for her. She told me to kiss her, again and again, to move my hand a little higher and that no one could see us. That even if they could she didn't care, and that she wondered what we looked like together, not just then but all the time.

"Do you think they know?" she whispered, her fingers filtering through my hair.

"Know what?" I asked, just as softly, pressing a kiss to her nose, the flush in her cheek.

"That you're kind of my thing too."

We laughed and talked until she fell asleep with her face pressed into my neck. I carried her to bed and lingered there. I didn't want to leave. I was beginning to hate the moments I spent away from Brooke.

All of them. Each miserable second.

But I knew what would happen if I stayed. If I slid beside her and kissed her some more, touched her where we both wanted. If I allowed my urges to overwhelm me, I wouldn't be able to stop. My resistance had been wavering all night and was close to being non-existent. And Brooke, among being unconcerned with her affection for me, was drunk.

She was open and comfortable, sweet and warm . . . and very, very drunk.

So I left, but fuck, it was bloody difficult, knowing the next time I saw her she would be different. Not as showy with her fondness. Still a bit tentative and unsure.

She seemed okay yesterday when we spoke on the phone. Hungover and regretting those cocktails, but still my Brooke. Laughing and willing. Even this morning when we met for coffee, there was no sign of the woman I'm currently observing.

I need to find out what's gotten her like this. Why she's so shut-off from me now.

What the hell could have happened in the span of five hours?

Taking the coffees as they are held out for me over the bar, I thank the barista and walk over to the seating area, moving between oversized lounge chairs and a leather sofa.

Floor-to-ceiling windows span across the front of the shop, offering a spectacular view of the bustling city, but I doubt she's noticed yet. Brooke's barely lifted her head since she sat down.

"Here you go, gorgeous." I set her coffee on the round high-top table and claim the stool across from her. "I got you a mocha this time, since you had white chocolate this morning. Figured you'd be due for a bit of a change." I take a sip of my black coffee and watch her above the brim.

Her hands slowly wrap around the paper cup. She clears her throat. "Thank you. How much do I owe for this?"

"Nothing."

I give her a strange look when she finally glances up at me.

How much does she owe? Is she being serious?

Sighing, I set my cup down and brace my weight on my elbows. "You're not paying me back for something I asked you out for, Brooke. That's never happening. This was my idea. I will always treat you, yeah?"

"You shouldn't keep paying for me when we do stuff, Mason."

"Why the hell not?"

"Because it's not like we're . . ." she pauses, her lips pinching together through a frown. Her shoulders sag, then with a much quieter voice, she continues. "I mean, we're just having fun, you know? When we hang out like this?"

I feel my jaw clench. I roughly scrub at my face, then stare at her, trying to figure out where this is all coming from. "Yeah . . . no, I don't fucking know, Brooke. We're just having fun? This is news to me."

She leans back a bit. Her teeth drag across her plump bottom lip.

I take in a deep breath, remembering how all of this started for her. What she was solely after in the beginning before I got her to consider trying things my way.

Just having fun was her main interest then. A quick root and then nothing. I thought we were past this absurdity.

"What's going on with you? What happened?" I ask, trying to keep my voice even and not at all accusing.

She looks away. "Nothing."

"Bullshit."

Her worried eyes flick back to mine.

"Don't do that," I tell her, straightening up. "Don't shut me out when something obviously happened, Brooke. You were just calling me your boyfriend and crying about it on the footpath, and now suddenly we're just having fun. Help me understand why you're being like this. Talk to me."

She looks down at her cup, her hands still wrapped around it. She sighs through a heavy blink. "Everyone keeps asking me what we are, or what we're doing. I don't know what to tell them because *I* don't know. I don't know what this is."

"Who is everyone?"

"Joey. Dylan." She pops the tab on her lid but doesn't take a sip. "They've been bugging me about it all morning. Non-stop. They want me to admit things. Label it. Us. I don't feel like I should have to. It's nobody's business what I'm feeling, or what I'm not feeling."

Our eyes meet. My hand curls into a fist on the table.

What she's not feeling?

"That's complete bullshit," I want to say, but I don't. I didn't coax her to sit with me and practically beg her to talk just to have an argument.

But I know she feels something. I know this changed for her too. I don't buy her denial.

She's freaked out *because* she knows what this is. Not because she doesn't.

Brooke looks away again, tapping her fingers on the cup.

I force my hand to relax and slide it into my lap. "All right, then don't. Don't explain it," I suggest, catching her cautious attention. "Why do we have to be labeled anything? Why can't we just continue doing what we're doing, 'cause I thought it was pretty fucking great."

"But everyone . . ."

"Who cares about everyone?" I ask, my voice growing a decibel louder. "Am I asking you to tell me what this is? Or if you could start referring to me as your boyfriend?"

Fucking hell. Not that I don't love hearing she did that. Why couldn't I have been present for that little offhand comment?

She frowns. "No, but you're asking other things of me, Mason. Things I don't do."

"And you're doing them."

"I know that!" She startles at her own voice, her eyes round and regretful as she looks around us, at the attention we've possibly drawn, but I wouldn't know for certain if that's the case.

I can only look at Brooke. The anxiousness radiating off her in thick waves. I can practically feel it on my skin.

She shakes her head, drops her elbows to the glossy table-top, and begins rubbing at her temple. "I *know* that. God, do you think I don't?" she asks much quieter, looking across the small table at me. Her hands lower. "Do you have any idea how strange this is for me? How confusing this must be, *for me*? Do you? Or are you just caught up in getting me to do things your way? As long as I'm agreeing to shit, that's all that matters, right?"

I give her a hard look. "What? No, of course not."

"Yeah, okay," she remarks coldly, averting her gaze.

My brow furrows as I observe her.

Jesus Christ. Women are mysterious creatures.

I force myself to calm down, once again. The beginnings of one hell of a headache builds behind my eyes.

Just pull her aside and tell her you love her.

I pinch the bridge of my nose.

Right. Because she's not already freaked out enough. Bombarding her with that confession will surely do her in.

I absorb the idea of Brooke having a complete nervous breakdown. Right here. Right now. Being too distraught to talk or even move after I've divulged my deepest feelings for her.

Will I be permitted to visit her in the hospital while she's under clinical observation? Surely the staff won't know exactly why she's in there. That is, if she isn't talking . . .

Reaching out, I brush my fingers against the back of her wrist. Her eyes follow my calming gesture. "I see how hesitant you are, Brooke, but I also see how you relax around me. How playful and fucking adorable you get when we're together, and not just when you're pissed. Though I do enjoy that version of you a good bit."

Her head lifts. She winces at the memory. "Christ, that hangover was epic. I thought I was dying."

We share a brief, quiet laugh. Hers more fleeting than mine.

She's still too anxious to soften for me.

I slide my fingers lower and gently squeeze her hand. "I know I ask a lot of you. I know I have since the beginning, but I think you rather enjoy yourself when you stop thinking so much about what this is and just fucking be with me. Stop thinking, Brooke."

"I can't," she whispers, tugging her hand away, her gaze drifting to the table. "I can't stop thinking. Trust me, I'm trying, okay? But it's not happening. Not today." She bites at her lip and slouches against the back of her stool. "I just need . . ."

"A minute?" I suggest, drawing her eyes back to my face. I faintly smile.

I hear you, baby.

She stares at me, frowning. "Yeah," she replies through a small nod, her voice incredibly quiet. "A minute."

I push at her cup, sliding it closer.

An offer of coffee and company, minus the conversation. Somehow I think this is a better option for Brooke rather than what I've been working around to this entire time.

Talking until she understands how ridiculous her worries are. How she doesn't need to label us if she doesn't want to yet, just as long as she acknowledges and admits to everyone in this bloody coffee shop that she is mine as much as I am hers. Once she's done that, we can take her announcement to the street, let the general population know. Venture out to neighboring cities and alert the media . . .

Okay, maybe that last part is a bit of a pipe dream. I'll be fucking ecstatic with one broad declaration to the masses.

Or to me. Hearing her tell *me* will be enough.

Brooke regards the coffee, her expression soft and timid. Finally reaching out with both hands, she brings it to her mouth and takes a long sip. I do the same with mine, watching her, wanting to be closer so I can smell her hair and that vanilla cupcake body lotion she slathers on herself.

She turns her head and reveals the long slope of her neck. Her pale throat.

Desire hums in my blood.

Fuck, I love kissing her there.

I swallow a heaping gulp of coffee.

She needs a minute? I need a bloody minute.

Clearing all indecency from my thoughts and willing my cock not to react, I watch her dimple cave in with her next sip.

Time passes. We embrace the silence between us, only it's not contented or easy like it's always been. I can practically hear her mind analyzing and overanalyzing, considering labels and then dismissing them with dishonest perception.

I have to bite my tongue to keep from speaking. I know how easily I can shoot this nonsense down. How concluding my argument is.

I'm in love with you. We're damn near perfect together, and you know it. Stop fighting this and come home with me.

Brooke taps on the side of her cup and stares between the window and the phone she places in front of her, every few minutes or so noting the time.

I finish my coffee and debate on getting another. I have a feeling my afternoon classes will be demanding and unusually difficult to focus on. Maybe a massive caffeine boost will help. My attention already wanders absentmindedly to thoughts of Brooke when I'm supposed to be instructing.

The curve of her hips. Her cute laugh. The way her tongue always tastes of sugar.

Knowing she's across the street questioning us might be enough to distract me entirely.

Might be? Who am I kidding? I'm tempted to clear out my schedule and spend the rest of the day convincing her. Erase all doubt from her mind as my hands roam her body, as I press the most vulgar words I can think of into the flush of her skin.

That sounds like a brilliant plan.

Licking the mocha off her lips, Brooke checks the time again, abruptly standing and palming her device. She grabs her nearly empty coffee. "I need to get back before I lose my job. Dylan already has cause to fire me. I accidentally yelled at her earlier." She looks away, muttering, "I'm yelling at everyone."

I touch her wrist. She quickly jerks her hand up and adjusts her pony.

A subtle, yet not so subtle move to keep me from touching her?

I'm not sure. Maybe I'm just becoming paranoid.

"All right then." I stand and toss my cup into a nearby rubbish bin. Following her to the door, I hold it open and allow her to walk out ahead of me.

She steps onto the footpath. When she glances in my direction, I gesture down the street.

"I'm just down there. Where did you park? I'll walk you."

"Um." She looks up at me, her eyes careful. Both of her hands holding her cup. "Maybe you don't?" she quietly suggests.

Maybe I don't?

I feel my eyebrows raise in surprise, my lips slowly part, though I'm not sure why. I should be expecting this.

She said so in the coffee shop. In so many words, with her stiff, averse body language, she needs me to back off a bit. Give her some time. *Her minute.* Honestly, it's the last thing I want to do, but what choice do I have here? I want Brooke to acknowledge on her own what this is for her.

What I am to her.

I need her to say it. I won't force the words I've been waiting for out of Brooke. I won't push her when she's obviously struggling more than ever with this right now.

I won't push her like I did this past weekend. Never again.

I have to rely on what I feel, how bloody sure I am of us. That's the only way I'm going to be able to step off and leave her be while she takes her minute, which apparently begins right fucking now.

She wants time? I can give her time, if it'll help move this along.

I'll give her whatever she wants.

I push a rough hand through my hair. My fingers slide down to my neck where I grip harshly at the skin. "Right. I almost forgot. I can't do our breakfast tomorrow."

Our breakfast.

Jesus Christ. I'm bailing on this again. I can't catch a break with this fucking day.

Brooke studies me, lowering her coffee after taking a sip. Her mouth pulls into a frown.

She looks . . . disappointed?

No. That can't be. Why would she look disappointed? Taking a bloody minute involves distance. I'm giving her that.

I drop my hand and continue with my lie. *This fucking sucks.* "Since I canceled classes on Saturday while we were away camping, I decided to add on a few early ones this week to make up for it. I didn't want to lose any potential clients. It would've been bad business not to offer."

In my mind, I try and remember the names of some of my attendees who requested classes before sunrise. There was at least a handful of them, business women who work long hours in the city and have difficulty getting home at a decent time. Weekends are usually spent with family, so they inquired about something before work. I told them I would consider it.

Maybe I could quickly throw something together for tomorrow so I don't feel so terrible about making this up.

I rub at my jaw.

Come on, mate. She wants a breather. Look at her. Look how she's acting. She would've canceled on you anyway.

"That's really early. People are insane wanting to workout instead of sleep." Brooke looks down the footpath, her gaze possibly following the couple who just strolled past, hand in hand. Making it look simple.

We can have that. Be that.

All too quickly, she lowers her eyes back to her cup.

"Mm." I look away and observe the world around us.

Cars go zipping down the street and a few bicyclists zoom past in a blur. The sun peers out from behind a cloud. Warmth spreads across my neck and down my forearms.

It's a gorgeous day, but I'm too tense now to enjoy it. My shoulders are tight and my back aches. Hopefully my next four classes will help with that.

"Well." Brooke turns her head, her pony flopping against her shoulder. She lifts her cup and weakly smiles up at me. "Thanks for the coffee. I should go."

Instinctively, and just because I really fucking want to, I move to lean in and kiss her, but catch myself before she seems to notice my intentions. Straightening and shoving my hands in my pockets, I give her a quick nod. "I'll see you around then."

I think I see something, maybe a glint of a distaste for my bullshit impersonal goodbye. Whatever it is, it's gone before I can analyze it, and so is Brooke.

She turns without saying another word. Without giving me another glance.

I watch the soft sway of her hips until she disappears around a corner. I saunter in the direction of my car, my hands curling in my pockets. Tensing, releasing, and tensing again. I think about how else I could've responded to Brooke's irresolution just now. How I could've reacted differently, and if it would've mattered.

I think about it all afternoon.

Through four classes, while I struggle to keep my attention off the studio window and the bakery across the street, I picture Brooke's face on the footpath when I first found her out there.

Those big, rolling tears wetting her cheeks. Her quivering lip. The way she startled when I approached her.

I remember the feel of her hands on my chest as she shoved me off, yelling about how she doesn't know men like me.

Good, I recall thinking. I want to be the only one. *Her* only one.

Seven o'clock rolls around. Stragglers from the last class finally gather their towels and water bottles and exit the studio. I shut and lock the door, allowing myself one glance across the street.

One more glance.

The lights are off in the bakery. Brooke's probably home by now. Or out, erasing me from her memory. Replacing me . . .

The thought makes me nauseous. I take a long, hot shower and heat up some soup for dinner.

Sitting at my kitchen table with my bowl in front of me, my laptop opened, I update my website and send out a newsletter via email, informing subscribers of the additional class tomorrow morning.

Maybe I'll at least have one person show. That's enough to transform this lie into a truth.

I swirl my spoon around the bottom of the bowl, stirring up the vegetables. Just as I'm about to close out of my email, a new message shows up in my inbox. The sender, *PageOne@gmail.com*, heightens my intrigue.

The small bookstore down the street.

I move the mouse and open up the message, quickly scanning the short paragraph.

Trish, the owner I met a few weeks back, has mentioned my class to her daughter, who in turn informed her roommates. Excitement is brewing. They are all interested in attending and are hoping for something this week. Maybe something permanent, if they all enjoy it.

My first smile in hours stretches across my mouth. A lightness moves through me.

I type out my response, my suggestion of a day and time. I allude to my enthusiasm as well, and welcome any parents or siblings, offering my standard 'first class on me' discount. I send the email and grab my phone to shoot out a quick text to my sister, Ellie, as I pad toward my bed.

She'll be so excited about this.

I sit on the edge of the mattress with my phone in my hand. Instead of opening up a new text, my thumb hovers over the last message from Brooke. I hesitate, then press on the screen to enlarge it.

> *Brooke: I'm a genius. Let's camp out in your loft! That way I can enjoy the tent (and you) and I won't even have to be outside. FANFUCKINGTASTIC idea, yeah? ;)*

Leaning forward, I rest my elbows on my legs and stare at the screen. I read the message two more times. I breathe deeply, evenly as I picture Brooke admiring the tent pitched in the corner of my room.

By the window, obviously. I'd like her to see the stars.

She climbs in excitedly and tugs on my hand. We tumble down together onto the soft, billowy sleeping bag and clutch at each other. Clothes are stripped. I taste her skin, nuzzling my mouth between her legs. My hands fit to her curves, squeezing her hips, her breasts. She explores my body with her eyes and wild touch, dragging her nails across my back, arching off the floor and writhing against my tongue.

Our wanting is vigorous. Our desire frenzied.

I fall back onto the bed, closing my eyes and reliving that moment as if it were real.

As if it still could be real.

Chapter Fifteen

Brooke

AFTER MY EMOTIONAL COLLAPSE IN the middle of the city, I leave Mason on the sidewalk and hurry to my car.

I just want to keep to myself the rest of the day. I need space to think, to get a hold on things. Calm the fuck down and breathe a little.

If I had any sick leave left, which I don't, thanks to my bout of pneumonia this past winter, I would fake an illness and head home instead of back to the bakery.

I don't want to talk . . . to anyone.

I'm expecting Joey and Dylan to bombard me with questions and clever little comments when I step through the door, but surprisingly, they leave me alone. I don't have to ask. It's strange. Maybe they can hear my tangle of thoughts. Maybe they received a call from Vince and he's filled them in on my enormously unprofessional outburst, or maybe I just look two seconds away from needing a straitjacket.

If I yell at one more person today, someone might actually have me committed.

Whatever their reasoning for backing off, I seem to settle in my solitary. My mind grows quiet and I busy myself with work. The rest of the afternoon goes by in a blur of baking timers and detailed decorating.

At home, after inhaling some leftovers, I pop my headphones in and listen to my playlist while I change my nail color. I stay in my room all night with the door shut. No one disturbs me. Smart move on their part. I am still irritated with Joey, though not as much as I was before my run-in with Mason, and hardly at all after I make a decision about him while I'm lying on my bed, reading through our old text messages.

Mason: I apologize for staring at your chest like that this morning. Did your mates notice?

Me: . . . .

Mason: What does that mean? Yes?

Me: That was my 'one second while I ask them' text. They didn't notice. But now they know you were all up in my boobs and will be watching for it tomorrow. Your cover has been blown.

Mason: Did you notice?

Me: Yes.

Mason: Hmm. I like to think I'm pretty covert with my obsession, but your tits in that top did me in. I nearly lost my mind a little.

Me: Really? I don't think they look any better today than they normally do. I am wearing a new bra. Maybe that's it.

Mason: What store did you purchase it from? The bra and the shirt. I want to send a thank you gift.

Me: Shut up.

Mason: Maybe a nice bottle of wine? Or jewellery? With a note attached detailing my appreciation.

Mason: I suppose I should go to church and thank God as well. Your tits are some of his best work.

Me: Well, while you're there, go ahead and give him props from me.

Mason: For what, sweetheart? My cock?

Me: Yup! Your PERFECT cock. I'll say a few hallelujahs for that masterpiece. I'll even drop to my knees . . . to worship.

Me: And by worship I mean suck your dick, just in case that didn't translate in Aussie speak.

Mason: Right. Getting hard. Not a good thing before class. I'll see you later, yeah? Take care of those tits for me. If they need a good squeeze, I'm just across the street.

I muffle my laugh against my hand. I trace my smile with the tip of my finger.

I make a decision, and God, it's easy. It's so easy to choose him. To choose *this*.

I don't care anymore. I don't care what anyone has to say about what I'm doing with Mason. Friends. Family. I'm not going to allow their opinions or remarks to get to me. I'm also going to stop overthinking everything and freaking out in the middle of the day. This is making me happy, and that should be the only thing that matters.

It *is* the only thing that matters.

Yes, I still have no idea what I'm doing, because this is completely new to me. Being this happy and not having sex with the person who is making me this happy, wanting to be around the same person all the time and it having absolutely nothing to do with my desire to sleep with them. It's confusing and unexpected.

But I can't stop smiling.

I can't stop smiling.

Damn him and his adorable little yeahs. I'm completely caught up in this guy.

After my shower, I wait for Mason's nightly FaceTime call, but it never comes. I'm half expecting not to hear from him. It's what I asked for. My little minute.

The other half of me wonders if he's staring at his screen as much as I am.

I fall asleep hugging my body pillow, my hand clutching my phone. I wake with it tangled up in the sheets and the battery nearly dead.

God bless car chargers.

When I step inside the coffee shop Tuesday morning, I find myself searching for Mason amongst the crowd.

It's a habit now, seeking him out. He always beats me here.

His tall, lean frame usually perched against a wall while he skims a newspaper. When he spots me, he sets the paper on top of the stack next to the registers and bends to kiss my cheek. We joke about which absurdly sweetened coffee drink I'll be ordering today. Cavities are a risk I'm willing to take. I wrinkle my nose when he drops a tiny pad of butter into his black coffee, turning down his offer to taste it.

Butter in coffee? And he thinks I'm crazy for requesting a nonfat latte with extra whipped cream and chocolate drizzle. Please.

This has become our routine. I pay for Joey, Reese, and Dylan's coffees, while Mason insists on paying for mine. We walk together to the bakery and chat for a few minutes before he tells me he'll see me later, takes the treats I offer him, the ones I now know go uneaten, and crosses the street.

I watch him slip inside the studio. Joey and Dylan watch me watch Mason slip inside the studio. The three of us exchange teasing looks, then we all proceed to get to work.

But Mason isn't here today, and I knew he wouldn't be. After breaking our breakfast plans due to a work obligation, I knew I'd be going through this morning ritual alone.

So why am I still looking for him? Why am I still expecting to see him leaning against that wall in loose shorts and a T-shirt that clings to his muscles, his hair still damp from a shower, casually unkempt in a mess of waves on top of his head. His blue eyes bright and engaging, and that charming smirk lifting his mouth.

It's odd, how I expect him. It's automatic. I want him to be here, and he's not.

I carry my order down Fayette street, my eyes shifting between the sidewalk ahead and the studio as it comes into view. Cars and large delivery trucks obscure my sight. When a break in traffic comes, I strain to catch a glimpse of Mason, teaching his class, but the brutal glare of the sun blinds me.

Oh, well. I'm sure I'll see him later.

I step inside the bakery and smile half-heartedly at Dylan as she works her fingers through Ryan's blonde wavy locks.

I still feel like an asshole for yelling at her like I did. I regret not sending another apology via text last night.

And one early this morning.

She lifts her head and grins back at me, all casual and pleasant, as if nothing unusual happened yesterday. "Hey. Where's Mason?" Her eyes trail over my shoulder.

Okay. I guess this here is all good. I can probably get rid of those classifieds I swiped from the recycling bin last night.

I sit the coffee carrier on the display case next to Ryan. She swings her legs in the air, her pink ballet slippers catching in the light and sparkling. "He had a class really early today," I explain, dropping my hand to Ryan's knee and giving it a light squeeze. "Hey, girlfriend."

She stops chewing her muffin, looking up at me, her cheeks stuffed with food. "Hi, Aunt Bwooke," she mumbles, spitting bits of blueberry onto her dress.

"We have that cupcake order that's going to be picked up at eleven. Five dozen red velvet. Can you get started on them?" Dylan asks in a tone that suggests I do as she says.

Her questions regarding work-related duties are never to be interpreted as questions. They are always commands.

Do these or I will fire you.

Roger that.

I nod and grab my coffee. "Sure."

"I'll be back to help you as soon as I get this mess fixed." She sighs exhaustedly, staring at the back of Ryan's head as she struggles to work out a knot. "No more letting Daddy braid your hair, baby, okay? He has no idea what he's doing."

I wave at Ryan and slip into the back, sidling up to the worktop. I set my coffee down and begin pulling supplies off the shelves.

Mixing bowls. Cupcake tins. A few spoons and spatulas.

Reese enters the kitchen with Drew in the infant carrier, his free hand straightening out his tie.

"I hear you suck at braids. What's up with that?"

He stops short and gives me a puzzled look.

I laugh and point to the doorway. "Ryan. Your wife is in there untangling her hair. With two girls you really need to step up your game. Watch a YouTube video or something."

His eyes widen. "They have videos like that on YouTube? Hair braiding tutorials?"

"Yup."

"Huh." He looks down at Drew, his hand flattening down his tie. "All right. Thanks. I'll check it out."

I watch him exit the kitchen, smiling at the idea of Reese, Mister Serious, hovering over his laptop late at night without Dylan's knowledge, because knowing him, he will want this to be a surprise. He becomes a hair braiding expert overnight and twists Ryan's hair into some elaborate pattern, completely flooring his wife.

I can also see him getting extremely frustrated when he can't figure it out after countless tries and leaving heated comments below the videos, explaining his aggravation.

> *NumbersGuy: This tutorial is too complex. You need to break this down better and explain your steps as you go through them. No one can follow this. The image quality is also quite terrible. Do better.*

Either scenario makes for a funny story.

I retrieve my apron off the wall and slip it over my head, wrapping the long strings around the front of me and tying them together into a loose bow.

A gift from Joey when I first started working here. Right after we first made nice.

I run my fingertips over my embroidered name, remembering how excited I was when I first put this on.

Did I know then that I'd be making a career out of this job? Or how much I'd end up loving it here?

My phone beeps from the back pocket of my jeans, breaking into my little moment of nostalgia. I pull the device out and open up the new text.

> *Mason: Sorry I had to cancel breakfast.*

I go over the message twice. Slowly.

There's nothing unusual about it. A standard apology, but it reads strange. No sweet introductory greeting. No nickname thrown in, sweetheart or gorgeous or little devil.

I like that one. I like thinking I'm Mason's greatest temptation. His only sin, he once said.

But this message isn't his typical style at all. It seems too impersonal for him. Something he might send a stranger, or someone he doesn't bother to give nicknames to.

What gives?

I quickly type my reply.

> *Me: That's okay. How was class?*

> *Mason: Great.*

Great . . . that's it?

Huh.

I stare at the screen, expecting more. More than just one word. I'm certain it's coming. Maybe a 'Let's do breakfast tomorrow instead', or a 'Can I have you for lunch?' to which I will then respond with something overtly sexual, and he will confirm that he does indeed mean lunch in the true meaning of the word, and also the implied innuendo.

'You eat your strange French toast. I eat you, yeah?'

Warmth spreads low in my belly, until my screen fades to black.

What? Really?

I light up my screen again, confusion pinching my brow.

Well, this is different.

Maybe he's really busy at the moment? No time to elaborate because . . .

Reasoning settles over me like a thick fog.

Class. He must be starting another class. His typical first one of the day. He can't text *and* instruct a class.

Of course. This makes perfect sense. *God, Brooke. Use your head.*

I convince myself of this completely logical explanation and set my phone on the worktop.

He'll probably text later, like he usually does. Or stop in at some point.

I smile at the thought.

The front door chimes as I'm setting out my ingredients for the five dozen cupcakes. Movement catches my attention. Joey steps through the doorway wearing dark washed jeans and a bright blue polo. He stares at me, his expression unreadable as he moves across the kitchen.

I open my mouth to utter a greeting, something to ease us back into our regular everyday banter, when he halts me with a hand in the air.

"Let me just start off by saying how much I hate not speaking to you," he announces, stepping closer and lowering his hand.

My grip tightens on the bag of flour. *He does?*

"I know this is all my doing. I should've apologized to you

yesterday but I felt like maybe it would be better if I left you alone. Teasing you like that wasn't . . . right of me. I regret doing it. I saw how upset I made you and it fucked with my emotions." He leans a hip against the worktop, his arms tightening across his chest.

Typical Joey. Even in an apology, he makes it all about him. He's lucky I like him that way.

I cock my head. "Oh, really? It fucked with *your* emotions?"

"Yes," he snaps. "I barely ate last night and turned down a quickie in the shower. I hope you realize how little that happens. And by little, I mean never. Billy thought I was coming down with some weird virus that diminished my sex drive. He wanted to take me to the hospital."

My mouth twitches. I open up the bag of flour. A white cloud of dust bursts onto the back of my hands and sprinkles the wood. "Good Lord. You two are dramatic."

"Brooke." Joey squeezes my shoulder, prompting me to look up at him. His sky-blue eyes are sorrowful. "I'm really fucking sorry, okay?"

I feel my throat tighten. "Okay," I quietly reply.

"It's like when I fight with Dylan. I can't handle it. And I fucking hate the whole silent treatment routine." He removes his hand from my shoulder and flicks his head, tousling his blonde hair. "Let's never do that mess again."

"Don't be an asshole and we won't."

His eyes narrow. I let out a quiet laugh, and so does he. Spinning around, he rests his elbows on the worktop and leans into it, exhaling a rushed breath. "Can I be blunt with my opinion for a second?"

"When aren't you blunt with your opinion?"

"Tuesdays, usually."

We exchange mocking smiles. I dip a measuring cup into the bag of flour and level out a scoop, dumping it into a large mixing bowl.

Joey looks down at the wood, moving his finger through some spilled flour and making tiny circular patterns. "You're different with this guy, Brooke. Really different. Don't take this the wrong way, but you're usually more like a puppy with men."

I wince, dumping more flour into the bowl. "What?"

"A puppy. A cute one. Relax. Like those teacup ones you carry around in your purse."

"Really? They're so yappy."

"I know," he says playfully, lifting his head. He smiles at my tight expression. "Anyway, you get this new toy, right? One of those bones that squeak."

"Only when you bite down on them."

A slow grin pulls across his mouth. "Girl, you have no idea."

I chuckle under my breath.

"Okay, so new toy. You're really excited to play with it, but you don't just want *one* toy. You want every toy, 'cause you're a puppy, and the minute another toy is placed in front of you, you're dropping the first one and lunging for the other. That's not happening with Mason. You aren't even looking at other toys."

I brush my hands off.

A puppy? Give me a break. They pee everywhere.

"Okay."

I slide the sugar and salt in front of me and palm a measuring spoon. I bite my tongue, keeping any comments that might derail this conversation to myself. I am curious to see where Joey is going with this. Some analogy . . .

Not all that inaccurate though. I do like my toys.

"I just know that sometimes new shit can be scary. You have no idea what's going on or how to explain it, and that makes some people bolt. Yesterday, when I was getting on you about it . . ." he pauses to straighten up. His hands flatten to the wood. "Look, I just don't want you to do that. Bolt. I think if you did, it would be a huge mistake. He's good for you. Great for you, actually, and you know I would say something if I thought you could do better. I don't think there is better."

Biting the inside of my cheek, I think about all the men I've been with, the ones worth remembering anyway. All of them pale in comparison to Mason. I never wanted to have any sort of real conversation with them. I never thought about them in scenarios that didn't involve sex.

Did I ever even laugh with them? Or stay up late at night talking for hours until one of us passed out on the line?

Would any of them have been able to convince me to go camping?

Fuck no. Only him.

I nod, conveying my agreement with Joey as I measure out some salt and pour it into the bowl. "I'm not bolting."

"You're not?" He sounds surprised.

"No. I mean, don't get me wrong. It is different. Really different for me, which when I think about it, I get a little freaked out, but that's okay. I'm okay with that." I look up at him. "I don't want to bolt. I like Mason. I like what we're doing. I called him my boyfriend yesterday and he . . ."

"Whoa." Joey waves his hand. "Wait a hot damn minute. You called him your boyfriend?"

"Yes."

"To who?"

I make a distasteful sound in the back of my throat, dropping my head and the measuring spoon. I slowly peer up at Joey. "You know the building I delivered to yesterday? Do you remember us going there last year, and the guy who hit on me?" Joey nods. "To him. He tried to get me to sleep with him again while I was there."

He grimaces. "Go home, Vince."

I shove at his shoulder. "You remember his name?" I ask, laughing. "I didn't. I had no idea."

He shrugs, his mouth twitching with a smile. "I lost my virginity to a Vince. That name is burned in my memory. Plus, I remember you telling me how he was uncircumcised and you thought his foreskin looked strange."

I scrunch up my face in disgust. "We talk about the weirdest shit."

"Word."

"Anyway, I ran into Mason right after that, and I told him what I said, that I called him my boyfriend, and his face, Joey." I frown, leaning my hip against the wood. My cheeks burn. "He looked so happy to hear me say that. I mean, I was literally *freaking out*, but he was just so ready, you know? Like *yes, say it again. Again, Brooke. Please*. I could practically hear his thoughts."

Joey smiles gently. "I bet. So, are we calling him your boyfriend now? Please say yes."

I shrug, turning back to the ingredients I laid out. "I'm just going with it. Whatever this is, I like it, so . . . yeah, I guess. I guess he's my boyfriend. I have a boyfriend." I let out a nervous giggle. My eyes widen. Joey regards me with barely contained jubilance. "Um, yeah I just had a tickle." I touch my throat, swallowing thickly. "That was weird."

Oh, my God. I just turned into a preteen.

"Weird indeed," Joey remarks, wiggling his brows.

The front door chimes again, followed by the loud tapping of heels striking on tile. Dylan steps into the kitchen with my sister close behind.

Juls used to be a regular in the bakery up until last year when she popped out her second kid. Now she's a full-time mommy, part-time wedding planner, and hardly has a minute to spare for visits that aren't work related.

"Good morning, everyone," she sings, circling the worktop and wrapping her arms around Joey. "Mm. You smell nice. Is that new cologne?"

"It's Billy's. I ran out." Joey leans back, releasing her from the hug. "Do you like it better than mine?"

Dylan chuckles from her stool. "Oh, Jesus. Here we go."

"What?" Joey cranks his neck around to stare at her. "I'm just asking. I'm secure, bitch. I know I smell fantastic in my own fragrance."

"Excuse me? Shouldn't you be manning the front, *bitch*?" Dylan affronts. "Don't piss me off, Joey. My blood pressure is already off the fucking charts lately."

"Is it?" I ask, dropping my gaze to the top of her protruding belly.

Dylan lets out a rushed breath, then gathers her hair off her neck and secures it into a messy pony. Juls and Joey loom closer. "Yes. I have a doctor's appointment tomorrow. Reese bought one of those home blood pressure monitors the other day when I felt really anxious. We've been taking it every night. It's pretty elevated."

"Other than that, do you feel okay?" Joey asks, rubbing Dylan's back and shoulders. "Nothing's going on with the baby?"

"No. I feel fine. Enormous and constantly sweaty, but fine." She drops her head back and smiles at him. "Thanks. That feels really good."

"Anytime, cupcake."

"Women having elevated blood pressure when they're pregnant is common," Juls says. "It's probably just something you need to keep an eye on. Maybe try and stay off your feet as much as possible."

Dylan closes her eyes. "That's what I'm worried about," she murmurs, rolling her head to the side as Joey moves up to her neck.

Jesus. I can't imagine Dylan staying off her feet any more than she already does. She's always planted on a stool back here, and I can tell it drives her crazy. She wants to be up, running her business. I get that. She's a very proud woman.

Juls reaches across the table and squeezes Dylan's hand. "I'm sure it'll be fine, sweets."

Dylan smiles, her eyes remaining closed.

Turning her attention on me, Juls walks around the worktop to stand closer. "I see you survived camping."

I roll my eyes. "Barely. Some tick nearly took me out."

She gasps appallingly. "Oh, gross. See? That's why I always shoot down Ian's weekend retreat ideas. I'm not picking ticks off the kids."

Dylan and Joey both start giggling. I pinch my lips together, fighting my own amusement at the idea of Ian roughing it as Juls looks across the worktop at the two of them.

"Something funny?" she asks, hands flying to her hips.

Joey moves to stand beside Dylan. "Ian wants to spend the weekend outdoors? Where in the world will he plug in his hairdryer?"

Wow. He took the words right out of my mouth.

Dylan's eyes go round, her cheeks lifting.

Juls glares around the room, remaining silent, seemingly pissed, until her shoulders start shaking and she covers her mouth. "I know. God, I know," she giggles, shaking her head. "He would be so miserable. I don't know why he keeps suggesting it. My man is crazy high maintenance, but I don't care. He's so sexy, isn't he?"

"No comment. We're practically related." I shuffle over to the shelf to grab some cupcake liners.

Juls glances down at her watch. "Oo, I gotta go. Hey, dinner this Friday, right?"

I give her a thumbs up.

She quickly says her goodbyes, bending down to speak softly to Dylan's belly before she slips out the front door. I grab the two mixers and set them on the worktop. The bakery officially opens, and Joey disappears upfront, while Dylan slides some of the ingredients in front of her and begins making her own batch of cupcakes.

As my batter is mixing, I hit the button on my phone and light up my screen again. It's possible that my text alert function is on the fritz. Maybe I missed something from Mason.

I note the time, and the pink glittered wallpaper set for my lock screen.

No messages.

I check the ring volume before pushing my phone aside and focusing on work.

At least until the cupcakes go in the oven.

Strolling up front after cleaning up the mess, I stand at the window and peer across the street, standing on my toes to see above the occasional car. I can feel Joey's eyes on me.

"I'm surprised he hasn't stopped in yet," he proclaims, echoing my exact thoughts.

I chew on my thumb nail, jerking my shoulder as I strain to see through his large studio window. The distance and projection of the sun make that impossible. His entire studio front is washed out by the glare.

"He canceled classes so we could go camping. Maybe he's squeezing them all in today to make up for it. He texted me earlier."

And it was weird.

I push that thought out of my head.

It wasn't weird, he was busy. He's allowed to be busy.

He's just really fucking busy.

I repeat this same rational justification for Mason's nonexistence today as the hours pass. I repeat it so much that it seems to transfer into my own reality.

After the cupcake order is picked up, a frantic mother rushes into the shop in tears because she forgot to order her son's birthday cake last week. She needs it by five-thirty tonight for his party. Doable, until the woman explains what exactly her son is requesting for his fourth birthday.

An elaborate Old McDonald style cake with a tall red barn and at least five of his favorite animals.

Have I mentioned how much I hate working with fondant? It's the devil.

Dylan and Joey exchange worried looks as the woman waits anxiously for the verdict. I can tell which way this decision is leaning, and no child should be disappointed on their birthday. Even little Timmy, or whatever the Hell this kid's name is, who had to go all out for his big day. We should at least attempt this.

"I think we can knock this out," I say, earning a leery look from Dylan. "What?" I mouth.

The woman pulls me into a grateful hug.

Dylan smiles at me, telling her there is no guarantee, and that she needs to be prepared to settle on birthday cupcakes in case this doesn't work out.

She agrees. "Yes. Yes, of course. Thank you so much!" And rushes out of the shop.

We immediately get to work.

Dylan stays off her feet as much as possible. I'm all over the place, pulling ingredients and supplies off the shelves, darting upstairs to grab some paper so we can sketch this out. Our design is promising. Whether or not we can pull of sculpting these fucking farm animals is another thing.

I work through lunch. Joey steps into the back after two o'clock and holds out a sandwich for me to take bites of as I roll out some fondant. Dylan takes several breaks and moves into a more comfortable seat when her back starts to hurt. We check her blood pressure twice. That whole thing worries me. I forget all about my phone and Mason in general as I mold fat little farm animals and place them around the barn.

The cake is completed with only minutes to spare. Dylan can't believe it. I'm too exhausted to offer my opinion on the ordeal and collapse onto a stool. It only registers that I haven't spoken to Mason at all today when I'm gathering up my things at the end of the day.

"Still nothing?" Joey asks as we step out of the bakery together.

I glance across the street. The studio lights are off. "No. Um . . ." I check my phone again and frown at the screen. No Mason.

Disappointment prickles deep in my chest.

Joey bumps against my shoulder, then throws his arm around me and pulls me along the sidewalk. "Early night, maybe? If he had extra classes today, he's probably beat. As am I. Jesus. Just watching you and Dylan back there knocking out that cake was enough to wipe me out. Of course, I barely slept last night due to our little lover's quarrel."

I feel the corner of my mouth twitch.

"Pizza and beer for dinner sounds fucking perfect right about now. I need carbs and booze. You in?"

Craning my neck, I watch the studio grow smaller behind us as we continue down the sidewalk.

Early night, maybe? I cling to Joey's reasoning for Mason's continued silence. I accept it as explanation.

Extra classes. Right. He's probably beat, that's all.

"Yeah, sure," I agree, looking ahead and tucking away my phone. "That does sound perfect."

Or at least I think it does.

By the time that option is actually laid out in front of me, an hour later back at the condo, my appetite is deficient and I can only manage to consume half of my slice of Hawaiian pizza and nurse a third of my beer. I pick off the pineapple chunks and stack them on the plate. The ham slivers next.

Billy asks me if I'm okay, if I'm feeling well.

"Just tired," I mumble, standing and carrying my plate to the sink.

Probably beat.

I can't explain my mood, or what exactly it is I'm feeling as I turn in early and take a hot shower.

Disappointment? Disbelief? It's odd, not hearing from Mason, but it's easily explainable, and that's what I tell myself again and again as I towel off and slip into an oversized T-shirt and a pair of black lace panties.

No reason to overreact. Or react at all, right?

God, when did I become spoiled by our daily conversations? I feel like a huge chunk of me is missing.

I comb out my hair and grab my phone before sliding under the cool sheets covering my bed. The dim light of my screen casts over my pillow as I hold it next to me, my shoulder digging into the mattress. My thumb hovers over the FaceTime icon.

I scowl at my own desperation.

He's asleep, Brooke. Early night. Really fucking busy, remember?

With a heavy exhale, I let the phone drop out of my hand. I curl my body against my pillow and force my eyes to close.

I force myself to stop worrying, and to chase after sleep.

And the next morning, when Mason doesn't show up for coffee, again, or stop in for a quick hello, I force myself to focus on my job, and not the man across the street who is confusing the fuck out of me right now.

Oh, and also, making it damn near impossible to *focus* on anything.

"Goddamn it." I pick up the now empty container off the floor and slam it onto the worktop. A mound of sugar collects near my feet, with a trail streaking across the floor. The granules shimmering along the wood.

Well, this is just perfect. And exactly how you get ants.

Snatching up the broom, I sweep up my mess as Joey steps into the back.

"I think you need a break. Your language is getting a bit out of control back here." He bends down to hold the pan for me, dumping what he collects into the trash.

"It is not," I scoff, sweeping another pile into the pan, although I am a fool to argue. I know how loose my tongue has been today.

"The last customer heard you."

I wince, my grip tightening on the handle as Joey straightens. *Shit.* "Oh."

"Yeah."

Leaning the broom back against the wall in the corner, I brush my hands down my apron. The hard edge of my silent, might as well be dead, phone scrapes against my palm. My teeth clench.

"Unfuckingbelievable," I utter, ripping off my apron and tossing it against the wall below the hooks. It falls into a crumpled pile on the floor.

"Strange that he still hasn't stopped over here." Joey leans against the worktop. "Are we sure he's alive?"

Oh, I'm sure. His car is parked in a different spot than it was yesterday. That means he went out last night, or at least some point before I made it in to work today.

Early night, my ass.

"Being too busy to call or stop over here yesterday is one thing, but standing me up for coffee and then not communicating with me all morning is bullshit. Especially when he's always over here, and always texting me cute, funny little messages. Now I get nothing? No contact? What the hell?"

"What happened the last time you saw him? After your delivery that day, did he act weird?"

I pinch my lips together.

No. No, he didn't act weird. I acted weird.

The room swirls around me as I begin to pace. Adrenaline surges through my body. "I told him I needed a minute. I couldn't . . . think. It might have been a panic attack. I don't know. I was freaking out, Joey. You know that, I told you. But I said a minute. Not two fucking days."

I shake my hands out at my sides. My feet carry me from one side of the kitchen to the other, and back again.

Where are you?

"Maybe a minute in Australia is longer?"

I stop near the fridge, glaring at Joey. "Really?"

He gives me an even look. "What? It's possible. Have you called him?"

When I don't answer, he shakes his head, muttering, "Of course you haven't. Because that would be the logical thing to do, right? Contact him and figure out what's going on."

Figure out what's going on. Contact him.

Call him? No. I'll do one better.

If he's changed his mind, he can tell me to my fucking face.

With determination fueling my steps, I grab some cash out of my wallet and dart out of the kitchen. "I'm taking my lunch!" I yell out, pushing through the door and stepping out onto the sidewalk.

Joey calls out something behind me, something motivating.

My spine straightens.

Yes. Feminine power. Why didn't I do this earlier?

I sprint across the street, grateful for my choice of flat, comfortable footwear, and pull on the studio door handle.

Locked.

"You have got to be kidding me."

I knock several times on the glass. I pound on it. Maybe he's upstairs hanging out between classes. Hiding out from me.

Pulling away. Needing his own minute.

Growling when he doesn't materialize in front of me with a believable explanation for his sudden absence from my life, I tug my phone from my pocket and dial his number.

It doesn't ring. His voicemail picks up.

"Oh, really? Is that how we're going to play this?"

Anger sizzles in my blood. I'm furious. With myself, for not contacting him yesterday. With him. More myself though, and that only dials up my rage. I asked for this, and now I'm reacting because he's only giving me what I thought I wanted.

He couldn't fight me a little? Show some defiance?

Damn him for being so understanding.

Stowing my phone away after deciding against leaving a message, I head down the sidewalk toward the restaurants, my feet commanding on the pavement.

Not that I need to eat. I've inhaled half of my weight in cupcakes already and it's only one o'clock. My mouth still tastes like raspberry mousse.

I blame men for any weight I might gain today. All men. The entire race.

Especially ones with sexy accents and stunning physiques.

The warm sun presses into my skin as I walk around the corner. I push up the sleeves of my silk blouse above my elbows and pop another button.

I decide on Grinders for lunch, a little sandwich shop Joey turned me on to years ago. It's the closest in proximity to the bakery, which will allow me to return back to my perch and watch out for Mason so I can have it out with him sooner rather than later.

Stepping under the green awning, I move through the busy outside seating area and head for the door, stepping aside for customers carrying trays. I follow behind a group of business men in suits. When I'm nearly inside the cafe, a laugh turns my head in the direction of the tables and chairs in front of the other half of the building.

A familiar laugh.

I stop, causing someone to bump into my back.

"Sorry," I mutter, stepping aside and searching the crowd. It only takes me another second to focus on Mason as he laughs again, his head falling back with his obvious enjoyment.

My stomach flutters.

I move closer, through the line of people filing at the door. My eyes lock on the person he's laughing with, sharing a table with, a meal with.

A date with?

A woman. A young woman, with red hair and striking beauty, laughs with a napkin to her mouth. Her attention wrapped up in Mason. Her eyes trained on his. The two of them are sitting alone at a table in the corner by the wrought iron fence that wraps around the cafe. An intimate spot, maybe?

It sure as fuck looks like it.

My jaw aches as I grind my teeth. My nostrils flare. I cross the pavement with heavy steps and stop next to their table.

Their table.

Mason looks up at me, surprise manifesting in his eyes. He opens his mouth to speak.

I don't let him.

"Who the hell is this?" I point my finger in the general direction of the redhead. I can't look away. My eyes stay glued to his. "Are you sleeping with her?"

The woman gasps, then goes completely silent.

Mason winces. "What?"

"What?" I echo, leaning down, keeping my finger extended in

the air. My hand shakes. "I said, are you sleeping with her? Is that what you've been doing the past two days? Fucking someone who isn't me? Fucking *anyone*?"

My voice cracks and my eyes sting. I lean away as Mason stands from the table.

"Come here." He reaches for my arm. His voice is hard, angry.

Like he has a right.

I step back. "No! You tell me right now where you've been! Where have you been, Mason? With her? Where!"

Tears spill down my cheeks in heavy drops. My lip trembles.

It's strange how quickly your mind can conjure up the worst possible scenario. Self-harm at its finest. Mason and this woman, images of them together, intimate, laughing. It's all I can imagine when I look at him right now.

In a movement too fast for me to avoid, he grabs my arm above my elbow with one hand while his other seals to my waist. "You're making a scene. There are children around," he whispers harshly against my hair, moving me across the pavement.

I hear the soft click of the iron gate opening.

Turning my head, I look back at the sea of eyes on me as Mason pulls me away from the seating area. Away from *her*.

"Like I give a fuck. Who is she?" I growl, trying to get away, pushing against his chest and, at the same time, wanting to bury my face there and cry this out. "Where have you been? What the fuck is this?"

He presses my back against the heated brick covering the side of the building. I look around us, at the building behind Mason. I inhale the dank, musky air.

He's pulled me into the alley. An alley, just like before, when he first kissed me.

Bending down, he flattens his hands on either side of my face and closes in on me. "What's the problem, Brooke? Are you upset?"

I inhale a sharp breath. *What the fuck?*

"Am I upset? Are you kidding?"

"No, I'm not. Do you think I'm with that woman? Do you care that I am?"

"What?" I whisper, fresh tears rimming my eyelids as I look up at him. "Are you?"

Bile rises in my throat.

He stares at me, not answering, his eyes distant and detached, but underneath them, dark smudges shadow his skin.

Instinctively, I go to reach for him, but flatten my hand against my side when I remember what he's put me through. "Where have you been?" I ask, my cheeks burning. "You just disappeared on me."

"You said you needed a minute." His voice is cold. Impassive.

That bloody fucking minute.

I break, sending more tears down my face, my hands drawing into fists and pounding against his solid chest. "A minute, Mason. A minute! Not two days. Fuck you! You were my best friend and you just stopped talking to me. Why did you do that?"

He flinches, his eyes as round as quarters as they search my face. Grabbing my wrists, which go limp in response to his touch, he presses closer.

"What else was I to you? Was that it?" he asks.

I shake my head. "No," I whisper, my body melting against the brick. I feel like I could collapse right now.

"What else?" He wipes a tear from my cheek. His breath bathes my face. "Fuck, Brooke. Tell me. What else was I?"

"Mine."

The word shocks us both. Him more than me. I swear he stops breathing. I accepted this possessiveness over Mason two nights ago. This right to him. I know what I want. But saying it, hearing it out loud when I've never felt this way before, that's what startles me.

Hearing my feelings at all is what startles him.

I drop my gaze to his dark cotton tee. "And I thought I was yours. I want to be." I squeeze his hip, pushing off the wall. It's my turn to press closer. Selfishly, my hands travel up his sides and around his back, dipping under his shirt.

Mine.

God, I missed his body. Two days feels like two years.

I stroke the hard curves of his muscles and the trail of his spine. I flatten my cheek to his chest. "Am I?" I quietly ask. "Am I yours?"

"Fuck," he moans, crushing me against him, his long arms

snaking around my body. Muscles tensing in relief and longing. With a sharp exhale, he nuzzles my hair. "You're mine, sweet girl. So fucking mine. I just wanted to hear you say it."

I close my eyes. Relief weighs down my frame, forming me to him. I'm so close but I want closer.

"You didn't even call me."

"I know. It's not because I didn't want to. Trust me. After that text the other day, I turned my phone off so I wouldn't. I needed you to come to me, Brooke. I wanted you to admit what this was."

"You were just going to wait?"

"Yeah. But only until Friday." He leans back and cups my cheek. "I gave your stubbornness a deadline. I wouldn't be able to wait any longer than that."

Friday? Jesus, what would I have looked like by then?

I fist his shirt, going up on my toes, not giving him an option one way or the other as I whisper across his lips, "kiss me."

I'm taking this.

With a growl, Mason seals our mouths together, our bodies. His length hardening against my stomach. He sucks on my tongue and kneads my ass, fingers digging at my flesh.

I gasp and arch further into him.

"Say it again," he begs, kissing my jaw. "God, Brooke. Say it."

I moan when he bites my neck. "That you're my best friend?"

He leans away, and I giggle at his expression.

Fuck, he's so adorable. Moody Mason.

I lunge at him again and wrap my arms around his neck, my feet dangling in the air.

He grumbles against my mouth.

"Oh. That you're mine? And I'm yours? Is that what you want me to say?"

He nods. "Baby, please."

"I am yours," I whisper between soft kisses. "I have been. It just took me a minute."

Laughing, he leans back and drops his forehead against mine. "Longest fucking minute of my life. You had me worried."

"I had *you* worried?" I twitch in his arms until he lowers me. "Who the fuck is that redhead?" I ask, poking him in the chest.

His mouth falls open. "Ah, fuck. I forgot. Come on." He grabs my hand and pulls me out of the alley.

"Erection," I grate out behind him.

He turns his head. "What's that?"

"You have an erection." I tug on his hand.

"Shit." He spins around just before we reach the fence and the herd of people. He winks at me as he discreetly adjusts himself. "Thanks, gorgeous. That could've been embarrassing, yeah?"

My heart melts at that one stupid word. I grab his face and kiss him hard.

"Mm," he moans and squeezes my shoulders, gently easing me off. "Now you're just making things worse."

Smiling through a shrug, I take his hand again and allow him to willingly pull me this time through the crowded seating area outside the café. We stop at the table he was occupying before my outburst.

I look at the redhead, and the man now sitting next to her. His arm thrown behind her back. Her hand resting on his thigh.

Oh.

Nice, Brooke. Very nice.

Mason gestures at the couple. "These are some mates of mine from Alabama. Tessa, and her boyfriend, Luke. They came up to see my studio and do some sightseeing." He looks down at me, smirking. "You remember me mentioning Tessa, right, sweetheart?"

"Mm." I nod through tightly pinched lips.

Chuckling, Mason wraps his arm around my waist and pulls me against his side. He looks at his friends. "And this is my Brooke."

My heart thumps loudly in my chest, echoing in my bones.

His Brooke.

I release the slowest, calmest breath of my life as Tessa and Luke regard me familiarly.

For the first time since I've met Mason, I don't feel unsure. The expectant worry that usually accompanies being this public with him is gone. Vanished. There's no trace of it.

This is easy. God, it's so easy standing here with him, being his, and it's undeniably everything I want. I realize this is what it feels like to be someone's only. To want to be that. And to hear someone declare their love for you just in the way they acquaint you with others.

A dizzying sensation moves through me like a coiling stream. I feel fuller and weightless all at once.

He loves me. Wow. That's what this feels like.

Raising a limp hand, I smile apologetically at the two of them, more so at Tessa. "It's nice to meet you. Sorry about earlier. I'm not usually like that."

She tilts her head. "No? I've heard you're a bit ballsy. It's all good. I would've done the same thing."

"Babe, you have," Luke adds, laughing. "Who are you kidding?" He holds out his hand and shakes mine. "Sorry I missed the show. I was grabbing drinks."

"Yeah, me too. Way to be absent. I'm probably banned from eating here now."

We all share a laugh, and I notice Tessa smiling up at Mason.

"Can you stay?" he asks, sliding his hand to my back as I spin to face him.

I shake my head. "No. Dylan's at a doctor's appointment so it's just me and Joey running the shop. I really need to grab some food and get back."

He presses a kiss to my temple. "I'll go inside with you."

I say my goodbyes and another round of apologies to Luke and Tessa. Mason keeps his arms around me as we wait in line to place my order. I bury my face in his neck. We laugh about how we've become one of *those* couples, and we both agree we don't really give a fuck.

He insists on paying for my food and walks me to the corner of the street where he grabs my face and presses hot, hungry kisses to my mouth and neck.

"I gotta go," I plead, but my hand holds tight to his shirt, my lips still moving against his.

He kisses me once more and leans away. "Can you come by after you get off? I'm teaching this special class tonight I want you to see."

"Special?" I flash him a devilish smile. "As in private?"

He laughs. "More private than usual, yes. Will you come?"

I giggle at his innuendo. He swats at my ass.

God, yes. I will be coming.

AFTER WAVING GOODBYE TO JOEY after work and telling him to *not* wait up for me at all tonight, I cross the street and open the door to Mason's studio.

I'm expecting my skin to prick with sweat the minute I step inside. My lungs to adjust to the sultry air. That's the first difference I notice.

The temperature is comfortable. How it is when Mason isn't teaching a class. A cool seventy degrees. The second thing I notice is the panel of spectators standing off to the side observing. Some of them snapping pictures.

Older people, mostly. Parents, by the looks of it. They look proud. I'm quickly reminded of my own mom and dad when I used to compete in cheerleading competitions.

I step further into the room and avert my attention to the actual group participating in the lesson. A profound awareness builds around me. Mason's invitation takes on an entirely different meaning as I smile at the young adults posed on their mats, most of them probably close to my age. All of them sharing similar physical characteristics.

I suddenly feel like the biggest asshole for interpreting his request the way I did.

God, Brooke. Tact. Learn it.

I spot Mason toward the back of the room. He's helping a young woman hold a pose where her body is forming an upside down V. Her hands and feet flat on the mat. She giggles and drops to her knees, then rolls to her hip. Her laughter is infectious, and soon others join in.

The woman beside me laughs quietly and whispers to the woman standing next to her.

"He's so great, isn't he? Look how much they're all enjoying this!"

I slide closer along the wall, keeping my attention on Mason as he convinces the girl to try again. She shakes her head, grinning, but ultimately going for it and stretching into the pose.

"I know. I was so excited when Kendall wanted to give this a try. Trish said he's offering this once a week, with a substantial discount. More than half-off. If they like it, I'm all for it, you know? It's good for them."

The woman beside me makes an appreciative humming noise. "The world needs more people like him."

More people like him.

Mason.

With a sigh, my head hits the wall. I gaze across the room at the one person who has completely surprised me in every possible way. From his unconventional dating method, to his irresistible persistence, to his sweet soul he shares with the world.

My Mason.

I begin to take in quick, shallow breaths the longer I stand here. Something shifts, my lungs and other organs making room for my heart to expand and take over.

Who cares, right? Adore him now, stabilize my breathing later.

What? That's crazy. I need to breathe. More than anything else, I need to keep breathing.

I close my eyes. *Breathe, Brooke.* I feel myself slipping, sliding under the water and sinking to the bottom.

This is madness. Beautiful, terrifying madness.

I can't breathe.

I love him.

My eyes fly open. Mason smiles at me. My heart reacts without pause, battering against my sternum.

What.

The.

Fuck . . .

I love him. He made me fall in love with him. That's exactly what happened. He didn't give me a choice in this. I've never had any control in this situation. From the beginning, it's been all him.

I bet this was his plan all along. Pull me in. Pull me under.

Well, now I'm fucking drowning, you gorgeous bastard.

In a panic, I move off from the wall and grab Mason's attention again, waving goodbye and ignoring his puzzled look. Pushing through the door, I dart down the sidewalk in the opposite direction of my car.

I run, and run and run and run.

To the nearest liquor store.

If I'm sinking with this guy, I'm going down my way.

Chapter Sixteen

Mason

"NEXT WEEK, THEN. HAVE A good night."

I wave to everyone, parents and attendees as they leave the studio after class. Trish gives me a gracious look on her way out, silently thanking me for the third time tonight for orchestrating this.

She doesn't need to thank me. I've wanted to get something like this started for years, and without her help spreading the word I'm not sure when or if it would've happened. I'm the one who's grateful. Elated, actually. I'm running on a mysterious energy. The best kind of high. What a difference from yesterday and the day before when I tortured myself by avoiding all contact with Brooke.

Now, I don't need to avoid her. I just need to find her.

Where the hell did she run off to?

I take the stairs two at a time and burst through the door, stepping out into my loft. After turning on the nearby lamp, I swipe my phone off the table and dial her number. It rings until her voicemail clicks over. My eyes pinch shut.

For fuck's sake, Brooke.

Worry pricks at my encouraging mood. Is she having a minor freak out? Over-thinking things again? And so soon . . . I was at least hoping for a few days of bliss with her before I had to talk her off another ledge.

I shoot her a quick text, asking if everything is all right, then strip off my shirt and toss it onto a chair.

I step into the bathroom and splash some cold water on my face. I run my wet hands through my hair and along the back of my neck. My reflection stares back at me, one I recognize from the past two days. Laden with uncertainty and tension.

Fucking hell. She *ran* out of here. She ran away from *me*.

As I debate on taking an actual shower to keep myself here and not pacing the streets, a habit I've acquired as of recently, a knock sounds on the front door, startling me. I move swiftly through the room and tug on the handle.

Brooke pushes past me the second the door swings open. I inhale a lung full of soft vanilla.

She's here. That's a good sign. I begin to breathe a bit easier, my anxious mind starting to settle.

"Hey. You had me worried. I thought maybe you were changing your mind." I close the door and watch her move into the kitchen.

She sets a bottle on the table. Tall, amber in color. Tequila.

Our eyes lock.

All right. Instead of pulling away, I'm now driving her to drink? Not sure this classifies as progress or not.

"Everything all right, Brooke?"

A small laugh bubbles on her lips. She unscrews the bottle, bringing it to her mouth for a taste. "I am so mad at you right now."

I watch her take a sip, then another. "Why?"

"Why?" she echoes, pointing at me with the bottle in her hand. Her eyes narrow. "You know exactly why." Taking another sip, she moves around the room with the bottle, gesturing with her free hand. "How long have you been planning this for, Mason? Since that first day, in front of your studio? Or maybe in the alley when I made you lay it all out there for me? Was this always your motive?"

She takes another sip of tequila as she paces in front of the window.

I rub my jaw, moving closer to the bed. I have no idea what she's referring to. "Brooke, what exactly . . ."

"I mean, you knew!" she yells, not in anger though. Disbelief maybe? Her voice breaks with a short burst of laughter. "You knew from that first day what I wanted out of this. From that *first day*. It wasn't a secret. Then you go and convince me to try things your way, with false intentions, I might add."

She lifts her head, stopping, staring at me from across the room. Her shoulders relaxing with the breath she expels.

"I only wanted to have sex with you. That's it. But the more time we spent together, the less I thought about what I wanted. And *you*, your entire argument was you wanted us to know each other before that happened. To really know each other, right? But you knew me when we went camping. You knew me then, Mason, didn't you?"

I think about how close I felt to Brooke that weekend, including during her unfortunate tick encounter and the mess that followed. Our talk in the tent before we crashed that first night, and our adventure together the next day.

She's right. I knew her. Well enough to take things where we both wanted.

"Yeah," I reply, nodding.

There's no point in lying about this.

"And you didn't give in. You didn't take me that weekend."

She doesn't allow me to respond. I don't really need to anyway. We were both there.

"That's not all you were waiting for," she concludes with a keen arch of her brow.

"No."

"This was never just about us knowing each other."

"No."

Shaking her head through a tight laugh, she takes one last swig of the tequila before setting it on the window ledge. "Who else?" she asks quietly, facing away from me.

I know what she means. I don't need to ask for clarification on this.

When all of this started with Brooke, I told her I didn't do a meaningless fuck anymore, but I never told her I didn't plead for this with anyone else. Or that I never wanted it this bad with someone before.

"No one," I confess.

I see the quick jerk of her head. I hear her mutter something that sounds an awful lot like "good." Her voice sounding slightly pacified.

Spinning around, with a steadiness in her eyes, she holds her hands out in front of her. "Well, you did it. Congratulations."

My eyebrows draw together. I search her face for understanding.

She sighs, staring me down. "I love you, you fucking perfect bastard. You got what you wanted. I'm completely and absolutely in love with you and your little 'yeahs.' They kill me. And for the record, I'm pretty sure I loved you that night in the tent so," she waves her hand. "Opportunity missed. You totally could've fucked a cheerleader."

I feel my lips part, a rush of fervency pitting in the center of my chest and blooming there.

She loves me. My Brooke . . . fuck. Finally.

With a quick exhale, she runs her hands down her face, pressing her palms flat to her cheeks. "Holy shit. Wow. That's what it feels like to say it." She blinks, her teeth gnawing at her lip. "Wow," she whispers.

I cross the room in quick strides, grabbing her face and kissing her harshly. She moans and melts in my arms. The bitter scratch of tequila bursts in my mouth.

"You make me feel crazy," I tell her.

"Good. You fucking deserve it. I only wanted sex, and now I'm completely screwed. I have no idea what to do with this, you jerk."

I laugh, taking her mouth again. My tongue moving against hers. My hands roaming down her back and cupping her arse.

"Should I have told you my intentions? Would you have agreed to this if I did?"

"I don't know."

We stare at each other. Brooke frowns, her hand flattening to my chest.

"I love how this happened, Mason. How you got me here. I wouldn't want to change any of that. You made falling in love with you so easy, I didn't realize I was doing it until it was too late. I think if you would've given me a heads up about it happening I might've told you to fuck off, and I don't want to imagine not knowing you. You're my best friend." She stands on her toes and kisses me. "And I'm yours, I think."

Sighing, I crush her against me. "You're mine. Fuck, you're everything, Brooke. Tell me again."

"I love you." She squeezes my neck, sucking on my lip. "I love you, and I'm not scared. I'm not. Just don't let go of me, okay?"

"Never." I bend down and kiss her neck. Her hands curl around my waist. "Touch me."

"Where?"

"You know where."

She laughs softly. "Mm. Okay, um, can you . . ." With shaky hands, she tugs at my shorts. Her breath bursts against my hair. "Pull it out?"

I turn us, backing her up until her legs hit the bed, my mouth still savoring her skin.

She sits on the edge and peels off her shirt, keeping her eyes lowered and focused on my hands as I jerk down my shorts and boxers, kicking them off along with my runners and pulling off my socks. I grip the base of my thick length, stroking it a little, watching the lust bloom in her eyes and her pink tongue dart out to wet her lips.

I stare at her full tits, pressed high together in a black lace bra. Her nipples hard against the sheer, see-through material.

"Do you want to see them?" she asks, unhooking the clasp around her back. "I think you do." She slides the straps down her arms and drops the lingerie onto the floor near my feet.

"Fuck." I step forward, reaching for her hand. "Touch me."

She wraps around my cock and tests her grip, giving slow, gentle tugs, her usual urgency for my body vanished. She looks timid.

I moan. My legs feel ready to give out. Just her hand and I'm struggling not to break.

"Mason," she whispers, lifting her gaze as she swipes her thumb across the head. "How bad have you wanted this? Show me." She leans forward and licks a drop of precum off my dick, watching me.

Owning me.

Jesus fucking Christ.

How bad have I wanted this? She's about to find out.

"Baby. Come here." I grab her legs and hoist her up the bed until she's stretched out on her back. Topless. Her tits bouncing lusciously with the jerky movement. Her dark hair fanning against my sheets just like I've imagined countless times.

Beautiful.

I pull off her shoes and socks, kissing the tops of her feet. I tug off her jeans and panties. I look down at her, my girl, naked, stretched out on my bed. Giving me this.

Giving.

Me.

This.

Fuck me. Moving here was the best damn decision of my life.

With my hands spread on her inner thighs, I push her legs open and lay my body between them, my cock rubbing against the mattress. I finger her slit.

"I want you so fucking bad. This. I want to taste this before I fuck it."

"Oh, God," she moans as I slip a digit inside, my lips toying with her clit. I suck it into my mouth and she shudders.

"I've dreamed of you in this bed, just like this, moaning for me while I lick you here." I palm her arse and move my face between her legs, roughly consuming her. Getting her in my throat the way I like.

She arches off the bed, fingers clawing at the sheet and tugging my hair, mumbling incoherent words between obscenities.

I suck on her lips, dragging my tongue between them. Up and down, slowly savoring her.

"So wet. You're dripping down my chin, Brooke. Do you like that?"

"Shit." She digs her heels into my back. With heavy-lidded eyes, she watches me rub my nose against her clit and fuck her with my tongue. "Mason, please."

"I want you," I tell her.

She swallows, nodding. "Yes."

"I want you more than I've ever wanted anything. Anyone." I slip three fingers inside her, pumping them in and out.

Fast. Faster.

She writhes against the sheet and grinds on my palm, moaning and softly begging.

"Please, yes, yes. Oh, fuck. Oh, God, fuck."

"I ache for you. My body. My soul," I whisper against her clit, licking it gently. "I lie here every night thinking about you. Getting off to this. Your body. This sweet little cunt. Fuck, Brooke. You have no idea how badly I want this. I can't put it into words."

She strokes my cheek, gasping. "Show me. Make me," her eyes roll shut. "Come. Make me come."

"Like this?" I ask, not waiting for an answer as I move my fingers in and out of her, sucking on her smooth pebble of nerves with earnest until my cheeks hollow and she cries out above me, whimpering a mix of my name and more and fuck, over and over and over.

When her climax subsides and her limbs shiver in aftermath, she wraps her legs around my back, drawing me closer and higher up her body, her hands gripping my shoulders, my back.

I kiss her soft stomach and the curve of her ribs. I lick her nipple, pulling it into my mouth as she watches me with those pouty lips parted.

"Ready?" I ask her, pushing off the bed and digging in my night table drawer for a condom.

Brooke sits up. "Wait. Wait, I," she stammers, pressing her fingers to her mouth. Her eyes dancing between the drawer and my face. "Um. I've never . . ."

"Fucked?" I smile roguishly. "Baby, I had no idea. I'll be sweet, yeah?"

She giggles as she lowers her hand, drawing her knees up. "Shut up. No, I've never done it without a condom. Ever. I've never really wanted to." She looks down at my cock, her gaze burning. "I want to now."

"Yeah?"

She nods, sucking on her lip. "I have an IUD."

I slam the drawer closed. Brooke startles, a laugh bursting from her throat.

I can't deny I want her this way. That I've always wanted Brooke this way. There's something about this woman that turns me into a possessive Neanderthal. I'm greedy with her. Selfish. I want my cum inside her, filling her, dripping down her leg. I want her to feel it and to tell me how it feels. And I sure as fuck want to be the only man who's had her like this.

Only me.

Condoms? No, we won't be needing condoms. I'll be tossing that pack into the rubbish.

Crawling back onto the bed, I drag my cock up her leg, the tip oozing, smearing over her skin. I kiss between her tits, sucking and licking as I settle my hips against hers.

"Mason." Brooke spreads her legs wider, lifting up, bracing her weight on her hands and looking down between us. "I want to watch you."

I follow her gaze, understanding.

She wants to watch me enter her. Fuck, yes. She can watch me all night.

"Baby."

I grip my cock with one hand, her hip with the other. I slide the tip in slowly, so fucking slowly, stretching her, watching the pleasure build in her eyes, her mouth falling open with a gasp and her teeth biting her lip through a moan.

An overwhelming, earth-shattering heat surges in my veins, burning up my spine. My thighs tense as I lean forward and push in.

Further.

Further.

That's it . . .

"So good," I tell her, releasing my cock and grabbing her neck, both of us watching as the last inch disappears inside her tight, slick pussy.

So tight. So fucking slick.

Sweet fucking Christ.

"Mason," she groans, shifting her hips against me. "Oh, God, please."

I tilt her head and take her mouth. She falls back. I go with her, laying my body over hers and pumping my hips.

"Fuck, Brooke."

I kiss her hard, sliding my tongue into her mouth, her soft body melting into me and pressing closer.

"I want to make you feel so good. So fucking good." I lean back, my forearms taking my weight as I watch her below me.

Her sweet lips parting with shallow breaths. Her cheeks deep in color. And those gorgeous eyes round and realizing exactly what this is.

Us, making love. This isn't just fucking.

I thrust forward in a slow, heavy rhythm, my gaze never leaving hers. Desperate noises escaping me. Tight, hoarse moans.

I sound frantic to come. I feel frantic to love her, to keep her, to make this last.

To go even slower, show restraint, my thighs burning as I stay unhurried. Brooke's legs shaking against my hips. Slower . . . *good, God, fuck. I can't. I can't . . .*

My hips begin bucking wildly, the smooth walls of her sex gripping me, tightening around me the harder I fuck.

"Brooke, baby . . ."

Her hand touches my ribs. Her other rubbing along my back. My sides. Her nails clawing at my arse.

I drop my lips to her ear and tell her how amazing she feels. How perfect she is for me. How close I am to coming, and how badly I want to fill her.

"Only you," I whisper, and she sighs, wrapping her hands around my neck and pressing her bare chest to mine.

She sucks on my jaw, my neck, dragging her teeth along my skin and biting my flesh.

I run my hands up her legs to her hips, pinning her to the bed when she begs me to make her come, to fuck her harder.

To fuck her like I love her.

I pound into her relentlessly, swearing and moaning, telling her to come on my cock and to take it. Me. Everything. That every part of me is hers and it has been since that first day on the footpath.

"God, you owned me. Did you know?" I ask her, laughing through a growl when she's too delirious with pleasure to answer me. Her eyes closed and her hands seeking anchor.

I palm her tits, squeezing and sucking, pinching her nipples. Biting down when she tugs ruthlessly on my hair.

"Oh, my God," she pants as she pulls her legs higher, gasping when I reach between us and rub her clit with my thumb.

"Mason," she moans, clawing at my skin. "Come in me. Come."

I surge forward, grabbing her face and dropping my head to look at her.

Her pussy clenches around me, and with her lips pressing against mine she falls, gasping and swearing into my mouth.

I fuck her through her climax, my limbs trembling. She tells me she needs to feel me come, "I need it. Please," and hearing that I break, exploding seconds after she does, a strangled cry catching in my throat.

"Brooke," I moan, collapsing on top of her, my face rubbing against her neck where I kiss her sweet skin. "Jesus Christ. You've wrecked me."

She giggles, stroking my hair. "You never said it."

My brow furrows. Curious, I lean back, pushing her sweaty hair off her face.

"I love you." She smiles lazily, her hands rubbing my shoulders. "I thought for sure you were going to tell me at some point during all that. In the throes of passion. At least while you were coming."

I lower my gaze to her chin, searching my memory and reeling from the best sex of my life.

"Are you sure I didn't say it? I feel like I was screaming it just now."

Her lips pinch tightly together, fighting a grin. She shakes her head. "You didn't say it."

"Well." I slowly kiss her mouth. "Do you know?" I ask.

"Yes."

"I've known for a while now. You may have loved me in that tent, but I think I loved you before that."

I sit back and slide my cock out of her. Cum oozes from her

body, down her slit. My cum. Her thighs glisten with a mixture of our desire.

"Fucking hell," I groan, rubbing at my mouth, staring. I can't look away from this.

Something inside of me begins to ache. A strange, foreign need to lay claim to someone, to have a right to them, but not just someone. Brooke. Only Brooke. This sweet, beautiful thing staring up at me. Sexy as shit and unquestionably the most challenging and defiant woman I've ever met.

"You're looking at me like you love me," she whispers, smiling, her eyes fluttering as she stretches her arms above her.

"Yeah."

Grabbing her thighs, I wrench her closer, smiling at her precious squeal. I push my hips between her legs again, leaning over her, filling her with one hard thrust.

She gasps, arching off the bed. "God, Mason."

"Let me show you how I love you, sweet girl."

Nodding, she grabs my face and kisses me hard and fast, soft and slow.

Just like how I take her.

Chapter Seventeen

Brooke

I OPEN MY EYES AS I stretch, searching the room for a clock.

I don't remember falling asleep, and I have no idea how long I've been out, but I know it's late. The curtains amplifying the darkness behind them, casting a heavy shadow over one side of the room. The other lightly illuminated by a lamp on the dresser.

I look over at Mason sleeping beside me.

He's lying on his back, one arm tucked beneath the pillow under his head, the other relaxed across his stomach, his face turned away. My eyes linger on the lines of his body. The slope of his neck. The smooth swell of his muscles, his trim waist, and the bulge of his cock against the satin sheet.

Mercy. I'm sharing the bed with an Adonis. *Again . . . how is this guy even real?*

My thighs pinch together. An ache gathers there. It's nearly painful. I can't remember how many times Mason and I have fucked tonight. I lost count after he bent me over the kitchen table and spanked me until I came.

My cheeks burn as the memory of his desperate voice fills my ears.

"Oh . . . fuck, Brooke. Fuck! Your pussy . . . ah, God. I need to come. Baby . . . Baby."

A shiver runs down my spine.

Damn, I love him like that. Wild for me. Fucking like a man depraved, and still giving me those tender moments in between where he kisses my cheek and whispers across my skin.

"You are loved, Brooke Wicks. My adoration for you is endless."

I smile against my fingers.

I want to absorb him, every flavor of Mason. His sweetness and his ferocity. The gentle planes and sharp, savage angles of his passion.

Why did it take me this long to choose him? To be okay with this? I'm so happy I could burst.

Sliding out from underneath the covers, I pad around to the other side of the bed and grab my jeans, tugging my phone out of my pocket. I note the time.

Eleven-forty-two P.M. .

I flatten a hand to my stomach. Geez. No wonder I'm starving. I skipped dinner. The only thing I've had since lunch is a banana fosters cupcake and some tequila.

Grabbing Mason's shirt off the chair on my way across the room, I slide my arms through the soft cotton and slip it over my head. The hem reaches my thighs. It smells like detergent and a faint hint of cologne. I bury my face in the collar.

Yummy.

I step into the bathroom to relieve myself and wash my hands. I gape at my reflection.

Jesus. Did we fuck in the middle of a tornado?

My hair looks atrocious. Matted and sticking out every which way. Some pieces still damp with sweat.

I tame the long strands with my fingers and gather them over one shoulder into a braid, securing the end with the elastic band around my wrist. I rub underneath my eyes to remove the smudges of makeup and pinch my cheeks.

There. Major improvement.

When I open the door and step back out into the loft, Mason is awake, lying on his side facing the kitchen, his weight braced on his elbow and the sheet gathered around his waist.

A plate of food sits on the bed in front of him. Grapes and cheese, by the looks of it. Maybe some raisins.

He pops a piece of fruit into his mouth and sucks on his finger. "Nice shirt," he says, smiling.

I tug on the hem. "Yeah, you know. If we're doing this whole boyfriend/girlfriend thing, I'm allowed full access to your wardrobe. Don't be surprised if several comfortable pieces go missing."

"If?" He tilts his head. "You love me, and there's still an if?"

The peaceful look on his face doesn't mask the restlessness in his voice. The tension crusting his words. I hear it. He worries I'm still unsure, or maybe that I'm slowly backing off and changing my mind, but I'm not.

And I hate that his brain automatically goes to that place.

"No. No if's. We're doing it." I move across the room and climb onto the bed, kneeling beside him. I snag a grape off the plate. "Don't tell Joey because he'll never shut up about it, but he was right." I shrug. "I want to keep you."

The biggest, most contented smile pulls across Mason's face.

I laugh around my grape.

God, he's adorable.

"Say that again."

I lean forward and kiss his mouth. "I want to keep you."

"Mm."

"And I really, *really* want to suck your massive cock."

He moans, sliding his hand to my neck. "*Jesus*. You just got me real fucking hard, Brooke."

"But, I want to eat first."

I jerk away, smiling at the look on Mason's face. The heaviness in his eyes and the slack in his jaw.

I pop a cube of cheese into my mouth and gesture at his crotch. "Let me know if things become painful for you. I can eat fast when motivated."

He presses a hand against the sheet. "Fuck. My balls. What's wrong with you?"

Throwing my head back, I laugh and then squeak when he squeezes my side. "Oh, my God. Do you hate me? I'm sorry. I'm just so hungry right now. Here." I feed him a grape. He begrudgingly takes it. "Eat up. Your balls will be fine."

Grabbing my wrist, he presses a kiss to my palm. "Let's hope."

We eat the food he's set out for us, pulling another bunch of grapes out of the fridge when we run out. Mason laughs when I make a pile for myself on the plate, stealing all the cheddar cubes and leaving him with the remaining raisins.

"I don't eat those," I tell him. "Unless they're covered in chocolate."

"Kind of defeats the purpose, doesn't it?"

I struggle to contain my amusement. "Oh, God. You were that kid at the birthday parties who hovered over the veggie tray, weren't you? Trying to get your little mates to eat carrots instead of chips and cookies. Bless you. Were you bullied, sweet boy?"

He pulls me against him and tickles my side until my eyes water and I cry out for mercy. He kisses my cheek and steals a cheese cube, grinning.

I grab a water for us to share and return to the bed.

"So, that class tonight. Have you taught something like that before?" I ask, washing down my grape.

"No, but I've wanted to. My sister, Ellie has Down Syndrome. She's the reason I got started in yoga."

I lower the bottle to my lap, searching my memory for the information Mason's already given me on his family.

Seven sisters. Mason being the baby of the group.

I know he's mentioned Ellie. I remember her name, but he's never told me much more than the fact that he's close with her.

"I've never met anyone . . ." I pause, considering my wording. "With that before. How is she?" I shake my head, my hand covering half my face.

Christ, she isn't sick, Brooke.

"Sorry. I don't know a lot about that."

His face softens with a gentle smile. “She’s good. Really good. She lives close to my parents’ house with a few roommates. That way she has her support, but also her independence. It’s good for her. My mum drove her a little nuts, I think.”

“Mums can do that,” I chuckle, offering him the water after he sets the empty plate on the night stand. “How did Ellie get you interested in yoga? Does she do it too?”

“She did. Once.” He takes a sip of the water, making a face. “Not really her thing. But, when she wanted to try it out, I gave her a lift to the studio. She didn’t have her license.”

“That was your first class too?”

“I just watched. It was for people with disabilities. But I signed up for my own class the next day.”

“How old were you?”

“Eighteen.”

I smile, thinking about a younger version of the man I’m staring at. A sweet boy helping his sister, and in the process, discovering a passion that would lead to a career.

I imagine Mason’s face as he takes on the role of spectator, watching a class like the ones he teaches from a perch on the wall. His blue eyes magnetic, engrossed in the movement and discipline of the instructor. Soaking it all in and connecting with it.

“I think it’s really great, what you did. Amazing, actually.” I kiss his jaw and fall back onto the bed, my head hitting the pillow. “Does Ellie like cupcakes? Or does she eat like a caveman too?”

He smiles, capping the water and tossing it. “She loves cupcakes.”

“Mm.”

Maybe if we ever visit Australia together, I can make her some.

“So, speaking of sisters, Juls is having me over for dinner Friday night. Do you want to go with me? It could be our official coming out as a couple debut, or whatever. If you’re busy, that’s okay. It isn’t a big deal or anything. It’s just dinner.”

I stare at my fingers as they twist together on my stomach.

Way to play down your looming sadness, Brooke.

Geez. Why do I already feel disappointed? As if the possibility of Mason having other plans that don’t involve me is too depressing to even consider. We don't have to spend every weekend together. He's allowed to have a life without me. Visit his own family without me . . .

Or, he could opt for *not* having a life without me and that would be terrific too.

Mason rolls over, kneeling between my legs, his large hands pushing up my shirt, *his* shirt, and stroking my torso.

"Brooke, do you have any idea how desperate I was to know you? To spend time together when this all started between us? That hasn't changed. I'm quite obsessed with you, if you haven't noticed. I want anything you're willing to give me, especially if it's something you're asking me to take." He squeezes my hips and rubs my thighs. He bends to kiss my stomach. "I'm yours. My body, my soul. All of my time is yours."

I slide my fingers through his hair. "Okay," I quietly reply, my heart beating so loudly I barely hear my own voice.

"And anything involving you is a big deal to me." He looks up, a playful smirk lifting one side of his mouth. "You were worried I'd be busy?"

I shake my head, fighting a smile. "Maybe."

"You think too much, Brooke. You make yourself nervous and unsure when you don't need to be." He kisses my rib. "Ask me again while you're sucking my dick."

"What?" I laugh, watching him push back onto his knees. *Ask him again?* "You already said yes."

"Pretend I didn't. You won't be so worried about my answer if you're focused on making me come." He fists his shaft. "Plus, I just really want you to suck me. Ever since you put that image in my head about fucking your pretty little mouth." He moans, pulling on his cock. His eyes burning down my body and lingering between my legs. "Come on, sweetheart. Before I flip you over and take you on your knees."

I inhale sharply.

Shit. To stall or to act. Suck him off or be fucked.

Both options seem equally compelling, but the longer I stare at Mason stroking his cock, the easier my decision becomes.

"Lie down. You're going to want to be on your back for this." I sit up and strip off my shirt, tossing it off the bed.

Mason slides his hand possessively over my breasts as we switch positions. He settles on his back, feet crossed at the ankles, his arms tucked beneath his head, and his cock lying heavy on his stomach.

I fist him at the base, spreading his legs wide with my knees. "How do you like it? Rough? A little teeth? Do you like your balls played with?" I take him into my mouth as much as I can. I cup his balls and fondle them.

If he doesn't like it, he will by the end of this.

"Fuck," Mason hisses through a groan, his body tensing.

He runs his hand along my cheek, pressing his thumb to the corner of my mouth and sliding it inside, feeling his cock against my tongue. His lips part.

I lick the underside of his shaft, swirling my tongue around the head and wetting him fully. I slide my hand up and down his glistening cock as I lap at his balls.

"Ah . . . God, Brooke."

"Mm," I moan, taking him into my mouth again and sucking vigorously.

He hits the back of my throat, again and again, cursing with his hands fisting my hair. Tugging gently.

I suckle at the head and smear a drop of precum on my lips, slowly licking it off.

His thighs jump. His chest rising and falling swiftly. I look up into his eyes and gasp around his length. He looks wracked. His eyes are electric, round with shock. The blue irises swelling and blackening with desire.

He told me his body was mine and this is what he meant. I own him right now. He isn't fighting his pleasure. He isn't holding back his reaction to me and what I'm doing to him. I ask Mason what he likes and he curses while staring, mesmerized, marveling in the wet seal of my flesh with his.

He's giving me this. Trusting me with this part of him. With every part. Knowing I'll care and adore him in the way he deserves, or at least hoping I will.

I will. God, I will. I want him overwhelmed. As far gone as he makes me feel. And I won't stop until I get him there.

I gently press my teeth into his length. He thrusts off the mattress.

"Fuck!"

"You like that?" I teasingly ask, wrapping my hand around his cock and slapping it against my tongue. "What about this?" I lean over his body and rub his slick head over my nipple. The hardened peak shimmers with saliva. The soft skin between my legs grows wet. My breath catches. "Oh, God, Mason, do you like this?"

He fists my hair and growls. "Baby."

"It's okay. It's okay," I whisper, kissing his shaft. Licking it. "You want to come? I know you do. Let's see what we can do about that."

I drop back down and swallow him, raking my nails up his stomach to his ribs while I bob my head. I work fast, then faster, sucking hard and taking him deep. His thick member swells in my mouth, hitting the back of my throat. I gasp when he tugs my hair and smile when his hips begin jerking in tiny movements off the bed.

"Brooke," he groans, thrusting more boldly now. His cock fucking my mouth in earnest.

I reach between my legs and brush my clit. My quiet moans don't go undetected.

"Fuck, yeah. God, do it, baby. Look at you. Rub that pretty little pussy for me."

Mason's filthy mouth, the throbbing of his cock against my tongue, and the hoarse way he says my name gets me there in record time. My desire drips down my hand. Releasing his shaft with my other, I stroke over his balls and press my finger against the smooth skin just below.

He inhales a sharp breath. His body arches off the bed. "Ah, God . . . fuck! Fuck, I'm gonna come. Baby, I'm gonna come."

I move my fingers against my clit until my legs shake and my climax burns up my spine. Mason pulls my hair and floods my mouth. I swallow between moans and whimpers, sucking on his head.

Holy fuck, I think.

"Holy fuck," he says, breathing heavily and rubbing my scalp.

With a heavy sigh, I collapse on top of him, my head lifeless on his thigh and my body half sprawled across his legs and half tangled up in the sheets. I close my eyes, sighing when he wraps me up and pulls me to his chest, cradling me there.

"Filthy girl," he whispers, pressing gentle kisses to my mouth and cheek. "My filthy fucking girl. I'll go to dinner with you. I'll go anywhere, yeah? You don't need to ask."

I squeeze his neck. I bury my face there and smile. "It's 'cause I can suck a good dick, right?"

Laughing, he pulls the covers over us, tucking me close.

Mason never argues my lighthearted reasoning. Or maybe he does and I'm too drunk with happiness to hear him.

So drunk I feel dizzy, spinning more and more out of control. Falling further into this blind madness where, as long as he holds on to me, I feel safe and steady.

OUR USUAL COFFEE TIME TOGETHER is skipped the next morning. For good reason.

Every time I attempt to get dressed, Mason bites my neck or pinches my nipple, stripping off my clothes and entering me in one hard thrust. We fuck on the bed, in the chair, against the wall by the window. Minutes turn into an hour, and after he leisurely fingers me against the shower wall and comes on my ass, we stumble out together and frantically scramble into our clothes.

Him, loose shorts and a fitted gray tee.

Me, my jeans and blouse from yesterday.

Nothing screams wild sex all night like the repeat of an outfit. At least I wear it well.

After kissing Mason goodbye, and then *really* kissing Mason goodbye, with frantic mouths and greedy hands pulling at clothes, again, I cross the street and enter the bakery just before it's time to open.

Joey looks up from behind the display case. He grins at my

attire. "Ah, you know, I miss the days of a good hoe stroll. I used to rock those back in my early twenties."

I roll my eyes and move through the shop. "Did you deliver?"

He holds up a pink cinch bag.

Sweet. My clothes.

"Thank you so, sooo much. You brought me panties, right?"

Joey hands me the bag. He lifts an eyebrow. "Yes, I brought you panties. There are jeans in there. Freeballin' and denim doesn't mix. Trust me."

"Tell me about it."

I shift on my feet, wincing at the odd sensation between my legs. Joey laughs quietly beside me.

"I'm going to go upstairs and change. Where's Dylan?"

I roam into the kitchen and look around the room, expecting to see her sitting at the worktop since she's not up front like she usually is in the mornings. I haven't seen her since before she left for her doctor's appointment yesterday.

Joey trails behind me. "She's upstairs. She's been waiting on you to get here so she can talk to us."

I glance back over my shoulder. "What? Why?"

"Fuck if I know. I tried getting it out of her when I got here this morning but she wouldn't open the door for me up there. Can you believe that? She sent me a text saying she's only saying this once, whatever it is. Shouty capping me and shit. Girl, please. I don't need that kind of attitude before seven A.M. ."

I climb the stairs with Joey following, my mind trying to come up with a scenario that would explain Dylan not being present in her bakery.

I remember when she was pregnant with Drew and it was nearing her delivery date. She was exhausted all the time, mean to everyone, walking around here like a slap-happy zombie. Joey and I convinced her to sleep in a couple days a week and leave the morning baking to me. I thought she was going to fire us both for that suggestion, but she must've been past her breaking point and too tired to argue. With little convincing needed, she agreed and soon became much more pleasurable. Everyone was happy.

Reese especially. Lord, was she cranky around him. Threatening his manhood with notes she made Pete deliver. Swearing up and down that she was not having any more kids.

And now look at her. Kid number three on the way. Reese pushing for more. They're both gluttons for punishment, in my opinion.

I knock on the door at the top of the stairs. Dylan mumbles something from behind it, and I twist the knob, swinging it open and stepping into her loft.

"Oh, *now* it's unlocked. I see how it is," Joey spits behind me.

Dylan lifts her head from the magazine she's reading.

She's in what looks to be one of Reeses' shirts, a baggy University of Chicago tee that stretches across her belly. Her back is against the headboard of her bed. Her feet still under the covers.

Huh. Maybe she is opting for lazy mornings around here. But shouldn't she be asleep?

"What's up, cupcake?" Joey leans his back against the wall, crossing his arms over his chest. He jerks his head. "Why aren't you dressed?"

"What's the point?" Dylan quietly asks, pinching her eyes shut through a slow shake of her head. She looks between the two of us. "I've been ordered to stay off my feet. Permanently."

"What?" I move closer to the bed. My bag of clothes hits the floor. "What do you mean, stay off your feet permanently? You aren't allowed to come downstairs at all?"

"Seriously?" Joey questions behind me.

How can she stay off her feet? She runs the bakery. She's Dylan, of Dylan's Sweet Tooth. She does all the wedding cakes and every other awesome thing we produce.

Oh, no. This won't work at all.

"Nope. I'm stuck in this bed for the next two weeks. I can only get up to pee." She tosses the magazine beside her, dropping her head back with an annoyed grunt. "The doctor is concerned about my blood pressure spiking the way it is. He said Blake is fine, but apparently keeping to a stool most of the day isn't doing enough. I have to be completely off my feet. That means no baking, no coffee time with you two, nothing. I'm going to go crazy up here."

"Aw, cupcake. It won't be so bad." Joey walks over and sits on the edge of the bed. He takes Dylan's hand. "It's only for two weeks. The shop will be fine. You know Brooke and I can handle things. And I'll load you up with gossip magazines and your favorite snacks. Don't worry."

Dylan weakly smiles. "I know you two can handle everything. I'm not worried about that. I'll just be bored up here and missing out on all the fun."

Handle everything? *Everything*? Is she insane?

I move to the foot of the bed so they both can see me. My hands squeezing my hips. My face pinched in disbelief.

"Excuse me? You're not worried? Why not? You should be worried. What about the wedding cake scheduled for next weekend? Now that poor bride is going to have to find someone to fit her in on short notice. That's not happening. The only person around here who does that is you. She won't have a cake. And you know she'll tell all her friends about the bakery that canceled on her last minute. We'll be ruined."

Dylan looks from Joey, back to me. Not a trace of anxiety in her casually amused smile. "She *could* have a cake."

Joey nods in agreement.

What? WHAT?

My mouth falls open. "Oh, really? Is Ryan making it? Did you pass all your stellar decorating genes down to her?"

"Brooke, come on." Joey angles his body so he's facing me. "You're fabulous at baking. You can totally knock out a wedding cake by yourself. There's no need to cancel."

"Are you both out of your mind?"

They must be. There is no way I can tackle a wedding cake by myself. Nor do I want to. I can't imagine disappointing someone on the day most girls dream about. I'll be heartbroken if they hate it.

"You make cakes all the time." Joey waves his hand. "This one will just be taller and with more flare. I don't see the big deal."

I glare at him. His blue eyes widen.

"I make birthday cakes, Joey. Farm animal ones, with fat ass pigs and cows with cute little faces. I don't do shit like you'd see on The Knot. I can't do spun sugar and delicate piping. Christ, all the edible flowers I've ever made, Dylan has gone behind me and redone."

"That's only because you get frustrated with yourself and eat them."

I turn my attention to Dylan after she speaks. My teeth clenching. "Because they look horrible!"

"You are seriously overreacting." Joey stands from the bed and winks at Dylan. "I'm heading downstairs to open. If you need anything, text me. Don't get up." He motions in my direction. "And calm her ass down please. She played the crazy card yesterday and cussed out a bunch of kids at Grinders. We don't need a replay of that."

I scoff and stare at the wall. "I wasn't directing it at them."

I would never do that. Not unless they were really pissing me the fuck off.

The loft door squeaks open, followed by the sound of Joey's heavy footsteps trailing off.

With a closed fist, I press against my forehead, my eyes shutting as I remember how amazing this morning started out. Stress-free and filled with mine and Mason's hungry moans.

Now I'm so anxious I'm ready to chew my fingers off. Awesome.

"All right. If you don't think you can do it, then I guess we'll have to cancel," Dylan says, staring at me with her eyebrow raised.

My stomach tightens and drops. I lower my arm to my side but keep the fist.

"But, I personally don't think we need to. I know you can do this, Brooke. I've seen some of the cakes you've created, and your detail work is beautiful. Joey's right. You are a fabulous baker. You're just nervous."

"I'm more than nervous."

Tasting bile in my throat, I begin pacing the room, feeling Dylan's eyes on me as I wring my hands out.

I'm a fabulous baker. My detail work is beautiful. I can do this.

I swallow thickly and repeat her words in my head like a mantra, hoping for confidence but only butting against my own self-doubt.

This is insane. How can this be happening? How can either one of them think I can handle this? I'm not Dylan.

I am not Dylan.

I think about the bride on her big day, without a cake. I imagine her disappointment and her anger, her sadness and the memories I'm keeping from her with just a simple phone call and some regretful words.

"We're so sorry," I will say. "We just can't do it. Medical reasons. It's just not possible. Please don't hate me."

She'll cry into my ear or curse me out. Maybe both. Probably both.

I continue to pace, my eyes losing focus somewhere on the floor passing under my feet. "God, I can't cancel on her. I can't. It's her wedding day. I would feel *awful*." I rub at my chest, pressing my palm against my heart. It flutters wildly.

"Brooke."

I can't cancel. There it is. My decision made, and one that comes with a mound of stress, knowing how easily I can still end up ruining this woman's wedding day by screwing up this cake. But canceling? I just . . . I can't do that. I will never do that to someone.

Maybe she'll be so deliriously happy on Saturday, she won't notice my blunder in the corner of the reception hall?

I bite at my thumb nail and squint at the floor, the wall. I force air into my lungs and will my pulse to slow.

If I have a stroke right now and Dylan has to go against doctors' orders and get up to call an ambulance, everyone will hate me for dying.

"*Brooke*."

Turning my head at the sharp sound of my name, I focus on Dylan's face and halt near the window. I lower my hand. "Huh?"

She smiles hesitantly. "Why don't you do a practice run this weekend? The whole cake. That way if you have any issues or difficulty with any of it, you can figure it out ahead of time. Plus, I'll be right upstairs if you have questions." She rolls her eyes, sighing. "You know I'm not going anywhere."

My spine straightens. A practice run?

I can work on the cake until I get it right. Until I get it perfect.

"Really? Dylan, really?" I move around the bed and stop to stand beside it. "You don't mind if I stay and work on it after hours?

And Sunday?"

"Not if you clean up your mess."

"I will!" My own excitement startles me. I place a hand to my mouth, a rush of hot breath bursting against my fingers. "Sorry," I murmur, blushing as I spin to grab my bag. "Okay. Yeah . . . okay, I'm just going to go get changed now."

Dylan laughs quietly, reaching for her magazine again.

After dressing quickly in my dark washed jeans and a print v-neck top, I pull my hair back into a haphazard bun and dart down the stairs, stowing my bag away before rushing into the main bakery up front.

I have so much to do now that Dylan is bedridden. But first things first.

Joey eyes me curiously while he helps a customer, nudging against my hip as I reach for the design binder on the shelf.

"What are you doing?" he murmurs.

I open the binder on top of the display case and flip to the special orders paperwork we keep in the back flap.

"I want to see what I'm up against with this cake. I'm going to do it. Dylan suggested I practice it this weekend. I want to be prepared."

"Wow, really? You're actually going to make a wedding cake by yourself? You?"

I glance up when I hear the disbelief in his voice, then fake glare at him for obviously playing it up. His spirited smile beams at me.

"I have all the faith in you. Rock it out, girl."

Taking the money being held out for him, Joey hands the woman behind the counter her purchase while I search for the order form for next weekend. The woman takes her change and exits the shop.

"Here." I slide out the form after matching up the dates and lay it out flat on the open page of the binder. I drag my finger down the thin paper to the bottom where the description is scrolled in Dylan's handwriting.

Three-tiered almond cake with a chocolate

ganache filling and a mocha buttercream

Okay. I can do that. Three-tiered is better than five-tiered. See, Brooke? No big deal. You got this.

I continue reading the notes on the design.

Sugared gardenias cascading down the cake and adorning the top. Tons of gardenias! Bride isn't using a cake topper. Wants the flowers to really stand out. Make them epic.

Edible flowers. Tons of them . . .

Make them epic?

Oh, God, no. No. No. No. No.

I drop my head into my hands, groaning. "Fuuuck. Why couldn't she have wanted farm animals or something? I hear country weddings are all the rage. Shit!"

"Don't believe what you hear. I went to a country themed wedding one time. We all sat on hay bales during the ceremony and drank out of mason jars. Talk about slumming it. I was itchy the entire night." Joey's body presses into mine as he leans closer. "Oh . . . gardenias," he quietly observes. "Dylan's really good at those."

I slowly look up at him, my scowl unforgiving.

Flinching, he steps back. "You know, I think I'm going to go get my coffee now."

"Good idea."

As Joey hurries out of the bakery, I lean against the case and rub my temple, digging my fingers into my flesh. I stare down at the order form and fight off tears when my eyes begin to sting.

This is it. This is how I'm going to get fired. Taken out by the mother of all baked goods.

Tugging out my phone, I sniffle and type out a message as tears dampen my cheeks.

Me: Hi.

God, I need him to talk me through this. To tell me I'm not going to fail.

His reply comes within seconds.

Mason: Hello, gorgeous. How are you?

Me: Freaking out.

My stomach coils and my hands shake. I wipe at my face and wait for his response, staring at the screen, waiting for those little bubbles to appear.

I wait.

And wait.

They never come.

The bakery door chimes open. I look up, expecting to see a customer, or Joey returning with his coffee and hopefully something alcoholic for me.

I've never needed a drink so badly before in my life. Screw unprofessionalism. If I'm getting canned, I might as well spend my last week of employment drunk and oblivious.

To my surprise, Mason steps inside the shop, looking more keyed up than I feel, if that's even possible.

His fretful gaze slams on me as he clutches his cell in his one hand and rakes through his sweaty hair with the other. The muscles in his arm swelling and glistening. His chest heaving.

"Brooke," he rasps, some emotion tightening his voice.

I study him. The apprehension in his eyes. His distraught demeanor. It confuses me. I don't understand it.

Until I glance down at the phone in my hand and read the last message I sent.

Chapter Eighteen

Mason

SHE'S CRYING. *FUCK.* SHE'S FREAKING out, and she's crying. *Fuck!*

What happened? It's barely been an hour. What the fuck? Did someone say something to her again? Get inside her head and cause Brooke to over think this and the way it makes her feel? The way *I* make her feel. She was fine.

No. Fine is cheapening it. She was much more than fine. So much more.

She was fucking perfect with me this morning. Unreserved. Laughing and completely open. Free with her affection. Then she comes here and reverts back to those old familiar habits. Drawing in on herself and slipping behind that shield of uncertainty.

Baby . . . God, don't do this.

What do I need to do? Pull each one of her friends and family aside and tell them to back the hell off? Fine, if that's what it takes. Their opinion of me notwithstanding, this is between me and

Brooke.

No one else.

I take a step closer just as she looks up from the phone in her hand.

"Oh, Mason, no," she says, shaking her head. Her eyes filling with new tears. "No, this . . . I didn't mean us. I'm not freaking out because of us. God, I'm sorry. That's what you're thinking, right?" She sits her phone down and wipes at her face. "I'm not. I promise, I'm not. I'm with you." Lifting her eyes, she captures me with the steadiest look I think she's ever showed me.

"I'm with you."

Relief loosens my tongue and slows my rapid pulse. I move across the shop and around the counter, need filling me.

"Baby." I grab her face and kiss her full, pink lips, tasting the juice she had with me this morning and the faint hint of tears.

She's with me.

"I'm sorry," she whispers. "I'm sorry I made you think that. I should've explained in the text. God, I'm so stupid."

"Stop." I lean away and cup her cheek. The corner of her mouth twitches. "You're upset. Tell me why so I can fix it and get back to my class."

Her eyes widen. "You left your class?"

"Yeah. They're taking a water break. It's fine."

"Mason."

She shakes her head at me, fighting hard against a smile, with puffy eyes and tears still beading on her lashes. Her skin flushed red and blotchy.

Damn. I can't stop looking at her.

How can someone look so sad and so beautiful at the same time? I don't understand it.

"You're crazy," she tells me with a soft voice.

I shrug, straightening and dropping my hand to her waist. "It's possible. I'm a twenty-nine year old who has a stuffed koala in his bedroom. An animal I bloody hate, I might add. I keep copious amounts of baked goods in my refrigerator that I never plan on consuming. And I abandon my class when my girl needs me. I don't know. Does that make me barking mad? I'm fine if it does."

"You love that koala. Don't lie," she chuckles, sniffing and rubbing at her eyes. Smiling up at me.

I feel my blood warm. God, I love hearing her laugh. And that timid smile . . . *fuck.*

Progress. This is progress.

Brooke seems better. Marginally, at least. She's no longer crying, and she doesn't look as troubled as she did when I stepped in here. However, I still need to find out what brought this on. I don't like seeing her upset about anything, and something definitely upset her.

I run my hand along her spine, bending to get closer. "Really, what's going on, sweetheart? I do need to get back."

With a heavy sigh, she turns to face the counter. "It's nothing you can fix. Though, given how amazing you seem to be at everything, foreign languages included, I wouldn't be surprised if you had a hidden talent for baking. Care to try your hand at it?"

We exchange looks. Mine, puzzled and struggling to follow her meaning.

Baking? She wants me to bake her something?

She waves off my confusion. "Never mind. Dylan's been put on bedrest for the next two weeks until she delivers, which isn't a *huge* deal, except for the fact that we have this freaking wedding next weekend and now I'm in charge of making the cake." She lifts a piece of paper off the counter and holds it between us. "And it's covered in flowers. Covered, Mason, like all over the damn thing. Look. She doesn't even want a cake topper. I have to put flowers up there too. Like this." Setting the paper down, she flips through the binder on the counter and stops on a picture of a cake, jabbing her finger at it. "See? Look at these little fuckers. This is what I have to make."

I lean over the binder to examine the picture.

Looks pretty standard for a wedding cake. I think my sister had one similar at hers a few years back.

"All right. And this particular design gets you upset?"

"I can't do it." Brooke slams the binder closed. Her head lowers. "I can't make flowers look like that. And there's so many of them. The bride wants them to be the focus of her cake, and I'm worried I'm going to screw it up and ruin everything."

She looks away and bites at her lip. Her fingers knot together on the counter.

Hmm. This is new. Brooke's normally so proud of her work. She practically glows when she's handing off her treats to me or discussing her day and what all she created. It's one of the things I love most about her. Her passion. I'm not accustomed to seeing any lack of confidence in this woman. Not with her career or anything else.

She's really worried she'll fail at this.

I reach for her, tugging at her hand and pulling her close. I want Brooke in my arms so bad but my shirt is soaked with sweat and she looks so damn pretty right now. I'd hate to ruin her clothes.

"I'm sure you'll do fantastic, Brooke," I say, tipping her chin up, our bodies barely touching.

She blinks up at me. Her eyes reddened from her tears. Her cheeks blooming with color again.

"I'm so stressed out about this. Making a cake like that on my own is going to be nerve wracking enough. I told you, I don't do those. That's all Dylan."

"But you *can* do them. You don't but you can. I believe you can." I run my finger along her jaw. "Don't doubt yourself. You might be better at this than Dylan. Who knows?"

"It has to be perfect, Mason. I'll see the look on the bride's face when I deliver it, and if she hates it I'll never forgive myself."

"So, make it perfect."

Her shoulders drop. Her brows pull together.

Damn, she's adorable in her confusion. That cute little wrinkle in her nose kills me.

Smiling, I bend to kiss her forehead. "You can practice on those little fuckers, yeah?" I ask quietly. "The flowers, I mean."

A laugh bubbles in her throat and bursts from her lips. She flattens her hand to my chest. "Yes. I can practice on them. I'm assembling the whole cake this weekend to see if I can do it. I just wish those little fuckers weren't on it."

She seems to relax a bit more, giving me an easy smile, touching the hem of my shirt and exploring my skin underneath with tentative fingers.

"Well, there you go. Work at it until you're happy. What you deliver next weekend will be exactly what this woman is asking for. You'll impress her, I bet."

"You seem so sure."

"I am sure."

My confidence in Brooke is unwavering. There's no doubt in my mind she will create something beyond what she thinks she is capable of. I've seen her work. I know how dedicated she is to this job. How driven. She will perfect this cake until she can make it in her sleep, but right now, she's crippled by her own insecurity. Blinded by it. Always letting that little voice inside her head speak louder than it ever should.

"You can do this."

She stares up at me, looking at my eyes, my mouth, and finally lowering her gaze to my neck. She wets her lips and swallows hard.

"I just don't want to disappoint anyone."

She looks so sad. So small.

Fuck, I want to hold her. Why did I have to make it so goddamn hot in that studio?

I squeeze her hips, hoping this small touch will give her some comfort.

"I know you don't. You care, Brooke. And that's why you're going to do something amazing. Just breathe a little, yeah? Try not to worry so much."

Her mouth tics—the hint of a smile. Letting her eyes slip closed, she takes in a deep breath, filling her lungs to capacity before releasing it slowly through her nose. She seems to slide closer.

"Better?" I ask, moving my thumb over her jeans.

She nods, her hands moving around my waist as she stares at my chest. "You know this means I'll be tied up all weekend except for the dinner. We won't really see each other."

I dismiss her underlying apology. "No worries. I have a few classes to teach. I'll just be across the street for distractions and words of encouragement, if needed."

"Yeah." Her voice comes out quiet and swift. She tugs at my shorts, her nails scrapping across my skin. "Mason?"

"Mm?"

She looks up. I recognize the shift in her eyes. Desire.

With her small, very capable hands, she glides up my arms, slowly, squeezing my muscles and wrapping her grip around my neck. Our bodies press together.

She doesn't mind my appearance?

"You're all sweaty and sweet. Just like last night," she whispers, standing on her toes to kiss me, crushing her perfect tits to my chest.

Jesus.

"Do you really think I can do this?"

I moan when she rubs her hip against my slowly hardening length. My hands rest on her waist. "Are we still talking about cakes?"

"Yes." She smiles against my mouth. "What else would we be talking about?"

"You're touching my cock. I have no idea what we're talking about anymore."

Laughing, she twists and brushes against me again.

"Baby," I moan. "I need to go."

"And I need to come."

Ah, fuck.

I groan and suck on her tongue a little, touching her arse, feeling my reserve and all responsibility for the business I own fading to nothing.

Maybe I can make this quick? Maybe my attendees will understand my weakness for this woman and wait me out?

Maybe I don't need to make this quick?

With a soft moan, Brooke pulls away so it's only her hands on my hips and nothing else. She looks up, a softness pooling in her eyes.

"Thank you for coming over and talking to me. I'm sorry I worried you with my text. I wasn't thinking."

Christ, that text. I nearly got run over by a delivery truck sprinting over here like I did.

I frown. "It's fine."

"I'm with you." She touches my face.

My breath catches in my chest. *Brooke.* I lean into her hand, my throat tightening as I try to swallow. "Yeah."

"I'm with you, Mason," she slowly repeats, her lip trembling, tears brimming her eyes again, but her voice so fucking sure it shatters any wall or shield she ever put up between us. Obliterating every hesitation and uncertainty. Every whispering doubt in my ear.

Gone. She's mine, and I am so fucking hers I don't remember the person I was before this.

"Baby." I crush her against me, kissing her, giving her my racing heart and my urgent touch and every breath I will ever take. "With you," I tell her.

She nods and breaks away to kiss my jaw and my cheek, pressing her lips all over my face.

We embrace each other, just holding, until our bodies steady and the pressing urge to touch and kiss and fuck lessens to a sufferable longing.

"Okay," Brooke whispers against my mouth. "Go, before you lose half your class."

"I don't care."

"Mason," she laughs, kissing me hard and then with a firm hand, pushing against my shoulder, shoving me in the direction of the door. She gives me an incredulous look.

I don't care . . . fuck, that's a bit mad. A truth, nonetheless.

This is Brooke. My Brooke. She's finally mine and she's with me.

She's with me.

I stop at the door. "Say it again."

Lifting her head from the attention she's giving the paper on the counter, a contented look shadows her face. Her hazel eyes appearing brighter now. Bigger, as she looks me straight on, standing taller, holding my gaze with that swelling confidence I'm used to seeing on her.

"I'm with you."

Her sweet voice lifts in the air, her words soaking into me, saturating my heart, my bones, and somehow going deeper than that. I feel them absorbing into my blood and taking on the life of my pulse, beating . . .

I'm with you.
Beating . . .
I'm with you.

Chapter Nineteen

Brooke

I'M EXCITED FOR TONIGHT. MORE than excited, actually. And not a bit nervous.

Wait . . . I'm not nervous at all?

I hold my hands out in front of me, turning them over in the air, watching for any signs of panic.

They're steady. No tremble to my fingers. Not even a slight twitch.

Huh. Look at that.

I press two fingers to the inside of my wrist. My pulse is stable, and my stomach doesn't feel like I just stepped off the world's scariest rollercoaster.

I'm not sweating.

I'm not pacing my bedroom or annihilating every sweet in this condo.

I'm not trying to talk my way out of tonight, or making up an excuse as to why I can't make it.

This is a big deal. A huge deal, and the only reason why I'm anxious is because I'm ready for it to happen.

I'm ready. So fucking ready.

Bringing Mason with me to dinner at Juls and Ian's house, officially stepping out with him as a couple, introducing him as my boyfriend. Any one of these would usually send me into a fit where I'd be locking myself in my room and blowing everyone off, refusing to answer my phone or faking an illness. I normally don't do stuff like this. I never do stuff like this.

But something is different. I'm different.

Maybe it's seeing the look on Mason's face when I tell him he's not alone in his feelings. Maybe it's the fact that he's become more than just a man I'm interested in. He's a man I want to be with all the time, doing everything with, including breakfast dates and dinners at my sister's house. Camping and late night drives through the city.

Or maybe it's just him. No one else could've gotten me here. I'm sure of it.

Mason went from being a guy I wanted to fuck, to a man I wanted to know, to the only person I care to be around.

The only person . . .

I sure as hell didn't see this coming, but I want it, and I'm not nervous.

I'm ready.

As I'm tying my navy cinch dress and securing the loose bow at my hip, my phone rings from on top of my dresser. I run my fingers through my loose curls before hitting the speaker phone button.

"Hey. I'm just finishing up getting ready. Mason should be here any minute."

Picking up my gloss, I apply a thin coat of the shimmery peach shade and press my lips together as I stare at my reflection in the mirror.

"Change of plans. I think Jake has chicken pox," Juls says.

"What?" I look down at the phone. "Are you sure? How did he get it?"

She sighs. "I don't know. Playground, I guess. Ian was giving him a bath and saw the blisters on his stomach. My poor guy."

Poor Jake is right.

"Well, shit. That sucks." I toss the tube of gloss into my make-up case and carry the phone over to the bed. I plop down on the mattress. "You know Izzy will probably get it now."

"I know. I'm almost hoping she does, that way I can just get them both out of the way at the same time. God, does that make me a horrible mother? Wishing a miserable infection on my child? Ian thinks I'm crazy."

Juls, a horrible mother? Please. She kills it. She's that mom other mom's hate because she's so fucking good at life.

She's organized. Her kids are perfectly behaved and always look like they hopped out of a Children's Place catalog. She still looks like a pin-up girl after two babies, and she rocks heels every day.

Every day. Even at the playground.

I stare at my feet. "Makes sense to me. I wish mom would've done that with us, that way I could still come over with Mason, assuming he's had chicken pox before." I feel a smile lifting my mouth. "I wonder if they call that something different in Australia. Like koala pox or spots down under."

"That second one sounds like an STD."

We both laugh. I pull my knees up and brace my heels on the wooden frame.

"I am bummed though. I was really looking forward to tonight. All of us hanging out." I pick at the hem of my dress.

How long does chicken pox last? A week? Several? Is there a period where it isn't contagious?

I bring up Google and do a search while keeping Juls on the line.

"Aw, me too. You know how excited I was. And the kids. Especially since you were bringing Mason. I really wanted to see you two together." She pauses as I skim the page on WebMD. "Can I . . . okay, I want to ask you something, but you can't get all Brooke on me."

I huff. "What does that mean?"

All Brooke . . .

All awesome and sexy as hell? Because that's unavoidable.

"You know exactly what it means. You can't bite my head off or hang up on me because I'm bringing up mushy shit you don't usually like to talk about. It's not nice. I want your word that you'll at least give me an honest response."

I exit out of the search on my phone and stare at the screen.

I have a feeling I know where this conversation is going. Mason. Juls wants details, which isn't surprising. I really haven't given her any. In fact, the last time we spoke about this I'm pretty sure I bit her head off and hung up.

I definitely hung up.

I sink back onto the bed, resting my phone beside my ear. "I promise."

"Really?" Juls whispers in complete disbelief. I smile and stare at the ceiling.

"Yes. Hurry up before I change my mind."

She clears her throat. "Wow. Okay. Well . . ." a soft, shuffling noise comes through the phone.

"Oh, my God, Juls. Do you have notes?"

Little Miss Wedding Planner. I can totally see her having a list of topic points for this discussion.

"What?" she asks, sounding startled. "No, no I'm just reading a magazine. Glamour or something."

Thud.

A notepad getting tossed, perhaps?

"Right," I laugh.

"Anyway, I was just wondering how serious this is with you and him. I mean, obviously you're willing to admit you're dating, since you planned on bringing him with you tonight."

"Mm mmm."

"And that in itself is a miracle," she chuckles softly. "Headline news. But, I didn't know if this is just something you are doing for fun, or if it's more than that. If you even know what it is."

"I love him."

She gasps. My stomach does a strange little flip.

"What? You do? Really?"

"Yeah." Grinning, I grab the phone and set it on my chest. I lift my hair up and let the cool comforter chill the back of my neck. "I really, *really* love him. I think I just got butterflies from saying it. So apparently those are real."

"Brooke, that's wonderful." Her voice grows exceedingly quiet.

I listen to her soft sniffles. My sister, ever the emotional wreck when it comes to anything even slightly romantic.

"Oh, my God. I was not expecting you to say that. Does he know?"

"I told him last night, right after I figured it out." I pinch my thighs together. "Then we had wild, shameless sex into the wee hours."

Juls shrieks. "I'm so happy for you! On both counts, obviously. And I know he loves you too. God, I saw it that night at The Tavern. The way he spoke about you while you were in the bathroom. He was so in love then."

"What?" I scoff. "No, he wasn't. That was before we even knew each other at all."

Is she insane? How he could he have loved me then? I met him two minutes before that night.

"So? I went out with Ian one time and I knew I was going to marry him. One date and that was it. Boom. Why should it take longer? Your soul is recognizing who it belongs to. Knowing should be immediate. It's like seeing a familiar face in a crowd."

I press my lips together, holding in my programmed skeptical remark.

Hmm. Maybe Juls is right? Maybe it isn't entirely strange for it to happen in an instant for some people. I remember what she was like after meeting Ian. Lord, she never shut up about the guy.

And now I never shut up about the guy.

"Maybe," I quietly reply, thinking back to that night at the bar.

Mason's face when he walked over. His engaging stare. The way he cared more about hearing me than staying and having a few drinks.

Did he love me then? God, that seems completely senseless.

"Is this like, it for you? Is he the one?"

"Jesus, Juls." I sit up and hold my phone out. "Would you get out of wedding planner mode please? I told you I loved him. I didn't ask your opinion on venues or centerpieces."

Now I know she's taking notes. I'm sure she has her planner open and is looking at potential dates. So typical.

"Did I ask about venues and centerpieces? No, I asked if you thought Mason was the one. A completely logical question considering your feelings for him."

"Crazy about Dylan being on bed rest, huh? Can you believe it?"

"Brooke," Juls snaps. "Don't change the subject."

I exhale a slow breath, leaning on my knees and running my thumb over my toenail polish. "The one," I repeat quietly, contemplating this foreign idea of forever with the same person. A concept I've never considered.

But I also never gave a second thought to loving someone. I never imagined any of this happening.

Mason is my wild card. He's that unexpected storm that hits when you're outside on a beautiful day, and at first you don't want it. You were enjoying the sun and the heat on your skin. That's what makes you happy. Then the sky darkens and the temperature drops a little, and you think 'okay, this breeze is nice'. You wait it out, thinking it'll pass, but the rain starts to fall. The first drop hits your shoulder. Another soaks into your hair. It startles you, but it feels good. You were too hot anyway. Then before you know it, it's pouring, saturating your clothes and pooling on the earth. A giggle bubbles in your throat. Where is this coming from? It's so sudden and surprising, and in a matter of seconds, you're drenched from head to toe. Your beautiful day is ruined, and you can't stop laughing.

You can't stop laughing.

The sun is overrated anyway. Give me a sweet storm when I least expect it.

Juls hums impatiently in my ear as I smile against my fingers.

"I . . ."

A knock on the door interrupts me. My heart thumps against my ribs.

Mason.

I leap off the bed and breeze through the condo. "Juls, hey, I gotta go. Mason is here."

"What? No! Yes or no. Yes or no. Give me something."

"I have to go," I laugh, stepping up to the door and peering through the peep-hole, grinning at the gorgeous sight of the man on the other side.

Mason looks so damn good in a gray dress shirt, the button undone at the collar, revealing his tanned neck and the thick protuberance of his Adam's apple.

Fuck, I want to lick him there.

He stares straight ahead, straight at me, as if he knows I'm looking at him. Admiring. A smirk playing on his lips and his blue eyes bright.

"Brooke," Juls says in my ear, her voice insistent.

I feel a surge of heat blossom in my chest. My toes curl on the carpet.

"Yes." I disconnect the call, cutting off her exuberant reply. I wrench the door open and hurl myself into Mason's arms.

I cling to him, kissing his jaw and inhaling his warm skin.

Jesus. Do all Australians smell this good? Like sunshine and impending orgasms. Mercy.

"Hey." He squeezes me back, wrapping his arms around my waist and lifting me off the ground. The pressure of his hold is paramount.

Did he hear me through the door? Does he know I just chose him as my forever?

I press my face against his neck, concealing my burning cheeks. "Hi," I whisper.

He laughs quietly, then leans back to kiss my temple. "Little devil. Ready to go?"

"Change of plans." I wiggle out of his arms and grab his hand, tugging him inside. I kick the door closed. "My nephew has the chicken pox. Juls just called. I've never had them so I can't go over there. God, can you imagine if I got them now? With Dylan laid up? Joey would be in charge of the bakery." I make a face. "Everything would be cream filled."

Mason smirks, then lowers his eyes to my attire, focusing on the crisscross of fabric over my breasts. His chest moves with a deep inhale. "Yeah? No dinner?"

I shrug. “Well, no meal with my family. We can eat something here. Or go out.”

“Mm.” He reaches for the door and turns the lock. His eyes darken.

Oh. Ohhhh. Eat something here. Right. Excellent choice.

“Anyone else home, sweetheart?”

I watch Mason’s hands lower to his belt. My neck warms.

“No,” I answer, shaking my head as he steps closer. “No, they went out. They won’t be back for a while.”

“Good. I’ve been hard all day.”

My gaze flicks up to his. “You have?”

The sound of the belt loosening draws my attention back down. The sharp whip of leather.

Mason grabs my hand and presses it against his cock through the fabric of his pants. He moans. The stiff organ twitches in my palm.

“Oh,” I gasp, molding my hand to him. “God . . .”

“Ever since this morning, Brooke.”

He tips my chin up, looking at me while he uses my hand to stroke his length. The front of his pants becomes restrictive. My pulse quickens to a galloping pace.

“I keep hearing your voice telling me you’re with me, and I get so fucking hard.”

I grip his shirt, reaching for a kiss. “I’m with you.”

His breath bursts across my mouth. “Brooke.”

“Take me. Here. Right here.”

He grabs my breast roughly and squeezes, giving me the briefest of kisses before my head rolls to the side with a moan.

“I want you wet,” he says, kissing the line of my neck. Moving his breath over my skin. I shudder when I feel teeth. “So wet that when I bend down and lick that sweet pussy you drip down the back of my throat.”

“Mason, Jesus.” My hand goes stagnant against his cock. My other squeezing his waist. “That won’t be a problem.”

God, what his filthy mouth does to me. I’m worried my legs might give out soon.

He backs me against the bar counter, his thumb rubbing

mercilessly over my nipple through the thin fabric of my dress.

I make quiet little noises against his shirt when he tugs on the hardened peak.

"I want you to milk my cock with these." He runs his hand between my breasts. "And this." He smooths his thumb over my mouth, then slides his hand beneath my dress and cups my throbbing sex.

His eyes flicker. I nearly shoot off the ground.

"Mm. Think I might start with this."

"Fuck. Please."

I grab his face and kiss him, and it becomes a battle of who can kiss harder, firmer, who can steal the other's breath away faster as both of our hands fumble between us, him popping the button on his pants and my fingers tugging on the zipper. He frees his cock. I hike up my dress. My thong stays in place, Mason slipping his finger under the wet fabric and tugging it aside. He runs his digit through my slit.

"Jesus," he moans. His eyes lowering as mine threaten to roll back in my head. "Tits out, gorgeous."

I pull the neckline of my dress down.

Bossy Mason. Yummy.

My breasts pop free, the cool air of the condo assaulting my nipples. I squeak when he grips the back of my thighs and lifts me, bringing us chest to chest, my hands gripping his hair and his palming my ass and squeezing.

He buries his face in my neck. "Want you. Want you so fucking bad I can't think."

"Take me. Please," I groan, biting my lip when he slowly lowers me onto his cock. My legs shake as he stretches me. "*Mason . . . oh, fuck.*"

He bounces me up and down, fucking me in the middle of my friends' condo, with our clothes still on and the cold metal of his zipper rubbing against my clit. Biting at my flesh. It hurts and it's heaven. Fuck, he's so big I fear he might rip me in half, but even the threat of death wouldn't stop me from taking this. From allowing him to use my body for his pleasure, which is exactly what he's doing. I have no control right now. He's manipulating my weight, lowering me onto his cock at the pace and ferocity he wants, and every time I gasp in shock or squirm in his arms, he revels in my response by giving it to me harder. Faster. Squeezing my thighs until they sting as he shows me how fierce his need is for me, which only solidifies my longing for him.

I've kept him hard since this morning. He's punishing me in the sweetest way for it.

Take me. Take me. Just don't let me go.

With parted lips he looks into my eyes, our faces inches apart as his shallow breaths bathe my skin and absorb into my lungs.

I feel drugged.

I want to taste him in my soul. I want to feel him moving in my blood. I want to consume and be consumed by this man. Only him.

Love is a madness I will willingly accept if he's the one pulling me under.

"Brooke . . . *goddamn*." He thrusts his hips steadily. "So good. So good, baby."

God, I love it when he calls me that.

My fingers tug at Mason's hair as I lean forward and moan into his mouth. I feel my orgasm tickling my spine. "I'm close. Where do you want to come?" I ask, watching the sweat bead on his brow. His nostrils flaring.

He keeps me on the tip of his cock, slowly lowering and lifting me. He sucks on my lips. "Where can I?" His voice is strained. He's close too.

"Anywhere."

"Anywhere?" He leans back and studies my face.

I smirk. I can't help myself.

Tensing my thighs, I arch into him and reach behind me, fisting his cock. I position him at my back entrance.

He sucks in a breath. His eyes as round as quarters as he stares at me. "Brooke."

"Anywhere," I whisper against his mouth, slowly applying pressure to the head of his cock, easing him past that tight ring of muscle.

I take in slow, deep breaths, controlling my breathing.

Mason isn't controlling much of anything.

"Baby," he rasps, his shoulders and arms tensing, his chest heaving as he slips inside, just an inch, maybe not even that much. Growling like a caged animal, the cords in his neck threatening to burst, he lifts me off his cock and reaches between us, stroking himself furiously against my clit. "Ah, fuck . . . Brooke, fuck!" he yells, the first spurts of cum hitting my stomach and the bunched material of my dress. The rest of his desire coating my sex and his fingers.

Bliss.

"Wow," I breathe, dragging my lips along his cheek, moaning at the warm sensation between my legs. "That was crazy."

And hot.

Mason snarls, leaning away and looking down between us. I swear he sways on his feet.

"Shit, Brooke. Fuck. I'm sorry. I'm sorry. I got it on your dress."

"Shh." I reach down and grab his dick, pressing it where I ache the most. Our eyes lock. "Need to come."

Huffing out a breath, he moves us to a nearby stool and sits me on it. His cock wet and heavy against my thigh. With his hand between my legs and his lips moving across my skin, he brings me to orgasm within seconds, pressing sweet words against my cheek and dirty ones into my ear.

He tells me I'm beautiful, the most beautiful woman he's ever seen, and that he'll be coming in my ass soon enough.

My tight, fuckable ass.

I moan against his shirt, panting as I come down from my climax. He grabs my face and kisses me.

"You." He smiles against my mouth. "A little warning next time, yeah? Give a bloke some time to prepare."

"Ah, come on. Where's the fun in that?" I giggle, stroking his face and pushing his hair back. I take a long look at him. "You're beautiful too, Mason. Your heart and your body. Your soul. I'm so lucky."

His eyes appear dimmer as he stares back at me. A dulled shadow passing over him.

Maybe he feels drugged too?

"Sweet girl, come on."

He scoops me up and carries me into the bedroom, my bare feet kicking out. He strips off my dress and we both clean up between kisses and lingering touches.

"Will that come out I hope?" Mason tightens his belt and watches me rinse my dress in the bathroom sink. Our gazes lock in the mirror. He looks regretful. "Really, really sorry." He bends down and kisses the side of my head.

I smile, wringing out the material and turning off the water. "I'm going to get it dry-cleaned. That'll be a fun stain to illuminate on." I pretend I'm handing off the garment. "My boyfriend got a little excited during anal. Can you press this for me?"

Mason rubs at his face, groaning.

Lord, his embarrassment is adorable.

I laugh and elbow his stomach as I move past him.

"Wanna watch a movie? We can order take-out and stay in."

He nods. "Yeah, all right. What movie?"

"I don't care. I have a bunch out there in my room if you wanna look. There's more out by the T.V."

I throw my dress over the shower curtain rod so it will dry. I can drop it off at the cleaners tomorrow when I go to work.

"I'm just going to use the bathroom and then I'll be out."

He jerks his chin and steps out into my bedroom, pulling the door closed behind him.

I use the toilet, looking up at my dress.

My boyfriend got a little excited during anal.

Or . . .

The man I want to spend forever with got a little excited during anal.

Mm, yes. I like that better.

After washing my hands, I stand in front of the bathroom mirror and run my fingers through my messy hair. It looks lifeless. I tug on the ends and my curls spring back. I twist the front pieces. A sticky substance clings to the pads of my fingers.

"What the . . ." I hold my hand in front of my face, grimacing. "Really?"

I grab my shampoo out of the shower. Gathering my hair over one shoulder, I bend over the sink and scrub my ends, rinsing out the suds and semen.

Only you, Brooke. Only you would get cum in your hair after spending hours styling it.

I laugh when I think about Mason finding out he got his spunk in my hair.

Would he be as apologetic as he was for my dress?

I towel dry the ends a bit so they aren't dripping and tuck the front pieces behind my ears. I pinch my cheeks and apply some chapstick from the drawer before padding out into my room.

"Finding anything? I'm in the mood for something funny," I yell out, grabbing a new pair of panties out of my dresser and slipping them on.

Mason doesn't answer. He's probably engrossed in whatever it is he picked out.

I open another drawer and pull out a pair of linen shorts and a tank, tossing them on my bed. I apply another layer of vanilla body lotion to my arms, legs, and neck before getting dressed and moving through the doorway.

Mason's back is to me as he stands beside the couch, blocking my view of the T.V., the remote in his hand.

Nothing is playing. At least I don't hear anything.

Why didn't he answer me?

I come up behind him and slide my hands around his waist. His body tenses.

"Hey," I whisper. "Pick something out?"

"Yeah, sure did." He quickly steps out of my arms and moves beside me, freeing up my sight. "Care to explain this?"

Startled at his abrupt pull-away and the tone icing his voice, I glance up at the T.V., at the stilled image of myself, naked and straddling another man. The camera angled on me from the side.

I remember setting it on the hamper before I crawled on the bed.

Fuck, I forgot about this.

Fuck! How much has he watched?

"You made a sex tape, Brooke? Are you fucking kidding me?" His voice booms through the condo, echoing off the ceiling.

The hairs on my neck stand up. I've never heard him this angry before.

I've never heard him angry at all.

Lowering my hand from my mouth, I turn to Mason. "Where did you find this?" I ask, moving closer.

"Your room. It had your name on it. I thought it was a home video or something."

His shoulders stay hunched forward. His gaze straight ahead, burning into the screen.

I picture the disc on my shelf. I had stuck it up there and left it. I haven't touched it since.

"You as a kid, or with your mates. I wanted to see that," he adds, rubbing at his mouth. "Not this," he mumbles.

I pinch my eyes shut, then shake my head, looking up. "I forgot it was in there. I'm so, so sorry. Here. Turn it off."

He wrenches his arm away when I reach for him. His cold eyes send a shiver through me. "Don't."

I pull back. *He doesn't want me to touch him?* "Mason."

"You were in there awhile. I got to watch the whole thing. You and him." He jerks his head at the T.V. .

The pain in his voice distorts his accent a bit. His words sound stiff. Fully pronounced, unlike the lazy, sluggish speech I'm used to hearing and loving.

I press my fingers to my mouth, shaking slightly.

Oh, God. He watched the whole thing.

"No," I whisper.

Any part of this, a second or a glimpse is too much for him to see. But all of it?

He slowly turns his head, his blue eyes so dark they almost look black. "The whole fucking thing, Brooke."

My stomach drops. "Mason, I . . . just, turn it off." I reach out again. "Let's get rid of this. You shouldn't keep looking at it."

"Why not?"

He tosses the remote. It hits the coffee table with a loud pang.

I jump. "*Mason*."

"Why the fuck not? I've watched it. It's out in the open now. It's no longer a secret."

"It was never a secret."

"Yeah? Everyone knew about it but me, huh? When was this

taken, Brooke?" he asks, looming over me. His pain shifting to a louder reaction. Anger. "When I wasn't fucking you? Did you go out and get it somewhere else?"

"W-What?" I blink up at him, my voice sounding miles away.

Is he seriously implying I've been screwing around on him?

"No! This was months ago. Before I met you. How could you say that?"

"How could I say that?" he laughs darkly. His lips curling against his teeth. "I don't know. Maybe because that's all you've cared about this entire time. I was just a hard dick you wanted, right? And you weren't getting it."

"No, you weren't . . ." My voice shakes. Tears well up in my eyes.

What is happening?

"No?" he asks, disbelieving. He runs a rough hand down his face. I catch the slight tremble in it. "Jesus Christ. Why do you even have this? Do you fucking watch it? Do you and your mates sit around and get off on this together?"

I gape at him, expecting him to recoil at his own words. To apologize and take them back, but he doesn't. He stares at me with nothing but disgust and anger swelling in his eyes. Maybe a hint of sadness. A shred of what I'm feeling.

I'm having a nightmare. This can't be real.

I ball up my fists as tears spill onto my cheeks. "No, we don't. I have it so *he* doesn't have it. I took it months ago, after it was filmed, *months ago*. I've never watched it. What is wrong with you?"

He gestures at the T.V., bending to get closer. "I just watched you getting fucked by someone else. *You*. And you're going to ask what's wrong with me? I just saw another man having his hands on you, his dick in you, and the woman I care about more than anything getting off on it. I just watched you fucking come!"

"You were never supposed to see that! I forgot I even had it. Jesus Christ," I cry, wiping at my face, my entire body trembling. "I don't even remember that guy's name."

I regret it the second the words fall past my lips.

I know how this sounds. Careless. Even worse than that.

His eyes widen. Mouth slack as he straightens a bit. "Well, that makes me feel a whole lot better, Brooke. You make these tapes with just anyone, yeah? Are there more in your room? Or do you keep them out here for everyone to watch?"

Flinching, I look away. "Stop," I plead, whimpering quietly against my hand.

Please, stop.

"Christ. Did you . . ." Mason's harsh voice trails off. He moves to turn away but I grip his shoulder, forcing him to look at me.

I know. I don't know how, but I know what he wants to ask me. And if he has the balls to think it, he can fucking . . .

"Say it," I urge, my lip quivering, my rage consuming me. "What were you going to say? Say it!"

My hands push and pull at his chest. I can't decide what I want, him closer or far enough away I can't hit him. I'm so mad, so shattered. I want him to comfort me and then stand there and take my abuse.

"Fucking say it, Mason!"

Fat tears stream steadily down my face.

He looks down at me, his own eyes brimming now. "Did you tell me all of that just so I would fuck you?"

"What do you think?" I ask him, but I can't hear my own voice. It's so quiet compared to the blood rushing in my veins. To my heartbeat pounding in my skull.

I want to scream and scream. I want to wake up.

Wake up! Wake up! Wake up!

Mason looks away. He doesn't say a word, but the answer I hear is so fucking loud it rings in my ears and reminds me just how real this is. I'm not stuck in a dream, or a nightmare.

I'm awake. I'm awake and I'm alone. Drowning.

I cry silently, my shoulders shaking. "I did," I whisper, grabbing his stare, which goes from shock to crippling grief in an instant.

Why? I'm only confirming what he thinks.

I tilt my wobbling chin up to get closer. "I did. It was all a lie. All of it. Everything I said to you. Everything I gave. When I chose you . . ." I sob, sniffing and weeping in my sorrow.

I don't even care. God, let him see me like this. Let him see what he's done.

He nods, turning away and wiping at his own face now. "Fine." He moves with purpose toward the door, his feet heavy on the carpet.

I follow behind. "You think it. It must be true. Nothing mattered to me. Our dates and that night in the tent. Yesterday and the day before and the day before that. So go! Leave! Get out knowing you meant nothing and I hate you! I will hate you for this!"

He pauses at the door, his head lowered and his hand gripping the knob. His shoulders lifted in tension. His back shaking.

This is it. That one second we have to take everything back. To tell the truth and admit our wrongs. To forgive and move forward.

To make this nothing more than a nightmare.

Reach for me. Reach for me. Take me. Don't let me go.

I open my mouth to speak but nothing comes out. Nothing, but a whimpering cry.

Without a sound, without giving me another look or word or pleading glance, Mason swings the door open and exits the condo.

Probably for the last time.

I dart across the room and fling myself into bed, letting my tears fall. I cry for hours, clutching at my pillow, biting and screaming into it until my voice cracks and my throat burns.

The pain, God, the pain in my chest. This ache. I feel like I'm dying.

How could he say those things? How could he even think them?

Mason.

I sob, picturing his face, staring at that T.V. like a man possessed, ready to explode. Scream or cry, I couldn't tell. Then, the disgust simmering in his eyes when he told me what he watched. The hurt. Tears welling up and threatening when he asked me if I ever really loved him, and the agony on his face when I lied.

I gasp and clutch at my chest.

God, someone rip this out of me. Take it away so I don't feel anything anymore.

"Brooke, sweetie, are you okay?"

I hear Billy's voice hours later, after the darkness rolls into my bedroom and blankets me. I open my swollen eyes, trying to see through the tears. Light from the outside room spills across the ceiling. I squint, focusing on Joey's face as he sits beside me. Billy looks on, standing next to the bed.

"What's going on?" Joey asks, studying me. His hand squeezing my shoulder. "And what the hell is that out there on the T.V.? Is that you?"

I cover my face and wail, sobbing into my hands.

How do I still have any tears left?

"Oh, no. What happened?" Joey rubs my arm. "Is it Mason? Did you two get into a fight?"

I sit up and draw my knees against my chest. I wipe the wetness from my cheeks even though it's pointless. New tears fall.

"Yes, we got into a fight. A huge fucking fight. He found that disc in my room and he watched it. All of it. I didn't know until it was too late. I forgot I even had it."

Joey's eyes go wide. "From like, six months ago? The Cuban guy?"

"Yes!" I shriek. *Thank you!* Both men startle. "Yes, from six months ago! Mason accused me of making that after him and I started hanging out. He said I only cared about fucking and since I wasn't getting it from him, I probably went somewhere else." My lip trembles. "He said so much," I whisper, remembering everything and feeling that pain in the center of my chest swelling inside me. "He was so mad, and mean. God, he was mean. He made me feel like a," I pause, biting my tongue and shaking my head.

No. No, I won't say it. Don't even think it.

Whore.

My eyes sting.

"You know he didn't mean any of that," Billy says, moving closer and tugging at the knot in his tie. "He was reacting, Brooke. How I'm sure a lot of us would react if we saw what he saw. He loves you."

"It still doesn't make it acceptable," Joey snaps. He waves a hand in my direction. "Look at her. Look at how upset she is."

"I'm sure he was just as upset, if not more."

"He *was* upset," I whisper, feeling two sets of eyes on me as I stare at the comforter. "Seeing that, it hurt him."

"Good."

I look up at Joey, then at Billy. Both of them reacting two different ways to this.

Staring at them is like physically being able to dig my heart out of my chest and look at it in my hands. There would be a line drawn down the middle. Two bleeding sides of me, reacting with equal passion and reason.

I hate Mason for what he said, but I get what pushed him to say it.

I love him. *I love him*, but I want him to feel what I'm feeling right now.

Sighing, feeling like every muscle in my body has been stretched and pummeled with a thousand fists, with my eyes burning and tears leaking and dripping down my face, I scoot down the bed and curl against my pillow again, clutching it to my chest.

A hand strokes my leg. "It'll be okay, Brooke. It will. I promise," Billy reassures me.

I wish I can take comfort in that. Maybe tomorrow he can tell me again and it'll sink in.

Joey pushes my hair off my face and kisses my forehead. "Is there anything you want me to do? Issue a few death threats? Egg someone's fancy new studio?"

I close my eyes. "Just get me out of bed tomorrow. I need to practice on that wedding cake."

"You got it."

I hear his footsteps trailing away.

"Oh, and Joey?" I lift my head.

He braces himself in the doorway, raising an expectant eyebrow.

"Get rid of that fucking disc."

Chapter Twenty

Joey (OMG)

I DRUM MY FINGERS ON the counter as my last ounce of patience is stretched thin.

This bitch right here. If she doesn't move her snippy ass along, I'm going to have to search for the number to those window repair men we used a few years back. I am not above violence today. Not after the weekend I've had. But only classy violence, of course. A nice hard shove in the right direction never hurt anyone. If she happens to go sailing through a window in the process, that's on her. I am merely directing her toward the exit she can't seem to locate on her own.

Firmly directing her.

Tapping her manicured finger on her chin, the woman in front of me, who has been debating on her selection for the past thirty-seven minutes, admires the left side of the case.

Again.

For the sixth time.

"These muffins right here." She points at a tray while glaring at me from overtop of her glasses. "Are those raisins?"

"The ones labeled cranberry *raisin* muffins?" I arch my eyebrow. "Yes, those are indeed raisins. We try not to lie to customers here as much as we can. What with allergies and everybody wanting to sue everybody."

"Mm." She pinches her heavily lined lips together. "I'm not sure about raisins. They tend to make whatever dough they're in a bit on the dry side."

"Nothing in this bakery is dry, I assure you."

Except for your vagina. When was the last time that thing saw any action? Prohibition?

I watch her walk along the counter. Back and forth. Back and forth. She leans in close, admires a treat or two while pinching the side of her glasses, then pulls back and resumes her leisurely as fuck perusal.

Breathe, Joey. Keep your fabulous shit together. No mauling the customers. They pay you. You love them.

Stopping directly across from me, the woman glances up. She looks bored out of her mind. "I don't see any gluten free options available. That's a shame. You know, Whipped over on Madison offers an alternative menu for people who have digestive troubles."

I tilt my head. "Whipped also caters to rodents. They were busted two weeks ago by the health department for a rat infestation."

Her eyes flicker a hair wider. "Oh, I . . . wasn't aware of that." She clears her throat, studying the case again.

Tension builds in my shoulders. I close my eyes and think of my happy place.

Billy on his knees, his finger probing my ass and his sweet mouth wrapped around my . . .

A loud clanging noise arises from the kitchen.

My head snaps in the direction of the doorway, then back at the woman who startles, a little too dramatically even for my taste, slapping a hand to her heaving chest as her eyes shift frantically around the room.

"What in the world was that?"

I grit my teeth.

Brooke. Poor thing is on the verge of a complete, epic meltdown back there. She has three modes I've seen her in the past three days—hysterically crying, angrier than my mother when she doesn't get a drink by noon, and so utterly stressed she paces around the kitchen, shaking and talking to herself.

Christ, it's only Monday. Between the Mason incident and this goddamn wedding, Brooke might need serious therapy by the end of the week.

I also might need some serious therapy by the end of the week.

Laughing off the disruption from the kitchen, I wave my hand in the air. "By the sound of it, I'm going to guess a sheet tray hitting the floor. I apologize for that. We're just so busy back there making things that *aren't* dry."

The woman adjusts her glasses, cutting a look at me.

I flick a few strands of hair off my forehead.

Bitch.

My phone beeps in my pocket. I tug it out as the woman continues wasting my time.

> *Dylan: What was that? Is Brooke breaking shit now? I know she's upset but she needs to remember where she is, Joey. HANDLE IT.*

Sweet Christ. Why couldn't she be on bed rest at her mother's?

> *Me: Ease up on the shouty caps, cupcake. Everything is under control.*

> *Dylan: BETTER BE. (I love you)*

> *Me: BITCH. (love you too)*

"Is this all fresh? When were these pastries made?" The woman taps two fingers aggressively on top of the glass. "They don't look as moist as they should."

I breathe in deeply through my nose, feeling the veins in my neck bulging, reminding myself again how much I love this job and the woman upstairs I don't want to piss off by murdering someone in the middle of her shop.

The woman sighs exhaustedly. "Do you offer any beverages here? Coffee, at least? Most upscale bakeries do nowadays."

That's it. Fuck her and the stick up her ass. I am done.

Forcing the fakest smile I've ever worn, I put my phone away and gesture at the case. "No, no coffee. This is a *bakery*, not a Starbucks. And everything in front of you is fresh and made daily. We here at Dylan's Sweet Tooth are all big fans of *moist* things. I myself am like a ripe peach, if you know what I'm saying."

Her overly plucked eyebrows pull together. "Excuse me?"

I glance at the clock on the wall. "A peach. You know, the fruit. I'm sure you've noticed the tarts on the middle tray in the case you've been staring at for the past forty-five minutes. Those are indeed peaches right there. Now, if I can interest you in a cupcake or *anything* today, please let me know. Otherwise, I'm going to have to ask you to take your fresh little attitude and that knock-off Coach . . ."

She gasps.

"Yeah, I see you . . . and head on down the street. This here is an establishment where people come in and purchase things. I know, I am stunning, but unfortunately I am not an exhibit, and neither are the treats in front of me."

The woman blinks rapidly, looking affronted.

I feel like I just came.

"Well." She tightens her grip on her handbag and glares at me, her nostrils flaring with her breathing. "I suppose if I'm being rushed, I'll take three of the mocha chocolate cupcakes," she huffs, tipping her chin. "Those look the most appealing."

Grinning, I grab a box. "Excellent."

After taking her money and walking her to the door, just to make sure she gets the fuck out, I spin around and head for the kitchen.

Brooke is sitting on a stool, her head lowered and her fingers rubbing in slow circles against her temple. The sheet tray I thought I heard is on the floor near the supply shelf. As for the rest of the kitchen, it's a mess. The worktop is covered in baking materials.

Flour is spilled. A stool is turned over. Brooke's practice wedding cake, which looked pretty damn perfect yesterday, now has a chunk missing out of the top tier.

Did she eat some of it? I wouldn't be surprised.

I notice as I move further into the room the tiny flower petals made out of gum paste dropped on the floor near the tray. A few are still on it. She must've been trying to construct the gardenias again. Each attempt she makes leaves her more and more frustrated and doubtful of herself.

Her head isn't in this. That's the problem. It's across the street.

"Hey. You need me to help with anything back here?" I ask, picking up the stool and righting it. I brush some flour off the wood and scoop it into my hand, dumping it in the nearby trash bin.

Brooke shakes her head. She lowers her hands to her lap and looks down. "How are we doing on treats? Do I need to make more?"

"Not right now. We're good."

"And they're . . . people are buying them? They want what I made?"

"I'm going to pretend I didn't just hear you say that."

She slowly looks up at me.

Sighing, I move around the worktop and stand beside her. "Everything out there is fabulous. Including me. We are selling as good as we always sell, because you are an exceptional baker. In fact, don't tell Dylan this, but I actually think your red velvet icing tastes a little better than hers."

I quickly glance behind me. The stairs are vacant. Good. She isn't disobeying doctor's orders and hearing my blasphemy.

"Yeah, right." Brooke gazes up at me skeptically. Shadowy smudges line her eyes, which appear dull and lifeless. Her face is pale and a bit puffy.

How much has she cried today? Too much, I'm guessing. It's all she's been doing. Here. At the condo. In her bed. In mine.

She isn't the only one running on minimal sleep. Three people to a queen bed isn't the most comfortable arrangement.

I've suggested a king to Billy. He seems to think Brooke won't be spooning with us for much longer.

I'm doubtful.

"Do I look as shitty as I feel?" Brooke asks, her chin trembling and tears threatening to fall, her hair a mess all around her, some of it tied back haphazardly while chunks tangle together along her back.

Does she look a hot mess? Yes, absolutely. But having two women as my best friends has taught me a very valuable lesson over the past decade.

Lie when you need to. And lie good. The truth is not worth the headache sometimes.

I rub her back. "You look amazing, as do I. I was actually thinking of taking a few selfies later if you want in. Capturing our first day together as a dynamic duo running this shit like we were born to do it."

"If you put a phone in my face, I will smash it against the wall," Brooke growls. "And then I will stab you with something for suggesting we capture this god awful moment."

Inhaling slowly, I slide my hand off her back. "Noted. And for the record, you are definitely becoming more and more like my little cupcake upstairs."

For fuck's sake. How many times have I been threatened in this shop?

"Actually, I'm not. That's the problem." Brooke stands from her stool and picks up the sheet tray. "You see, Dylan would be able to construct these stupid fucking flowers with no problem. I can't. I've tried, and I've tried." She drops the tray on the wood. "And I've tried. None of mine are turning out right. That bride is going to be getting a cake with no flowers on it on Saturday because of me. Her cake will end up being the most boring looking wedding cake in the history of wedding cakes, *because* of me. And bonus, it could also taste like shit. Happy fucking wedding day."

I walk over and grab her shoulders. "I think it's time for a little break."

She shrugs away from me. "A break? And where would I go on this break, Joey?" Brooke grabs a large mixing bowl off the shelf and tosses it onto the worktop. "The coffee shop? Where Mason isn't waiting for me? Or maybe I could go to that park he took me to with the water fountain. Or the campsite. That seems like a nice break spot." She goes about retying her apron, although I'm not sure she needs to. It seems pretty damn secure. "Or maybe I'll just march across the street and take my break over there? See if he looks as bad as I do. See if he's feeling anything even close to what I'm feeling, because he fucking should! He should be the one crying, and losing sleep, and," she gives up on the trying to tie the apron and rips it off, tossing it on the floor. "And heartbroken. He should feel like he's dying, because that's how I feel!"

Oh shit.

She huffs out a breath and wipes at her face. "Jesus Christ. I didn't even want this!"

I watch Brooke turn away from me, her shoulders hunched forward, her hands coming up to cradle her face as she cries and cries and cries.

Fuck! I can't take this! I can't take anymore more of this. It's killing me. I love Brooke. Wild, crazy, fun to be around, Brooke. This isn't her. This isn't even a dulled out version of her. I have no idea who the shattered woman is in front of me, but I know who's responsible for it.

And that asshole is about to get a little visit from yours truly.

I pick up her apron and lay it across the stool. "Take a minute to get yourself together. I'm going to turn the sign on the door and step out to get something to drink. You're amazing. I love you. Remember that."

Spinning around, not giving her a chance to argue or me a chance to see any more of her devastation, I move into the front of the shop and flip the sign on the door, push it open to get outside, and cross the street, sprinting to avoid traffic.

I pull on the door handle.

Locked.

"Really? No classes today, Mister Hemsworth?"

Cupping my hand on the glass, I peer inside the dark studio.

I know Mason lives upstairs. Brooke told me his set-up is similar to Dylan's. There's a chance he isn't here.

There's also a chance he is.

I dig into my back pocket and pull out my wallet, fishing through for the bobby pin I keep inside.

Billy likes to cuff me. I like to get out of them without him knowing and pounce unexpectedly like a tiger in heat.

I always get off first. Those are the rules my baby likes to forget.

Straightening the pin, I slide it inside the lock and work the mechanism. It takes less than a minute until I'm rewarded with the soft click. The swift glide of metal. I pull the door open and lock it behind me, crossing the room and bounding up the stairs. I'm ready to use the pin again when I test the knob of the next door.

Surprisingly, it turns without any resistance.

I step out into the loft. The room is darkened, courtesy of the drawn curtains, but I can make out the large figure on the bed.

Face down, breathing heavily and clutching a bottle of what looks to be tequila, Mason seems to be out cold, fully clothed and still wearing his shoes. I'm willing to bet he's going to be waking up with the hangover of his life.

Perfect.

I flip the switch on the wall. Light bathes the room, but the man on the bed remains motionless. Stepping over dirty clothes and other shit on the floor, beer bottles, a few books, and what looks to be camping gear, I move into the kitchen and grab two saucepans from a cabinet.

And then I bang the fucking shit out of them.

Mason's head snaps up. He blinks fast, alarm and confusion in his dimmed gaze as he attempts to focus on me. The bottle in his hand rolls off the bed and onto the floor, spilling amber liquid. He covers his one ear and buries his face into the pillow, groaning.

I toss the pans in the sink and brush off my hands.

Ah, that felt good.

"What the hell? What are you doing?" Mason grunts.

"Oh, I'm sorry. I got so hungry on my walk over here I thought about making something, and then I remembered that I don't really cook. My boo does. Thought I'd make some music instead. Did you enjoy that?"

He grumbles something I don't make out. He slides his hand off his ear and turns his head to look at me through half-lidded eyes.

"Afternoon," I sing, smiling as I move closer. "I gotta say, you know, I am a bit disappointed in you, Mason. I mean, for years I have been let down by American men doing dumbass shit, but you have managed to prove to me on an international level that the majority of the male race are complete fucking idiots. Way to represent your country there. Bravo."

"What . . . how did you get in here?" he asks, still looking just as disordered, trying to sit up and then moaning, collapsing back onto his stomach. "Fuck. My head. Can you switch that light off?"

I study my nails. "Nah. And to answer your question, I picked the lock. This building is like a billion years old. A monkey could get in here if he wanted to."

Mason grabs a pillow and covers his head with it.

"You know I was rooting for you, right? Really rooting for you. And now I look like the shitty friend who pushed a guy who was *not* who we all thought he was on someone I really care about." I kick the mattress, jarring his body a little. "Thanks for that. I doubt Brooke will ever take my advice again."

Mason lifts his head, snatching the pillow off and glaring at me, until his sudden movement registers in pain across his face and he winces. "Could you . . . please stop talking? Please."

I bend down. "No. I have a lot to say, and you're going to hear every word of it."

Groaning, he rests his head back on the pillow, his eyes open but unfocused. "Fine. Get on with it then."

"Gladly." I cross my arms over my chest. A large object in the corner by the window grabs my attention. "Why do you have a tent set up in your room?"

Mason pinches his eyes shut, breathing deeply.

"Never mind. That's not important. What you did, saying those things to Brooke and making her feel the way she does right now was beyond fucked up. We all have skeletons in our closet, Mason. I'm sure you've been with other women. You knew Brooke wasn't a virgin when you first met her. That wasn't something she kept from you. Getting on her about shit that happened before she even met you is a complete dick move. Yeah, it sucks that you saw it. I'm sure anyone would've reacted the way you did, but it doesn't make it right."

"Sucks?" He blinks up at me. "It more than sucks, mate. All right?"

We stare at each other for a moment, and it's then I see how ragged he looks.

His blonde hair is a mess. Pieces sticking straight out and the rest plastered to his skull. His beard is grown out several days worth. It's thick and dark. He looks older. The same shadowy smudges I just saw across the street on Brooke line his tired eyes. His clothes are wrinkled. I'm guessing they've been worn a couple days in a row now.

Jesus. He's as miserable as she is.

"Is this what you've been doing all weekend?" I ask, gesturing around the room, picking up the tequila bottle and setting it on his night stand. "Getting drunk and then passing out?"

He nods slightly, barely a jerk of his head.

"You know what she's been doing?"

Mason flicks his weak stare to me.

"Crying."

It darts away again.

"She's messed up over you. Really messed up, which is only adding to her stress. This fucking wedding she's got . . ."

"Why?" he gruffly asks, cutting me off. His gaze still lost on something in front of him. "Why is she messed up? She shouldn't care. She doesn't love me. She said it herself. None of this ever mattered to her. I never mattered."

Bending down, I get close enough to his face, he has no choice but to look at me. "You believe that? 'Cause if you do, you're more of an idiot than I thought."

He grits his teeth. "She said she hates me."

"I'd hate you too if you made me feel like a whore."

His eyes go wide, as round as saucers. "What?" he asks, his voice eerily quiet.

Oh, for fuck's sake. Of course he has no idea that's how she would take all that. God, sometimes I wonder why I love men as much as I do.

Cock.

Yup. That's why. That's definitely why.

I straighten my spine. "I heard what you said. The whole 'are there more of these tapes? Does everyone watch them?' bullshit. How the fuck do you think she would feel after hearing that? And from *you*? The one person she cares about more than anything? Yeah, I'm sure she does hate you. But that isn't all she feels."

He swallows heavily. "I would never think that of her. I was just . . ." his voice trails off as he rubs a hand over his face. "Fuck, I was . . ."

"You were mad and upset, and you said some shit you didn't mean."

He releases a stiff breath, nodding, his jaw locked tight.

I squat beside the bed. He looks at me, the pain searing in his eyes. The guilt. I'm happy it's there. He should feel really fucking sorry for this.

He made me commit a felony.

"And Brooke was upset, crushed actually, and said some shit she didn't mean," I tell him, watching his nostrils flare, his throat shuddering with the breath he takes. "We all have people in our past, Mason. Some of us more than others. I say, who the fuck cares? I know Billy's been with other men. But you know what? I fucking have him. They don't. He chose *me*. Brooke might've made that tape with someone else, but she never gave anyone what she gave you. To be honest, she never even came close. Forget about the tape and think about that. You got her. She chose *you*. Everyone else? Fuck em'."

I stand to my feet, Mason's eyes following my movement. I glance once more around the room. "You know, I always pictured you as a neat guy. This is quite a disappointment. Unless this is all the aftermath of Friday night then, okay, I can understand that. I've wallowed in filth when I've been on the outs with my man. Pretty normal reaction to heartbreak." I look down at him. "The tent I still don't get though. You've lost me there."

He shifts on the bed, turning onto his back and immediately clutching at his head and wincing in pain, his breath seething through his teeth.

"Brooke joked once about camping in here instead of outside. That's where I've slept the past two nights. Pretending she's with me."

My chest tightens.

Oh, my God. If I wasn't so irritated with this man, I'd give him the kiss of his life right now.

Smiling, I move away from the bed. "Aw, that's sweet. I appreciate your misery. I do. I am a full supporter of karma, and you deserve that bitch's wrath right now."

"Thanks," he mumbles.

"Anytime. Oh, and Mason?" Halfway out the door, I turn back, waiting for him to look up at me before I speak. "She loves you. Fix it, or you will have me as your enemy. And I can get all kinds of crazy up in here. Breaking into a business is nothing. You won't have one when I'm finished."

He gives me a troubled look.

I wink, pulling the door shut behind me.

God, I am fucking fabulous. Someone should really write a book about me.

Chapter Twenty-One

Mason

THE DOOR CLOSES BEHIND JOEY.

Wincing through the pain tightening in my skull, I try and sit up, try and get out of this godforsaken bed and into the shower I desperately need, but the knife prying my head apart twists an inch deeper, lighting a fire along my scalp.

"Fucking hell," I groan, grinding the heels of my hands into my eyelids and falling back onto the bed.

This bloody hangover. I can't remember ever having one this awful before. Not even during the three years I spent at university.

Think you've outdone yourself, mate. And over the woman you love. Good on ya.

I close my eyes, hard, needing to see her, giving into this agony. I can't fight it. I don't want to.

Brooke touches my hand, looking up at me, smiling the way she always does with those dimples caving in her cheeks and that warm flush blooming across her face. Her big hazel eyes burning, the gold flecks dancing in the sunlight. She slides her hand along my palm, moving her fingers between mine and squeezing.

Squeezing.

Taking and laying claim.

Mine, she's saying.

My breath grows thicker, slow moving in and out of my lungs. My pulse is wild. I need to hold her.

Reaching out, lifting her chin so I can see that sweet face again, I startle at her appearance.

Big tears fall down her face, her lip trembles. She lets go of my hand and we're suddenly feet apart. I'm at the door, my hand on the knob, my body shaking so badly the hinges rattle. I hear her voice behind me, words broken apart by sobs, telling me I never mattered and that this meant nothing. She hates me.

"I will hate you for this!"

My eyes flash open. Wetness beads on my lashes. I wipe it away and flip over, groaning into the pillow and breathing anxiously against the sheet.

She said it. I didn't imagine that. She said it after confirming my biggest fear, that she never loved me. That it was all a lie, and I believed her.

Hell, it makes sense. Brooke was fighting me from the beginning. We wanted different things. She knew what I was after, and she figured out what she had to do to get the one thing she cared about.

Only . . .

It felt different. Pretty early on, it felt like maybe sex wasn't the only thing she cared about.

She wasn't pushing it. She wasn't grabbing my hand and hurrying us, getting what she wanted and getting rid of me. She was holding on and standing still, letting me lead her, trusting me, hesitating at first but finally opening up and slowly becoming the one to reach out. Saying things to me I was feeling. Even when I limited what we did because I knew my willpower with her was and always will be shit, she kept our pace. She was with me. She was willing.

She was mine, or she was a damn good liar.

Why would she tell me I never meant anything if it wasn't true?

Because I hurt her? Because I reacted?

That disc. God, fuck, that disc. I never should've picked it up. Never should've played it, not without asking Brooke what it was first. Just knowing about it, I could've gotten past that and enjoyed my night with her. I could've pretended it didn't exist.

Maybe.

The truth is, I don't like thinking about Brooke with anyone else. Ever. I don't want to know about it. I don't want to run into some drunk tosser who's been with Brooke and makes it bloody known he's been with her, and I sure as fuck don't want to see it happening.

Watching her with some other bloke, seeing his hands on her, touching what's mine, thinking in that moment he has her when he never fucking came close, yeah, I reacted. I reacted how anyone would react seeing something like that.

Seeing someone you love taking pleasure you aren't giving.

I was angry. Murderous. Rage running in my blood, and the pain, fuck, that was the worst of it. I ached in my bones. There was a hole in my chest, I was sure of it. Bile singed the back of my throat. I couldn't breathe.

I looked at Brooke and all I could see was her with him.

I looked at Brooke, and all I could see was the woman on that disc, not the one I knew.

Not the soft, vulnerable woman I had in the alley. Or the shy one giving me a first in that photo booth. Not the Brooke who laughed and played with me, or the one who told me she loved me and that she was mine.

"Yours," she said that day. *"I thought I was yours. I want to be."*

Did I imagine it all? Did I imagine the hold she had around my heart and the tie I felt to hers? Did I imagine *this* Brooke?

I looked at her, and I couldn't breathe. I couldn't think. I gave her my anger and my pain. I spoke without consideration. I reacted.

I reacted, asking something I was sure of minutes before.

I was sure.

She was crying. I knew she was, but I barely saw her tears. I couldn't focus on that. Then she spoke and her answer gutted me.

Her truth.

Only . . .

What if it wasn't? What if Joey is right? What if we were both saying shit we didn't mean, both of us reacting, being rash and thoughtless of the other person. Not seeing each other's pain and only feeling our own.

Is it possible?

Fuck . . . is it?

He said she's been crying all weekend, that she's messed up over this. Why would she be messed up if I mean nothing to her? If *this* was always nothing?

Closing my eyes again, I see her face, her broken, agony-stricken face, covered in tears I'm now focusing on for the first time. Really focusing on. Her pink lips trembling and her entire body shaking.

Shaking like mine.

She was shattered. Fuck, she was. I couldn't see her suffering. Not while feeling my own. It blinded me, but now I see it. She was crushed. Devastated. Because of how I spoke, how I looked at her. My reaction ripping her apart, and my question . . .

My question destroying her.

"What do you think?" she asked me, begging me with her eyes to speak the truth for her. The only truth she wanted to say, but I didn't. I gave her nothing because I couldn't. I couldn't see her.

I couldn't see my Brooke.

"She loves you. Fix it."

I gave her nothing, and she gave me everything. Me. No one else. She chose me.

She chose me.

A shuddering breath bursts from my mouth, blowing hot against my face.

My Brooke.

My Brooke . . . she chose me. She loves me.

Loves. Me.

And I'm the one who made her feel like she never mattered. I'm the one who treated her as if she meant nothing that day.

I'm the one who made her feel like a whore.

Pain sears in my jaw as I grit my teeth.

What have I done? What the fuck have I done?

WHAT THE FUCK HAVE I DONE?

I need to see her. Need to talk to her. Need to hold her.

Groaning, feeling a thousand needles stabbing my skull and acid churning in my gut, shredding the lining of my stomach and burning my intestines, I ball my fists and try and push off from the bed.

I get an inch. Maybe. Pain doubles me over. Scorching pain behind my eyes, in the center of my chest, blooming out to my limbs, my fingers. I feel it everywhere. I roll onto my side and hold my head. I taste bile in my throat.

I have been doing nothing but drinking the past two days. Drinking and missing Brooke. Drinking and wondering if she was always too wild for me. If maybe we were doomed from the start.

Was the sole purpose of meeting this woman to show me everything I ever wanted, and everything I would never have? Is the universe that fucking cruel?

I couldn't answer that this weekend, or maybe I didn't want to. Fear bonded to my tongue and imprisoned my mind.

I have no problem answering now.

Impossible.

Impossible, because I love her wild. It was always part of the attraction with Brooke. I love her rough edges and her sharp tongue. I love the woman who pulled me into that photo booth as much as I love the one who shyly came against my mouth. The sheep and the wolf. It has always been *everything* about this woman, her unbridled desire and the soft, sweet way she gentles for me. Her darkness and her light. I want them both.

I will always want them both.

We were never doomed. I didn't move to Chicago to open my own studio. That's not what brought me here. I moved to Chicago so I could find her.

That disc, it means nothing. He never had her. No one has ever had Brooke the way I have. No one ever came close.

I pinch my eyes shut and stay on my side, not moving. I breathe tensely through my nose. The pain decreases to a bearable throb.

A few minutes pass and I'm trying again, sitting up and then immediately collapsing back down when the room starts to spin mercilessly.

"Fuck!"

I roll onto my stomach and bury my face into the pillow. I feel my heart everywhere. In my skull, pounding, the echo radiating along my scalp and down my spine. In my chest where it aches, it doesn't beat. It won't beat there, not until she's with me.

Not until I have her.

It's probably for the best that I'm too sick to move. I know I look like shit. Probably worse than I feel. If I were able to get out of this bed, there wouldn't be anything stopping me from going to Brooke right now, not waiting and getting myself together. A change of clothes at least.

No. I wouldn't wait for clothes.

She deserves better than this version of me coming to her and begging for forgiveness. I need to sober up first. Shower. Fucking shave.

Christ, I'll probably scare her looking like I do.

I need to do this right. I won't be selfish right now. This is for her, not me.

Tonight. Tonight will be better. Or tomorrow after I get a decent night's sleep and go long enough without a drink that I don't reek of alcohol. I can see her in the morning, first thing. I can meet her at work, or at the coffee shop, or . . .

My gut tightens. Rosie's.

Yes. Fuck, yes, tomorrow is Tuesday. Our breakfast, the one morning Brooke agreed to give me.

I still want it. Does she? Will she show up? Will she be hoping I'm there, even though I hurt her and she has every right to hate me?

Anxiety soaks into my bones. My heart rattles in my chest.

God, if she's there . . .

Fuck it. I might ask her to marry me before I get my apology out. I won't be able to stop myself.

No. Come on, mate, she deserves to know how sorry you are. Give her that first.

An extraordinary serenity warms my skin. I'm so close. So

close to seeing her. If she shows up at Rosie's or not, this unbearable agony ripping me apart from the inside out is nearly extinguished because either way, I'm getting my girl back tomorrow.

And I'm never letting her go.

Swiping my arm along the bed, I grab the furry leg of the bastard stuffed koala and pull him against my side, squeezing him.

Only one more night in the tent without her.

Chapter Twenty-Two

Brooke

I DON'T KNOW WHAT I'M doing.

I know what I *should* be doing. I should be sleeping, or at least trying to sleep. I could use more than what I've been getting, which is turning out to be only a few hours a night. Not nearly enough. I'm exhausted. Physically and mentally. It distracts me from the pain a little so I'm okay with being too tired to care about how I look, and nearly too tired to care about anything. But since I am awake, and showered, at least half-way put together, I should be walking in the opposite direction on Fayette street and heading into work, but I'm not.

I'm walking past the coffee shop, down the street a little further toward those yellow umbrellas.

Why? Why am I doing this? I need all of the practice I can get, every spare minute I have to work on those flowers, and instead I'm wasting my time going to Rosie's because it's Tuesday.

It's Tuesday.

Mason wanted this day so badly, this breakfast. Me, early in the morning, and I know he isn't here. I know it. I know it just like I know that at some point today I'm going to hear that door chime and hope that it's him, and it won't be. And then I'm going to cry, and throw something, and scream a little. I'm going to miss him and hate him and love him because I can't turn that off yet, and I'm afraid I won't ever be able to.

I'm more afraid I'll never want to turn it off, and I'll keep doing this.

I know he isn't here, but I can't turn around. I can't stop myself from crossing the street and stepping up onto the sidewalk. It's programmed in me to look for him, to hope that he'll be here. To hope that he's still with me.

A shuddering breath fills my lungs. My eyes won't stop watering. I can avoid this torment. It isn't too late . . .

My body moves without thought. I scan the line wrapping around the building before stepping inside the busy café.

The young hostess looks up from her podium, ready to greet me, but I avoid her eyes and shift my attention around the room.

"Good morning. Is your party already seated?"

I hear her question as I study the faces in the booths along the window and the tables spread out along the floor.

Be here. Please, be here.

I take a step closer to look again, and again. One last time.

He isn't here, and I knew he wouldn't be, so why am I crying? Why?

The first tear slides down my cheek. I focus on the hostess and shake my head, biting at my lip. She gives me a concerned look. I need to get out of here before this becomes yesterday at the coffee shop all over again, where I sobbed uncontrollably the entire time I waited for my order.

I got a free muffin out of it, which was nice. Not that I had the appetite to eat it.

Spinning around, I push through the door and run straight into someone, bumping into their chest.

"I'm s-sorry," I mumble, wiping at my face and moving to

sidestep them.

Large hands squeeze my shoulders. "Brooke."

My stomach drops. I look up at the person holding onto me, but I don't need to. I know that voice. That low, relaxed voice. It pours over me like sap sticking to a tree. My bones suddenly feel heavier.

Mason studies me with parted lips and absorbing eyes. "God, I'm . . ." he pauses, moving his hands down my arms, squeezing gently. "It's really good to see you."

I blink up at him. "You're here," I whisper in disbelief, looking all over his face, waiting for him to vanish and for this to be just another layer of my nightmare. A cruel joke my heart is playing on me.

"Where else would I be?" he asks, smiling a little. "It's Tuesday."

My lip quivers. I don't know what to make of this.

He's here. He's here, and he's touching me. He's smiling. The man who wouldn't listen to me, who would barely look at me three nights ago.

The man who believes I never loved him and that everything I said was a lie. He's here.

I wished and wished and wished for this, and now I suddenly can't breathe.

I step back and his hands fall away.

"I can't do this," I utter, pushing past him and darting across the street.

I don't know how to do this.

"Brooke!" Mason's voice calls out behind me. He sounds urgent. I know he's following.

And I run faster.

I pass the coffee shop, dashing in between people walking on the sidewalk. Knocking into several of them and blurting out an apology between hasty breaths.

Mason calls out again behind me. He sounds closer.

Tears sting my eyes as I push myself to move, to not let him catch up.

What am I supposed to say to him? I want to collapse into his arms and I want to scream into his face. I want him to hold me and I can't stomach the thought of him touching me. I'm so confused. He isn't supposed to be here.

Why is he here?

My breath is stolen from my lungs when my toe catches on something. The crack in the sidewalk. I don't see it. I go down hard, smacking the concrete with my hands bracing my weight and my knee dragging along the cement.

"Ow, ow, ow, ow, ow," I cry, rolling onto my side and pulling my knee to my chest. The pain is instant and unforgiving. Flesh is torn open. My hands burning and cut up from the concrete, blood beading on my palms, but my knee, Jesus, my knee feels like it's on fire.

"Fuck! Ow. Ow. Ow."

Mason crouches down beside me, a bit winded. Concern tightening his features.

"Shit. You all right? Let me see. Come here." He tries to slide my jeans up my leg, my bloody knee visible through the hole ripped in it.

I brush his hands away, sitting up and wincing. "Stop. I'm fine. It's n-nothing."

Mason grabs my ankle. "Brooke, you're bleeding. Let me just check it. You hit the ground pretty hard. I won't hurt you, I promise. I just need to see your leg and make sure this isn't serious."

My chest shudders. I drop my hands to my lap, my palms burning.

"You already hurt me," I quietly reply, surrendering and slowly stretching out my leg for him.

His lips pinch together. We stare at each other, and he looks like he wants to say something in response but he doesn't.

Using gentle hands, he pulls my jeans up my leg and over my knee, making sure to keep the material away from my broken skin. He bunches my pants on my thigh.

I inhale a sharp breath when his warm hands hold my leg, his thumbs pressing and sliding around the tender area.

The world blurs around us. Heat blooms at the base of my spine.

God, this shouldn't feel good. I'm injured. This really fucking hurts.

Focus on that, Brooke. You could've died. The sidewalk almost killed you.

This hurts. This hurts. This hurts. You're not enjoying any part of this.

I repeat that mantra in my head as he continues to examine my leg. *Thoroughly* examine it.

He massages my ankle, my calf. He pops my sneaker off and presses against the bones in my foot.

My toes curl. *What is he doing? I didn't hurt my foot.*

"Mason." I try and pull my leg back.

"Just checking," he says, smirking a little and popping my shoe back on.

Bending down, he squeezes my leg and blows softly against my cut, watching me with those bright blue eyes while he does it.

My breathing quickens. I don't know whether to cry or moan. I decide on a strange mix of both, which luckily goes unnoticed thanks to the car horn down the street.

"This hurt?" he asks, forcing my knee to bend and then straightening it. He repeats the motion.

I shake my head. "No. It just stings where it's bleeding. And it hurts around my knee-cap."

He nods slightly. "Good. It looks like it's just scraped really bad. You might've bruised the bone a little. You should be fine. No major surgery needed, I'm willing to bet."

"Okay." I pull my leg out of his lap and attempt to stand. "I need to go."

I shift my weight on the ground, trying to maneuver this on my own.

Getting to my feet on a bum leg and without the use of my hands quickly proves to be a hopeless endeavor. Not only because there's no way I'm going to be able to do this without any assistance, but also because Mason doesn't allow me much time to struggle.

"Let's get you cleaned up."

Leaning over, he scoops me into his arms and stands effortlessly, taking my weight.

Oh, my God. What is happening?

I squeak, flailing a little. "Put me down! What are you doing? I can walk."

"You think you can walk?" he asks doubtfully. "Relax, sweetheart. I have you. It's a bit of a hike across the street to my studio anyway. Rest your leg."

Sweetheart? HIS STUDIO?

He sounds so cavalier, like nothing monumentally destructive happened between us three nights ago.

Did I imagine it all? Jesus Christ, am I going crazy?

I tilt my head to look at him.

Clean shaven, freshly showered, no signs of distress or obvious heartache in his eyes. He appears well rested and as stunningly attractive as ever.

I barely brushed my hair this morning and I'm not even sure my clothes match.

All of the pain I'm feeling shifts and centralizes in my chest. I squirm in his arms.

"Put me down right now! God, look at you! You should be destroyed! You should be the one crying and miserable, and instead you look like this? Get off of me! I said I can walk. I can walk."

His eyes widen. Agony slips over him like a cloak.

I mentally question if I just slapped him in the face somehow, flailing about like I did.

That's exactly how he looks.

"I am," he whispers harshly, his body tensing against mine.

I still in his arms.

"I am miserable. I have been, but I'm holding you. I'm touching you and I can't help the way my heart reacts to that. I'm sorry. Know that I've been in Hell, Brooke. Know that the past few days have been the darkest of my life. Every second we've been apart, I've been drowning."

"But you look fine," I tell him. "You don't look miserable."

You don't look like me.

"That's only because I know something you don't."

"What?"

His lip twitches. "Let's get you cleaned up first. That cut needs some cleaning out. I have that first aid kit in my loft. It has what we need." He cradles me closer, dropping his head to breathe in my hair. "I have so much I want to say to you. So much I need to say. Let me do this first, yeah? Let me heal you, Brooke."

Let him heal me. Is it even possible? I feel damaged beyond repair.

Closing my eyes and surrendering once again, I let my head fall against his chest.

The ground moves beneath me. I feel like I'm floating. Mason's hold is gentle yet secure, preventing any bumping or jarring as he maneuvers us. I hear the light traffic on the street, the soft scrape of a key fitting into a lock. I smell the earthy scent of the studio and Mason's clean soap.

I tilt my head up and rub my face into his neck. Fuck it. If it turns out I'm dreaming, I want this to be a really good fucking dream.

He ascends the stairs, shifting his arm underneath my knees. The door opens. I lift my head and look around his loft as he carries me to the bed.

It looks how it always looks. Tidy. I'm not sure you can see the floor of my bedroom anymore. I've stopped caring about neatness and organization. I'm barely sleeping in there anyway.

One thing seems out of place and catches my attention as he sits me on the edge of the mattress.

I stare at the tent in the corner of the room. It takes up the majority of the floor space near the window and bends awkwardly against the ceiling.

"Have you been sleeping in that?" I ask, wincing when I push my palms against the mattress, forgetting about my injuries. "Ow."

"Yeah. I might get rid of my bed. I rather like it in there." Mason grabs my wrists, turning my hands over to examine me. "Let me grab my kit. Don't move."

I watch him pad into the bathroom, his running shorts hanging low on his hips. He returns seconds later with his kit and a bottle of disinfectant.

"Would you really get rid of your bed?"

He kneels in front of me, pouring some of the liquid onto a square piece of gauze. "Depends."

"On?" I hiss through my teeth when he presses the cold gauze against my knee. My leg jerks. "Shit. That stings."

"Sorry. I need to clean it out. You might have dirt in it." He lifts the gauze and blows over my knee again. Our eyes lock. "Better?"

Christ, it just got a thousand degrees hotter in here.

Swallowing thickly, I nod. "Mm. A little."

"I'll be quick."

He presses the pad against my skin again, lifting and moving it over my knee. I pinch my eyes shut and grit my teeth.

"You said it depends. What does it depend on?" I ask again, blowing out quick breaths and distracting my mind from the pain.

I am curious. Maybe it depends on him needing a new mattress and he doesn't feel like purchasing another one. Maybe he's debating on going rogue and drifting away from all uses of modern civilization.

Why would someone give up a bed for a tent?

"Depends on you," he answers casually.

The sound of something tearing opens my eyes, or maybe it's his response. He applies a bandage over my knee and looks up.

"Why would it depend on me?" I ask.

I watch his neck roll with a heavy swallow. He grabs another piece of gauze and pours some disinfectant on it, then holds onto the back of my hand as he presses the gauze against my palm.

It doesn't sting nearly as bad as my knee did. I barely react to it, or maybe I'm just too engrossed in the vague man in front of me.

"Mason," I press him.

He clears his throat. "If you want us to have a bed, or if you're happier in the tent," he explains as he cleans out my cut and moves to my other hand. His eyes focused on his task. "I'm not sure we can have both in here and be able to move around easily. It's a bit tight in that corner. And I was thinking, if we got rid of the bed and set the tent up over here, we can fit your dresser and anything else you want to have. Whatever you want."

I blink several times, trying to absorb and understand what he's just said, but there's no way . . . is he really suggesting what I think he's suggesting?

He looks up at me after he's finished and discarded the gauze. "Do you want bandages on your hands too? I wasn't sure."

"Did you just ask me to move in with you?"

Mason stares at me, his expression indecipherable. He doesn't respond.

I swallow and blush instantly. My gaze lowers to my lap.

Oh, my God. It's official. I'm crazy. I'm imagining conversations now.

"I did," Mason finally says after what feels like an eternity of silence.

I slowly look up.

"That's what I'm asking. I mean, it makes sense, yeah? I'm going to spend my life with you. You're my forever, and I thought this would be a good way to ease you into agreeing to marry me, just in case that idea terrifies you. I'll do it proper, I swear, Brooke. You deserve that. I'm just warming you up to it."

My mouth falls open. Heat floods my face and my neck as my eyes struggle to focus on anything in front of me. "I think I need to sit down."

"You are sitting down."

"Well, then maybe I should stand up."

He pushes lightly against my shoulder. "Your knee. Rest it for a minute."

Frustrated, I swat at his hand. "Stop! Just stop, okay?" I yell, startling him a bit.

He drops his hand and nods, looking cautious.

Tears fill my eyes as I slowly fall apart. "I don't understand what's happening. Friday you let go of me. You promised you would never let go of me, Mason, and then I don't hear anything from you for days. I thought this was over." I shove against his chest. "I thought this was over! I've been dying and what the fuck have you been doing? Planning our life together? Are you serious?" I blink, sending fat tears down my face.

Hesitantly, he reaches up and wipes his knuckles along my cheek. "I've been dying too."

"How?" I ask, watching him shift closer.

"The only time I left this room was to go to the liquor store," he tells me in a somber voice, brushing my hair out of my face. "I've been drunk up through yesterday, Brooke. Black-out drunk. I don't remember most of it. I canceled all of my classes and smashed my phone against the wall."

"Why? So I wouldn't call you?"

He shakes his head. "So I wouldn't call *you*. God, I would've been bloody ecstatic if you would've called me. I came close. I nearly texted you a few times and I knew I shouldn't. You hated me, but I missed you so fucking much." He holds my face, tears brimming his eyes now. "So fucking much, Brooke. Every second you were away from me I longed for you. That distance killed me."

I sniffle, thinking back to that night, to all the things that were said and the question that broke us.

"I fucked up," Mason whispers, blinking and sending his own tears down his face, moving so close to me I can feel his breath on my skin. "I saw that disc, what was on it, and I . . . I lost it. Baby, I lost it. I couldn't see you. I couldn't hear what I was saying or how it sounded. I have never felt any of the things I feel for you for anyone else. I've never felt possessive before, but that night I wanted to find that guy and kill him for touching you. I would've killed him, Brooke."

"Mason." I clutch at his shirt, crying harder.

"You're mine, and I saw you with someone else and that fucked with my head. I know I have no right to be that way. I know you were with him before you even met me, but fuck, Brooke, I feel like you've been mine for longer than we've known each other. You brought me here." His hold on me tightens. "*You brought me here*."

The devastation, the agony and regret in his voice, it's ripping me apart. I can't help but feel some blame for this.

And I missed him too.

I slide my hands to his face, ignoring the burn in my palms. "I'm sorry about that disc."

"No." He wipes away more of my tears. "I'm the one who's sorry, Brooke. More sorry than I will ever be able to express to you. This is on me. I hate what I've done. I hate that I made you feel any less than how I think of you. I hate that you thought this was over. It could never be over for me. God, even when you said this never mattered and I meant nothing, I still loved you. That will never change. I will never let go of you."

I drop my head, letting more tears fall. "I only said those things because I thought that was what you believed. I didn't mean them."

"I didn't mean what I said either, sweetheart."

Mason guides my chin up, sliding his body between my legs, cupping my face and making sure I look at him.

"I will never let go of you, Brooke. I told you the day we met that I wouldn't be able to. I warned you then. You remember?"

"Yes," I quietly reply, tears dripping off my jaw. "You made me so nervous. I think my heart knew who you were that day and it scared me."

"Baby," he murmurs, sliding his mouth over mine and pressing, melting us together.

He guides my head with his hand, tilting me to deepen the kiss, licking along my lip and moaning when I open for him.

We kiss and we kiss and we kiss, but it's so much more than that. I can feel his apology on his mouth. I can taste it on his tongue. His sadness and his guilt, I swallow it and give him my own.

It's the best and worst kiss of my life, because I know what we went through to have it.

I fist Mason's shirt and pull him closer. "I like that tent," I tell him, sucking on his lip. "Maybe enough to give up the bed."

He smiles. "It's so lonely in there without you."

"Take me in there now."

"Yeah?" He leans away. "Can your injury handle my lovin'?"

Laughing, I kiss his jaw. "You can be sweet, yeah?"

Smiling that gorgeous smile that nearly stops my heart at the same time as filling it, he stands and helps me to my feet.

"I can be sweet for you."

Mason assists me to the tent. I can put most of my weight on my knee, but not all of it. I have a small limp. Nothing that would prevent me from doing my job.

Thank Christ.

With some assistance, I push the flap aside on the tent and hobble inside. Falling onto my hip, I grab the stuffed koala off the sleeping bag and hug him to my chest.

Oh, my God. Has he been sleeping with this? My heart might burst.

Mason ducks his head and steps inside the tent. He taps the

koala on the head. "He's not so bad. Seems docile compared to his mates."

I'm smiling, laughing through my pinched lips, until Mason reaches behind him and strips off his shirt.

His shoes and socks follow.

I loosen my hold on the koala and it rolls out of my lap and onto the tent floor. I gaze down at the impressive bulge in Mason's shorts.

My mouth waters. I am literally salivating at the thought of his cock in or anywhere near my body.

Preferably in. At least touching. I mean, I'll look at that masterpiece all goddamn day, but here, right now, I need to feel it.

Mason crouches beside me and kisses just below my ear.

"I love you," he whispers. "You with me, sweet girl?"

I close my eyes, nodding, fighting the biggest smile of my life.

"Yes."

I raise my arms and he strips my shirt over my head. My bra follows.

"Lie back," he instructs, popping the button on my jeans as I stretch out beneath him.

He's careful not to brush against my knee as he pulls down my pants. My jeans are discarded. I lift my hips, tugging at the string of my thong, biting my lip when Mason slides them down my legs and tosses them over his head.

He crawls over me. I tuck my fingers inside the waistband of his shorts and tug them down to mid thigh, my toes helping. My breath bursts against his neck. I lick and bite it, running my tongue up to his jaw.

His cock slides against my slit. I feel his hand between my legs, positioning himself.

My legs tremble.

"You're dripping," he murmurs, kissing my cheek as he slides in the first inch. "You feel how hard I am?"

I gasp, nodding and clawing at his back. He fills me slowly, stretching me perfectly. I squeeze his neck and lift my legs higher.

The pain in my knee is forgotten. Goose bumps break out across my flesh.

Mason thrusts into me, his pace measured and adoring. He

whispers his sorry over and over against my lips, his voice growing incredibly quiet. When I stop hearing it, I close my eyes and feel his mouth moving the words his soul is screaming at me.

No apology has ever been felt like this.

He tells me he's mine, his body, his heart. I worship him with my hands, roaming over the beautiful planes of his back, squeezing and rubbing his muscles, his trim hips and his ass. I press my lips everywhere, his face, his neck, his shoulders. I tell him that I'm his and I always have been. When he hears my declaration, he moans and fucks me harder. My pussy clenches around him and soaks his cock. Wetness leaks to my ass.

Mason drops his head and circles my nipple with his tongue. He sucks on the other, lifting and squeezing my breast, using his teeth when I beg him for it.

I fist his hair and cry out, arching away from the floor.

"Baby. Missed you," he rasps, grabbing my face and kissing me hard, rocking into me more steadily, drawing my orgasm. "It killed me being apart, Brooke. I need you here. Need you with me."

"Forever?"

"Fuck yes, forever. I love you. I will never love anyone else."

"Mason," I groan, gasping into his mouth. "If you ask me, I'll say yes. I'm not scared. I will always say yes to you."

I feel the rhythm of his heart change.

He growls, leaning back to look at me with wild eyes, his breathing heavy and desperate between us, his jaw clenched tight and sweat dripping down his face. I can see him struggling, trying to slow down the fervent drag of his cock while the muscles in his arms flex and swell on either side of my face.

He loses the battle.

Swearing and moaning my name, Mason pistons his hips and releases inside of me. His orgasm is exquisite, the tensing of his stomach, the noises he makes. He drops his head against my shoulder and pants in hot breaths, only contented for a few seconds before he's sliding down my body and nuzzling his mouth against my clit.

"Oh . . . oh, God."

I reach blindly for his hair, my eyes closed in bliss. I feel his hands take mine and link us together on either side of my body, his fingers pressing into the tops of my hands.

My legs shake against his head as he sucks and sucks on my clit. I moan when he blows lightly across it.

"You'll say yes?" he asks, and I know he's smiling. I can practically feel it against my skin he's so close to me.

"Yes," I breathe.

He squeezes my hands. He rolls his tongue heavily over that smooth bundle of nerves, and I wait, I wait for him to ask while my body tightens and warms all over. I wait while blood rushes in my ears. I strain to hear his voice. *Is he asking?* The only thing I can hear is my own heartbeat and my answer, over and over as my orgasm pulls me apart.

"Yes, yes, yes, yes, yes."

I collapse against the sleeping bag, my skin slick with sweat. I feel Mason's lips on my thigh as he presses them there.

"Will you marry me?" he asks.

Smiling, I look down my body between my legs.

Mason raises his head. He looks so unsure for a man who just got his answer multiple times.

Was I not loud enough?

I sit up and grab his shoulders, pulling him until he's on top of me. I kiss his mouth. "I'm sorry. What was that? I couldn't hear you."

His lip twitches. Leaning back a bit, he stares down at me, smoothing his hand over my cheek. "Will you?" he asks, staring at my mouth, waiting for that one word I will never make him wait for.

"Yes."

He collapses, burying his face in my neck. "Baby."

"Don't let go of me."

I feel the slight shake of his head, his lips on my skin and the wetness leaking from his eyes.

"Never."

Epilogue

Brooke

MY HANDS ARE SHAKING. SWEAT builds up on my palms.

Jesus. How hot are these people trying to make this fucking wedding?

I suppose there's a bright side to sweating my ass off standing here. If the bride hates the cake, it'll probably end up melting before she cuts into it anyway.

I'm doing this delivery alone. I wanted it this way, until last night when I cried to Mason and begged him to cancel his classes this morning so he could be here to support me. I took it back immediately when it actually occurred to me that he *would* do that.

I won't have him missing anymore classes because of me. He's missed enough.

Turning my head, I glance at the cake on the table beside me as I wait for the bride. To my standards, I think it looks . . . okay. Maybe better than okay, but I'm not the one getting married.

Yet.

My thumb twists the engagement ring around my finger.

The flowers look as realistic as I was able to get them. The icing is flawless. This morning when I snapped a picture of the finished product and sent it to Dylan she called me and squealed in my ear.

I begged her to stop. Reese really begged her to stop. She still has another week to go before Blake is due to arrive and if she goes into early labor because of me, I might as well pack up my apron.

Reese will fire me himself.

As I'm looking up the stairway leading to the bridal suite, my phone beeps in my back pocket. I slide it out and read the message.

Mason: How's it going, sweetheart? You doing okay?

A door closes at the top of the stairs. I glance up and see the bride and a woman walking with her in my direction. I look down and quickly type my response.

Me: I'll let you know in a minute.

I tuck my phone away. Standing beside the table, I clasp my hands in front of me and concentrate on remembering to breathe. It's a challenging task, and one I might benefit from disregarding.

Passing out right now does have it's allure. I'll miss the rejection.

The bride gasps, raising a hand to her mouth when she gets halfway down the stairs. Her eyes glued to the cake.

I don't know what to do. I debate on giving this disaster a right shove and fleeing out the doors behind me.

"Oh, my God. Look at it, Mom!" She hurries down the remaining steps and stops in front of the table. She fans her face. "Shit! I'm going to cry. I can't cry." She cuts me a look. "Don't make me cry!"

"Okay? Um . . ." I gesture at the cake. I pray I don't vomit all over it. "I'm s-so sorry. The flowers weren't the easiest for me, but I'm very certain it tastes good. It's at least edible."

"What?" she laughs, moving quickly and throwing her arms around me. "You're so funny. I love it!"

"You do?"

"Yes!" She releases me and admires her cake. "The flowers are perfect. They look just like my bouquet, right, Mom?"

The older woman beside her nods. "Absolutely stunning." She gives me a warm smile. "You have a real talent, young lady."

I look from the woman, to the bride, then back again. "Um . . . thank you. Dylan, our main baker, is on bedrest so I did this by myself. I was really nervous. I ate some of the practice one I did."

"It's perfect. All of it. God, thank you again." The bride squeezes my hand, then grabs her mother and flees back up the stairs.

I stand there for a moment staring at the cake. My cake.

I did it.

Holy fuck, I did it.

Pressing my hands against my cheeks, I spin around to walk toward the door. A figure halts my steps.

Mason stands in the doorway of the estate house, smiling at me, still in his sleeveless tank and running shorts. His phone in his hand.

I sprint across the marble floor and hurl myself into his arms.

"You're here! Did you see?" I lean back to see his face, my feet dangling in the air. "She loved it. She thought it was perfect. Even the flowers."

"They match her bouquet," he adds, kissing me sweetly.

"You saw." I squeeze him tighter. "What are you doing here? What about your class?"

He puts me down and walks me outside, resting his hand on my lower back.

"I don't have any until this afternoon."

After stepping off the last stair, I look up at him. "What? You canceled them again?"

"No. I never had any scheduled until later. I just let you think I did. I knew you wanted to do this alone. I just wanted to be here if you needed me."

I tug on his hand, pulling him against me. I press a kiss to his chest. "I love you."

"Yeah? Wanna get married?"

My laugh cuts with a squeal when thunder claps over our heads. My hands immediately fly to my ears. I slide closer to Mason and lower my arms.

"Oh, my God. That was so loud."

He looks up at the rapidly darkening sky.

The first few drops of rain pelt against my face. The wind picks up around us.

"We should get going, yeah? It's coming fast."

Mason tugs on my hand and we dart through the parking lot.

There is no gradual incline of precipitation. The rain goes from a few sprinkles darkening the asphalt to buckets being dumped from the heavens.

I shriek, staying close to Mason as he humorously tries to shield me with his T-shirt. My hair sticks to the sides of my face and water pools in my sneakers. We're both drenched by the time we reach the delivery van around the side of the building.

I tug my keys out of my pocket.

"Out of nowhere. It was so nice today too. The sun was out."

I look up at Mason after he speaks, watching as he wipes his hand over his face and pushes back his wet hair.

He gives me an odd look. "What is it?"

Buckling over with my hand clutching my stomach, I fall into a fit of laughter as the rain continues to beat down on us.

"Something funny, gorgeous? You've lost me here."

I grab his face and stand on my toes to kiss him. "It was beautiful today. All day, and now it's raining."

"Yeah," he replies, still confused. "That it is."

"It feels good, doesn't it? I love sweet storms like this."

Lightning flashes across the sky, startling me again. We both look up, then at each other.

"We need to get in the van," he tells me. "With lightning, we'll be safe in there. Come on."

A wicked little thought pops into my head. Biting my lip, I grab his arm and lead him around the back of the vehicle. I quickly unlock the door and climb inside.

"What are you doing?" he asks, looking around the open space.

I reach for him, fisting his shirt. "I'm willing to bet you've never had sex in a delivery van before."

He arches his brow. Rain beads up on it. "Can't say I have."

"Me either."

I tug and he tumbles on top of me, pinning me beneath him, or maybe he lunges for me when he hears I'm giving him another one of my firsts.

I'm too happy to care how I get him. He's mine.
You hear that, bitches? MINE.

The End

Playlist

Overjoyed by Matchbox Twenty

More Than Anyone by Gavin Degraw

Come Around by Rosi Golan

Replay by Zendaya

Sugar by Maroon 5

Clumsy by Fergie

Somewhere Only We Know by Keane

Acknowledgements

MR. DANIELS, THANK YOU FOR being my best friend, for being an amazing husband and father, and for your steady support as we navigate through this crazy world together. Your face is my favorite face of all faces.

To my betas, thank you ladies for reading Sweet Obsession, and for going through this writing process with me and being my little voices of encouragement when I needed you. Beth Cranford, on top of everything else you do for me, thank you for sitting down with this story at the end and proofing it, timeline checking, and making sure Joey stays as fabulous as he should be. Kellie Richardson, Pwincess, thank you for your amazing teasers, and for loving this series almost as much as them Bama Boys. (Now that I think about it, Ben should've been in this. He could've arrested Paul at the bar.)

To my agent, Kimberly Brower, thank you for your countless emails and unwavering support. To Ellie McLove, I know . . . I need to give you more time, but you secretly like the ridiculously short turn-around schedule I throw at you, right?

My heartfelt thanks to all the bloggers who supported Sweet Obsession, for your reviews and messages you send me, and for helping me reach more readers than I could ever imagine. To Kylie with Give Me Books, thank you for everything you do for me. Please come to the states so I can hug you!

To my Instagram girls, there are way too many of you to list here. Know that each and every one of you mean the world to me. Thank you for everything.

Finally, my biggest thanks goes to my readers. Thank you all for your excitement and patience with Mason & Brooke's story. I hope you enjoyed reading it as much as I enjoyed writing it. Now, about that Joey book . . .

Xo, J

SWEET ADDICTION SERIES

Sweet Addiction

Sweet Possession

Sweet Obsession

ALABAMA SUMMER SERIES

Where I Belong

All I Want

When I Fall

Where We Belong

What I Need ~ Coming Soon

DIRTY DEEDS SERIES

Four Letter Word ~ Coming Soon

Hit the Spot ~ Coming Soon

About the Author

J. DANIELS IS THE NEW YORK Times and USA Today Bestselling author of the Sweet Addiction series and the Alabama Summer series.

She loves curling up with a good book, drinking a ridiculous amount of coffee, and writing stories her children will never read. J grew up in Baltimore and resides in Maryland with her family.

Website
www.authorjdaniels.com
Facebook
www.facebook.com/jdanielsauthor
Twitter
@JDanielsbooks
Instagram
authorjdaniels
Goodreads
www.goodreads.com/author/show/8184331.J_Daniels

CPSIA information can be obtained
at www.ICGtesting.com
Printed in the USA
BVOW03s1707040117
472614BV00006B/266/P